PRAISE FOR THE KILLER
FASHION MYSTERY SERIES

"A solid cozy...Readers in the mood for a low-stakes whodunit will be charmed."
  -*Publishers Weekly*

"...the book is enriched by the author's cleverly phrased prose and convincing characterization. The surprise ending will satisfy and delight many mystery fans. A diverting mystery that offers laughs and chills."
  -*Kirkus Reviews*

"Fashion is always at the forefront, but never at the cost of excellent writing, humorous dialogue, or a compelling story."
  -*Kings River Life*

"an impressive cozy mystery from a promising author."
  -*Mystery Tribune*

"Samantha Kidd is an engaging amateur sleuth."
  -*Mysterious Reviews*

"Diane Vallere takes the reader through this cozy mystery with her signature wit and humor."
  -Mary Marks, *NY Journal of Books*

"A captivating new mystery voice, Vallere has stitched together haute couture and murder in a stylish mystery. Dirty Laundry has never been so engrossing!"

THE KIDD STAYS

IN THE PICTURE

DIANE VALLERE

Polyester Press

READING, PA

THE KIDD STAYS IN THE PICTURE

DIANE VALLERE

Polyester Press

READING, PA

THE KIDD STAYS IN THE PICTURE

KILLER FASHION BOX #2

This edition includes books 4-6 in the Killer Fashion mystery series.

SOME LIKE IT HAUTE

1

PAPER PAJAMAS

THE SMELL TOLD ME I WASN'T AT HOME. BEFORE I OPENED MY EYES and saw the two concerned faces staring at me, before I heard the sounds of the monitors and medical equipment that sat close by, before I felt the scratchy sheets on the bed, I was assaulted by the scent of antiseptic cherry cleanser.

The faces were familiar. There was Eddie Adams, my close friend and confidant. And behind him, diverting her eyes, was Amanda Ries.

Not a confidant. Not even a sometimes friend.

She was my ex-boyfriend's maybe-former girlfriend.

Eddie and Amanda looked at me with a mixture of concern, fear, and embarrassment.

"She's awake," Eddie said when my eyes focused on him. "Dude, are you okay?"

I scanned the room, taking in the medical equipment, heart-rate monitor machines, and curtain that had been pulled back so I could see my visitors. I glanced down at my outfit.

Paper pajamas.

"Is this a hospital room?" I asked.

"Yes," Eddie said.

"Am I the patient?"

"Yes."

"Did I come here in an ambulance?"

"Yes."

"Then I don't think I'm okay."

Amanda burst into tears.

Twenty-Four Hours Earlier...

Ridiculously tall and thin girls surrounded me. Ridiculously tall and thin women. Ridiculously tall and thin *something*. They were so unlike the people I usually spent time with that I didn't know what to call them.

They were models.

They pranced around in stick-on bras and barely-there panties, waiting to be pinned and taped and glued and tied into the fashions that they would wear at the upcoming Amanda Ries runway show. Tonight was the dress rehearsal to check fittings, practice walking the runway, and generally make sure nothing had been left to chance. It was Fashion Week—or the closest thing that existed outside of New York City. Thanks to its proximity to the Big Apple, our little town of Ribbon, Pennsylvania, hosted its own version of Fashion Week, often convincing buyers to make the two-hour trek and check out the talent. It didn't matter that we weren't in the fashion capital of the country but rather about 150 miles west. Fashion Week adjacent, if you will.

"Miss Kidd, where do we go after we're done with our fittings?" one of the waifish models asked. A flashbulb popped in my face. I blinked several times, trying to restore my eyesight. "Miss Kidd?" she asked again.

"It's Samantha, not Miss Kidd," I lectured. I wasn't that much older than they were. Well, maybe I was, but admitting your age at a fashion show wasn't unlike telling your herd of cattle that you were the weak one. I pointed down a narrow hallway with walls covered in bulletin boards. "Last room on the right."

I felt a tug on my sleeve. "Excuse me, ma'am?" said a little-girl voice. "I think there's been a mistake with my second look."

Ma'am? She couldn't be talking to me. I looked at the model. Wide blue eyes, long blond hair, and a body of angles and bones. Sixteen years old was my best guess, only because anything younger would have been illegal.

I climbed up on a small step stool. "Can I have everyone's attention?" I hollered. Someone shushed, and the crowd quieted down. "I am Samantha. Not Miss Kidd, not ma'am. If you have a question for me, and you expect me to answer, you need to call me Samantha."

I hopped down from the step stool and pushed it under the nearest table.

"She's turning this place into a circus," said a voice next to me. An attractive man in an unstructured black-and-white tweed jacket and a porkpie hat stood next to me. His thick gray hair seemed out of place against his youthful olive skin. "Warehouse Five used to be an artists' studio. Now it's a joke."

"You don't think fashion design is a form of art?" I asked.

He watched the models. "It's a money-making machine. Look at these people. Acting like any of this is important. They're clothes. They'll be in style for a couple of months, and then everybody will forget about them. That's not art." He turned to me. "Are you part of the problem?"

"I'm here to help out, if that's what you mean. Samantha Kidd," I said, holding out my hand.

"Santangelo Toma."

"You're an artist?"

He nodded. "I do portraits and nudes. My studio is down the hall. Ever since these clowns showed up, I can barely hear myself think. It's an insult to the rest of us that they've been allowed to take over."

"The show's tomorrow night, and then it'll all be done."

"For good, hopefully. I started a petition to make sure something like this doesn't happen again." He glared at the models and then turned around and left.

One more stressor for Amanda. The last thing a designer would want in the panicked days before her first major fashion show was to learn the tenants of the building wanted her out.

The shy stick figure who'd called me ma'am was still next to me. She tugged on my sleeve again. "I'm sorry to bother you, but I think there's been a mistake."

The outfit in question was a silver lamé kimono. It hung open, exposing her skinny torso and flesh-colored panties. There wasn't a high price placed on modesty backstage at a runway show, with models often parading around half clothed, but this girl didn't have any goods to show off even if someone was interested. She held her arms out to the side, palms up, and raised her shoulders. Her hands were completely hidden by sleeves that were too long for her limbs, sleeves that hung down to the floor.

I sighed. "Let's go ask someone." I looked around, over, and under bust forms, mannequins, and rolling rods, until I found an imposing black man who stood head and shoulders above the (ridiculously tall) models. He had a tailor's tape draped over his shoulders and was dressed in a vest and trousers over a pressed dress shirt and navy blue plaid tie. We headed his way.

"Can you help her? This kimono doesn't seem to fit right," I said.

A few of the girls laughed amongst themselves. The man asked, "Are you Harper?"

The model nodded. The man turned to me. "All of the samples have been fitted and approved. That is how it's going down the runway. Harper was specifically requested to wear it."

The other models snickered again. Harper's eyes filled with tears, and she turned away from them.

I didn't have the energy for this. If Amanda wanted Harper to wear the oversized and poorly fitting kimono, then who was I to override that decision? Just the unassuming ex-girlfriend of the designer's maybe-former boyfriend. But I didn't have time to think about that. I had a model in the throes of an emotional breakdown and no Twizzlers in sight.

"If you have a problem, then you have to ask Amanda," the man said. "It's her show."

Again, I scanned the warehouse for the designer. The man pointed toward the back of the stage. Amanda was partially visible. She was talking to a person I couldn't see. Amanda's straight black hair hung in a thick, glossy sheath between her shoulder blades. She ran her hand over the top, smoothing strands that had probably never been out of place in their life.

I bet nobody called her ma'am.

I headed toward Amanda with Harper close to my heels. When we reached the designer, I saw who was on the other side of the conversation. Amanda's financial partner, a six-foot-tall Amazonian named Tiny Anderson. Tiny, as I'd come to learn, wore some version of the same outfit everyday: white oxford shirt, gray sweater, dark-wash men's jeans, and brogues. Both unisex and unflattering, her uniform served the dual purpose of letting her blend into the crowd while being sure that nobody mistook her for anybody else.

I waited for an appropriate pause in their conversation so I could interrupt.

"When is Nick getting here with the shoes?" Tiny asked.

"Nick isn't bringing the shoes tonight," Amanda said.

"We still have to do a hem check." Tiny gestured toward the models with a hand holding several spools of metallic thread. A row of silver straight pins lined the hem of her sweater. "I thought he knew how important it was that we had everything here for the run-through." Tiny glared down at Amanda.

"Nick didn't want to show up today because of—" She stopped mid-sentence. The two of them turned and looked directly at me.

This had been one of the worst months of my life. And that's counting the times when I'd happened upon dead bodies, stood face-to-face with murderers, and almost gotten killed. This was worse than all of that.

Somehow, after breaking up with my shoe-designer boyfriend Nick Taylor, I'd gotten myself in the position of helping his ex-girlfriend Amanda Ries coordinate her runway show.

2

SHOW NO SIGNS OF WEAKNESS

Breakup Rule #1: Show no signs of weakness to your ex's friends. That's why I arrived, on time, on that first day of scheduling. Amanda had hired me for my fashion experience and professionalism, and I was prepared to bring it. I wasn't going to give her fuel for any fodder about me.

But it was painfully obvious that Amanda wouldn't be singing my praises to anybody. Her show was being railroaded because Nick wanted to avoid me.

"I'm sorry to interrupt," I said. I thought it best to pretend I hadn't overheard them. "Harper has a problem with the sleeves on her kimono. They're too long. There must have been a mistake."

Tiny was the one to talk. "We picked every model's looks based on their measurements and coloring. There is no room for error, and considering these decisions were made by us"—she used her hand to make a sweeping gesture that included herself and Amanda—"I highly doubt there's been any mistake. Remind the girl she's supposed to be a professional, and that she has about five seconds to decide if she can do that before we replace her."

"But look at this," I said. I grabbed one of Harper's wrists and held her arm out. The fabric at the bottom of the sleeve pooled onto the ground. I turned toward Amanda. "Is this what you wanted?"

Tiny didn't give Amanda a chance to answer. "She's wearing the kimono. End of story."

I dropped my voice and said to Harper, "If you don't want to do this job, you better say so now and get your things. But I need to tell you, you won't be getting a positive referral from Amanda, and you might want to rethink your decision to get into modeling if this bothers you so much."

Tears spilled down Harper's cheeks and dripped onto the silver lamé. The drops rolled down the surface. I held out a box of tissues, and she pulled three out in quick succession. Up close, she looked even younger than I'd originally thought.

"Tell you what," Tiny said to Harper. "I'll look at it after I finish dealing with our shoe emergency." Tiny glared at me, her momentary expression of compassion instantly replaced with annoyance. "Apparently you had something to do with that too."

Harper blew her nose loudly and dabbed at her eyes. Tiny's response had done little to make Harper feel like she had been right to speak up. She'd treated her more like a robot than a human. The models—all of them—had been on their own since the day they'd first shown up. No one was looking out for these women.

Harper straightened up to her five-foot-nine-in-bare-feet height. "If Amanda wants me to wear the kimono, I'll wear the kimono, but only because Samantha stood up for me," she said to Tiny.

Tiny looked back and forth between the two of us and then walked away. Amanda went the other direction.

"I didn't stand up for you," I said to Harper. "I just asked the question."

"You went to Tiny. No one goes to Tiny."

I patted her arm in a soothing manner. "It's going to be okay. You have to admit she and Amanda seem to be leaving no room for error. That means they think you're going to rock that kimono better than anybody else here. Right?"

"I guess so." She sniffed twice in quick succession and blinked away more tears.

"I'll give you a couple of minutes to get it together. Amanda's having a meeting at quarter after six." I checked the wall clock. "That's in about ten minutes. Can you make it? I think it would be best if you're there and no one knows how you felt about this."

She blew her nose again. "I'll be there." Then her voice turned nasty. "I just wish Tiny wouldn't."

"You might be in luck. I think she's going out to get the shoes."

Harper looked up. "Mr. Taylor isn't coming here?"

"No."

"Oh. I like it when he comes. He makes everybody happy."

Now it was my turn for a tissue.

Harper left in the direction of the other models. She bent over her duffle bag and came up with a small makeup pouch. She pulled a bottle of eye drops and a compact from it and went to work on her red eyes and nose.

A flashbulb went off next to me. I blinked a couple of times to make the black dots in front of my eyes go away. Someone with a camera had to be there, but the flash had temporarily blinded me. "Who are you and why are you taking my picture?" I asked.

"Clive Barrington." The dots faded, and I made out a silhouette of a man with his hand held out. I shook it. "Freelance photojournalist. Amanda agreed to let me document her show. I'm taking background shots tonight to flesh out the behind-the-scenes aspect."

Santangelo Toma had been right. This *was* turning into a circus.

Clive leaned against a cutting table. He was a moderately built man who I'd place in his forties. Longish golden blond hair was parted on the side and tucked behind his ears. His camera dangled from a black strap around his neck. He wore a T-shirt, plaid blazer, cuffed jeans, and green bucks. Those were nice. I wonder where you got a pair of green bucks these days? I was getting distracted. I looked back up at his face, and he winked at me.

"I think we might want to talk to Tiny about the pictures you're taking. I don't think she'd be too pleased with your presence here."

"Tiny left to get the shoes," Amanda said, having materialized from out of nowhere. "But Samantha's right. Maybe you've taken enough pictures for tonight."

Clive adjusted his lens. "A few more shots, and I'll be out of your hair."

"Keep it brief. The models don't need any more distractions."

"I'm going to sit in front of the runway." Clive turned to me. "Where are you going to be?"

"I can't see how that matters."

Amanda, who had started to walk away, stopped and turned back. "Samantha, maybe it's you who should leave."

I was tired and didn't mind the idea of going home and collapsing in bed. "What time should I be here tomorrow?"

"You don't need to come tomorrow. We've got it under control."

"But tomorrow is the show," I said.

"That's right. You can pick up your check at my studio on Monday." Amanda spoke with a finality that cut me to the quick. With one hand, she tossed her shiny black hair behind her shoulder.

I felt like I'd been stung center mass by a swarm of angry

bumblebees. It was bad enough to have spent the past six weeks pushing aside petty jealousy to work with Amanda, but worse yet, she was firing me. If my back and knees and feet and shoulders didn't hurt so much, and if the caffeine from the pot of coffee I'd finished a few hours ago wasn't wearing off, then maybe I would have tried to establish my role backstage. But all things considered...

"Fine. I'll get my handbag and coat. Good luck," I said with as much dignity as I could muster. None of this had been easy. Nor appreciated, it seemed.

I weaved through the same labyrinth of rolling rods, mannequins, and fabric bolts that I'd worked around for the past few weeks and collected my belongings. I bundled up into a wool coat and hat and braced myself for the blast of cold from outside. Good riddance.

The main portion of Warehouse Five was connected to the front foyer and adjoining galleries of other artists by a hallway that ran the length of the building. I turned right and headed past the picked-over food service table toward the exit. Closer to the door, the lights were out. I flicked the switch on the wall next to the lavatories a few times, but nothing happened. *No worries,* I thought, as I trudged toward the glowing Exit sign.

And then I noticed a figure hovering in the parking lot. Fear folded around me like a blanket. *Act natural,* I coached myself. *Just keep walking. Your car is right outside the door.*

I fumbled for my keys, mentally kicking myself for not having them in hand already. The figure slunk back into the shadow. Adrenaline replaced the numbness of being dismissed, and the hair on the back of my neck stood up. I turned around to see if there was anybody else in the hallway with me. There wasn't. I pushed forward and then out the exit doors, with my head down. My car wasn't far.

And then a flicker of light caught my eye. I turned to look at the source, and quicker than you can say "supermodel," a trail of fire ignited a path from the edge of the parking lot to where I stood. I jumped away, too slowly. The flame licked my boot and climbed the hem of my pants. I swatted at my cuff, and the fire went out.

A figure in a puffy down coat stepped out of the shadows. I couldn't make out if it was a man or woman. He or she swung a lumpy bag that connected with my midsection, and I doubled over, my wool winter coat only absorbing some of the blow.

"Stay out of this," said a distorted voice. The person swung the bag again. I fell to the ground. My attacker ignited the bag with a match. The eerie orange light cast shadows over a face mostly hidden by a thick scarf.

The flaming bag struck me again and again. The ground was cold through my coat, and I could barely move. The fire went out. I squeezed my eyes shut. Fabric tore, and round objects pelted me. I rolled to the side, my face wet with the tears of pain.

3

TRYING TO DISTRACT ME

"And that's where I found you," said Amanda from her seat next to the hospital bed. She wrung her hands as she spoke. She had just told us about finding me curled up in the parking lot, surrounded by burnt fruit, unable to stand or get help for myself. My memories of the previous evening had ended shortly after the beating stopped.

She'd done the right thing, calling 911 to get an ambulance for me and not letting anyone else into the area. When the EMTs arrived, I'd been taken to the hospital, where I relayed what little I could remember to a police officer after being poked, prodded, and X-rayed. My version had been told under the influence of painkillers and may have included a few extra details, but the overall gist was the same. I'd been attacked in the parking lot between the Warehouse Five exit and my car. I'd been beaten with a bag of oranges and set on fire. I'd been left to die or freeze, whichever came first. And now, thanks to Amanda, I lay recovering from internal bruising and second-degree burns. My left hand was wrapped in a gauze bandage, and it hurt to take deep breaths.

"What time did you find her?" Eddie asked.

"It was a little after eleven. I went to the parking lot when some of the girls left. I wanted to see what was taking so long."

Eddie voiced my thoughts. "So nobody knows what happened."

"No."

I sat up and spoke in a raspy voice. "Somebody set me on fire and beat me. That's what happened."

"That's what you keep saying, but nobody saw anything. Tiny had to go meet Nick—" Amanda paused mid-sentence and looked at me. A tension-riddled silence ballooned into the small hospital room while every one of us wondered if I would react to the mention of Nick.

For the past six weeks, the name "Nick" had been a largely unspoken four-letter word. Our breakup had been unexpected; my ability to move on had been overestimated. The week I let it all sink in, I'd bought out the local grocery store's supply of frozen chicken tenders and subsisted on them, vanilla ice cream, and waffles for a week. I gained seven pounds, dropped out of society, and spent much of my time with my cat.

I love my cat, but there are some who might say my behavior was not entirely healthy. Still, there was no way I was going to let Amanda, Nick's maybe-former girlfriend, know how I felt.

Eddie took control of the conversation. "You said Tiny went out?" he asked.

"She went to pick up the samples at Nick's showroom. It seemed like a long time, but that's because we were at a standstill until she got back. I mean, there were little things for us to do like tack seams and steam samples and go over the order of the show, but I was keeping the models there so we could do a walk-through, and that cost us money. We couldn't do anything without the shoes."

"You were there late. The models were there late. Who else?" Eddie asked. In the background, the vital sign monitor beeped like the Atari videogame I'd gotten for Christmas in 1981.

"Interns and assistants, hair and makeup."

"What about other artists who rent space in the building?" Eddie pressed. In the past, it had been me asking the questions in circumstances like this. Tonight, I was happy to let Eddie step in while I listened.

"They were gone for the night."

"You're sure?"

"The last one to leave was an artist. He complained to Tiny about the noise before he left."

I strained to speak. "What about the photographer, Clive Barrington? Was he still there?" The effort of speaking made me cough.

Amanda averted her eyes. In that moment, I recognized the look. It wasn't guilt. It wasn't appreciation. It wasn't sympathy. It was pity.

"Clive, Amanda. Was he there?" I asked again, this time with more conviction.

"I don't know if he was there or not. He said he wanted to get a few pictures of the models walking the runway, but I don't think he knew we'd keep him waiting for hours."

"Who does he report to?" I asked.

"Nobody. He comes and goes as he pleases. When he started, he made a point of telling us he needed unlimited access if he was going to capture my story. Tiny agreed as long as she got picture approval before anybody else saw them. That was her demand. That we see the photos before any of them went public."

"Was there anyone else there that you remember?" Eddie asked Amanda. "Or you?" he asked me.

I watched Amanda, not knowing if she was going to return the eye contact. She didn't. She stared at her hands and fidgeted with her bracelet. If I hadn't noticed a slight movement at her temple, I might not have recognized that she was clenching and unclenching her teeth.

"I would have to think about it," I said. "Everyone I remember had a legitimate reason for being there. Do you agree, Amanda?"

She nodded her head. Something buzzed in her red crocodile handbag. We all watched as she fished it out and looked at the display. She hit a button that stopped the sound and tossed it back inside then looked up to find us all looking at her.

"It's not important," she said. Her handbag buzzed again. She ignored it, but the buzzing continued. After several buzzes, text message alerts, and vibrations, Eddie stated the obvious.

"Someone seems to disagree with you."

She stood and gathered her coat. "I need to get back to Warehouse Five. There's a lot to do before the show." She walked to the door and then stopped and turned back around. "I should have known something like this would happen." Then she left.

Breakup Rule #2: Don't be seen as a victim. I'd been hired to help Amanda at Nick's request, and I'd gotten attacked. It was her runway debut, her big show, her production. I'd only shown up that first day to honor my commitment and make sure nothing outside of positive things could be said about my character when she spoke to Nick about me. Now, I was unmade-up, with hospital hair, in paper pajamas. There was no way she could keep this story from him. Seeing as how I was at the center of the drama—through no fault of my own—there was a good chance Nick would see things the way Amanda would paint them: with me at the epicenter. I'd become an unanticipated inconvenience to her carefully scheduled timetables.

I waited for the door to shut and then turned to Eddie. "You have to get me out of here. It's going to take me longer than usual to get ready, but there's no way I'm going to miss her show."

"Are you nuts?" he asked.

"We both know I'm going to her show. We both know you're going to help me. Go get a nurse, and find out how I get out of here."

"Dude, you can try to talk me into helping you, and there's a chance you might be successful. That's why I'm leaving you here in the hands of the professionals."

"Eddie, I don't have insurance. I can't afford to get a bill for whatever they might do if they keep me here."

"You're not invincible. You were beat up with a bag of fruit. Who does that?"

"It was a warning. Like a scene from *The Grifters.*" I hadn't given much thought to the choice of fruit as weapon. But in that movie, a bag of oranges had been used to beat up Angelica Houston because it caused internal injuries with minimal external bruising. I held my hands out and traced the burns on my left hand with the fingers on my right. "I don't get the fire, though. If somebody wanted to attack me without leaving evidence, why go with an open flame?"

"I know what you're doing," Eddie said. "You're trying to distract me with movie references and words like 'evidence.' It's not going to work. You're in a hospital bed, suffering from internal injuries and second-degree burns. For real. This isn't a movie. I know you like danger, but this is probably the safest place you can be."

"I don't like danger," I said.

Eddie raised one eyebrow. "I'm not going to help you get out of here before you're ready." He pulled on his bomber jacket and left.

There was a tap on my door, and a nurse entered. She took my blood pressure and asked if I needed anything.

"May I use the phone?"

She carried the old desk set to the table next to my bed. "Privacy?"

I nodded.

She left, and I called a number from memory. "Hello, Dante? It's Samantha Kidd. Are you free tonight?"

4

SMART, SAFE, AND SENSIBLE

Dante Lestes was a somewhat mysterious photographer from Philadelphia. I'd met him when a promotional contest in town inspired me to plan a heist. Dante had surprised me in the past by helping me when others wanted me to play it safe. He accepted that I ran head-on into impossible situations, and he'd given me the tools to protect myself. He had experience working for a private investigator, and while I was far from being a detective, I paid attention when he shared his knowledge with me. I might never be Kinsey Millhone, but I was a quick study.

Dante was everything Nick wasn't: dangerous, tattooed, and accepting of my lifestyle choices. In the past, he'd hinted that he was interested in getting to know me better. I, being of post-breakup mental fragility, hadn't followed up on those hints. But tonight, I figured a fashion show was a perfect place to set a new ball in motion. Keeping things on my turf, so to speak.

The tests at the hospital showed nothing that wouldn't heal in time. The doctor gave me the option of staying another night, an offer that came with pain medication and all the green Jell-O I could eat or going home. Even though it hurt to breathe, and some of my skin was blistered and red, I chose to leave. If I'd had insurance, I might have seen things differently, but that's the glamorous life of a fashion-industry professional with a recently spotty work history.

My plan wasn't completely foolproof, but I'd worked through the important issues. My car was still at Warehouse Five, but there wasn't time to retrieve it now. I took a taxi back to my house, filled Logan's bowl with cat chow, showered, and thought about how I would gain entry to the show. Having spent considerable time working there, I planned to talk my way past whoever was working the door. No way would Amanda have thought to ban me.

The shower, makeup, and hair-drying process kept me preoccupied, but by the time I had to choose an outfit, I had second thoughts about leaving the house. The local cable channel would broadcast the show. I'd already set up a recording. Maybe that would be the smart, safe, sensible thing to do.

I pulled on a loose-fitting black jersey trapeze dress, thigh-high stockings, and kitten-heeled boots. My ribs were still tender, and I didn't want to fuss with a waistband. I pulled my long hair up into a high ponytail and clipped a conical gold piece around the base of it then added gold hoop earrings and an arm filled with bangles. My injuries were hidden. Only I knew they were there.

Only I would know that someone had waited in the parking lot for me, lit me on fire, and pummeled me with a bag of fruit like a prison warning. I had to know why.

Screw smart, safe, and sensible.

By the time Dante arrived, I was ready. I opened the door. Dante stood in front of me. His amber eyes locked onto mine then slowly traveled down to my lips then my body, where they lingered for a moment too long before he looked back into my eyes. I felt heat coming off him, heat coming off me. I held onto the door, taking shallow breaths, partly because it hurt to take bigger ones, and partially because being around Dante left me out of breath.

I guess being alone with Dante wasn't terribly smart, safe, or sensible either.

"So, we're going to your friend's fashion show, right?"

I didn't bother explaining the nuanced relationship between me and the designer-slash-maybe-former girlfriend of my ex and simply nodded.

Dante had traded his motorcycle for a late-seventies Corvette Stingray with orange flames. Not only were we going, but we were going to arrive in style.

I gave Dante directions to the warehouse district. It was in a stretch of five abandoned factories that had been bought out by a special interest group and subleased as gallery space to local artists. Quilters, painters, jewelry designers, and other creative types shared room in the converted building, occasionally banding together for open houses and community activities. Officially, the building was named after the investors, but locally they were referred to by the faded numbers that had long ago been painted on the exteriors. Warehouses one through four sat vacant.

Dante wasn't one to fill the air with chatter, but I'd learned that his silences didn't mean he was bored. There were times when I'd seen him in action, and I wondered if he had the same need for excitement that I did. I didn't ask. Tonight, I thought it best to keep him in the dark about my recent attack. I didn't want another lecture, and I certainly didn't want him to turn the car around.

The parking lot was close to full. Dante handed the car keys to a valet attendant. I got out of the car. A cold wind snapped at my face and ankles. I pulled my coat around me and caught the door that was being held open from inside. The person holding the door was Nick.

The last time Nick and I had been face to face had been six weeks ago, outside my house, discussing the merits/flaws of my personality. At the time, I'd been acting as his office manager by day and his girlfriend by night. A few days after that conversation, he'd reached the conclusion that my working for him wasn't a great idea. He replaced me with a recent college grad and suggested I work with Amanda.

Clearly, that had worked out well.

"Kidd," he said. His voice was soft and warm, like honey dissolving into a mug of hot tea. "I didn't expect to see you here tonight."

I hadn't expected to see him either, a fact made painfully clear by the reaction of my nervous system. I tipped my head to the side and pulled my ponytail over one shoulder. "Hi," I said.

Nick had thick, curly brown hair that he kept trimmed in a neat business-like style. He'd taken to wearing it differently. Longer and slightly unkempt, which gave him a boyish look. Instead of a shirt and tie like he normally wore for industry events, he was in a long-sleeved T-shirt, jeans, and Converse sneakers. He looked more like one of the interns running around backstage than a highly respected shoe designer.

"I heard about the attack. Are you okay?" he asked. Behind him, Amanda watched us. For as many times as I'd wondered how I'd react the next time I saw Nick, I'd never thought it would be twenty-four hours after being released from the hospital while his maybe-former girlfriend glared at us from twenty feet away. At least I was wearing lipstick.

We were a foot apart. He smelled like clean sheets and freshly baked doughnuts and New Year's Eve. I looked away from his root-beer-barrel-colored eyes to his T-shirt. A piece of lint clung to his sleeve. I picked it off. He reached out for my hand, but a shock of electricity sparked at his touch, and we both pulled away.

"Samantha?" Dante said behind me. I looked over my shoulder at him and then back at Nick.

The two eyed each other. When it seemed obvious I wasn't going to make an introduction, Dante held out his hand. "Dante Lestes," he said.

"Nick Taylor." They shook. Nick turned back to me. "You shouldn't be here. Not after what happened."

I didn't say anything, and the tension grew to an uncomfortable level. Someone opened the door next to us, and a gust of cold air entered. I stepped away from Nick. "Hope everything goes well tonight," I said. I left him in the hallway and followed Dante through the crowd.

The setup of the show wasn't all that different from other runway shows I'd attended. Rows of collapsible white chairs were set up on either side of a raised white platform. A screen occupied the end of the runway, and Amanda's name was mounted on it in large silver vinyl letters. Colorful lights cast an ethereal orange, red, and yellow glow across the audience. Large urns of orange roses sat on tall cocktail tables at the back of the room, and thousands of orange rose petals were strewn down the runway. Dante followed me as I weaved through the crowd, selecting two seats by the back. I didn't need to be in front. I didn't need to be noticed.

I looked for familiar faces. Buyers from Tradava, Ribbon's own department store where Eddie worked, sat in front-row seats along the right-hand side. As was the norm for a fashion show, a couple of pop stars were mixed into the crowd with an actress who was going to be starring in a new political drama. For a show two-plus hours west of New York, Amanda had drawn an impressive crowd.

Dante tipped his head closer to mine. "If I'd have known you were going to ignore me, I might not have accepted your invitation."

I blushed. "I'm sorry. I get distracted at these things, looking for people I know."

"Me too." He pointed to the end of the platform. "There's one."

I followed his finger and saw Clive snapping pictures of the crowd.

"You know Clive Barrington?"

Dante chuckled. "'Clive Barrington.' I never heard anybody use his full name before. We used to call him Bare. We competed for a few jobs, but Bare always had a taste for the ladies and eventually it got him into trouble."

"What trouble?"

"Underage girl at an unchaperoned photo shoot. Turned into a he-said-she-said thing. Nobody knows what happened, but he couldn't get a job after that. To tell you the truth, I didn't know he'd resurfaced."

"I wonder how he hooked up with Amanda?"

"Who knows? Looks pretty much the same as he did back then. A little older, a little less hair. The glamorous life is taking its toll on him. Back in the day, he wouldn't have been caught dead with highlights."

It had never occurred to me that Dante might know anyone at the show tonight. I watched him watch Clive and wondered what he was thinking. Before I had a chance to ask more questions, the lights went down.

Loud Japanese pop songs filled the air. A Godzilla movie was projected onto the back of the stage, above Amanda's name. A model walked out, dressed in a silver leather motorcycle jacket over a red pantsuit. Her hair was bright red at the roots, fading to orange then yellow, and cut in a bob with heavy bangs. She sauntered down the runway, posed at the end, then turned. Even from the back row I could make out the intricate red embroidery on the back of her jacket. The crowd applauded eagerly.

The next model started down the runway. She wore a black leather corset over a silver pantsuit. Her orange wig was pulled back into a chignon, secured with silver chopsticks.

The third girl stomped down the runway in a red Lycra halter dress. Her wig was yellow.

By the time the fifth model came out, it was clear that the audience was sitting up and taking notice of what Amanda was showing. Did it matter that her choice of venue was a downtown warehouse in Ribbon? Who was to say. More and more designers who had neither the money nor the connections to pull off a major event in New York City were orchestrating pop-up fashion shows, inviting as many industry insiders as they knew, and hoping for the best.

But this was not Amanda's first rodeo. She'd spent years interning for a famous designer before parting ways and taking a job with a local department store. On the side, she focused on her own collection, slowly building a name for herself by reinventing the classics. What I saw tonight was more than a slight departure from the styles that had originally gotten her noticed. But what was fashion without risk? And who ever said that a futuristic silver jumpsuit wouldn't one day be a classic?

A familiar figure stepped onto the stage. It was Harper, the reticent model in the ill-fitting kimono. Her silver wig was cut in a blunt bob like the first model. Her lips, painted tomato red, were shaped in a pout. The kimono still didn't fit, but tonight Harper showed she was the professional they'd wanted. Her sleeves hung down to the floor, making her look like a child playing dress up. She sashayed down the platform, hips swinging from side to side, creating the illusion of sex appeal even though I knew her to be mostly skin and bones. A trail of smoke followed her.

A smattering of applause filled the auditorium as if what we were watching was part of the show. But something wasn't right. A thin orange stripe appeared to hover just above the rose petals that scattered over the ground as Harper walked. First one then another of the rose petals ignited like small bursts of glowing light. And then a whole bunch of the petals caught fire in a path that followed Harper.

And then suddenly, her kimono erupted in flames.

5

MAKE-OUT POINT

The house lights came on. The sudden change of illumination temporarily blinded me. Someone screamed. As my eyes adjusted, I followed the screaming to Harper. She fumbled with the sash on the kimono. Flames climbed the sleeves from the ground up and wrapped her like a special effect in a movie. She clawed at the fabric. Smoke filled the air, compromising visibility.

Nick appeared from behind the screen where Amanda's name was printed. He ran toward Harper and yanked the kimono from her shoulders. She left it in a burning pile and ran toward an exit. The flames caught onto the rest of the rose petals that covered the runway. More screams, now from the crowd. People stampeded toward the exits, bottlenecking the doorways with bodies trying to get outside. The fire grew, feeding off the fabric and oxygen in the room. I lost sight of Nick.

Dante tugged me the opposite direction of the crowd. "This way," he said.

I took his hand and barely kept up as we weaved past the frantic audience. We stumbled over flipped chairs and discarded drinks that now littered the floor. The fire had flashed over, climbing the walls and the ceiling. Sweat dripped from my hairline despite the cold night air. Within seconds, sprays of water shot out of the sprinkler system. We reached a set of double doors. He stepped back and pushed me through them.

We made it to the exit and fell outside. Fire trucks flooded the parking lot, sirens blaring. Professionals went to work on the fire. In the pandemonium, Dante took his keys from the valet booth. He scooped me up, one arm behind my head, the other under my knees, carried me to his car, and set me in the passenger seat. I closed my eyes while he drove us away from the scene. It wasn't until I heard the engine turn off that I opened them and saw that he hadn't taken me home.

We were parked in a vacant lot that overlooked a spectacular view of Ribbon. Lights from the streetlamps that illuminated the grid of downtown created a dense glow that slowly expanded into less and less, until it became the nothingness of the neighboring towns. In high school, we called this Make-Out Point.

"You want to tell me why your ex-boyfriend said you shouldn't have gone to the show?"

"He was worried about me, that's all."

"Does he have a reason to worry?"

I played with the gold bracelets on my wrist. "I had an incident yesterday."

"Samantha, don't beat around the bush with me."

"I've been helping Amanda with her show. Yesterday there was a fire outside of Warehouse Five. I don't know how it started. It came right to me across the parking lot to where I stood, and I caught on fire. I dropped and rolled to put out the flames, and while I was down someone approached me. They were bundled up in an oversized coat, and from my spot on the ground, they looked humungous. They told me to stay out of it, but I don't know what 'it' is. And then they beat me with a sack of fruit and set me on fire."

"Fruit?"

"Oranges, tangelos, and clementines. When Amanda found me curled up in the parking lot, they were scattered around me."

"What happened after that?"

"I spent the night in the hospital."

"Why did you call me?"

I looked down at my hands. I didn't want to make eye contact when I said this part. "Everybody else told me to stay home. They thought it was too dangerous for me to come here tonight." I snuck a peek at his face but couldn't tell what he was thinking.

"Do you know who attacked you?" he asked.

"No."

"Someone involved with the show?"

"Maybe. I don't know."

"Are you in pain right now?"

"Yes."

He started up the car. "I'm taking you home."

"No. My car is still at the warehouse," I said. "Take me back there. Please." It had been too much activity for one day. My ribs ached, and I couldn't breathe. I needed to sit down, lie down, rest, sleep. My internal injuries throbbed, and even if the hospital had determined that none of them were serious, they hurt. Badly.

Dante reached for my handbag and found my prescription inside. He shook a tablet into his palm and handed it to me.

"You're in pain. Take this." He handed me a bottle of water from the cup holder.

I swallowed the pill and sank back against his bucket seats, trying to keep the seatbelt from digging into my midsection. The tension from the runway show, the medication for the pain, and the overall exhaustion of my life combined, and the world went dark as I fell asleep in the car.

Breakup Rule #3: Don't wake up in another man's bed. The bed was comfortable enough, but it wasn't mine. It took me a second to recognize whose bed it was. Dante's.

Dante lived in a studio apartment on Duryea Drive, on the side of a mountain off the beaten path of Ribbon. He'd once explained it as the place he kept here when not living in Philadelphia. I'd been here before but never on a sleepover.

Being a studio apartment, the interior wasn't divided up into separate rooms. It was one large room that split off to the right into a modest kitchen and to the left into a modest bathroom and makeshift closet. The bed that I currently occupied was of the futon variety. Which meant there wasn't any place else to sleep, which meant even though I was alone now, I probably hadn't been last night.

Not sure how I felt about that.

There was a tap on the front door, and then Dante entered. He carried a bag from the grocery store. I pulled the comforter up around me.

"You're awake," he said.

"I am."

"You want breakfast? Bacon? Eggs?"

"Sure." Things were getting curiouser and curiouser. But I was already slightly down the rabbit hole. Why not get some bacon while there?

I peeked under the sheet and saw that I'd slept in a T-shirt and sweatpants, neither of which were mine. I stood up and hopped across the cold hardwood floor to the bathroom. My dress, smelling faintly of wet ash, hung over the curtain rod. I found an empty hanger in Dante's closet and hung the dress up, did other bathroom-type things, and rejoined him.

The futon had been folded up, and a small table with a large plate of bacon and eggs sat on a table in front of it. There were forks poised on either side of the plate. Dante patted the seat next to him. Rocky and Bullwinkle filled the screen. I pinched a piece of bacon and ate it before sitting.

"You should have told me about the attack," he said.

I figured we'd get around to this sooner or later. "I don't always make the best decisions."

"That's a very mature thing to admit."

I shrugged. (I couldn't say anything else. My mouth was full.)

"I talked to my sister this morning," he said.

Dante's sister, Cat, traveled in the same fashion circles that I did. "How is Cat?"

"She's great. She's in Paris on a buying trip." He continued. "She filled me in on your recent history. Helps explain last night."

My initial antagonistic relationship with Cat had morphed first into acquaintances and then into friendship. She knew about my employment issues since moving to Ribbon, about my frequent run-ins with the law, and about my recent breakup with Nick. If you needed gossip on me, she could give you the Cliff Notes version.

"I don't question the fact that you wanted to go to the show. Your ex and I have very different ideas on letting you live your life, regardless of what appears to be questionable judgment. But like I said, you should have told me."

"What did you expect me to say? 'Somebody put me in the hospital at a fashion show rehearsal, and now I need help figuring out who it was'? You were going to pretend that was normal?"

"You think asking me out on a date was normal?"

"What's so abnormal about that?"

"You were set on fire outside of the rehearsal, and there was a fire at the show last night. Somebody put a lot of people in jeopardy. If you hadn't been attacked, it might have seemed like an accident. But connect the two, and there's forethought. Somebody intended to hit that show. That same somebody thinks you're a threat."

It was true. Hearing him spell it out made it all the more real and scary. I couldn't pretend everything was okay. I set the bacon back on the plate.

"I keep trying to figure out what I know. Somebody attacked me. Me. Not anybody else connected to that show. All I've been doing for the past month is showing up at Warehouse Five to help Amanda get the show ready. I agreed to do it for reasons I don't want to get into. It was important to me to fulfill my obligation and protect my reputation. I didn't threaten anybody, I didn't see anything shady, and I didn't have any confrontations. I was the perfect employee. And if you must know, Amanda basically fired me before I was attacked."

"That may all be true, but somebody still set the show on fire. What else do you remember about what happened?"

"The warning. 'Stay out of it.' What is 'it?' How can I stay out of 'it' if I don't know what 'it' is?" I tried to stand but doubled over as a flash of pain shot through my torso.

"Slow down, Samantha. You might not be in the hospital anymore, but it's going to take time for you to heal. For now, you'll have to rely on me for whatever you need."

"I'm not moving in with you."

"Don't worry. It's temporary. And I'm not the babysitting type. Can you drive a motorcycle?"

"No."

He tossed me a set of keys. The key fob was shaped like a flame. "Looks like the Stingray is your ride for the next couple of days, but for the record, I think it's best that you stay away from the places you usually go."

"Why?"

"You don't know who attacked you or why. You might be able to explain it away as wrong place, wrong time, but I'm not a big believer in coincidence."

"You think someone might still be after me?"

He nodded once. The thought, now verbalized, was troubling. I wanted to discount his theory, but at my core, I agreed with him.

After breakfast was finished, Dante shrugged into his black leather jacket and left the house. As soon as his motorcycle disappeared around the curve of Duryea Drive, I tossed the dirty dishes in the sink and changed the channel to the local news. I'd expected the fire to be the top story. It wasn't.

In typical obsessed-with-celebrity nature, the top story was about how the rising star in the modeling world had been spotted on a plane that landed in Mexico last night.

Somehow, in the middle of all the chaos, Harper had managed to skip town.

6

GODZILLA ON THE MOON

Grainy footage of Harper stepping off a plane filled the screen. The clip was only a few seconds long and seemed to have been filmed from someone's cell phone. Harper's hair was pulled back into a ponytail, and she wore an oversized black topcoat and jeans. A duffle bag hung over one shoulder, the only luggage she appeared to have with her. She looked directly at the person filming her, hoisted the duffle bag strap higher, and hustled the other direction. The clip repeated as the reporter spoke.

"A vacationer headed to Cancun captured this footage after recognizing Harper Ashton when she boarded the plane. He said she arrived in full makeup but removed it during the flight. Ms. Ashton had left the ill-fated runway show of designer Amanda Ries. I believe we have a report on that show as well."

The footage switched to a view of Warehouse Five. An investigative reporter stood about a hundred feet in front of the now-abandoned warehouse. Fire had ravaged the building, leaving black stains on the outer edge of doorways and windows, like fake eyelashes that had clumped. The camera panned the exterior of the building.

"Last night a fire at Warehouse Five threatened to take the lives of many fashion insiders. The city of Ribbon has been offering tax incentives to local businesses, and Amanda Ries, local designer, had taken them up on that. Her runway show had been widely publicized from here to New York City, drawing buyers of major department stores who were eager to see this new collection. Touted as Godzilla on the Moon, Ries's show promised a departure from her early classic style. Only six looks walked the runway before an unexpected fire broke out, causing the warehouse to be evacuated. We have not been able to reach a representative from Amanda Ries's studio for comment."

I felt sick. The bacon churned in my stomach, and an acidic taste gurgled up into my throat. I filled a glass of water, chugged it, and then sat back down and clicked off the TV.

Only six looks had come down the runway. The sixth was Harper's kimono. There had been something off about that garment from the start. The poor fit, the assignation to Harper, and the refusal to alter it. The rest of the show had gone off as fashion shows do. Which made me think that someone had planned all along to use the kimono to start the fire.

Was that why I'd been attacked? Because someone didn't like the fact that I spoke up on behalf of Harper and asked for it to be altered? Because maybe someone had been planning all along to sabotage the show, and the kimono had been the trigger?

But rigging a garment to ignite on the runway in the middle of a show was a pretty out-there concept. I couldn't help thinking how many people had a stake in a fashion show's success: designer, financial backer, models, model management, venue, press. And every single one of these people had not only been there but had access. Would one of them gain more by destroying the show than helping to create it? What secret had been hidden amongst the garments and the shoes and the rose petals?

This wasn't the first disastrous runway show in fashion history. The year Lindsay Lohan was affiliated with Ungaro and failed to appear was bad. So was an early Michael Kors show when plaster fell from the ceiling of the loft where the show took place and landed on the heads of some high-profile models. But neither was this bad. A collection that quite literally went up in flames.

Amanda wasn't the luckiest of designers. A little over a year ago, she'd been favored to win a local design competition that never took place because one of the judges was killed. While she missed out on the cash prize, the publicity helped her land financial backers who funded her debut runway collection tonight. But like I said, luck wasn't on her side. People knew her name but little more. There might be no such thing as bad press, but for a designer, sooner or later you've got to prove your worth. Otherwise you're little more than a runner-up on a canceled reality show. No one quite remembers who you are.

It didn't take long for me to find out what everyone was talking about even though I was squirreled away at Dante's house. The local news, the internet, and the *Ribbon Times* fed me information. None of which compared to what I could find out from Eddie. I found my phone sitting on an end table and called him.

"Hey, dude," he said. "How are you feeling?"

"A little banged up but mostly okay."

"You heard about Amanda's show?"

I paused for a second, weighing the pros and cons of admitting that I'd ignored his cautionary words and had gone to Warehouse Five anyway. "I heard," I said.

"It was crazy, dude. People went nuts. I didn't think I was going to get out of there alive."

"You were there?"

"Tradava arranged for me to attend. I got there right when the lights went down."

Tradava was the reason I'd left my job as Senior Buyer for designer shoes at Bentley's New York. Well, maybe the chance to start over was the reason, but Tradava was the enabler. I wouldn't have quit my job in New York without something lined up in Ribbon, and when I'd landed that job, I'd felt the planets aligning to give me a chance to get on the road less traveled. It was either my greatest spontaneous decision or my greatest mistake; the jury was still out on which.

After landing the trend specialist job at Tradava, the fashion director who hired me was murdered, and everything went downhill from there. A year into my relocated life in Ribbon, I didn't know if I wanted to work for a company who had shown little (no) interest in employing me once the murder was cleared up. Still, they had benefits.

"Do you think you could do me a favor?" I asked.

"Sure. Are you still at the hospital? Need me to sneak in a meatball sandwich?"

"No. I—I went to the show last night too. With Dante. And now I'm at his apartment. Can you swing by my house and check on Logan?"

"I'm not sure which part of that to comment on first. You went home with Dante?"

"Yes, but it's not like that."

"I'm reminded of a phrase that includes frying pans and fires, but in light of what happened last night, to say it out loud might be in poor taste. Let's just say I hope you know what you're doing," he said. "And yes, I'll check on your cat on my lunch break."

"Thank you," I said. Tires crunched in the driveway out front. I peeked out the window. Dante's motorcycle pulled onto the bottom of the gravel-covered driveway and slowly snaked up to the house. "I'll call you back," I said and hung up.

I opened and shut a few drawers in Dante's kitchen, looking for a scrap of paper and a pen. I needed to take notes of what I remembered from Warehouse Five last night while the memories were still fresh. At home, I knew where I kept everything. In Dante's apartment, I was at a loss.

The third drawer down was filled with an assortment of cards and photos. And the photo on the top was of Dante, a pretty blonde, and a young boy. I flipped the photo over. In green pen was the caption "Dante, Linda, and Jameson."

I should stop. I knew I should stop. I should put the photo back in the drawer, close the drawer, take a Sharpie out of one of the cups next to sofa and write my notes on a napkin. But instead, I pulled out the next several photos. The blonde and the boy by a birthday cake. Jameson's 6th birthday. And one of Dante and the boy fishing. Happiness—and similar bone structure—evident in both of their faces.

The click of the door hijacked my attention, and the photo floated to the floor.

"I forgot my wallet," Dante said from the doorway.

"I was looking for a piece of paper," I said.

"Paper's in the bottom drawer."

"I didn't get to that one yet."

He walked over and scooped the photo from the floor. The open drawer was next to my thigh. He dropped the photo into the drawer and pushed it closed with his knee. I didn't move. When he stood, he was inches away from me.

"I have a son. He's seven now. He and his mom live in Philly."

I tried to act nonchalant, to pretend I wasn't curious or surprised, but I felt the heat climb my face and suspected that I was failing miserably. "I thought when you weren't here, you lived in Philly."

"I do."

"You're not married, are you?"

"No."

"Were you?"

"She and I didn't work. It's about what's best for Jameson."

"Do you see him often?"

"Weekends, mostly."

"But today is a weekend, and you're here."

"Something else came up."

I looked away, embarrassed. I was suddenly overwhelmed with questions that I had no right to ask.

"I'm sorry about the violation of your privacy," I said.

"No worries." He stepped away from me and glanced down at my T-shirt. I crossed my arms over my chest. He smiled. "How's the pain?"

"I'll deal. It'll get better."

"In time. With rest."

"And what happens in the meantime? Whoever did this gets away with it?"

"Gets away with what?" Dante prodded.

"I don't know."

"I've been thinking about it myself."

"And?"

"And I haven't reached any conclusions. You look like you have a couple of theories. Use me," he said, and cocked an eyebrow, "as a sounding board. Unless you want to use me for something else."

"We are not going to have that conversation while I have an assortment of internal injuries around my midsection."

"That's fair." He did a poor job of stifling a grin.

As much as Dante knew from his work with a private

investigator, this wasn't his world. It was mine. And I could use a
fresh perspective.

Ever since moving to Ribbon, I'd surrounded myself with
people who knew what the fashion world was like. Nick was a shoe
designer. Eddie was the visual director at Tradava. Cat owned an
off-price designer boutique. Every one of us accepted the
peculiarities of the industry as if they were normal. But here we
were, with a sabotaged fashion show in our own backyard. Nothing
normal about that. There was a possibility that Dante would listen
to me, that he'd help me see something I hadn't seen so far.

Or there was the possibility that he was playing with me the
way Logan played with the occasional chipmunk he caught in the
yard. Swat them, let them run a few steps away, then catch them
and swat at them again. I saw what Logan's game did to the
chipmunks. I didn't want that to happen to me.

Dante turned on the sink water and washed the dishes. He
transferred them to a drying rack that sat on his counter. "I can tell
you're wrestling with something," he said. "Let me know when you
want to talk."

I bit my lip and stared at the coffee table. I still had too many
questions I needed to work out.

"I'm going to take a shower," I said.

"Go crazy."

When I was done, I spritzed last night's dress with Dante's
cologne and put it back on. I dried my hair, pulled it into a low
ponytail, and then capped it with a gray houndstooth fedora from
the Justin Timberlake part of Dante's closet.

When I returned to the living room, Dante was on the sofa,
inspecting a camera and a couple of lenses on the table in front of
him. "Is that my hat?"

"It is."

"Looks good on you."

"Thanks." I scooped up the keys, pulled on my black wool coat, and headed to the front door.

"Where are you going?"

"Out." I paused by the door, not sure if he was going to tell me when to be back, or if I was going to tell him where I was headed. A few seconds passed, and I left.

I have never driven a sports car before in my life. The concept of being handed the keys to a Corvette Stingray, no strings attached, was slightly beyond my grasp. I sat in the soft leather bucket seat and ran my hands over the steering wheel several times before starting the car. The engine roared to life the way the lion roars at the beginning and end of MGM movies. I undid the parking break, put the car in gear, and coasted down the driveway. I pulled onto Duryea Drive and followed the winding road until eventually I made it out to the streets of downtown Ribbon. Minutes later, I parked in front of Amanda Ries's workroom.

What was I doing here? I wasn't sure. What I was sure of was that Amanda did not want to see me or talk to me. After the way she'd dismissed me the night before the show, and after her reaction to me at the hospital, it had been clear that we weren't destined to become friends who braid each other's hair. But I'd been attacked because of my affiliation with her. Maybe nobody else was trying to find out who had assaulted me, but I wasn't willing to let it go.

I got out of the car and locked the doors then followed the sidewalk up to the front entrance. I paused in front of the white front door and tried on greetings and explanations as to why I was there. Much like bathing-suit shopping after the holidays, none of them fit. Before I came up with the perfect salutation, the front door opened inward. Tiny stood in front of me, barely contained in the frame of the door.

"Don't just stand there," she said. "Come on in. We've been expecting you since last night."

7

____

AN UNATTRACTIVE
SHADE OF GREEN

I stepped backward and glanced at the sign mounted to the left of the front door. "ARS | Amanda Ries Studios," it read. I tried to look around Tiny but was unsuccessful.

"What do you mean you've been expecting me? Nobody knew I was coming here." *I* didn't even know I was coming here. "Who is 'we'?"

"Your reputation precedes you. Amanda knew you'd show up sooner or later." She handed the door to me and headed inside. She turned around again. "Coffee?" she asked.

"Sure."

She went into the next room. I unbuttoned my coat but left it on. The only time I'd been here before, Amanda hadn't invited me inside. She'd met me at the front door with a rolling rack of garment bags filled with samples and closed the door behind me.

This time I was inside and more than a little curious. I couldn't say what it was about Amanda that got to me, unless I did a little soul searching and acknowledged a basal jealousy that left me feeling an unattractive shade of green.

Amanda had attended I-FAD, the Institute of Fashion, Art, and Design, with Nick. I didn't know how much intimacy was included in their college history, but they had remained close long after graduation. Amanda was gorgeous, with sleek, long black hair parted on the side, her perfect size-four figure, her five-foot-nine frame in flats, though she rarely wore them. She could have been one of the models walking the runway like Harper instead of the designer producing the clothes, and the fact that she'd chosen the more creative of the two paths, and showed every indication of being successful at it, seemed an unfair bounty of talent. At least, that's what a petty person would think. I was doing my best not to be petty. For now.

Amanda's waiting area was a study in black and white. The carpet was black and ran wall-to-wall. The walls were a crisp contrast. Abstract paintings on unframed canvases filled the walls. A vintage bust form, covered in black patent leather, sat by the front window, as if to welcome visitors with its limbless figure.

"Here's your coffee," Tiny said. "Cream, no sugar. Right?"

"Right. How'd you know?"

"I watched you make it every day for the past six weeks."

I wondered what else Tiny might have noticed about me in those weeks. Did she think I'd seen something I shouldn't have seen? Did she have reason to want to scare me off? Tiny might have been over six feet tall, but that didn't mean she was above suspicion. I took the mug from her outstretched hand and blew on the hot liquid.

"Sam, before Amanda comes out here, I want to say something. We both appreciate the work you did on the show. Neither one of us considers you in any way responsible. I don't know if that was ever made clear."

"Responsible for what?"

"Your little stunt brought on some bad publicity. The day before the show, claiming to have been attacked in the parking lot."

"I was attacked."

Tiny held up her hands, palm-side out. "I guess we'll never know the truth, will we?" She crossed her arms over her gray sweater. The cuffs on her white oxford had been unbuttoned and folded back, exposing a black utilitarian sports watch. Whatever jovial vibe she'd started out with had been replaced. "Like I said, Amanda and I expected you to show up. What's your take on the fire?"

"Somebody sent me to the hospital the night before the show. I don't know who, and I don't know why. A day later, a fire at the warehouse destroyed Amanda's show. I don't believe that fire was an accident. When I was attacked, I was warned to 'stay out of it.' The only business I've been involved with for the past six weeks is Amanda's business."

"You'd do well to walk away from the whole thing," Tiny said.

"You said my reputation preceded me. That means you know I'm not going to leave this alone."

"I don't get people like you," she said, shaking her head. "You make things far more complicated than they need to be. Nobody's asking you to be a hero. Why not just get on with your life?"

It was in high school that I first learned that people don't expect you to take the hard way. I was on the track-and-field team. Before each meet, our coach would gather us in the gymnasium and call out the different events. If we planned to compete in one, we called out our last name and he wrote us in.

I was one of six girls who had been tagged long-distance runners. There were only two events for us: half mile and mile. Nobody wanted to run the mile. Ever. But one day I decided I would. Coach called out "mile," and I called out "Kidd." He looked up from his clipboard and held my expression for a few seconds. I shrugged in a "why not?" gesture. He smiled and wrote down my name. From that day on, I ran the mile every time we had a competition.

If I was going to do something, I was going to go the distance.

"Tiny, I'm not going to let this go until I have answers."

"If you won't walk away for yourself, then walk away for Amanda."

It was at that moment that Amanda appeared from the kitchen. "Tiny, you're wrong. If anybody can help me, it's Samantha."

"You're making a big mistake," Tiny said. She grabbed a cross-body nylon bag that was propped along the wall and stormed out the front door without a coat. I watched through the front window as she hunched her shoulders against the wind and climbed into a black SUV then drove away.

Amanda lowered herself into a leather chair behind her large glass-topped desk. A vase filled with orange roses like the ones at her runway show sat on the corner. She held out a white business-sized envelope. "This is probably what you came here for. Your check. Take it. You earned it."

I took the envelope, folded it in half, and tucked it into my handbag. "Amanda, I didn't have anything to do with the fire," I said. "But I'm not going to forget that somebody jumped me."

She stared at me with a sort of curiously distaste, like a first-timer to Paris when presented with frog legs. "I don't know who attacked you," she said. "But you must know something I don't. Something that will help me figure out what's going on."

"The way Tiny just stormed out of here. Was that normal?" I asked.

"What's normal these days? I found you barely conscious in the parking lot outside of Warehouse Five. Twenty-four hours later my show went up in flames. It's hard to believe the two aren't connected. Tiny's convinced you had something to do with the fire. When you pulled up out front, she wanted me to call the cops."

"What possible reason could I have for wanting to make myself look like a victim and then burn down your show?"

Amanda opened a different drawer and pulled out a tri-folded piece of paper. "Maybe you should take a look at this."

She held the paper between her first two fingers the way Mae West would have held up an unlit cigarette. I took the paper and unfolded it. In mismatched letters that looked like they'd been cut from magazines, glued to the page, and then run through a copier, the paper said:

AMANDA RIES: BURN, BABY, BURN!

8

REMARKABLY NORMAL

I sank into one of the chairs across from Amanda's desk. "When did you get this?" I asked.

"The first one came about a month ago."

"There are more?"

Amanda dropped her eyes to the glass desktop. She pulled her sleeve over her hand and wiped in circles at a ring from a mug that hadn't been set on a coaster. When she finished, she pulled the bottom drawer of her desk open and pulled out a small stack of white papers bound with a yellow rubber band. When she looked at me again, her face was the picture of worry.

"So far there are six."

"May I?" I asked.

She nodded, and I took the pile. After pulling the rubber band off, I flipped through the pages. Each one held a threat spelled out in mismatched letters like the first. I ran my finger over the smooth paper. I couldn't picture Fonts.com having an option that looked like a pre-technology cut-and-paste blackmail note. Whoever had painstakingly assembled these pages of threats had access to fashion magazines and a lot of time on their hands. Whoever had done this was making a point. I doubted it was coincidental that fashion was Amanda's business.

"Take them. I don't want to look at them anymore," she said.

"Does Tiny know about the letters?" I asked.

"No."

"Do the cops?"

"Whatever you might think of me, you need to know one thing. I am remarkably normal. When I get a cold, I go to the doctor. When I drive through a shady part of town, I lock the doors and roll up the windows. And if I receive threats that look like the work of someone with a screw loose, I go to the police. I don't share your attraction to danger."

"I wish people would stop saying that."

"It's true. You get off on the thrill in a way I don't understand."

I stood up and pushed my sleeves back so she could see the burn marks on my wrists. "Do you see this?" I asked. "This would never have happened if I wasn't at your dress rehearsal helping you with your runway show. It never would have happened if you weren't trying to get me to leave. I'm not here because I get off on the thrill of being hospitalized for doing you a favor. I'm here because I don't want the person who did this to me to get away with it."

"Samantha, I never dreamed you would get hurt. Of all people, you. The day before the show gets sabotaged too. If you would have stayed in the hospital, you wouldn't even have been there."

"What are you saying, Amanda? You don't believe me, do you?"

She leaned back and crossed her arms. "Why did you agree to work for me? I might have understood if you and Nick were still dating, but you broke up. Nobody would have judged you if you'd said no, considering the circumstances."

"You know that's not true. Everyone would have judged me.

Including you. If I hadn't shown up to help you after I said I would, you would have talked trash about me. And despite what you may or may not have heard, I have integrity. I know the fashion industry and was prepared to help you. And I did. End of story."

"A lot of people think the only reason you showed up was because you wanted to use me to get Nick back."

"If I were trying to get him back, the last place I'd be is here. Nick doesn't support my need to find answers."

"That doesn't affect you, does it? That he worries about you and the decisions you make?"

"I'm worried about the fact that I was attacked two nights ago. That's what I worry about."

Amanda dropped her eyes to the desk. She was hiding something. Did she know more about my attack but didn't want to tell me?

I pressed on. "There's an artist who rents space at Warehouse Five. He's been trying to get you banned from the building."

"Santangelo Toma. Tiny told me she'd take care of him."

"Take care of him how?"

"The same way she appeased the rest of the tenants. She offered them comp tickets to the show. Most of them were happy to accept."

"And Santangelo?"

"He tore up the tickets and threw them at her."

There was something hinky about Santangelo's behavior. I could understand him not being happy about the chaos Amanda and company brought to his studio space, but his animosity seemed disproportionate to the situation.

Before I could ask any more questions, a car pulled into the front driveway. I turned around and followed Amanda's stare out the picture window. The tall black man who'd been working with the models the night I was attacked got out of a midnight-blue

BMW. He slammed the door and walked to the Corvette. He stopped by the driver's side window and bent down to peer inside.

"He was backstage on Friday night. Who is he?" I asked.

"Oscar LeVay. He owns OLV model management. Tiny worked with him to cast the show."

"Which means he was there the night of the show too?"

"Yes. He's been there every night this week."

I couldn't tell if Amanda was thinking what I was thinking, but the word "opportunity" was flashing through my brain like it was the name of a new show in Vegas.

"Were you expecting him?"

"No."

"Then I want to stick around and hear what he has to say. Where can I hide?"

The doorbell rang. Before she made a move toward it, she reached out and put her hand on my forearm. "You can't tell anybody about this conversation." There was open desperation in her voice.

We stood two feet apart, eyes locked in a face-off where lines were drawn and crossed. If this had been a western, there would have been tumbleweed and the cry of a coyote.

"Done," I said. I scanned the interior of her studio and noticed a hinged wicker screen that partitioned off the corner of the studio by a rolling rack. "What's behind the screen?"

"Nothing. That's where models change when there's mixed company."

I moved to the corner and stepped behind the screen. "Let that guy in, and pretend I'm not here."

"Why?"

"Just do it."

I ducked behind the screen and wedged myself onto the floor behind a round wicker hamper. I hadn't noticed if the lighting created a telltale shadow that would give away my presence, but I figured it couldn't hurt to be as indiscreet as possible.

I heard Amanda open the door. "Oscar, hi. Tiny just left. Is there something I can help you with?"

Heavy footsteps marched into the room. The door closed. I pictured the well-appointed man in the room with Amanda and wondered how she could possibly hold her own against someone as imposing as him.

"Amanda, I took a chance by hiring out Harper to your show and look what happened. She was my top girl. Now she's fled the country. Do you know what this will do to my business? She's been with me since she was fourteen. I've spent years grooming her for the big time. Every day I face a firing squad of mothers who are afraid to trust their girls to me, and I've built my fortune on being able to maintain the safety of every model in my charge. I've lost that reputation because of you."

"Oscar, my collection was ruined. *My* reputation took a hit, not yours."

"And your name is in every news outlet from here to Manhattan. Publicity stunts only work once, my dear. I don't care what circumstances there were, I expect you to pay in full." His voice grew louder, and I imagined the effect his words and attitude had on Amanda. I wished I could see, but there was no way to do so without giving myself away.

Or was there?

Amanda had a large mirror hanging on the outside of the powder room, and the door was partially open because the room was vacant. I strained my neck until I picked up the reflection of the two of them in the middle of the room.

Oscar was a good six inches taller than Amanda. An ivory pashmina scarf was draped around his neck and tucked into the front of his coat. He held a tweed hat, shifting it from one hand to the other.

"Oscar, be reasonable. Tiny manages the billing."

"I don't trust her. She's been nickel and diming me over the models' fees since we started casting this show. You had twenty of my girls. They get two fifty an hour with a minimum five-hour booking per day. That's twenty-five grand for the fittings, twenty-five grand for the rehearsal, and twenty-five grand for the show."

Seventy-five thousand for models for the runway show? I knew the fashion industry was lucrative for lots of parties involved but not in towns like Ribbon. I didn't believe Tiny would have agreed to those rates and not renegotiated the event as a total. Unless Tiny was getting a kickback on the side from the arrangement. Regardless of the models' height, I had a feeling they were getting short shrift.

Oscar continued to rant. Even from a short distance I could see a gloss of sweat beading on his shiny forehead. "I should sue you for the damage you've done to my business. Harper was booked for the next year, and I'm going to lose those commissions."

Amanda's face went whiter than it had been. "Oscar, please calm down. I'll talk to Tiny when she returns, and I'll have her call you to discuss the situation."

"When will that be?"

"This afternoon."

"If I don't hear from her by three, I'm starting legal action against your company."

"That won't be necessary."

The doorbell rang. I couldn't see who had arrived, but I assumed if it was Tiny, she wouldn't have rung the bell.

"Excuse me," Amanda said. She disappeared from my sight.

Oscar moved closer to her desk. I ducked back, behind the screen, and held my breath. Had I left evidence of my presence behind? No. But there was one thing that I knew had been left on Amanda's desk: the threatening letters that she'd been mailed.

Maybe Oscar wouldn't see them. Maybe they'd be lost among the piles of invoices and sketches and notes scattered on the surface. "Oscar, I have to cut your visit short," Amanda said. "My lunch date is here."

"Tell Tiny I expect to be paid by the end of the week."

Footsteps sounded across the floor, and then the front door opened and shut. I stood up and stepped out from behind the screen.

The letters were missing.

9

───────

A JOKE AT MY EXPENSE

"Samantha, get back behind the screen. Now," Amanda whispered urgently. Something about her tone told me to act first and ask questions later. The door opened again, and before I could twist around and look in the mirror to see who had arrived, she spoke in a falsely bright, unexpectedly loud voice. "Nick, you're early for lunch. Let me get my things. Bye, Oscar!"

Amanda had said nothing about Nick being on his way.

This was bad. No, this was beyond bad. Wearing the clothes I'd worn last night, now scented with Dante's cologne, I might be sending signals that could be misinterpreted. I also realized that hiding in Amanda's studio, discussing the threat on her company, could be considered me seeking danger. This wasn't the time or the place for me to debate the merits of my personality. Even my signals were sending signals.

Amanda knew I was hiding behind the screen. I doubted she'd out me. I ducked further into the corner and slouched behind the hamper. I didn't need to see anything else. What I needed was an invisible cape.

The door shut. "Were we planning on lunch? I don't remember that," Nick said.

"Oscar was here to meet with Tiny, but she went out. I didn't want him to stay indefinitely, so I said that for his benefit. Have you already eaten?"

"We're actually going to lunch?"

"I think it'll look bad if we don't leave. I mean, we said we were going out. If he's watching, he'll expect us to leave. We should. Leave. We should leave so we don't look suspicious."

For the briefest moment, I was proud of Amanda. She was right. I didn't know what to make of Oscar's tirade, and I didn't yet know how he fit into the bigger picture, but she was thinking like I would have thought. Good for you, Amanda.

Nick didn't say anything at first, and I had to fight every impulse to lean forward to see his expression. "Sure, okay. You're right. Let's get some lunch."

"What's wrong? You're acting like I said something funny."

"Your reasoning reminded me of someone else." He paused. "That's the first time that ever happened."

"Do I want to know who?" Amanda asked.

"Probably not."

I gave them a ten-minute lead and then left out the back door. I stood by the side of the building until Nick's truck pulled out of the driveway, then I snuck to the Corvette and left.

While I drove, my mind wandered back to Oscar's insensitivity. He'd been more concerned about money than the wellbeing of his clients. Now I had four people I didn't trust: Tiny, Clive, Santangelo, and Oscar. It would have been easy for any of them to set both fires, the one that ignited me and the one that destroyed Amanda.

My mind wandered back to the threats Amanda had received. Had Oscar pocketed them? It was curious that she'd even shown them to me, but it was also painfully clear that she had unspoken reasons not to trust anybody else. I needed to find out more about everybody who had access to Amanda's show.

Without putting much thought into it, I ended up at Warehouse Five.

Amanda had negotiated use of several adjoining rooms and the main hall for the runway show. I wondered how many people had been put out of business thanks to the fire, and how favorably she'd be viewed for upcoming events. It was odd that Santangelo appeared to be more upset than the rest of the artists who used space at the warehouse to showcase their creations. I wondered if there was something else behind the resentment he'd shown toward Amanda.

I parked at the far end of the lot and approached the building. The recent cold weather had long ago killed any plant life that had grown around the perimeter of the building, leaving only loose pebbles and broken chunks of concrete scattered on top of the macadam. Yellow caution tape had been wound around rusted-out poles that marked the edges of the lot. The tape had broken, and two ends now snapped in the wind.

The first set of doors I tried was locked, as was the second. By the third, I concluded that the building hadn't reopened after the fire. I pressed my face up to the glass and squinted, trying to make out the interior. A bright pop of a flash bulb blinded me. I stood up straight and blinked several times, waiting for the dots in front of my eyes to clear. The door to the building opened, and Clive Barrington leaned out.

"Just don't stand there. Come in, if you're coming in."

"What are you doing here?" I asked. "As far as I can tell the building is locked up."

"Documenting the aftermath," he said, tapping his camera. "'Model Sizzles On and Off Runway,'" he said. "Or maybe 'Designer

Turns Up the Heat.' My contract gave me access to a much bigger story than documenting her twee show."

"Amanda knows what you have in mind?"

"I have unrestricted access and the freedom to do what I choose with the footage."

"I can't imagine anybody was happy about giving you access to come back today."

"Happy, no. I can't say they were either," Clive said with a grin.

"But yet, here you are."

"I can go anywhere Amanda went on one condition."

"What's that?"

"I turn over a copy of my photos to my new friend."

"Anybody I know?" I asked. Clive tipped his head toward a man who stood by the end of the building.

He was tall and thin and wore a tan sport coat over a white shirt and brown sweater. A brown, gray, and camel wool scarf was wrapped around his neck, and a camel tweed cap covered his head. The sleeves on his jacket were too short, as were the hems on his pants. Ichabod Crane came to mind. He stared at the windows of the building for a few seconds and then spoke into his phone.

"Who's he?"

"Arson investigator. He came with the cop."

That's when a second man stepped into view. Detective Loncar.

The detective appeared not to notice me at first, odd considering I'd been on his radar almost since the first day I arrived in Ribbon. Loncar and I had a history established through a couple of homicides. During at least one investigation, he'd filed me in the Person of Interest column. Considering my recent turn as victim, I thought the best tack was to let bygones be bygones and say hello. I excused myself from Clive and started across the loose gravel parking lot, wishing I had more practical shoes than the kitten-heeled boots I'd worn last night.

"Ms. Kidd. Why am I not surprised to see you here?" Loncar said before I reached him.

"Nice to see you, too, Detective," I called out. I walked past two orange cones and stepped over a white concrete beam that marked off a parking space. Loncar stayed where he was, looking at the exterior of the building. Unlike the arson investigator, Loncar wore a coat over his suit. The shoulders of his coat extended beyond his own shoulder line and sloped down above his arms. The cuffs of his pants broke across the front of his rubber-soled shoes. Considering his thick midsection, I would have suggested he avoid cuffs in the future, but he didn't appear to be in the mood for unsolicited fashion advice.

The arson investigator stepped forward and put his arms out on either side of him. "This is a restricted area. No access for the public."

Loncar turned to him. "It's okay," he said. "I got this one." He bowed slightly and held his hand out toward the parking lot. "Lead the way, Ms. Kidd."

I looked at the lot and back at him then carefully stepped over the loose gravel in my heels. When I reached the macadam, I turned to face the detective. "Do you have any leads?"

He didn't answer right away. Instead, he turned and looked at the building, then at the arson investigator, and Clive.

"What brings you here?" he asked when he finally turned his attention back to me.

"The fire. I was here when it happened. I thought I'd come back, look around, see if anything stood out to me as being off."

He crossed his arms. "Ms. Kidd, perhaps you'd like me to sponsor your application to the police academy?" Before I could answer, he continued. "Because otherwise I can't figure out why you keep showing up at my crime scenes."

It seemed we'd furthered our relationship. Detective Loncar made a joke at my expense.

"Detective, you should talk to me about this. I could help you."

"Ms. Kidd, we've been over this. The city of Ribbon employs me to perform a job. If you want to join my team, feel free to go through the proper channels. Otherwise, it's best if you learn that I'm not going to share information with you."

I glared at him for a few seconds and then walked away. He could certainly point out that he wasn't going to tell me anything, but to ignore my attack and the possible connection to the fire was a new level of cold. If he wasn't going to help me find answers, I was going to find them myself.

I approached Clive, who had continued to take pictures while I was gone.

"How much is Amanda paying you?" I asked.

"We worked out a special rate." He smiled with half of his mouth and glanced down at my body, as if he were implying that the exchange involved something other than money. "I could work out the same rate for you if you're interested."

I wouldn't have minded learning some dirt about Amanda but considering how high Clive rated on my Sleaze-O-Meter, I could hardly believe what he was insinuating.

"Is there any way I could get a copy of your film too?" I asked.

"Not bloody likely. I'm afraid that's not in my power to negotiate. Hello, Inspector Gigger," he finished.

I turned to my left. The arson investigator had approached when I wasn't looking and now stood by my elbow. Loncar stood to his side and didn't look happy. Not that he usually exuded sunshine and daisies, but today, his attitude was more gutters and weeds than usual.

Ichabod Crane spoke up. "Mr. Barrington, I don't know what you're discussing with this woman, but I think it's important to point out that the photos you're taking are part of my arson investigation and are no longer your property."

"I can appreciate your position, Inspector. I'd rather give my film to you than to her any day. But I am a bit baffled as to why you don't want to talk to her."

"Why would we want to talk to her?"

"She's had as much access to the scene as I have."

Inspector Gigger looked at me with new interest. Clive pointed his camera at the building and the shutter clicked several times.

"He's right," I said. "I'm Samantha Kidd. Detective Loncar knows me. I've been working with Amanda Ries on her runway show. And before you think I had something to do with the fire, let me assure you, my only interest is in finding out who attacked me the night before the show."

Loncar scratched his head. "You were attacked, here, two nights ago?"

"Yes."

"If I go back to the station, will I find a police report?"

"Yes."

Clive stepped closer. "Go ahead and tell the detective how you were the victim in all of this. That's what you want everybody to believe, right?" He elbowed me in the ribs, and I doubled over in pain.

I coughed twice, blinked back tears, and fought waves of nausea. Clive stepped back and looked surprised. I felt Loncar's hand on my back.

"You okay?"

I held up my hand, and then slowly, I stood. "I'll survive."

"You're done here," Loncar said to Clive.

"I'll expect copies of your photos in my inbox this afternoon," Gigger added.

Clive looked back and forth between their faces. "That's not the arrangement. You can't revoke my access."

"Mr. Barrington, I've been over your contract. Page four, third paragraph. Ms. Ries retained the right to replace you," Loncar said. For the briefest of moments, I saw him as my hero and overlooked his unfortunate cuff choice.

"That's right. If she wants to replace me, she's the one who has to do it. Not you," Clive said. "And not him." He pointed to Gigger.

A light bulb went off in my head. "Amanda already retained a new photographer." All three men looked at me. "Dante Lestes. I know you saw him at the show. He was sitting next to me when you took the photos before the show started. You waved at him, and then you went backstage. Come to think of it, that was right before the fire started."

"If Amanda wants to replace me, she should have told me."

Clive's elbow-to-the-injury move had left me angry and vindictive, and I hit him where it hurt. "She did. Maybe you were mad at her and set the fire yourself? As a way to get back at her?"

Clive looked like he'd bitten into a rotten lemon. He turned and spit onto the gravel behind him. "I don't have to listen to your accusations." He put his camera in a black nylon duffle bag.

Loncar looked at me. "Do I know this Mr. Lestes?"

"I don't think so. But I can arrange an introduction if you'd like."

Loncar studied me for a few seconds and then turned to Clive. "Mr. Barrington, I'm going to follow up with Ms. Ries, and I suggest you do the same."

The cockiness that had come with Clive's all-access pass vanished, and in its place was a scowl. I thought back to what Dante had told me about Clive. Was he a predator among the models? Most of them could take care of themselves, but Harper had been the loner. Had he been after her? Would my constant interference have angered him enough to assault me in the parking lot?

I knew he'd be calling Amanda sooner rather than later, and if she was in a vulnerable state, he would convince her she needed him. I had to get to her first and explain why it would be a very bad idea for Clive Barrington to remain part of her inner circle. The good news was Dante could step in without missing a beat, as long as he had nothing else on his plate.

"Detective, you don't need me to stick around, do you?" I asked Loncar. He looked at me like he thought I was nuts. "I just remembered I have to make a couple of phone calls, and you probably have things to do here. I imagine you don't want anybody who isn't on the force hanging around trying to figure things out on their own."

"Not so fast," he said. He looked past me at Clive and didn't speak until after the photographer had backed out of his space, turned around to glare at us, and driven away. "I'm going to get Ms. Kidd's statement," he said to Gigger. The arson investigator nodded and walked away.

"New partner?" I asked.

"Ms. Kidd, my superiors think last night's fire was an accident. I don't want to encourage you, but I don't agree with them."

"How would that encourage me?"

"I have no authority here. Inspector Gigger is an arson investigator for the Pennsylvania Arsonists Association. He's using my office and my resources. He has full cooperation from the department. As far as my captain is concerned, there is no ongoing criminal investigation from our office."

"There was a fire here last night, and Amanda told me about the threats to her company."

"What threats?"

"Letters that somebody's been sending her. She said she told the police about them."

"First I've heard of them."

"Amanda showed them to me. I don't know if it's related, but two nights ago I was attacked backstage at her rehearsal. Then there was the fire. I think the two things are connected. Even if she hadn't confided in me, I'd be looking for answers."

"She confided in you? Why would she do that?"

"I don't think she trusts anybody else. No offense."

A few beats of silence passed between us. I hadn't planned on making it sound like Loncar couldn't do his job. Truth was, I knew he could, but now hardly seemed the time to offer an apology. Perhaps a nice manly arrangement of flowers delivered to the precinct tomorrow would be better.

"I can advise you to mind your own business, but since there's no investigation, I can't do much about it if you don't."

"You always tell me to mind my own business. You tell me to steer clear of your investigation for my own good. This time, I've already been attacked and hospitalized before there even was an investigation."

He wiped his arm across his brow. "Officially, I have nothing to say. Unofficially? You're in dangerous territory, and there's pretty much nothing I can do about it."

10

SHOULD HAVE SAID NO

"You just said you had no authority here, but I bet you want to know what happened, right?" I said. "I was here. I've been here all along. Whoever attacked me told me to stay out of it. That means somebody thinks I know something about something. And I bet that something has to do with whatever happened here. I bet I could help you. Ask me something. Go ahead, ask."

He glared at me. "As much as I hate to admit it, you've got a knack for this stuff. And after that article on you in the paper, my boss won't get near you with a ten-foot pole. He says you're making us look bad. Just do me a favor? If you figure anything out, keep me in the loop."

I'd experienced a certain amount of notoriety since moving back to Ribbon, and what at first seemed like a case of bad timing had turned into a mild celebrity status. Carl Collins, reporter for the *Ribbon Times*, had done a small profile on me after I'd saved the local museum considerable embarrassment over an exhibit of hats on loan from a Hollywood actress. I leveraged my newfound local fame into a side gig. When not working for Amanda, I acted as personal shopper and stylist to Ribbon's fashion challenged. It covered my immediate budgetary needs and allowed me to splurge on the occasional heavily discounted off-season garment at the Ribbon Outlet Center. Even Logan had traded up in his quality of life, his kitty bed now lined in cast-off cashmere sweaters beyond repair.

"No problem." I looked behind me at where Clive's car had been. My announcement that he'd been replaced had started a ticking clock, and I needed to talk to Amanda and Dante. "Detective, I have to go," I said. I waited another second to see if he had any last words of warning for me and hopped back and forth from foot to foot so he'd think I had to pee.

"Be careful, Ms. Kidd," he said.

I drove half a mile down the street, pulled the car over to the shoulder, and called Amanda. After four rings, her service picked up. I hesitated before talking. What if Nick was still there? What if Tiny heard the message? I hung up and redialed. This time she answered.

"Amanda Ries Studio," she said.

"This is Samantha. Can you talk?"

"What is this in reference to?" Her tone was curt.

I guessed from her answer that she was not alone. "I found Clive Barrington lurking around Warehouse Five. There were cops too. One I know. The other was an arson investigator. I sort of made it sound like you had replaced Clive with another photographer."

"Please hold," she said. I was treated to a soft jazz version of a Billy Idol song, which was almost as offensive as her rudeness. She picked back up before the song ended. "I'm back. I'm sorry about that back there, but Nick was here. I told him it was Tiny on the phone."

"Where is he now?"

"He just left. Tell me what's going on."

"Okay." I told Amanda about Clive's presence at Warehouse Five but left out the part about Detective Loncar having no authority at the crime scene. Loncar felt like an unlikely ally, but in a way, I felt a loyalty to him. Weird. "Clive said you granted him unlimited access. Is that true?"

"Yes. When we started the whole thing. Tiny set it up. She said, depending on what pictures he took, we could use them for publicity. She had to get him access to the warehouse for when we weren't there, too, because he said there would be times when he wanted the quiet before the storm, you know, when none of us were there. There's not much he hasn't seen."

"That means Clive could have gotten into the warehouse and rigged the platform before your show."

"Why would he do that?"

"I'm not asking why yet. I'm just asking if he could."

"Sure, he could. But so could a lot of people. Your friend Eddie had access too. Tradava loaned me the mannequins that sat in the lobby. And the food service people came in early, and there are other artists that show their work in Warehouse Five, so they could have gotten in—"

"I only want to know about Clive right now. Has he given you any footage so far? Any preliminary photos to approve?"

"He gave Tiny some preliminary backstage shots to use early on. She handled everything that didn't involve the actual collection so I wouldn't have to be bogged down in details. She has his contract."

"Can you get it to me?"

"Sure. Is that all?"

"No. Dante Lestes is going to be your new photographer." I chewed my lower lip and debated whether to tell Amanda the truth about Dante. "He's a legitimate photographer, and you can trust him." I arranged to come by her office tomorrow morning and ended the call. Phase one, complete.

I started the Stingray and headed back to my house. The smell of my clothes was making me ill. Or maybe it was something else. Maybe it was the truth about my life starting to sink in.

Since the breakup with Nick, I'd been keeping myself busy, trying not to think about how things had gone wrong. But trading one relationship for another didn't feel right either. I hadn't mourned Nick and my breakup, and a part of me wondered if a meltdown was lingering under the surface.

Six weeks ago, things had been great. Nick and I had moved into steady-date-Saturday-night territory, and I'd stupidly traded on our relationship and asked him to put me on his payroll.

Nick was a high-end shoe designer. He had started his career working for a few top designers and eventually landed a position as creative director for a French couture house which was expanding from apparel into the accessories market. After he'd built up a name for himself, he literally sold off that name to a couple of financiers. He'd received professional recognition and cemented his fan base but felt he'd lost some of his creative control.

Nick had been one of the designers in my vendor matrix when I worked for Bentley's New York. There'd been chemistry from the first time we met in front of his showroom, but our positions in the industry kept us on our respective sides of the don't-cross line. It wasn't until after I left Bentley's and moved to Ribbon that we reconnected. He had bought back distribution of his company and invested every dime he had into a relaunch of his brand. I'd given up my lucrative career at Bentley's to become the trend specialist at Tradava. By all measures, we were both experiencing new beginnings, and the timing for a relationship finally seemed right.

And then we'd found the body of the man who had hired me, and I spent some time wondering if Nick was capable of murder.

Turns out that's a biggie when it comes to determining if a relationship is on the horizon.

After that was cleared up—and after the six months he spent in Italy—I was ready to address my affections. Things were fine until I started working for him. Too much togetherness. Ultimately, we broke up.

And then he told me he'd given my name to Amanda to help with her runway show.

And now, forty-four days later, I was dealing with the aftermath.

Amanda Ries was everything I wasn't: classically beautiful, financially successful, and an upstanding law-abiding citizen who didn't question authority. She and Nick had gone to design school together. I still didn't quite believe him when he said they never had a romantic relationship. She was Barbie-doll pretty, with sleek black hair that fell to her waist and proportions that didn't come from pizza and meatball sandwiches. I couldn't compete with someone like that. And because I wanted to prove that I was a class act, despite every instinct I had, I took the job.

The ironic thing was that I had to turn away business to fulfill my commitment. But that's not what this was all about. Nick had asked me to help Amanda, and that had felt good. He'd probably expected me to say no.

I should have said no.

I should have said no, pretended he'd never asked, and gone about my business.

But I didn't. Because Amanda, aside from being Nick's maybe-former girlfriend, was a talented designer, and after a year of false starts in jobs that fell short of my own expectations, I recognized that working with her would allow me to fall back on my passion for the industry. I had a high-taste level, proven instincts on trends, and was a good at multitasking. Besides, confronting my pettiness about Amanda's relationship with Nick was like putting a pin in it. At least that's what I'd hoped.

I pulled up in front of my house. I'd been planning to park the Stingray in the garage, but a brown minivan was in the driveway. I drove past the house, pulled into my neighbor's driveway, backed out, and parked by my mailbox.

A disheveled woman in a hooded coat stood by the door to my garage. "Samantha Kidd?" she asked.

"Yes."

She pushed the hood off her head. "I'm Molly Diers. I need help. I would have made an appointment, but I finally got a sitter, and it's an emergency. Can we do this?"

It took the better part of a minute for my brain to switch gears from arson and attack to the styling needs of my small town. If the woman in front of me hadn't appeared so in need of fashion help, I might not have ever made the connection.

Molly Diers wore an oversized olive-green snorkel coat over a pair of pants printed with superheroes. Her feet were shod in dirty camel Ugg boots that had seen better days, and there was a smudge of something green on her cheek.

"Follow me," I said. I unlocked the garage door and walked across the concrete floor to the door that opened at the top of the basement. A wooden staircase led down to my converted home office.

When I first moved back into the house, the basement had held several mismatched bookcases filled with magazines, memorabilia, and paint cans. The basement had flooded, thanks to my parents never having the foundation sealed, and most of the contents had been damaged to the point of ruin. I'd arranged for a trash pick-up and tossed everything but the clothes I made in high school.

Once emptied, I was left with a twenty-foot-long room with exposed brick walls. Five packs of yellow rubber gloves, several bottles of vinegar, a jug of bleach, and an industrial fan had removed traces of the flooding. Now the walls were decorated with fashion sketches, the room where my dad had brewed his homemade wine had been turned into a fitting room, and the rest of the space had been outfitted with bars for clothing samples and shelves for accessories. A discarded architect's table served as my desk.

Molly followed me down the stairs. I flipped to a blank page on a yellow legal pad.

"Have a seat. Let's talk about what you want."

"That's easy. I want to look good again. You should have seen me back in the day. Fashion was my life. I've been married for seven years, and the bastard left me. After two boys, I don't even feel like a woman anymore."

I jotted *single mother-seven years-woman* on the legal pad and underlined "woman" three times. "Tell me about your daily routine."

"I get up, feed the hellions, get them off to school. Five hours later I pick them up."

"What do you do all day?"

"I pick Cheerios out of my hair." I considered writing that part down. "Do you have kids?" she asked.

"No."

"Then you don't understand. You have no idea what a terror two boys can be. They wreck everything. Everything. Meanwhile, my rat ex-husband already has a new girlfriend half his age. He gets the boys every other weekend and the boys think he's a god. What do I do all day? Once I get them off to school, the house is quiet. I can relax. I have five hours to pretend my life turned out differently."

Molly Diers didn't need a stylist, she needed a therapist. "How do you dress now?" I asked.

"You're looking at it. If it doesn't have an elastic waist, I'm not interested."

I felt like I was on the *Punk'd* version of *What Not to Wear*.

"I have to be honest, Molly. I don't think we're going to be much of a match, style-wise."

"You can't turn me away. I need tough love. I read about you in the paper. You take on killers and whackos and police, and you lived in New York. When I was fourteen, I used to walk around my house with a book on my head. These days, high fashion is a T-shirt without a stain. Besides, the boys are back in school, and I need to look like I can hold down a job. I need you."

Already I felt bad for turning her down. I looked at my calendar. Amanda's name had been written in, but that job ended with the runway show. I flipped the page to next week and the week after that. All clear. If it wasn't for Molly Diers, what would I be doing? Looking for arsonists, flirting with Dante, and pining away over Nick.

Maybe I needed Molly Diers too.

"Fill out this questionnaire, and then let's set up a schedule for you."

I handed her a clipboard with a couple sheets of paper on it. Molly looked relieved. I pulled three tissues out of a box on the corner of my desk and handed them to her. "There's something green on your cheek."

"There's always something green on my cheek." She scrubbed her cheekbone until the green went away, leaving fresh pink skin.

I didn't know how other personal stylists worked, but when I hung out my shingle, I assumed I could figure it out as I went. I compiled binders of looks that represented the fashion identities I'd once learned from a Cosmo quiz: Casual, Fashion Forward, Bohemian, and Powerful. My personal style ran along the lines of whimsy, but my goal wasn't to have my clients dress like me.

I sat Molly in a comfy purple velvet chair and handed her a stack of binders. Day One involved identifying the way she wanted to dress, the sizes she wore, and the budget she had in mind. I'd shop and put together what I felt was the basis for a new wardrobe to suit her needs. My take was ten percent of her spend.

While she was busy with the binders, I snuck off to the back corner of the basement and called Dante.

"Where are you?" he asked.

"I'm at my house."

"I thought we had an arrangement."

"No, you had an arrangement. I had a need to change my clothes and see my cat. I'll be done here soon." I glanced at Molly. She had her nose buried in Bohemian. "Can you come over in about an hour?"

"Sure."

Molly and I finished our first consultation, and she wrote me a check to cover my initial consulting fee. I thanked her, we set up an appointment three days away, and I walked her out. Dante's motorcycle pulled into the driveway next to her car as we were saying goodbye.

"Is he yours?" she asked.

"I'm not sure."

"I don't think I'll ever be ready for a man like that."

That made two of us.

11

—————

ULTERIOR MOTIVES

I waited until Molly drove away before I led Dante into the house.

"You rang?" he asked.

I held my finger up in a just-a-minute gesture. I was hungry. I opened and closed cabinets looking for food and came up with a box of Snyder's of Hanover sourdough pretzels. I pulled a fat pretzel out and held the box toward Dante. He waved them off. I bit into the round loop of a full pretzel and leaned back against the counter.

"I talked to Amanda today," I said. "She's been getting threats at her studio."

"What threats?"

"Written. They look like old-fashioned ransom notes with letters cut out of magazines, but whoever made them kept the original and sent her a copy. I'm guessing it's because whoever did it didn't want to leave fingerprints."

"Nobody's going to take the time to cut letters out of a magazine."

"They did. I saw them. The most recent said 'Burn, baby, burn!' I don't think it's much of a coincidence that her runway show went up in a blaze of glory."

Dante leaned back against the chair. "Why are you still helping Amanda?"

"Because I said I would. I made a commitment."

"The job is over."

Breakup Rule #4: Don't get into your last relationship problems with the potential new guy. Logan was the only one who heard the gory post-breakup details. Maybe if Dante and Logan bonded enough, I could leave the explanation to my cat.

"The fire investigator is trying to determine whether the runway fire was an accident or arson. Even if it was intentional, nobody was hurt, so it's not a homicide investigation."

"Have you talked to any of the models?"

"No."

"Not even Harper? Weren't you two close?"

"Harper was a loner among the girls. We weren't close, but she didn't seem to have any other friends. Besides, Harper is in Mexico. Why?"

"Samantha, I can understand your desire to figure this out, but there's something else driving you here, and you're not telling me what it is."

I looked down at my hands. "The attack was personal. Someone was in the parking lot waiting for me. Someone wanted to hurt me, and I don't know why."

"You might never know why."

"How am I supposed to move on if I don't know if it'll happen again? How do I know somebody isn't watching me every time I leave my house?"

"All the more reason to stay at my place."

"I'm not going to hide," I said. "But I can't live my life constantly looking over my shoulder either. I don't know how anybody could expect me to."

"What's your plan?"

"My plan?"

"I figure after your meeting with Amanda you came up with a plan. You asked me here because I'm a part of it." He stared at me for a few seconds. Logan climbed from the table onto Dante's leg and then onto the ground. Dante never broke eye contact with me. "Unless I'm wrong, and I wouldn't mind being wrong."

I felt my face grow warm. "I told Amanda to fire Clive and bring you on as her photographer. I need somebody on the inside. Clive was at Warehouse Five today—"

"You went to Warehouse Five? That's a crime scene."

"I know. Detective Loncar was there with an arson investigator."

"I can't imagine either one of them was happy with you walking around."

"Happy? No, but after Clive elbowed me in the ribs, Loncar took my side."

"He what?" Dante gripped the table and his knuckles turned white. His sleeves rode up, and the flame tattoos around his wrists throbbed with his pulse.

I waved my hand. "It's good that he did. I don't think the detective believed me until he saw I was in pain."

Dante looked like he wanted to put his fist through something. Maybe a wall, maybe Clive's face.

"He's out of the picture. You're in his place. Can you do that?"

"You said Clive was hired to document the show from inception to completion? Sure, I can step in."

"You'll need to get pictures of whatever you can if we're going to crack this thing."

He leaned back. "I'll get pictures of samples, sketches, and

Amanda's showroom. If she'll give me a list of everybody she employed, I'll get interviews on film. Clive probably turned something over to her already. That's standard procedure."

I didn't know what to say. I'd gotten so used to everybody telling me I shouldn't be involved that I wasn't prepared for Dante to take me seriously. "Is that okay?" Dante asked.

"Sure."

"Great. I'll tell her I need to see whatever he's done so I can stay true to the style of the initial photography and keep the change of photographers seamless." He sat back in the chair and put his hands behind his head. "That should give us a good start if we're going to 'crack this thing.'" He smiled.

"Take pictures of everything you can. The fire happened after the attack. Did I see something backstage, and the fire was set to cover it up, or was someone planning to set the fire, and they wanted me gone before it happened?"

"You need to be careful. If you're right and somebody targeted you, they're not going to like knowing you're poking around their business."

"I know."

We stared at each other for a few seconds, until I broke eye contact and focused on my pretzel. I snapped off the other loop and bit into it. Pretzel dust covered the front of my shirt. I dusted it off, chewed, and swallowed the lump of dough. I felt better already.

"What now?" Dante asked.

"You need to go to Amanda's studio, introduce yourself, and get the lay of the land. She doesn't know I confided in you. Right now, she thinks you're a fashion photographer who can replace Clive."

"I'm your man on the inside."

"That's what I'm counting on. Be on the lookout for Tiny, Amanda's business manager, and anybody else who comes along.

There was a tall black man there today named Oscar LeVay. He owns the agency where Tiny hired the models, and he expects Amanda to pay him seventy-five grand for the show even though it didn't take place. He may have taken the letters from Amanda's desk."

Dante's eyebrows went up.

"I was hiding behind a screen when Oscar arrived. When he left, the letters were gone."

"If she went to the police about the letters, they would have kept them."

"Maybe that's why the ones I saw were copies."

"Did you see this Oscar guy take them?"

"No. I don't even know if he saw them. But if he saw them, and he was responsible for sending them in the first place, he might take them to hide the evidence."

"Did you tell Amanda that?"

"No."

"Why not?"

Because Nick was there. "The timing wasn't right," I said out loud.

"Anything else you can tell me?"

"Clive wasn't happy when I dropped your name."

"You leave Clive to me."

I walked Dante to the front door. "Thank you for helping me," I said.

"Samantha, just because I'm helping you doesn't mean I don't have ulterior motives."

"Meaning?"

He put his fingers on my chin, tipped my head back, and kissed me. On the few occasions when I thought about what it would be like to kiss Dante, I imagined heat-of-the-moment, back-up-against-a-wall type stuff. Like kissing Brando in *The Wild One.*

It was just like I'd imagined.

The world melted into nothingness, and the room spun, leaving me dizzy. It was enough to make me forget the name of that shoe designer who'd been on my mind a lot lately. When Dante pulled away, he looked me straight in the eyes. I blinked twice and then looked down at his chest. He pulled on his motorcycle helmet, flipped the visor down, and left.

I took a shower, put on clean undies, and checked my reflection in the foggy mirror. My injuries, though invisible, felt like a corset around my waist, and the elastic on my panties dug into my chicken finger, ice cream, and waffle weight gain. I moved my gaze from my torso to my face. The person staring back at me looked like a stranger. Where was the happy- go-lucky buyer who turned projects in on time and hit her end-of-quarter target inventory levels? Where was the overachiever who met sell-through expectations and gross margin goals? Where was the woman who could travel three cities on the contents of one carry-on suitcase and stay under the company per diem of sixty dollars a day?

She was gone, a distant memory. In her place was an unemployed job seeker with a muffin top.

Since moving to Ribbon, I'd been suspected of murder, used as a plant in a counterfeiting ring, and trapped in a museum. I'd started a relationship I had long daydreamed about and was pretty much responsible for sabotaging it before it got off the ground. My friends had gone ignored since the attack. Life as I knew it was out of control. I hadn't even called my parents in California to tell them I'd been hospitalized. I didn't want to give anybody any reason to criticize my life. I was becoming isolated. And somewhere along the way, that had become okay.

As the fog cleared from the mirror, I focused on my reflection. I looked older than I had when I worked at Bentley's, and it had only been a little over a year. My brown hair hung past my shoulders, limp, unkempt. I'd gone from maintenance trims every six weeks to pulling it into a ponytail and ignoring it. My eyes looked tired. My brows needed shaping. My skin looked dull. And don't get me started on my pedicure.

I ran a thick comb through my hair and secured it into two low ponytails on either side of my head. Without stopping to overthink things, I picked up a pair of scissors and sliced through the hair on the left side of my head. *Whack!* Right below chin level. The hair bobbed up around my face. The right side of my hair was long, serious, and staid in comparison.

I held my hand up to cover the left hand side of the mirror. The person who stared back at me with long straight hair was a stranger. She had seen things I never expected to see and had lived through things I never expected to live through. She looked light-years older than I'd been when I moved back into this house.

I moved my hand to cover the right-hand side of the mirror. The woman I saw looked fresh. Perky. Ready for anything. Unfettered by straightening irons and blow driers and the fight against killers and naturally curly hair.

I took the scissors to the ponytail on the right and snipped through the wet hair. The natural curls sprung up, making the hair instantly wavy. I squirted a handful of mousse into my palm and rubbed it onto my strands. I followed with a tinted moisturizer, mascara, and dark red lipstick, and blow-dried my hair upside down. When I flipped back up, I looked at the stranger in front of me. She looked like someone who didn't care so much that she'd been in the hospital two nights ago. She looked like she might have a plan. I didn't have a plan, so I liked the girl in the mirror even more.

I dressed in pajamas and went to the kitchen for a glass of wine. So what if it was only three thirty? That was practically happy hour.

I downed the first glass and poured a refill. After the second, I had a good idea. I would call Nick. Just to say hi.

I ignored the voice that said two glasses of wine plus one call to an ex-boyfriend was not only a not good idea, it was plain old bad math. When his message came on, I pulled myself together. "Hi, Nick. It's Samantha." I stopped. What was I thinking? I ended the call and stared at the phone.

That went well. Not.

Seconds later my cell buzzed with a text: *Sorry didn't answer. At Brothers Pizza. Come join if you're not busy.*

I tried to text back something that communicated that I missed him and was looking forward to seeing him but not let on that I'd kissed Dante. I ended up going with: *See you soon.*

I stood up and stumbled. Maybe it hadn't been a good idea to drink wine on a stomach filled only with pretzels. And maybe it wouldn't be a good idea to drive to Brothers Pizza. How far away was it? I rolled my eyes up while I tried to calculate if I could walk, lost balance, and landed on the sofa. No, maybe it wasn't a good idea to walk either.

I called Eddie. "Yo," I said when he answered. "Do you want to go to Brothers?"

"Can't. I'm pulling an all-nighter at Tradava. Pizza does sound good, though."

"I'm meeting Nick, and I could use some backup."

"Did he call you, or did you call him?"

"I called him."

"And?"

"And he texted back and told me to join him." I waved my hand around, not necessary since he couldn't see me. "I just want to talk to him."

"About what?"

"Nothing."

"Are you okay?"

I spun around and caught my reflection in the microwave. The stranger who might have a plan looked back at me. "I'm great. I chopped off all my hair," I said. And then I hiccupped.

"Dude, don't go anywhere. I'll be there in ten minutes."

12

CAKE WITHOUT ICING

Eddie arrived quickly. When I opened the door, his eyes moved around to the left, right, and top of my head.

"You weren't kidding," he said. "Follow me." He charged inside and started up the stairs.

"Aren't we getting pizza?"

"Not yet."

"Where are we going?"

"The bathroom." I stopped halfway up the stairs. He reached the landing and turned around. "How to put this gently," he said, drumming his fingers on his chin. "The right side of your hair is an inch shorter than the left. Come on."

I climbed the remaining stairs and entered the bathroom behind him. My two chopped-off ponytails lay next to the sink like a sacrifice to the beauty gods. Eddie stared at them for a few seconds, shut the lid of the toilet, and instructed me to sit facing the wall. He combed my hair and separated it into sections. I felt him tug on the length, and then I heard a series of snip, snip, snips. He repeated the process toward the back left of my head and then the back right.

"Aren't you going to ask me why I did it?" I asked.

"Dude, someone put you in the hospital a couple of days ago, you almost got burned down at Amanda's runway show, and you're fresh from a breakup with Nick. So you freaked out. I'm surprised you didn't dye it purple."

He tipped my head forward, and I felt the cold metal scissor blades against the back of my neck.

"Do you know what you're doing?" I asked.

"I style the mannequin wigs at Tradava. Now, sit still and shut up."

Eddie lined up the jagged edges of my butchered haircut. I hiccupped again.

"What have you eaten today?"

"Wine and pretzels. Are you almost done back there?" I waved my hand around behind my head, feeling the layers.

He swatted my hand away and set the comb and scissors on the counter. Like an expert stylist, he threaded his fingers into the back of my hair and shook it from side to side. "Turned out pretty well, all things considered."

"Great. Let's go." I stood up and swung my leg over the toilet seat like I was dismounting a horse.

"You might want to put on clothes first," he said, pointing to my pajamas.

I went to my bedroom while Eddie went downstairs. In my closet, I shoved my collection of candy-colored pumps to the side and stared at a pair of Doc Martens I'd bought in the nineties. Black leather lined in red plaid. They were tough. They were don't-mess-with-me shoes. That's what I needed. I also needed a don't-mess-with-me outfit.

I changed into an oversized red V-neck sweater that I turned backward, and a pair of black skinny jeans. I looked in the mirror at my reflection. My hair was already mostly dry, hanging in waves around my head.

Something was off. I found a black beaded necklace shaped to look like a peter pan collar and tied it around my neck. Long black ribbons dangled down my exposed back. I folded the cuffs of the Docs down so the red plaid lining showed.

"What's taking you so long?" Eddie called up the stairs.

I knew exactly what was taking me so long. The wine buzz was wearing off, and in its place was self-consciousness. What had I intended to accomplish by calling Nick? If I was being honest with myself, I'd say I wanted attention. I wasn't ready to be honest just yet.

I jogged down the stairs, gave Logan a can of Fancy Feast, ate another pretzel to calm my nerves, and we left.

It took seven minutes to get to Brothers Pizza. On a good day, when the lights cooperated with my need for cheese and dough, I could get there in four. Tonight, I welcomed the additional three. They gave me a chance to cycle through all the potentially disastrous outcomes for the evening.

"Why did I think this was a good idea?" I said to Eddie.

"Because you like drama, and you thrive on chaos."

"It was a rhetorical question."

We crossed the lot and went inside. Eddie wasn't used to me walking so fast (thank you, Docs) and had to jog to keep up with me. I pulled the door open and waited a second for my eyes to adjust to the dim interior.

Brothers was my favorite pizza place in all of Ribbon. They had opened in 1971 and appealed to every generation of locals since then. The interior was classic old-school Italian, with Chianti flasks and plastic ivy hanging from the ceiling. The wallpaper was pink flocked with burgundy. The configuration was long and narrow, with booths on the right-hand side, tables on the left, and a couple of pinball machines next to sliding-glass doors that led to the outside seating. An internet juke box, the only modern addition to the place, stood next to the bar, halfway to the back.

Booths were red vinyl and tables were wood. Initials, expressions, and a couple of phone numbers were carved into most of them. The seven pizza ovens were in constant use and contributed to the scent of tangy tomato sauce, oregano, and basil. They probably had the fixings for a salad around somewhere, but I'd never seen anyone order one.

"Shoe designer, ten o'clock," Eddie said. "Oh no, he didn't. Let's go." Eddie grabbed my arm and tried to spin me around. The treads on my boots made me unspinnable.

"What?" I asked. I scanned the interior and spotted Nick and Amanda together by the Ms. Pac-Man machine. I had the top score on that back in high school. Focus, Samantha. "He brought Amanda? He didn't say anything about her being here with him."

"What exactly did he say?"

I pulled out my phone and scrolled through the texts. "At Brothers. Come join."

"That's what I thought. You know, because texting is so good for nailing down specifics of a post-breakup rendezvous." He took my phone, deleted the text, and handed it back. "You wanted this, right?" He gave me a push.

I turned away and grabbed his bicep. "I don't want it to look like I called you for moral support. I'm going to play it cool. Pretend we met up in the parking lot and you're getting takeout."

"Fine." Eddie split off from me and stood in line at the ordering counter. I watched Nick and Amanda. They appeared not to have noticed me yet. He said something to her, and she laughed. He put his hand on her shoulder. She didn't shrug it off.

No way was I going over there now. Not gonna happen.

I turned and headed back to the exit. Eddie stood in a crowd by the ordering counter. I flashed him a look and jerked my thumb toward the door. He shook his head no and pointed to the pizza oven and then at his watch. I turned around and went outside.

A blast of cool air hit my face. I couldn't leave; Eddie had driven me. And I wasn't about to walk the two miles home, even if I was wearing comfortable shoes. I looked at the moon and then looked at my phone. There was one other option.

I texted Dante and suggested if he wasn't busy, he join me for pizza. He texted back almost immediately. Now, all I had to do was wait outside until he showed up. And then, I'd be on a date too.

The door to Brothers opened, and Nick came outside. "Kidd," he said.

"Taylor," I said back, opting to act like we were in fifth grade.

"I almost didn't recognize you. You look different." He smiled, and the crinkles at the corners of his root-beer-barrel-colored eyes deepened. "New haircut," he added.

"I needed a change."

"Change can be good."

He reached up as if he were going to push my hair away from my face like he'd done so many times before. I put my hand palm-side out and stopped him before he touched me. The smile dropped from his face. We stared at each other as if there was something to be said, but neither one of us knew where to start.

"How's the job hunt going?" he asked.

"Great. But I'm guessing I shouldn't count on you for a reference."

"Come on. You know it wasn't like that."

"No, I guess it wasn't. But hey, thanks for recommending me to Amanda." I held both thumbs up and gave him a fake smile. "That's sure to head somewhere great."

He grabbed my wrist and pulled me around the side of the

building. I looked over my shoulder at the parking lot. No signs of Dante.

"If you have something you want to say, then go ahead and say it," he said.

"Me? What could I have to say? The last actual conversation we had was you telling me to turn my back on Eddie in his time of need. But now it's your friend with the crisis. What do you want me to do now, Nick? Ignore Amanda's problems and watch somebody destroy her business?"

Nick's eyes flashed. "It's not the same thing."

"You're right. It's not. Because this time you *asked* me to help her."

"And I've felt guilty about that ever since."

"Well, don't. None of this is for you or for her. I'm only trying to figure out who attacked me. Maybe nobody else cares about that, but I do. Saving Amanda's business would be icing on the cake, but you know something?" I put both hands on his chest and pushed him back. "I can totally eat cake without icing."

He looked at me as if I'd turned blue and told him I planned to live under a mushroom. "Kidd, you're not making any sense."

Did I just say something about eating cake without icing?

I sensed that righteous indignation was a limited resource that would soon give way to tears. I would not let Nick see me cry. I would not let him know how I'd felt when the days after our last conversation turned into weeks. When I'd been in the hospital and he hadn't even sent me a card.

"Samantha?" Dante said behind me. I looked over my shoulder and smiled. He approached us and put his hands on either side of my waist. "You didn't have to wait outside for me." He looked at Nick and then back at me. "How about I go get us a booth?"

"Sure. I'll be done in a second."

The bells over the door chimed as Dante disappeared inside. I turned back to Nick. The crinkles were gone from his eyes. "Kidd," he said. "I never expected things to get so complicated." He bent down and kissed my cheek. "Take care of yourself."

He went back in, leaving me out front. Seconds later, Eddie came outside with a white pizza box.

"Dude? Are you okay?"

A single tear dropped from my eye and left a cold track over my cheek. I swiped it away. "I know you have to get back to Tradava, but I'm not ready to leave yet."

"I saw Dante come in. Are you responsible for that too?"

I nodded. "Go. I'll be fine. I'll catch a ride home with him."

"I hope you know what you're doing."

I pushed through the doors, scanned the interior, and found Dante seated at a booth in the back. I snaked through the crowd and lowered myself onto the opposite side. The wine buzz from earlier was wearing off, but under the circumstances, I knew it would be a good idea to order something to eat.

"Hey," I said.

"Hey yourself," he answered. "New look?"

I reached up and felt the new shorter ends of my hair. "I needed a change."

"With just your hair or with other things too?"

"I'm considering a total lifestyle overhaul."

A beer sat on a cardboard Bud Light coaster on the table. The glass was more full than empty. I glanced at it and then at him.

"Why'd you want me to meet you here, Samantha?"

I shrugged. "I needed an excuse to get out of the house."

"I don't think that's the reason."

"Okay, fine. I like their pizza."

"You picked a fine time to start telling the truth." This time he smiled.

A waiter carried a silver tray to our table. "Large round with cheese, right?" he said to me.

"This can't be ours. We haven't ordered yet."

The waiter set the pizza on the table. "Missy, you've been ordering the same thing since you were in high school." He looked at Dante. "Good luck with this one. She's been breaking hearts for two decades." He left.

Dante transferred a slice onto a beige plastic plate for me and then for himself. I shook on a generous amount of oregano and bit into the tip of the slice. Too hot. Burnt my mouth. I reached for the water and guzzled half of the glass. Dante watched me. I set my slice down and looked at him.

"It's hot," I said.

"I hear some like it hot."

"I heard that too."

"What about you, Samantha? How do you like it?"

"I like it room temperature."

He raised one eyebrow.

"Are we still talking about pizza?" I asked.

He smiled. "For now."

"I can live with that." I turned my attention back to the slice. I was reaching for my third when I realized Dante's second still sat on his plate.

"Go for it," he said.

"I can't eat a third slice if you're not going to at least pretend to finish your second."

"I have a better idea. Let's get a to-go box and get out of here."

"But—"

"Your friend Eddie asked if I could give you a ride home. And I said I would, but there's someplace we have to go first."

After packing the pizza up, I followed Dante out of Brothers. Out of the corner of my eye, I looked for Nick or Amanda but saw neither one. It was just as well. I wasn't sure what Dante had in mind, but I thought it best not to have the image of Nick in my mind when it happened.

Dante led me to a black sedan. He beeped a remote at it, and the lights flickered once.

"Isn't this your sister's car?" I asked.

"Yes. I don't want to draw attention to ourselves."

"What exactly do you have in mind?"

"We're working a case, Samantha." He rested his forearms on the top of the car and looked across the hood at me. "We're going back to the scene of the crime."

13

THE MAIN EVENT

ALL OVER THE WORLD, COUPLES WERE HEADING OUT TO DANCE CLUBS, bars, and restaurants for date night. Dante and I were headed to a crime scene.

Samantha Kidd, this is your life.

While I wondered what Dante's sister would say about the scent of pizza that would most certainly cling to the interior of her otherwise pristine car, Dante drove us to Warehouse Five. It was dark, and the roads were crowded. He parked the car under a streetlamp about a hundred feet away from the gravel lot I'd stood in earlier. The aches and pains I'd been ignoring all day were catching up to me, and I moved slowly. Dante was halfway to the building when he realized I was still by the car. He doubled back.

"You okay?"

"I'll manage. I think I'm getting stiffer as the night goes on."

"You need to exercise. Stretch. Stay limber."

"I exercise plenty," I lied. "I'll be fine. Let's go."

He reached for my hand and guided me forward. My initial instinct was to shake him off, but I found it comforting to hold onto him. Even though he was ahead of me, he walked at a pace that I could match. He didn't let go when we reached the lot, and suddenly it seemed awkward to stand in a faintly lit parking lot with Dante holding my hand, like maybe this rendezvous was about more than searching for overlooked clues.

"You said Clive was here today?" Dante asked. I nodded. "Was he paying special attention to anything?"

"Hard to say. The building was locked, but he was inside. When he came out, he took pictures of the back door and windows. We're not going to be able to see anything he was looking at."

He turned toward the building, and I followed. Together we stumbled over the loose gravel, getting farther and farther from the car. Dante pulled a leather glove out of the inside pocket of his motorcycle jacket, let go of my hand, and pulled it on. He reached for the doorknob and jiggled it. Locked. He pulled on another glove and leaned close to the window, framing the light away from his eyes so he could see inside.

I stood on my tiptoes behind him and peeked over his shoulder. The only thing visible was a faint stationary light coming from somewhere to the left.

Dante looked at me. "See anything?"

"How am I supposed to see anything? It's dark out, and you're in my way. That's why I came here when there was daylight."

He unzipped his jacket and lifted a camera that hung around his neck.

"There was a guy in high school who wore a camera around his neck," I said. "I think it was a Warhol thing. Were you like that? The guy at the parties who caught all the embarrassing stuff on film? Or were you the *Sex, Lies, and Videotape* guy who…" I felt my face flush. "Never mind."

"When I went to a party, I wasn't all that concerned with taking pictures."

"Then why bring a camera tonight?"

"I'm on the job, see?" he said out of the corner of his mouth. He fiddled with the dial around the lens and aimed the camera at me. The shutter clicked a few times but there was no flash.

"Hey!" I said. "Stop that."

He faced the building, and the shutter clicked a few more times.

"Don't you want to turn on the flash or something?"

"Don't need to. I'm using infrared film."

"And this is good for us why?"

"This film captures a picture of the infrared spectrum, not what you see with your eyes. I can't develop it until I'm in a darkroom, but there's a chance we'll catch something nobody else will see either. Every day that goes by is a chance for the scene to get disrupted. Critters, wind, weather. If there's a clue here to whatever happened, we have to find it sooner rather than later. We're already working against a ticking clock."

"This film is going to help you figure out if Clive saw something before Detective Loncar asked him to leave."

"Yes."

"Have you been planning this all night?"

"I admit, your invitation took me by surprise, but after that, yes."

I didn't know if it was the solitude of the parking lot, the forethought of Dante's infrared camera plan, or the lingering romance of having shared a pizza, but I stepped closer to him. "Do you have anything else planned for tonight?" I asked quietly.

He stared at me for a second before he leaned down and kissed me. What I'd gotten earlier that day had been little more than a preview. Tonight, I was treated to the main event.

My arms went up, around the back of his neck, and pulled him closer. I parted my lips and felt his teeth gently bite at my lower lip. I tipped my head back and he kissed down the side of my neck and then back up to my ear lobe. If I hadn't been holding on to him, my legs would have given way underneath me.

He unbuttoned my coat and slipped his arms around me. I flinched when he touched a bruise. He pulled his arms away.

"Did I hurt you?" he asked in a low voice.

"The jerk who jumped me hurt me."

Dante held my hand and lowered himself to the gravel. He lifted the hem of my oversized red sweater with his gloved fingers and kissed the bruised flesh to the left and right of my navel. I closed my eyes. We were in the middle of a public parking lot, but it felt like the most secluded place in the world. I put my hands on his head and tipped it back so he was looking at my face.

"I'm not as tough as I act," I said.

He nodded a few times and looked again at my waist. He pulled the right glove off with his left hand and used his index finger to trace a line across my tummy. After about a minute, he pushed himself up to a standing position, put his bent knuckle under my chin, and tipped my head back again.

"That's why you've been breaking hearts since high school."

I expected him to kiss me again. He didn't. Instead, he took my hand and pulled me ever so gently toward the building. "I'm going to take as many pictures as I can. You said the police kicked Clive away from here and secured the scene?"

Dante's gears had shifted from romantic interlude to investigator on the job, and it took me a second to shake off the thought of his lips on mine and focus on his question. "Clive was inside the building when I got here. He must have seen me before I saw him. I walked up to the door, and he opened it and startled me. He didn't say where he'd been or what he was doing. I bet that camera gives him access to a lot of places, no questions asked."

Dante put his hand on his own camera. "That's what we're

counting on." He looked up at the building. "What's on the other side?"

"The parking lot. I'm going to check on my car while we're here."

Truth was, I needed a couple of minutes away from Dante. His tender kisses had been unexpected, and now I was more mixed up than ever. I'd been attracted to him since our first meeting, but I'd been in a relationship with Nick. Now I wasn't. Or was I?

We'd broken up. And then I'd fallen apart. Now it seemed like there was a second shoe that still hadn't dropped. What did that scene at Brothers mean? Was he in or was he out?

I didn't know. I didn't like that I didn't know, but I didn't think it was a good idea to race from one man to another as long as I was confused about my feelings for both of them. Nobody said I had to decide tonight. Healing takes time, and if I gave myself enough time, the answer was bound to present itself. At least that's what this month's advice column in *Elle* magazine said.

The corners of the parking lot were marked off with streetlamps, but the bulbs were out in two of them. The lot was dark. I knew I should be doing what Dante was doing: looking for clues related to the fire. But morbid curiosity led me to the exit I'd walked through before getting attacked.

I stood with my back pressed up against the solid metal door. Other entrances were more inviting; this one was intended for deliveries and crew members. The frame was flush with the door's surface. It would have disappeared into the exterior wall if not for the brass lock and partially rusted doorknob that now jutted into my left butt cheek.

I closed my eyes and thought back to the attack two days ago. What did I remember? I had been on my way outside. A few steps into the lot, and the flicker of a fire had caught my attention. Within seconds—or faster, maybe—the fire had connected with my foot like someone had drawn a line on the macadam. From that point, I hadn't had time to think. I'd swatted at the flames while a stranger approached and had been unprepared for the sudden beating with the bag of fruit.

I hadn't spent much time thinking about the choice of fruit as a weapon. Fruit would have been easy enough to come by. The food service table at Warehouse Five was filled with fresh fruit, raw vegetables, and Coke Zero. The soda went first then the vegetables. I'd heard a few of the girls whispering about the high sugar content in fruit and whether someone was trying to ruin their careers. I almost heard their minds blow the day I arrived with a hoagie.

But soft citrus as a weapon was intended to inflict injuries that could not be traced. Which told me whoever assaulted me hadn't been all that concerned with my wellbeing. If they'd hit a major organ, that warning might as well have been a death threat.

I walked to the edge of the lot where the paved parking spaces met with dirt and loose gravel. The lights were out, except for the glow of the red-orange Exit sign. If someone had determined a path for the fire from a pre-drawn trail of accelerant, would I be able to see it? Or would the traces of that trail have been eradicated by the firemen who had doused the building with water to put out the fire?

Dante was using infrared film to catch things we couldn't see, but there had to be other answers here. What else couldn't I see with my own eyes?

I dropped down to the ground and ran my gloved hand over the macadam. I lifted it to my nose and sniffed, expecting the scent of gasoline. All I got was a nose full of silvery cobwebs and gravel that stuck to my glove.

I stood up and slapped my hands together to rid them of the shiny, silk-like threads and pebbles. Again, I was struck with questions about my knowledge of Amanda's show and how that would make someone see me as a threat. I played out my last few hours as part of Amanda's team. Had Oscar been angered by how I lobbied on behalf of the models? Had Clive been using his position as photographer to conduct some other nefarious business? Had Santangelo arranged the attack because I was a part of Amanda's team? Had Amanda herself been planning a publicity stunt?

I opened my eyes and looked at my black Honda del Sol. The plastic top was in place, and the windshield was covered with colorful flyers and coupons for upcoming art shows, discount car washes, and at least a dozen other advertisements. It didn't seem like a good idea to leave the vehicle parked in the lot. I felt around in my handbag for my keys and unlocked the driver's side door. I cleared the flyers off the windshield and threw them onto the passenger-side seat.

It took a couple of tries to get the cold engine to turn over. When it caught, I put it into gear and locked the doors. Movement at the edge of the lot caught my eyes. I rolled down the dirty windows to get an unobstructed view outside.

Just like at the runway show, I smelled the fire before I saw it. I drove to the dumpster at the edge of the lot. Flames leapt up from inside the receptacle.

I saw a leg jutting out of the top a moment later.

14

―――

PINKY SWEAR

I slammed on the brakes and jumped out of the car. Despite the cold of the night air, heat from the fire licked at my face and coated me in sticky, desperate fear.

"Samantha! Get away from the dumpster!" Dante called out. He ran toward me and waved his hand to the side.

"There's someone inside!" I yelled, pointing as close as I could to the leg.

"Get back!" He threw his arms around me from behind and turned me away from the fire. I screamed from the pain of his arms against my bruises. He half carried, half dragged me several feet away.

An explosion cracked like a boom of thunder. Pieces of trash sprayed through the air. Dante pulled me down to the gravel and shielded me with his shoulder. I pushed him away and scrambled to my feet. I pulled my cell phone from my bag and called 911.

The fire truck arrived before the police. Men in khaki jumpsuits with yellow reflective tape climbed from the vehicle, uncoiled a hose, and put out the flames. Dante sat next to me on the hood of my car. We were wrapped in a blanket I'd found in the trunk. Two black and whites pulled into the lot from the left, and the policemen conferred with the firemen. A dark brown sedan entered from the right, and Detective Loncar got out. He stared at the dumpster for a few seconds and then walked over to us.

"Let me do the talking," I said to Dante.

"Ms. Kidd, Mr. ..." Loncar paused.

"This is Dante Lestes. Dante, this is Detective Loncar. Dante is the photographer I was telling you about earlier today. The man who's going to take over for Clive Barrington."

Dante freed his arm from the blanket and shook Loncar's hand.

"Ms. Kidd, I know you know this is a crime scene. Care to tell me what you two are doing here?"

"I know you're not happy to see me, but before we get to that, you should know that there's a body in the dumpster. I was over there," I said, pointing behind me, "and I saw something move over there." I pointed to the trash receptacle. "I didn't see the flames until I got close. I also saw a leg. I called for Dante, and the dumpster went up like the Fourth of July."

Loncar patted his pockets until he found his small spiral-bound notebook. He scribbled something inside. "You say you saw movement before you saw the fire?"

"Yes. Honestly, I didn't even know that's what it was. That's why I went closer. When I saw the leg, I knew whoever was in there would get burned."

"How long would you say it was between you seeing something and the explosion?"

My eyes rolled up while I ran the memory through my mind like an editor reviewing first rushes. "A minute, maybe. It happened quickly."

A shiny silver car pulled into the lot and parked catty-corner to Loncar's dirty sedan. Inspector Gigger got out. Loncar said something unrepeatable and told us to wait where we were. When he was a couple of steps away from us, I turned to Dante.

"The guy who looks like Ichabod Crane is in charge of the arson investigation at the fashion show. I don't think Loncar likes him. I don't like him either. At least with Loncar, I know where I stand."

"Where's that?"

"If he had his way, it would be a couple of miles from the crime scene."

"You don't seem to respect his wishes."

"I'm not the one who brought us here," I said.

"Point taken."

Loncar pointed to Dante and me, and Inspector Gigger looked at us, his expression unreadable. He popped his trunk, pulled out two bottles of water, and crossed the lot to where we sat on the hood of my car. Before he spoke, he handed each of us a bottle. I didn't realize how thirsty I was until I gulped down half the contents.

"Thank you," I said. I looked at Dante. He set his bottle next to him. It remained unopened.

After a lightning round of introductions, Gigger turned his attention to me. "Ms. Kidd, Detective Loncar tells me you were the one to call 911. Can you tell me what you saw?"

"I already told Detective Loncar everything I saw."

"But Detective Loncar isn't me, so why don't you go through it again?" he said. He flashed a tight smile that vanished as quickly as it had appeared. If I'd been on the fence about him earlier, there was no confusion now. Like Loncar, I didn't like the man, but there were bigger issues at present than a tally of Gigger's popularity votes.

"I came around the back of the building to check on my car. It's been here since the night I was attacked. Something by the dumpster caught my eye. I don't know what it was. I drove closer to check it out, and that's when I saw the flames. I yelled to Dante to meet me around the back—"

"Why?" he interjected.

"What?"

"Why did you call to your boyfriend?"

"He's not my boyfriend." I looked at Dante, who studied Gigger. "I saw movement by the dumpster. I thought maybe somebody needed help."

I felt Dante press his thigh into mine ever so slightly. It was a warning.

"Did you see anybody who might need help?" Gigger asked Dante.

"The bin exploded before I got close enough," he said.

"Yes or no. Did you see anybody?"

"No."

Gigger turned toward the dumpster and crossed his arms. "It's dark outside. You probably saw a rat."

I jumped down from the car and threw the blanket off my shoulders. "It wasn't a rat, Inspector. I don't like rats. If I saw one, I would have run the other way."

He stared at me for an uncomfortable number of seconds. I wanted to uncap my water and throw what was left of it in his face, but there wasn't enough to have any impact. Maybe that's why Dante was saving his.

Gigger turned to Dante. "You can't corroborate Ms. Kidd's statement. Is that correct?" Dante shook his head slowly. Gigger nodded at each of us and walked back to Loncar.

The firemen put out the fire. When they finished, they put the hose on the truck and stood around in the lot. I counted twelve men. Twelve pairs of thick men's boots stomping around the gravel close to the dumpster. Twelve pairs of size-twelve feet destroying any evidence that might have been left behind by the person who started the fire. I was thankful for the firemen's timely arrival and attention to detail in the form of putting out the flames, but I knew if there was something to be found, chances were, it had been destroyed.

Dante fussed with the zipper on his motorcycle jacket underneath the blanket. I climbed back up and wrapped the other side of the blanket around me. We sat side by side on the hood of the car, watching the scene in front of us. Gigger nodded to the head fireman and approached the dumpster. His hands were behind his back and his face was aimed at the ground. Slowly he walked around the base of the trash bin, swinging his head from left to right with each step he took.

"Tell me exactly what you saw," Dante said to me. "Start with what you were doing when you left my sight. Take your time."

I stared straight ahead and tried to find my chi. Since I didn't do yoga and wasn't sure what my chi was, I defaulted to a couple of calming breaths before speaking. Maybe yoga would be a good idea.

"I wanted to retrace my steps from the night I was attacked. I stood in the doorway with my back to the door and looked at my car and then slowly walked toward it. When I got there, I unlocked the door and put the flyers that were under the windshield wipers onto the passenger-side seat. I got in. Something by the dumpster caught my eye. I drove closer and rolled down the windows. I smelled something burning. Then the fire showed up from the top of the dumpster, and I saw the leg."

"I hate to have to ask this, but do you know if the leg was attached to a person?"

"You think it was just a leg? Sticking out of the dumpster?" Realization of what Dante suggested made me shudder like a team of cats had clawed a chalkboard nearby. "What if it's not there anymore? Do you think that's why someone set the fire? They amputated someone's leg, and they wanted to destroy the evidence? Should I tell Gigger?"

"Shhh," Dante said. "You told Loncar. Do you trust him?"

"I don't know if trust applies here. I think he'll follow up on what I said, but if Gigger is keeping him out of the investigation, then he's in pretty much the same boat as us. Unless—"

"Unless what?" Dante asked.

I reached inside the neckline of Dante's jacket and fingered the black nylon strap that held his camera around his head. "I would think the investigating officer would be very interested in the photos you took."

"That is a good point."

"But I think, since nobody asked us if we had any photos to share, that it might be best for us to see what's on your film before telling anybody."

"There are people who might say that's withholding evidence."

"Yes, but none of those people are here, right?" I searched Dante's face. "And I'll give the pictures to Loncar. You don't even know if there's anything to show him. It's not like you were back here taking pictures. You were on the other side of the building. Wouldn't it be worse if you told him you had evidence, and it turned out there was nothing there?"

"I don't think 'worse' is the word you want."

"You know what I mean."

"Unfortunately, I do," he said.

"Then we're agreed? We'll see what's on the film, and then we'll turn it over to Loncar."

"You're not going to make me take a pinky swear, are you?"

"You think I'm the pinky-swear type?"

"The more I get to know you, the surer I am that you're a type all your own."

"I'm going to take that as a compliment," I said.

"Your choice."

Loncar pulled away from the group of firemen and rejoined us. "Ms. Kidd, I'm going to ask you a favor. Have Mr. Lestes drive you home."

"But my car's been here for two days now."

"I understand. I can't tell you not to drive it home, but until we have a chance to go over the scene in daylight, I'd prefer you left it here."

This was a different side of Detective Loncar. In the past, we'd gone round and round, me proclaiming what I knew, him testing me to see if I was making up a story. There had been times we collaborated, and there had been times when I'd gone rogue and caught a killer in his backyard.

This was the first time he had acted like I had some control over whether to grant his request. It might have been the effect of Gigger's condescending attitude, or it might have been the late hour. Or maybe Loncar was warming to me.

"Mr. Lestes, I think we have everything we need from you tonight." He pulled two cards with contact info from his wallet and held them out.

I waved the card off. "I still have the ones from the other investigations, thanks."

Dante took the card and slipped it into the inside pocket of his leather jacket. Loncar took down Dante's contact info and walked away.

"So now you have a choice," Dante said. "Let me take you home, or ignore the detective's request and drive yourself. What's it going to be, Samantha?"

15

AN UNDERSTANDING

Breakup Rule #5: Try not to repeat broken rules.

I woke up on the right side of the bed. The sheets were in a jumble, and Logan stared at me from the left.

"Don't judge," I said. "Detective Loncar had a bad night. I thought doing what he asked was the upright-citizen thing."

Logan meowed.

I rolled over and stared at the ceiling. This was the second time Dante and I had spent a night under the same roof. Exhaustion and injuries kept me from engaging in any hanky-panky, but judging from the state of the sheets, I'd either had a very restless night or I hadn't slept alone.

I couldn't help wondering what I was doing. It didn't feel like things were over with Nick. I closed my eyes, and Logan climbed onto my chest and lowered himself. He pushed his paws out in front of him, tickling the bottom of my chin. I turned my head to the left, and he stretched out more. One of his claws scraped my jaw.

"Ow!" I said. I rolled to my side, and he scooted off and head-butted me. I freed a hand and ran it over his head, smoothing down the fur. He purred and curled himself into the nook created by my chest and my bent knees. I lowered my head to the pillowcase and rested my arm loosely around him. "You're being a very good cat through all of this," I said.

He lifted his head and opened one eye, blinked, and lay his head back down.

"I don't need Nick, and I don't need Dante, but I need you," I said, and kissed him between his ears. He purred.

I dozed off again, waking to the sound of knuckles rapping against the doorframe.

"Rise and shine, sleepyhead," Dante said.

"What time is it?"

"Nine thirty."

I sat up in bed and immediately pulled the covers up to my chest when I realized I wasn't wearing a bra under my pajamas. Dante smiled. "I'll go out for coffee while you get dressed. It's going to be a busy day."

I waited until I heard the front door close and the car engine start. I re-dressed in the sweater and jeans from last night and went to the kitchen. I ate a piece of cold pizza left over from Brothers.

A strange sound came from the living room. It was the VCR I'd had since college, and I only used it when I found something that was important enough to tape. It sounded like it might be dying a slow death. I hit the eject button, and a tape popped out. And I remembered what I had thought important enough to tape: the local cable channel that had planned to broadcast Amanda's runway show.

Not being skilled in the art of video enhancement, duplication, or transfer, pretty much the only thing I could do with the tape was watch it. I rewound the brittle twenty-year-old tape and crossed my fingers that it would stay in viewable condition long enough for me to check it out. I pressed play.

The cable company hadn't made much of an effort for Amanda. A camera had been set up at the end of the runway. I picked out Dante and me on the left side of the screen, and after scanning the rest of the patrons, I found Clive on the right. Twenty-seven seconds in, I saw a man in a pork pie hat slip past the crowd and duck backstage.

Santangelo Toma. Despite his very public refusal of the comped tickets he'd been offered prior to the show, he attended. Which meant he'd been there, and his actions suggested an alibi.

When the lights dimmed and the loud Japanese pop music started, everything dissolved in darkness except for the runway. The graphics from the Godzilla movie were projected on the backdrop right above Amanda's name, and the first model walked out. She wore the China-chop wig that faded from red roots to orange to yellow ends, and she was dressed in the silver leather motorcycle jacket over a red pantsuit. She posed at the end of the runway and turned. The intricate embroidery I remembered on the back of her jacket was distorted by the grainy quality of the video.

Five models walked the runway before Harper appeared. Her wig was silver. The sleeves on her kimono dragged on the ground as she walked. I freeze-framed the video and stared at her face. Gone was the shy, nervous model who had asked for my help earlier. She looked confident, like she had a secret.

From this angle I didn't see the smoke behind her like I had at the live showing. I watched her work the kimono, and then it went up in flames. Someone in the audience screamed. The music was cut, and the house lights turned on. Harper struggled to get the kimono off. Nick appeared and tore it from her shoulders, and she ran backstage. The kimono was left in a burning heap on the runway. The fire caught onto the trail of rose petals. Seconds later, the fire was everywhere: walls, ceiling, chairs, backdrop. Guests fled from their seats. Someone knocked the camera over, and the video went to fuzz.

The early reports on the news hadn't shown any footage from the show, but if I was watching this much, then certainly Gigger and company had seen it too. I kept watching, hoping the image would return. Within seconds the screen defaulted to color bars, and then a message that said the programming had been interrupted. The counter on the VCR continued to advance, so I knew I'd gotten everything the cable channel had filmed.

Rewind. Watch again. Rewind. Fiddle with the remote. Zoom. Rewind. After close scrutiny of the crowd, I picked out Eddie and a few others from Tradava. I never saw Tiny or Amanda, but it made sense that they were both backstage, where I would have been if I hadn't been let go the night before the show.

I sat up straight. Nobody who worked at the show had been attacked. Not prior to me, not after me. Only me. Maybe the plan all along had been to set fire to Harper's kimono, and the warning was meant to keep me from paying too much attention to what had been going on.

I thought back to the day Harper had come to me about the ill-fitting garment. The sleeves had been long enough to drag on the ground, but when I'd first inquired about the need for alterations, Oscar had dismissed us, saying that Harper had specifically been chosen to wear that kimono. Now I knew why. Someone had planned for her kimono to catch fire. I interfered with that plan when Harper came to me and I ultimately went to Amanda. But Amanda couldn't be the one responsible for destroying her own show. It didn't fit. Which took me back to motivation. To create a stir? To gain publicity? To destroy the show? Or to get Harper?

I dug my cell phone out of my handbag, tapped the screen to

cue up my contacts, and flipped to the Fs. Under Fuzz, I found the detective's number. I called.

"Loncar," he said.

"Detective, this is Samantha Kidd." I waited a beat then forged ahead. "I've been reviewing footage of the runway show, and I had a couple of questions."

"When you say you were reviewing footage of the runway show, what exactly do you mean?" he asked.

"I set my VCR up to record the show." The phone went silent, and I imagined Loncar cursing the day my parents put the house up for sale. "I figure you've seen this same footage. Maybe it would help to bounce theories off each other? Since we're practically working together on this. I feel like we have an understanding."

"You might be confused about that."

"Did you check out the report of my attack?"

"Yes."

"Then you know I'm the victim here. I'm just trying to figure out who assaulted me."

"What are your questions?"

"Was anybody hurt in the fire?"

"No."

"Do you know how the fire was started?"

"We're working on that."

"Do you have any suspects?"

"Ms. Kidd, I think we've tapped out the limits of our understanding."

"Wait!" I paused for a second. "Are you still there?"

"Yes."

"The way I see it, this has to do with either Amanda Ries, the designer, or Harper, the model who was wearing the kimono. For all I know, I wasn't even supposed to be the target of the attack. I think I was at the wrong place at the wrong time."

"How do you figure that?"

"If it was about me, there would have been a second attack. I left the hospital and attended the show as a guest. I wasn't a threat from out front. Since I left the show, I've visited Amanda, gone to the crime scene, and gone home. If someone was after me, they would have had ample opportunity to get me. Which means whoever attacked me accomplished what they set out to do."

"Where were you when you were attacked?"

"I was on my way to my car. I was backstage, and then I walked past the food table to the exit. Nobody else was attacked, and nobody claims to have seen anything."

"Is that all you got?"

I thought back to the fitting. "There's something else. Harper—she's the model in the kimono. Have you talked to her?"

"We can't reach her. She's out of the country."

"Still? Isn't that suspicious? That in the middle of the fire and the chaos, she managed to get out of there, get to an airport, and get to Mexico?"

"I'm not at liberty to comment on Ms. Ashton's role in the investigation."

"What about the kimono? Harper complained about the fit. Amanda specifically picked that garment for her. Do you have somebody at the lab analyzing it for clues?"

"Ms. Kidd, this is not a TV show. Besides, the samples were destroyed in the fire."

"Was anything else damaged?"

"We're looking at claims from Warehouse Five, the makeup people, and the designer. If we can't link this crime to someone, Ms. Ries is going to pay out a pretty penny in insurance."

"Did anybody else lose property? Amanda's show was in the main hall of the warehouse, but other artists show their work there. What about them?"

"Outside of the fashion show, everything went untouched. If damages were sustained to anybody else on the property, they haven't been filed."

16

FORWARD NOT BACKWARD

The rest of the tenants of Warehouse Five hadn't been impacted by the fire, but Amanda was at risk of losing everything. I hadn't been expecting that. "Thank you, Detective."

"You're welcome, Ms. Kidd."

Three fires at the same location: the one that was part of my attack, the runway show, and now the dumpster. It had to mean something, but what? What exactly did I know? Not much.

Could Gigger be right that the movement I'd seen was a rat? I shuddered. No, if I suspected it was a rodent big enough to catch my attention across the parking lot, I never would have driven over to see it. Someone had been back there. Either the person who set the fire or the person in the dumpster. I shuddered again.

Gigger might have assumed that I'd seen a rat, but Dante believed me. It was that belief that kept me focused on finding the truth. Last night, we'd been a team. Not the bumbling Keystone Cops type, but two people focused on finding answers. Already I could see that, when it came to investigation, Dante knew what he was doing. The cover story with Amanda, the camera with the infrared film, the wariness when giving a statement to Gigger all illustrated that. I could learn from him.

Dante hadn't chided me for the way I'd handled the police. He didn't warn me away from danger. Ever since I'd found evidence that he had a whole other life, one that had started long before he and I met, I wondered what else there was to get to know about him. But even that bothered me too. Was he just another mystery that I wanted to solve? And once I saw him as a real person, not a dangerous semi-stranger, would the attraction dissipate?

I hoped I wasn't that shallow.

More and more, as questions about the fire and subsequently the job with Amanda came up, I questioned my involvement. There was a bigger personal issue here, one that transcended the investigation and the dangerous situations in the past. It was my ongoing need to find where I fit in.

Giving up my job at Bentley's New York and moving back to Ribbon had been an intentional move to help me figure that out, but being back in the house where I'd grown up had had an unexpected side effect of grounding me somewhere in my childhood. Here I was, over a year into that move, and no closer to finding answers.

I loved the city of Ribbon, with its pretzel factories and Pennsylvania Dutch restaurants. What I didn't love was feeling like I'd somehow reverted back in time. In my professional life as a buyer, I'd known what I was doing. I had confidence in my abilities. And even though I knew I'd chosen to leave that job behind, it seemed I'd lost something of me in the process—something I hadn't known was there.

I hummed the Japanese pop song from Amanda's soundtrack that I suspected would be stuck in my head indefinitely and made a long-overdue phone call. Dante returned with the coffee a few minutes after I hung up.

"What were your plans for developing that film?" I asked.

"I'd like to get to it today, but first I need a darkroom."

"Take me to the crime scene so I can get my car. You can come back here. There's a small room in the basement where my dad used to make wine. I'll give you the keys, and you can do whatever you need to do to set it up as your darkroom."

"What are you going to be doing?"

"I have some personal business to attend to."

Dante didn't pry. I respected him a little more because of that. And even if he did ask, I wasn't sure I'd tell him where I was going.

Back to Bentley's New York to talk to my former boss. Because a year was long enough to flounder while trying to figure things out on my own. Life didn't seem to be headed the right direction, and there was a very small chance that I'd need to give up everything I thought I wanted in Ribbon and go back to the life I'd left behind.

After we retrieved my car from Warehouse Five, Dante followed me back to my house. I showed him the darkroom and left him alone while I showered and changed into a black leather skirt, black tights, and black over-the-knee boots. I pulled on a red motorcycle jacket, grabbed my keys, and took off.

Two and a half hours later, I pulled into a public parking lot across from Bentley's New York and spent more on parking than I had on a pizza last night. The air was pungent with the mixture of Chinese food and cigarette smoke. I held my breath and jogged to the customer entrance on Broadway. Once inside, a determined perfume sampler added a spritz of the latest Estée Lauder fragrance to the olfactory mix.

Good times.

As if an autopilot program had been activated, I bypassed displays of new merchandise and hopped into the up elevator. When I reached the fourteenth floor, I got out, climbed three steps, followed a long hallway, and turned left. My former boss's office was the third on the right.

"Knock, knock," I said, lightly rapping my knuckles against the nameplate that read Marcia Dann. Marcia looked up from her computer and smiled.

"Well, hello, stranger," she said. "Come on in."

"Do you mind if I shut the door?" I asked.

"Go right ahead." She didn't seem surprised that I'd asked. "How's life in the small town?"

"I've found the simple life not so simple." I smiled. "It would appear I'm having a hard time transitioning from being a city mouse."

"Personally or professionally?"

"Both."

"Have you talked to your parents about this?"

"My parents told me to sell the house and move in with them until I figure things out."

"You're not moving in with your parents. Life is about moving forward, not backward."

"I guess that means you don't think I should ask for my old job back?"

She leaned back and tapped a soft pink sculptured nail on her desk. "You could have asked me that question over the phone. What's the real reason you drove a hundred and fifty miles to see me?"

I collected my thoughts for a few seconds while fragmented memories of my nine years at Bentley's filtered through my mind. "You took a chance on hiring me, and I learned more working for you than any other time in my life—at least until I moved back to Ribbon."

"Yes, I imagine three homicide investigations can do that to a person." She smiled. "Samantha, do you remember the year I hired you?"

I nodded.

"You didn't know everything there was to know about being a buyer. In fact, you didn't know much about being a buyer at all. But you had a certain skill set: creative and analytical. You watched the other buyers. And you learned fast. By the time you resigned, you were the person other buyers watched."

"It's just that, now, something is holding me back. The job at Tradava didn't work out, and then the job at Heist didn't last, and, well, something's got to give."

"You wanted to leave Bentley's. Coming back here isn't going to give you any satisfaction. You thrive when there are problems to be solved. You already know how to solve the problems of retail. Three-month projections, overstocked inventory, assorting a department, making advertising choices. You need to apply that same analytical thinking that served you as a buyer to your own life."

"Do you think it's that easy?"

"Nothing good in life is easy. But people do things so they can grow. If you haven't grown from this move, then you haven't figured out why you went there to begin with." She leaned back. "Let me ask you this: why did you want to work at Tradava?"

"I was in Ribbon, my parents were moving, and Patrick found me sitting in the parking lot with my cat. We talked for five minutes, and we clicked. It felt like a sign."

"Patrick was a genius, and he would have made a good mentor, but you were overqualified for the job. If that had worked out, you would have been so bored you'd have asked for your old job back a year ago."

She slid the top drawer of her desk open and pulled out a red business card that said *Retrofit Magazine.* "A friend of mine is starting up her own magazine. She's looking for a fashion director, someone who can recognize trends and work independently. We're not talking comfortable little job here, Samantha. We're talking international travel for Fashion Week. Discovering new talent. Getting in on the ground floor of something new." She tapped the card on the desk. "You could do this if you wanted."

She held out the card. This was it. This was the opportunity I wanted.

I took the card. "Thank you, Marcia," I said.

She held her hands up. "Don't thank me. I have no say on whether or not you get the job. There are probably a hundred fashion bloggers out there who would sell off half of their closet for this opportunity. If you want it, you're going to have to go for it. And I mean that literally—she's going to need to see what you can do."

"Anybody who would sell off half of their closet for this opportunity should rethink the clothes they've been hoarding all these years."

"That's why I'm giving you the card."

We caught up on industry gossip before she headed to a meeting, and I left. I had driven over two hours for a thirty-minute meeting that restored my self-confidence and recharged my core values. I left Bentley's feeling more inspired than I had twenty-four hours ago and more resolute that my decision to leave had been the right one.

It was a little after two. Traffic would become an issue by three, although there was no good time to drive in Manhattan. Still, I couldn't resist a quick trip to Figaro for an afternoon chocolate soufflé. It's important to recognize the special things in life. And it was right around the corner.

I walked to the corner of 57th and Broadway. Figaro was a small European restaurant nestled in the middle of an otherwise residential street. A chalkboard out front listed the specials. It was the only indication that an eatery resided below street level. The chocolate soufflés were legendary to those in the know and took twenty minutes to rise. The hostess led me to a window table, where I placed my order without looking at the menu.

Eleven minutes of staring out the window while waiting, I saw a familiar person walking down the opposite side of the street.

What was Nick doing in New York City?

He crossed to my side of the street. I picked up my handbag, coat, and scarf and asked the hostess where the restroom was. I gave him five minutes to get past Figaro before coming out.

When I left the restroom, he was being seated.

I glanced at my table. My soufflé sat, alone, next to my water glass. The soufflé was already starting to fall.

Crap. The only reason I knew about this restaurant was because Nick and I used to have business dinners here during Market Week.

My options were limited. I ducked behind a ficus tree and leaned forward, flagging down the hostess. She didn't look at me until after I resorted to *"Psst!"*

"Can I help you?" she asked.

I kept my voice low. "I have to leave. That's my soufflé on the table over there." I pointed. Nick looked up, and I ducked behind the tree again. "Can I get it wrapped up to go?" I whispered.

"There's no way to transfer it from the clay pot to the takeout container. Plus, they have to be eaten right away," she said.

"Do what you can. It's an emergency." I pulled a twenty-dollar bill from my wallet and thrust it at her. "I'll be waiting outside."

The fallen soufflé was gone by the time I returned to Ribbon. I'd like to say it helped me feel better, but it didn't. The only thing it accomplished was making my skirt feel tight in the waist.

17

MEATLOAF

I pulled into my driveway at six thirty. My spontaneous tell-me-why-I'm-fabulous trip had taken most of the day thanks to my chocolate soufflé-and-Nick surprise, but a particular clarity often follows a quenched chocolate craving. I'd been able to focus on the matters at hand while driving. And, as I'd come to organize them while sitting in traffic, the matters at hand were as follows:

1.Get job.

2.Find out who's out to get Amanda and why I was attacked in the process.

3.Buy Logan one of those As-Seen-on-TV cat toys.

4a. Analyze feelings about Nick and

4b. Determine how they pertain to feelings about Dante.

5.Start exercise regime!

During the last twenty minutes of traffic I'd taken time to rank them in order of importance.

I didn't know if I would be coming home to company or not. My self-confidence detour through New York had left me with a feeling of independence and purpose I'd sorely needed to find. I hadn't called Dante to check in. It wasn't until my car was safely parked in my garage that it occurred to me that he hadn't checked in with me either.

There was a note taped to the TV. *Samantha, photos are in the darkroom. I leave it up to you to review and share with your detective friend.*

I filled Logan's water dish and shook a few extra cat kibbles into his bowl. He buried his face in his food as soon as I set it down. I left him alone in the kitchen, figuring we'd have time to catch up later.

I jogged down the stairs and went into the darkroom. The room, originally designed to be little more than a large storage closet, was lined on the right with built-in counter tops that wrapped around to the back wall. Basins of liquid sat next to each other along the counter. Light bulbs were suspended above them from cords that were duct-taped to the wall to keep them out of the way.

The left-hand side of the small closet was filled with metal baker's racks that held cast-off games, toys, and empty glass bottles that my dad had at one time planned to use for his homemade beer and wine. An old scuba suit hung from the corner of one fixture. The mask, snorkel, and flippers sat in a pile on the floor.

I approached the right side of the room. Hanging above the basins of liquid was a length of twine, strung from wall to wall like a clothes line. Small black binder clips secured 8x10 photos of the crime scene onto the twine. I scanned the lot of them, wondering what, if anything, I'd notice.

I spotted the silver wig in the fourth picture. The wig Harper had worn.

The composition of the photo caught the corner of the warehouse. I glanced at the preceding photos and saw what Dante had done. He had started with his back to the building and taken the first picture and then snapped additional pictures as he slowly turned around. In an aerial view of the lot, his pictures would make up one o'clock, three o'clock, nine, and eleven. The photo with the wig was at nine. The wig was on the ground next to a somewhat-rusted tin trash can.

Since being involved in a homicide when I first moved to Ribbon, I'd tried to make up for what I lacked in common sense when it came to crime scenes. I read *Forensics for Dummies* and watched *Adam-12* marathons when I was alone. It was no citizen's police academy, but it was something. It made me think that, if a crime had been committed at this warehouse days ago, the police would have searched through the trash to look for clues.

Which meant the trash overflowing from this can was new.

Which told me someone from the fashion show had returned to Warehouse Five after the fire and thrown the wig out.

What it didn't tell me was why.

I started back at the beginning and followed the narrative. They told a story that continued around the perimeter of the building to the other side of the lot where I'd been. A few photos included me, approaching the dumpster. The last one was me, turned around, yelling for Dante. After that, he must have let the camera dangle from his neck when he ran to where I was.

If I hadn't yelled for him, he might have crept closer. He might have photographed evidence of whatever—or whoever—I'd seen by the dumpster. He might have seen it too.

Whoever started the fire had taken a big chance in doing so while we were on the property. They could have been spotted. Either the fire had been for our benefit, or someone had been trying to destroy evidence before we discovered it. Had that someone been watching us the entire time we were there?

It would take a remote detonator to start a fire from a distance. How far of a distance? I didn't know. But assuming the arsonist had been watching me approach the dumpster, there was a chance he didn't know about Dante, who had been on the other side of the building. That meant the arsonist didn't know about the existence of the photos.

Suddenly, it seemed very important that I set up a meeting with Detective Loncar.

I unclipped the photos and carried them upstairs. The mailman had delivered my auto-insurance documents last week, and I slid them out of the envelope and replaced them with the pictures. I called Loncar. It was seven thirty, and I wondered briefly if his wife ever questioned his off-hour phone activity.

When he answered, I identified myself. "Detective Loncar, this is Samantha Kidd. I know you weren't expecting to hear from me, but I have some information I need to give you."

"Ms. Kidd, I'm about to sit down to dinner. Can this wait until tomorrow?"

"Okay, sure," I said. "I'll come to your office. What time?"

There was a pause. "What's this information in reference to?"

"The Warehouse Five explosion last night. I have pictures that I think you should see, unless you'd rather I take them to Inspector Gigger—"

"Where'd you get these pictures?"

There was no way to skirt the issue and expect the detective to take me seriously, but I didn't want to drag Dante into anything he shouldn't be a part of. "The pictures are legitimate. Anything more will have to wait until we meet."

He made a noise that might have been accompanied by a shake of the head or an eye roll. "Ms. Kidd, where are you?"

"At my house."

"Same address?"

"Same address."

"Hold on." I heard muffled sounds, as if he was holding his

hand over the receiver. Seconds later he returned. "You planning on going out any time soon?"

"No."

"I'm on my way."

By the time Loncar arrived, I had the photos scattered around the living room. They started on the gray sofa and worked their way around the floor to the black-and-white armchairs that sat in front of the blue tweed curtains. The last few were on the chrome-and-glass coffee table, resting on top of the latest book on Halston. There was probably a more standard way to assemble them, but I wanted Loncar to see the photos in the same order I had.

"Hi, Detective. Come on in," I said after greeting him at the door.

He leaned into my house and looked around first and then wiped his feet on the Welcome mat and crossed the threshold.

The last time Detective Loncar had been inside of my house was the day he'd taken me to the police station for suspicion of murdering my boss. I liked to think we'd come a long way since then. Maybe I should have picked up some champagne to celebrate.

"I'm sorry to pull you away from your family time and your dinner."

"Don't mention it."

"No, this could probably have waited—"

"My wife made meatloaf. The last three times she made it, it was still raw in the middle. There's not enough ketchup in the world to save raw meatloaf."

Considering my culinary skills—or rather the lack thereof—I filed that bit of info away for future reference. Who knew ketchup was part of the meatloaf-serving process?

He looked at the photos strewn around the room. "So, what do you have?" he asked.

In the thirteen minutes after hanging up with Loncar and determining the layout of the photos, I convinced myself to tell him where the pictures had come from. I'd started looking into this whole thing because I'd been attacked, but after seeing a body part in the dumpster, I knew that attack was minor compared to whatever was going on.

"Remember the photographer I introduced you to last night? Dante Lestes?" Loncar nodded. "He took these pictures while we were there."

"You didn't mention these last night."

"Dante was on the other side of the warehouse. I didn't know what he was doing over there. He ran around to my side when I saw the fire—and the leg—and the—"

"Explosion. I remember your statement." He shoved his hands into the pockets of his brown coat and looked at the layout of photos.

"Start here," I said, and led him to the first photo. I stood back and watched him move from one to the next, occasionally looking back. When he reached the photo of the trash can by the back door, he picked it up and looked at the back left corner.

"Look at the—"

He cut me off with a hand held palm-side out. I bit my bottom lip and waited for him to say something.

He pulled his cell phone out, thumbed the screen, and held it up to his head. "Yo, chief. Remember those photos from the fire at the warehouse last week? Uh-huh, uh-huh, uh-huh. Find me the one on the north side of the building and check if there was any trash in the bin. They did? Where's it now?"

I stepped forward and opened my eyes wide like I wanted him to tell me what was going on. He turned his back to me. "Uh-huh. Good. Yep. Tomorrow." He hung up.

"Ms. Kidd, tell me what made you notice this particular photo."

"Well, there shouldn't be any trash in the bin, right? Your guys would have emptied whatever was in there the day after the fire. Why's it full? I could understand maybe a couple of paper cups or something, but full? That tells me someone was there after the fire. Someone who had enough to throw out that they filled that trash can."

He nodded.

"And then there's the wig," I added.

"The wig?"

"Right there, that silver thing on the ground. That's the wig Harper Ashton wore in the fashion show the night of the fire. What's it doing in the trash now? Why wasn't it there two days ago? Who threw it away?"

"You're sure Harper wore the silver wig?"

"Yes. I was there. I saw it. Detective, I think somebody's been back to Warehouse Five. I think last night's fire was about destroying evidence."

He picked up the photos from the black-and-white chair closest to the door and sank into it. "Ms. Kidd, we looked in the dumpster after you left last night. We didn't find evidence of a body. The dumpster contents were pretty much destroyed by the time the fire was out, and without a body, there's no homicide. There's no investigation."

"You think I'm making all of this up?"

"No." He set the stack of photos on the coffee table. "We did find one thing on the ground by the edge of the property."

"What?"

"A key card to the warehouse. Photo ID on it says it belongs to Santangelo Toma."

18

———

MAGNET FOR TROUBLE

"Santangelo Toma is an artist who rents space inside Warehouse Five," I said.

"What else do you know about him?" Detective Loncar asked.

"Just that he didn't like how Amanda's team took over the warehouse. He said he hadn't been able to concentrate since they started setting everything up, and he couldn't wait until the show was over. He called it a circus and was unhappy about the whole thing."

Loncar leaned forward. "How unhappy? Are we talking annoyed or angry?"

"He filed a complaint with the building management, but they ignored him. The money Amanda's show was expected to pull in far outweighed the rent of any of the other tenants, so his complaints fell on deaf ears."

"Was he the only one who complained?"

"I think so. He said he started a petition to get her kicked out of the warehouse, but nobody wanted to sign it. Tiny arranged for the rest of the tenants to see the show. Ribbon isn't the biggest town in the world, and most of them were excited about the idea that a major fashion show was going to take place where they worked."

"She excluded him?"

"No, he tore up the tickets and threw them back at her. But he was there. I saw him go backstage before the show. It's on the video. Do you want to see?"

Detective Loncar glanced at my ancient VCR. "I've got my own copy. Thanks." He picked up the stack of photos and tapped the edge along the glass coffee table. "Did you have any personal beef with Mr. Toma?"

"Not that I'm aware of. Do you think he was burning a body in the dumpster?" I shuddered.

"Ms. Kidd, The human body is 90 percent water. It's very difficult to cremate one in an open fire. If there was a body in there, which I'm not saying there was, it wouldn't have burned through all the way."

"What are you saying?"

"It's highly unlikely that what you saw was a human body."

I sat on the arm of the sofa where Logan had been sitting. He sprung out of my way to the back and walked along the top of the cushions like it was a catwalk. Which, considering he was a cat, it was.

"Ms. Kidd, is there anything else you want to tell me?"

"Like what?"

"I'm not the lead on this investigation. Inspector Gigger is. He's taken over everything that we've found and cut us out of the loop. His goal is to find the arsonist. Your statement made it seem like there might have been a murder vic in the dumpster, but we found no evidence of that. Our clues either went up in smoke or were washed down a sewer drain by the firefighters. If you got a theory, I'm willing to listen."

I turned my head and looked at Logan. He was in a ball, his fur spiking up and back. He watched Loncar out of the corner of his eyes, like he knew this man wasn't a regular visitor to our house. I turned my attention from Logan to the detective and saw him watching my cat too.

"Black cats aren't bad luck," I said.

"I know. I have three of them."

As if that was what he needed to hear, Logan stood up and skulked across the length of the sofa, down the arm, to the floor. He sat six inches from the sole of the detective's boot and started to clean his private parts.

"I think whoever started last night's fire was trying to destroy something. Even if he saw me, he might not have known Dante was on the other side of the building. That might be the movement I saw: someone setting fire to the bin. When I went over to investigate, he took off. You just said if it wasn't for me, you wouldn't have even known about that fire."

"You keep saying 'he.' I'm not convinced that the presence of Mr. Toma's ID means he's the arsonist. You got any reason to think it's a man?"

"No. The person who attacked me could have been a man. And I don't mean to sound sexist, but starting fires just seems like more of a man thing. You know, from the caveman days."

He smiled and then tried, too late, to stifle it. "For someone who pulls this stuff out of thin air, you're not too far off. Most arsonists are men. But until we figure out why he's setting these fires, there's not much more a profiler can do."

"I have a theory on that too," I said, bolstered by his compliment. "If this were a serial arsonist—someone who gets their kicks by scaring people—he wouldn't target Amanda, would he? But so far, I was attacked in that parking lot, Amanda's runway show went up in flames, and now a fire was started behind the warehouse. It seems like too much coincidence to be random."

"You think this is someone with a bone to pick with Ms. Ries?"

"She did get those threatening letters," I said.

"You mentioned these letters once before. Tell me about them."

"Come on, Detective, you knew about them before I did."

"Humor me."

"Fine. Two days ago, I went to Amanda's studio. I didn't plan to go there, and I can't say why I went there, but I did. After her partner left, she showed me the letters. There were six of them. Threats. Someone had been trying to scare her before the show. 'Burn, baby, burn,' 'All's well that burns well,' 'If you can't stand the heat, get off the runway.' Stuff like that. They were made from letters cut out of fashion magazines."

"How do you know that?"

"Give me some credit. I can recognize the B in 'Harper's Bazaar' from twenty feet."

He sat up and stared at me while I talked. "Where are these letters now?"

"I figured your department had the originals. I saw copies. I don't know where the copies are now, but there's a chance that Oscar LeVay took them from Amanda's desk."

Loncar stood up and walked away from me. He pulled his phone out and made another call, his voice low and hard to understand. I heard "Ms. Ries" and "letters" and "last week." Then a series of "uh-huhs," a "yeah," and a "got it." He hung up and shoved his phone back into his pocket before turning back around. He sat in the chair opposite me and leaned forward.

"Guy at the desk remembers Ms. Ries coming in last week. She asked what we would do if we found out someone was threatening her. She didn't mention the letters, but the timing fits."

"What did your guy tell her?"

"The truth. The problem with threats is we can't act on them. If we get a chance, we can keep an eye out for suspicious behavior, but other than that, we're stuck until a crime is committed."

"You're saying I could put threatening notes in my neighbor's mailbox—"

Loncar held up his hand. "Putting something in a mailbox is a federal offense."

"Humor me. I could leave her nasty notes to say I was out to get her, and even if she knew the notes were from me, you couldn't do anything?"

"Do you have a beef with your neighbor?"

"She doesn't have to spy on me so much, but other than that, we're good. So?"

"If you threatened your neighbor, and she came to us, there would be a record of her complaint, but unless you acted on that threat, there's not much we can do."

"In Amanda's case, first she was threatened, and then I was attacked. Wasn't that enough?"

He leaned back. His shirt was unbuttoned at the neck and his tie was slightly askew, as if he'd thrown it back on before he came to my house. One of these days I was going to set Detective Loncar up with a personal shopper, just to see what would happen if he dressed in clothes that fit.

"Here's how it goes. Ms. Ries comes to the station and tells the desk sergeant somebody's been threatening her. This isn't the first time she's been at the center of a scandal, and this time she has a runway show coming up. Could be a ploy for publicity. But she's a pretty lady, and she seemed scared, so the desk sergeant answers her questions and tells her to come back when something happens."

"Right. But what about me?"

"See, that's a problem too. Your attack wasn't connected with Ms. Ries. You were assaulted in a public area. You were hospitalized. The report on you went to a different division. Assault charges by unknown assailant. A couple of the beat cops took that report and filed it."

"You checked it out?"

He nodded. "Then there's this fire at Ms. Ries's show. Now Gigger gets called in. His job is to find out who set the fire and stop him before he sets another one. Arsonists prey on people's fears. Even without a murder, you're looking at a lot of heat on the precinct."

"And you were shut out of the investigation. But if—"

"If there had been a body last night, I'd be looking at a homicide investigation. Instead, everything about this case has been departmentalized. I'm looking at a fraction of the big picture. And Gigger's not the sharing type. His one goal is to catch this arsonist before he strikes again."

He leaned back in his chair and smoothed his tie down to his ample belly. "Ms. Kidd, what's your interest in this? I don't mean to get too personal, but it never seemed to me like you and Ms. Ries were close friends."

"Somebody attacked me. Maybe everybody else is willing to dismiss it, but I'm not."

"Most people would take some time to recover, maybe get out of town for a few days."

"I'm not most people."

"Yeah, I figured that out already."

"Detective, I know you think I'm a nuisance. Somebody who showed up in your backyard and has been in the middle of three of your investigations. You might even call me a magnet for trouble, but you'd be wrong. All of this trouble, it was here before I ever came back to Ribbon. I checked. This city's crime has been on the rise for the past decade. I moved here because I had fond memories of the city where I grew up, but the city I'm living in now isn't the one I remember."

Loncar's expression changed. His eyes narrowed slightly, and his lips pursed, like he was considering how far he'd let me insult the city he was charged with protecting. Only thing was, it was my city now too.

"How long have you lived here?" I asked.

His head tipped to the side. He didn't answer right away. Logan stood up and walked past him, rubbing his back against the detective's pant leg.

"I was in Harrisburg five years ago. Picked up a lead on a trail that had gone cold. Couple of kids broke into a row home in center city and killed a man for kicks. I never saw anything like that." He shook his head. "Punks wrote messages on the walls in the victim's blood."

"Like *The Shining*," I said.

"Yeah, only they couldn't spell. The walls looked like something those Chick-fil-A cows might have written. Woulda been a joke if it hadn't been real. That's when it hit home that bad people weren't restricted to big cities."

"That's when you transferred to Ribbon?"

"Yep. Moved when the transfer came through."

"And crime's been on the rise ever since?"

"Yep."

"Maybe *you're* the magnet for trouble," I said.

Loncar smiled.

"Detective, you wanted to know my interest in this. Here it is. I moved back here so I could figure out a more satisfying life for myself. New York City is great for a lot of people, but it wasn't right for me. But since I've been back, I've been framed for murder and almost killed. I volunteered at the exhibit at the museum because I thought it would lead to a job opportunity, but we both know how that turned out. The only job with any security was the one I worked when you asked me to rat on my employers. I'm not trying to prove anything to anybody but myself."

He ran his palms down the thighs of his trousers twice and then rested his hands on his knees. "About that. You got a knack for figuring things out. Now normally, I wouldn't want to encourage you, but it seems I owe you one. You surprised me by showing me these photos. Gigger doesn't have these photos." He held his hand up to keep me from interjecting. "I'm going to share them with him, because that's how this works. But I appreciate you calling and not just because you got me out of meatloaf."

"I'd offer you something to eat, but I don't cook," I said.

"That doesn't surprise me."

"I could if I wanted to. I just have other priorities, that's all."

He stood up. "Ms. Kidd, I'm going to ask you for a favor."

The hair on the back of my neck stood up.

"If you find out anything else that you think relates to any of this, you call me. Deal?"

"That's your favor?"

"I'm not asking you to look for evidence. I'm asking for you to call me if you think you figured something out."

In that one moment, something shifted. I knew it, and Loncar must have known it, but we both acted like everything was the same.

"Sure," I said. He turned to leave, and I followed him to the door. He was halfway to his car before I called out after him. "Hey, Detective?" He turned around. "I think this is the beginning of a beautiful friendship."

"I had a feeling you were going to say something like that," he grumbled. He got into his car and drove away.

19

OPPORTUNITY KNOCKING

THE FIRST THING I DID WHEN I WOKE UP ON TUESDAY MORNING WAS to find the business card for *Retrofit Magazine*. I propped it on the kitchen counter, filled Logan's bowls, and brewed a pot of coffee. I didn't feel my professional self until I showered and dressed, which was eight thirty. I finished off a cup of coffee and called Eddie at Tradava.

"Yo," he answered.

"In thirty seconds or less, can you tell me what's so great about me?"

"Why? You didn't buy purple hair dye, did you?"

"No! I—I'm going for a job today. A bonafide job that isn't working for someone I know and isn't—hopefully—connected to any sociopathic business people."

"You're serious?"

"As a heart attack," I said.

"Dude, it's about time." He paused for a second. "Okay, highlights: you know seven ways to tie an Hermes scarf. You can get ready in fourteen minutes. You are the only woman I know who can wear a necktie and not look butch. And you can eat an entire order of onion rings yourself."

"Those are the highlights?"

"Ask another guy, get another answer."

"Fine. What are my weaknesses?"

"There's no polite way to answer that."

"It's an interview question. She's going to ask. What are my weaknesses?"

"You're incapable of seeing your faults."

"Ha, ha."

"What do you want? You're a Taurus. You're stubborn, self-indulgent, materialistic, and possessive."

"I'm not feeling so good about the onion ring thing anymore."

"Dude. We work in fashion. Of course you're materialistic. And the self-indulgent part? It could be a lot worse."

"What about possessive?"

"Let's just say you still call the trend-specialist job at Tradava yours, and it's been, like, over a year."

"Do you think I can't move on?"

"Here comes the stubborn thing. You think I'm telling you that you can't move on. Now you're going to move on to prove to me that you can. But when you get down to it, I just want you to find whatever it is that's going to make you happy."

"What if what makes me happy takes me back to New York?"

"What can I say? I'm a Gemini. I want everybody to be happy."

"Okay, thanks. I have to go put on shoes and make this phone call."

"You can make a phone call in your bare feet."

"Not if I want the job, I can't."

"Dude." He hung up.

It was two minutes to nine when I called Nancie Townsend. This time she answered.

"Nancie, hi, this is Samantha Kidd. I'm calling about the job at *Retrofit*. Marcia Dann from Bentley's New York sent me. Not sent me. Told me. About you. About the job. I'm it. I'm your gal. I can finish an entire order of onion rings in one sitting."

Did I say that?

Nancie cleared her throat. "Samantha Kidd. You worked at Bentley's New York? For how long?"

"I was with Bentley's for nine years."

"Experience at a major New York luxe retailer. That's perfection."

We spent the next twenty minutes on the phone, talking about orange being the new pink and green being great for food with 30 percent less fat and awful for magazine covers. She laughed at my joke about culottes making a comeback and wanted to know what I thought about country-western as an emerging trend. I said something about suede fringes being acceptable for five minutes every ten years, and she didn't hang up. Things were going well.

I knew what was coming. I knew the inevitable "where are you working now?" question was on the horizon. And aside from a rundown of the dead ends I'd had over the past year, there was no way to distract her, so I headed her off at the pass.

"Nancie, here's the thing. I want this job. I'm qualified for this job. I've had a spotty work history since leaving Bentley's, but I've managed to keep myself connected to the fashion industry. As a matter of fact," I said, my self-indulgent Taurus side directing me, "I've been working with Amanda Ries recently. Her name has been in the news a lot lately."

"I've seen the coverage. That's one heck of a story. From what I saw, the clothes were amazing. Could you get an exclusive?"

"Let me ask her. She's been open to a lot of my suggestions," I exaggerated.

Big mistake. Huge.

"Perfection! Get me an exposé, something about Amanda's troubles. I want it all. The struggles, the collection, the fire. Oh—this will be fabulous. I can see a regular feature: 'designers in the hot seat.' Backstage with designers who are about to have a make-it-or-break-it show. How soon can you get it to me?"

I chewed my bottom lip and turned my back on Logan, who looked suspiciously like he was judging me. "Nancie, you do know that there have been more incidents since her show, right? Maybe instead of focusing on the fire, it's best to let the police find some answers."

"The police? As in, the fashion police?"

"No, as in the police-police. Men with badges who carry guns."

Her voice dropped to a whisper. "Do you know these men? Could we could do an article about them?"

"These police aren't the kind you'd want to feature in a fashion magazine," I said as an image of Gigger as Ichabod Crane popped into my head. "But I tell you what. I'll write a story about Amanda—about the collection and what it was like behind the scenes of the runway show—and email it to you."

"Perfection. But I want film, and I want it to be good. Have the article—with pictures—in my inbox by Friday morning. If it's good, I'll pay you freelance rates to run it, and you'll be the frontrunner for the job."

"Deal."

I took down her email address, and we said goodbye. I turned around to face Logan. "If you didn't like expensive cat food, I wouldn't have to worry so much about things like paychecks and jobs."

He stuck his paw in the air and swatted at a piece of lint and then turned around and disappeared through the narrow opening to the basement.

Now you've done it, I thought to myself. You leveraged your

connection to your ex-boyfriend's maybe-former girlfriend's arson-tainted collection for a possible job opportunity.

One of these days I was going to take the easy road.

Okay, fine. Write an article about Amanda's show. I could do that. I'd spent time working backstage prior to the incident. I knew firsthand what went on before the show started, and I bet a lot of people would find that interesting. Forget the attack. Forget the fire. Forget the mysterious leg sticking out of the dumpster.

I shivered. None of that was going to be easy.

And on top of everything else, I'd promised Nancie photos.

First, I pulled a carton of Neapolitan ice cream out of the freezer. It was slightly less than half full. I ate a scoop and called Amanda. Tiny answered.

"Hi, Tiny. This is Samantha."

"Sam, hey. It's been a couple of days. How are you feeling?"

I cringed. I did prefer 'Samantha.' "Better. The first couple of days were painful, but the doctors said I'll heal. Thanks for asking," I added.

"The doctors gave you a clean bill of health? Which doctors? I'll follow up with them."

I misunderstood her. "I didn't accrue any major medical bills, but thanks for the offer." The phone was silent. "Tiny?" I prompted.

She laughed. "Medical bills. That's funny." She cleared her throat, and I realized the laughter had been forced for impact. "You were attacked in the parking lot. We don't carry liability insurance for accidents that take place in public areas."

"You thought I was going to sue you?"

"Just try it. I doubt you'll get far." There was an awkward pause. "Listen. Sorry about the accusations. Things have been tense around here ever since the fire. First your attack then the fire. It's a never-ending stream of bad publicity. I'd give my right arm for some good press right now."

"You can't honestly tell me that nobody from the media has contacted you about all of this. Somebody must have offered to run a puff piece in order to get an inside scoop."

"That's just it. I don't want a puff piece. I don't want the fire to be the focus. This is a business. Amanda needs coverage that's going to get us orders. Everything else is a distraction."

If I wasn't mistaking, that knocking sound I heard was opportunity standing at my door.

"Tiny, I might be able to help you with that. I spoke to a contact in the industry earlier today, and she's interested in a feature on Amanda's collection. Any chance you can talk her into giving me an exclusive?"

20

HAIL MARY

"Whᴀᴛ's ᴛʜᴇ ғᴇᴀᴛᴜʀᴇ?" Tɪɴʏ ᴀsᴋᴇᴅ.

"Backstage at a runway show, glamour of fashion, the hype of a new designer. That sort of thing."

"She could use something like that. Where will it be syndicated?"

"I can't say."

"Can't or won't?"

"Tiny, somebody's going to write about this sooner or later. Clive Barrington is bound to sell off his photos to the highest bidder. Amanda has a better chance of a fair story with me writing it than with a stranger. I can do the story based on my experiences prior to the show, but it'll be best if I write about the whole thing, fire and all."

I let my words dangle in the air for a few seconds. It was harder to not fill the silence with words than it was to sleep on my side with a midsection full of bruises. Finally, she spoke.

"Can you play ball with Clive?"

"If you give me his number."

She rattled off his digits, and I wrote them on the side of the ice cream carton.

"Be here in an hour. Oscar LeVay is coming for a meeting with Amanda. After that, you're up."

"See you soon." I hung up and grabbed my handbag. No way was I going to pass up a chance to watch Amanda interact with Oscar. I still suspected that he'd taken the threatening letters from her desk, and I wanted to know why.

I shrugged into my coat, wrapped a scarf around my neck, and whipped the front door open. Standing on my doorstep was Molly Diers, my sad-wardrobe client.

She wore the same olive-green snorkel coat she'd worn the first day we met. A brown stain had been added to the front. On her legs were heather-gray sweatpants that ended in elasticized cuffs right above thick white socks and neon cross trainers.

"I'm sorry I'm late," she said. "I had a last-minute yoga class this morning. Did I miss my whole appointment?"

In the mix of everything that had happened—the arson, the date-not-date with Dante, the trip to New York, the potential new job, and the visit with Detective Loncar—I'd completely forgotten about Molly's need for a makeover. The problem was, Molly was in need.

Really, really in need.

"I'm sorry you came all this way. Something came up, and I have to leave. It's an emergency."

"A fashion emergency? Bigger than me?"

I looked her over again. "Can you come back this afternoon?"

"The kids will be out of school at two forty-five. If I can come at four, I could focus more."

"Four. Sure." The only thing I had planned for the day was to go to Amanda's showroom and then come home and write an article for Nancie. I could do that in five hours, right? "Four o'clock. Meet me here, and we'll have another consultation."

"I don't need another consultation. I need clothes. I thought you were going to have something for me to look at today. My ex-husband is coming in for his parents' fiftieth anniversary, and he's bringing Lolita!"

"His new girlfriend's name is Lolita?"

"It might as well be. I can't see him like this." She looked down at the green snorkel coat and picked at a clump of what appeared to be dried-on scrambled eggs.

I did some mental calculation. Go to Amanda's, stop at Tradava on the way home to pick up clothes for Molly, and then come home and write the article. It would be tight, but I could do it. And in the category of keeping myself busy so I didn't think about Nick or Dante, it was just what the doctor would have ordered if there'd been a doctor in this scenario).

"I'll have everything ready when you get here."

"Great. Thank you, Samantha. You are a lifesaver," she said. She pulled a Kleenex from her pocket and dabbed at her nose. I wanted to spin her around and give her a push toward her car, but that seemed rude. Patiently, I stood on my porch and waited for her to put away the soiled Kleenex, pull flotsam out of her other pocket, and dig through it for her car keys. Two sourball candies wrapped in plastic and a pack of matches fell to the porch before she looped her finger through the key ring. I was afraid if she bent down to collect them she'd drop everything else in her hand.

"I'll get it," I said and stooped down. I closed a gloved hand around the candies and picked up the plain white matchbook with my other hand. "Do you smoke?" I asked.

"No, why?"

"I don't see a lot of people with matchbooks these days."

"It's a memento. The last time a stranger hit on me in a bar."

I put my hand on her upper arm and gently turned her around. "Molly, things will get better for you. I don't know how long it's been, but you'll get back out there again."

"What do you mean?"

"I don't know how long you've been carrying around this packet of matches, but your confidence will come back. Before you know it, the nights when strangers hit on you will all run together."

She turned back to face me. "It was this past Saturday night," she said. She glanced at the matches. "He was a creep who was looking for a nude model. Do I look like model material?" She waved her hand up and down the length of her stained snorkel coat. "When my ex left me for a younger woman, I decided to teach my kids something about integrity. But please." She paused. "Do something about this." She left me on the porch and drove away.

I glanced down at the matchbook. It seemed silly that such a small thing could give Molly a confidence boost. It wasn't the matches themselves. It was what they represented.

I was about to toss them when I noticed something written on the inside. I flipped the package open and saw a phone number, followed by the letters C. B. I knew of a C. B. In fact, I knew of a C. B. who was just seedy enough to use a pickup line about models. I raced back inside and pulled the Neapolitan ice cream out of the freezer. The number I'd written on the side matched.

Clive Barrington had given away a pack of matches after the fire at Amanda's show. Did it mean something? I intended to find out. I called the number.

"Clive Barrington," he answered.

"This is Samantha Kidd."

"Ah, love, to what do I owe the pleasure?"

"I was talking to one of my clients, and she just so happened to have a pack of matches with your number on them." I paused for effect. "It struck me as curious that you had a pack of matches on you and that you gave them away the day after the fire at Amanda's show. Perhaps trying to rid yourself of evidence?"

"I hardly think I'd write my name and number inside matches that were used to start a fire. Come on, love. I expected more from you."

And I'd expected less of him. "She said you asked her to model for you. Is that the best pickup line you have?"

"I wouldn't resort to using something so mundane. The models I shoot aren't amateurs. Although I'd make an exception in your case. How about it, Ms. Kidd? Care to let me take artistic photographs of you?"

"No thanks." I hung up without saying goodbye. I tossed the matches on the counter and left.

Even with the sidetracks of Molly's appearance and the conversation with Clive, I still hoped to arrive at Amanda's before Oscar left. I'd have a better chance of getting film for my article if I showed up with a photographer than if I asked permission first. There was only one photographer I had a chance of getting on short notice.

"Dante, this is Samantha. Meet me at Amanda's showroom as soon as you can. Bring your photography equipment." I left the address on his voicemail and disconnected. I nestled the phone into the cup holder next to the list I'd made yesterday while driving home from the Big Apple. "Get job" was at the top. *Stay focused, Samantha. This article is about getting paid, not about the investigation.* And if—no, *when*—I got the job, I'd celebrate by buying Logan that fancy cat toy. Productivity was my middle name.

I parked in the driveway next to a shiny black sedan. It was the same car that had parked next to the Corvette the first day I came to Amanda's studio. I followed the sidewalk to the front door and listened before knocking. The door was too thick. I bent down and crept under the front windows and then peered into the corner.

Oscar stood facing Amanda. Today he wore a navy blue three-piece suit with a paisley necktie. "Thank you for understanding," he said.

"Had she mentioned that she was going to Mexico?" Amanda asked.

"Harper was a loner. She didn't have friends at the agency. The only person she listened to was her sister. If anything, I'd think the others were jealous of her rise. Perhaps that made things more difficult for her. Perhaps that's why she left without telling anyone."

I strained to keep up with their conversation, plugging one finger into my right ear and pressing my left closer to the glass. The voices stopped. After a few seconds, the front door opened. Amanda looked at me standing under the window.

"You're early," she said.

"I was already on my way."

She leaned forward and looked at the patch of lawn where I'd been standing and then turned around and went inside. I followed.

"Have a seat. Oscar and I are finishing up."

Oscar wasn't in the room, and I hardly suspected him of hiding behind the wicker screen like I'd done days before. "Where is he?" Just then, a toilet flushed. "Oh."

The tall man came out of the powder room. He saw me and then asked Amanda, "We've reached an understanding?" She nodded. He lifted a wool cape from a peg on the wall and draped it around his broad shoulders. He picked up his hat from a chair and tipped it my direction before putting it on and leaving.

"Is everything okay?" I asked.

"'Okay' is hardly the term I'd use."

"Is he still demanding payment?"

"Yes," she said. "And Tiny said I have to pay if I want to come out of this with my reputation intact."

"Where is Tiny? I expected her to be here."

"She's at the bank. Nobody wants anything from me except for money."

"Amanda, this article can help you with that. I don't know how much Tiny told you, but I saw the collection at the showroom. I know the vibe you were going for. I'm a good person to make this happen because of that. If you're interested, let me get a few shots around here. Your office, your inspiration boards, your samples. What didn't make the runway show and why? That sort of thing."

She sipped her coffee and the silence ballooned. I waited her out. Finally, she set the mug down on her desk and crossed her arms. "This collection was inspired by Kaiju movies and outer space."

"But prior to this collection, you were known for classic silhouettes. You interned for Maries Paulson—"

"Tiny doesn't want me to talk about that collaboration."

"Why not?"

"She says I have to make a name for myself, not rely on the names of people I worked for."

I didn't understand Tiny's motivation. Amanda's past collaborations and internships would separate her from a pack of recent design school graduates. Her experience would show that she had more than what you can teach in a classroom. Tiny sounded like she wanted to negate all of that. It seemed to me that Amanda didn't need a business partner. She needed a publicist.

"When you graduated from design school, your first solo collection was ice-cream factory meets Ralph Lauren. Lilac turtlenecks and riding pants, pink satin ball skirts with fitted T-shirts and cropped bouclé jackets, robin's-egg blue wool blazers with matching suede elbow patches. How do you go from that to Godzilla on the moon?" I waved my hand around the part of the showroom filled with racks of cast-off garments.

"My preppy stuff wasn't getting me noticed. Tiny said I needed a

Hail Mary. That's what this collection was. A big risk that could have potentially changed everything. I had appointments with editors from all the major magazines lined up to view the samples after the show."

"What happens now?"

"No samples, no appointments." She waved toward a rack. "These are new. Tiny pushed me to make a second set of samples to show the buyers who showed interest." She stepped away from the fixture and looked over my shoulder. "Who are you?" she said suddenly.

I turned around. Dante stood inside the room.

"I'm the new photographer. Samantha asked me to meet her here." He pulled a business card from inside his leather jacket and handed it to her. She studied it for a couple of seconds and then stuffed it into her pocket.

"Tiny didn't say you were bringing a photographer," she said to me.

"Amanda, consider this a second chance to make that Hail-Mary pass that Tiny talked about. I'm here. He's here. We'll take photos. You can use them to shop the collection to whomever you want." I held my breath. Her eyes bounced back and forth between my left eye and my right, like she'd discovered that they were two different colors. (They weren't.)

"Your photographer isn't prepared for a full-on photo shoot."

"I have everything I need in the car," Dante said.

Now her eyes bounced back and forth between him and me. "You're not going to get a better chance than this one," I said. "Especially one that won't cost you an arm and a leg."

She pulled her phone out of her pocket and scrolled through her contacts. Before making a call, she looked up. "One model, one hour."

"I have a better idea," Dante said. "Let Samantha try on the samples. Save you money on a model and the time it would take her to get here. You'll be here the whole time, so you'll see everything I see."

Before I had a chance to point out that I wasn't exactly a model size, Dante pinched my arm. I didn't know him well enough to know what he was thinking, but I hoped he had more of a plan than embarrassing me with a split seam.

"That'll work," Amanda finally said.

"I'll get my equipment," he said. "Samantha, you want to help?"

"Samantha can get undressed. I'll help." She pointed to the small scrim that I'd hidden behind when Oscar LeVay had first stormed into the showroom. "Change behind that. Samples are on this rack. Considering the sizes, you might want to start with the kimonos."

I made a face at her behind her back and then, when the front door closed, grabbed a garment and disappeared behind the scrim. Within seconds my motorcycle jacket, sweater, skirt, tights, and boots were on the floor, and I was clothed in a thin red cotton robe. The showroom was colder than I would have liked, and as soon as Amanda and Dante returned, it would be obvious to everybody in the room.

While Dante's plan had the possibly intended goal of embarrassing me, it had also left me alone in Amanda's showroom until they returned.

First thing I did was look through her desk drawers for the threatening letters. With one hand holding the robe shut, I made slow progress. I needed both hands. I let go of the neckline and dug through her desk. Five pairs of scissors, a couple of tape measures, a stack of sketch pads. Paper clips, Post-its, pencils and pens and highlighters. I was so absorbed in the search of her desk that I didn't hear her come back inside.

"Just what the heck do you think you're doing?" Amanda asked.

21

BOW ON THE BACK

BREAKUP RULE #6: KEEP WEARING GOOD UNDERWEAR.

The red cotton robe flew open. Dante's camera snapped several shots. I pulled the robe closed and glared at him.

"I was looking for the letters," I said.

Amanda crossed the room and slammed her desk drawers shut. "You weren't supposed to tell anybody about those," she hissed. She looked at Dante and then back at me.

"I'm only trying to help."

"Then do what you said you were coming here to do." She disappeared into the back room.

Dante stepped closer to me. I looked up at him, my knuckles turning white as I clutched the robe shut. "Thanks for the heads up. I thought you were going to be lugging in a bunch of equipment?"

"I said 'equipment.' I never said 'a bunch.'" He glanced down at my white knuckles. "I know you're cold, but you're going to have to relax for the photos."

"Fine. Tell Amanda to turn up the heat."

He slipped his hand inside the collar of the robe, bent down, and kissed the side of my neck. Cold was no longer an issue.

I stepped back. "Let's do this."

One hour and seventeen costume changes later, I was back in my turtleneck, skirt, and boots. Dante had used one large overhead light as a spot above me. I rested in a chair opposite Amanda's desk while he packed it up.

"I'm curious," Amanda said. "Why do you use film when you could go digital?"

"Film captures reality," Dante said. "It takes more than a point-and-click mentality to get the shot. You know those Hollywood glamour photos from the thirties and forties? Film. One overhead light, just like we used here. The light defines the angles of the face. No need for retouching. You might want to consider it for your catalog."

"You're not going to touch these up?" I asked in a panic.

"I'll use a white pencil to bring out the highlights. I won't need more than that."

I found an empty hanger and rehung the red robe. It had served as my between-outfits costume, keeping the secret that I couldn't close most of Amanda's samples. Amanda glanced at me and stood up. "Can I talk to Samantha alone for a second?"

"Sure." I gave Dante an I-don't-know-what-this-is-about look. He hoisted his bag onto his shoulder, saluted us, and then left.

As soon as the door was shut, she held out her hand. "I'd like those letters back," she said.

"I don't have them."

"Where are they?"

"You left them on your desk the day you showed them to me. I hid behind the screen when Oscar showed up, and when I came out, they were gone."

Her hand flew to her mouth. "Oscar took them? Why didn't you say anything?"

"I thought maybe you had the foresight to put them away before you let him in. If you didn't, then I think it's safe to assume he took them. You didn't think anything when they were missing?"

"Like I said, I thought you took them." Her eyes were wide with fear. "This is bad."

"Amanda, he only has a copy. Tell the police. They have the originals, right?"

"What are the police going to do?"

"They'll ask him about them. That'll keep you from being involved. Let Detective Loncar do his job," I finished.

Amanda shooed me out of her studio, and I found Dante waiting by the Corvette. "You were pretty good in there," he said.

"Yeah, well, don't do that to me again."

"What? I thought you'd like having a chance to examine the samples up close. I can't think of anything closer than getting you inside them."

"In case you didn't notice, I didn't entirely fit inside them," I said, remembering the strapless red gown that didn't zip up the back. Thanks to Dante's suggestion that I step in as a model, Amanda had gotten an unexpected peek at my underwear. Hard to maintain post-breakup moral high ground around the maybe-former girlfriend when she knows you have a bow on the back of your panties.

"Come on. I'll buy you lunch to make up for it."

"No thanks," I said. "I'm going to skip lunch. Too much to do. You should get back to the darkroom to develop the film."

He slung his bag over one shoulder and tipped his head. "Just because the red gown didn't zip up over your hips doesn't mean you have to give up food," he said.

"You think the fact that I didn't fit in a sample-sized dress is going to make me give up food? You have a lot to learn about me."

"I guess I do."

I zipped up my coat. The air was cold and wet, like the gas around a fresh tray of ice cubes when you first pull them out of the freezer. I stopped by my car, closed my eyes, and took a deep breath. I held it in for a few seconds and then exhaled. The crispness invigorated me. I'd always loved the first cold snaps of the season, the promise of impending flurries, and the beauty of a fresh blanket of white snow when it covered the streets and yards.

A series of clicks sounded. I opened my eyes and found Dante aiming the camera at me. I threw my hand up in front of my face. "What are you doing? The photo shoot is over."

"Just thought I deserved something for my hard work."

"I think you got that something when my kimono opened up."

"I didn't look," he said. He kept a straight face, and I almost believed him.

I unlocked the car and tossed my bag on the passenger-side seat. "I have a client coming this afternoon, and I don't want any distractions."

"A distraction, huh? I was wondering how you compartmentalized me."

"I don't compartmentalize people," I said. Real classy, I thought. That's the equivalent to did not/did too on the fourth-grade playground.

Dante folded his arms on the top of the Corvette and leaned on them. The black leather of his motorcycle jacket tightened around his muscles. A blast of wind tossed my hair around my face. Dante's jet-black Elvis-style hair barely moved, except for the strands that dusted his forehead.

"Samantha, I don't judge you for who you are, but that doesn't mean I don't see who you are. You put people in boxes to keep them separate from each other. It's like you're protecting your relationships so they're there when you need them. Friends go here." He stood up straight and pantomimed something on his left side. "Bad guys go here." He pantomimed to his right. "I don't know where you tried to file your last boyfriend. I don't even know if he's still in the picture." He walked around the Corvette and stopped when he was facing me. He reached a hand out and tugged on the collar of my coat. "I'm waiting to see where you file me."

"I can't offer you anything other than what we have right now," I said.

He picked up my hand and pressed my fingers to his lips. "You'll tell me when you figure things out?"

"I'll tell you when I figure things out."

He nodded and put his equipment in the Corvette. I got into my car, backed out of Amanda's driveway, and left. As I reached the corner, I glanced in the rearview mirror. Dante was still standing by the Corvette, watching me drive away. I turned right at the corner, turned right again at the stop sign, and pulled over into the red zone.

I wasn't anywhere close to figuring things out.

Since leaving Dante's apartment yesterday morning, I'd gone to New York, reconnected with my boss, talked my way into a job opportunity, and established a working relationship with Detective Loncar. These were all people who served a purpose. Was Dante right? Did I compartmentalize the people in my life so they'd be there when I needed them?

I didn't like how that sounded. Even if, for the first time since leaving New York, I felt like I had something to focus on. If not for the arsons, things would have been looking good. Why? Because I'd pushed thoughts of Dante and of Nick out of my mind for twenty-four hours and focused on me? Or because I had temporarily surrounded myself with people who could offer me a boost when I sorely needed it?

That's it. I didn't want to be someone who used her friends. I thought back to Molly Diers's desperation this morning. She was counting on me to make things a little better when she had to face her ex and his new young girlfriend. I could do that. Starting now—right now—I was going to do something for someone else—for her.

Work history notwithstanding, Tradava was as good a place as any to start building Molly's new wardrobe. I went in a side door, past juniors, to the coffee counter. I found Eddie on the top rung of a six-foot-tall ladder, a hot glue gun in one hand and a fist full of glue sticks in the other.

As visual director for the store, Eddie oversaw the various displays that showcased designers, trends, and colors. Most people didn't recognize the effort that went into maintaining the newness of a store that had been around for several decades.

A row of white mannequins, clothed in ensembles of red, orange, and winter white, lined the wall usually occupied by a display of chocolates. I adopted a pose at the end of the row and stood still. Eddie climbed down the ladder and stood back, assessing the work he'd finished. He turned around and scanned the row of mannequins. When he got to me, he shook his head. Glue dribbled from the glue gun and left a trail down the side of his paint-stained jeans.

"If you're trying to get lost in a crowd, you might want to find a different crowd."

"You're saying I'm not mannequin material?" I asked. I put a hand on the arm of the mannequin next to me, and she rocked dangerously to the left.

"Dude!" Eddie said. He shoved the glue gun into his pocket,

raced forward, and caught her. "These mannequins cost a grand a piece."

"For real?"

"New mannequins are either fiberglass or plastic, and they are the definition of cheap. I'm trying to maintain a tiny shred of nostalgia in an ever-changing world of hot pants and prom dresses."

Suddenly he hopped on his left foot and kicked his right foot like there was a mouse in his pant leg. He made a *woop woop woop* sound like Curly from the Three Stooges and hopped in a circle. The cord from the glue gun wrapped around his leg. Now tangled, he lost his balance and fell forward. His hands connected with the mannequin on the end and knocked her over. Her arm popped off, slid out of the sleeve, and landed on the ground. The plaster broke by her elbow, but the arm didn't fall off. I yanked the cord to the glue gun out of the wall.

"You're supposed to unplug it when it's not in use," I said. "Unless you know something I don't."

He picked up the plaster arm from the floor. There was a half-inch space between the components that had broken, and in the middle was a steel rod.

"Another one bites the dust," he said.

"Why didn't it fall apart?"

"There's a steel frame inside the plaster."

"Can you shoot a bunch of hot glue in the middle and squeeze it shut?"

"I wish. When these old ones break, they have to be destroyed. There's too much chance of them cracking more and causing an accident around customers."

"You're going to send her off to the mannequin graveyard?"

"Worse. Broken mannequins have to be destroyed. Security arranges a pickup with a special trash-removal company. And I can't yell at anybody over this one because it was my fault." He suddenly looked at me. I held my hands up in front of my waist palm-side out.

"Don't even think about blaming this on me."

His shoulders fell, dejected. He pulled the large black radio off his belt. "Walt, this is Eddie. I got a broken mannequin on one, by the coffee shop. Nothing dangerous, but it's one of the old ones. It's gonna have to be burned."

My head snapped up. "Why do you have to burn it?"

He waved me silent and held the radio up to his mouth again. "Not the whole thing. Broken arm. Sure, I might have another lying around. I'll put it behind the coffee counter. Get it when you're ready." He hooked the radio back to his belt.

"Why do you have to burn them?"

"You see how big this thing is? Imagine how much space it would take up in the trash. And like I said, they're expensive. The iron framework inside can be recycled, but the plaster has to be burned off, and then the iron has to cool and be professionally cleaned before the company can start over. We get back like a tenth of the price of the mannequin, but it's something."

"Who burns them?"

"I don't know. Some company with a big incinerator. What do you care?"

I chewed on my lip and remembered the mannequins that were staged by the entrance of Amanda's show. "I have to call Detective Loncar. I think somebody might have been burning a mannequin in the dumpster behind Warehouse Five."

22

TOPEKA

BUT BEFORE I CALLED THE DETECTIVE, I NEEDED TO KNOW WHAT I was talking about. "You said these mannequins were made of plaster. What else are they made of?" I asked Eddie.

"Horse hair and cotton fibers to make them stronger."

That's exactly what I'd started to suspect. I didn't know much about the flammability of plaster, but when you added in the content of cotton fibers, you had something that would burn. And if someone burned a plaster mannequin leg, the only thing left would be the steel rods inside.

I called Loncar. "Detective, remember how I saw a leg in the dumpster at Warehouse Five? But you found no evidence of a body? And how Ichabod—I mean, Inspector Gigger—didn't believe me?"

There was a sound on the other end of the phone like a chuckle.

"Gigger was right." I continued. "There wasn't a person in the dumpster. There was a mannequin. Maybe not a whole mannequin but a part of one. If you can come to my house tonight, we can go over my theory in more detail. I have an appointment at four that should last an hour, and that's my priority. And I have to write an article, but I can work on that after you leave. So, seven? Can you come then?"

"Fine," he repeated. "See you tonight."

MOLLY DIERS'S car was in my driveway when I returned home. I pulled in behind her minivan, backed out, and parked next to the mailbox. After wrestling with the merchandise I'd bought at Tradava after I called Loncar, I shut the door with my hip and headed toward the house. Molly was on my front porch with two boys. Logan sat inside the big picture window staring out, and one of the boys had his face pressed against the window staring in. The other boy sat on the swing next to Molly, his head buried in a book.

"I hope you don't mind. I was late picking the boys up from school and didn't have time to take them home." Her eyes cut to the packages draped over my arm. "Are those for me?"

"A couple of last-minute items," I said. "Why are you waiting outside? You must be freezing."

"They wouldn't stop bothering each other in the car. The rule was they could get out if they didn't talk."

I looked at the one with the book and the one antagonizing Logan. They looked angelic enough. If Molly could deal with her two boys sitting in the background while she tried on clothes, then I was going to deal with her two boys sitting in the background while she tried on clothes. I threw the bags over my left arm and unlocked the front door.

"Follow me," I said to Molly.

"Is she a witch?" the non-book-reading boy asked. "She has a black cat."

"She's not a witch, dummy," said the boy reading the book. "She's probably a pagan."

"Joseph!" Molly said. "You take that back."

"I take it back," Joseph said. "Maybe she *is* a witch."

I let Molly lead the way to my basement/studio and carried the shopping bags down the steps behind the trio. Not-Joseph sat on a folding chair, swinging his legs above the exposed cement floor. Joseph set his book down on the chair next to his brother and wandered to the bookcases against the back wall.

"Molly, are you sure you still want to do this today?" I asked.

"I told you this morning. I need a dress for this weekend, and I'm running out of time."

"But if you're busy keeping track of the boys—"

"Do you have any puzzles? They love puzzles. Any puzzles."

I scrounged around and came up with two unsolved Rubik's cubes. Within thirty seconds the only sound was the click of plastic against plastic.

First crisis averted.

"Today is about determining what shapes look good on you and what you like. We might not agree on everything. I'll give you an honest opinion, but ultimately it's your money, so you have to feel good about spending it," I said. It was the same speech I gave every client. I had a feeling Molly would take it more seriously than most.

"I can't believe this is my life. I used to know about stuff like this, and now I'm paying you to make sure I don't walk out of here looking like a fool," she said. "The things we do for family."

I hung the shopping bags on an empty rolling rack and tore the plastic down from the hangers. I handed the first round of clothes to Molly and lowered my voice.

"Remember those matches you dropped the other day? Is there anything else you can tell me about the guy who gave them to you?"

Her lips curled into a frown. "Why do you keep asking about him? He was a nobody."

"You kept the matches, which meant something,"

"Yeah, it meant I wanted to light some candles in my apartment." She grabbed the black dress in my hand and turned away.

"Molly, don't sell yourself short. You're a beautiful woman, and when we're done here, everybody is going to see it."

She looked at me for a second, and her expression softened. "He told me I reminded him of a model he used to work with," she said. "It was just a line that a creep in a bar probably uses on every woman who walks in, but I liked the way it sounded."

"It's the accent," I said. "Makes everything sound good."

"What accent?"

I narrowed my eyes and looked at her. Something didn't make sense. She took the clothes and undergarments that I held out to her and carried them to the darkroom I'd indicated for her fitting room. A moment later, the door opened back up, and she came out, her face bright red. Dante was behind her.

"I'm sorry," he said to Molly. "You surprised me as much as I surprised you."

Molly looked at him and then me. "Was that part of the plan—send me into a dark closet with a sexy man?"

"Nope. Not part of the plan." I glared at Dante and then turned back to face her. "This is Dante. He's a photographer. He sometimes uses that room to develop photos."

Behind me, Joseph spoke. "That's probably where she casts her spells."

"Mom! Don't go in there!" Not-Joseph cried out.

The look that I gave the two boys probably didn't do much to prove I wasn't a witch.

I turned back to Molly. "The room is empty now. You can go in and change."

She leaned into the doorway, more tentatively this time. When she was convinced no more tattooed bikers were lurking about inside, she closed the door behind her.

"What are you doing here?" I hissed at him.

"You told me to come here and develop the film, remember?"

"Are you finished?"

"The prints are drying. Who is this woman? Do you trust her? Because every photo I took today is hanging in there."

"She's a client." The door opened slowly, and Molly poked her head out. "Samantha, can I ask you something in private?"

I left Dante and crossed the room to her. "Yes?"

"These photos of you. What are they from?"

"I'm writing an article on a local designer and needed some art. Last-minute thing—no time to hire a model."

"That man is your photographer? Do you trust him?"

I looked at Dante, who was fiddling with one of the Rubik's cubes while the boys watched.

"More than I probably should," I said.

"I wish I met men I could trust." She shut the door again, and I went back to Dante.

"This woman just went through a nasty divorce. Her ex-husband has a girlfriend half his age, and her in-laws invited her and the kids to their golden anniversary party this weekend."

"I know you're not seriously leading up to asking me to be her date."

"God, no!" The clicking of the plastic toys in the background stopped. I froze and looked at Dante. He looked behind me. He smiled at them. The clicking started again. "If I'm going to help her,

I need her undivided attention. That means no you and no them." I tipped my head toward Joseph and Not-Joseph. "As in, can you make them go away? Like, to the kitchen?"

"You think their mom is going to let me take her kids?"

"I think their mom would pay you to take her kids."

The door behind me opened, and I turned to look at Molly's head, poking out from behind the door. She looked nervous.

"Come on out," I said.

She walked to the center of the room wearing a close-fitting jersey wrap dress. Until today, I hadn't realized what kind of body Molly had under that snorkel coat. The jersey molded to her long, lean torso, nipping in at the waist where she'd cinched the wrap-around tie. Behind me, I heard the click of a shutter. Molly copped a couple of poses and pouted, and Dante clicked a few more frames.

"You're a natural," Dante said.

"It's the dress," Molly said. She stepped in front of the full-length mirror and studied herself.

"Molly, if it's okay with you, Dante can take the boys to the kitchen for a snack, and that'll give us a chance to concentrate."

"Yes, please," she said to Dante. He said something to the boys. They looked at him in awe. He tipped his head toward the stairs. "I hope you guys like ice cream and pretzels." He looked at me. I made a face. Not-Joseph giggled, and then the boys followed Dante.

"Who is he, the Pied Piper?" she asked.

"He's a friend."

"You think he's busy this Saturday night?"

"If I were you, I'd make other arrangements."

The impending in-law anniversary celebration had shifted Molly's priorities from single mother getting by to wardrobe overhaul. By the time we were finished, she chose two-thirds of what I'd assembled during my high-speed shopping trip at

Tradava, including a paisley printed tunic, several pairs of boot-cut pants, an amber cowl-neck sweater with an asymmetric hem, two suede skirts, and the jersey wrap dress for the party. She wanted to pair it with fishnets and stilettos. Not entirely appropriate for a fifty-year wedding celebration, but if it was between that and her snorkel coat, I knew which way I'd cast my vote.

After Molly left with her boys in tow (freshly tattooed thanks to Dante's skills with a waterproof eyeliner pen), I opened and closed the cabinets looking for food. I wasn't known for going long stretches of time without a meal, and turning down Dante's lunch invite had left me hungry. And when I was hungry, I had a hard time focusing. I pulled a package of frozen chicken breasts out of the freezer and set them in the sink and then stared out the window into the yard next door.

"Topeka," Dante said, joining me in the kitchen.

"What?"

"Topeka. Capital of Kansas. The way you were staring out the window, I figured you were doing some mental gymnastics. For me, that's either state capitals or times tables."

"Why'd you say Topeka?"

"Most people get stuck on Kansas."

"I'm good with Kansas. I get lost in the M states."

He grinned. "The photos from today are in your basement. You want to go look at them? I didn't see anything abnormal, but I don't know what you're looking for."

"Sure." I went down the stairs with Dante behind me. The rack of clothes from Tradava stood in the middle of the basement, covered in cast-offs that Molly hadn't rehung. An ivory dress had fallen from the plastic hanger and lay in a pool of wool jersey on the floor. I tossed it over the top of the bar and then went into the darkroom.

Dante had clipped large photos to rope strung along the wall, photos that held images of me in Amanda's samples, photos that captured the interior of Amanda's studio. More than one captured the unflattering view of the unzipped back of the too-small red gown. If Dante hadn't been the one who took the pictures, I might have tried arguing that it wasn't me. But now two people knew about the bow on the back of my panties.

He slipped his arms around me, and I leaned back against his chest. "It's getting late. I've developed most of the photos. I can come back tomorrow to finish the rest. Unless you want me to stay..." His hands glided upward, and his lips brushed against the side of my hair.

I turned around and boosted myself up onto one of the unused counters, legs dangling down the cabinet like Joseph's legs had dangled from the folding chair out front. The red glow from the bulbs and the intimate setting of the darkroom were navigating our conversation in a direction that made me nervous. Not bad-nervous. Ramped-up-pulse nervous.

Dante's heat was palpable. His eyes were dark and mysterious. His black rockabilly pompadour gleamed with the red lights reflecting off it, and his lips were fuller than I'd noticed until now. And they were about two inches from my own.

I remembered how it had felt to kiss him last night. Soft. Tender. He placed a hand on the counter on either side of my hips and leaned in so far that his lips almost touched mine. I leaned forward and nipped at his lower lip. His fingers reached under my sweater.

A knock on the door of the garage interrupted us.

I pulled back. "That must be the detective," I said in a raspy voice. "I asked him to come over tonight."

Dante hung his head down, his hands still planted on either side of me. "Great," he said in a voice that matched my own. "We can show him the photos."

I hopped down from the counter and left. Dante followed. But when I got to the garage door and looked out the window, I knew it wasn't great at all.

Detective Loncar wasn't alone. The person with him was Amanda.

23

IT'S COLD OUT THERE

"What's Amanda Ries doing here? With my detective?" I asked out loud. To myself I added *while Dante and I were about to cross a line I wasn't sure I was ready to cross?* while also taking note of the possessive pronoun I'd applied to Loncar.

"Only one way to find out," Dante said.

I opened the door to the garage and motioned them in. Loncar's breath came out in puffs thanks to the drop in temperature. The air felt moist and cold. Like snow was on its way.

"Ms. Ries came to the police station to talk to me. I think you should hear what she has to say." He looked over my shoulder at Dante. I turned and looked at Dante too.

"I was just leaving," he said. The four of us walked through the garage and into the house. Loncar and Amanda waited in the kitchen. Dante shrugged into his motorcycle jacket and zipped it up. I walked him to the door.

"You don't have to leave," I said.

"I think I do. You went stiffer than a surfboard the second you saw Amanda, and I'd place money on what you were thinking. I don't think it had much to do with the arson investigation. You're not over the shoe guy yet."

I blushed and turned away. The coat closet was opposite the front door, and I reached inside and pulled out a black plaid wool scarf. I draped it around Dante's neck and kept my hands on the ends. "It's cold out there."

"I'm not all that worried about the weather. Good night, Samantha."

He left. I stood by the door and watched him straddle his motorcycle, pull on his helmet, and back the bike off its kickstand. When he was out of my driveway, he cranked the engine and took off.

Breakup Rule #7: Recognize when you're not ready to move on. Amanda knew Dante was working with me in the capacity of photographer. She'd fired Clive and brought him on based on my recommendation. Catching him here at my house must have triggered questions about my real relationship with him. And while I doubted she and Detective Loncar had gotten into a discussion of my love life, Loncar had seen Dante and me together at Warehouse Five. Finding him here, after dark, might compromise my story about Dante being the official new photographer for Amanda's collection.

I joined Loncar and Amanda in the kitchen. "Can I get either of you anything?" I asked, hoping the answer was wine, pretzels, or ice cream, assuming Dante and the boys hadn't finished off two out of those three.

"No thanks," Amanda said. Loncar just shook his head.

We moved to the living room. Amanda sat in one of the arm chairs, her back to the window. Loncar kept his hand on the back of the other chair but did not sit. I, being of the why-stand-when-you-can-sit philosophy, took the sofa.

"Did something happen?" I asked.

Loncar looked at Amanda. Amanda looked at the floor.

"Ms. Ries, I assume you came here to tell Ms. Kidd what you told me earlier. Why don't you go first?"

Amanda stared at her hands like she'd just discovered they were there. She wore a set of gold rings on her left hand, and with her right she slid them up to her knuckle and back into place.

Whatever it was Loncar wanted her to tell me, she wasn't eager to share. I stared at the top of her head while she played with her jewelry. The clinking of the gold rings against each other was the only sound in the house. She looked up at me, her face pale and gaunt. "Can I use your restroom?"

"Sure. It's the room directly at the top of the stairs," I said.

She moved quickly. Soon after the door shut, I heard her retching.

"Detective, what's going on? Why did you bring Amanda with you?"

"I didn't. She must have come here after she came to me. We met up in front of your house."

"What's going on?"

Logan stuck his head out from under the sofa. The detective held his hand down, and Logan sniffed it. "Ms. Kidd, I came here to talk to you about the fire in the dumpster outside of Warehouse Five."

"Did you check it out? Did you find anything?"

"Gigger had the contents of the dumpster bagged. They're at his office. You want to tell me what I'm looking for?"

I picked up a piece of paper and made a quick sketch of the steel disc that I'd seen by the arm hole of Eddie's mannequin "About three inches in diameter, with a hole in the middle. There are openings like triangles. It'll look like the bomb-shelter-fallout signs from the fifties."

Loncar stood up and turned his back to me. He wandered into

the kitchen and made a call. When he came back, he was looking at the face of his phone, swiping through photos.

"Is this what you're talking about?" He handed me his phone.

The image on the screen matched the steel disc on the inside of the plaster mannequin joint I'd seen at Tradava.

"Yes," I said. "It's a piece of metal from a plaster mannequin. It fits around the arm holes and leg holes, so you can snap the limbs into place. That disc says that somebody burned a mannequin. But why? Why throw it out in the first place?"

"You were pretty sure you saw a leg."

"Don't you see? I did see a leg. It wasn't a person's leg. It was a mannequin leg. That's why you didn't find evidence of a person inside the dumpster."

He stared at the picture on his phone and nodded. I studied his face, looking for signs of exasperation or disbelief. There was no eye rolling. No shaking head. No rescinding his offer to listen to my theories.

I continued. "Amanda's show was at Warehouse Five, and she had mannequins in the lobby before the show."

"The mannequins at the mall are plastic. We would have smelled the burning plastic when the dumpster went up in flames. You were close to the fire. You probably would have had some fluorocarbon poisoning."

"New mannequins are plastic, but not these. They're made of plaster and metal. They're a lot heavier than the new ones. More durable too. Someone would have to be pretty strong to get one into the dumpster."

"How do you know so much about mannequins?"

"My friend Eddie Adams told me. You remember him, right? Tradava's visual director who worked the hat exhibit at the museum?"

Loncar nodded.

"When these mannequins get broken, Tradava calls a special company to dispose of them. They incinerate the mannequin and recycle the steel rods inside the torso and limbs."

"Whoever tried to burn the mannequin must not have known about the steel frame inside."

"Or whoever tried to burn the mannequin didn't care so much about destroying it. They cared about destroying whatever it was wearing."

Loncar looked up. "You think this was about destroying the clothes?"

"The rest of the clothes from Amanda's show were destroyed, weren't they?"

The water turned on upstairs, and the toilet flushed. The door opened and then shut. More throwing up.

"I think I should see if she's okay," I said.

"When I feel like that I want to be alone."

"Do you know why she feels like that?"

"I get the feeling she's not entirely happy about the reason she's here."

"Are you going to tell me what it is?"

"It's her business to tell you, not mine." He stood up. "I'm going to follow up on this mannequin lead." He waved the page with my sketches. "I'll let you know if anything comes of it."

Loncar didn't have to tell me anything if he didn't want to, and we both knew it. "I appreciate it," I said.

He nodded once and let himself out.

I went to the kitchen and filled a glass with ice and ginger ale. After climbing the stairs, I tapped gently on the bathroom door.

"Amanda, it's Samantha. The detective left." I waited a beat. She didn't respond. "I brought you ginger ale."

"Come in," she said.

Of all the places I could have imagined spending time with

Amanda, my bathroom wasn't one of them. She sat on the fluffy pink carpet square by the base of the toilet with her back leaning against the wall. Her glossy black hair had been pulled back and tucked into the collar of her sweater. Her eyes were bloodshot and framed in circles that had gotten darker since she'd arrived. I held out the glass. She waved it off. She stood up and rinsed her mouth with tap water, dried her face on a hand towel, and sat back down.

"You must love this," she said. "Homicide detectives showing up at your door and me throwing up in your bathroom. Can I ask you a question?"

"Shoot."

"Why did you keep showing up to help me?"

"Because after a year of trying to do things I wasn't so good at, I wanted to do something I was."

She picked at the pink carpet fibers. "I thought I was good at designing clothes. If I'd thought for a second my career would go this way, I never would have bothered."

"Amanda, you're a fashion designer. It's a stressful job. Not arsonists-and-attackers stressful, but it's not like you spend your day in a glass cage with kittens. No matter what happens, you have to find a way to deal with the stress."

I lowered myself until I was sitting across from her. She took a sip of the ginger ale. "Is this how you felt when you first moved here? Like the walls were closing in around you and there was no way out?"

"A little."

"I didn't make things any better for you. I thought you were trouble. When Nick suggested I have you work on the show, I was afraid of what would happen."

"Are you accusing me of something?"

"No. But I was afraid that your presence would make things

more difficult. My best friend's ex-girlfriend. Not exactly the qualifications I would have written up on the want ad."

"You wanted my help. And after the fire, when I came to your studio, you confided in me about those letters."

"That's what I'm trying to tell you, Samantha. That wasn't real. Everything Nick had told me about you said you weren't going to walk away when you were attacked. I couldn't deal with that, too, so I sent you on the trail of an imaginary bad guy." Her face went even more ashen. "Don't you see? There's no anonymous threat."

"But your show went up in flames, and the threats in those letters—"

"Samantha, please, listen to me. I made those letters myself."

24

THREE INGREDIENTS

I heard what she said, but I didn't believe her. We stared at each other for a few seconds before she spoke.

"I made all six of them. I cut the letters out of fashion magazines and glued them to a piece of paper and ran off a copy and showed them to you."

"But you said you gave them to the police—"

"I said if someone sent me threatening letters I would take them to the police. You misinterpreted that. All I wanted to do was to distract you from the fact that you were attacked outside of my show. I felt guilty. Especially since I'd basically just fired you. When the fire happened, he said you'd try to figure out who did it, so I made up the letters as a distraction. I would have told you about them sooner. I was going to tell you about them the day you came over for the interview, but you brought the photographer. And then I found out you told the police about them. Why? Normal people go to the police. You don't. I know you don't, because Nick told me you don't."

A part of me wondered what else Nick had told her about me.

"Then nobody's been threatening your business?"

"No." Her eyes filled with tears, and she buried her face in her hands.

Amanda was in a dark place. She was on the brink of losing everything: her business, her credibility, her future. She'd spent half an hour throwing up in my bathroom and, even though I'd been too polite to comment on it, there was a clump of vomit in her hair.

She was teetering on the edge of rock bottom.

Tentatively, I put my hand on her arm to console her. She tried to stifle her sobs, but the tears weren't going to stop anytime soon. I reached for a box of tissues and handed them to her and then sat and waited while she pulled herself together. Of all the questions that I could have asked, I avoided the biggest one of all: if Nick was her best friend, why wasn't he helping her through this crisis?

She blew her nose for the seventeenth time and set the tissue in a neat pile with the others. Her nose was red and swollen, and her eyes were puffy.

"Amanda, there's a very good chance the person who put me in the hospital was the same person who started the fire that destroyed your show. I need you to be honest with me and tell me what you told the arson investigator."

"The tall man with the short pants?" she said. For the first time since we'd met, we shared a smile. "I gave him a statement, but I didn't have much to say. The fire started on the runway. I was backstage, making sure the models were perfect before they went out. You probably saw more than I did."

"I have the show on videotape. Do you want to see what you missed?"

In a move of extreme compassion, I offered Amanda the use of my shower before we watched the video. I was still reeling from her confession. The self-proclaimed normal woman with the model appearance and the glamorous business had gone a little crazy. I guess we all go a little crazy sometimes.

While she was showering, I went downstairs. There was still the matter of food—or lack of food—to be dealt with, and even though Amanda and I were forging new ground in how we related to each other, I wasn't yet ready to let her see my shortcomings. There was only one person I could call.

"Yo," I said when Eddie answered. "I'm in over my head, and I need your help."

"Are you okay? Where are you?"

"I'm at home, but I'm not alone."

"Which one? Nick or Dante?"

"Neither." I held my breath and glanced up the stairs. "Amanda."

"Is Mercury in retrograde?"

"We don't have enough time for the full explanation. Here's the problem. She's in a bad way, and I don't think she should be alone. But I haven't eaten since nine o'clock this morning, and that was a bowl of ice cream. And I know this is petty of me, but I feel like I have a chance to prove something about myself to her, and I don't want to order delivery."

"I'm pulling an all-nighter on these displays. I can't bring you food. Tell me what we have to work with."

"I have two partially defrosted chicken breasts, a bag of baby carrots, less than a third of a half gallon of Neapolitan ice cream, three bags of pretzels, and a box of wine."

"How close have you guys gotten since she's been there?"

"Uncharted territory."

"Okay, so save the pretzels and the wine and get out a large stockpot. I'm going to tell you how to make chicken soup."

"Sounds complicated."

"How complicated can it be? You have three ingredients."

"Good point." I got out the stockpot and came back to the phone.

"Bring four cups of water to a boil. Hopefully your chicken will be defrosted by this point. Add the chicken and chopped-up carrots. Throw in some salt and pepper, cover, and let it simmer for half an hour."

"And then what?"

"And then you pour it into a bowl and eat it."

"That's it?"

"Dude, we are going to work on this. Now, is everything else okay?"

"Not even close."

After hanging up, I put the water on to boil and submerged the package of chicken breasts in warm water to get them fully defrosted. My mind wandered to Amanda's motivation while I chopped the baby carrots. When the water in the stock pot was boiling, I added the chicken breasts and the carrots, shook in some salt and pepper, and closed the lid again. I set the microwave timer for thirty minutes and poured myself a generous glass of wine. I'd earned it.

Ten minutes later, Amanda came downstairs and joined me in the living room. "Something smells good," she said.

"I'm making chicken soup. I thought it might make you feel better." I didn't mention that it was either that or pretzels, and that I didn't consider her worthy of my pretzel stash.

"I thought you didn't cook?" she asked.

"I can cook when I have to," I said defensively. The timer beeped, and I stood. "Have a seat. We can eat out here and watch the video. I'll be right back."

We traded spaces, and I went into the kitchen, returning with a wooden tray that held two bowls of soup. "I don't have any crackers," I said.

"This is already more than I expected. Thank you."

Amanda swept her hair back over her left shoulder. She wasn't one to overdo her makeup routine, but without any, she was still a knockout. She balanced her bowl on her lap and scooped dainty mouthfuls of broth to her lips. If she hadn't been sitting in my living room, I would have held the bowl up to my lips and drank. Heck, if she hadn't been there, I would have bribed Eddie to show up with hoagies.

I hit play on the remote, and the screen filled with the image from the stationary camera at the end of Amanda's runway. She looked up and froze for a moment, her spoon halfway to her mouth. The broth dribbled from the spoon and spilled onto her camel trousers. She glanced down at the spreading wet spot but didn't dab it.

This was the fifth time I'd watch it, and I hoped to see something I'd missed the first four. There were Dante and I on the left. There was Clive on the right. At the twenty-seven second mark, there was Santangelo sneaking in. I glanced at Amanda to see if she'd noticed, but she did not.

The lights went down, the pop music started, and the runway came alive. Godzilla graphics illuminated the back wall above Amanda's name. And then five models came down the runway before Harper in the silver wig and kimono.

"She complained that her kimono didn't fit. Remember?" I said. "But aside from how the sleeves are dragging on the floor, it looks great on her."

Amanda leaned forward. "It's going to happen now, isn't it?" she asked quietly.

I nodded.

I knew where to look for the smoke. It appeared on the left first, by the hem of the kimono, a whisper of something, and then flames. It was that fast. Screams replaced music. The house lights went on. Harper struggled to take off the kimono. Nick stepped out from behind the backdrop and helped her. The fire blazed a trail through the rose petals on the ground and spread to the rest of the room. Someone knocked the camera over, and the video went to static.

"So that's what happened," Amanda said when it was done. "We couldn't see anything. We didn't know. One second I was adjusting a collar on one of the girls, and the next, Harper was screaming."

"How did Nick know Harper needed his help? If you were all so busy backstage, how come he knew to come out and help her out of the kimono?"

"There was a small video feed on a monitor in the back. Tiny watched the monitor to keep up with the pace and make sure there weren't any problems out front. Nick must have been watching too."

"Where was Clive Barrington through all of this?"

"I don't know, and I know how that sounds, but you know what it's like backstage at a runway show. It's chaos! I love the excitement, but I had to concentrate on the problem in front of me. Otherwise I get overwhelmed by how little I can control. That's why I have Tiny watching the monitor and the interns to help dress the models and Nick to oversee the accessories. There's almost too much to do, but it would be worse to have people helping who I can't trust."

"That's why you let me go on Friday night, isn't it?" I asked. She looked up at me, and we locked eyes. "You didn't know if you could trust me. You knew how stressful it would be, and you knew I knew the collection. There was no good reason for you to let me go before the show. And if you hadn't fired me, I wouldn't have left when I did, and I might not have been attacked."

"I've been over that decision a hundred times since then. Honestly, Samantha, I didn't want to let you go."

"Then why did you?"

"Because I couldn't stand what it was doing to Nick. I'm not sure how much more he can handle."

"What does Nick have to do with you letting me go?"

She pushed her soup bowl away and sat back. "You don't know, do you?"

"Know what?"

"Nick's father is in the hospital."

25

REALITY BITES

MY HEART STOPPED. TEARS BUILT UP A WALL BEHIND MY EYES. I SET
the soup bowl down. "When?"

"A few weeks ago. He's been splitting his time between Ribbon
and New York."

"What happened?"

"His dad fell and broke his hip."

"Is he going to be okay?"

"It's still too soon to tell."

"Why didn't Nick say anything?"

"What did you want him to say? You broke his heart, and you
moved on like nothing happened."

"That's what you think? Is that what Nick thinks?"

"What do you want us to think? You brought a date to my
runway show. You told Nick you needed a change. And the guy
you're dating is my new photographer."

"He used to work for a private investigator. He's a good person
to have on the inside."

"Depends on what you're trying to accomplish."

I looked at my soup bowl for a few seconds. "Me working with you after Nick fired me—that wasn't his idea, was it? It was yours."

She shrugged. "You two were making each other crazy. At least that's how it sounded to me."

"He talked to you about me?"

"Don't you talk to Eddie about Nick?"

"That's different."

"How?"

How to tell her that I had an irrational jealousy of her because I didn't know the details of her past with Nick? That even though I'd known him for nine years, I secretly hated that she'd known him longer? That some might say people who ate ice cream for breakfast weren't in the same league as she was? I went with "Maybe it isn't different. It just feels like it is."

"He wanted to make sure you were going to be okay."

"Does he know about the letters?"

"No. That was—that was my own idea. He's dealing with a lot right now, and I thought if I could keep you preoccupied, you'd be one less thing for him to worry about."

"How is his dad?"

She shrugged. "I don't know. We haven't talked much over this past week. He has his problems, and I have mine." She tucked her feet under her and picked at the carpet fibers. "I went to design school so I could get into fashion. One thing led to another, and now here I am. I guess you never know when the bottom's going to drop out of your life."

"Amanda, you have a gift. Don't let any of this stop you from using it. This," I gestured toward the screen, "is all a set-back, sure, but don't let it get in the way of what you want out of life."

The longer Amanda sat on my sofa, the less jealousy I felt toward her. She'd relied on the people around her to see her vision through, and she found herself alone. Did she have a chance at success if she was willing to hand control of her business over to others? Was it possible for her to succeed if she didn't?

Amanda yawned, and then so did I. I'd lost all track of time, but I suspected it was late. Hours had passed since Loncar and Amanda showed up and Dante had left, and for a moment I wished I could pretend that none of this had happened. But I couldn't. Because all of it had. The breakup. The attack. The fire. And now, Nick's dad. Things had gotten very, very real.

Something had happened since the breakup. Somewhere between learning that Dante had a son, Detective Loncar had a wife who made uncooked meatloaf, and Amanda had a nervous stomach, I realized that I'd kept myself from seeing reality when it came to Nick. I'd projected my feelings onto him, the daydreams that I'd had when he was a shoe designer and I was a buyer, when we couldn't do much more than casually flirt over chocolate soufflés at Market Week.

And once we'd started dating, I wanted him to see me as perfect girlfriend material. The reality? He was coping with the very real crisis of his father's declining health, while I was with his maybe-former girlfriend eating three-ingredient chicken soup.

Reality bites.

I carried the empty bowls to the kitchen so Amanda wouldn't see the sadness on my face. The clock read eleven thirty. Dante's developed photos awaited me in the darkroom, but they felt less important now that I knew the threats against Amanda had been fake.

I was working up the best way to politely suggest that playtime was over when I returned to the living room and found her asleep on the sofa. I pulled a spare comforter out of the closet and covered her. I pointed a finger at the ceiling. "I get extra credit for this, you got that?"

It was well past my bedtime, and my body was tired and achy. I climbed into bed. I dreamt about fires and woke up in a sweat with the covers kicked onto the floor. I'd been so buried in details about Amanda's samples that I hadn't stopped to ask the most obvious question of all: How had someone started the fire in the middle of a runway show in the first place?

26

GOLD STAR FOR
PERSONAL GROWTH

THE NEXT MORNING, I WOKE UP ALONE IN THE HOUSE. AMANDA HAD left a note on the coffee table thanking me for my generosity. That was it. No acknowledgment of the fake letters. No apology for firing me on the eve of her runway show. No mention of the homemade chicken soup. I peeked out the front window to confirm her departure. Her car was gone.

I showered and dressed in a man's white button-down oxford under a chunky gray knit sweater with a Union Jack on the front, a short, pleated gray-and-navy plaid skirt, tights layered with argyle knee socks, and black leather riding boots. I slipped on black fingerless gloves for the simple reason that they made me feel tough.

I opened and shut the freezer and refrigerator. Now that I'd cooked the chicken breasts and the carrots, the only thing left was a carton of Cool Whip left over from a Labor Day party. Surprisingly, it looked exactly as it had months ago. I dragged my index finger though the white fluffy substance and tasted it. Seemed fresh enough. But then I thought of last night. I'd made chicken soup from scratch. In personal growth terms, wouldn't it be taking a step backward to have Cool Whip for breakfast?

I called Eddie. "How'd things go at Tradava last night?"

"I wrapped up around two thirty."

"I thought when you got promoted to visual director, you'd be able to delegate a little?"

"Dude, I'm not management material. I got into creative work so I could be creative. Telling other people what to do isn't my style."

"Funny, I don't remember you having a problem with it when I helped you out at the museum," I said. "Where are you?" I asked.

"Home. Why?"

"Can you pick up breakfast and come over here? I need to talk out a few things."

"Do these things include your slumber party with Amanda?"

"Yes."

"I'll be there in twenty."

To hear Eddie say it, you could get from any point of Ribbon to any other point in precisely twenty minutes. The estimation was surprisingly accurate. The doorbell rang about twenty minutes later. I checked the peephole. Eddie was on the porch, holding a brown paper bag.

He handed it to me, and I pulled out two breakfast sandwiches wrapped in wax paper. They appeared to be the same, so I handed him one.

He looked at the wrapper and swapped them out. "Trust me," he said.

I poured two mugs full of coffee and joined him at the dining-room table.

"You are not going to believe what Amanda told me last night. Get this: after the fire, she showed me these threatening letters against her company. She made them up to send me off on the trail of a criminal who didn't exist."

"Which you're doing, so it worked."

"It started out with me wanting to know who jumped me. That turned into wanting to know who set the fire at the show, because I think the two things are related. But then there was a fire in the dumpster outside of Warehouse Five the day after the show. I can't figure that out. Was someone trying to destroy evidence? Or did they know I was there and wanted to scare me?"

"Dude, you've been busy. Back up. What's this about another fire?"

"After you left me at Brothers, Dante and I went to Warehouse Five. It was his idea," I added before he could make any more comments about me doing exactly what Amanda suspected. "He thought we might notice something."

"Did you?"

"That's the thing. He was on one side of the building taking pictures. I went to the other side because that's where I was attacked. My car had been sitting in the lot the whole time. I moved the flyers from the windshield to the front passenger side and sat inside. Something moved near the dumpster. I drove closer to check it out and smelled smoke. Right after I saw a leg sticking out, the dumpster caught on fire."

"A leg?" he said.

"A mannequin leg."

"That's why you got all juiced up when I told you about the mannequins."

"I told Loncar about it. At first, I thought it was a body or an amputated limb. He said they didn't find any evidence of a body inside, and the fire hadn't been burning long enough to completely destroy a corpse."

Eddie set down his sandwich and his face turned a greenish shade. He pulled a pill vial out of his pocket and swallowed a white tablet. "Dramamine. It'll help with the nausea."

"Are you getting sick?"

"I'm trying to eat while you're talking about disembodied limbs burning up in dumpsters. A little nausea is normal."

Eddie was right. I hadn't even flinched at Amanda being sick last night, and now my best friend was popping anti-nausea pills like Skittles. Were dismembered limbs and dead bodies becoming yet another thing that I compartmentalized?

"We don't have to talk about this," I said. "Let's talk about something else. What's going on with you?"

"Me? The usual. Working round the clock to get the store ready. Nab four or five hours of sleep and then do it all over again."

"All work and no play makes Eddie a dull boy," I said.

"I've got a two-week vacation coming up. Going to Miami Beach. I'll make up for lost time as soon as that plane lands."

"You're okay with that? Work like a crazy person, go away to recharge, and come back and do it all over again?"

"That's how life works. At least since you moved here, there's a new element to the mix."

"Yep, that's me. All fun and games until somebody gets hurt." I swallowed a disturbing amount of coffee and coughed.

"The Dramamine has taken effect. Hit me with whatever you have."

I leaned forward and tapped my index finger on the table. "Here's what I want to know. Why would someone want to attack me? Was I the target all along? I don't think so. The fact that there have been no other physical attacks makes me think my attack was a message to Amanda. One of her staffers gets hospitalized. Warning!" I made jazz hands on either side of my head. "Somebody wants you to fail!"

"It *is* starting to look like somebody's had it in for Amanda all along."

"That's what I thought, but mostly because of the threats she made up. Now I need to come up with a different angle." I ticked off what I knew on my fingers. "First I was attacked, and there was a fire. Then the second fire during her show. Third in the parking lot outside of the venue where she held her show. The fire on the runway would have been enough to ruin her. I don't know why someone set the third fire."

"Do you have to? I mean, this is Amanda Ries we're talking about. She fired you. She faked evidence to send you chasing after phantoms. And she's Nick's ex-girlfriend."

"We don't know that last part. We only suspect it."

"Dude, this isn't the time to play dumb," he said.

"Fine. She's Nick's ex-girlfriend. But the woman spent an hour throwing up in my bathroom last night. Did I sneak in and take blackmail photos? No. I made her chicken soup."

"Great. You get a gold star for personal growth. That doesn't mean you have to solve her problems for her."

"I know I don't owe her anything. I know I should just walk away. And I know the fact that I don't proves everything everybody says about me is right."

We stared at each other for a few seconds, an entire conversation of acceptance and understanding taking place between a raised eyebrow, a smile, and a shrug. Then Eddie turned his head to the side. "Do you smell burnt toast?"

I sniffed the air. "Yes."

"Okay, good. I thought it was my imagination." He picked up his breakfast sandwich and took another bite.

"Why do we both smell burnt toast? We're not making breakfast."

We turned our heads toward the front of the house. Through the picture window I saw orange flames shooting out from an open trash can sitting in the middle of my driveway.

27

STOP WASTING MY TIME

"FIRE!" I YELLED. I RAN OUT THE FRONT DOOR. EDDIE FOLLOWED.

The trash can sat behind Eddie's VW Bug. I crept closer to see what was burning inside, but the heat from the flames kept me back.

"Call someone," I said. I raced back inside for the fire extinguisher that was under the kitchen sink and returned. My cold fingers fumbled with the pin. I pulled it loose. I aimed the nozzle at the fire and squeezed the handle. A blast of compressed carbon dioxide shot out like a cloud of snow. The pressure caught me by surprise, and I was knocked off balance. I scrambled to my feet and started again. The spray covered the inside of the metal can until the flames were extinguished. I stepped back and dropped the canister. Across the street, Mrs. Iova's curtains opened, and she looked out. I was shaking too badly to make a face or a rude gesture like the other neighbors did when they caught her spying.

Minutes later, I heard a siren growing close. A red fire truck turned at the corner and raced toward my house. Several men jumped down and uncoiled the hose, ready to act.

"Where's the fire?" one asked.

"It was in there." I pointed at the trash can.

He crept forward and looked inside the receptacle. "How'd it start?"

"I don't know."

"Where were you?"

"Inside my house."

"You throw away anything flammable?"

"I didn't throw away anything at all. This isn't my trash can." He looked at me like I was a nuisance. "Can you call Inspector Gigger or Detective Loncar at the Ribbon Police?"

"You know them?"

"Yes. I'm helping"—no, that wouldn't go over all that well—"I've been a witness at other fires in Ribbon. I think I should talk to them."

He stood a few feet away from me, suited up in his fireman garb. His fellow firefighters scattered around the end of my driveway, their testosterone and adrenaline levels in need of a release. I felt like I was throwing a party for twenty and only had one cupcake to serve for dessert.

Eddie stood on the front porch with Logan over one shoulder. Eddie's eyes were wide. He set Logan inside the house and pulled the front door shut. He sat on the front porch step, and I joined him. The sudden fear of fire had kept me from noticing the chill in the air, but now that I stopped and sat, I felt the cold through to my bones. I went inside and pulled two wool blankets from the hall closet and returned outside, handing one to Eddie.

Inspector Gigger's shiny silver car pulled up behind the fire truck. He approached the group of men and exchanged words with the chief and then strode across the lot to us. Pieces of ash flitted through the air like gray snow flurries. I stood up and wrapped the blanket around me tighter.

"Ms. Kidd," he said. "What can you tell me about this fire?"

"My friend Eddie and I were inside the house. We smelled something burning. As soon as we saw the flames in the trash can, I came back in for my fire extinguisher, and Eddie called the fire department."

"How do you think this fire got started?"

"I don't know."

"What was in the trash can?"

"I don't know. It's not my trash can."

"Where did it come from?"

This was getting tiring. "I don't know."

"Ms. Kidd, it's a stretch to think you didn't have anything to do with this, so stop wasting my time. I want to know how you started the fire. Timing device? Remote detonator? Or perhaps your friend did it for you?"

"That doesn't even make sense! We were inside. Ask my neighbors. Somebody must have seen us run outside and put out the fire. Ask Mrs. Iova over there. She spies on everybody. She must have seen something."

"I find it hard to believe your trash can spontaneously combusted."

I jumped up, and the blanket fell from my shoulders. "Inspector Gigger," I said, taking a step toward him, "I don't know what you've heard about me, but I am not in the habit of setting fires to get attention."

"But you do like the attention you get from playing amateur sleuth, don't you?" He reached inside his coat and pulled out a newspaper clipping. Deliberately, he unfolded it and held it so it was facing me. It was the article that had run about me after my involvement in the recent museum murder.

"That is a human-interest story that grew out of the fact that I did something good."

"That is true." He glanced at the newspaper. "Nice photo, by the way." He folded the newspaper clipping up and put it back into his pocket. "But arson is a crime of attention seeking. Three fires, Ms. Kidd. Three fires where you've been present. Four if we count your so-called attack. It raises questions."

"It wasn't so-called, it was! And what about the mannequin leg in the dumpster at the warehouse? I know you must know by now that it was a mannequin leg. I called Detective Loncar as soon as I figured that out. He confirmed that I was right."

"Ms. Kidd, you're friends with the visual director of a store that uses mannequins. There's another way that you could have been right about that without using your considerable powers of deduction."

It was worse to hear him insinuate that Eddie was involved too. "I don't need to listen to this," I said. "Someone set a fire in my driveway, and I called 911. If I'd done anything other than that, people would have wondered why. But I do exactly what I'm supposed to do, and I get accused of rigging fires all over town?"

Loncar's unwashed car pulled up behind Gigger's silver one. As soon as the detective was out of the car, he scanned the scene. I pointed at him. "From now on, I will only talk to him." I stormed past Eddie and into the house. I didn't bother slamming the door. Whoever wanted to follow me could.

A few minutes later, the detective came inside with the head fireman. He closed the door, and Logan came out from under the sofa and ran his head against the detective's trouser leg. Loncar picked him up, scratched his ears, and set him back down. Logan took off up the carpeted stairs to the bedrooms.

The head fireman stayed by Loncar's side. He looked to be about fifty-something, with deep creases by his eyes and mouth. His hair was mostly gray, matted to his head from the fire helmet he now held in his hand.

"Where's Eddie?" I asked.

"He's giving his statement to Gigger," Loncar said. "Why don't you get me caught up?"

"Eddie and I were in the kitchen talking about Amanda." I met Loncar's stare. "Oh, come on. She's my ex-boyfriend's maybe-former girlfriend. If I didn't talk about her behind her back, people would think there was something wrong with me."

"Go on."

"We smelled something burning. Eddie described it as burnt toast. I was facing the windows and saw the flames out of the top of the trash can. I tried to get close to see what was inside, but it was too hot. I got my fire extinguisher from the kitchen, and Eddie called 911. Gigger can probably tell you the rest."

"You did a good job putting out the flames," the fireman said.

"It's not my first time with a fire extinguisher," I said, thinking back to an unsuccessful attempt at deep frying. "Do you know what was burning?"

The fireman shook his head. "There's nothing left. Whatever was on fire is now a pile of ash. You say your friend smelled burnt toast?"

"That's what he said. I smelled something burning, but I didn't connect it with anything in particular except maybe the time I scorched my pajamas with a flat iron."

The fireman's eyes moved to my newly bobbed hair. "You gave up the flat iron?"

"Temporarily." I settled in on the sofa. "We might have assumed that someone burned their breakfast if we hadn't seen the flames. They were big, like three feet higher than the top of the trash can. I wouldn't swear by it, but the flames seemed smaller by the time I came back and put it out. Like it would have put itself out without my help."

"You might be right. The aluminum trash can contained the fire pretty well. Since there's nothing left inside to tell us what was burning, it could be that the ignited object burned away completely. No scent of chemicals means it was organic."

"You're not going to say it was an accident, are you?"

"No. But if the arsonist rigged things to burn themselves out, he probably didn't want to stick around to see how it unfolded. Makes me think it was a message."

"Your men seemed a little annoyed when they got here."

"Not annoyed. There's a certain adrenaline rush that helps them act fast and minimize the threat of an open fire. When they arrived and the fire was out, they were left with all this adrenaline and nothing to act on."

Loncar's turn to ask questions. "You put out the fire, the firemen arrived, and then what?"

"Then nothing. Gigger arrived and accused me of being the common thread at all the fires. You showed up somewhere around there."

"He's right, you know. You were present each time." He held up his hand palm-side out. "I'm not saying you set the fires. I'm not saying it's anything more than coincidence. But you best think about that, because there's a chance you can offer us a lead we don't have."

I leaned forward and held my head in my hands. The room went silent while they waited for me to come up with a theory. "I don't know what lead you think I can come up with. This fire was in front of a private residence. It was a message because it's *my* private residence, but that doesn't mean it makes any more sense."

"Ms. Kidd, if there's anything you remember from any of the other fires, I'd like to hear it. I think the fire captain would like to hear it too."

I looked back and forth between Loncar and the captain's faces. They weren't treating me like I was a nuisance. Instead of ridiculous accusations like Gigger's, Loncar had asked me for help. Politely too!

Before I could say anything, a fireman burst through the front door. His helmet was back in place, and his chest was puffed out like a cage fighter at go time.

"Yo, Cap, we gotta leave. There's been another fire downtown." He rattled off an address. The captain jumped up and ran out of my house.

And I sat on the sofa, feeling like someone had dumped a ten-pound bag of ice down the back of my shirt.

The new fire was at Amanda's studio.

28

NONE OF IT HELPED

Within seconds the firemen were gone. Gigger put a Kojak light on top of his car and sped away from the curb. Eddie stood with Loncar and me on the front step.

"Aren't you going with them?" I asked Loncar.

"No. I'm going to stay here and find out what caused that light bulb to go off over your head when you heard the address of the fire."

The detective was getting very good at reading my expressions.

I turned and went into the living room. Loncar and Eddie followed. Eddie and I shared the sofa, and Loncar sat in one of the arm chairs.

"What's your theory, Ms. Kidd?"

"That's Amanda Ries's studio," I said. "You wanted a theory? What about this: Amanda spent the night here after you left." I sat up, and my eyes darted around at various items in the living room while I thought. "I don't know when she left. I woke up, and there was a note on the table. Either I was sound asleep, or she was abnormally quiet. Maybe whoever set this fire thinks she lives here.

Which would make Amanda the common thread, if you consider that there have now been fires at her show, in the parking lot outside of where her show was, here, and now at her studio."

"Any thoughts on why someone would be out to get Ms. Ries?"

"None. She's the most law-abiding citizen I could imagine." Eddie nodded his head in agreement. "But it seems like somebody is keeping tabs on her whereabouts. Did you ever follow up with Santangelo Toma? About the ID that you found by the dumpster outside of the warehouse? Or the fire? Either fire?"

"Yes."

"And?" A new thought hit me. "His name is San-TANGELO. Tangelos are a close cousin of oranges. Like what were used to beat me up. Are you following me?"

Eddie's eyes went wide. "Dude, that's creepy."

"I know. It's like a calling card or something."

Loncar crossed his arms over his coat and cleared his throat. We turned our attention to him.

"We confirmed with Ms. Ries that the fruit she found around you was part of the food service for the staff and models."

"Santangelo has a studio at Warehouse Five. He could have swiped the fruit and jumped me. It could have been him."

"Mr. Toma is not your man." Loncar stood up. "Thank you for your cooperation, Ms. Kidd. Be careful."

I stood up too. "Detective, I'm curious. If I graduated from your citizen's police academy, would you take me more seriously?"

"Trust me, I take you very seriously." He buttoned two buttons on his wrinkled coat and left. Eddie followed him out the door and drove off behind him.

I wandered around the living room, straightening magazines on the table, moving coffee cups into the kitchen. At one point I loaded and started the dishwasher, and then I vacuumed.

None of it helped.

I pulled a navy blue pea coat over my sweater and skirt and went outside. The aluminum trash can was out of the way. I crossed the driveway and looked inside. The only thing left from the fire was a small residue of ash in the bottom center. I went back inside and found a mostly-empty eye-shadow compact in the bathroom. I tapped the remaining clump of purple powder loose and went back to the trash can to retrieve a sample of the ash. I was only able to come up with two pinches, but for my purposes, it would do. I clicked the eye-shadow case shut.

Back inside, I went to the darkroom and pulled my old chemistry set from the baker's rack. A giant spider, startled by the sudden activity, sprung to life from the pile of photos. I screamed, jumped backward, banged my hip on the corner of the counter behind me, and screamed again. I didn't know where the spider had disappeared to, so I had to be quick.

The last time I used this chemistry set was when I was ten. Although my dad had high hopes of me following in his scientific footsteps, I'd traded the lure of the beaker and microscope for the mall at an early age, and the only chemicals I was interested in were the ones that straightened my naturally curly hair. The chemistry set had been shelved and forgotten. I swatted at the box with a broom handle as a warning to any other bugs living inside, and when nothing appeared, carried the box upstairs.

On the second floor of the house, my bedroom sat to the right, the bathroom sat directly in front of me, and my sister's old room was to my left. I'd had the notion to convert it to a closet a few months ago, lining the perimeter with cheap white floor-to-ceiling bookcases that housed off-season shoes, handbags, scarves, and jewelry. A rolling rod had been pushed to the back wall. It held two dozen sleeveless dresses that wouldn't see the light of day until sometime in May.

I set the microscope on the desk and found a clean glass slide.

With the tweezers that came with the set, I pinched a small amount of ash from the eye-shadow compact and placed it onto the glass. The glass went under the microscope, and I put my eye on the lens. Mixed with purple granules that could only be residue eye shadow were lots of gray stringy things and a long golden thread with a black stripe down the center.

I twisted around and scanned the clothes on the rack. A red sheath dress by the end of the rack had a torn hem. I pulled at a loose thread until it snapped off, and I set that on a new slide. The color was different, but the texture was similar to the gray stringy things. I found an empty beaker in the box and dropped the red thread in and then ran downstairs for the grill lighter that I used to ignite the wicks in burned-down candles. Back upstairs, I lit the red thread and watched it curl up and then dissolve into ash. I put the ash on the slide and looked at that.

It was pretty darn close to the gray stringy things.

So, the gray stringy things were threads. Then what was the golden rod with the black core? I had a hunch.

When Eddie had evened out my hair, he'd suggested that I donate what I chopped off to a wigmaker. It sounded like a good idea, the kind of thing I'd like to be thought of as doing. I'd put my chopped-off ponytails in a one-gallon plastic bag and left it on the sink.

The other thing I was thought of as doing was procrastinating, which was why the bag of my hair was still where I'd left it. I pulled a strand out of the bag and carried it to my desk. I knew what I wanted to see when I looked at it under the microscope.

It was the same structure as the golden thread. Which meant it wasn't a thread. It was a strand of hair. Golden hair.

A quick Google search told me that dark hair that's been chemically treated maintains its original color at the center. The golden strand with the dark core came from a not-natural blond.

Clive Barrington wasn't a natural blond. Dante had made a comment about Clive's hair color before the runway show.

I went back into the house and called my dad. We weren't the sort of family to talk every day, but I'd learned to balance my I'm-involved-in-a-murder-investigation-again calls with questions about house maintenance so he and my mom wouldn't worry too much about me. To them, I'd been frozen in time around ten years old. My older sister had been the one with babysitting jobs and child-in-charge responsibilities. I'd never been trusted with anything, not because I couldn't handle it, but because, to them, I'd always be "the kid." A shrink would probably theorize that the sense of never having grown up was why it had been so important for me to buy this particular house. I couldn't disagree, which was why I never started therapy.

"Hi Dad, it's the kid," I said.

"Hey, kid, what's up? Everything okay in the ol' PA?" he asked. He'd started speaking in rhyme since moving to California. I attributed it to the side effect of all that constant sun.

"I have a science question for you. Would a brown hair and a blond hair look the same under a microscope?"

"Nope."

"Do you mean no, or did you just say 'nope' because it rhymed with 'microscope?'"

He chuckled into the phone, and then his tone turned from Dr. Seuss to scientist. "You have to consider different factors. Is the hair color treated? If so, how long ago? Environment plays a factor, too, as does genetics. And then consider what people put on their hair: gel, mousse, hair spray—"

I wanted information, but I could already see that this could go on for a while. I cut him off. "I'm looking at a hair under a microscope. At least I think it's a hair. It's long and gold, but it has a black core."

"Where'd you get the microscope?"

"It's the one you gave me for my tenth birthday." I paused for a second, wondering if he would be impressed. My next thought was about why he'd kept it all these years. Maybe this was the very moment he'd been waiting for.

"Did you check the hair against a control group?"

"I looked at one of my own hairs under the microscope. It's the same texture, but it's dark all the way through."

"What's your conclusion?"

"I think they're both human hairs, but the gold one was dyed."

"Does that information tell you anything?"

"It sure does. Thanks for helping me, Dad, but I have to go."

"Hey, kid?" His tone shifted from scientist to dad. "How come you didn't want to play with the chemistry set when I bought it for you?"

It only took a second to answer. "Because maybe I had to grow up before I saw the value in figuring things out on my own."

29

OUR CASE

After assuring my dad that I wasn't in trouble, I called Amanda's studio. No answer. I called her cell. No answer. I called Detective Loncar, whom I had reprogrammed from "Fuzz" to "Partner?"

"Loncar," he answered.

"Detective, hi, it's Samantha Kidd. I have more information to show you."

"I'm at the station."

"I'm on my way."

I grabbed the photos and placed the hair samples in a plastic bag in my handbag. I didn't pack my childhood microscope. There was something about the Fisher-Price logo that might have made Loncar take me less seriously.

I parked in a visitor space. Even though this wasn't the first time I'd gone to the police station to provide information, the idea of walking in still made me nervous.

Once inside, I checked in with the desk sergeant. He pressed a couple of buttons on his phone and mumbled something into the receiver. Seconds later, Loncar came to the lobby to greet me. I followed him over the freshly-mopped-yet-not-clean linoleum tile floor, through a door marked Questioning, to his office. He sat behind the worn wooden desk, and I lowered myself into the worn vinyl chair facing him. Since the last time I'd been here, a plastic bowl filled with individually wrapped sour balls sat on the corner of his desk. He caught me looking at them.

"Take one if you want. They're sugar free. My wife's on a health kick, and everything I like is off limits."

"No, thank you." I stared at the sour balls. Something about them bothered me.

He opened the bottom drawer of his desk and pulled out a bag of carrot sticks. "Sugar-free candy and carrot sticks. This is my life."

"Did you know if you chop up carrots and boil them with a chicken and salt and pepper, you get soup?" I asked.

"I thought you didn't cook," he said.

I changed the subject. "Do you think it's strange that I keep getting involved in criminal investigations around Ribbon?"

He looked surprised but not taken aback. "It's not how the rest of the residents live," he said.

"That's not what I mean. Does it indicate a personality flaw?"

"That you like to figure things out? No." He uncrossed his arms and folded his hands on top of his desk. "I have a daughter around your age. You two"—he paused—"have some things in common. Then again, in some ways you couldn't be more different." He leaned back. "Are you close to your family?"

It was a good question. Living in the house where I'd grown up made me feel close to my family, but truth was, our lives were separate.

"We Kidds are an independent lot. We're like gypsies."

"I don't know many gypsies who move back to the town where they grew up in order to ground themselves."

Darn that Detective Loncar. He had a point. "When my parents told me they were moving to California and selling the house, I realized this was the last place I'd lived where I felt like I belonged to something. Now they're living their life, and I'm trying to live mine."

"If you got into trouble—real trouble—would you turn to them for help?"

"I like to think if I needed them, they'd be there for me."

"Five years ago, my daughter was engaged and had a good job. Now she's pregnant and alone. She won't talk about who the father is. She won't talk about why she broke things off. She's back in touch with her ex, but I'm pretty sure he's not the guy. Besides, he's moved on. She acts like my wife and I are going to punish her for making bad decisions."

"Are you?"

"She's our daughter. We want her to be happy." He stared out the window for a few seconds. "You said you figured something out. What do you have for me?"

Back to business. "That fire in the trash can in front of my house. I think it was set by Clive Barrington."

"Is that an accusation or a fact?"

"Back up for a second," I said, considering the scientific approach of my dad. I pulled the envelope of ash out from my handbag and set it on Loncar's desk. "Inside that envelope is a sample of hair that I found in the bottom of the trash bin from my driveway. I analyzed it and determined that it's been dyed blond. That is a fact. Clive Barrington has highlights, which would look the same as dark hair that's been lightened. That is also a fact. I concluded that Clive may have been the person to set the fire."

Loncar took the envelope. "That is a good piece of deduction, Ms. Kidd. There's only one problem with your theory."

"What's that?"

"Clive Barrington is in Tahiti."

"When did he leave Ribbon?"

"Yesterday. He's on a photo shoot. He checked in with us before he left because he knew he was part of an open investigation."

How very considerate of him. "What if he checked in with you to make sure you knew he had an alibi, and then he arranged for more fires while he was gone? Wouldn't that throw you off his scent?"

"Would that be the scent of burnt toast?" he asked.

"Burnt crumpets is more like it," I said, even though I don't think he expected an answer.

"Ms. Kidd, I appreciate that you brought this information to me, but answer this. How would Mr. Barrington's hair have gotten into the trash can if he wasn't at the scene?"

"Maybe it was his trash can."

Loncar leaned back. For the first time since we'd met, the buttons on his shirt did not strain over his belly.

"Let me get this straight," I said. "You're not even considering Clive as a suspect in your investigation?"

"Ms. Kidd, do I need to remind you that there has been no body? There have been no reported deaths. My only role in this is to help Inspector Gigger find an arsonist before somebody dies. We've had four fires so far, and nobody's been injured. I'd like to keep it that way."

"Nobody's been injured except *me*."

"You weren't injured in a fire."

"The attack on me is being considered separate from the arsons? Even though everything is Amanda centric?"

"Unless you can provide additional information about that attack, I'm afraid we don't have any leads to work with."

A red button lit on Loncar's phone. He held his hand in a hold-on-a-minute gesture and answered. He told the person on the other end that he was finishing up now. He hung up and caught me trying to read the incoming call number upside down.

"Ms. Kidd, this job isn't all hotlines and anonymous tips. Sometimes a phone call is just a phone call."

"So that wasn't related to our case?"

He crossed his arms again. "You got anything else for me?"

"Nope."

He stood, and I followed suit. "Thank you for your cooperation. I'll share your findings with Ichabod." He cracked a smile.

Loncar followed me out of his office. I stopped at the exit doors. "You never did tell me what you found out about Santangelo Toma," I said.

"Goodbye, Ms. Kidd."

I DROVE TO WAREHOUSE FIVE. Detective Loncar might have thought he was doing me a favor by ignoring my question, but as far as favors went, his was up there with gifting me brussels sprouts for my birthday.

I parked by the front lobby doors of the warehouse and went inside. If I'd expected someone to stop me, they didn't. There was nobody at the information desk, and most of the doors to the studios were shut. I wandered down the hallway and tried a few of the knobs. They were locked.

When I returned to the lobby, I spotted a man on a ladder. He was taking measurements from the ceiling down. He called them down to another man who stood by the window. The man on the floor wore white gloves. Sketches and paintings of a woman's figure were propped along the base of the room. Something about the sketches felt familiar. I stepped closer. The man on the ladder twisted around and yelled at me.

"Hey, you! You're not supposed to be in here," he said. "The building's closed for an installation."

I ignored his warning and stepped closer to the nearest painting. The image was of the back of a naked woman. Her hands were behind her, over her backside. The most striking thing about her was her silver hair.

"Who did these paintings and sketches?" I asked the man.

"One of the residents. We rotate the front gallery each month so everybody gets equal exposure."

"But there was a fashion show here last week, and this whole front gallery was empty except for a couple of mannequins."

"Yeah, funny how things work out. This guy raised the biggest stink about that show, and now he gets the lobby the month before the holidays."

"These are by Santangelo Toma, aren't they?" I asked. The man nodded. "Do you know where I can find him?"

"Sure. He's in his studio. Third door down on the right."

I thanked him and followed his directions. Like the rest of the hallway, the door to Santangelo's studio was closed. I tapped a few times and then tried the knob. It opened easily. Inside I found the artist sitting on a stool, staring at a half-finished canvas.

Smudges of charcoal were on his fingers and cheek. His clothes looked rumpled, as if he'd slept in them. Red suspenders were clipped to his loose-fitting trousers over a stained waffle-weave long-john top. His pork pie hat rested on the floor on top of a pair of shoes. His feet were bare.

Despite the cold temperature outside, the studio was warm. A small space heater was plugged into an outlet in the corner. A low table next to it held brushes and paints, a glass of cloudy water, and an assortment of oil pencils.

"Santangelo," I said, making my presence known.

He was startled. He crossed the room and pulled a tarp over the painting, but it was too late. I already knew who it was, and I knew what he'd done.

"That's Harper, isn't it?"

"I didn't make her do it. What's it to you?"

"You wanted the fashion people to be kicked out of the warehouse. You started a petition to get rid of Amanda. Explain to me how Harper being your model factored into that equation? If you got your wish and Amanda was evicted, you wouldn't have had access to Harper."

"She didn't want to be a part of that life anymore. She told me. I'm the only one who knew she was going to leave town."

"She told you she was going to Mexico?"

"She said she was going away. She felt bad because my paintings weren't finished. It was her idea for me to use the mannequins."

Instinctively, I turned and faced the part of the building where the installation was taking place. The woman's figure in the silver wig. That's why the silver wig was in the trash can the night Dante and I had come back. The image in the painting wasn't Harper; it was a mannequin.

I turned back and stepped closer to Santangelo. I put one hand out on his forearm. "The night of the fire, you took one of the mannequins, didn't you? From the lobby. You brought it in here."

"Amanda Ries's show made it so I couldn't concentrate. The only good thing that came out of it was meeting Harper. She said she liked the way I painted her. Real. Not like the fashion magazines. Not all airbrushed and Photoshopped. She said when it was all over, that's how she wanted to be remembered. But then everything got crazy, and she left."

"What do you mean, everything got crazy?"

"That photographer went after her. He wouldn't leave her

alone. On her all the time, saying her career would be over if she didn't sleep with him. She couldn't take the pressure."

Dante had mentioned something about that when he first told me he knew Clive. A scandal. An underage model. A ruined career.

The Harper Ashton I knew was a sixteen-year-old girl on the edge of cracking. I'd seen it in her eyes. The demands of her job, the ill-fitting garments, the way she'd been treated more like an object than a person. She'd been too young to know how to deal with the demands of the industry, and she'd fled.

"Why did you try to burn the mannequin?" I asked.

He looked up at me. Whatever he'd hoped to gain by going against Amanda and Tiny had left him with little energy and even less spirit.

"After the fire, I knew somebody would find it in my studio and link me to the arson. I didn't need a lot of time, just a couple of days so I could finish my painting. But the investigators were poking around, and I couldn't concentrate. And I thought if somebody saw that mannequin, they'd think I was responsible. It was bad enough that I was so outspoken with my complaints and started that petition nobody wanted to sign. I might as well have put a neon sign over my head that said 'I'm a suspect.'"

"Detective Loncar is surprisingly understanding when it comes to stuff like that," I said.

Santangelo studied me. "You saw me. The night I set fire to the mannequin in the dumpster. I would have put it out, but you saw me. I had to get out of there. I couldn't risk my reputation, my show, my paintings. Not now."

I felt like I'd slipped into a world where people were commodities and creative pursuits were paramount. Somewhere along the way the humanity of life had been traded for fame and fortune, for false niceties that hid felonious rationalization. In all of my years in fashion, I'd never encountered people like this, who saw destruction and vandalism as justifiable when it came to protecting their art.

I backed away from Santangelo. His words said that he was sorry for what he'd done, but his actions told me he'd do it all again. If anybody was a victim in all of this, it wasn't him. It wasn't Harper. It wasn't me. It was Amanda.

I fled Warehouse Five for home. Santangelo had given me more information than I could process on an empty stomach. After finishing the Neapolitan ice cream directly from the carton, I slowed down. Sure, the artist in residency had screwy motivation, but he'd done little more than try to protect himself. The person who had been out for himself all along was Clive.

I spun the empty carton of ice cream until I found Clive's number. He answered after several rings. I hadn't calculated the time change, but Tahiti was on the other side of California, so it was earlier than here, and I wouldn't have minded waking the British bum up.

"'Allo, darling. How are you? Enjoying a bit of a rest now that you've some time on your hands?"

"You might have fooled everybody else, but you haven't fooled me. I know about your history with the minor. Your career was almost destroyed. What did you offer to Amanda to get her to hire you?"

"Amanda gave me an opportunity to redeem myself, and I gave her legitimacy. My documentary would have done for her what *Unzipped* did for Isaac Mizrahi. She would have been more than a designer. She would have been a star."

"But you risked it all by making a play for Harper."

"I'd like to see you prove that bit of rubbish. Amanda and I had an arrangement. A couple of hours in the editing booth, and I'm certain to have a magnificent narrative of what happened."

"But there wasn't any show, and Amanda can't want your photos now."

"I have no loyalty to Amanda. I've spoken to editors at the major magazines, and there's extreme interest in what I shot. Ten different galleries are bidding on the opportunity to showcase the images, and the tabloids are talking six figures per image. Why shouldn't I take advantage of the situation? Exclusive footage of fashion in flames. Much better than what I might have gotten if the show went off without a hitch. You might say I got lucky."

"If the fire inspector can link you to the arson, I wouldn't call it lucky."

"Ms. Kidd, a photographer needs to know how to chase the light. That's what I did. Chased the light."

"And if someone had gotten injured in the process of you chasing it?"

"Then I'd have sold my film to the highest bidder and walked away. But alas, that wasn't to be the day I struck gold."

Again I thought of the strand of dyed-blond hair. "Is your hair color natural?"

"I hardly think that's relevant," he said.

"The police can link a person with dyed-blond hair to the fire," I said boldly. I didn't say which fire.

"A little Sun-In can hardly be called dyed. Now, if you're done with your interrogation, Ms. Kidd, I have sixteen swimsuit models waiting for me on a white-sand beach. You do know I'm in Tahiti, don't you? Where I've been for twenty-four hours. I've spoken to Inspector Gigger and Detective Loncar. If they were content to let me do my job, I suppose you should be too."

I made a fist and punched the cushion on the back of the sofa. "Thank you for your time," I said with as much cordiality as I could muster.

"Cheerio, lass," he said in return and disconnected.

Clive stood to make a lot of money from those photos, and if he'd been pressuring Harper for sexual favors, then he surely had no moral compass and would destroy Amanda in the process of getting rich. If he was telling the truth about being able to sell the photos, then my suggestion that Amanda replace him with Dante had created a situation for her. It had made things worse. Amanda Ries might have fabricated some of her troubles, but as far as I was concerned, they were far from over.

I remembered the photos in the basement. Fine, I thought. Clive thinks he can make money by selling his photos? They'd lose all value once Nancie Townsend published Dante's photos in her new magazine. I'd show Clive the meaning of exclusive.

I called Nancie. "Nancie, this is Samantha Kidd."

"Samantha, I was just thinking about you. How's the article coming?"

"Better than expected. I'm pretty sure I can have something to you by tomorrow."

"Perfection. Do you have art?"

"I have art like you wouldn't believe."

"You're not toying with me, are you?"

"Here's what you need to know about me. When I say I'll deliver something, I deliver it. Deadlines are not a problem. Are you still interviewing other candidates for your full-time position?"

"There are a few people on my radar, but I tell you what. I'll blow them off until tomorrow at five. If your article is as good as you say it is, you've got yourself a job."

I brought the photos upstairs to the computer and sat down to write the exposé of all exposés.

SOME LIKE IT HAUTE

by

Samantha Kidd

The world of haute couture is fickle. Too long in the spotlight, and a designer can get burned. For emerging talent Amanda Ries, the burns didn't come from the spotlight. They came at the hands of an arsonist.

Details of the fire at the recent Amanda Ries runway show can be found in the newspapers and online, but what's missing from those reports is a description of the true stars of the show: the clothes. Why? Because aside from the first six runway looks, the audience didn't have a chance to see them. This reporter gained backstage access prior to the show and followed up with a visit to the showroom to document the full collection.

Formerly known for an ice-cream-sherbet color palette of All-American classics, Ries tried her hand at something new. Shades of orange, red, yellow, and silver decorated futuristic jumpsuits, motorcycle jackets, and kimonos. While other designers gravitate toward a post-apocalyptic future, Ries shows us an exuberant vision. Her woman of the future is strong, confident, and fashion forward, a merging of sixties space age and nineties minimalism with a dash of Harajuku thrown into the mix.

I chewed on my fingertip and read over what I'd written. So far, so good. Already I'd managed to plug my credentials and pull the rug out from under Clive's supposed exclusive by having art of my own.

Before continuing, I picked up the stack of images and flipped through them. It was about the clothes, not about me being in the clothes, so I ignored how I looked and focused on the garments. I selected four images and then prepared to send them. Here was the one flaw with Dante's shoot-on-film decision. What was I to do? Scan in these pictures and email them?

I hadn't talked to Dante since Tuesday night, when Loncar and Amanda had shown up. He claimed I went stiff as a board when Amanda showed up. And he took it to mean that I wasn't over Nick.

He was right. But this didn't have to do with Nick. This had to do with an investigation that we'd started together.

I called him. "I need to email some of these photos that you took. How should I do that?"

"Whoa, slow down. No 'Hi, Dante'? No 'How was your day?'"

"Hi, Dante. How was your day?" I said.

"It was good. I took the bike to Jersey. Stared at the ocean for a couple of hours. Cleared my mind."

"Do you do that often?"

"Whenever I need some clarity. You should try it sometime."

"I don't have a bike."

"Anytime you want to go, all you have to do is ask."

I twirled a lock of hair around my index finger but said nothing.

After a few seconds, he spoke again. "So, what's this about photos?"

"I'm working on that article about Amanda, and I need the art. Your photos are on film, and they haven't been touched up."

"They don't need to be touched up. There's truth in them."

There was that word again. Truth. The same word Santangelo had used. It made me uncomfortable because I knew I'd been avoiding it. But there was no time like the present to acknowledge the truth about my own life.

"Can you come over tonight?" I asked.

"What for, Samantha?"

"So we can talk."

30

HALLUCINATION OF SILVER LAMÉ

I WAS WIRED WITH NERVOUS ENERGY, SO I CLEANED. SCRUBBED THE grout in the bathroom with a toothbrush and sponged down the baseboards. Even dusted the pages of the books on the bookcase. Fueled with romantic frustration, concern about Nick's father's health, and anxiety over the arsons around town, I might as well have hung drywall in the basement. The past week had taught me a lot about myself, and I was determined not to become one of those never-happy people even if it killed me.

By the time Dante arrived, I'd picked up a couple of smudges of dust and dirt on my sweater and plaid skirt. I didn't bother to change. He gave my outfit a quick glance but said nothing. I held the door open and let him in.

"I'd offer you something to drink, but your options are limited to water. Sparkling or tap."

He waved my offer off. "I have a feeling this isn't a purely social visit."

"It's semi-social. Come with me." I went upstairs to the spare bedroom and cued up my article on Amanda's show. "This is an article about Amanda. It could lead to a job. I need your permission to use the photos. You'll get full credit, of course."

He fanned the stack of photos out and paused for a second over the one in the red dress. "You could have asked me that over the phone," he said.

"I need your signature."

"You didn't ask me here to get my signature on a release form."

"No, I didn't."

Dante leaned against the wall and crossed one foot over the other. He crossed his arms as well. The sleeves of his black leather jacket rode up, exposing his tattoos. "What's on your mind, Samantha?"

I chickened out. "Clive Barrington," I said.

"Clive? What's he done now?" He relaxed his arms, as though he'd been expecting a different subject.

"Someone set a fire in a trash can in front of my house." At the look of anger on his face, I continued. "I was able to put it out with an extinguisher before the fire department arrived. I found some ash in the bottom and looked at it under the microscope." I waved toward the Fisher-Price toy. "There was evidence of dyed blond hairs. You told me Clive dyed his hair. I thought it might have been him, except I confirmed he's been in Tahiti. He couldn't have set the fire."

He followed my gesture to the Fisher-Price microscope, and a hint of a smile tugged at his lips before he grew serious again.

"Clive Barrington is not a nice guy. He was always a part of the scene, not just the photographer, but on the party circuit. There was a rumor about him making advances toward the models, even those who were underage. He promised to help make careers. More than one mother looked the other way and left him alone with their daughters."

"Did any of the accusations stick?"

"Nope. The guy's like Teflon. He's an opportunistic bastard who looks out for himself."

"Does he have it in him to do any of this?"

"I wouldn't put it past him, but I can't see the upside. Clive Barrington doesn't do anything unless it benefits Clive Barrington."

"I called him earlier today. He's negotiating with some industry gossip magazines to showcase the fires. 'Fashion in Flames,' he called it. He said something about how a good photographer chases the light."

Dante leaned forward and flipped through the photos again. "If Clive let it be known to the right people that his footage was for sale, he could start a bidding war. I'm thinking he'd get six figures, maybe even seven. Fashion, emerging designer, arson. Could bring his name back into the limelight. Make him hot again. Make people forget about the accusations."

"There's a motive. And he was there. He had the opportunity. If only I could figure out how he started the fire."

Dante waved his camera. "There's a few more shots on this roll of film. I can develop them now if you want."

"Sure," I said.

"Come with me. It's been a long time since I had a photography assistant."

We went down two flights of stairs to the basement and entered the darkroom. Dante closed the door behind us. I turned to face him. He put his hands on my hips. I closed my eyes and stood there for a second, smelling cinnamon on his breath, before reaching up and moving his hands away.

"I appreciate you helping me with the investigation, but I'm not ready to do this," I said.

I wanted Dante to nod his understanding, but he didn't. He didn't walk away or say something cliché about being friends or toss out a light comment about timing or calling him if I needed a distraction. My words hung in the air with no acknowledgment that I had made a conscious decision to close this door without fully knowing what was behind it.

Finally, he spoke. "The new photos will be ready in an hour. No worries on using them. Email me the waiver. I'll sign it and get it back to you."

"Thank you," I said.

I left the room and went back upstairs to work on the article. After a short while, I heard footsteps downstairs. Seconds later, the garage door opened and shut, and a motorcycle drove away.

I emailed the finished article to Nancie with a note that photographer approval would be following soon. Next, I called Amanda's studio. Tiny answered.

"This is Samantha. I finished the article on Amanda. Any chance you or she would be available for a follow-up?"

"I told her that article was a bad idea, but her business is her business now. We parted company earlier today."

"She fired you?"

"I quit. If I don't get out soon, no amount of press in the world will save my reputation."

"But what about her? Amanda Ries Designs and her being on the verge of breaking out?"

"Sometimes you have to know when to cut ties from a sinking ship."

Amanda had surrounded herself with people to protect her from the details of running her business, and everybody was moving on. I wondered how she was taking it.

"Is Amanda there? Can I talk to her?"

"She's at Warehouse Five, wrapping up business with the insurance company. You can probably catch her if you get there soon."

Before she could hang up, I blurted out, "Oscar LeVay."

"Excuse me?" she asked.

"Have you paid him for the models at the show?"

"How is that any of your business?"

"I guess it isn't."

"That's right. Anything else?"

"Nope."

"Good. See ya around, Sam. I'd like to say it's been a pleasure, but that would be a lie." She hung up.

I stuck my tongue out at the phone and then looked up OLV Model Management and called the main number. A receptionist said Oscar was in a meeting and offered to take a message.

"This is Samantha Kidd. K-i-d-d. I'm working with Amanda Ries to resolve any outstanding issues related to her recent show. Do you know if Mr. LeVay received payment for the models yet? If not, I can arrange for a check to be delivered this afternoon."

"Mr. LeVay would probably want to talk to you about that. Hold, please," she said. She clicked me to a silent line for the briefest of moments, and then Oscar picked up.

"Tiny?" he asked.

"No, this is Samantha Kidd. I'm calling on behalf of Amanda Ries. Tiny is no longer with the company."

"Is this a joke?"

"No, sir. I'm helping Amanda clear up any outstanding issues that resulted from the fire, and I came upon your invoices. Where do we stand on them?"

"I'm not sure. Tiny claimed to have cut a check, but until I see it, I'm not going to believe it."

"Why don't I deliver payment in full? If I can verify that a second check has been cut, I'll put a stop payment on it."

He agreed. I verified his address and made arrangements to meet him before the close of business. I had a little over an hour.

Oscar was the only person still waiting for something from

Amanda. It stood to reason that whoever was trying to destroy her wouldn't do so unless they got what they wanted. I'd give Oscar what he wanted and see what he did next.

My check from Amanda was still in my handbag. I scanned it into the computer and used the resulting jpeg to mock up a fake check with a suitably computer-looking font and a made-up account number. After a ten-minute diversion to look up the penalties for check fraud, I called Detective Loncar.

"This is Samantha Kidd. I'm about to deliver a fake check. I thought I'd tell you first."

"Ms. Kidd, intent to commit check fraud is a crime. Depending on the amount of the check, you could be looking at misdemeanor or felony charges. I thought you were smarter than that."

"Detective, I skewed the dimensions of the check by a quarter of an inch and signed it 'Diana Vreeland.' The routing number says 'gotcha' in a simple number-letter replacement code, and the currency of the check is listed as doubloons. I hardly think I could be accused of intent to commit fraud."

"Where are you?"

"I'm at my house, and I'm going to OLV Model Management. Oscar LeVay expects me to bring him a check on behalf of Amanda Ries."

"Don't do this, Ms. Kidd."

I retrieved the stack of photos that Dante had developed and set them by the door. Next, I showered and changed into a red turtleneck and matching wool cape, narrow black pants, and riding boots. I wrapped a plaid scarf around my neck, pulled on black leather gloves, grabbed a handbag, and left.

OLV Model Management was in West Ribbon. There was a noticeable change to the buildings once you passed through downtown. Houses looked more imposing, streets were cleaner, and new office buildings were interspersed with old ones. I parked close to the building entrance and let myself inside.

The first thing I noticed was the large glass vase that sat on the receptionist's desk. Instead of flowers, it was filled with bright oranges. I was so thrown off that I forgot why I was there.

"They're pretty, aren't they?" The receptionist smiled. "I love Clementine season."

"Clementines," I repeated. "Smaller and sweeter than oranges, aren't they?"

"Easier to peel too." She stood up and leaned over the vase, taking a deep breath over the vase. "They smell good too. Go ahead. Give them a whiff."

I tentatively stepped closer to the vase. From a distance of two feet away, I breathed in the scent. It took me back to the attack. Right before I was hit. I pushed away from the desk and yelled, "No!"

The receptionist, not willing to have a potentially deranged stranger hanging around her lobby, stood from her desk and very quickly escorted me to Oscar's office on the third floor. He appeared to be waiting for me.

"You must be Samantha. Come in," he said. "Care for a drink?" he asked. A fully stocked bar cart sat to the right of his desk.

Knocking back a shot of vodka wouldn't do much in the way of making me feel better. I considered asking if he had any meatball sandwiches lying around, but instead politely declined his offer.

Before diving directly into felony-committing mode, I set my belongings on the table and looked at Oscar's office. If hints to his personality were hidden in the room, I wasn't seeing them. The walls were lined with images of airbrushed models and not much more. His desk was immaculate, as were his bookshelves. Knickknacks were kept to a minimum, which seemed a nice gesture to the cleaning service.

Nope, if I was going to engage Oscar LeVay in any secret-spilling banter, I was going to have to play the cards I was dealt.

"Mr. LeVay, I wondered if I could trouble you for an opinion," I said. I eased the stack of Dante's photos out of the envelope. "You're a respected expert in discovering models. I recently had these photos taken. Do you think I have a future in the business?"

He took the photos and studied the one on top. The red dress. He flipped to the next one and the one after that. "You have a certain charm. Perhaps catalog modeling for the plus-size market."

"Excuse me?"

"Plus-size models are in the ten-to-twelve range. You're—how tall? Five six?"

"Seven. Five seven. And a half."

"A bit on the short side, and a little old for this line of work, but there's a place for big-boned girls like you."

My cheeks flushed red. The last time I'd checked, I was below the national weight average for women in the United States, but thirty seconds with Oscar, and I felt like an undesirable. Was this how he spoke to everybody who walked into his office asking about their chances for success?

Focus, Samantha.

"What about Harper Ashton? She's one of your top models, isn't she?"

"Was. I expected her to work for me for a long time. All she had to do was steer clear of the darkness of the industry, and she could have become one of the greats. Like Christie and Linda. Bring back the all-American look."

"I never thought about it, but she would have been perfect for Amanda's other collections. Before she went with Godzilla on the moon."

"You're right. She was to become the centerpiece of Amanda's collection. Classic American sportswear on a classic American beauty. The two could have helped each other, made each other famous. But then Amanda had this"—he waved his fingertips by his temples— "this hallucination of silver lamé. I tried to get Harper pulled from the show. She didn't need to be a part of Amanda's train wreck."

"You said 'was.' Isn't Harper with your agency anymore?"

"Harper disappeared after the show. I exhausted countless resources trying to make sure she wasn't injured or in any danger. There was a lot at stake. And then she sends a postcard from Mexico. No apology. No explanation. But I know who was behind it."

"Who?"

"Her sister."

"Harper has a sister?"

Oscar opened a leather-bound binder that sat on the corner of his desk and flipped through several pages of photos. He stopped on the second one from the end, pulled the glossy image out of its plastic sleeve, and held it up. "Her sister. Molly Diers."

31

PUTTING THE BAND
BACK TOGETHER

THE FACE THAT STARED BACK AT ME WAS ONLY SLIGHTLY FAMILIAR. IT was a different Molly than the one who needed my help to find an outfit for her in-laws' family gathering. The woman in the photo was airbrushed and glamorous in a minimalistic, late-70s way. Even in her modeling days, Molly Diers was into the bohemian look.

Oscar set the photo down and stared at the image. "Molly had the body and the attitude, but after the incident, she was over."

I rested my butt on the arm of the chair across from Oscar's desk. "What incident?" I asked.

"Molly took a job nobody knew about. It was a closed set and involved a bit of nudity. She was just a girl. There should have been a guardian, but there wasn't. Molly claimed abuse. Her mother, who denied giving permission for the job, came after me for sending a girl her age into an adult situation without supervision, and Molly dropped out of sight. The photographer left the country and only worked abroad until recently."

"Let me guess. The photographer was Clive Barrington."

"Yes." Oscar had been speaking from a collection of memories too strong to keep suppressed, but my interjection pulled him back to the present. He took in how I was resting on the arm of his probably very expensive office chair and stood to his full imposing height. I stood up straight, too, even though five foot seven and a half wasn't particularly imposing.

"Samantha, I believe you are here to deliver a check." He tapped the edges of my photos on his desk to line them up and handed them to me.

I tucked them under my arm while I felt around in my handbag for the envelope containing the check. As soon as he had it, I would be dismissed. Which was fine, because I had to get out of there.

I set it on the corner of his desk. He picked it up and looked inside. Satisfied with what a cursory glance told him, he looked up. "Let me know if you'd like help putting your portfolio together."

Sure. The next time I needed someone to pummel my self-esteem, I'd be sure to give him a call.

I threw the car into gear and peeled out of the parking lot. There was no way Molly Diers's arrival on my doorstep had been a coincidence. Especially now that I knew something had happened between Molly and Clive in the past. Add in that Oscar had represented Molly at the time of the incident.

Molly had dropped out of the modeling world, gotten married, let herself go, and gotten divorced. Three people who had a connection to Amanda's ill-fated runway show were at the same place at the same time. It seemed like someone was putting the band back together, and at the top of the list of potential organizers was Molly Diers.

According to the police, the only crime to be investigated was that of arson. Could Molly be guilty of setting the fires around town? She had motive: create a diversion to get her sister away from Clive Barrington. If Molly had taken note of the photos in the darkroom, then the fire at my house could have been a deterrent.

Like the attack on me the night before the show. A message for me to mind my own business.

I drove to Warehouse Five. Traffic was light, and I arrived quickly. Two cars were parked in the lot: Amanda's little black coupe and a gold sedan with a dent on the rear passenger side. I pulled into the space next to Amanda's and got out.

Someone had propped the door open with a brick. I entered. Charred air perfumed the interior. I stood still and listened for the sound of voices. There were none. There was only the leftover smell of burnt building. My stomach turned. I moved forward.

The auditorium where Amanda's show was to have taken place was on the left-hand side of the building. I assumed that's where I'd find Amanda. I assumed wrong. The room was empty.

Although I'd been back at Warehouse Five to talk to Santangelo Toma, this was the first time I'd been inside the auditorium since the night of the show.

The room remained largely untouched from the chaos that had ensued. Chairs had been tipped over and pushed to the side to make way for patrons to flee. Scars of soot marred the walls. Burnt bits of rose petals crunched under my feet like discarded cornflakes.

Curiosity got the better of me, and I climbed up onto the catwalk. The original white plastic floor covering had melted in the fire and was fused to the damaged platform underneath. The smell was unbearable and probably toxic. I knotted my scarf around my neck and spun the knot to the back like a robber in an old western and then pulled the wool up over my mouth and breathed through it. Not much better.

I dropped down to all fours and ran my hand across the surface of the floor. I still didn't understand how the fire had started. I sat for a second and closed my eyes to recall what I'd seen both in person and on the videotape. Five models had walked down that catwalk before Harper. Nothing had happened to any of them. And then Harper had strutted her stuff, oversized kimono sleeves dragging along the floor behind her. The kimono went up in flames.

The *kimono* went up in flames. The flames started at the tip of the sleeves and climbed the garment.

I concentrated harder on the memory. The fire had been started at ground level. What was it? A trigger wire under the flooring? I scoured the floor for signs of platform tampering with low expectations for success. The fire inspector had been through here looking for this very thing, and it was a given he actually knew what a trigger wire looked like. If evidence had been left behind, it would have been found by now. By Gigger or Amanda or Tiny or an insurance agent who wanted to prove that someone else was responsible for the fire. The only thing left for me to see were melted plastic and long strands of metallic thread. The threads clung to the wool of my coat like sticky cobwebs. I'd seen these metallic threads before. They'd clung to my glove the night I'd felt around the macadam of the parking lot.

I reached down and peeled a strand of the metallic thread from my coat. I tried to tear it but couldn't. It wasn't thread at all. It was a thin, flexible wick. A few stray threads that matched those of Harper's kimono clung to the end as though the two had been connected.

And I knew. This was how the fire had been started. The long, barely visible wick had been attached to the oversized, dragging sleeves of the kimono and lit from backstage. The fire traveled the length of it until it reached the sleeve of the kimono. If I had a chance to examine that garment, I'd bet something had been hidden in the edges of the sleeves to make it combust.

Molly hadn't had the opportunity to tamper with Harper's kimono.

Tiny had.

The night I'd gone to Tiny about Harper's kimono, she'd been holding spools of metallic thread. She said she'd look at the ill-fitting garment if there was time. She hadn't been willing to make alterations. Her only concern had been making sure the wick remained intact. She'd planned all along to use that kimono to set fire to the show.

I tucked the cluster of metallic threads into my bra, not wanting to take a chance on them falling from a pocket. I climbed down from the platform and went backstage. The fire had destroyed most of the room, leaving an empty cavern. Anything that burned had been consumed by the flames, leaving exposed metal frames of the furniture. The walls looked like a graffiti artist had airbrushed on black soot marks, growing increasingly darker around the windows and the door.

The smell of the fire was stronger back here. Almost a week had passed, and just standing here, I could see the fire, smell the fire, feel the fire. The memory was as strong as it had been the night of the show.

That's when I realized I wasn't reliving a memory. A new fire had been set and was burning down what was left of Warehouse Five.

32

———

ANOTHER PRETTY FACE

Smoke trickled into the room from around a closed door at the rear. Worse, sounds came from inside. The same sounds I'd listened for when I first arrived.

I moved closer and reached out for the knob. The heat burned my fingers before contact. I dumped the contents of my handbag and turned it inside out and then used it like an oven mitt to grab at the knob. It opened. Smoke poured out of the door as it swung open. And then, something caught my ankle. I screamed and kicked away. The cloudy air made it difficult to see, but I squinted through the smoke to see what it was. A hand.

Tears clouded my vision. The scarf was no match for the smoke. I had to get outside where the air was clear. Phone, wallet, everything that had been in my handbag now lay scattered on the floor. All of that could be replaced. My life could not. Neither could the life of the person in the closet.

I looked down at the person on the ground. It was Amanda.

"Get out of here!" I called. I grabbed her hand and pulled her toward me. She fought my efforts.

She panted for air and coughed. I pulled the scarf down from my face so she could hear me. "You have to get out of here. Now!" I dragged her toward the back door. She stumbled through it and got about ten feet away from the building before collapsing onto the gravel, knees first. She turned over onto her back and coughed like a thirty-year smoker.

I stumbled away from the building and saw a car partially hidden down the road. It faced me. I ran toward it. My legs gave way halfway there. I fell. I scrambled back up to my feet. The engine started, and the car backed away.

Tiny's face laughed at me through the windshield. She was going to get away.

I dove onto the hood and grabbed the antenna. The car backed up, and I slid, my grip on the thin metal spoke the only thing that kept me tethered to the car. The antenna snapped off. Tiny twisted the steering wheel hard. My fingers hooked into the exhaust vents. Tiny's face was red with rage.

My body, sore from residual bruises and new injuries, couldn't take this for long. I couldn't even scream, my voice hoarse from inhaling so much smoke. Tiny arced the wheel hard and spun the car the opposite direction. I clung to the car. She cursed. The brakes slammed on. She reversed and drove, reversed and drove. I gripped tighter.

The car swerved into the woods. Silent screams tore at my throat. My cold fingers cramped. Branches scraped against me as she drove. The car skidded on a patch of sludge and spun across the road. My fingers released, and I flew off the car. I landed on hard, cold dirt, knocking the wind out of me. Tiny rolled her window down and smiled.

"Like I told you, you should have stayed out of it. Nobody would have suspected me. Not after people started digging into Clive's background with Harper's sister."

"You knew about that?" I choked out.

"Of course, I knew about it. I hired them both. I set the stage for little sister to follow in her big sister's shoes and for Clive Barrington to be suspect number one."

"You used Harper as a diversion? She could have been killed."

"Boohoo. The industry loses another pretty face. There's a hundred girls like her waiting in the wings." She spat out the window onto the cold, dry ground, barely missing my head.

"But why did you do it?" I asked in little over a whisper. Pain came at me like ice picks. I wanted to close my eyes and give up, but I had to hold on a little longer.

"Amanda was never going to be more than a two-bit designer, not with this collection."

"You convinced her to take a risk. You told her she needed a Hail Mary."

"All part of the plan. It was my money that backed her. My investment. I insured her company for ten-million dollars when I came on board. I needed her to believe that she was at the end of the line. All I needed was for the whole collection to go up in flames and be ruled an accident. Ten-million dollars paid to me."

"But why the rest of the fires? Why not just the one?"

"I got the idea when I saw the threatening letters."

I pushed myself up to hide the pain I was in. "Amanda—didn't tell you—about the letters," I panted.

"She didn't, but Oscar did." She smiled. "He demanded to know what was going on and threatened to leak the information to the media if we didn't pay him for the show."

"The rest of the fires—all to look—someone after Amanda?" My chest heaved and fell with each painful breath. "You made— fake letters—real?"

"I found the file on her computer. She made up the notes. Once I knew she invented them, I knew she'd never go to the police. It was perfect. But then you came along. You were never supposed to get involved. Why did you? She's your ex-boyfriend's ex-girlfriend. You should hate her as much as I do."

I coughed several times. Conscious and unconscious thoughts twisted in my mind. I had to fight to stay with her. I couldn't let her see how close I was to letting go, giving up, drifting into darkness. I channeled the Dread Pirate Roberts and addressed her while I conserved my strength. "Don't compare yourself to me. We're nothing alike." *I wouldn't be caught dead in men's jeans.* "You won't get away with any of this. You'll never see a dime of insurance money once the arson investor learns you're the person behind the fire."

"Prove it." She smiled at me. Tiny was no less intimidating when she smiled.

With every ounce of energy that I had left, I reached inside my bra and pulled out the cluster of thread that I'd found inside the warehouse. I held it up.

"This isn't thread like everybody thinks. It's a wick. You had it trail from the sleeves of Harper's kimono, and you lit it from backstage. When the fire caught up to the garment, it erupted."

Her smile froze. She opened the car door and stepped out. I couldn't let her take it from me. This was the only evidence that I had.

I wrapped my arms around the tree next to me and pulled myself up. Lights from an oncoming car indicated we had company. Tiny's car blocked the road, but her lights were off. The oncoming car would have to stop. She turned around and shielded her eyes.

When she turned back to face me, I slugged her with everything I had in me.

And then the approaching car slammed into hers, knocking it off the road. The car hit Tiny, Tiny hit me, and we all crashed to the ground.

33

WRONG

My new hospital room was pink. Despite the charming hue, I wasn't any less freaked out than the last time I'd woken up in one. A curtain had been pulled shut between me and the other bed in the room, but I didn't know if I was alone or not. A few feet from the wall was a table that held a tray filled with food. If it wasn't a meatball sandwich, I wasn't interested.

A woman in scrubs printed with little crowns and tiaras walked in and checked my vital signs. "Are you up for visitors? A couple of people have been waiting to see you."

"Sure."

If I'd known my first visitor would be Detective Loncar, I might have given a different answer.

"Don't ask me what happened, because I don't remember," I said.

"Maybe I can fill in some of your gaps." He sat down in the chair next to the bed. "Tiny was arrested on suspicion of setting multiple fires around Ribbon."

"I was sure it was Molly Diers. She has a history with Clive Barrington. Did you know she's Harper's sister?"

"We knew all about Ms. Diers."

"You didn't tell me."

"She came to us in confidence. There was nothing illegal about her arranging for her sister to leave the country, but she wanted us to know in the event rumors about Harper's disappearance created a diversion from the arson investigation."

"That's where she got the sourballs. She took them from the bowl on your desk." It was the tiniest connection, but if I'd been paying attention, I might have realized it sooner. "How did you know where to find me? Last time we talked, you didn't say anything about suspecting Tiny. I only figured it out at Warehouse Five."

"When the report came in of the fire, I knew something was up. I called Inspector Gigger. He found the two of you on the ground about a mile from the warehouse. Nobody's sure how you got there considering the condition you were in. You were holding some metallic thread."

"It's what Tiny used as the wick to light the kimono. I should have noticed it earlier. It was on the parking lot macadam by my car. I thought they were cobwebs."

"Gigger recognized it for what it was. Amanda gave him permission to examine the garments at her showroom, and he found the same threads. We pulled in a computer guy who found an invoice on Tiny's computer for two dozen spools of microscopic metallic wicks. They were paid for with her personal credit card. It was enough to connect Tiny to the garments in the showroom, the garments at the show, and the garments that returned to the showroom. And the fire that took place two nights ago."

"Is that all?"

"No, that's not all. I thought you'd be interested in knowing that

Ms. Anderson legally changed her name to Tiny several years ago. Prior to that, it was a nickname."

"What's her real name?"

"Clementine."

I closed my eyes. It was exactly the calling card I'd suspected, only Santangelo wasn't the culprit. Tiny had played off my injuries as if I'd made them up. Refusing to acknowledge that the attack had happened had been the perfect cover for her considering she was the responsible one. I tried to relax against the flat hospital pillow, but every position brought on pain.

"We followed up with Oscar LeVay too. Doubloons," he said, shaking his head. "That was a good one."

"What about Molly and Harper and Clive?"

"The statute of limitations on Ms. Diers's accusations has long since run out. Mr. Barrington is free to do as he sees fit. As for Ms. Diers and her sister, I think they're officially out of the business. Ms. Diers gave us an address for San Francisco."

Bohemian capital of the country. Figured.

"Ms. Kidd," Loncar said, "I appreciate your help on this. That last fire would have destroyed any evidence left. I'm not sure we would have put it together if it wasn't for you."

I swiped the tears from my face and tried to act like his praise didn't affect me. Loncar stood up and held out his hand. I shook it. He left the room.

Amanda walked in with a vase of orange roses. "I don't know how to repay you," she said. "You saved my life."

"You would have done the same for me."

"Let's hope it never comes to that." She set the flowers on the table next to the bed. "Nancie Townsend called with a couple of follow-up questions to your article. When I heard about the new magazine, I told her she'd be a fool not to hire you." She picked at the corner of the hospital sheet and then stopped when she realized what she was doing. "If I were smart, I'd hire you myself. I'm looking for a new business manager."

"Amanda, don't take this the wrong way, but that's the worst idea you've ever had."

She smiled. "You're probably right." She pulled a pink envelope out of her handbag and tucked it under the vase of roses and then left.

Seconds later, Eddie took her place by my bed. I sat forward and looked toward the door. "Exactly how many people are out there?" I asked.

"I let them go first. It's all me until they kick me out." His blond hair was unkempt, pushed to one side and tucked behind his ears. He wore a Berlin concert T-shirt under a gray hoodie under a faded denim jacket. His cargo pants were weighted down by the contents of the pockets by his knees. He pulled two foil-wrapped items out of the pockets and set them on the table between us. The scent of meatball sub filled the room. "The commissary loves me. I've been buying meatball sandwiches every day just waiting for you to wake up."

I peeled back the paper and bit into the sandwich. Mozzarella cheese, soft meatballs, hard roll, yes. It was good to be alive.

"The stories in the waiting room describe a David-and-Goliath-style fight, but I'm having trouble picturing how it all went down. You were on foot. She was in a car. Care to tell me how you walked away?"

I looked at my hand and slowly made a fist. My skin was red, raw, and chapped, and a greenish-yellow bruise had formed by the knuckles. I ran my left fingers over the discoloration and remembered the moment when I'd slugged Tiny. A shudder wracked my body at the memory.

"Dude?" Eddie prompted.

"I guess she just caught me on the wrong day."

I didn't read Amanda's card until after Eddie had left. It was a generic Get Well, with balloons on the front and a sappy message printed on the inside. But under the message, in Amanda's neat handwriting, was Nick's name, followed by a New York phone number. I asked the nurse if I could use a phone.

Nick answered on the second ring. "Hello?"

"Hey Taylor, it's Kidd."

"Kidd," he said. "I didn't recognize the number."

If he didn't know about what had happened, he would soon, but that wasn't why I was calling. "I know you're probably busy, but I just called to tell you I was wrong."

"About what?" he asked.

I let a beat of silence pass before answering. "About cake. Nobody should have to eat cake without icing."

We spent the next forty-five minutes talking about this and that and nothing important at all.

It was exactly how I liked it.

GRAND THEFT RETRO

1

THE SEVENTIES

There were seven and a half reasons why it was a bad idea. If I had listened to my inner voice, the one that tabulated those seven and a half reasons, I might have spent the weeks surrounding my birthday enjoying myself. I might have spent my days at my job writing editorials about style from decades past. I might have had a date for Saturday night. Instead, I was hanging from the side of a building. The last thing on my mind was cake.

And as much as I've been trying to distract myself from my current situation, it's getting harder and harder to ignore the truth. Being on the cusp of a birthday might not be my biggest concern.

Yeah, possibly falling three stories to my death trumps any concerns I have about my age.

One day earlier...

It was closing in on eleven o'clock at night. The sun had gone down hours ago, taking with it my desire to stay at the office working on editorial content and retweeting #OOTD (outfit of the day) and #FashionFail (white socks with sandals) under the *Retrofit* Twitter account. Unfortunately, I wasn't a farmer, and the rise and set of the sun had nothing to do with my workload. *I could be a farmer,* I thought, gazing out the window at the pitch-black sky and the mostly empty parking lot. *I could wear Wellingtons and overalls and raise chickens.* Someone knocked on the doorframe. I whirled around. "Chickens," I said.

Our newest intern to take on the role of office manager and schedule coordinator looked startled. "Um, sure. Chickens. Listen, Samantha, Nancie's finishing up with the manager of the auction house. She said as soon as they're done, she wants to see you in the boardroom. You know what that means." She grabbed both ends of the scarf that had been wound around her neck and adjusted it so the ends were closer to even, and then went back to her tiny desk out front.

I did know what it meant. If my boss, the owner of *Retrofit*, the e-zine where I'd held a job for four months, had requested my presence in the boardroom at eleven o'clock at night, it meant she wanted to go home. Which meant the rest of us could finally go home, too.

"I'm on it," I said to myself.

I left my cubicle and walked down the hall to Nancie's office. *Retrofit* had been started on a shoestring budget, but thanks to Nancie's ability to talk people out of their advertising dollars, she'd catapulted us from fashion blogger territory into becoming a regular website with tens of thousands of page views a day. The concept was simple: how to take yesterday's trash and modernize it into today's world of style.

Fashionistas checked in with us on how to incorporate vintage finds into their daily wardrobes. Collectors searched our databases to see if that pair of culottes they scored at a yard sale over the weekend had a chance of coming back into style. *Retrofit* had been cited by more than one industry professional as a website to watch. Our online subscribers doubled almost daily. We were one of the fastest growing style-dedicated websites on the internet.

The past few months had all but erased the memory of the spotty work experience I'd had after I gave up my job in New York and moved back to Ribbon. Four months at *Retrofit* had gone a long way toward restoring my instincts and making me feel like I was part of something that appeared to be successful.

I arrived at the boardroom and tapped on the door before going inside. Nancie stood with her back to me, talking to a tall man. He was attractive in a boldly masculine way. He had jet-black hair and strong features and wore a white collared shirt under an unstructured navy-blue jacket, and jeans. His skin tone, a shade I needed a steady stream of appointments at a tanning salon to achieve, glowed against the white of his shirt. He had a look of determination about him, probably thanks to the fact that his two eyebrows almost connected above the bridge of his nose.

Nancie turned toward me. "Sam," she said. "This is Tahoma Hunt. He works at an auction house. We'll be working closely with him on our next project." She turned to Tahoma. "This is Sam Kidd. She's my right hand around here."

He held out his hand. "Tahoma Hunt. Executive Director, Bethany House."

"Samantha Kidd," I said while clasping his grip. "Nancie's right hand."

He smiled as though I'd said something funny. He put his left hand on top of our handshake, making a hand sandwich. Not a naturally touchy-feely person by nature, I stiffened at the contact but held my smile in place.

Tahoma turned to face Nancie. "Call me when your team is on

board," he said. "I'll make the necessary arrangements to help your project succeed."

"Perfection!" Nancie said. She put her hand on his shoulder. He dropped my hands and stood very straight. I could tell from his posture that he was both physically fit and proud of his build. "Sam, wait here. I'll be back after I see Tahoma out."

I stifled a yawn and dropped into one of the vacant chairs that sat around the boardroom table. The wall in front of me was filled with colorful Post-its. Nancie liked to work out ideas this way, shifting colors from the left to the right and back again. I claimed not to understand her system, though I suspected it was a problem-solving technique she'd read about in whatever recent *How To Succeed* book was at the top of the bestseller lists. Nancie was a self-taught dynamo when it came to running *Retrofit*, and far be it from me to criticize her methods.

About a minute after she'd left me alone, she returned. She took a swig from her environmentally friendly travel mug and set it on the table with a *thunk*. "Sam, I know it's late. We're going to call it a night soon. But first, I need to know if you're in or you're out."

I searched her expression for clues to what she was talking about and then tried to rewind my thoughts to a place where maybe she'd offered me an opportunity. The only thing I could think of were chicken coops.

"I need to hear more before I decide," I said.

She sat in the chair opposite me and leaned forward. The white cuffs of her crisp cotton shirt were flipped back over her black sweater dress. Nancie ignored the trends we covered in *Retrofit* and embraced a simple black-and-white dress code and low maintenance beauty routine. Even her jet-black hair was never out of place, thanks to a Japanese treatment and a turbo-powered flat iron.

"As you know, *Retrofit*'s subscriptions are on the rise. You know what that means?"

"I'm thinking it's good—"

"It's perfection! Except that just last week five new fashion blogs started up. We must stay ahead of the curve. Be new. Different. Risky. Do you know what that means?"

"I'm thinking you want more content—"

"We have to beat everybody else at the game we started. Change. Be aggressive. We've built a database of over a hundred thousand names in a little over four months, and we show no signs of slowing down. Those names are our future. They're gold. They're money in the bank. And you know what you do with money in the bank?"

"Save it?"

"Leverage it to make more! I've been talking to a team of investors. They're interested in taking *Retrofit* to the next level." She stopped talking and looked at me. Was I supposed to say something now? She hadn't asked me a question.

"I feel like I'm supposed to know where this is going," I said.

"Here's where it's going. *Retrofit* is going to produce a trend magazine. Print. National distribution. This is the big leagues, Sam. This is what I always dreamed of. But I can't do it alone. What do you say? You convinced me to take a chance on you when I started this thing. Are you still with me?"

I felt the old familiar one-two punch that I used to feel when I worked in a corporate setting as a buyer. The immediate fear of a near-impossible challenge and the subsequent sparks of excitement to figure out how to get it done. "Nancie, that's big. Huge, even. But how are you—we—going to produce a magazine? There's two of us. Four, if you count the interns, but they change every couple months. I like the idea, but I think maybe there's a little more involved than we can handle."

"I thought you might say that. Pritchard, you can come out."

The door at the back of the boardroom opened, and a man in a three-piece suit entered. He had glossy dark-blond hair parted deeply on one side in a comb-over. He wore both tie pin and cuff links, and when he reached his hands up to smooth the sides of his hair with his palms, I saw the chain of a pocket watch draped across his vest.

"Sam, this is Pritchard Smith. He's joining the *Retrofit* team. He comes with a long list of contacts in the industry just like you."

"It's Samantha," I corrected.

I knew the reasons my employment history had brought me to *Retrofit*: my degree in the history of fashion, coupled with nine years as a buyer and then two as a mostly unemployed job seeker. My mentor in New York had told me about this opportunity, and I'd out-interviewed at least a dozen fashion bloggers to get it. Nancie and I spent long hours working to ensure *Retrofit*'s success. Pritchard's interest in a relatively small start-up might be a sign that we'd done something right and were poised for expansion.

I looked at Pritchard. He crossed his arms and studied me. A half smile pulled at the left corner of his mouth, and I wondered if there was something else that brought him to our door.

Nancie picked up a two-inch-thick spiral-bound notebook from the table. She looked lovingly at the cover, and then pushed it in front of me. It was about nine inches by twelve, and on the bottom right-hand corner a sticker had been placed that said *Retrofit Trend Magazine, Vol. 1*. I started to open it, but Nancie put her hand on top and kept it closed.

"That's my baby. My dream. I've been working on it since before you came on board. From the first day we started the e-zine, *Retrofit* has been about focusing on previous decades and teaching people how to understand the evolution of style. This is going to work in tandem with what we've already built. Two issues a year. Comprehensive style tips, history, tutorials, and anything else we can brainstorm. Each issue will focus on a different decade."

"Isn't that what we do now?" I asked.

"We'll do it times a thousand. We'll go back in time and highlight the designers who influenced that decade, give brief histories. Publish never-seen runway photos, collection sketches, anything we can get our hands on. Find the designers to whom they've passed the torch. We'll highlight individual trends and provide how-to guides on styling vintage clothes while staying modern. Mix and match. Create a look with a knowledge of fashion history."

"That sounds pretty amazing, but—"

She continued. "Every page of the premiere issue has been laid out. Editorial. Fads. Accessory highlights. Sidebars. It's all there." She tapped the top of the notebook. "What we need is the content."

I had a suspicion where Nancie was planning on getting content. I looked at Pritchard. He confirmed my suspicion with a smug smile.

Nancie tapped the notebook again. "I want you and Pritchard to put your heads together and come up with concepts. We're not going to do the whole 'what's hot/what's not' thing most magazines do. Instead of telling people their horoscopes, we're going to show people how to *dress* for their horoscope. I want to teach women how to discover their personal style by showing them the icons who changed the way we see clothes today."

"Go retro," I said.

"That's it! How to go retro and find the fit that flatters you. Build a look from the inside out. Are you taking notes? You should be taking notes."

"I don't have a pen," I said.

Pritchard reached inside his suit jacket and pulled out a sleek silver ballpoint pen. "Take mine."

"See? Already working together. Perfection!"

Reluctantly, I accepted it. The pen had a nice weight. I clicked it up and down twice, made loopy circles on a blank sheet of paper that Nancie thrust in front of me, and then turned the circles into a giant flower doodle. Next to it, I wrote *New Retrofit project.*

Nancie turned her spiral-bound notebook around so it faced me. She picked up the corner of the cover and opened it. Inside was one line: *Retrofit: the Seventies.*

The Seventies?

"The Seventies have been having a moment for years. We'd be foolish not to get on the bandwagon. Mock something up while I'm out selling ad space. Once we lay out your concept, you can start contacting designers, pulling samples, and setting up the shoot. Bethany House has agreed to give us unrestricted access to their archives. It's going to take real commitment on your end, Sam. I know this is more than you signed up for, so back to my question. Are you in or are you out?"

This time I didn't look at Pritchard. I didn't have to. For the first time since I'd left my high-profile job as senior buyer of ladies' designer shoes at Bentley's New York, I could pay my bills. I'd weathered a storm of personal danger with more close calls than I wanted to count. I had a fully stocked pantry and a regular schedule for the dry cleaning. I had enough money left over after paying my bills to buy new shoes. And just last week I'd bought a two-hundred-dollar luxury cat condo for Logan. I wasn't about to give it all up.

"I'm in," I said.

Nancie glowed. "My power team—perfection!" She tapped my hand. "Now, go home and get some rest. We're going to attack this first thing in the morning."

And that's how it happened that I jumped into the deep end of Seventies fashion.

The story of how I ended up hanging from the side of a building is a little more complicated.

2

FLARED, FRINGED, AND FUNKY

The morning after Nancie announced her project, I rose with the sun and put myself into the correct Seventies mindset by dressing in an amber velvet pantsuit with particularly wide lapels. It was a few seasons old but channeled the proper aesthetic. As in, modern with a hint of groovy. I found a navy-blue shawl with chocolate-brown fringe on the end and draped it over one shoulder, and then tied the two ends together by my opposite hip. I stepped into brown heels, gave my Logan a fresh bowl of cat food and a kiss on the head, and was out front by the time my carpool arrived. And by carpool, I mean Eddie.

Eddie Adams was the visual director for Tradava, the local department store in Ribbon, Pennsylvania. He was also one of the few people in Ribbon who knew me in high school when I'd lived here the first time. I like to think he's my voice of reason, but he's been known go to a little crazy himself. Mostly, he keeps me in check and accepts my unique wardrobe choices.

On any given day, Eddie was dressed in a version of 80s skateboard dude meets sign painter. Today he had on a Blondie T-shirt and a pair of black Dickies with colorful painted handprints down the front of the legs. I often wondered if he spent his free nights coming up with new and interesting ways to customize the workpants he bought at Sherwin Williams.

"Dude. You're up? And dressed?" He looked behind me. "Is there something going on that I don't know about?"

I looked behind me, too. Logan had jumped onto the windowsill in the living room and watched us. The window was framed with long blue tweed curtains, and Logan's shiny black fur made a stark contrast against it. Perhaps he, too, was curious about my early-morning rise.

"New project at *Retrofit*."

Eddie had not put his VW Bug into reverse. We sat in the driveway, the engine idling. "It's seven o'clock. You're never ready by seven. I figured I'd come in and make coffee."

"Nancie sprung the project on me last night. And there's a new guy, too. I can already tell he's the competitive type. I want to get a jump start and make sure he doesn't try to railroad me into taking the crap jobs."

"How long were you at the office? Your car was still in the lot when I left Tradava."

"I left a little after eleven." I yawned. "I got about five and a half hours of sleep. Drop me off and then go to the coffee drive-thru in the parking lot behind Bowl-O-Rama." I yawned again.

He put the car into gear and backed up, sighing heavily. Eddie, like the rest of the world, relied heavily on Starbucks and Keurig to provide him with caffeine on demand. Somewhere along the line he'd become enamored of my Mr. Coffee, left behind by my parents when I bought the house from them. He swore it made the best coffee in Ribbon. Under normal circumstances when I took an extra ten minutes deciding on my accessories, it worked out well, as I came downstairs to a freshly brewed pot.

Eddie drove the less-than-a-mile distance to the strip mall. I'd often considered walking to work (not in these shoes) but the distance between thought and action seemed particularly far when it came to anything resembling exercise. While Eddie drove, I filled him in on the assignment.

"I get it now," he said.

"What?"

"The velvet suit. You don't wear anything without the proper motivation."

"I'll have you know this amber velvet suit is brand-new, and it's fabulous."

"Brand-new to you, but more like three years old from a designer discount store," he said. "You know as well as I do how long it takes designer merchandise to go from the runway to off-price, and I saw that very same suit hanging in Cat's store last week."

"I cut the tags off this morning, and that should count for something."

He laughed. "Seventies, huh? Dude, if you don't watch it you're going to be knee-deep in Evel Knievel jumpsuits and Indian princess headdresses."

"Not that we're going that direction, but I believe every look from the Seventies had its place. You can make fun of feathers if you want, but you can't deny Cher rocked them during the Half Breed years."

"You don't get to use Cher to defend every trend of the Seventies. She's rocked everything she's ever worn. She's Cher." He tore open the plastic package of a cheese Danish with his teeth and made a *puh* sound with his mouth to blow away the piece of plastic wrapper that stuck to his lip. With the hand not driving, he squeezed the bottom of the package to make the Danish pop out the top. "Find me a modern-day interpretation of an Evel Knievel studded jumpsuit and I'll give up coffee for a week."

I love a challenge as much as the next girl, but nobody wanted to see that.

Eddie pulled up to the curb in front of *Retrofit* and bit into his pastry. At the rate he was going, his cargo pants were going to be tight by the end of the week.

"I'm working on a major installation in the denim department. Probably going to take all night. Do you want to call me when you're done?"

"Sure. Later." I hopped out of the Bug and strode inside, ready to start my plan of acing Pritchard Smith.

To the rest of the world, *Retrofit* was like any other storefront in the Ribbon East Shopping Center. We were sandwiched between a vitamin supply store and a Hallmark. The office was narrow and deep. Individual offices had been formed using ten-foot-tall wooden walls on castors. The results were glorified cubicles, glorified because the ten-foot-tall height made it impossible to spy on anybody who occupied the space next to yours. For the past four months, it had been Nancie, me, and a rotating stable of interns from the local college. Any curiosity about what someone else was doing was satisfied by a holler into the hallway.

The lobby of *Retrofit* was a makeshift desk where our intern-of-the-month sat across from a low sofa and coffee table where visitors waited. I passed through the doors, down the hall to my desk, mentally prepared to start my new challenge of showing my coworker the meaning of dedication and commitment.

But even at 7:15 in the morning, Pritchard had beaten me to the punch.

SK: I'm in the field. See what you can dig up on the internet and we'll compare notes. —PS

He was "in the field" at seven fifteen in the morning? Doing what? Fashion doesn't wake up at seven fifteen. Fashion barely rolls out of bed by ten.

"Sam!" Nancie said behind me. "Wow. You and Pritchard must be as excited about this project as I am. Both of you up and at 'em before eight o'clock. Perfection."

"Where *is* Pritchard?" I asked. "We were supposed to meet this morning, but he's not here."

"He didn't say anything about waiting for you." She shrugged. "He's at a private residence in Amity. About a half a mile past the old doll museum. He said something about a rare chance to talk to the owner of a massive vintage wardrobe. I don't think he mentioned her name. Did he tell you more than that?"

"No, that's just about all he told me too," I lied. "I must have misunderstood him when he said where to meet. I better not waste any more time. Don't want to be the slacker on your Dream Team!" I said and raced out the front door.

My heels slowed me down, but I caught up with Eddie at the coffee drive-thru. I yanked the passenger-side door open, shifted the massive pile of mini donuts and individually packaged cheese Danishes to my lap, and got in.

"I need a ride to a house in Amity," I said. "Like, immediately."

"Dude, I think you sat on my Pop Tarts."

I felt around under my bottom and pulled out a squashed package. He snatched it from my hand and tossed it onto the back seat. "That was blueberry. My favorite."

"I'll buy you a whole box if you step on it."

He collected his change and his large coffee from the attendant and peeled out of the lot onto Perkiomen Avenue heading east. We'd gone two miles before he asked the obvious question.

"Do I want to know what happened in the past five minutes?"

"This Pritchard Smith guy is trying to make me look bad. We just got the assignment last night—last night! I walked into the office at seven fifteen and he was already gone. And there was a note on my desk. 'SK—'"

"He addressed the note to 'SK'?"

"Yes. It's bad enough that Nancie calls me 'Sam,' but SK is worse. I met this guy yesterday. How do you go from, 'Hi, I'm Samantha Kidd, nice to meet you, happy that we'll be working together,' to 'SK—stay here and work while I visit rich people and peruse their closets'?"

"That's what the note said?"

"Close enough."

He laughed. "So, you're hopped up on the Seventies. What does that have to do with your new best friend?"

"Nancie revealed this big project last night right before we left. We're going to put out a semi-annual print magazine to accompany the content we feature on the website. The first issue is dedicated to the Seventies."

"That's a huge undertaking. Does Nancie know what she's in for? Once she goes from internet content to print, her expenses are going to go through the roof. Our print catalog at Tradava is about a hundred pages long and it costs us about a thousand dollars a page to produce."

"That's how Bentley's was too." Bentley's New York was the luxury department store where I'd built my career until I'd decided that my life, while glamorous on the surface, wasn't what I wanted. I didn't miss the long hours or the life-in-a-carry-on during fashion week, but I'd learned to appreciate the industry education I'd received over the nine years I worked there. "We co-opted the page expenses with the designers."

"If your magalog is dedicated to the Seventies, most of your designers are dead."

He had a point. "I figured Pritchard, Nancie, and I would brainstorm today and come up with a plan of attack. But noooo.

He's already at some private collector's house looking at clothes. And he expects me to sit around the office pulling background info. Pull over."

"What?"

I grabbed the steering wheel and yanked it toward the side of the road. Eddie slammed on the brakes. The air filled with the scent of burnt rubber from his skid marks on the road. "*Never* grab the driver," he said.

"Yes, dad." I pointed to the driveway entrance on the opposite side of the street. "That's the address."

Eddie waited until there was a break in traffic and he pulled onto the road, did a U-turn, and turned into the driveway. The house was about a football-field-distance from the driveway turn-in and still looked massive.

"Do me a favor?" I said. "Stick around for a couple of minutes. I'm not sure how well my showing up is going to go over, and truthfully, I don't even know the person who lives here. There's a very good chance I'm not going to be as welcome as I should be."

Eddie shook his head. "I was going to have a solid hour of alone time in the office before my staff came to work," he said to himself. "I was going to have a chance to figure out exactly how to design a wall of denim before the phone started ringing. I was going to—"

"Gorge yourself on Danishes and Pop Tarts and donuts without anybody knowing." I picked up a package of chocolate-covered mini donuts and shook it at him. "There's something up with you because you don't eat like this. I do. Don't think we aren't going to talk about that when we have more time." I tossed the donuts onto the back seat next to the flattened blueberry Pop-Tarts.

"You make a compelling argument for me wanting to stick around and wait for you."

"Please?"

"I'll give you fifteen minutes."

I blew him a kiss and got out.

The private residence in question was a three-story colonial, red brick. I rang the bell twice to no answer. I knocked, and the door eased open without the help of someone on the other side.

Curious.

"Pritchard?" I called inside. "Pritchard, it's Samantha Kidd. Nancie told me where to find you. Are you here?"

I bent forward and peeked in. Two cats, a white Persian and a gray-and-white Scottish fold, sat on the otherwise empty divan in front of me. The Persian jumped down and headed toward me. I blocked the door with my foot. "Hello?" I called again.

No answer.

I turned around and held up a *just a minute* finger to Eddie, and then stepped inside and shut the front door behind me. The fluffy white cat buzzed against my velvet pant leg, leaving behind a coating of cat hair.

The layout was remarkably similar to my house, although the decorating style was big budget/discerning eye vs. my visual sale/whimsical-yet-frugal-fashionista aesthetic. I followed the scent of cigarettes and coffee through the living room, turned to my right, and climbed the first two steps of the staircase.

"Pritchard?" I called up. A calico cat poked her head around the corner and then scampered across the landing above me. Slowly, I scaled the stairs and looked side to side at the various doors that opened onto the landing. No one appeared to be here. I opened the door to my immediate left and climbed a second flight of stairs. In my house, those stairs led to the third-floor attic that my parents had converted into my childhood bedroom. Aside from the creepy factor that came after I'd read *Flowers in the Attic*, I loved it.

But not as much as I loved this room.

The room was about twenty feet square but felt much smaller because it was filled with chrome racks like the kind department stores use to deliver new merchandise to the selling floor every morning. Each rack was packed full of clothing, some partially removed from plastic garment bags. On the floor between the racks were large black trunks with brass hinges and corners. Two trunks were closed but one lay open, exposing a fluffy interior of ecru lace scarves, paisley shawls, and at least four satin dusters trimmed with long piano fringe not unlike the trim on my shawl. Two maple dressers were propped along the wall on either side of a four-foot-tall window that opened out onto what appeared to be a balcony.

What the heck was this place?

I crept closer. Feathers, velvet, beads. Shades of amber like my suit. Mustard yellow, avocado green, chocolate, and teal side by side with paisley prints and batik prints. I recognized a few pieces that I'd seen in the old fashion magazines Nancie kept in the offices for our reference, and a quick peek at the labels confirmed that these weren't knockoffs. They weren't a few years old. This was the real deal—flared, fringed, and funky. Judging from the condition of the garments and the photos hanging around the top of each hanger, these were samples from fashion shows that had taken place decades earlier. *This* was what Pritchard Smith had come to see without me.

I fingered the silk of a yellow-and-blue paisley caftan then ran my open palm over a suede blazer and matching tiered skirt. I'd never gone in much for western, but this was exquisite. I slipped off my shawl and velvet blazer, dropped them on top of the open trunk of scarves, and had my right arm halfway into the sleeve of a turquoise silk peasant blouse with hand-painted feathers and Indian beadwork at the neckline and hem when I heard a voice.

"I'm telling you, I heard her call my name." The voice was unmistakably Pritchard Smith. I froze in place. The turquoise silk peasant blouse slipped from my fingers and landed on the floor. My brain scrambled to find a cover story for why I was there but came up empty. There was a stretch of silence, and then Pritchard spoke again. "I don't know. But she can't find out what we know. I risked enough to get here. If she ruins this, I'll take her out of the equation."

Suddenly, I was a whole lot less concerned with finding Prichard Smith. But I was trapped in a room filled with clothes. A fashion time capsule. Hiding in the closet wasn't an option because the whole room was a closet.

Pritchard's voice grew nearer. "I'll know in a minute. Hold on." The one-sided conversation indicated that he was on the phone, but his choice of words didn't inspire me to stick around.

In the past two years, I have hidden behind a scrim, behind library shelves, and even—once—in a tree outside of a fashion industry event. But never have I gone out a window, three floors up from the ground.

"All I can tell you is that if she finds out, it's over." The hinges on the door below creaked, and I sprang into action.

There's a first time for everything.

3

MAD SPIDERMAN SKILLS

I SCOOPED MY CLOTHES AND SHOVED THEM INTO MY OVERSIZED HOBO bag, threw the strap over my shoulder, and ran for the window. Truth be told, I'd hoped for a balcony. What I got was barely a ledge. I went through the open window. By the time Pritchard had reached the room, I was dangling by a shutter. Which brings us to reason #1 why spying on my coworker was a bad idea: Spying leads to impulsive exit strategies, and impulsive exit strategies rarely work out well.

My fingers curled through the bottom slats of the shutter, and I strained to hear the voices in the room. "She's not here." Pause. "No, I'm not going to calm down. Do you not realize what's at stake?" Pritchard cursed. From my spot outside of the window, I heard what sounded like hangers moving along a rack and trunks being slammed shut. Whatever Pritchard didn't want me to find was in that room, and I must have practically stumbled onto it. First chance I got—

The screws that attached the upper hinge of the shutter to the brick exterior broke.

As if in slow motion, the rectangular panel of slatted wood slowly pulled away from the building. The shutter moved diagonally, my weight pulling it off-center. Which would have been fine if the particular screech that comes from a metal hinge scraping a brick building hadn't coincided with the movement.

"Who's there?" Pritchard asked. I pictured him charging to the window and looking down at me, dangling from a shutter in my amber velvet suit. I didn't want to get caught, but I couldn't jump. The ground was three stories down and the fear of broken bones was high, as was acute humiliation. My heart raced, and adrenaline coursed through my arms and legs. This can't be it, I thought. I hadn't been particularly eager to turn another year older, but the reality of *not* turning another year older seemed a trifle worse.

I braced myself and looked up, hoping a plausible story would spring to mind. Instead of the angry face of Pritchard, the window casing slammed shut and the latch clicked into the locked position.

His voice became muffled and barely understandable. Even if I could climb my way back to the frame, there would be no way in without breaking the glass.

I positioned the toe of my chocolate-brown shoe into the mortar joint of the exterior brick and pressed ever so slightly, seeking leverage. I barely succeeded, but barely was good enough. I grabbed the ledge under the window, shifted my weight, and inched my feet along the brick. Underneath me, a car horn beeped. I turned my head and saw Eddie's VW Bug idling next to the house.

Reason #2 spying on my coworker was a bad idea: The need to develop a cover story.

"You can't tell Nick," I said to Eddie.

"Tell him what? That you told me to give you fifteen minutes, and right before I drove away you popped out the third-floor window and scaled the side of a building? Not that I'm not impressed by your mad Spiderman skills, but I'm not sure that story could work in Hollywood, let alone Ribbon, Pennsylvania. Do you want to tell me again what happened?"

"The front door was open. I went through the house looking for Pritchard. I ended up in the attic. I heard him tell someone he thought I was there, and I got the feeling it would be a very bad idea for me to be in the room when he entered. I went out the window because I thought I could get your attention from the balcony. There wasn't a balcony. End of story."

Eddie shook his head. "There are so many things wrong with that scenario that I don't know where to start."

"Well I do. Promise me you won't tell Nick. He's been worried about his dad since he broke his hip, and I don't need to be another thing for him to worry about. My role as his potential girlfriend is to be a calming presence in his life."

"Did you get that from the 'how to be a potential girlfriend' guidebook?"

"I've been reading a lot of romantic comedies, and I've noticed a trend. Do we have a deal?"

"Deal."

I sat back and rubbed my palms against each other. Somewhere after the window slamming, I'd discovered the gutter that ran alongside of the house. Nothing like a little shinny down the drainpipe to make a girl feel spry. Once I was back on the ground, I pulled my blazer out of the handbag and put it on, hiding the scratches I'd incurred along the way. Unfortunately, my velvet pants were torn in three different places, one of which exposed the frilly lace trim on the side of my pink panties.

"What now?" Eddie asked.

I tucked the edges of my shawl deep into my hobo bag. "Take me back to *Retrofit*. There's something going on with Pritchard, and I'd like to see what I can find out."

"Translation: as long as he's at that house, you have a window of time to snoop around his cubicle."

Clearly, I hadn't fully embraced the reasons why snooping was a bad idea just yet because it did seem like a good idea.

Eddie's best efforts to get to work early had been dashed thanks to me and my hanging-from-a-building act, so I couldn't complain about the fact that he drove directly to his job instead of dropping me off in front of mine.

The parking lot was mostly empty, but instead of cutting across the vacant spaces, I stuck to the sidewalk. It was a Wednesday in May, and it seemed the residents of Ribbon had better things to do than go shopping. I entered *Retrofit* and went to my cubicle.

Before *Retrofit* had become *Retrofit*, the offices where we ran the magazine had been a storefront for a local bakery. I imagined the scent of various and sundry breads coming from the back of the offices where Nancie Townsend had set up the boardroom. During particularly long meetings, I would have paid good money for someone to deliver freshly baked loaves of sourdough.

Once the bakery moved out and Nancie obtained the keys, she'd taken it upon herself to convert the property to a business. The permanent walls had been painted yellow, the linoleum tiled floors had been covered in throw rugs, the counter had been taken out and replaced with moveable walls that created the perception of individual offices. The intern who worked as our receptionist and general Johnny-on-the-spot sat at a small desk out front. There weren't a lot of jobs that included shopping on eBay for old copies of *Vogue* in mint condition, and while I knew our rotating door of interns were unpaid, the sheer novelty of the job kept local fashion students in line for the next vacant position.

Keys jangled outside of the offices. Moments later, Nancie stood in my doorway.

"Sam, great, you're here." She pushed the sleeves of her black-

and-white blazer up over her forearms. "I got a concerned message from Pritchard. I was worried that you might have tried to go with him today."

"I haven't seen Pritchard all morning," I said truthfully. "Didn't you say he had an appointment with a collector?"

"Yes. Local clotheshorse. Pritchard wanted to see what she had before acting on behalf of *Retrofit*, but he heard rumors that her collection was worth a look. He might persuade her to loan it to us for a special feature."

The garments that I'd seen were in pristine condition. The vibe was exactly what we needed. With the correct accessories, we could style the outfits two ways: as they were shown forty years ago, and how to wear them today. It would be unlike anything the fashion magazines did, because they focused exclusively on new collections. And I was capable of styling it myself.

"I have an idea." Forgetting about Prichard for the moment, I outlined the concept to Nancie. "What if we had a feature that broke down exact items from the Seventies—maybe even the complete head-to-toe look that a designer showed on the runway or how it was featured in *Vogue*—as close as we can get it." I made a quick sketch of a female figure on the left half of a piece of paper and wrote "Literal Translation" under it. "On the right, we take one key item from the look and style it for now. Pair it with jeans, or leggings, or all white. Modernize the jewelry, hair, makeup. Make it today." Under the right sketch, I wrote "Modern Translation." I pushed the paper toward Nancie.

She picked it up and looked back and forth between the two sketches. With the hand not holding the paper, she flicked the page, leaving a dent in the middle. "Perfection!" she said. "This is exactly what we need to give our magazine its identity. I'm going to call Pritchard and tell him. Depending on what this collector has, he can pull looks and shoot them so we can at least have placeholders before we put them on a figure."

"But don't you think that's a two-person job? To help identify what we should and shouldn't use?"

"Sam, Pritchard is a Godsend. I can't expect you to run all over town on a project of this magnitude. Let him do the legwork while you get started on editorial." She left my cubicle muttering, "dream team."

I bit back my response. I knew my idea was good. I knew it would possibly be what made our first issue a collector's item. But the person who put the outfits together would get stylist credit on the pages of the magazine. The person who wrote the editorial would have one listing in the front on a page nobody looks at because the font is painfully small.

The four months I'd been working with Nancie had been enough to show her what I brought to the table. I didn't know what Pritchard was up to, but I wasn't going to let him take sole credit for finding our source and styling the clothes. That would turn my dream job into a nightmare. No way was I going to play second fiddle to a middle-aged guy with a comb-over.

But I couldn't help wondering who he'd been talking to. What was he hoping to find in the attic, and what would he have done if he'd found me there? His words had sounded threatening but could have been just a figure of speech. I'd worked with competitive colleagues before, and I could do it again. If Pritchard was going to throw down the gauntlet of who-is-a-better-employee, I would accept the challenge.

I spent the next few hours making a list of major trends of the Seventies so we'd know what to find for our literal translation. Caftan, bohemian, patchwork, beading, long vests, prairie skirt. It was a start. I was eager to get going on the idea-to-execution stage. I was anxious, too. The longer Pritchard spent away from the office, the more I wondered how well he'd take to running with my idea. *If she ruins this, I'll take her out of the equation.* I still wasn't sure what he'd meant, but I couldn't afford to lose this job.

Nancie returned to my cubicle in the late afternoon. "Pritchard called. He's been looking at that collection all day." She pulled a pair of square black sunglasses out of her handbag and perched them on top of her head. "Make sure he knows he can rely on you. I don't want him to feel like he has to do everything."

I felt the heat climb my neck. "I'll make sure it's a fifty-fifty partnership," I said.

"Perfection." She hiked her quilted Chanel 2.55 handbag onto her shoulder. "I'm heading out for a teeth cleaning. Don't work too hard. Wait—you're working for me. Work as hard as you want!" She laughed at her passive management style and left.

I sorted unwanted emails into the trash folder and listened for Nancie's keys in the lock. When I was sure she was gone, I grabbed a notepad and went to Pritchard's cubicle. I didn't know how much time I had, so if I was going to snoop, I had to be quick.

Long ago I'd heard that a messy desk was the sign of an organized mind, and seeing how I was probably the only person who could follow my logic of notebooks and paper stacks, I liked to think it was true. But if my desk indicated that I had an organized mind, Pritchard's indicated the opposite. His desk was neat. Clean. Empty. It was as if he'd spent the last hour of last night removing all signs that he worked there.

Weird.

His desk, like mine, was a white laminated table. A black metal inbox tray sat on the corner. A matching pencil holder sat next to it. It was filled with several dozen retractable black ballpoint gel pens. I pulled one out of his cup holder, clicked to reveal the point, and clicked it to retract.

A row of small, white, build-them-yourself bookcases ran along the far wall. They were mostly empty. Pritchard was new to the team, and he hadn't brought much in the way of decoration, personal effects, or distractions. Which was good, because as far as snooping around his office went, there wasn't a lot of time.

I opened the file manager on his computer and scanned his files. They were as clean as his desk. Each was neatly labeled in all caps. Subfolders were capitalized, and sub-sub folders were in lowercase. His master folders were labeled by decade. I clicked on the Seventies. Inside were two nestled folders: designers and private collections. I clicked on "designer" and found a subdirectory of every major fashion player who'd contributed to the look of the decade. Halston, Biba, Bonnie Cashin, and more.

I closed out of his computer and stood, ready to leave. I was halfway out the door when I stopped and turned around again, this time spotting a briefcase hidden on the bottom shelf of his bookcase.

Searching Pritchard's company-owned computer was one thing. But his briefcase? That was a violation of personal property. How would I feel if he broke into my office and went through my things?

You're above this, I told myself. Go back to your office and do your job. It's natural to feel threatened by the new guy. Nancie will recognize your dedication and hard work.

There was an email from Nancie on my computer when I sat back at my desk. *Sam—I talked to Pritchard. He loves your idea and said he'll run with it. What else ya got?*

The jerk was going to take credit for my idea. Not. Fair. I leaned back and felt the tear in my pants widen. The tear in my pants caused from dangling from a shutter while Pritchard made more than one statement that some might call threatening. This wasn't about workplace politics. It was about self-preservation.

I returned to Pritchard's office, took the briefcase off the shelf, and set it on the desk. Once I had it open, it took another couple of seconds to realize that Pritchard Smith was not who he seemed.

4

BOYISH CHARM

You would have thought someone who traveled with an assortment of fake identification would make more of an effort to hide it. But the briefcase opened easily, and right on the top of a stack of files and envelopes were four ID cards with Pritchard's photo. The names on the cards varied: Pritchard Smith, Smith Pritchard, Pritchard Whitbee, and Gene Smith. Each card was from a different state. There was one from New York, one from Delaware, one from Florida, and one from Utah.

The birth year fit Pritchard's appearance. The cities and states told me nothing. You could apply for identification anywhere with proof of residence. All that would take was a credit check and an approved rental application, and in some cities a hundred-dollar bill passed under the table might stand in for both.

The phone rang. We used a universal number in the *Retrofit* offices, so the only way to know who the call was for was to answer and ask. I picked up Pritchard's phone. "*Retrofit* Magazine," I said.

"Hey, Kidd."

It didn't take more than two words for me to identify the speaker: Nick Taylor. Shoe designer, former business affiliate, on again/off again relationship with my finger poised on the switch, ready to flip it on.

Nick's voice was low and rich and deep, and when he wanted to, he could infuse those two words—"Hey, Kidd"—with a variety of emotions. Tonight, he'd selected sexy and casual from his arsenal. My knees grew weak, and my heart rate picked up.

"Hey, Nick," I said.

"Working late?"

"I hadn't planned to, but something came up. Why?"

"I know this is last minute, but I thought maybe you'd like to come over."

Over the course of the nine years that I was a buyer for Bentley's, Nick and I had maintained a business relationship that approached but never quite crossed the line of flirtation. I assumed he had his share of attention from the other female buyers in the market. There aren't many straight men in fashion, and even if there were, Nick would have been ahead of the curve. Curly brown hair and root-beer-barrel colored eyes that crinkled in the corners when he smiled. He even had dimples. He was a grown-up man with boyish charm, stylish in a metrosexual way that was on the right side of masculine. If Duran Duran ever needed an American stand-in, he'd be perfect.

After I left Bentley's, we ran into each other again. With no workplace politics in our way, we'd even started to date. But the usual relationship challenges cropped up: ex-girlfriends, hot bikers, and life-threatening murder investigations, and we never quite got the car into drive. During the six months when we'd acknowledged that we were in a relationship, there'd been an almost feverish need to establish a physical connection, but something had kept us from advancing past Go and collecting two hundred dollars.

Recently life came at both of us with an agenda. We stepped back, recalibrated, and started over. Nick's dad had broken his hip. I'd been hospitalized after a psycho attacked me in a parking lot. Living on the edge lost some of its luster.

Neither one of us voiced a conscious decision to back up, slow down, and start over, but that's pretty much what we did. Nick oversaw his dad's recovery, temporarily living in New York. I put my energy into proving myself at *Retrofit*. In our spare time, we spent hours on the phone, talking about everything from past fashions to current events. We even managed a few long-distance dinner dates, preparing the same meal and watching the same movie, connected by our cell phones. I hadn't been alone with Nick in four months. And here he was, inviting me over.

"It's a little late for me to drive to New York," I said.

"I'm not in New York. I'm in Ribbon."

"You're here?" A zing of adrenaline coursed through me while I tried to remember if I'd shaved my legs that morning. The long distance had lulled me into a safe zone, and I wasn't sure if I was ready.

I stared at the various ID cards in front of me while my head and heart (and a spot a little lower) waged a debate over what I should do. My head won control of my voice, though my heart might have tried harder if not for the torn pants. "I'm sort of busy. Nancie has me on a new project and I just discovered some interesting information." My heart wasn't happy and pounded more aggressively in my chest.

"Breaking news in the world of retro fashion? Let me guess: Diane von Furstenberg copied the idea for the wrap dress from her next-door neighbor."

"Nothing that shocking." I chuckled. "There's this new guy working here, Pritchard Smith."

"That's good, isn't it? *Retrofit* must be successful if your boss is expanding the team."

"I guess so. Nancie loves him, says he has all kinds of contacts to help us, but there's something off about him."

"Kidd, you're not going to turn this into—you're not going to—hold on." There was a muffled sound, as if Nick had put his hand over the receiver for a moment. He came back moments later. "This project that Nancie has you working on—is it urgent? Because there's something I'd like to talk to you about."

First an invitation to go to his place. Now a pending conversation. Two curious things. If I were a cat, it would have only taken one.

My heart sucker punched my head and spoke up. "I'd love to," I said. "But I'm stranded at *Retrofit*. Eddie gave me a ride."

"I can pick you up."

"I can be done here in about five minutes," I said.

"I'll meet you by the curb."

I hung up the phone and glanced back down at the ID cards. Maybe this was a sign. Maybe I should talk it over with Nick. It might distract him from the fact that my velvet pants were torn in three places.

Thoughts of the torn pants led me back to the memory of hanging off the side of the building earlier, which led me to Pritchard's threats and the discovery of his secret identity which led me to:

Reason #3 why spying on your coworker was a bad idea: When you stick your nose into other people's business, you sometimes discover things you'd rather not know.

I took the ID cards to the scanner and made a copy for myself. I returned the cards to the briefcase and returned the briefcase to the corner of the bookshelf where I'd found it. I lowered myself into a squat behind Pritchard's computer and jiggled the mouse to wake the monitor. It was logged into his *Retrofit* email. *Retrofit* had been my employer long before it had been Pritchard's, and darned if I was going to let him get important information before I did. It took a few clicks to forward his email to mine. I wasn't going to let him undermine my four months of tenure.

I didn't know who Pritchard Smith was, but I intended to find out. Assuming I survived an evening with Nick.

Nick's white pickup truck idled next to the curb by the time I left the office. It had been months since I'd seen him in person. Even through the tinted glass of his windows, I could make out his gleaming white smile. I locked the doors to the office, tucked the key into my handbag, and double-checked that my copies of Pritchard's fake IDs weren't sticking out the top. I wasn't taking any chances by leaving evidence of my snooping behind.

I climbed into the cab of Nick's truck. Set my handbag on the floor by my feet. Pulled the car door shut. Buckled the seat belt. All because I was nervous. Like I was fifteen and going on my first date.

"Kidd," Nick said in a low, husky voice.

I turned and looked at him. "Taylor," I said back, though mine sorta squeaked. The streetlights cast a glow that illuminated the amber in his eyes into the cab of the truck. His curly brown hair moved with a breeze that wafted through the window. He put his hand on my hand and curled his fingers over mine. I flipped my hand upside down so our palms were against each other. A flush of warmth courtesy of the body parts below my heart coursed through me, and I pulled my hand away in embarrassment.

He smiled. "Long time no see."

"I was just thinking about that."

He put the truck into gear and drove through the mostly empty lot until he reached the exit. His showroom wasn't far from *Retrofit*, but instead of slowing down and turning right at the light by the Dairy Queen, he breezed through the intersection.

"You just passed your store," I said.

"We're not going to my store." He reached over and threaded his fingers through mine again. Two blocks later, he picked my hand up and pressed it to his lips in a gentle kiss. I might not have known what to expect from him, but the subtle signals conveyed a shift between us. My decision to say yes to his invitation had been partially predicated on the fact that maybe we were just going to talk like we had been doing long distance. But the kiss indicated otherwise. My heartbeat picked up, and I squirmed in the seat. Nick hadn't mentioned my torn pants. He hadn't cursed when we hit four consecutive yellow lights. He kept his eyes on the road, but for the rest of the drive he didn't let go.

"Do I want to know where we're going?"

"I don't know," he said. "Do I want to know why your pants are torn? Not that I mind the view of your panties."

I pulled my hand away and tugged on the bottom of my blazer. "Surprise me."

Nick kept an apartment in Italy, where he lived six months out of the year. After moving his base of operations from New York to Ribbon a few years ago, he'd rented a furnished apartment in Ribbon where I'd heard he sometimes stayed. When his father broke his hip, Nick had put his business on hold, sublet the apartment, and moved back to New York to help care for his dad. None of which helped me figure out where he was taking me, but running through the possibilities did serve the side benefit of distracting me before we arrived.

We drove through downtown Ribbon, past streets of run-down Victorian row homes. He turned left at a church and after a few blocks turned right and right again. He eased his truck up to a private garage, fed a plastic card into an automated parking teller, and when the garage gate opened, pulled forward into a space by the elevator marked "Reserved."

"Surprise," he said. We got out, and I followed him to the elevator wells.

"You live here?"

"Yes."

"How long have you known you were moving to Ribbon?"

"A couple of months."

"Why'd you keep it a secret?"

"I had plans to throw you a surprise party."

"Nice try. Why would I get a surprise party when you were the one who moved?"

"New York was inconvenient. There are lots of reasons why I wanted to find something bigger. Truth is, it took some time to find an apartment I liked, and when I found this one, I didn't want to jinx it."

We got onto the elevator. "Am I one of the reasons?" I asked.

He reached for my hand and ran his fingertips over mine. "You're the main reason," he said softly. He tipped his head down and kissed me.

Whether it was instinct or memory of kissing Nick in our on-again times, I didn't know, but I grabbed the lapels of his jacket and pulled him close. This time when our lips met, there was no mistaking my intention or his response.

"I want more, Kidd," he said after the kiss. "My dad's accident made me realize what's important in life. I hope—I think—it just feels right." His brown eyes intensified.

The elevator stopped, and we got out. I ran my finger around my lips to fix any smudged lipstick. Nick walked to apartment 2001, but before he could insert his keys into the lock, the door opened.

An older man who bore more than a passing resemblance to

Nick leaned on a cane in the hall in front of us. He looked at me, then at Nick, then back at me.

"Is this her?" the man asked.

Nick rested his hand on the small of my back. "Samantha Kidd, I'd like you to meet my new roommate. Nick Taylor, Senior."

Nick hadn't invited me over for hanky-panky. He'd invited me over to formally meet his dad.

5

LIFE'S LITTLE CURVEBALLS

I'D FIRST SEEN NICK'S DAD A LITTLE OVER A DECADE AGO. I DIDN'T know if Nick Senior knew I was the same girl who had walked into Nick's showroom and slipped my sample-sized foot into one of the shoes on display. Truthfully? It didn't matter. You gotta love the universe. Just when you think you know where your life is headed, you learn that your coworker has an alias and your possible love interest has moved in with his dad.

Life's little curveballs.

"Mr. Taylor, nice to meet you," I said.

"I know you," he said. "When was it—ten years ago? You were a buyer from Bentley's. Didn't want me to see you trying on the samples in Junior's showroom. I always wondered what happened to you. Did you know your pants are torn?"

"I—um—"

He looked at Nick. "Real conversationalist, this one." He turned back to me. "Call me Nick." He held out his hand.

I shook his hand. "I can't call you Nick. I call him Nick."

"You can call him Junior like I do."

Nick's eyebrows went up. "She's not going to call me Junior."

"Suit yourself. Anybody want a beer?" Nick Senior turned around and went to the kitchen.

I started to follow him, but Nick put his hands on my waist and pulled me backward. "From that kiss in the elevator, I don't think hanging out with my dad is what you had in mind." Now that was an understatement. "And it's not exactly what I have in mind either." He turned me around and stared directly into my eyes. "This is my life now, Kidd, and I want you to be a part of it. Is that okay?"

"Sure," I said. Nick put his hands on my upper arms and studied my face. I hoped for another whammy of a kiss before his dad returned. Instead, he pulled me in for a hug.

More than anybody else, I knew that it's better to be involved in life than to sit on the sidelines. Nick's invitation to his new residence spoke volumes about how he felt. While I was unsure of a lot of things, I knew he wouldn't have brought me here if he didn't want me to be here. I was an adult. I could learn to act like one. Plus, I was curiously optimistic that Nick's dad would retire to his bedroom for an early night and we'd have a chance to spend some time alone together.

Behind me I heard a beer can open. I pulled away from Nick and turned around again. "There's a documentary on about the Son of Sam. You two want to watch?" Nick Senior asked.

"Sure," I said again, feeling the optimism slide away.

The documentary outlasted Nick Senior. Nick and I maintained our first-date-with-the-parents position, side by side, holding hands. When the credits rolled, he turned to me. "You probably have a full day tomorrow. How about I take you home?"

"Sure."

We covered the four miles in a matter of minutes. Nick pulled into my driveway and threw the car into park. "Thanks for being a good sport, Kidd," Nick said. "Sorry the Son of Sam monopolized our evening. You never got to tell me about this work project."

I had hit overload on the amount of information I was capable of processing in one night. "It can wait."

We sat like that for a few moments, just watching each other, saying nothing. I wondered what he was thinking. If he'd asked me about my thoughts, I don't think I could have articulated them. Finally, I reached over and put my hand on his. "Good night, Junior," I said. I got out of the car and went inside. He didn't drive away until the door was locked behind me.

I woke the next morning with Logan chewing on my hair. Two swats and one attempt to bury my head under the pillowcase proved ineffective against his feline determination. I pushed back the covers and went downstairs to feed him. I found my hobo bag on the floor, half of the contents spilled across the blue-and-white linoleum tile. Both my hobo bag and the folded copies of Pritchard's many ID cards had a regurgitated blob on top of them.

"What is this?" I asked Logan. He looked up at me and meowed, as if asking me why I'd made photocopies of my coworker's questionable ID cards in the first place. "Oh, come on. The man is hiding something. Who fakes an ID from Utah?" I pulled several paper towels from the roll and wiped the gunk from them and from the handbag. Both now had wet spots that didn't smell particularly fresh.

Recently I'd noticed that Logan had put on a little bit of weight. The vet suggested I switch him to diet cat food, which had not proven to be a popular lifestyle change. My diet was far from an infomercial for weight loss, and it never seemed fair to enjoy the savory delight of meatball sandwiches and cheesesteaks alone, so while Logan now dined on reduced-calorie kitty vittles, he also enjoyed the occasional meatball or chicken finger. I suspected the hairball was a message.

I went back upstairs, showered, brushed my teeth, and dressed in a black turtleneck, black flared pants, and a paisley caftan. I blow dried my hair upside down and tied a paisley scarf around my head Rhoda-style. Chunky heeled boots gave me a couple of additional inches of height. I dug a black fringed handbag out of the closet and carried it downstairs.

When I got back to the kitchen, I put my wallet, lip glosses, and phone into the fringed handbag and opened a can of diet cat food for Logan. He looked at the bowl and then at me and meowed. "It's diet cat food or nothing." I opened the freezer and pulled out a box of frozen waffles. He meowed again. I looked back and forth between the waffles and his bowl. "Fine," I said. "I'll eat Bran Flakes. Are you happy?"

Logan sniffed the bowl of food, gave me the saddest (most manipulative) look, and gagged a few times until another mess came up. After cleaning it, I left a message for Nancie that I'd be late getting to the office and took Logan directly to the vet.

"WHAT HAVE WE HERE?" Nancie asked when she entered my cubicle several hours later. Logan, doped from the vet visit, was sacked out on the carpet. He opened one eye and made a noise that sounded like sandpaper on a piece of bark, and then laid his head back on his paw and fell asleep.

"My cat is having trouble adjusting to his new diet food. The higher fiber content upsets his stomach. I took him to the vet this morning. He's drowsy because he just got a shot to relax him."

She ran her hand over his head. "Is the poor baby sick? Did the ittle bitty baby swallow something icky?"

Logan opened one eye again. Logan was neither ittle or bitty. He was a far cry from a baby too. He might have been sick, but the look he gave Nancie conveyed everything I was thinking. And then he stood up and gagged a few times, just to make sure she got the point.

She stood upright and stepped back. "New shoes. Suede. Can't take a chance." She backed away toward the opening to my cubicle but stopped before leaving. "How's the research going?"

"Research?"

"For the magazine. I heard from Pritchard this morning. He said he struck the mother lode of Seventies fashion at that private collector's house."

"What's the collector's name?"

"Jennie Mae Tome."

"How did Pritchard find her?"

"He's resourceful. And good for us! That boy is going to ensure this whole project succeeds. Make sure you carry your weight, Sam. I know you know we're a team, but there's no point in working at odds."

I wish Logan *had* thrown up on Nancie's new suede shoes. What had Pritchard done so far? Not much, as far as I'd seen. And the fact that Pritchard wasn't Pritchard didn't help matters. Whatever he was doing on the payroll at *Retrofit* was a mystery.

"Nancie, how well do you know Pritchard?"

"Trust me, he's qualified. I already told you, you two are my dynamic duo. A perfect complement to each other's skills. Don't get lost in the boys-versus-girls thing, Sam. Fashion doesn't discriminate between the sexes. It discriminates between those who have taste and those who do not. Hey, that's good. I should write that down." She laughed and then left.

I wasn't in the mood to spend my afternoon in front of my computer digging up background material on designers from the Seventies, but as long as Nancie stayed at her desk, I didn't have much of a choice. What started as a Word doc of cut-and-pasted info resulted in several hours on Wikipedia and a series of secret boards on Pinterest. I called the public library and set up an appointment to dig through their archives of vintage magazines and filled my Netflix queue with *Love Story, The Getaway, Annie Hall,* and *The Eyes of Laura Mars.* No way would I let Nancie think I was phoning it in while Pritchard was in the field. Until this project was done, I was going to live, breathe, eat, and sleep the Seventies.

It was going to be dy-no-mite.

NANCIE TOOK her customary break at quarter after twelve. She stopped by my cubicle. "How's it going?"

"I'm on a roll."

"Perfection! Pritchard emailed some info. First thing tomorrow, I want a sit-down to see where we're at."

Nancie left. I waited three whole seconds after the door shut behind her to see what Pritchard had thought important enough to send her.

You work with the skills that you have (or have learned). At any other job, the punishment for hijacking my boss's email and forwarding it into mine would be somewhere between clerical duty and termination. But Nancie had established a shared info policy. Plus, she had only three employees, and I was one of them. I could talk my way out of this if I had to. I could blame it on the tech guy who set up her office equipment.

Nancie was right; Pritchard had been busy. What he lacked in actual get-it-done work ethic, he made up for in schmoozing. His email said: *spending the afternoon with Jennie Mae Tome. She's granted me an exclusive before she finds an auction house to sell her collection. Twelve runway looks coming via email attachment. More later.*

How was I supposed to compete with that?

I scanned the other unread emails in her inbox. One popped out at me. The subject read: *Need to talk to you about Pritchard Smith.* It was from 123@fashion.net I clicked the email, but the body of it was blank.

I clicked reply and wrote: *Nancie asked me to follow up on this. When can we meet?* I added my name, email, and phone number. I waited ten minutes, but there was no reply.

Our *Retrofit* computers were on the same network so we could access each other's work without difficulty. Nancie wasn't nearly as organized as Pritchard, and it took me almost an hour to find the files related to our project. When I did find *Retrofit* Mag 70s (filed under "Projects," in a folder called "*Retrofit* Dream Projects," sandwiched between "Rags to Riches" and "Romeo Must Die") (???), I realized why Nancie had been singing Prichard's praises.

The photos he'd sent were simple but effective. Each picture contained an outfit completely accessorized. To the left of each hanging outfit was a sheet of paper with a handwritten number. All in all, there were photos of outfits 1-37.

The mother lode, indeed.

I scrolled through the pictures, recognizing items that I'd seen while doing my research. He'd labeled each photo with the number, which was perfectly fine in terms of organization, but would require a lot of extra work to backtrack and determine the designer, the season, the year. A lot of work that would have to be done on the premises.

This project was not only good for Retrofit, but it would help me reestablish my place in the fashion community. If he didn't shut me out.

Again, I thought about the phone conversation I'd overheard. Pritchard had seemed intent on finding something in the attic and not letting me know about it. Whoever had been on the other end of the phone call was in on it.

Pritchard had no intention of asking me to the field to help him with Jennie Mae Tome's sample collection. Whatever he was up to, he planned to milk his side of the project for all it was worth, spending hours upon hours with his private collector friend, emailing bits and pieces of info that would keep me buried in busy work.

Not. Gonna. Happen.

What Pritchard hadn't taken into consideration was that I wasn't the type to sit back and let someone else get all the glory. Especially since:

A) I was just as qualified as he was, and

B) this was my first steady employment in over a year, and I had every intention of ensuring that "steady" meant more than four months.

I'd had my share of distractions in the form of criminal investigations. A niggling voice in my head had started to tune into the fact that my involvement in such situations wasn't coincidental —that I sought excitement the same way I used to seek out opportunities for risk-taking in business. But pinching pennies had changed my priorities, and I vowed to focus on my job. This project was the kind I could sink my teeth into, and I intended to do just that.

I grabbed my handbag, put out fresh water and a disposable litter box for Logan, and slid a portable white baby gate into place by the open door to my cubicle. "I'll be back in two hours," I told him. I texted Nancie that I changed my mind on lunch after all and told her Logan was best left alone while he slept off the narcotics the vet had given him. I locked the office doors and left.

It didn't take me long to arrive at the house where Pritchard was working. This time I followed the long, gravel driveway to the set of spaces at the right of the building. I parked my Honda del Sol and walked to the front door. I rang the bell by the screen door, even though the interior door was open. When no one answered, I leaned forward and pressed my ear against the screen, straining to hear conversation from inside.

Maybe that's why I jumped so high when I felt a hand on my shoulder.

6

HARD TO TELL

"MAY I HELP YOU?" ASKED A MOSTLY BALD GENTLEMAN. HE WAS formally dressed in a black suit with a white shirt and a gray vest. His face was lined with wrinkles that had been etched into his skin over time, and his nose turned up ever so slightly. He easily stood four inches taller than me, and I was wearing platform shoes.

"I don't know. I work for *Retrofit* Magazine, and I'm here to look at the collection of clothes."

The man raised his thick gray eyebrows but said nothing. He reached past me and opened the door. He stepped back and gestured with his other hand for me to go first. I did.

The room hadn't changed much since I'd been there yesterday. Heavy curtains hung by the large picture windows that faced the front, blocking the light. The man in the suit pushed the front door shut behind me, and the room went dark. It took a second for my eyes to adjust.

"Ahem."

I blinked a few times and scanned the room again. A woman

was seated on the divan. Beside her, round bolster pillows had been pushed aside, covering the tufting on the cushion. She was dressed in a loose paisley caftan, not dissimilar to mine. Both her legs and her arms were crossed, legs at the knee, arms at the wrist. She held a pair of glasses in one hand. She looked more curious than threatened by my presence in what appeared to be her house.

"I wasn't expecting any visitors," she said. Her voice held a faint accent. Russian? Slovakian? It was hard to pinpoint.

"I'm Samantha Kidd," I said. "I work at *Retrofit* Magazine. I understand you gave permission for us to view your collection—"

The elegant woman stretched out her right hand. "Hello, Samantha Kidd. I'm Jennie Mae Tome." I shook her hand. Light tinkling sounds came from a collection of gold bangle bracelets on her wrist that rushed against each other. Judging from the way the gold shone, even in the dim room, I estimated them to be at least eighteen-karat gold. At a glance, I estimated that there were fifty of them. Whoever Jennie Mae Tome was, she wasn't poor.

"Mr. Charles, why don't you bring Miss Samantha and I some tea?" she said to the man in the suit. I looked at him and found him scowling at me. His expression changed slightly, though he didn't go out of his way to hide his opinion of my unannounced visit.

"Right away." He disappeared into the next room, presumably the kitchen. Jennie Mae gestured toward a rocking chair. "Please, have a seat."

I lowered myself onto the wooden chair and felt something brush my ankles. When I looked down, I saw a black-and-white cat skulk across the room, his tail pointed straight up in the air. Another cat sat in the corner by a large canister of six-foot-tall peacock feathers. A third came out from a narrow opening that I already knew led to the stairs that led to the attic.

Jennie Mae reached down and scratched the black-and-white

cat's head. "I hope you're not allergic," she said. "I've always loved cats. They keep me company in a way people don't."

I reached out and stroked a calico that jumped onto the arm of the divan. "I understand completely. My cat knows more about me than anybody else."

"Ah, you're a cat person too. And you have style." She smiled. It felt funny sitting in the dark with her, both of us dressed in caftans with head wraps. I wondered if this was what the Seventies were like. Surely more than one person dressed like Rhoda, didn't they? Did anybody care that while they sought individuality, they often weren't the most unique person in the room? Come to think of it, it wasn't that different from today.

"Now, what brings you here?" she asked.

"Like I said, I work at *Retrofit*," I said, expecting her to put two and two together. She didn't react, so I continued. "The online magazine that focuses on looking to the history of fashion in order to predict the future?"

"You enjoy fashion, don't you?" she asked.

"I do. It's what I've wanted to do as long as I can remember."

"I must admit, I've never heard of this magazine."

"I thought—I understood that you gave permission for us to view and photograph your collection."

She leaned back against the divan and ran her hand over the head of a fluffy white Persian cat. "My friend Mr. Charles must have arranged that. I leave anything involved in running the estate to him." She looked at the cat, who settled in next to her. "Tell me about this project."

"It's to be our first print magazine. The concept behind *Retrofit* is to show people how to take items from the past and incorporate them into the present. Our premiere issue is going to be dedicated to the style of the Seventies, highlighting the top designers, showing how things were worn then and how to interpret individual items now."

"It sounds fascinating," she said.

"We're relatively new. My boss officially launched it last year. But what Nancie has been able to accomplish in that time is amazing. She's a visionary. I'm lucky to be on her team."

Mr. Charles reappeared from the swinging doors. He held a tray filled with two teacups, a ceramic pot, and a small canister for sugar cubes and for milk. A saucer of lemon wedges sat next to a plate of sliced bread. From the scent, I guessed it was banana. He set the tray down between us.

"Will that be all, Jennie?" he asked.

"For now."

He looked at the tray, and then at me. His features looked less friendly than judgmental. I felt like he was trying to send me a message. It might have been don't-overstay-your-welcome, it might have been get-out-of-here now. Hard to tell.

He left the room through the door that led to the upstairs.

"Jennie, how well do you know Mr. Charles?" I asked, wondering how I was going to go about implying that her employee was possibly involved with Pritchard.

"I know him better than I've known anybody in my whole life." She patted the afghan on her lap, and the fluffy white cat woke up. "Have you been formally introduced to my kitties? This is Navajo." She scratched the cat's ears, and the cat tipped its head back, exposing an exquisite turquoise-and-red beaded choker around its neck. "The tabby is Harvest Gold, and the calico behind the piano is Bohemian Rhapsody." She smiled at them. "You can take the girl out of the Seventies, but you can't take the Seventies out of the girl."

Jennie Mae Tome was delightfully eccentric, and I felt relaxed in her company. "Has Mr. Charles been in your life all along?" I asked. Not that I didn't enjoy meeting the cats, but they took me off topic.

She poured the tea into her cup. "We lost touch for a long time. Quite by chance, he learned that I was living in Amity, and he looked me up. We discovered that a friendship remained in place of what we'd once had. Plus, he knows exactly how I like my afternoon tea," she said. "I hope it's not too strong for you."

"Strong? I've always been more of a coffee drinker, but I'm sure this'll be fine."

She filled my mug and set the pot back onto the tray. She added a few sugar cubes to her mug and stirred, and then took a sip. Her eyes closed, and she sat back against her chair with a smile on her face.

I reached for my mug and blew on the hot liquid. I set the cup on the saucer and looked at Jennie Mae.

Her smile grew wider. "A good cup of tea does make a difference, doesn't it? This is just the pick-me-up I needed." She took another sip, and then another. Before I'd even started my mug, hers was empty. She refilled her cup and drank half of her second mug.

That must be some good tea. I lifted the mug to my lips and swallowed a gulp.

Whoa! That wasn't tea, it was bourbon!

I coughed. Jennie Mae opened her eyes and tipped her head. "It's an acquired taste, I admit," she said. "But you'll soon find that no other tea compares." She drained her second mug and sat back. Navajo jumped onto her lap, and Jennie Mae closed her eyes and stroked the cat's fur.

Now, I'm not the type to judge people by their clothes, surroundings, or pets, but the combination of all three of these very things, in addition to the spiked tea, was making me wonder if I'd stumbled through the looking glass. I stood up and immediately felt the booze all the way to my knees. I sat down. Maybe it would be a good idea to eat something.

I ate two pieces of banana bread before I stood up again. The room spun. I was what the kids called "a lightweight," and drinking bourbon on a mostly empty stomach at one thirty in the afternoon was an unfamiliar experience. And on top of all of that, I had to pee.

"May I use your bathroom?" I asked.

"Of course," she said, keeping her eyes closed. "It's at the top of the stairs through the white door."

I carefully stepped around the furniture. My platform shoes made slight indentations in the plush carpeting. I kept one hand on the wall to steady myself until I reached the stairs and was able to grab the wooden banister. This didn't feel right. My head was cloudy, and my feet felt like they each weighed fifty pounds. I reached the landing. The bathroom was in front of me, just like in my house at home. But the staircase that led to the upstairs attic— the attic that Pritchard had chased me out of just yesterday—was right there.

Right. There.

Which brings us to reason #4: No good can come from spying while you're buzzed on bourbon.

I looked around. No signs of Mr. Charles. No signs of Pritchard Smith. No signs of Jennie Mae Tome. If everybody was so busy, where were they?

I opened the door that led to the staircase that led to the attic and listened. Nothing. If Pritchard was up there, then he was doing a very good job of pretending he wasn't. And why would he want to do that? Because he knew I was there, and he didn't want me to catch him doing whatever it was that he was there to do.

Slowly, I crept up the second set of stairs, careful to keep my footsteps silent as I ascended. I wanted the element of surprise when I reached the attic and discovered him.

But as it turns out, the element of surprise was for me. Because the fabulous attic-turned-walk-in-closet that I'd seen the first time I was there, jammed with racks, dressers, and trunks of vintage fashion, was empty.

7

WHAT HAPPENED
TO THE CLOTHES?

THE ATTIC WAS LARGER THAN IT HAD APPEARED WHEN FILLED WITH clothes. I crossed the floor, my shoes making soft *thud* sounds against the worn wood. I opened the window and leaned out, looking to my left first and then right, expecting to see something amiss. The view was much like the day before, or what I remembered before defenestrating myself. No moving vans were pulled up to the property. No shady-looking people hauling away garbage bags of fringes and gauchos. A truck of landscapers unloaded potted plants from the back. If Pritchard had packed everything up and taken it out of the building, Nancie would have told me.

I ran down the stairs. Nobody was on the second floor. Down the second flight of stairs, half running, half falling, mostly stumbling. Jennie Mae was resting on the divan snoring slightly. I knocked into a glass shelf that held vases of silk flowers. They fell, and colorful glass pebbles scattered out and pelted the carpet. I pushed through the swinging doors and found Mr. Charles in the kitchen.

I pointed my finger toward the ceiling. "What happened to the clothes?"

"What clothes?" he said.

"The clothes in the attic. They're gone." I stopped talking. Nobody knew I'd been in the attic, and if I were going to admit it to anybody, I didn't think Mr. Charles was going to be my first choice. "I heard from my coworker that Jennie Mae has a vast collection of clothing in her attic. I just peeked"—I turned, put a hand on one saloon door, and leaned forward, checking to see if Jennie Mae was still asleep— "but the attic is empty. I assume someone came for the collection?"

"No one came for the collection." The butler moved past me to the living room. He took the stairs two at a time. I lost sight of him after he hit the landing. Seconds later I heard him cry out, "No-no-no! We've been robbed!"

I picked up the wall-mounted phone and called 911. "Nine-one-one, please state your emergency," said a male voice.

"There's been a robbery," I said. I gave them the address even though I knew it was displayed on their screen. I heard a sound behind me and turned around. The saloon-style doors to the kitchen swung shut, as if someone had been holding them open. I stepped closer to them, but the short phone cord yanked me backward. The sudden movement, coupled with the bourbon, the empty attic, and the banana bread all came together in one giant nauseating punch to the gut, and I dropped the phone and threw up in the sink.

Reason #5: snooping eventually leads to the police.

I sat on the front step to Jennie Mae's house. The breeze picked up the edges of my caftan and blew them around. A uniformed officer looked at me and then gestured behind him to a man in white. "We need a medic over here," he said.

I held up a hand. "I'm fine."

"I'm not taking that chance." He instructed the medic to give me the once-over, and then he went inside the house. I followed the man in white to the medical van. After checking my blood pressure, pupil dilation, and pulse, he handed me a bottle of Muscle Milk and a straw. "You need protein. Drink this and wait here."

"I have to go back inside," I said.

"The cops won't like that," he said.

"They never do."

I downed the beverage and handed the empty carton to the medic. "Thank you. I feel better already."

I hoisted my caftan up around my waist and undid the button on my pants. It didn't help the have-to-pee situation.

I went back inside the house, leaving the front door open so sunlight could illuminate the dark house. Jennie Mae's chair was now occupied by the black-and-white cat. Detective Loncar, Ribbon's version of Columbo, stood next to the tray table that held the ceramic pot of tea and the empty glasses. He wore a neatly pressed olive-green suit with a white shirt and a yellow-and-olive-speckled tie. I'd grown used to the sight of his buttons stretching across his belly, but today they laid flat. He must have either lost weight or sized up.

"Ms. Kidd."

"Detective Loncar," I said.

"You don't look too good."

"Bourbon," I said.

"That's not like you."

"I know."

The detective used the end of his pen to lift the empty teacup and sniff the residue.

"That's where I got the bourbon," I said. He turned to me but didn't say anything, so I continued. "I thought it was tea."

"Where did it come from?"

"Mr. Charles brought it from the kitchen."

"Who's Mr. Charles?"

"The butler." Loncar crossed his arms over his chest. "I didn't say 'the butler did it.' I said the butler brought the tea from the kitchen. Those are two very different sentences."

"Where did the butler go after he served you this spiked tea?"

I looked in the direction of the stairs. "The last time I saw him, he went up there."

Loncar followed my gaze. "You went up with him?"

"No. I heard him holler something about being robbed, and I went to the kitchen to call you."

"Ms. Kidd, I would like nothing more than to tell you to stay out of this, but right now, you're about as in the middle of it as a person can get, so instead I'm going to tell you to answer my questions as honestly as you can. Withhold nothing. Do you understand?"

I held up my hand, palm-side out. "Before we do this thing that we do when I end up in these kinds of situations, can I go to the bathroom?"

"Sorry. The rest of the house is off-limits. Tell me again what you're doing here?"

"I'm here on a job. A paying job."

"Who's your employer?"

"*Retrofit* Magazine."

"Then your employer knows you're here."

I bit my lip. "Not exactly."

"Miss Kidd, have a seat. We need to talk."

IT TOOK Loncar's team several hours to secure the scene. Jennie Mae Tome's cats swarmed under the feet of officers who photographed the interior of the house. I watched from the doorway, since I'd been instructed to wait outside. In time, Loncar joined me.

"How are you feeling?" he asked.

"Better," I said.

"Can you call someone to pick you up?"

"I drove."

"I think it's best that you leave your car here for the night."

"You can search it if you want. I didn't take anything."

"I'm not accusing you of theft." He paused. "I'm not convinced you've sobered up enough to be safe behind the wheel."

I was about to argue when a hiccup escaped my mouth. "I'll call a taxi."

"I'll be in touch," he said.

The *Retrofit* offices were empty by the time the cab driver dropped me off. I would have gone straight home, except that I wanted to pick up Logan and my bathroom needs were off the charts. I went straight to the restroom, and then, after washing my hands, headed to my cubicle. "You are not going to believe the day I had," I said as I turned the corner.

"Try me," said a voice from behind my desk.

I jumped and turned to face my desk. Pritchard sat behind it, holding Logan in his arms.

8

———

ONE STEP CLOSER TO DEATH

A dark shadow was cast across Pritchard, making it difficult for me to see his face. I stepped forward, and he turned on a light and shined it into my eyes. I shielded them, too late. Spots of red filled my vision. "What are you doing in my office?" I asked.

He moved Logan from his lap to the desk. Logan let out a low, throaty growl. I closed the distance between us, scooped Logan into my arms, and retreated to the doorway.

"Don't be alarmed," Pritchard said. "I can assure you I didn't hurt your cat." He leaned back in my chair and smiled. Despite reassurances to the contrary, his presence felt threatening. "Silly girl. If you had done your job, you would have been left out of everything. If you had minded your business. But you didn't. People warned me about you."

"What do you want?" I asked.

"How much do you think Jennie Mae's wardrobe is worth?" he asked.

"I don't know. I don't know the extent of her collection."

"Oh, but you do know, Ess Kay. You saw it the day you went

looking for me in her attic. Too bad that shutter didn't give under your weight. This whole problem would have solved itself."

He knew that I'd been there. I shuddered at his detached description of what might have happened.

"In a wa-a-ay," he said, dragging the word "way" out into three syllables, "you set this whole thing into motion. And now there's a ticking clock." He tapped his index finger on the top of the desk as if keeping time. "How does that make you feel, Ess Kay? That there is a timer running in the background, a specific length of time in which certain acts will unfold?"

He stopped tapping. "You already know more about what is going on than you should, Ess Kay." He kept saying my initials phonetically. *Ess Kay.* He dragged the S sound out like a hiss. *Esssssssss.* It reminded me of the cobra in Rikki-Tikki-Tav *i.* "Yes, you know quite a bit more than I like. But I know a lot too. For example, I know you live on West 47th Street in a house you purchased from your parents. How charming."

Cold fear snaked up underneath my caftan, chilling my spine and climbing my neck. I hugged Logan tighter, and he didn't struggle.

Pritchard leaned back in the chair. "I know you have a cat," he continued. He waved his index finger at Logan's face. "Hello, Logan," he said. "I know you've had troubled employment since leaving Bentley's New York. Your family lives in California, except for your sister, who lives in Maryland. Bethesda, if I'm not mistaken."

How did Pritchard know so much about me? Worse, what would he do to the people I loved? My parents and my sister were all out of state. He couldn't get to them. And then an image of Nick flashed into my brain. *Nick,* I thought. *He doesn't know about Nick.*

"You're going to help me, Ess Kay. And if you help me like I ask, nobody will get hurt. There is something at the Tome house that I need. You're going to get it for me. I can't go back there, but you can. Our boss will insist on it. This might work out yet." He steepled his fingers and smiled, his lips pressed together. "Perfection," he added and chuckled to himself.

I started to tell him he was wrong, that someone had stolen the contents of Jennie Mae's attic, but I bit back my words. He claimed to still need something from her house. If Pritchard hadn't stolen the collection of samples, then who had?

He stood up. I backed away from him. He laughed again. "I'll be watching you, Ess Kay. And I'll be in touch." He reached out to pet Logan. I twisted around so his hand fell short. "No matter. We had plenty of time together before you arrived." He laughed again, picked up the brown leather briefcase with the gold PS monogram, and left.

As soon as the front doors closed behind him, I raced forward and locked them from the inside. I knew it didn't matter. Pritchard had been inside *Retrofit* when I'd arrived. Nancie had probably given him a set of keys. He could come and go as he wished.

The idea that someone could get to me so easily ignited my nerve endings, sending a buzz to the surface of my skin. I'd been in tight situations before but never with someone so confident that they'd sought me out in plain sight. The risks I'd taken in the past had been life-threatening, but because I'd actively pursued settings that put me face-to-face with killers. Even if I had learned my lesson, this time I had no choice.

My curious streak had led me into Jennie Mae's attic, and because I'd gone back, I was being manipulated into danger. While I'd been chatting with Detective Loncar, a crazy man had demonstrated how easily he could get to me by abducting my cat.

I spent a minute making sure Logan had not been harmed. He was still drowsy but showed signs of his regular personality. My brain went onto autopilot. *Get out of here*, screamed a voice in my head. I put him in his carrier, grabbed my things, and left before I realized I didn't have my car. It was still in Amity.

I ran to Tradava. Logan yowled with the jostling and shifted from one side of his carrier to the other. Until I knew what I was going to do, I was going to stay in very public places. I entered the store by the prom dress department and cut directly through juniors and past costume jewelry to the door that led to the stairs that ended right in front of Eddie's visual office. Eddie's back was to me. I stood, framed out by the doorway, clutching Logan's carrier to my chest, trying to figure out what to say.

"Meeeeeeeoooooooow," Logan said, making two syllables last about four beats.

Eddie turned around. "Dude, what are you doing here? Is that Logan? New question. What is Logan doing here?"

"I need a favor," I said. "A really big, enormous favor with no questions asked."

"Fine, I'll make you fried chicken for dinner."

"I need you to take Logan for a couple of days. Maybe more. I don't know how long."

He looked at me and then at the carrier. "Is everything okay?"

"Please. Don't tell anybody. He's a nice cat. He's supposed to be on a diet, but he likes the cat food with the cat that eats out of the crystal bowl. He'll need a litter box. I'll pay you back for whatever you buy."

"Dude, I know how to take care of a cat. What's up?"

"Work is—work is a little off-the-charts crazy right now, and you're probably not going to see me all that much until I'm past some of these deadlines. So please, don't come looking for me, don't call me, don't invite me over for dinner. Pretend I don't exist."

"Is this a birthday thing? Just because you're one step closer to death is no reason to shut out the world."

I started to deny the correlation but the fear of letting Eddie know and potentially putting him in danger stopped me. "I'm a little overwhelmed. Everything is going to go back to normal in a couple of weeks, okay?"

"Okay, but considering both your lifestyle and the alternative, you're lucky you *are* still around to celebrate another birthday."

"Thanks for that." I handed the cat carrier over to him and bent down, sticking my finger into the metal grid on the door. "Be a good cat," I said. "Do whatever Uncle Eddie tells you to do. I'll be back to get you as soon as I can."

Logan stretched his paw out and ran the little black pads on the bottom of it over the top of my finger. Tears sprung to my eyes, and I choked back a sob. I swallowed a lump. "Thank you," I said to Eddie. My throat constricted, and the words came out in a rasp. Before I could regret what I'd done or Eddie could change his mind, I turned around and left.

The taxi driver dropped me off in front of my house. I gave him a healthy tip, and he gave me his card. "I am Mohammed Jones. My company tells me about you. You like to ride in taxis, correct? Please, take my card. I am new to the taxi world. I will drive you where you want to go." His English was very proper, as if he'd learned it in a classroom and not on the street.

I thanked him, asked him not to leave until I was inside the house, and got out. Surprisingly, he waited. I secured his card to the refrigerator under a magnet shaped like the Liberty Bell. Perhaps we could work out a deal.

I locked the front door, closed and locked the windows, and spent the next hour going through the house making sure I was alone. It was a slow and systematic process that left me wondering what exactly I would do if I'd found someone on the premises. By the time I'd finished, I had a shopping list of things that would make me feel safe. Pepper spray. Security alarm. Bull horn. Police on speed dial. Possible adoption of pit bull.

I opened a bag of Unique Splitz pretzel shells and a bottle of birch beer and sat at the kitchen table. What had happened today? I didn't know. I'd gone to work. I'd left work and gone to Jennie Mae's house. It was very possible that while I was enjoying spiked tea with the lady of the house, she was being robbed. Had she known the tea was bourbon? Or had the tea been spiked for my benefit? Jennie Mae appeared to trust Mr. Charles, but I didn't.

And then there was Pritchard's behavior. Not only had he acted suspicious the day I'd overheard him in the attic, but after Jennie Mae's sample wardrobe had gone missing, he'd shown up in my office and doled out thinly veiled threats. He was after something, and despite the missing clothes, it sounded like he still hadn't found it.

Which left a whole lot of what I didn't know: what was Pritchard after? Where did he come from? What had happened to Jennie Mae's collection? Was Mr. Charles on the up-and-up? And who was going to take care of all those cats?

And the niggling question that didn't seem to relate to anything but was at the center of it all was what did any of this have to do with my job at *Retrofit*?

The house felt quiet. Scary in its solitude. In the past, when I'd gotten mixed up in less than savory situations, I'd always been able to come home to Logan. He'd been my rock, my companion, ever since I'd adopted him when I lived in New York. He'd watched me date my way through three different deli counter employees (I blame it on my love of cured lunch meats), work sixty-five-hour weeks while I climbed the corporate ladder at Bentley's, and gained and lost the same twenty pounds depending on the year. He'd stood by me through my rocky new start in Ribbon even when one particularly harrowing adventure had put him in harm's way. He hadn't judged when I dated not one but two men since relocating: Nick, who he'd been hearing about for years, and Dante Lestes, a hot (with a name like Dante, how could he not be?) private investigator who felt it was his duty to make me his protégé. Logan hadn't even shown a preference for either man, leaving the choice up to me.

Since Nick and I had slowly reconnected after our abrupt break-up, Dante had become a faint memory. After I'd made it clear that I wasn't over Nick, Dante had left town. And I'd been okay with that. Dante's attention felt good, but it also felt dangerous. Like living too close to a flame. Nick's attention was exciting, too, in a different way. When we were in the same room, it was like nobody else mattered.

But now, I had to distance myself from him too. The hair on my arms stood up as I remembered the way Pritchard had listed off details about my life, my parents, my sister, my cat. I didn't know how much he knew about me or what he was trying to protect by scaring me into submission, but I wasn't willing to put people I loved at risk.

I finished my birch beer and nuked a frozen pizza. In the time it took to finish heating and eating, I reached a few conclusions. Pritchard Smith's arrival on the job at *Retrofit* had not been an accident. He'd had knowledge of something in Jennie Mae Tome's attic, something that he'd tried to keep me from discovering. Whatever that knowledge was, I was close to exposing it, and now, the lives of the people I cared about were in danger.

And since there was nobody around to protect me from him, I was going to have to learn to take care of myself. Which is exactly how I found myself at the police station the next morning.

9

———

SPOTTY HISTORY

"I'D LIKE TO FILL OUT AN APPLICATION TO THE CITIZEN'S POLICE academy," I told the officer behind the desk. He was dressed in the standard Ribbon PD uniform: navy-blue shirt and trousers made from fabric so thick it might have been recycled from discarded water bottles. His name, Kent Callahan, was embroidered above his left breast pocket in neat block letters. On the opposite side was a patch in the shape of a badge. It had a picture of intersecting ribbons circled by the words *Ribbon Police Department. To Protect and Serve.*

As a counterpoint to his official police uniform, I was dressed in a maize-colored peasant blouse and a pair of chocolate-brown wide-legged pants that hid my platform shoes. Oversized gold hoop earrings swung on either side of my face.

Officer Callahan didn't bat an eye at my request or my outfit. He opened a metal file cabinet, flipped partway back, and pulled out a sheet of paper. "Fill this out and bring it back in."

"Can I fill it out here?"

"If you want."

I carried the sheet of paper to one of the empty chairs in the lobby. There was no table to use as a desk, so I pulled Pritchard's pen out of my handbag and then used my handbag as a lap desk. The point of the pen went through the paper twice before I got the hang of it.

The questions were easy enough. I breezed through the expected name/address/driver's license fields and the "Have you ever been arrested?" (thankfully, close calls don't count). Next: How did you hear about Citizen's Police Academy? I chewed the end of the pen while I considered the pros and cons of writing Detective Loncar's name. I could come back to that.

The bottom portion of the form was a series of yes-and-no questions that required Xs in the proper boxes. In the military? No. Been convicted of a felony? No. Relative in law enforcement? No. This was easy. I was a shoe-in.

The second page, however, gave me pause. What is your current occupation? Editor for online fashion magazine. Why are you interested in Citizen's Police Academy? I have an ongoing interest in establishing a healthy working relationship with the local police. (I wasn't even in class and already I was trying to butter up my instructors.)

The last question was optional. What are your goals in the community upon graduation?

There wasn't nearly enough space for a proper answer.

I completed the application and returned to the desk. Officer Callahan didn't notice me until I cleared my throat. He looked up. "Yes?"

"I'm finished." I held out the papers.

"Congratulations. Wait here while I get you a badge," he said sarcastically.

"Do you get a lot of applicants?" I asked.

Callahan took the paper and set it facedown on a copy

machine. "Fair share. The background check weeds out anybody with a criminal history. Most quit before it's over. A couple turn in the paperwork and don't bother showing up again. Why do you want to do it?"

"Detective Loncar suggested it to me once."

The copier spat out a piece of paper. The officer picked it up and looked at it. Then he looked at me. I held his stare for at least two solid seconds. "Wait here," he said.

Five minutes later, I was seated across the desk from Detective Loncar. This wasn't the first time I'd been in his office. It wasn't even the second. But since the last time, he'd replaced the bowl of sugar-free candy that had sat on the corner of his desk with a tray of partially solved Rubik's cubes.

"My desk sergeant tells me you want to sign up for the citizen's police academy," he said. "You want to tell me what that's about?"

"It was your idea," I said. His forehead broke out in a series of deep horizontal lines as he frowned. "Remember? It was back when you were investigating those arsons around Ribbon?"

"That was a joke, Ms. Kidd."

"See, here I thought you were telling me that you respected my interest in the law. All this time, I took it as a compliment. Like I was the daughter you never had."

"I have a daughter. You know that."

"Yes, but she doesn't share your interest in police work like I do."

"Small miracle."

"Detective, I'm serious about signing up. I think it's time I learned what goes into law enforcement and stop getting in your way."

He had a pencil in his hand, and he put it eraser-side down on top of my application. He slid the pencil side to side, which moved the paper back and forth with it. He had a habit of doing these little, mindless, annoying things. Clicking pens, spinning cups, and now shifting my paper.

I leaned forward and put my hand on the sheet. "Stop that."

"What?"

"That. Whenever I'm in here, you do stuff like that. Like clicking your pens or tapping your wedding ring on the chair." I looked at his hand. "Where's your wedding ring?" I asked.

"My wife asked me to move out. She said she can't handle this life anymore."

I was shocked at the timing. "But your daughter just had a baby," I said. I looked at Loncar a little more closely. The circles under his eyes were two shades darker than the rest of his face. "I thought babies pulled family together."

"You'd think so, right?" He shook his head from side to side. "My daughter is living in my house with my wife, and I'm living at the Motel 6."

"Interesting choice."

"The department gets a discounted rate."

I didn't know what to say, so I said nothing. Loncar set the pencil down and leaned back. "Why did you really fill this paperwork out?"

I wanted to tell him about the crazy man who had threatened me and my loved ones, that I was scared, and that I had a newfound respect for people who had taken an oath to protect and serve. But two things stopped me:

1. Claiming my coworker had broken into my office at a fashion magazine to threaten me to possibly help him steal an attic filled with forty-year-old clothes sounded crazy and
2. Loncar and I had a spotty history.

Detective Loncar had arrested me, interrogated me, used me as a decoy, ignored me, and most recently, saved my life. Did that mean he was at risk too? How deep did Pritchard Smith's dirt on me run?

"It's something I felt like I had to do."

He nodded slowly, like he knew there was more thought behind my words. Or maybe it was because he slept under an open window and woke up with a stiff neck. He pulled a pen out of the mug on his desk and signed the bottom of the form. "You're in," he said. "First class is on Monday."

"What should I wear?" I asked.

"Sweats."

"I don't wear sweats in public."

"I'm sure you'll figure it out." He pushed the paper toward me. "Give this to Callahan." I took the paper and started to leave. "Ms. Kidd," he called behind me. I turned around in the doorway. "You remember anything else you want to tell me about what happened yesterday?"

"Not yet," I answered truthfully. Until I felt like I could take care of myself, I wasn't saying anything to anybody.

I called Mohammed and asked if he was driving his cab. He was. When I told him I was at the police station, he went silent. "I didn't do anything wrong," I told him. "I was visiting a friend." Oddly, it felt almost true. "I'll walk to the sandwich shop at the end of the strip mall. Can you pick me up there?"

"Yes. I will be there in one minute," he said.

True to his word, he pulled the yellow sedan into the parking lot outside of the sandwich shop about sixty seconds later.

"Thank you, Mohammed," I said.

"You may call me Mo," he said. "Please sit and buckle in your body. I cannot drive until you are secure."

IT WAS AFTER ELEVEN. I asked Mo to keep the meter running while I ran into the sandwich shop and ordered a hoagie. My favorite sandwich shop, B&S, had opened a second location, and I felt it was my duty to support them in their endeavors. Their primary location was a few doors down from Nick's showroom, which, considering my current plan to distance myself from everybody I knew, seemed a little risky.

"Do you want me to take you to your address, Miss Kidd?" Mo asked.

"If I'm going to call you Mo, you need to call me Samantha," I said. "We're not going to my house today. I left my car at a—a friend's house." I gave him the address to Jennie Mae's residence.

When we arrived, he drove his taxi down the long gravel driveway. "That is your car?" he asked. "It is funny looking. What is it?"

"It's a Honda del Sol. I bought it in the nineties, but it spent most of the time parked in a lot in New York City."

"I have not seen a car like that. It is very shiny. And it is very nice. No." He paused and appeared to concentrate for a moment. "It is very shiny and very nice. Like my new taxi. Yes."

"I thought this taxi looked different. What happened to your old taxi? The one you drove yesterday?"

"I have worked hard. I now afford new taxi. My old taxi is in graveyard."

I stifled a giggle. Mo had been making great effort to use the correct words, and I didn't want him to think I was laughing at him. "I think you used the wrong word. 'Graveyard' is a burial ground."

"Taxi graveyard, that is what the other drivers call it."

"Taxi graveyard. That's a new one," I said. I suspected the other cab drivers were having fun at Mo's expense.

"No, it is a place for old taxis. When a driver can buy new taxi, an old taxi is retired. It is parked into the lot behind the Ribbon High School until it is auctioned off or demolished. That is taxi graveyard. Lots and lots of old yellow taxis. It is sad to see them except that they have done their jobs well. I applaud them."

"That's a nice thought," I said. I leaned back against the gray fabric interior and relaxed my head against the head rest. "The old taxis have done their jobs well," I repeated to myself. "You're unique, Mohammed. You'll be successful because people will remember you."

"You are also unique, Samantha. I think people will remember you too."

I met his smile. "I'm unique because of the way I dress. If I put on regular clothes like everybody else, I'd blend into the crowd."

"But your car would not blend in, so you would still be unique."

I barely heard what he said, because another, more important thought had hijacked my attention. Mo was right. If I dressed like I dressed and drove what I drove, I would be easy to track. But if I didn't, if I changed my appearance, my vehicle, my residence—drastically—I would blend in. I could come and go, and Pritchard Smith might not be the wiser.

"Mo, if I wanted to not stand out and be unique and maybe borrow a taxi from the graveyard, do you know how I could make that happen?"

Mo beamed at me from the rearview mirror. "My brother owns the taxi graveyard." His face turned sad. "But if you drive a dead taxi, I can no longer drive you as a client."

I smiled. "I think we can work something out."

IT DIDN'T TAKE MUCH for me to convince Mo that I would still need a driver from time to time. It took even less to convince him to give me the keys to his newly retired cab. He followed me and my Honda del Sol back to my house and waited in the driveway out front while I filled a suitcase with items from the box of painting clothes my parents had left behind. They were relics of former decades: jeans printed with seashells, sweatshirts with cigarette logos, T-shirts featuring Starsky and Hutch, and *Royal Tenenbaums*-esque jog suits with contrasting stripes down the sleeve and pants. I was hoping Nancie would grant me a little leeway on the dress code. It might not be work attire, but no way would Pritchard recognize me dressed like this.

I left my car in the garage and climbed into Mo's taxi. He drove me to the taxi graveyard and wished me luck. His old vehicle was easy to identify; it was the cleanest of the bunch. If Mo took half as good care of his new taxi as he did his old one, it wouldn't go to the graveyard for a very long time.

I pulled on a baseball hat and followed Mo out of the parking lot. He waved to me before we turned different directions at the light. It was still early. I drove to Tradava and parked behind the store. Inside, I went directly to the sporting goods section and picked out several sweatshirts and sweatpants in shades of gray, maroon, hunter green, and navy blue. I added a rust-colored nylon backpack and stuffed my purchases into it after I paid. I left out a different door than I'd entered and strode across the parking lot to *Retrofit*.

I hadn't given much thought to how Nancie would react to the news about Pritchard. She'd made no secret of the fact that she thought he was fantastic, and here we were, her dynamic duo, on seemingly opposite sides of the law.

I'd given a little thought to the curious case of Pritchard Smith and had reached one conclusion: if he'd intended to fly under the radar and wheedle himself into Jennie Mae's good graces, then my showing up at her house and discovering the empty attic had put a crimp in his plans. The cops knew about the theft. So did the media. Once the Ribbon website was updated and the local news went on the air, the whole town would have heard about it. Jennie Mae's collection was vital to our premiere issue. I expected to find Nancie in full-on panic mode.

Sounds from the back of the offices indicated that I wasn't alone. "Nancie?" I called. There was no response. Something didn't feel right. I regretted having called out because if the interns or Nancie were there, they would have answered. Whoever was in the offices with me wasn't feeling chatty.

I tossed my backpack in my cubicle and crept down the hallway to the back of the *Retrofit* offices. I kept my back to the moveable walls, one hand in front of me and one behind, and took small steps down the makeshift hallway. As I approached, I confirmed that the person in Nancie's office wasn't Nancie.

It was Tahoma Hunt, the executive director of Bethany House, who had been meeting with Nancie the night she'd first told me about the Seventies magalog.

10

TRYING NOT TO BE NOTICED

I HOVERED IN THE HALLWAY, WATCHING TAHOMA MOVE ABOUT Nancie's office. If he knew I was there, he was doing a good job of ignoring me. Today he wore a loose, faded, army-green jacket over camouflage pants in shades of desert sand, day-old avocado, and baby puke. His head was covered by a red knit hat pulled low over his strong forehead. The hat was the one shot of color in an otherwise drab outfit.

He appeared to be searching Nancie's office for something, working slowly and systematically, returning everything he touched to the spot where he'd found it.

I was too close to get away without alerting him to my presence, so I leveraged the element of surprise. "Where's Nancie?" I asked with more courage than I felt.

Tahoma looked up, startled. For a fraction of a second, we locked eyes. I tensed, not willing to guess at his next move. His hands rested on top of a spiral-bound notebook on Nancie's desk. It was the *Retrofit* bible that she had shown us the night she pitched the project. It contained every ad, every story, every column, every concept she hoped to incorporate in her vision. Nothing about the way she'd presented it to Pritchard and me had indicated that it was anything less than top secret.

"I don't know where Nancie, is," he said, pulling the red knit hat off his head and stuffing it into his pocket. "We had an appointment. I've been waiting for her for a few minutes now." He stood up straight and hooked his thumbs into the pockets of his camo pants.

"How did you get in?"

"The door was open. I figured she ran out for a second and intended to return right away."

"That sounds like Nancie," I lied. It sounded nothing like Nancie, but warning bells sounded in my head. We were alone in the *Retrofit* offices, and it seemed better to play along. I reached across the desk and slid the bible toward me. I held it up and smiled. "This is what I needed." I clutched it to my chest. "Do you want me to call her? See what's holding her up from your meeting?"

His eyes didn't leave the bible. "No, that's not necessary. I'll reschedule with her for another day."

I stepped backward and left room for him to pass me. He paused for a moment and then left Nancie's office. I held my breath and watched his back as he went out the front door. On a whim, I ran after him. I didn't know which way he'd gone, left or right, but there was no sign of him. I went back inside and grabbed my backpack.

Nancie wouldn't leave the offices unlocked during the day, not with all our files and records here. And where were the interns? Something was very wrong. Very, very wrong. No way was I staying here.

If it had been a mere suspicion before, now I was sure. There was a connection between Nancie's Seventies project and the theft at Jennie Mae Tome's house. But for the life of me, I didn't know what it was. I left Nancie a note. *Nancie, Need to talk about project and PS. I have the bible. –Samantha*

I wanted to warn her that something was up, that because of her project, she might be in danger, but I didn't know how to convey it on a Post-it. I called her cell and left a message. I added *Be Careful* under my name, and then, I left.

IN ADDITION to Tradava and *Retrofit*, the Ribbon East strip mall included a movie theater, a vitamin store, a revolving door of local crafty businesses, and a pizza place called Brothers. They served the best pizza in all of Ribbon and had been the location of most of my high school dates. This was not the time to question the lack of imagination of the boys who had taken me out, nor was it the time to order a pizza. I found myself in need of a bathroom, but not for the obvious reasons.

The good thing about being something of a regular at a pizza place over the course of twenty-or-so years (give or take the time I'd spent at college and working in New York), was that they didn't kick you out when you went past the booths directly for the door marked "Ladies." The other good thing was that they didn't comment when you emerged in an entirely different outfit moments later. I left with my peasant blouse and brown bell-bottoms in my backpack, dressed in a new poly-cotton sweat suit, looking not unlike Danny Zuko the day he tried out for the gymnastics team in *Grease*. If I hadn't been able to come up with a movie reference for the outfit, I might never have come out of the stall. I walked straight to the dead taxi and drove away before anybody could recognize me. Incognito or not, I had a rep to protect.

There was a certain freedom in driving around in a taxi. Other drivers made way for me, as if expecting aggressive navigation from my vehicle. I drove home and parked in the driveway. Who cared if Pritchard saw it there? He'd assume I was being dropped off or picked up. He'd never guess that it was my new mode of transport.

I went inside and checked my messages. Most of the world had given up the idea of an answering machine. I kept mine because it reminded me of my parents, from whom I'd bought the house. It was an Eighties model, and like the phone, a sort of Hershey-bar brown. The red light blinked repeatedly. I pressed play and sat on a brown wooden barstool normally tucked under the counter.

Beep! Dude, it's Eddie. Thought you'd want to know Logan and I bonded over a Catwoman movie last night. All is well with the world. What's up with you?

Beep! Hey, Kidd. It was good to see you the other night. My dad's going to take my seat at my poker game tonight. Since the apartment will be empty, I thought maybe, you know. If you want to. Call me.

Nick played poker?

The tape in the machine let off a whiny squeal and then shut itself off. I opened the compartment and pulled out the tape. Strands of caramel-brown cassette tape innards had failed to retract into the opposite side of the tape and now created a knotted-up mess inside the player. My novelty answering machine had come to the end of the road.

I wound the strands of tape around the cassette and tossed it in the trash. Did anybody still sell answering machines? Did I need one? I had my cell phone. If someone wanted to find me, they could call that. If they didn't have the number, I probably didn't want to talk to them.

While Nick's message lingered I my mind (I knew exactly what Nick was implying, and yeah, I wanted to, but I also knew that meeting up with him would be a very bad idea), I called Detective Loncar.

"This is Samantha Kidd," I said. "I have some information for you."

"You remember something?"

"Not exactly. Is there a place I can meet you to talk? Not the police station."

He was silent for a moment, and I braced myself for one of his this-is-not-a-joke conversations. He surprised me. "Meet me in the lobby of the Motel 6 on Fairmount."

"Be there in twenty minutes." I pulled a Philadelphia Phillies baseball hat on over my ponytail, grabbed the keys to the dead taxi, and left.

Detective Loncar was sitting at a table in the back of the lunch buffet. On the wall behind him was a muted painting featuring a boat docked in a remote alcove, all shades of mint green and mauve. The table in front of him held a tray with a partially eaten hamburger, fries, and two chocolate chip cookies. Last I'd heard, his wife had put him on a restricted diet to control his diabetes and his weight. On one level, he'd found a way to appreciate the break from her too.

"That's a new look for you, isn't it?" he asked, glancing at my poly-cotton-blend sweat suit and Phillies hat.

"I'm trying not to be noticed." I slumped down a bit.

"Does this have to do with my investigation?"

I pulled the bill of the baseball hat down further over my eyes. "Yes." I looked side to side. "I thought you said the lobby?"

"This looks less suspicious."

"That was good thinking," I said.

"Not my first rodeo," the detective replied.

I couldn't help but laugh. Six months ago, if you'd have told me that I'd be sharing a table at a motel with Detective Loncar—

laughing, no less—I would have said you were crazy. My life had changed in immeasurable ways, and crazy was the new normal.

"Whaddya got for me?" Loncar asked.

I took a deep breath and exhaled. The only thing it accomplished was to distract me with the scent of his burger. I looked at the salad bar. They had chicken wings and potato skins, and, "Is that a nacho station?"

Loncar cleared his throat.

"Oh, right. Sorry." I shifted my attention from the food to the detective. "Like I told you, I'm currently working at *Retrofit* Magazine. So far, it's been an online publication, but my boss got the idea for us to put together a print magazine. Our whole concept is to look to past decades for fashion inspiration and then teach people how to interpret the trends."

He took a pull of his coffee. It was the exact shade of beige that I liked. "Go on," he finally said.

"There's a new guy at *Retrofit*. Pritchard Smith. He showed up on Tuesday. I don't know his background, but he appears to have connections in the industry. Two days ago, I followed him to Jennie Mae Tome's house. He was talking about the private collection in the attic with somebody, but I only heard one voice, so I think he was on the phone. I got the feeling that they thought it was valuable, or that something was hidden in it."

"Did you ask him?"

"He, um, didn't know I was there."

He studied me for a second and then nodded once, indicating that I should continue. I gave him points for not following up on that particular point.

"My boss doesn't know that I followed Pritchard. Nobody does. I didn't think he knew I was there, either. I was supposed to be working on research while he was on his appointment, but I didn't like that arrangement, so I took it upon myself to become familiar with whatever was in the attic."

"This was Wednesday?" he asked.

"Yes."

"Ms. Kidd, you'd get into a lot less trouble if you minded your business. You know that, right?"

Let's call that reason #6.

"My business—my job—is to work on this magazine. Thanks to the guy I'm working with, I was chained to a computer and he was looking at a highly sought-after sample collection. Now it seems like he had an ulterior motive."

"Let's cut to the chase. You went to Ms. Tome's house. Mr. Smith was at Ms. Tome's house. You suspect him of stealing the clothes from her attic. Do you have anything to back this suspicion up? Or is this a case of you confusing workplace competition with burglary?" He balled up his napkin and tossed it on his plate on top of the untouched cookies. That was just wrong.

"Here's where things get weird. Pritchard threatened me in my office yesterday, *after* Jennie Mae was robbed."

"Then he wasn't involved in the theft."

"You're not listening to me. Pritchard Smith threatened me, my family, and my cat. He's out to get me." This time, I made direct eye contact. "And then today, I found someone else—the director of an auction house—in my boss's office. His name is Tahoma Hunt. You need to look into him too. He's tall, fit, dark skin. Longish black hair. Native American, I think. He had on a red knit hat, an army jacket, and a pair of camo pants."

"Good thing you remembered what he was wearing. It's not like he could change his outfit to blend in," he said, scanning my sweat suit again.

"You're going to follow up on everything I tell you, right? You're not just asking me to tell you everything to indulge me, are you?"

"Ms. Kidd, it's not my job to indulge you. It's my job to determine what you know and to act on that knowledge if it relates to an open investigation. Now, where was your boss during all this?"

"I don't know. Tahoma said the doors to the office were unlocked, but nobody was there. He had the bible of our project, and that's highly confidential. I think I caught him by surprise. When I took the bible from Nancie's desk, he seemed disappointed. He left even though he claimed he had an appointment with her. Whatever is going on is connected to this project, but I don't know what it is."

"Tell me about *Retrofit*."

"It's a start-up fashion magazine. Internet, at least at first."

"There are people who read this?"

"Fashion is big business," I said. "How long have you known me?"

He raised his eyebrows.

"I've been back in Ribbon for two years, and in that time, I've worked for two department stores, a museum exhibit, and a runway show. All of which ended poorly. You told me once you knew crime was on the rise in Ribbon when you took this job. Like it or not, the fashion industry is part of our city. There are factories here that designers can use. There are warehouses available for cheap. We're a train ride away from New York City, and a lot of people who work in the industry commute because the cost of living here is reasonable."

"Bringing new business to Ribbon should be a good thing, not an excuse for illegal behavior."

"You're missing my point. Fashion is big business, and it's a glamorous business. It draws all kinds of people, including the ones who see it as a way to get rich or get famous. Look closely at the crimes that I've been involved with. There's a pattern there.

Something is happening in our city and it's attracting the wrong people."

"This new job of yours. *Retrofit*. Why'd your boss set up shop here?"

"Same reason. You can run an online magazine from anywhere. We're close enough to New York that we can make a trip to photograph designer samples or wander Manhattan to catch up on street style."

"But your website has to do with old fashion."

"That's right. Nancie came up with a niche target: repurposing vintage pieces into current styles. We were ranked in the top twenty-five up-and-coming style websites last month."

"Tell me about this project."

Detective Loncar was a master of interrogation. The first time we'd been alone in a Q&A type situation, I'd tried my hand at keeping my mouth shut. When that failed, I'd moved on to selective truths. Eventually, he'd found a way to win my trust and I'd spilled the beans. His expertise lay in his minimal conversational approach. If he'd gone into Freudian psychoanalysis instead of police work, he'd ask me to tell him about my mother.

I reached into my bag and pulled out the *Retrofit* Seventies bible. I set it next to Loncar's plate and tapped the cover. "This is a mockup of what we've been working on. Nancie made this. She's been selling ad space to fund it, and she asked Pritchard and me to find interesting content for our editorials."

"What does she say about the theft at Ms. Tome's house and your suspicions of Mr. Smith?"

"I haven't seen Nancie in days."

"You find that suspicious?"

"She said she had meetings with advertisers around the clock." I hadn't given much thought to Nancie, but Loncar brought up an interesting question. Nancie had been MIA since before the theft. If I was so certain that there was a connection between the Seventies project and the theft, what made me think she *wasn't* involved?

11
———

TWO THOUSAND
CALORIES BEFORE LUNCH

"Ms. Kidd, I want you to walk away from this project," Loncar said.

"With all due respect, this 'project' is my job," I said. "It's the first real job I've had since moving to Ribbon. It's not like I haven't been trying, either. You have no idea how hard it is for a former fashion buyer to find work these days."

"You could always move back to New York City," he said.

"Are you trying to get rid of me?"

"It would sure make my life easier."

We both stood. Around us, a team of busboys in white aprons cleared the empty tables. I adjusted the hem of my sweatshirt and looked at Loncar. "Thank you for listening to me."

"Ms. Kidd, it's my job to listen to you. Anybody else and I'd give the info to one of my rookies and have them follow up with a few phone calls to try to locate this Mr. Smith. But you have a track record, so I'm going to follow up on this myself."

Implied but not said (by him): I sure hope this isn't a joke.

Not said but thought (by me): I really wish it was.

We went our separate ways: Loncar to the door marked Stairs and me past the front desk and out to the parking lot. The dead taxi was parked at the edge of the lot under the sign advertising room rates. *$39.99 Internet special, includes HBO and Breakfast Buffet.* No wonder the detective hadn't checked himself into the Westin.

I drove to my house, parked the dead taxi in front of my house, and went inside. The first thing I did was find a suitable hiding place for the *Retrofit* bible. (I stuck it in the pantry behind the Bran Flakes.) Next, I finished the second half of my hoagie and most of a bag of potato chips and then changed from my sweats into a cream ribbed poor boy sweater, long, rust suede maxi skirt, and a cropped brown-and-rust paisley vest trimmed with an elaborate silk cord that knotted in the front. I took the Phillies baseball hat off, scrunched some mousse into the ends of my hair, and pulled on a crocheted cap like the one Ali MacGraw wore in *Love Story.* There were times to lie low, and there were times to be seen. This was a time to be seen. I finished off the rest of the potato chips and then got into my car. I let the car idle for a moment while I dug around in my bag for my cell phone. I called Eddie.

"Yo," I said. "How's Logan?"

"Hello to you, too. I don't know what you've been feeding your cat, but he's been making good use of that litter box."

"Did he poop out anything interesting?" I asked.

"Dude."

"The vet said whatever he ate that made him sick has to come out before he'll feel better."

"I love your cat, but I'm not going through his poop."

"Point taken. But does he seem peppier?"

"He should be. He has to be a couple pounds lighter by now. Are you going to tell me what's going on with you?"

"Not yet. Are you going to tell me what's going on with you?"

"Dude, you're the one who handed over your cat and told me not to contact you."

"Yes, but you're the one who downed two thousand calories before lunch. Now ask yourself: which one of us is acting more out of character?"

"I'd say it's a toss-up."

I put the car into reverse. "Call me if anything happens and give Logan a kiss for me. Right on top of his head between his ears. And tell him I'll pick him up as soon as I can."

"I don't think he minds it here so much. I put 'Cat Scratch Fever' on repeat this afternoon, and tonight we're watching Val Lewton's *Cat People*."

"I think maybe when this is over you should get your own cat."

Another call beeped through. I pulled the phone away from my head and checked the display. It was Nick. I hadn't called him back after his "if you want to" message. I wanted to, no doubt about that, but I was afraid to pull him into this. I let the call go to voicemail and felt marginally guilty.

I said goodbye to Eddie and left my driveway. Traffic was lunch-hour heavy, and it was hard to tell if it was my imagination or an actual fact that someone had followed me. I drove to the strip mall where Nick's studio was located and cruised past but didn't stop. I spent five minutes in an automatic car wash at the corner of the parking lot, and then patronized the Dairy Queen drive-thru and treated myself to a vanilla shake. If Pritchard was following me, he'd see me doing all the things I usually did. I wanted him to believe nothing had changed.

I drove with my milkshake to the parking lot in front of *Retrofit*, finished the shake, and then got out and pretended to fuss with something in my trunk. After about a minute, I shut the trunk and headed for the entrance, as much for appearances' sake as for my personal agenda.

The front doors were locked. I let myself in and went to my cubicle. It looked just like it had yesterday. No daggers in the middle of my desk. No threatening messages written on my cabinets. My laptop docking station sat empty like I'd left it. But there was an eerie sense of quiet in the building. I set my handbag down on my desk chair and went down the hallway to Nancie's office. The portable wall dividers were slightly crooked, but that wasn't what alerted me that something was wrong. It wasn't until I reached her doorway that I understood what caused my sense of alarm.

Unlike my office, that appeared to be in much the same state that I'd left it in, Nancie's was the opposite. It was empty.

File cabinets had been yanked open, their drawers cleared of information. Closet doors hung wide, showcasing bare shelves. The laptop, docking station, mouse pad, and wireless keyboard, all gone. Even the wastepaper basket had been cleaned out.

I left Nancie's office and checked the boardroom, the coffee corner, and the supply closet. By the time I came to Pritchard's cubicle, I wasn't surprised. It was empty, just like everything else.

Retrofit had left the building.

12

BE INVISIBLE ALL THE TIME

I RETURNED TO NANCIE'S OFFICE AND DOUBLE-CHECKED THE cabinets. All signs that this office had recently been in use were gone. Even the carpet had been vacuumed. What had caused her to leave? My note? Or something more ominous? Had she been threatened, too? Or had she befallen an even worse fate than threats?

Or maybe it hadn't been fear that chased Nancie out of the office but a need to disappear.

Four months of working with Nancie had put her outside the scope of my suspicions, but she could have been the one on the other end of Pritchard's phone call. I'd seen her level of dedication when it came to the success of *Retrofit*, and I'd experienced her relentless drive in the face of the challenges of growth. Another person might have been happy with our accomplishments in such a limited time. But Nancie wanted more. The idea of the magalog had come from left field.

She'd been gung-ho about Pritchard and had cautioned me to stay put in the office while he did his thing in the field. Maybe they were working together. I'd bought into Nancie's passion about *Retrofit* when I first came to work with her and I didn't want to believe she had a hidden agenda, but to ignore the possibility in light of the ransacked office and the theft at Jennie Mae's house felt obtuse.

I backed out of the office slowly. When I'd entered, I hadn't paid much attention to the cleared-out desks that the interns used. They'd been taught to clear them each night, and the revolving door of unpaid help kept anybody from making their space overly personal. In fact, I remember Nancie instructing a few of the college students to respect the fact that the desk was theirs for the time that they occupied it.

But someone had gutted us of our files. Who? And why had they left my cubicle untouched? If it meant something, I didn't know what. Except that whoever had cleared out the *Retrofit* offices had gotten away with everything—everything but the bible I took when Tahoma was here. Aside from my office, the interior was as empty as Jennie Mae Tome's attic. Whoever was responsible had expected me to come back and find it like this.

They'd been watching me.

They were probably watching me right now.

All instinct to make myself visible vanished. I grabbed my handbag from my office and ran out the front door. I left rubber tire tracks in the parking lot in my haste to get out of there.

New plan: be invisible all the time.

I pulled the car into my garage and slammed the door down behind it. I found a half-empty can of spray paint on the work bench and sprayed it over the glass panes of the mechanical garage door, blacking them out from the inside. My hands shook, and the paint splattered on the inside of the door, leaving graffiti-like fuzz and, where I'd had a heavy hand, drips that looked like thick, black tears. The chemicals caused my eyes to sting and water, mimicking the paint that ran down the inside of the door.

I went inside the house. Minus one pudgy black cat, the whole of it felt too big, too empty, too much. I pulled the living room curtains shut and clipped them closed with binder clips. I followed with the drapes in the kitchen and the blinds by the back door. As I made my way upstairs, I peeled off the crocheted hat, the vest, the cream-colored sweater, and the rust suede maxi skirt, leaving them in a trail to the bedroom. I tore the tags off the navy poly-blend sweatshirt and pants, put on the baseball hat, pulled my hair through the loop in the back and tied on a pair of Converse sneakers. I put my wallet, phone, lipstick, keys, and laptop into a Tradava shopping bag and left.

This morning, I'd wanted to be seen. Samantha Kidd, fashionista, girl about town. Now, I wanted to go unnoticed. I was dressed like a bag lady, and I knew there was one place where I could work without interruption, one place where nobody would think twice about my appearance. I drove the dead taxi to the library.

On my way there, my cell phone rang. Another call from Nick. I was still shaking from the encounter at *Retrofit*, and despite my efforts to keep him out of danger, I wanted to hear his voice. I answered the call and put it on speaker while I drove.

"Nick, hi. Sorry I haven't called you back. Work's been busy."

"You're working?"

"Yes. Nancie has me buried in the Seventies. You wouldn't believe what I've learned. Did you know a blue leisure suit with white belt and shoes was called a Full Cleveland?"

"Did I see your car at the Dairy Queen earlier today?"

"You did. I needed a quick pick-me-up. Sorry I didn't come to your store to say hello, but like I said, she's got me working around the clock. I know you said something about us getting together, but I don't think you should count on seeing me for a while."

He was quiet for a moment. "Is this about my dad?" he finally asked.

"Your dad?" I repeated. "No." Did Nick think I was superficial enough that I couldn't handle him moving in with his dad while his dad recovered? Could I live with him thinking that if it helped protect him? It was a small price to pay. "I mean, not really. It's going to take me a little time to adjust, that's all. You two should spend time together, get to know each other." I took a quick hard left to throw off anybody who might be following me and then swerved into the next lane. A car horn beeped, and my phone slid from my thigh to the floor mat of the passenger side.

Nick's voice came out tinny and far away. "Kidd, he's my dad. I already know him. And if his accident taught me anything, it's that life is short. I don't want to waste any more time. I want to start reacquainting myself with *you*."

I wanted it too, but I couldn't risk his safety. I leaned toward the phone and raised my voice so it would carry. "I'm sorry, Nick. I'm on my way to the library to research some stuff for work. If I finish up early, I'll call you, but I think it's going to be a long night." The light in front of me turned yellow, and I slowed and then stopped. I ducked down and swatted at my phone until my fingertips connected. I pulled the phone closer until I was able to pick it up and put it in the cup holder. The light changed, and I pulled forward. "Hello?" I said. "Are you still there?"

It had taken Nick and me months of repair work to make up for the hurt over our break-up. Hours of phone conversations where we said nothing but communicated everything. Gradually, the pain had faded. And now here I was, willingly making myself look bad. Distancing myself from what could be.

Reason #7: Snooping on your coworkers can lead to complications in your love life.

Except that a very small part of me wondered why Nick was pushing for this now? The last few months had been sweet. Between his business and his father, his hands had been full. The last thing I would have thought he'd want was to ratchet up the romance factor between us.

"Don't work too hard," he said in a strained voice. "Call me if you finish early."

I tried to think of something to say. A few seconds passed, and the screen indicated that the call had dropped. I punched the steering wheel, and the horn sounded. The driver in front of me rolled down his window and gave me the finger. I hollered back at him even though he'd done nothing wrong.

Good times.

I arrived at the library and circled the block three times until a parking space opened up. I ignored every impulse that told me to call Nick back and do damage control and forced myself to go inside. The sooner I figured out what Pritchard was up to, the sooner everything could get back to normal.

Even though the library offered relative safety, I still looked to my left and right before approaching the front desk. I felt watched, vulnerable. The librarian barely looked up at me. "I'd like to reserve a computer," I said. I handed her my library card. "Preferably one in the back."

She punched a few buttons on the keyboard. "Second floor, by the restroom. Here's your password. There's a one-hour time limit. If you want more time, come back to me and we'll do this all over again."

My cell phone made a noise for an incoming text. She looked at it. "No cell phones allowed. Turn it off or you'll have to leave."

"Yes, ma'am," I said. I switched the ringer to silent and headed to my temporary office.

It took a few minutes to figure out the library's search system and access the online databases that cross-referenced articles from newspapers and magazines. In the past I'd had to locate issues of magazines and find them on the library archives. Since then, most periodicals had been digitized and I could find what I needed from the relative comfort of the plastic library chair. No wonder they enforced a one-hour limit.

The first person I looked up was Jennie Mae Tome. She and her walk-in closet seemed to fit all too well with the project at *Retrofit*. She was as good a place to start my research as any.

I pulled my small white lined notepad and Pritchard's pen out and scrolled through mentions in *Vogue, Harper's Bazaar,* and *Glamour,* pausing periodically to take notes.

Jennie Mae Tome was a wealthy retiree who had taken up residence in Ribbon, Pennsylvania after leaving the fashion industry in the early part of the millennium. As a teen, she'd gotten her start as a model, but that wasn't to become her career or her legacy. She'd been quick to spot ill-fitting garments on the other models before catalog shoots or runway shows and learned to make alterations with whatever was handy: tape, band-aids, bobby pins, and ultimately her makeshift sewing kit. When one designer spotted her lowering the hem of a miniskirt, he fired her. There'd been no time to undo her alteration before the show, though, and the mini—now a midi—had walked the runway of the local ladies' country club spring fashion show. The audience, delighted at the notion that there was an option for women whose knees appeared older than their well-cared-for faces and youthful wardrobes, placed orders for the skirt that broke records. The designer spent the next two days tracking down Jennie Mae Tome from the contact information on file with the modeling agency that employed her. It would have taken less time if Jennie Mae hadn't lied about her age or her address.

Jennie Mae quickly went from minor alterations to being asked for her opinion on new designs. Not one to conceive of clothes from scratch, she found it easier to tweak existing patterns than come up with entirely new ideas. She made samples of shirts with exaggerated sleeve fullness, culottes with wider legs, and skirts that dropped to the floor. Her suggested tweaks to existing designs contributed to the success of many collections. While the designers received the recognition and the sales, Jennie Mae received their sample collections. Which, instead of wearing like they'd hoped, she'd tucked away in storage.

Until now.

I stopped reading. Jennie Mae's vast wardrobe hadn't been curated by her personal sense of style. They'd been gifted to her, direct from the designers she had worked for. The value of those clothes, having been stored sight unseen, some for upwards of forty years, was incomprehensible. And until a few days ago, they'd been housed in the attic of her house in Amity.

My pen flew over the paper as I jotted the important details into my notepad and leaned back in the chair, thinking about what it meant. Jennie Mae hadn't worked exclusively for one designer. She'd been ahead of her time. She'd touched many collections. She'd left her mark. Her eye for proportion and detail had changed the way American women dressed. And almost nobody knew her name.

But for every bit of information I found about Jennie Mae the model and the influencer of trends, I came up short on mentions of her personal life.

Mere days ago, Nancie had spoken passionately about *Retrofit*'s first print magazine. Considering both she and Pritchard were MIA, it didn't seem likely to happen. But if it did happen, if the photos of clothing from Jennie Mae's archives became public, all of that would change. Jennie Mae would go from being a wealthy recluse to a cult figure. Was that a good thing? She must have thought it was. Everything that had happened had started after she gave Nancie the green light to use her clothes in our premiere issue.

Unless she hadn't granted permission at all. She herself had told me that her butler ran her estate. It was very possible that he was the one who had been dealing with everyone and she'd been left out of the decision.

I wondered, where was Mr. Charles on the day I showed up alone? Had he, too, seen me enter the attic or leave via the window? Had Loncar spoken to him yet?

Lost in my research, I didn't notice the passing of time until my phone alarm indicated that the one-hour time limit on the reserved computer was about to run out. The computer clock said it was quarter to seven. Even if I renewed the hold on the computer, I'd eventually have to decide where I was going next. It was getting late. I didn't want to drive the streets of Ribbon in the dark in a dead taxi with nowhere to go. The one thing I knew was that I wanted to go someplace I'd feel safe. And short of sleeping in the dead taxi in front of the police station, I didn't know where that safe place would be.

Except that there was one place...

I closed out the article I'd been reading and pulled up the website for the Motel 6. Minutes later I'd reserved a room through their online portal. I was about to check into a motel with nothing but the clothes on my back, which felt safer than going home. I'd reached a new low days before my birthday.

THE MOTEL 6 was marginally less welcoming at night. Approximately the same number of cars filled the lot as earlier today but now they occupied spaces under the various street lamps. I pulled the dead taxi into a space by the front office and went inside to check in. The front desk clerk did not comment on my lack of overnight belongings. He handed me the key to room 137 and told me it was next to the ice machine (and that I couldn't miss it). I found the gift shop (a corner of the lobby) and purchased a toothbrush, toothpaste, and a new sweatshirt that said *I Got Tied Up In Ribbon!* across the chest in fuzzy white letters.

I left the office and sought my room. The desk clerk had been right about the ice machine. The unit was set off by a glowing blue sign with ICE spelled out in eighteen-inch-tall letters. I bet you could see it from the street. The machine made an erratic electric buzzing sound. *Bzzzt. Bzzzt. Clunk. Bzzzzzzzt.* I unlocked my door and was about to enter when somebody grabbed me from behind.

13

SPENDING THE NIGHT TOGETHER

"What's going on, Kidd?" Nick asked. "Checking into a seedy motel without bags?"

He looked angry. And suspicious. And angry. My heart pounded against my rib cage while I tried to figure out the smartest way to handle him. "How did you find me?" I asked.

"You said you were going to be at the library. That it was going to be a late night. I wanted to surprise you."

"Surprise me how? I told you I was working."

"I was going to smuggle you a coffee and give you a thirty-second shoulder massage." Aw, that was sweet. My shoulders *were* a little tight. "But when you left, I thought you were headed to my apartment. I followed you—until I saw you pull in here. A motel, Kidd?" A car pulled into the lot, and Nick turned as if expecting to see a familiar face. A family of four got out and went into the lobby.

"It's not what you think," I said.

"Are you sure? Because I think you lied to me. You said you were working all night. You're driving around in a beat-up taxi, and now you're at a motel—"

"Okay, it is what you think. Mostly. But I can explain."

"I don't want excuses, Kidd. This—you and me—I thought we had a chance this time. But it's never going to work if I'm the only one who wants it." His voice rose steadily. His usually soft and comforting baritone voice was sharp, cutting through the otherwise quiet night.

"Nick, keep your voice down. People are going to notice."

He ignored me. "I'm dealing with my father at home—do you know what it's like to live with your father when you're an adult? It's crazy. I caught him binge-watching *Keeping up with the Kardashians* today."

"Shhhh!" I said. I grabbed at his hand, and he shook me off.

"I told him to get out of the house. I told my father to get out of the house. Because I wanted—no, I needed—one night to myself. For us. And you *lied* to me. And now I find you checking into a motel? Who is he, Kidd? That biker from Philly? I hope for your sake he's worth it."

The door to the room next to mine opened, and Detective Loncar came out. He was in a white crew-neck undershirt and jeans. White socks with yellow reinforced toes on his feet. His thinning hair stood up on one side, as if he'd been sleeping.

"What the hell is going on out here?" He looked at Nick.

Nick looked at me.

I looked at Nick and then at Detective Loncar. "I believe you two have already met," I said. I turned and led them into my motel room.

NICK SAT in the desk chair. Loncar brought a chair from his room into mine. I was the only one allowed on the bed. When we were all situated with plastic cups of ginger ale from the vending machine, I short-handed my explanation of events to the two of them as best as I could.

"Nick, I know you're mad, but I'm not sneaking around behind your back. I'm trying to protect everybody I know. I thought the best thing to do was to distance myself from you, at least until the detective and I figure out why Pritchard Smith is after me."

"Whoa," Loncar said. "We," he motioned back and forth between himself and me, "are not figuring out anything. You," he pointed at me, "are minding your own business."

"Minding my business is exactly how I got into this mess. I hardly think it's going to get me out of it. Besides, I start Citizen's Police Academy on Monday, so I'll be much more equipped to handle situations like this."

"About that," Loncar said, "I tore up your application." I inhaled sharply, ready to react. He held up his hand to keep me from talking. "That is not up for discussion. My job is to keep you safe. Not to help you graduate from the CPA. Letting you take that course would be bad judgment on my part."

"That's not fair."

"Life's not fair. You think I like sleeping in a motel while my wife and daughter coo over my granddaughter?"

Nick chimed in. "You think I like knowing my girlfriend would rather check into a motel than call me for help?"

I looked back and forth between their faces. "Do you think I like going out in public in sweatpants?" I asked.

Loncar stood up. "I'm not going to ask how you got the room next to mine or how you happen to be driving around in a retired taxi. What I am going to ask is that you don't leave the motel tonight. Got that?"

Before I could answer, Nick spoke up. "She's not going to leave the motel. I'll make sure of that."

"Just how do you plan to do that?" I asked, crossing my arms in front of me.

"We're spending the night together."

Loncar seemed to think that was his cue to leave. Funny, I would have figured him as the chaperone type.

Nine years working together. Nine years flirting with each other. Nine years of innuendo and then one year of foreplay. Sure, I'd dated other people during the time that I'd fantasized about Nick. But from that first day when I'd met him on a sludge-filled street in New York while he was unloading his truck of samples and I was out for my morning coffee, through the time we'd spent together at market (the week when buyers had appointments with designers to select their collections for the upcoming seasons), we both seemed to understand that there was a connection between us. That was a whole lot of anticipation to dump onto a blossoming relationship.

Maybe that's why we crashed and burned the first time. Never mind the slow courtship. The following year had been too much, too fast. Nick had bought back distribution of his shoe collection and was making a go of financing it himself. I'd been new to Ribbon, trying to reestablish myself in the town where I'd grown up. He'd spent six months in Milan working with his factories. I'd cycled through two jobs, three homicide investigations, brought down one knockoff ring, and saved his maybe-former-girlfriend from failure at the hands of an arsonist.

We'd both been busy.

But it wasn't just that. Since returning to Ribbon, I'd learned a lot about myself. The whole motivation for this move had been because I wasn't happy in my job—a job that most people would think was glamorous and enviable. I was seeking something, some satisfaction at the hands of my lifestyle strip-down and rebuild, and I still didn't know what it was. Deep, deep, deep down I was starting to fear that I was never going to be happy. That I was so busy looking for rush after rush after rush because it kept me from looking at the one thing I hadn't bothered to change since I'd given notice at Bentley's: myself.

I'd spent two years keeping myself busy with failed jobs and dangerous situations and living room rearrangements and closet cleaning that I hadn't stopped long enough to confront the important question: exactly what was it that I wanted?

The clock on the fake wood table next to the bed indicated that it was nine thirty. Until tomorrow morning, there was nothing to take my mind off the fact that Nick and I were alone in a hotel room. Not even a deck of cards.

"So, your dad is sitting in at your regular poker game?" I asked. I fished my toothpaste and toothbrush out of my bag and carried them to the bathroom. "I didn't know you played poker. What are the stakes? Maybe I should join."

"Kidd, I don't want to talk about my dad right now, and I don't want to talk about poker." He stood from the narrow chair and walked toward me.

"Okay. How's work? You're due for a trip to Milan soon, aren't you?"

He was right in front of me. I could smell his aftershave—Creed's Bois du Portugal, a heady mix of cedar and sandalwood. The heat from his body came off him in waves, reaching me even though there were inches between us. I held up my toothpaste in one hand and my toothbrush in the other. "You can use my toothpaste if you want, but I only bought one brush," I said quietly.

He put his hands on either side of my face. Slowly he leaned toward me, until his lips rested right above mine. I tipped my head up slightly. We kissed.

He didn't need toothpaste.

"Shhhh," he said when he pulled away. He put his finger on my lips to emphasize the point. "You're the most thoughtful person I've ever met. You're generous," he kissed me, "beautiful," he kissed me, "and sexy." He kissed me. "If you weren't a touch crazy, you'd be perfect."

"I'm not perfect," I whispered back.

"Oh, yeah? What's wrong with you?" His voice was barely audible. I leaned back against the bathroom sink for support. He put his hands on my hips, and his lips made a trail from my earlobe, to my cheek, down my neck.

"I have cellulite," I blurted.

He stood up and looked directly at me, the crinkles by his eyes deep with laugher. "It's going to take more than cellulite to scare me away this time," he said. His lips met mine again, and this time I felt it all the way to my toes.

We were interrupted by a knock on the door. Nick's hands tightened on my upper arms. "Shhhh," he said again, but this time it had a completely different tone.

"It's your neighbor," Loncar said through the door. "You guys want a pizza? I have leftovers."

Nick relaxed his grip and bent down, his forehead resting against mine. "You want his pizza, don't you?"

"I'm not going to turn it down," I said.

I stayed in the bathroom while Nick got the pizza from Loncar. The scent of his cologne was quickly replaced with tangy tomato, oregano, and pepperoni. No wonder Loncar's wife was trying to change his eating habits. They were practically the same as mine.

By the time the pizza was finished, I'd made a decision. "Nothing is going to happen tonight."

"That's why I'm staying here. To make sure you're safe," Nick said.

"That's not what I mean. We're in a motel room. Alone. We've never spent a night together before."

"You like to make up rules, don't you?"

"They're more like guidelines," I said.

"Okay, a guideline has been established. Nothing will happen tonight. But if you change your mind, nobody is going to judge us for giving in to temptation."

I closed my eyes, aware of his fingertips on my skin. Could I let go for one night? I opened my eyes. "Detective Loncar is on the other side of that wall. I'd rather not be preoccupied with him when we—if we—do that."

Nick looked at the wall between my room and Loncar's. "Good point. That leaves one question."

"What's that?"

"Which side of the bed do you want?"

We slept in our clothes. I woke to an infomercial for exercise equipment. Nick's arm was around me, and my face was pressed against the buttons on his shirt. Our legs were intertwined. We were both on his side of the bed.

He appeared to be sound asleep. This was going to be awkward.

What was I supposed to do? Extricate myself and pretend I'd stayed on my side of the bed? Or will myself to be still until he woke up and untangled himself from me? I felt a Charlie horse in my calf and moved my legs. He rolled toward me and put his other arm around me. "Mmmmm," he said, burying his face in my tangled hair. "I decided last night that I'm not a big fan of guidelines."

Okay, maybe it wasn't going to be awkward after all.

TWENTY MINUTES LATER, we were enjoying the complimentary breakfast buffet. Loncar came into the room, looked at us, and sat across the room. Maybe it was because he thought it best to keep his distance. Or because he saw me feed Nick a piece of bacon. You just never know with that one.

"So, I've been thinking," Nick said. He reached across the table and braided his fingers through mine. "Last night was...right?"

"Right," I said. "Except for the broken spring in the bed."

"I didn't notice it."

"It wasn't on your side."

He ran his thumb back and forth over mine. "It's going to be okay," he said. "You've had too many close calls since you've been back in Ribbon. I'm not going to let anything happen to you."

"I'm not going to let anything happen to you either," I said. The gravity of the situation hit me. Bacon or no bacon, this was it. This was real. I hadn't heard from Pritchard in days. Maybe he'd found what he was looking for and had forgotten all about me.

"I'm going to my apartment to shower and change," Nick said. "I'll bring my laptop back and work from here for the rest of the day. Do you want me to bring you anything?" he asked.

Even thought we'd spent the night together, I wasn't yet comfortable asking Nick to bring me clean underwear. "Nope, I'm fine," I said.

We left the lobby, and he walked me back to the room. I unlocked the door, but he didn't come in. "I'll be back in a couple of hours," he said.

Loncar came around the corner. I felt awkward, like my dad was watching the end of a date. I backed into the room.

"See you later," I said to Nick. I stepped all the way into my room and put the chain on the door.

Ten minutes later, Nick called. "Hi," I answered. "Sorry I acted funny. Loncar made me self-conscious."

"Kidd," he said. In one word, I knew something was wrong.

"Is everything okay?" The hair on my arms and neck stood up.

"Nothing's okay."

"Why? What happened?"

"It's what didn't happen. My dad never came back from the poker game last night."

14

———

UNPRECEDENTED

I forced myself to block the paranoid thoughts that fought for room in my imagination. "I'm sure it's fine. You said he took your seat at your poker game. Can you call the guys?"

"I left messages with everybody I know. This was a new group of players. They met at the bingo hall. Nobody shows up until after four," Nick said. I could hear the tension in his voice.

"What about his friends? Did any of them play?" My phone buzzed with an incoming call. I pulled the phone away from my head and looked at the display but didn't recognize the number. I put the phone back to my head. "Maybe he got up early and went out for breakfast."

"He didn't sleep in his bed," Nick said.

"Neither did you."

"This isn't funny."

"I didn't say it was funny. I'm just saying not to panic. Please, Nick, stay calm. There could be a logical explanation." Aside from the one I was thinking: that Pritchard was behind this. He wasn't done with me yet.

"I'll call you back," he said.

After he hung up, I dressed in the *I Got Tied Up In Ribbon!* sweatshirt and yesterday's sweatpants. My phone rang again, but by the time I found it, the caller had hung up. A few seconds later, the screen lit up, indicating a new message. I put it on speaker while I pulled my hair back into a tight ponytail. The voice was high and unnatural, as though the caller had been trying to mask their identity.

"You didn't play your cards right, Ess Kay. I wonder, was it worth the gamble?" The question was followed with laughter. It sounded fake, like the Joker in a Batman movie. But this was no joke. It had come from Pritchard Smith. And it meant one thing. He knew Nick had spent the night, and he'd taken that opportunity to kidnap Nick's dad.

I went outside and pounded on Loncar's door. He opened it seconds later. "They took Nick's dad," I said before he could tell me to go away.

Loncar grabbed my arm and pulled me inside. He slammed his door shut behind me and threw the dead bolt. "Tell me exactly what happened."

I cued up the message, put the phone on speaker, and played him the message. "Nick's dad went to a poker game last night. Playing my cards right. Did you hear that? And he asks if it was worth the gamble. Those are references to the poker game, see? He's making sure I know what he did. If Nick hadn't followed me here, his dad would be safe right now. But he isn't. He's in trouble and it's my fault!"

The tension that had been building from the first moment I'd heard Pritchard tell someone they had to keep what they were doing a secret snapped. *I* snapped. My voice cracked, and tears streamed down my face. It was my worst nightmare. I collapsed against Detective Loncar. He patted my back as I cried on his shoulder. He didn't say a word, just stood there while I bawled on his one decent suit jacket.

When my tears subsided, I pulled away. I looked at the bedspread. Loncar and I had gone head-to-head a few times. Crying on his shoulder in the same room where he'd slept was unprecedented, and I found it impossible to make eye contact.

"You stay here. In this room. Give me the keys to your house and your office. And the taxi. I want the keys to that retired taxi you've been driving. Until you hear from me, you are to go nowhere, you are to do nothing. You are not to answer the door after I leave. You are not to send up smoke signals or order takeout from the sandwich shop on the corner. Do you understand?"

"But I have to go home sometime."

"Not until I clear it."

"I have to check out."

"I'll check out for you."

"You're treating me like a child," I said.

"You're right. Until this case is solved, I'm going to treat you like a child. You wanted to be the daughter I never had, right? My daughter might not want to talk to me right now, so you're going to be her stand-in. You got that?"

"Yes."

"I am going to call you from your house. I trust you'll recognize the number?" He asked. I nodded. "Answer that call and that call only."

"But what about Nick? He needs to know about that message."

"I'll take care of Mr. Taylor. What did you leave in your room?"

"My backpack, my laptop, and my toothbrush."

He brought my belongings from my room into his and took my keys. "Lock the door behind me." And with that, he was gone.

Hotel rooms can get very boring very quickly. I showered, redressed, brushed my teeth, and blew dry my hair without benefit of a comb or a straightening iron. No makeup, no styling products, no nothing. My morning routine used up all of seven minutes.

When I came out of the bathroom, I checked my phone to see if I'd missed any calls. I hadn't. I checked my email. Nothing interesting. I spent the next two hours watching *Forensic Files*, pausing to order a case of Luminol on the internet. When I stopped to think what I might discover during Luminol spraying, I canceled my order and changed the channel to Hallmark. At least their mysteries came with a healthy dose of romance.

The rest of my afternoon went something like this:

12-2: Watched Hallmark Channel. Smiled at how well things went between Nick and me last night.

2:01: Picked up phone to call Nick.

2:01:30: Set down phone. No call made.

Aside from Loncar's instructions for me to stay put and not contact anybody, I didn't know what to say if Nick answered. He'd been here with me, trying to make sure I was safe, while a crazy person had kidnapped his dad. Because of me, his family unit was at risk. I didn't know if he'd forgive me if anything happened. If Nick had been asked, I didn't know if he'd think things between us had gone all that well.

Truth was, there were a lot of things I didn't know about Nick. I'd faked myself into believing that nine years as colleagues had shown me who he was, but they'd shown me one dimension of his personality. It was his charming side. I knew facts about him—his annual vacation in Hawaii, his penchant for martinis and Frank Sinatra music at the end of the day, and how he looked in a vintage tuxedo, but that was a façade. I'd never given him the opportunity to be vulnerable around me because I was the one who found trouble, not him. How did he react when the crisis in my life hit this close to home? Would he take it out on me by yelling or shutting down? Would he forgive me my involvement or hold it against me regardless of the outcome? Neither option was desirable.

During the past several months as we took things slow, I'd brushed the unresolved issues between us under the rug. I didn't bring up how he'd once given me an ultimatum. He didn't bring up —whatever it was that bothered him about me (if he had, I'd have an example). I thought about all the happy couples in the world, and how they seemed to make it work. Maybe not talking about problems was the secret.

2:16: Changed channel to *Gone Girl.*

4:00: Realized that maybe all those happy couples in the world are like the couple in that movie.

4:01: Clicked back to Hallmark.

4:27: Showered for second time. Came up with a plan to save Nick and potentially rescue his father. If Pritchard had kidnapped him to prove he could get to me through my circle, then Pritchard needed to think Nick and I were not together. Nick and I would have to stage a public fight.

4:55 (it was a long shower): Texted Nick. Debated the pros and cons of telling him my plan. Watched screen for two minutes straight waiting for response. Nothing.

4:57: Watched credits to Hallmark movie.

4:58: Ran background checks on Nancie Townsend and Tahoma Hunt.

5:37: (while waiting for report to show up in my inbox): Considered running background check on Nick.

5:37:30: Deleted partially filled-out form requesting background check on Nick and went back to third Hallmark Movie.

The reports on Nancie and Tahoma arrived in my inbox fifteen minutes later.

Aside from a fair portion of credit card debt and a problem with unpaid parking tickets, Nancie's background report seemed normal. She had seventeen different addresses attributed to her name, which seemed a bit odd, but sometimes it's hard to find the perfect place to live. She had no DUIs, no sex offenses, no liens against property (because she owned no property), and her credit score was slightly above average. Nothing that set off warning bells or internal alarms.

Tahoma Hunt was a different story.

15

RATIONALIZING

The first things I noticed were the felony convictions.
Tahoma Hunt might have a respectable title at Bethany House, but
from what I read, he was a repeat offender. The fourteen charges,
some multiple, ranged from property crime to larceny theft to
robbery and vandalism. Tahoma Hunt did not appear to be a very
good guy.

The second thing that hit me was his current address in Utah. It
shouldn't have meant anything. Lots of people chose to live in Utah.
But the two facts, coupled with his presence at *Retrofit* and the theft
at Jennie Mae's house, were too convenient. First Pritchard had a
fake ID from Utah, now I found that Tahoma lived there. What
could possibly be happening in Ribbon, PA to draw not one but two
men here from out of state?

I couldn't help but wonder how Nancie had met Tahoma. Had
he heard about our project and sought her out? Or had their
connection over the *Retrofit* project been a separate coincidence? I'd
learned a long time ago that one coincidence was just that; two was
a pattern. Now to find out what it meant.

BY NINE O'CLOCK, I was cleaner than I'd been in the past five years. I was also bored out of my mind and starved. Loncar hadn't called. Nick hadn't texted. And Hallmark had moved on to Christmas movies in May. Things were not looking up.

I rooted through my backpack, hoping for a candy bar or at least some mints but came up empty. What I did find, though, was Mohammad's business card. It featured a clear picture of him smiling for the camera, along with his cab license number, effective date, and phone number. Along the bottom was a separate number for the PA Department of Transportation and a website for the Licensed Cab Driver's Association.

If Mo was who he said he was, then he might be able to help me. But having run background checks on several people in the past few hours, it seemed prudent to be sure Mo was legit. Being well past the hours of nine and five, the first call to the PA Department of Transportation went unanswered. I returned to the computer and accessed LCDA.com, plugging Mo's name and license number into the required fields. After a minimal wait while the computer ran the info, his profile page popped up. It included the same photo, name, cab driver's license, and the valid to and from dates that were on his card. I clicked around the page looking for something to caution me against calling him, but his bright white smile looked just as cheerful on the page as it did in person. Maybe Mo was exactly who he said he was.

Detective Loncar had said something about smoke signals and ordering take-out, but technically he hadn't said I couldn't make calls from his room. (This isn't me being obtuse. It's me rationalizing that I was about to do something Loncar probably didn't want me to do.) I closed the internet window and called the number on Mo's card.

"Mo, this is Samantha Kidd."

"Miss Samantha. Is there a problem with the dead taxi?" he asked.

"No problem at all. It's been great. But I have a proposition for you."

"A proposition? I do not understand."

"An opportunity. I'm at the Motel 6 on Fairmont Avenue. I can't leave the hotel. Could you pick up a few things for me and deliver them? I'll pay you when you get here, and I'll pay your cab fare as if you were driving me around."

"This is an odd request," he said. "I usually charge when I have a passenger."

It didn't seem that odd to me, but something that he'd said gave me another idea, one that was far odder than the first. If we could create a decoy and make it look like Mo was driving me around, then I could come and go as I wanted.

"Miss Samantha?" he asked. "I am waiting for your shopping list."

"Change of plans," I said. "Let me call you back."

My next call was to Eddie. "Do you think I could borrow a mannequin? Not a whole one. Just a half? The top half. Dressed. Is that possible?"

"Dude, where are you? The doors to your office are locked and the *Retrofit* website hasn't been updated in two days. Did you relocate?"

"Not exactly. I'm—I can't tell you where I am. Top secret. It's connected to this project Nancie has me working on."

"You're still employed? That's good news."

"We'll see." About the employment or the news being good, I wasn't sure which. "But a mannequin. Do you have one I can borrow?"

"I have Torso Tess. She doesn't have a head or arms."

"No head? I need a head."

"Why do you want a mannequin?"

"You can't repeat this to anybody. Got that?"

"Dude, that's the basis of our entire friendship."

In five minutes of fast talking, I told Eddie that I was hiding out at a Motel 6 while Detective Loncar investigated the theft at the Tome house. I didn't mention the exact threat from Pritchard. I didn't have to.

"That's why you wanted me to watch Logan."

"How's he doing? Are—things—back to normal yet?"

"Hard to say what normal is. I feel like I clean that litter box three times a day. He does seem peppier."

I breathed a sigh of relief. "So, the mannequin?"

"I'll glue a Styrofoam wig head to her neck and stuff the sleeves of a sweater with tissue paper. That should work. Where do you want me to bring her?"

"I don't. I'm going to send a taxi to Tradava. Put her in the back of the taxi and send her off. The driver knows me. He'll bring her here and drop off a few things. Then we'll set her up in the back of his taxi so it looks like he picked me up and drove me away. If anybody is watching here or looking for me, they'll think she's me. I can go undercover, and nobody will know."

"Dude, she doesn't have legs."

"Just get the mannequin together. I'll work out the rest by the time Mo arrives."

I called Mo back and asked him to pick up a package from Tradava. I didn't tell him that it was a fake me. I had a feeling that would be lost in translation.

I checked the phone obsessively over the next hour and a half. The sun was down, and the motel, other than a few patrons here and there, was quiet. No word from Loncar or Nick.

At ten after ten, a bright-yellow taxi pulled into the parking lot.

I stood in the doorway to the hotel room and watched it snake past the rest of the parked cars and head in my direction. I went inside and grabbed the rust backpack. I scribbled a note to Loncar that I'd be back shortly (this was me directly going against police orders—I was fairly sure his warning to stay put was mostly to keep me out of his hair) and pulled the door shut behind me.

I got all the way to the bottom of the metal staircase before a spray of bullets let loose from the driver's side window.

16

A PLAN

It was too late to pretend I'd heeded Detective Loncar's advice. I dropped the backpack and ran toward the ice machine. My phone, wallet, and an assortment of lip glosses scattered into the parking lot. The shiny yellow taxi backed up, and then the tires squealed against the blacktop as the driver threw it into gear. Another taxi pulled into the lot, and I recognized Mohammed. I yanked the back door of the second taxi open and dove in.

"Drive!" I hollered.

I felt a bullet hit the side of the cab. It rocked with the impact. Mo swung the wheel, arced the vehicle in a one-hundred-eighty-degree turn, and left the lot twice as fast as he had entered. I hid behind the passenger seat. I didn't want to look up and see where we were going or acknowledge where we had been.

"Is he following us?" I finally asked.

"No, Miss Samantha. He is not with us. We are alone on the street."

I believed him, but I was afraid to move. Torso Tess was on the back seat, her Styrofoam eyes staring into mine. I tried to turn her away from me, and her head popped off. I set it on the seat next to her shoulder and pulled her jacket up over her stub of a neck.

"Miss Samantha, why would someone shoot at you?" Mo asked.

"It's a long story."

"Like *War and Peace?* That is a long story, too."

"No, not quite like that. Mo, I think you should take me to the police station."

"You have already been to the police station once, have you not?"

"Yes," I said. I'd gone to the police. I'd told Detective Loncar everything I knew. He said he was going to protect me. And then I'd been shot at in the one place where Loncar claimed I'd be safe.

"You are trying to avoid someone," Mo said. "I have an idea."

"But your new taxi was shot."

"I do not worry about my taxi. I have insurance."

I felt Mo accelerate through the streets of downtown Ribbon, turning here and there, stopping at the occasional traffic light. I didn't know where we were going. I watched through the back passenger windows and saw the facades of row homes pass by. It took me awhile to realize we were headed to the west side of town.

RIBBON AS A TOWN had pockets of suburbs that accommodated our different residents. There was the wealthy section, filled with Victorian houses, where old money lived. There was the factory district that had been converted into loft apartments, attracting urban hipsters and creative types. There were the residential suburbs like where I lived. And then there was West Ribbon, the melting pot of ethnicities.

I hadn't spent much time in West Ribbon as a child, largely because my friends lived in the same school district as I did. My interaction to other kids was limited to track meets and the occasional run-ins at the mall, but mostly, we stuck to ourselves. I hadn't thought much about where someone like Mohammed would live, but it made sense that he would live here.

He parked his taxi between two freshly washed minivans and turned off the engine. "Miss Samantha, I hope you don't mind, I bring you to my house where I live with my sister. It is safe here."

"Thank you, Mohammed, but I can't put you or your sister at risk."

"Miss Samantha, I think we can help you. Please come inside."

I had little choice but to acquiesce. Every contact I had with the outside world was scattered in that parking lot of the Motel 6. Mohammed was my lifeline.

The front foyer of his house was warm and inviting. The walls were painted soft powder blue. A wooden table sat under a painting of women weaving bowls out of straw. On the table was a similar bowl filled with potpourri. An oven door opened and closed, and soon a spicy scent filled the air.

"My sister is cooking," Mo said. "Are you hungry?"

"It's awfully late for dinner, isn't it?"

He laughed. "She is not making dinner. She is making crackling bread for tomorrow."

The air smelled great, but I didn't think I could eat. Not after having bullets fired at me. "Mo, may I use your phone?" I asked. "I need to make a couple of calls."

He held out his cell phone. "I will give you privacy." He left me alone and went to the kitchen.

I called the police station and left a message for Detective Loncar. "Tell him Samantha Kidd called. I'm okay, but I need to talk to him about the shooting at the motel. This isn't my phone. I'll call him tomorrow." I hung up. I hesitated for a few seconds before calling Nick. His was the one phone number I had committed to memory. He didn't answer. "It's Samantha," I said. "I'm checking in to see if you heard from your dad. I lost my phone so don't try to call me back. I'll call you tomorrow." I held the phone for a few additional seconds and then hung up.

A pretty, dark-skinned woman with bright green eyes and high cheekbones came out of the kitchen. She wore a loose tunic and baggy pants both cut from a batik-printed cotton fabric. "Hi'ya," she said. "I'm Keisha."

I held out my hand. "I'm Samantha." She wiped her hands on her apron and then shook mine. "You have a lovely home," I said.

Mo responded. "My sister is a hairdresser but cannot find work because she doesn't know English as well as I do. But she is good. She can help you," he said again.

"You said that before. I don't want to be any more trouble than I already have."

"You are not trouble," he said. He turned to Keisha and said something in a language I didn't recognize. Her face lit up and she looked at me. She answered him and then clapped her hands together. She said something to me, but I didn't understand. I looked at Mo.

"I'm sorry, I don't know what she said."

"It is simple solution. She needs head and you have one. I tell her she can have your head."

I stepped away from them and held my hands out in protest. "Nobody can have my head," I said.

Mo looked worried. "Your head. In the back of the car. It came off the body that your friend placed into my taxi. Is that not what it is called? Head with hair? My sister needs to practice. Head in taxi —*the* head in *the* taxi—would be perfect for her to practice."

"The mannequin head," I said. Relief flooded me. "Yes. That head is available."

Keisha, who had been looking concerned while Mo and I

clarified exactly whose head she was getting, bent down and lifted a large plastic tub filled with scissors, combs, flat irons, and blow driers. She pulled a long, flat case out of the side of the box and opened it up on the table. It was filled with thick, glossy black hair. She looked at me and then waved her hand up and down next to her shiny hair.

"Make hair longer," she said.

"Extensions," I said. "That's what we call them."

She tipped her head and assessed me. "Diff'rent for you, ya?"

"It would be different."

"Would ya like ta try?"

In light of having been shot at mere hours ago, "different" seemed like a good idea.

***

THE ADRENALINE CRASH, coupled with the soothing sensation of Keisha's nimble fingers weaving the extensions onto my head, made me sleepy. Nobody knew where I was, and that felt safe. It also felt solitary. I'd pushed everybody away to protect them. In twenty-four hours, I'd gone from sharing a bed with Nick to hiding out at a stranger's house. I'd given my cat to my best friend. Pritchard didn't have to come after me with a loaded gun. The isolation would destroy me instead.

After Keisha finished, she wrapped my head in paper towels and led me to the sofa. Mo had put out fluffy pillows and sheets. I took off my sneakers and sat down. Keisha held the paper towels around my head as I reclined, until my head rested on the pillow.

"Thank you," she said. "Is good to practice on live head."

I squeezed her hand. Considering the bullets that had been fired at me, having a dead head wasn't that far outside of the realm of possibility.

THE NEXT MORNING, OVER CRACKLIN' bread and black coffee, Mo, Keisha, and I watched the news on a small portable set. A reporter stood in the Motel 6 parking lot describing the scene.

"Reports of an altercation in the parking lot were brought to the attention of the hotel manager. Motel guests claimed to see a woman throw a backpack at a taxi driver and then leave in a separate cab. Police have also found evidence of gunfire, but no one claims to have heard shots fired. Guests have been moved to another, unnamed motel while local police investigate."

Not only would Loncar have been tasked to investigate the shooting, he'd be out of a place to stay. I needed to let him know what had happened. Except, aside from the gunfire, I didn't know what had happened.

I finished my breakfast in silence. There'd been no mention of finding my phone or my wallet. Was Pritchard the person who had shot at me? He had to be. Had he taken my things after I left? Did it matter? He knew I was staying at the motel. He had arrived in a taxi. He had known about my arrangements and that the person I trusted was a person driving a yellow cab.

And when he called this morning, he'd made not one but two references to the poker game where Nick's dad had supposedly been last night.

How had he known? The room must have been bugged. No—that wasn't likely. I'd been in Detective Loncar's room, and there was no way anybody could have known that we traded. The bug must have been on me the whole time.

I'd been so careful to change my appearance, to drive a different car, and to try to fake him out. I'd even been carrying around a backpack instead of a handbag. And the things I'd put into that bag were my wallet, my phone, my lipstick, and my pen.

The retractable pen that Pritchard gave me the night he'd first been at *Retrofit*.

I hated that pen.

On the bright side, the pen was now in one of three places: the shooter's possession, with the police, or in the Motel 6 parking lot. I didn't care which of those options was the right one. The thing I cared about was that the pen was no longer with me.

"Miss Samantha, I will take today off and drive you wherever you would like to go," Mo said while Keisha cleared the dishes.

"No," I said. "I appreciate all you've done. Both of you. But I can't involve you in this any further. Take care of your sister. Maybe you should go away for a few days. I'm going to be okay."

"This does not seem like a very good idea," he said. "You are unprepared for danger."

"Not for long. I have a plan."

THE RIDE I accepted from Mo was to a small shop that I'd passed about a hundred times and never paid attention to until now. It was between a used record store and a dry cleaner and had a wooden sign out front that simply said, "Spy Store." I thanked Mo profusely, brushed my new waist-length fake hair over my shoulder, and went inside.

The interior of the spy store was brighter than I'd expected. Rows of glass cases lined the perimeter, with room enough behind them for the salesman. He was dressed in a suit jacket over a T-shirt and jeans. His hair looked like a toupee, but considering I was about twelve hours into having thirty-inch-long extensions, I was less critical of his choice than I might have been otherwise.

He looked up at me and nodded his hello. "If you need something, let me know."

I scanned the case of merchandise in front of him and spotted an assortment of pens that looked just like the one from Pritchard's desk.

"I need something," I said.

He put down the magnifying glass and pushed his glasses further up the bridge of his nose.

"I need a couple somethings. There's one problem. I don't have my wallet or credit card. Maybe we can work something out?"

"Lady, this isn't that kind of a store."

I blushed. "That's not what I meant. Do you take internet orders?"

"All the time."

"If you had an order paid by credit card, you'd fulfill it, right?"

"Sure."

"What if the customer wanted to come in and pick it up in person? Would you do that?"

"Yeah."

"Okay. I know my credit card number by heart. If you let me use your computer, I'll place an internet order so you get paid, and then you can give me the stuff."

He looked skeptical. "This is a store that sells spy stuff. There are a lot of people who want to see me shut down. I can't take a chance that you're not who you say you are." He stood up and crossed his arms over his chest. "Who did you say you were?"

"Samantha Kidd." I leaned in and dropped my voice, hoping to play to his conspiratorial side. "I was shot at in the parking lot of the Motel 6 by Fairmont Avenue. You probably heard about it on the news, right?"

His expression, body language, entire demeanor changed. "Yeah, I heard about it."

"The guy who shot at me knew exactly where to find me. I think he had a bug planted on me. I think it was a pen. It looked like that one," I said, tapping the glass above the display of pens. "I'm going to need one of them. And some pepper spray. And a lock-picking tool. Do you have a lock-picking tool?"

By the time I left the spy store, I'd not only convinced the spy shop employee that I was who I said I was, (funny, he managed to not say his name the whole time) but that I wasn't going to rely on the police to help me and that men should not wear short-sleeved shirts under suit jackets. He must have believed me because he let me use the store phone, which he assured me had an anti-tracking, anti-bugging device on it. I'm not going to lie. As soon as Loncar told me my house was safe for residence, I was going to install one of them.

I'd made two phone calls. The first to Detective Loncar's direct line. "It's Samantha Kidd," I said.

He cursed. "Are you okay? I've been trying to find you since we heard about those gunshots at the motel."

"I'm okay. I left before your team showed up. I have information for you, but I need something first."

"What?"

I paused. "A ride to my house."

"Contrary to popular belief, this isn't a taxi service."

"There's a sheet of paper in the trash can in my kitchen. It's folded into fourths. You can fish it out of the trash yourself if you want, but my cat threw up on it, so you might want to wear gloves. It's a copy of four ID cards that I found in Pritchard Smith's briefcase at *Retrofit* before all of this happened. And in case you're interested, I'm pretty sure he's the person who shot at me at the motel. From the driver's seat of a yellow taxi cab, which explains why I'm not all that excited about calling a cab to drive me around town or taking my car."

"What about Uber?"

"Today's not the day to start accepting rides from strangers."

I pictured him in an internal debate over the pros and cons of chauffeuring me around town. "Tell me what you remember about yesterday morning."

"I made arrangements with a taxi driver to come to the motel—"

"I told you to stay put."

"He's been cleared of suspicion," I said. I forgot that the detective disliked when I used phrases I'd picked up from the movies. "I checked him out. He's a cab driver. Licensed with the cab drivers association and everything. Want to check yourself?"

"No."

"I was going to have him drive around town with a mannequin in the back seat of his taxi to throw off the scent of my trail."

"If you had stayed in the motel room like I asked, there'd be no trail to follow."

"All I wanted was some clean underwear. Is that such a big deal?"

Loncar was silent for a few beats. "Walk me through your morning."

"I was waiting for the taxi. I saw headlights and looked out front. A yellow taxi pulled into the parking lot. The car swung around, and the driver fired at me. I dropped my backpack and ran. Make sure your team goes over the building well. The gun didn't make a very loud noise, but there were a bunch of shots fired. One of them hit Mohammad's taxi."

"Who's Mohammed?"

"The taxi driver I called. He showed up right after the first taxi. I dropped my phone and ID in the parking lot, so right now, I have nothing."

Loncar coughed and then cleared his throat. "I'm not getting an address on this number. Where are you calling from?"

"The spy store on Casey Street."

"I know the place. Keep an eye out for me. Guy who works there isn't going to like it if I have to come inside."

The second call was to Nick. He answered halfway through the first ring, like he'd been waiting for the phone to ring. "Have you heard from your father yet?" I asked.

"No."

Wrong answer. If this was Pritchard's move, then I had to outsmart him. I bit my lip. Tell Nick my plan or not? I couldn't risk tipping my hand and having him say no. If I was going to pick a public fight to distance myself from him and keep him safe, I was going to have to keep him in the dark. "Nick, I've been thinking about last night, and I think we should talk about what's going on between us. Meet me in the parking lot outside of *Tradava* in twenty minutes."

"Kidd, I'm a little preoccupied. Can't this wait?"

I took a deep breath and steeled myself. "There isn't going to be a better time, Nick. We need to talk. Today."

17

VALUED IN THE MILLIONS

True to his word, Detective Loncar pulled up in front of the spy store not long after I'd called him. He didn't ask about the bag I carried, and I didn't volunteer information about its contents. Loncar navigated lefts and rights through West Ribbon until he turned onto my street. Soon enough, he pulled into my driveway.

"Can I have my keys?" I asked.

His expression changed. "They're in my desk drawer."

"What are they doing there?"

"Keeping you from entering your house."

"You know, you should be nicer to me. From what I heard on the news, you're out of a hotel room, and I have a spare sofa."

My new lock-picking tools would come in handy, but that didn't seem like the sort of thing Loncar would abide. Plus, there was another way in. I hoisted my bag of spy gear out of his car and carried it around back.

I'd once read that seventy-five percent of people hid a key to their house within five feet of the door. There had been a time when that was true for me too, but it had been Nick and Eddie who hid the key, not me. I'd never gone in much for conformity, so the last time I locked myself out of the house, it had been a challenge figuring out how to break in.

I set the bag down by the back door and walked to the picnic table. "Grab an end," I said to Loncar.

"What for?"

"I need to get to the second-floor window. The screen is bent, and if I can pop it out of the frame, I can disengage the faulty latch and raise the window enough to climb in."

Loncar looked up at the window for a few seconds. "You didn't just come up with this plan, did you." It wasn't a question.

"It'll work. Trust me."

We carried the picnic table to under the window and then stacked the benches on top of each other on top of it. I was happy to be in sneakers and not heels. I climbed the stack of furniture, removed the screen, and tossed it to the ground. It landed a few feet from the detective. The wooden bench under my foot snapped in half, and I grabbed the window to keep from falling.

Hanging from the side of the building was no less terrifying today than earlier in the week.

"You okay up there?" Loncar asked from the ground.

"Peachy." I pushed off what remained of the bench and hoisted myself into the window. What I hadn't wanted to tell him was that the window led to my bathroom. A sloppy landing would put me right in the middle of the commode. I pulled myself through the opening, used one hand to shut the toilet seat, and then eased my way through until I was resting on the thick aqua rug. I flipped over and stared at the ceiling, breathing in and out, in and out. I was starting to believe my house was cursed.

The door to the bathroom opened. Loncar stood, upside down.

I rolled over to my stomach, got onto all fours, and then stood up. "How'd you get inside?" I asked.

He held up his own set of lock-picking tools. "In case of emergency," he said. "When that bench broke, I figured I had your permission to enter the premises."

<hr>

I GAVE Loncar the copies of Pritchard Smith's various IDs, and he left. I changed out of the *I Got Tied Up In Ribbon!* sweatshirt and into a rust-colored jog suit my mom had scored when I was a kid. The patch on the sleeve was embroidered with the slogan, "You've Come A Long Way, Baby!" in marigold thread. She hadn't been a smoker, but the offer of a free sweat suit emblazoned with a positive message had been too good to pass up. After collecting barcodes from the cigarette packages of all her friends, she obtained the knit ensemble, wore it exactly one time, and then packed it away in a box in the attic. I found an old pair of Reeboks in the back of my closet and laced them on. I tied a yellow-and-rust paisley scarf over my new waist-length hair and left.

For the first time since I'd been back in Ribbon, I made the hike from my house to Tradava by foot. It was less than a mile, and whether it was the cigarette company slogan stitched to my arm or the emotional journey I'd traveled in the past few days, I felt like I'd accomplished something significant in addition to burning off a handful of calories.

Nick's white pickup truck was already in the lot, most likely because I was forty minutes late. I stood by the front of Tradava next to a bench that had been bolted into the sidewalk. The parking lot and store entrance were busy with shoppers, people headed to a matinee at the movie theater, and the late-lunch crowd. To me, they were witnesses. Nick got out of his truck and came toward me. A stray shopping cart from the grocery store nearby rolled into his path. He stepped around it and met me by the front-facing display windows. His eyes flicked from my face to my sweat suit to my hair extensions and back to my face.

I stepped back and put my hand up. "Don't," I said.

"What?"

I launched into what I'd rehearsed in my head. "I can't do this, Nick." I waved my hand back and forth between us. "You want me to be somebody I'm not. We've been over this and over this too many times. It's not going to work. It's never going to work."

"Kidd, I never said I wanted you to be somebody else. I want you to be you." His eyes jumped to my unnaturally long hair again. "Who are you today?"

"I'm me. That's just it. You think you know me because you've seen some of my clothes. Well, you don't know me. You know some of me. You know the me that wears heels and dresses and menswear—"

He cut me off. "And you know some of me too. That's all. I know you could rattle off five things about me if you needed to, but how well do we know each other? That's the point of a relationship. We have to get past what's on the surface before we'll ever know anything of substance."

Was that true?

He was distracting me! I stood up straight. "I know everything I need to know about you, Nick. You'll never be able to commit to me the way you've committed to your company." I cast a glance at the people closest to us to see if they were watching. So far, we hadn't attracted much attention.

"Where is this coming from? You've never had a problem with my being a shoe designer before. And having a job doesn't mean I can't have a personal life, too."

"That's right." I raised my voice. "All of your traveling to Europe and back, spending time with models and rich Italian women. How am I ever supposed to trust you?"

My throat hitched, and my sight blurred with tears. I didn't want to do this. I didn't want to drive Nick away. I didn't want to alienate him; I wanted to ask about his dad and tell him about the shooting. I wanted to feel like part of a team instead of trying to do everything myself. Last night had been a huge step forward in terms of trust, but if I confided in him now, I could be risking his life. The tears spilled onto my cheeks and dripped onto the rust cotton sweatshirt. I couldn't say anything I wanted to say, but I could barely stand behind the words I'd rehearsed in the car.

People were staring at us. Among them was Eddie. He pulled away from the crowd in front of Tradava and advanced toward us, but then stopped. He was the only one who had an inkling about what had been going on with me, and I was afraid to look at him, afraid that I'd give in to the truth, confess the entire scene was fake.

Nick's face turned red. "How are you supposed to *trust* me? The same way I'm supposed to trust that you don't call Dante Lestes to keep you company while I'm gone for six months of the year."

"Dante? There's nothing between me and Dante. The last time I saw him was after I saved your ex-girlfriend's life!"

Whatever I'd hoped to accomplish had gone from pretend fight to a public airing of our issues. I'd been surprised when Nick mentioned Dante at the motel, and now here was the subject again. Was Nick really that jealous? Was I? Pent-up nerves from everything that had happened exploded in anger, and I was too far gone to rein myself in. "This is never going to work, Nick. We want different things."

He took a couple of steps back and turned away, but then turned back and faced me. "I know you're under a lot of stress, Kidd. I thought I knew you well enough—I thought I knew you.

But right now?" He glanced down at my sweat suit again. "I don't have a clue."

"Don't judge me. If I want to wear sweats in public, then I'm going to wear sweats in public."

I needed to make this look convincing. I turned around and walked away.

Nick didn't follow.

BEHIND TRADAVA WAS A FIELD. Around the back of the field was a trail. At the end of the trail was a stop sign. And four blocks past the stop sign was my house. It wasn't the route I'd taken to get to the department store, but I sought the cover of overgrown weeds while I got my emotions in check.

There were no cars—taxi or otherwise—in the driveway. I couldn't see in the garage because I'd blacked out the windows with spray paint, but I assumed that my car was still there. I grabbed a rock and threw it through a pane of glass. The rock landed on the hood of my car, leaving a dent.

Despite the challenges of having hair straight off the cover of Crystal Gayle's Greatest Hits, I moved quickly. I packed an overnight kit, grabbed fresh underwear, and snatched my spare set of car keys from the junk drawer in the kitchen. Five minutes after I'd broken in, I drove away. I trusted that Loncar would know what to do about the window.

Sooner or later I'd have to come up with a plan for where to spend the night. If I played my cards right, that problem would solve itself. I drove to where the drama had all started in the hopes of figuring something out. I headed to Jennie Mae Tome's house.

She didn't seem surprised to see me. "Ms. Kidd, please, come in.

Mr. Charles just prepared my afternoon tea. Would you care to join me?"

"I'd love to join you, but not for tea," I said, remembering the last cup of tea I'd had at her place. "Jennie, in the past week, I've been drugged, threatened, and shot at. The one job I've managed to hold on to since moving to Ribbon is gone, and the connecting thread to all my problems is the assignment from *Retrofit* and the collection of clothes that were in your attic. So, I'm curious. What can you tell me about them?"

She looked at the mug of tea in front of her, picked it up and raised it to her lips, but didn't drink. Moments later, she set it down and leaned back in her chair.

"You know a thing or two about fashion, don't you?" she asked. "Not about what the kids wear today, but the history of fashion. That's how you found the job at *Retrofit*."

"Yes," I said. "I read about your history with designers and their runway shows in the Seventies. I know that you were instrumental in changing the way women dressed and that the clothes in your attic were payment for your work backstage."

"Then it should come as no surprise to you to hear that those clothes are worth, shall we say, more than one might expect from a couple of trunks of old clothing."

"No, I don't suppose that it does."

"Mr. Charles convinced me that I wasn't getting any younger and that, to care for my cats, I should have the clothes appraised. I contacted Bethany House and an appointment was made. The executive director seemed to think my collection of samples would be valued in the millions. He said there were private collectors, designers, and museums that would be interested in buying should I ever want to sell."

"Did Mr. Charles tell this to Detective Loncar?" I asked.

"I don't suppose he would have thought it pertinent. The appointment never happened."

Interesting, I thought. Tahoma was the Bethany House executive director. Bethany House would have the contacts to sell off Jennie Mae's wardrobe and make a lot of money, and a dishonest director could have done it on the side.

"Why didn't you wear the clothes?" I asked. "I'm sure that's what most of the designers had hoped for when they gifted them to you."

She went quiet for a moment, seemingly distracted by memories, not all good. "I had the body and the face for fashion, but not the lifestyle. I grew up in a small town and married young. My husband ran off and left me with nothing. At the time that I was given many of those items, I would have gladly turned them down and taken money instead."

Jennie Mae lifted her china cup and sipped her tea. She rested the saucer on her lap, covered in a burgundy afghan with harvest-gold edging. The color palette was not dissimilar to my Virginia Slims jog suit. Behind her, a collection of frog ceramics covered the surface of her piano and a series of shelves on either side of the windows.

She moved the china cup from her lap to the tray. "A woman from *Retrofit* called me. She said they were doing an article on Seventies fashion and she had tracked me down."

"That was my boss, Nancie," I interjected.

She nodded. "She asked if I would be interested in a feature story, a spotlight about my contribution to the look of the Seventies. I am not one to sit around hoping for attention. My modeling days are behind me, but I find that old garments are far more interesting than old people. I politely suggested that to her and mentioned the samples in the attic. She said she was going to send someone to the house for an interview, and would I mind if she took a few photos of the clothes for reference?"

"She?" I asked.

"Yes. Nancie said she would send her fashion editor. I got the impression that that person would be a woman."

I kept my immediate thoughts to myself so as not to interrupt her. Jennie Mae might not be aware, but *I* was Nancie's fashion editor. If Nancie had been planning on sending me out to examine the clothes, when had Pritchard come into play? Or had that been a convenient line on Nancie's part to put Jennie Mae at ease? Someone was working with Pritchard. And I hadn't heard from Nancie for days. If she was involved and working with Pritchard, she wouldn't be overly concerned with accurate job titles and pronouns, especially if using them could gain her access to something valuable.

"Being interviewed about my archives was a way for me to relive my past," she continued. "Once the clothes were featured in *Retrofit*, their value would increase. Bethany House would be able to get far more for them than if they'd remained in my attic, and that would allow me to provide for my cats should anything happen to me."

But now that the clothes had been stolen before any official appraisal had taken place, their value was unknown. Besides that, what channels could someone go through to make money off the clothes? The theft was public knowledge. It was the kind of story that could go viral once word got out. I doubted the motivation behind the theft had to do with shortchanging Jennie Mae Tome's feline companions of their inheritance, but unless Pritchard had a contact list of black-market wardrobe collectors in the back pocket of his three-piece suit, I couldn't figure out his angle.

"Were you surprised when that person turned out to be a man?" I asked, even though I already knew the answer.

"Was it a man? I never met him. I was," she looked at her tea service, "napping at the time. I assumed we missed the appointment. The next day, the woman—your boss—called, very excited. She said the magazine wanted to move forward with a feature and asked if I would grant exclusive access to my wardrobe to use in the editorial. She was very persuasive. She said that the exposure would validate the worth of my collection. I mentioned it in passing to Mr. Charles, and he agreed that it was a good idea."

"What day was this?" I asked.

"This past Wednesday."

Otherwise known as hanging-off-a-building day. Heat climbed my face. "Then you never saw anyone from *Retrofit*?"

"No. Does that matter?"

"I don't know. Nancie never asked me to come to your house, so I assume she changed her mind and asked Pritchard Smith to view your clothes instead."

She dropped her teacup. The calico cat by her feet jumped up and ran away. The teacup landed on the Oriental rug, and the liquid disappeared into the thick pile. Jennie Mae reached for the empty cup, and her hands shook. She balled both fists up and buried them into the fabric of her skirt.

"What was his name?" she asked.

"Pritchard Smith. Do you know him? Do you recognize the name?"

"I wish that I didn't," she said. "Pritchard Smith was my husband."

18

YES, DAD

IF I'D BEEN HOLDING A CHINA TEACUP, I WOULD HAVE DROPPED IT too. "I don't understand," I asked. Pritchard Smith was twenty years younger than Jennie Mae. The ages didn't fit, but I already knew from the fake ID that "Pritchard Smith" probably wasn't my coworker's real name.

She gripped her hands hard enough that the skin on her fingers turned white. "I was barely legal," she said. "I was a small-town girl suddenly living a very big life. My parents died four days after my eighteenth birthday. Pritchard and I had grown up as neighbors. He was a few years older than I, but in a small town, you get to know most everybody. We married in a quiet ceremony."

"Did you have children?"

"No. My lifestyle was such that children didn't enter into the equation." She looked at the cats, and I immediately understood how she felt. They weren't pets to her; they were children.

"How long were the two of you married?"

"Officially, we still are. I was on the road working, and he couldn't take that. He left me before our first anniversary. It was months before I could acknowledge that he wasn't coming back. I threw myself into work. It was 1972. That's when I was the busiest. As long as I wasn't at home, I wouldn't know he wasn't there either."

"Did you ever hear from him again?"

"No," she said. She reached a hand up and dabbed the corners of her eyes. "I waited for him to return for a long time. But as the years went by, the memories faded, and I learned to accept that he wasn't coming back."

I held myself very still. The story Jennie Mae recounted to me was more than a story to her. It wasn't a collection of facts she'd learned from an episode of a TV show, it was her life. I wanted her to continue but had to separate my morbid curiosity from the human need to protect her from reliving painful memories.

I rested my hand on top of hers. "Jennie Mae, I'm so sorry to have brought this up. Is there anything I can get you?"

She squeezed my hand and looked at me. Her clear green eyes were shot through with red, belying the efforts she'd made not to cry. "You said the man who came here was named Pritchard Smith. Could it be my husband? Could he have tracked me down to Pennsylvania?"

"I don't think so," I said. I didn't want to offer conjecture. "I'm trying to understand how it all fits. Would you mind if I looked in your attic again?"

"There's nothing there," she said. "The trunks, the samples, the clothes. It's all gone."

"And you don't suspect Mr. Charles?"

She shook her head. "He was just as stunned by the theft as I was. He notified all of the auction houses to be on the lookout for any garments that might come to them via off-channels and has been spending his spare time combing the internet and news, hoping the thief will show his hand."

I didn't like how often the butler's name kept coming up in

relation to the clothes in the attic. It wasn't the first time I'd wondered if he and Pritchard were in cahoots. If he'd been involved in the theft, he could have given Pritchard access, helped move the merchandise off the property, and claimed to be managing the loss. He'd have the same motivation to watch the news for mention of the clothes if he were guilty as if he were innocent.

At that moment, Mr. Charles rounded the corner from the kitchen and noticed the teacup on the carpet. He picked it up and placed it on the tray, and then picked up the tray and carried it into the kitchen. How much had he heard?

"Does Mr. Charles live here with you?" I asked in a lower voice.

"He stays in the guest house out back. We learned a long time ago that we lost our compatibility when we tried to live under the same roof."

"Compatible? I thought he was your butler."

"How very *Sunset Boulevard*." She laughed a full, throaty laugh. "We met years after Pritchard left me, but a relationship was doomed because without answers about my past, I couldn't commit to a future. Do you have a gentleman friend?" she asked.

"Sort of." I thought of the words Nick and I had shouted at each other in the middle of the Tradava parking lot. Even though I knew I'd picked the fight to protect him, the things we'd said still hurt. They erased the memory of him kissing me last night and of waking up next to him on his side of the bed.

"How well do you know this man?" Jennie Mae asked.

"I've known him for over a decade."

"It's not about how *long* you've known him, it's about how *well* you know him. If you want the relationship to work, you're going to have to put yourself aside and learn about him. That's the only way you'll ever know if you're compatible."

I looked away from her. She'd pretty much hit the nail on the head. I'd mistaken time for intimacy. I'd tried to maintain control, with my guidelines and boundaries. Nick had allowed me to have a hand in his business once. He'd let me see the challenges he faced in reclaiming his label, and he'd even invited me over to meet his dad. But because I was so afraid of what he'd say when he got to know what was under my designer clothes, I hadn't dropped my guard and let him in.

"Samantha, I hate to be rude, but it's time for me to garden. If you have no other pressing questions, I'm going to ask Mr. Charles to escort you to your car."

"That won't be necessary," I said. I thanked her for visiting with me and left.

My visit with Jennie Mae had been brief but informational. I was eager to talk to Loncar, to find out what he thought about the value of her wardrobe and tell him about the connection between the name Pritchard Smith and her. I didn't know why the man Nancie had hired was using that name, but the fact that he was here now, and had been inside Jennie Mae's house, was creepy. Jennie Mae

Tome had been a target long before Nancie had told me about this project.

I drove back to my house. The dead taxi was parked in the driveway, and the broken glass pane on the garage door had been taped over. I braced myself for the inevitable confrontation and rang the doorbell. Loncar answered.

"You're not supposed to be here," he said.

"And you are?" I glanced at the empty beer bottle on the coffee table. "What do you think this is, a bed and breakfast?"

"Ms. Kidd, I've heard about your cooking skills, so no, I would hardly mistake this for a bed and breakfast," he said, emphasizing the last word. It would have been insulting if it wasn't so accurate. "Get inside." Once I was in the living room, he shut and locked the door.

"I was bugged," I said. "I had my wallet, my phone, a lipstick, and a pen that Pritchard gave me. It had to be the pen. Pritchard knew where I was, he knew who I'd talked to. There was no other way he could have known Nick spent the night at the Motel 6. Or that you and I swapped rooms. Or that I was driving the dead taxi. Do you see now?"

"Where's this pen?"

"My bag spilled in the parking lot of the motel. I lost everything. Did your team recover anything?" He shook his head. "If you don't have it, then either he has it or it rolled under somebody's car. Did you ask the hotel if they had security cameras? Or if anybody reported anything? Did your team find the slugs in the exterior wall?"

"My team has remained on top of the investigation."

"What about my message? Did you go through the trash? Did you find the copy of the ID cards?"

"Ms. Kidd, where did you find those IDs?"

"In Pritchard Smith's briefcase." I diverted my eyes. "I'm not proud of this, but there was something about him that I didn't trust from the beginning, and his briefcase was right there in the office, and it wasn't locked, so I looked. And I was right, right? Four different IDs from four different states. And just now I was at Jennie Mae's house, and she told me—"

"You went to the Tome house?"

"You're not listening to me! She told me Pritchard Smith was her husband. She thought he left her. But think about it, the guy I work with has a bunch of different identification, and one of them has that name on it. He shows up here. He must know about the clothes. He goes to her house. Mr. Charles handled the arrangements, and I bet my coworker used a different identity so Mr. Charles wouldn't be suspicious."

"Ms. Tome told you all of this?"

"Yes."

Loncar ran his hand over his hair. He looked around the living room and then faced me again. He pointed both index fingers at me like Isaac from the opening credits of *The Love Boat*. "I told you to stay out of this."

"With all due respect, I tried to stay out of it and Nick's dad got kidnapped. Do you have an update on that? Has anybody heard from him?"

"Not yet." He dropped his hands, balled them up into fists, and then released. If he'd been a cartoon character, smoke would have come out of his ears.

"Where are you staying tonight?" he asked.

"I thought I'd stay here."

"You're not staying here."

"Are you?"

"Yes."

"Maybe I could stay with your wife and daughter?" He stepped toward me, and I stepped back and held up both hands. "Maybe not."

"Wait here," Loncar said. He pulled his phone from a pocket on his belt and went into the kitchen. A few seconds later, he came back. "I need privacy. Go to your room."

"Yes, dad," I said. I climbed the stairs, went into my bedroom, and slammed the door behind me.

There was no reason at all why I shouldn't stay at my house. Pritchard didn't know I was there, and even if he did, I had a police detective there to guard me. It should have been the safest place I could be.

I wandered around the bedroom, getting reacquainted with my belongings. Hello, dresser. Hello, jewelry box. Hello, closet.

Hello, brown suede hobo bag that Logan had thrown up on.

The same brown suede hobo bag I'd had with me the day I jumped out of Jennie Mae Tome's window.

In the middle of everything else that had happened since that day, I'd forgotten all about that bag. If I didn't do something about the spot on the suede, the smell would never go away.

I opened the bag and pulled out my navy-blue fringed shawl. Under it was a silk scarf and a round object wrapped in several layers of antiqued white tissue. I must have picked it up when I grabbed my clothes. The object was light. I unwrapped the tissue, layer after layer after layer. Before I'd finished unwrapping it, I knew what it was. The blood flow to my appendages slowed, leaving my arms and legs tingly and numb. I set the object down and went to the kitchen to find Loncar.

"I thought I told you I needed privacy," he said.

"I thought you should know I just found a skull in my bedroom."

I don't remember a whole lot after that.

19

———

JUST FOLLOWING ORDERS

ACCORDING TO THE MEDICAL EXAMINER WHO STOOD NEXT TO THE four policemen who showed up after Loncar revived me and called his precinct—possibly not in that order—the skull had been wrapped up for a long time. And if I hadn't grabbed it when I went out the window, it might still be wrapped up in a trunk. For all we knew, it might never have been found.

I'd been operating under the belief that the theft was about the clothes. But what if it wasn't? The skull must have been in the attic all along. Maybe *that's* what Pritchard had been talking about when I overheard him approaching the attic.

Now I had a whole new hobo bag of theories. Jennie Mae told me her husband had left her. But what if he hadn't had the chance to leave her because he was dead? She could have murdered him and hid the body. I shivered with the thought and shook my hands as if they'd encountered a decomposing corpse. Or what about Mr. Charles? Maybe the skull was his dirty little secret and Jennie Mae's closet was the perfect place to keep it from becoming discovered?

Loncar oversaw the transportation of the skull down the stairs, into the back of an ambulance. I did not point out that the skull was already dead.

"Do you want to hear my theories?" I asked Loncar.

"No."

"But—"

"No."

"Fine. But when you're not paying attention, I'm going to raid the liquor cabinet and make out with boys!" I said.

"What?"

"Sorry. I think I had a flashback to high school."

"God bless your parents."

He went into the kitchen, and I followed. "Now that we know what's going on, it's okay for me to sleep here, right?"

"We don't know what's going on, and no, it's not okay for you to sleep here."

"Come on, it's obvious. Somebody has been looking for the skull."

He crossed his arms. "Then why go to the trouble of stealing the entirety of her collection? Why provide evidence of a crime instead of working under the cover of magazine editor? Why allow the skull to reside in her attic for forty years? Why come looking for it now?"

"You don't think we know what's going on."

"No, I don't."

"Okay, fine. Where am I supposed to go?"

"About that. I made arrangements."

"This is my house. I pay to live here. It should be safe now that you're here. You're the police, right? Do your job and keep me safe."

The dad/daughter dynamic was stressing me out, and from the look on Loncar's face, he wanted this situation over more than I did.

"I thought you'd like to know that we heard from Mr. Taylor this afternoon. Seems his poker game went late. He was on a winning streak and wasn't willing to leave."

"But Nick called his dad a whole bunch of times and he never answered."

"Said the tables were running hot and he didn't want any distractions."

"Then Nick's dad is safe?"

"That's what I said."

"Did you talk to him? Or to Nick. Did you talk to Nick?"

"I'm not a messaging service."

Loncar made it sound like it had all been a misunderstanding. Nick's dad had been invited to Nick's poker game, and he'd gone, probably because he and Nick had been getting on each other's nerves. But Nick Senior stayed out later than expected because he was on a winning streak. What if someone had arranged the invitation, gotten him out of the house, manipulated the winnings, all to send a message to me? It sounded too self-involved to be true. But as soon as I staged the parking lot fight with Nick and made it clear that we were through, his dad called home with a reasonable explanation.

I didn't buy for a second that it had been a misunderstanding. Pritchard was behind this. Just like he'd been behind everything all along. And I was the only one who saw through him.

So why didn't I feel good about things? Because Loncar still didn't want to hear me out. He still didn't believe me about Pritchard. All he wanted was for me to go away to some place where I couldn't be involved. I bet his "arrangement" didn't involve pretzels.

"Get whatever you need for the night. Your ride is going to be here in five minutes."

"Let me guess. You're having me picked up by an unmarked police car and taken to the county jail."

"You know something? That's the first good idea you've had."

I went upstairs and dug my passport out from under my assortment of fishnets. My Crystal Gayle hair kept getting tangled in the strap of my bag, so I braided it quickly and then wound it around and around my scalp and secured it with a scarf, the tails hanging down the back. I put on a brown-and-orange floral tunic and brown flare bottom jeans. The jeans were too long, so I adjusted with a pair of platform shoes with wooden soles that I'd bought in the Nineties the first time Seventies style had threatened to make a comeback. One of my mentors had once shared this charming philosophy: Fashion comes around three times, and then you die. I hoped this current assignment wasn't accelerating my schedule.

Out front, a car honked. I looked out the window. A gray sedan sat in my driveway. Everything about it, from the four antennas on the back to the red and blue lights nestled under the front grill, said Police Car. I'd been right.

I stuffed a few more things into my bag and went downstairs. Loncar stood by the front door. "You're going to thank me for this, Ms. Kidd."

"Yeah, right. The laundry is overflowing. Detergent is under the sink. Washer and dryer are in the basement. Knock yourself out."

I left the house and got into the back seat of the sedan. I recognized the officer in the passenger seat from the day I'd filled out the Citizen's Police Academy application. "Officer Callahan," I said. "Nice to see you again." I looked at the second officer. "Hi, I'm Samantha Kidd." I reached my hand over the back of the seat, and he shook it.

Callahan gave his partner a critical look, and the partner shrugged. "What?" he said. "She's being polite."

"This is silly. You know that, right? You don't want to drive me around any more than I want you to drive me around. There are actual criminals out there that need to be caught."

"We're just following orders, ma'am," said Callahan.

"Don't 'ma'am' me," I said. I sank back against the seat and crossed my arms.

"Buckle up. It's the law," said the driver.

I straightened up and fastened the seat belt. Callahan backed the car out of the driveway and headed the opposite direction of the highway. We got up the hill, past the street where the Fourth of July parade took place each year, toward the defunct Ribbon Railroad train tracks. A dark-blue car sat by the train tracks, blocking our way. "What's he doing?" I asked. "Honk your horn."

"Looks like car trouble," Callahan said. He put the car in park and got out. The officer in the passenger seat got out too. They approached the blue car.

This didn't seem right. We were on an empty road with no other people in sight. No way was this the way things were supposed to go down. I felt around inside my bag from the spy store until my fingers closed around the canister of pepper spray. I unbuckled my seat belt and got out of the car. "Hey," I yelled. "What's going on?"

The officers got into the blue sedan. It pulled past me and drove off. I'd been so intent on watching the cops get into the car and drive off that I hadn't noticed that I wasn't alone.

A tall man in a plaid shirt, jeans, mirrored sunglasses, and a Duck Dynasty amount of facial hair came out of the woods. He grabbed me. He threw me into the back seat of the unmarked police car, jumped into the front, and peeled out.

20

EXTRAS IN A LOW-BUDGET PORN MOVIE

I LANDED FACEDOWN ON THE BAG FROM THE SPY STORE. AS THE CAR accelerated, I unsheathed the pepper spray and aimed it at the side of his face. The spray stung my hands, and I squeezed my eyes shut.

The driver screamed. The car swerved as he reached up to cover his eyes. "Damn it, Kidd!"

Damn it, Kidd? I knew those words. I knew that tone. I knew the voice. "Nick?"

He pulled off the aviators and tossed them to the floor. I reached for the steering wheel from the back. We were the lone car on the road. Whatever orders the two officers had been given, they didn't include sticking around after the car swap had taken place. I didn't have time to think about what had just taken place. I was busy making sure we didn't crash.

The car veered from one side of the road to the other. I did what I could to even it out, but we were going too fast for me to steer from the back seat. About a quarter mile later, we hit an incline and the car slowed considerably. I yanked the steering wheel to the side, and we eventually came to a stop thanks to a cornfield. Nick grabbed a bottle of water from the center console, tipped his head back, and poured the water on his face. Water splashed onto my arm. I dropped back into the back seat and waited for him to say something. The silence was interminable.

Tentatively, I spoke. "Are you okay?"

He wiped his eyes. "You sprayed me with pepper spray. Since when do you carry pepper spray?"

"Since this morning. I didn't know it was you. Since when do you have a beard and mustache?"

"Since this afternoon." He peeled the beard off and scratched his chin. "It's a lot itchier than I expected." He set the beard on the seat next to him but left the mustache and sideburns on.

"Do you want to tell me what just happened?" I asked.

"I called Loncar after I heard from my dad. He asked about you, and I told him about our fight." He went silent. I knew he was thinking about what we'd said to each other. "You staged that fight, didn't you? You did it to make sure whoever had my dad saw you and I weren't together."

"It worked, didn't it?"

"Come up here," he said quietly.

I didn't climb over the seat. I got out of the back and moved to the passenger side. As soon as I sat down, he reached out for me and slid me across the seat. He took my face in his hands and crushed my lips with a hot, wet, open-mouth kiss that erased anything he'd said earlier that day. His lips were soft and gentle, and if it wasn't for the prickly fake mustache and the residue from the pepper spray, the kiss would have been perfect. I put my arms around his neck and twisted my torso until I was pressed up against him. I would have straddled him if the steering wheel wasn't in the way. My heart raced, and the adrenaline that I'd felt since the car handoff kicked back into gear.

"I'm not going to lecture you about the decisions you make ever again," he whispered. "That's a promise."

"I don't want you to make promises you can't keep."

"Kidd, you and my dad are the two most important people in my life. What you did brought him back to me."

"Loncar doesn't think the two things are related," I said.

"Loncar has been known to be wrong in the past."

If Nick had suggested we curl up in the Crown Victoria in the middle of the cornfield and spend the night there, I would have said yes. At that moment, him acknowledging all the times Loncar and I had gone head-to-head, when Nick suggested that I leave things to the police, when my interactions had led to captured criminals, I would have done just about anything to preserve the moment.

"Let's get out of here," he said.

Or, there was always Plan B.

Nick put the car in reverse. I buckled my seat belt on and rested my head against his shoulder. He backed through the cornfield until we found the road, and then turned around and headed back the way we'd came. I didn't know where he was taking me, and I didn't care. For whatever reason, being with Nick felt safe (even if he was dressed a little bit like Paul Bunyan) (or maybe that's why). If the sense of security was all an illusion, I didn't want to destroy it.

He turned right at Perkiomen Avenue and drove a couple of miles east, and then took a right at a small used-car lot. Two blocks later, he pulled into the parking lot of an apartment complex.

"Where are we?" I asked.

"My old apartment. It's mostly empty, but the lease isn't up until the end of the month. I've been slowly moving myself out."

He hadn't been kidding about the "mostly empty" part. The furniture was a dining room table and an inflatable air mattress on the floor. Partially packed boxes lined the walls. A fancy coffee maker sat in the kitchen. A pizza box from Brother's sat on the counter.

"I don't have any chairs," he said. He went to the oven and pulled out a pizza. Nestled into the cheese were small birthday candles. He looked at me and then at the pizza. "Do you even know what day today is?"

"It's my birthday," I said. I hadn't thought twice about it since hanging from the shutter. I was officially one year older.

Nick lit the candles with a lighter and then set the pizza on the middle of the dining room table. He climbed up and sat on one side. I sat on the other.

"Happy birthday, Samantha," he said. "Make a wish."

I wish life would be normal for one day, I thought to myself and blew out the candles. Then again, what was normal?

We ate our pizza off paper towels, keeping pace slice for slice until it was gone. That was one of the things I'd missed about Nick after we'd stopped working together. That we could share a pizza or a couple of hot dogs from a New York City street vendor just as easily as we could dine in a five-star restaurant. That he'd order a side of potato chips as an appetizer and then fight me for the last one. We might not have dated for those nine years, but I knew from how well we'd gotten along that we were a lot alike.

"Do you ever think about raising chickens?" I asked.

"No," he said. He gave me a funny look and was quiet for a moment. "But sometimes I think about giving up everything and becoming a carpenter."

"You do?"

He shrugged. "There are days when that seems simpler."

"That's how I feel about raising chickens."

"You do know that the people who raise chickens don't raise them as pets, don't you?"

"I hadn't thought it through that far."

I climbed off the table and stretched my arms directly up over my head, and then I tipped my head from one side to the other. "I need to unwind. Decompress."

"You can relax here. It's safe. Have a glass of wine and let your hair down."

My hair. I reached up and untied the scarf that I'd secured around my new hair. Then I unwound the hair and undid the braid. I shook my fingers through the long locks and then draped them over my shoulders like Lady Godiva. Nick's root-beer-barrel-colored eyes grew darker.

"You look like a different person with that hair," he said. His voice was husky.

I reached up and ran my finger across his mustache. "I could say the same thing about you."

"It's like we're us, but we're not us," he said.

"There's a risk that maybe we'll do something we wouldn't normally do because we don't feel like ourselves," I said.

"That's what I was thinking."

I slowly unbuttoned my tunic. The second button got caught in my hair. I unwound the strand of hair, grabbed the hem, and pulled it over my head. It took a while to get my hair through the neck hole. When I finished, I tossed the tunic onto the floor. I was in my bra. Nick put his arms around my waist and pulled me close. My body pressed against his chest. I wrapped my arms around his neck and stood on my tiptoes. He started to kiss me, and I pulled away.

"Do you have any music?"

"Music. Sure. There's a docking station on the floor next to my sax."

"Your sax? You play the sax?" I asked, surprised.

"I did. Still do every now and then. Not as often as I'd like."

I handed him the docking station, and he cued up a mix of Seventies soft jazz and turned to me.

"Where were we?" he asked. This time his hands were a little higher. I ran my fingers through his thick curly hair. The corner of one of his sideburns stuck to my thumb. I twisted my wrist to unstick it and then smoothed it back into place.

We kissed through at least two songs. I was aware of his hands on my skin, his fingers gently strumming against my spine, until—

"Ow!" I said. "You pulled my hair."

"Sorry. It got caught in my watch." I turned around, and he untangled my hair. When he was finished, he pulled me against him. He kissed the side of my neck. I saw our reflection in the glass of the painting on the wall. His hands moved from my stomach to my—

"Lights," I said. I stepped away from him and looked around for a switch. There was a round dimmer on the wall by the front door. I spun it—nope, still too bright—and then pushed it so the room was mostly dark. When I turned around, Nick was in his underwear.

"You wear boxers?" I asked.

"What did you think I wore?"

I felt myself go red. When I'd pictured Nick without his clothes, his choice of underwear hadn't been the thing I'd focused on. Bolstered by the darkness, I swept my long extensions off my shoulder. They got caught in the ficus tree. I turned toward the tree and bent my head down to free my hair. When I was done, I turned to Nick. He was back in his jeans. He held his plaid flannel shirt toward me.

"I don't want to do this with an alternate version of you," he said. "I can wait if you can."

I looked back at our reflection in the glass of the painting on the wall. His eyes were still bloodshot from the pepper spray, and the upper portion of his cheeks were a little swollen, both of which made him look slightly strung out. Together, we looked like extras in a low-budget porn movie. "Deal," I said. I slipped the flannel shirt on over my bra and quickly buttoned it up. "I do have to ask you a favor, though."

"What's that?"

"Will you give me a haircut before we go to sleep?"

THE NEXT MORNING, Nick got back into disguise. He'd bought more than one plaid flannel shirt, so I didn't have to give up the one I was wearing. He reattached the sideburns but left the mustache on the sink. "Something to remember me by," he said. He left a key on the counter next to a container of protein powder and left.

Nick drank protein powder?

Truth was, there was a lot more to distract myself with here at Nick's partially vacated apartment than there'd been at the Motel 6, but that didn't change the fact that I didn't like being cooped up. An hour of getting acclimated with the place (aka snooping) was enough to trigger feelings of guilt. Was this sax-playing, boxer-wearing, protein-powder-drinking man my boyfriend? And was he the same guy who had a thousand-piece puzzle of the Sistine chapel in a closet next to the entire collection of Stephanie Plum mysteries? Signed?

When did Nick have the time to get Janet Evanovich to sign twenty-some books? Did he read them? Were they personalized?

The answer to the last question was yes. At least, the three that I pulled off the shelf were.

But just like last night, I knew I didn't want to get to know Nick because I'd gotten acclimated with his stuff. I stopped snooping (after I found his high school yearbook and read a few of the entries inside) and checked my email.

Whoa, Nellie.

Four days away from the internet plus two forwarded email accounts and one forgotten birthday left me with a very full inbox. I deleted half of it immediately and then scanned the names for anything of relevance. There were five from Eddie, varying from "Happy Birthday, Dude," to "You OK?"

The last one from Eddie was a picture of Logan curled up with a stuffed Godzilla toy. At least I knew they were both safe and out of harm's way.

I sent a cryptic thank-you and sorted through various birthday offers for free sandwiches and discounted appetizers. Buried on the third page was a reply to the one I'd sent from Nancie's inbox. I'd forgotten all about it.

The email was brief. *I have information about the man who claims to be Pritchard Smith. Meet me in the parking lot behind the dentist office on Penn Avenue.*

The note was not signed. There was no meeting time listed, no date listed. It was a simple call to action.

I wrote back. *Just saw this. Can you still meet?*

The reply came right away. *Yes.*

I wrote back again. *On my way.* I looked up the direction to the address listed. I found an online car service and booked a reservation. Ten minutes later, I was face-to-face with my source.

21

JENNIE MAE'S DRAWERS

The woman in front of me was in disguise. She wore a highlighted wig, a thin gold necklace, and a yellow sweater with a plunging V-neck. Her face was heavily made up, making it a different color than the skin on her cleavage. I placed her age somewhere in her forties, though she appeared to be in denial over the aging process. As lacking in taste as her outfit appeared, it was decidedly more flattering than Nick's flannel shirt.

"Took you long enough," she said. She took a drag on a long brown cigarette and exhaled smoke to the side of her face. The scent clung to the air. I waved my hand to make it go away. "Oh, please. You have worse things to worry about than a little secondhand smoke."

"What can you tell me about Pritchard Smith?"

"His name isn't Pritchard Smith."

"What is it?"

She took another pull of her cigarette. "You're going to have to find that out yourself. Here," she said. She handed me a neon-pink sealed envelope. "Sorry it's not more discreet. They were on sale at

Staples. Don't open it until after I'm gone." She threw her cigarette onto the ground and walked away.

As soon as she was out of view, I tore the envelope open. Inside were two pieces of paper. One was a copy of a driver's license that said Pritchard Smith. My Pritchard Smith. The second was another Pritchard Smith, born in 1937. The DL number was the same.

I'd given Detective Loncar the copies of the fake IDs that I'd found in Pritchard's suitcase, but aside from that, I had nothing. Now I had something again.

Having a personal driver was going to get very expensive very quickly. Add in the fact that I didn't have my wallet and could only spend money on the internet with my memorized credit card number, and I had limited options. It did seem that getting a replacement license should be at the top of my priority list, and considering I now had questions about how someone could go about getting a picture ID with someone else's info, a trip to the DMV seemed very two birds, one stone. I pulled out my phone and made another reservation with the car service company and then waited on the curb in front of the dentist's office. If my informant was watching me, I wanted her to see that I was leaving alone.

I arrived at the DMV, filled out the appropriate paperwork, and picked up a couple of brochures on identity theft. When I reached the window, a petite blonde behind bulletproof glass started on my paperwork.

"It's your birthday!" she said when she reached the date. She stopped typing and looked up at me. "You look good for your age."

How do you respond to that? I smiled and secretly hoped her shoes pinched her feet. "What can you tell me about identity theft?" I asked.

"There's information in the kiosk by the doors." I held up the brochure. "You already got that? Is that why you're here? Did somebody steal your ID?"

"Something like that," I said.

"You should call the credit card companies and turn off all of your cards. And change your online passwords. You don't shred your mail, do you? You need to shred your mail."

"It wasn't from the mail," I said. "My ID was stolen. But that mail thing—does that happen often?"

"It's one way these people work. Sometimes they steal credit card applications, establish credit in your name. I've heard of people stealing social media profiles, too. You need to go home and Google yourself to find out what else they got."

"What would somebody do with my social media profiles?"

She shrugged and typed something into her computer. "Who knows? Sometimes people just want to mess with your head."

"If somebody did that, opened credit cards in my name and took over my social media profile, could they come in here and get identification in my name?"

"You ask a lot of questions," she said. "Are you sure this is you?" she asked.

I could have cited the article that a local reporter had written for the *Ribbon Times* that mentioned me in conjunction with homicide investigations around town, but I didn't. There was one photo, and it had been a bad hair day.

"Did you hear about the shooting at the Motel 6 the other day?" I asked. When she nodded, I continued. "I'm the person who was shot at. I dropped my bag and ran and lost my ID, my phone, and my lip gloss."

"Bummer," she said. I couldn't tell if she was talking about the shooting, the loss of my ID and phone, or the lip gloss.

"Big time. And right before my birthday, too," I said, hoping to distract her. "I guess I never thought about identity theft until recently, and now I can't stop wondering how hard it would be?"

She leaned forward. "Don't quote me on this, but it's not all that hard to fake an ID," she said. "I mean, to make a real fake, yes, it's hard. But if all you want is something that can let you buy beer before you're twenty-one, that's easy. Not that you have to worry about that anymore," she said.

Mental note: stop telling people I just had a birthday.

"What if you want something better than a fake ID to buy beer. Something that is legit. How hard would that be?"

She dropped her voice even lower. "You're talking about a bigger operation. We hear about them in our employee newsletter every now and then. You can research it on the internet." She clicked a couple more keys on her keyboard and rolled the mouse around and clicked four times. A piece of paper chugged out of an ancient, asylum-beige printer. She snatched up the paper, stamped it with a red stamp, and initialed next to the fresh ink.

"Your new ID will arrive in about a week. In the meantime, keep this with you." She slid the paper through the narrow opening under the window.

"Thank you," I said. "Can I ask one more thing?"

"You can ask, but I probably can't answer. Besides, the guy behind you looks pretty annoyed that you're taking so long."

I left the office with paperwork validating my identity (don't think I didn't triple-check that it said Samantha Kidd and not anything else) and the humiliating realization that the photo on my replacement license was going to show me in a flannel shirt. Although one problem had been solved, I was still dealing with the very real crisis of how to get about town.

I called Mo. "It's Samantha Kidd."

"Miss Samantha!" he said. "My sister Keisha is very happy. She has been hired. She wants to say thank you for your head. She thought you might come back for dinner. Last night she made special goose eggs stew."

"Mo, I think it's best I don't spend too much time at your house, at least until this mess that I'm in is resolved."

"You are messy?" he asked.

"No, I'm not messy, but my life is."

"Do you need me to recommend a cleaning service? I know a woman whose husband cleans houses—"

I started to explain but gave up. "Thank you, Mo. If I need a cleaning service, you'll be the first person I call."

"Do you need a ride?"

"I wanted to see if I could borrow another dead taxi."

"Sure. Do you want the one that I loaned you before?"

"Do you have it?"

"Yes. Your friend brought it back to the graveyard. He asked a lot of questions."

I pictured Detective Loncar interrogating Mo about the retired taxis. I had a feeling Mo would hold up very well under interrogation. "Here's the thing, Mo. I can't get to the taxi graveyard because I don't have a car."

"This is easy problem to solve. I come to you and take you there as a thank-you for giving your head to my sister. No charge."

TEN MINUTES LATER, Mo dropped me off at the taxi graveyard with a fresh set of keys. I thanked him, assured him that I loved the extensions his sister had given me but the responsibility of having that much fabulous hair had been beyond the scope of my everyday beauty routine, and then left. I drove to my house to get a change of clothes.

Loncar had repaired the broken window from the garage door with a piece of wood. I said a silent thank-you to him, and then broke a pane from the door next to it and let myself inside. Out of habit, I locked the door behind me.

Evidence in the living room indicated that Loncar had been sleeping on my sofa. I clicked the TV on to see what channel he watched. ESPN. I clicked it off and went into the kitchen, where I found the trash can overflowing with empty bottles of Rolling Rock next to a brown bag from Burger King. Come on, detective, I thought. You can surely do better than that.

I went to my home office on the second floor and made copies of the copies of the information my source had given me. I wrote EVIDENCE! on one page and was about to leave when I spotted my *Retrofit* press card on my desk.

Nancie had given me a press card three months ago. It had been a joke at the time. What breaking news would an e-zine dedicated to decades-old fashion be required to cover? But when she started up *Retrofit*, she applied for everything that a magazine should get, and now that we were building a solid reputation among online fashion journals, the applications were being stamped APPROVED and the accreditations were flowing in. I'd worn my press pass around *Retrofit* for a week. I'd even Instagrammed a selfie and proclaimed it my new favorite accessory, until the day I realized it didn't go with my Hermes scarf. I'd left it on the desk here and forgotten about it.

I hung the cord around my neck. As far as I knew, there was a good story wrapped up in Jennie Mae Tome's collection in the attic. Intro Samantha Kidd, Girl Reporter.

I changed into a brown blazer, A-line skirt, and a pink blouse with a long matching scarf that knotted at the neck. I left my hair loose but pinned the front to the side with a barrette. It was about twelve inches shorter thanks to Nick but still halfway down my back. I finished with nude pantyhose (because it was both era accurate and I needed the control top to fit into my skirt) and chunky heeled shoes, dropped the copies of the IDs on the kitchen table for Loncar, and pulled the *Retrofit* bible out from behind the box of Bran Flakes.

When Nancie had given Pritchard and me the assignment for our first-ever print magazine, she'd been concerned with two things: us following the layout of her bible, and her selling ad space. I flipped through the spiral-bound notebook, waiting for something to strike me. It didn't. Nancie had been meticulous in the layout. Each page had a title, a collage of photos or notations that indicated what she wanted, and how she wanted to feature it. The only thing missing was exactly how she expected us to go about getting the content. She'd hinted at Pritchard's contacts, and had gone so far as to warn me to pull my weight. But maybe Pritchard didn't have a contact list of possible leads at his disposal. Maybe there had been one collection on his radar: Jennie Mae's.

That had to be it. Pritchard's whole reason for showing up in Ribbon had been to get into Jennie Mae's drawers.

If that was the case, then it wasn't a coincidence that he was elbowing me out of the way. If he was after something in Jenny Mae Tome's archives, then he'd been zeroing in on it long before he showed up at her house. I closed the bible, tucked it back behind the Bran Flakes, and left.

I drove the dead taxi to the library. Armed with my press pass and my temporary ID papers, I obtained a new library card. The librarian set me up on a computer on the first floor where there was no time limit. I pulled up a new search and typed in "Fake ID bust" and scrolled through the search results, looking for something I could use.

I found it on the fourth page of results: a small-town newspaper article from 1972 that wrote about an ID scam in Utah.

The first thing that struck me was the name of the suspect: Gene Whitbee. Where had I heard that before? I closed my eyes and concentrated. When it didn't come to me right away, I read the article. What I learned put everything in a whole new light.

Gene Whitbee was a small-time crook who operated out of a trailer in Utah. He and his partner mostly trafficked in stolen merchandise, but Gene ran a fake ID operation on the side. In time, the fake ID ring became easier with less overhead than what was required to run the fence, and Gene used the profits from one business to expand the other. When his partner found out that Gene had been taking control of the operation, he threatened to turn Gene over to the authorities. Gene wasn't going to go down without a fight. Rumors that he shot his partner abounded, though no body had ever been found.

The physical strain of working with photographic chemicals and the equipment needed to produce top-dollar fake IDs eventually took its toll on Gene. Unmarried and unloved, he died alone in a folding chair by the community pool. His body was found next to a pile of empty beer cans and a note: *PS: I'm sorry.*

It wasn't a postscript. It was an apology. Because, as it turned out, Gene Whitbee's partner had been Pritchard Smith.

22

NOT THE BAD GUY

I FELT LIKE I WAS TRYING TO COMPLETE A JIGSAW PUZZLE WITH PIECES from four different collections. If Pritchard's body had never been found, was it possible that the skull in the hobo bag was him? Let's not forget that the skull had been in Jennie Mae's attic. Had he really left her? Or had she been responsible for his death? Had her story about Pritchard leaving her been made up to cast her as the victim instead of a possible accomplice in a forty-year-old murder?

And who, exactly, was the person running around calling himself Pritchard Smith now?

I was surrounded with information, scattered around me like bird feed in a public park, but the years, the crimes, the evidence, and the motives didn't match.

I clicked onto a public internet browser and opened my email. The unread count was back over a thousand. I scrolled through the pages until I found the email I wanted.

To 123@fashion.net: *If Gene Whitbee murdered Pritchard Smith forty years ago, who have I been working with?*

The reply popped up almost immediately. *You have the wrong man.*

I wrote back: *who is the right man?*

There were no more replies.

What did she mean, the wrong man? That was a Hitchcock movie with Henry Fonda. Did she want me to rent the movie? I looked it up on IMDB. True story of an innocent man suspected of murder. My coworker was guilty of something, I just didn't know what. Maybe her response was merely an expression that had triggered a "there's a squirrel!" reaction in my already overtaxed brain.

Absentmindedly, I clicked through my emails, deleting most without opening them. Halfway down the second page, I stopped. There was an email from Nancie that I'd somehow missed.

Samantha: I'm heading to Bethany House to check out their archives. Call me to discuss.—Nancie

The email was dated three days ago—the last time I'd seen Nancie.

I looked up the phone number to Bethany House and pulled out my cell. The librarian eyed me suspiciously. I packed up everything I'd brought with me and went out front to make the call.

"Bethany House," answered a female voice.

"I'm calling on behalf of Nancie Townsend's office," I said. "She had an appointment on Friday?"

"Yes, she's been working in the vault for the past few days. There's no reception in there. I can give her a message when she comes out if you like."

I was already in the dead taxi by the time she finished her sentence. "That won't be necessary," I said. I hung up and peeled out of my parking space. I had no idea where Bethany House was located, but that wasn't going to stop me from getting there.

I called Eddie. He answered in his professional voice. "Visual Department, Eddie Adams."

"It's me. I need directions. Are you by your computer?"

"What do I look like, Google Maps? Use the GPS on your phone."

"This isn't my phone. It's an untraceable cell from the spy store. And before you say anything, 'untraceable' means 'no GPS.'"

"Dude, you are one maraschino cherry short of a banana split."

"That doesn't make any sense."

"It means you are both bananas and nuts."

"Listen to me. I just got on the highway heading east. I need to get to Bethany House. Which way do I go?"

"The auction house? I heard they have an awesome collection of vintage skateboards on display. Okay, hold on, I got it."

He gave me the directions and wished me good luck.

"How's Logan?" I asked.

"Back to normal. He slept on my head last night."

I felt a pang of jealousy. I didn't know if I was still being watched or not. After the release of Nick's dad, I felt like as long as I operated as a free agent, I could keep everybody safe. Nick's snatch-and-grab and his Jim Rockford disguise seemed to fool anybody who might be watching. There had been no threatening phone calls, no spray of bullets when I left, no attempts on my life for the past forty-two hours. Let's see if I could keep it that way.

After hanging up with Eddie, I drove through Pottstown, past Stowe, to Sanatoga. The view gradually changed from highway to residential to small town. I looked at the notes written on the back of the ID of Gene Whitbee. Third right after the correctional school for boys. I passed the school, counted out streets, and made the turn. In front of me sat a monumental three-story pink brick building with white trim. A small iron sign hung from a post in the front yard. Bethany House, it announced.

I parked by the front door, adjusted the bow tied around the neck of my mauve blouse, and got out of the car. The doors to the building opened, and Tahoma Hunt came out. I remained in place, unsure if I should approach him or get back in and drive away.

"Samantha," he called. "I've been trying to reach you. Have you talked to Nancie recently?"

I was wary of giving him information. "I don't know how you hooked up with Nancie or what it is you're planning on getting from her, but I know about your background. I know about the felony convictions in Utah. You need to leave Nancie—and me—alone."

His brows lowered over his eyes, casting a determined and angry expression to his face. "That is history. I need to talk to you about *Retrofit*. I think you might have gotten the wrong idea about what I was doing the day you spotted me in Nancie's office."

"I got the impression that you lied about having an appointment and were planning on stealing the master version of her project."

"That's what I thought you thought."

"Am I wrong? You do have a history of stealing things."

"You've looked into my background. I should have expected as much after our encounter." He stood tall, his height and broad shoulders emanating a sense of personal pride, not shame or deceit. "What I did in the past was for personal reasons and has nothing to do with my business at *Retrofit*. You're right that I was there for the bible, but you're wrong about why. Nancie sent me to get it for her."

"She did? When?"

"Nancie wasn't feeling well and wanted to work from home. I volunteered to pick it up for her."

"You didn't act like you were doing a favor for a friend. If what you're saying is true, you could have told me so that day."

"Nancie told me someone was after the bible and that she didn't want to leave it in the office. You startled me when you showed up. I didn't offer an explanation because I didn't know if I could trust you. When you took the bible, I realized you didn't trust *me*."

"Where is she now?" I asked.

"I don't know. I imagine she's home sick."

I didn't tell Tahoma that just hours ago, his receptionist had told me that she was working in the vault of his auction house.

"I'm curious about one thing," I said. "You said you've been trying to reach me. How did you know I was coming here?"

"Nancie told me." He smiled tentatively. "Our encounter had been bothering me, and I told her I wanted to clear things up."

Tahoma got into his SUV and started the engine. I stood next to the dead taxi, hoping to double back to the Bethany House after he drove away. He didn't drive away. I got into the taxi and drove to the gas station on the corner, going through the motions of filling up the tank until his SUV disappeared past several green lights. I hopped back into the dead taxi and returned to the Bethany House.

I parked in the same space and went inside. A woman with striking red hair and coral lipstick sat behind a small wooden table. She looked up at me. "I'm sorry, we're closed for the day," she said. Her voice was thick with a South Philly accent. "If you want information on membership, I can give you a pamphlet."

"I'd like to talk to someone about your vault of clothes from the Seventies for an article for *Retrofit* Magazine," I said. I reached inside my neckline and pulled out my press card. "I've been working closely with Pritchard Smith."

"Nobody told me anything about a Retro magazine or a Richard Smith," she said.

She was either a very good actress, or she didn't recognize his name. I changed tactics. "We both work for Nancie Townsend. I called earlier, and someone told me she was working in the vault."

"I didn't realize that was you. I was just about to tell her it's closing time. Come on, I'll take you there."

As the elevator descended, I thought about how well Nancie had taken care of me since I started working for her. I thought about how the opportunity to work at *Retrofit* had come through the recommendation of my boss at Bentley's, who had never steered me wrong. I thought about how dedicated Nancie was to the magazine, how she came in early and stayed late, and how her eyes had lit up when she first told Pritchard and me about her idea to do a special print edition.

Nancie would not have let *Retrofit* close overnight. If we'd lost our lease, she would have had us set up shop in her basement before giving up her dream. She wouldn't have asked Tahoma to go to our offices to pick up the bible. Cold or no cold, she would have done it herself.

Nancie was not going to turn out to be the bad guy here. Which meant one thing.

The elevator doors opened, and the receptionist reached inside and pressed the button marked Vault. Before I knew what was happening, she pushed me in. The doors shut, and the elevator descended with me in darkness.

23

THOSE SITUATIONS

"WHO'S THERE?" ASKED A VOICE I HADN'T HEARD FOR SEVERAL DAYS.

"Nancie? Is that you?"

"Sam?"

"Yes," I said. "Keep talking. My eyes haven't adjusted yet, and I don't know where I am." I felt around on the floor for my handbag. I found a lipstick, a Snickers bar, and the canister of pepper spray before I found the bag. Nothing else appeared to have fallen out. "I'm in front of the elevator doors. Where are you?" I asked.

"Turn to your right and follow the sound of my voice. Keep walking, keep walking, keep walking, okay, stop."

"Where are you?"

"On the floor."

I blinked a few more times but nothing happened. I pressed my eyes shut and counted to thirty. When I opened them, I was able to make out racks of clothing and shelves of shoes. Next to the shoes, I spotted Nancie. Now that I could see, I knew why she hadn't gotten up to meet me. She was tethered by a length of rope to the foot of a large wooden dresser. About ten feet past her, a door was partially open, exposing the faint silhouette of a toilet.

I rushed over to her. "Are you okay?" I asked.

"It's the strangest situation. I came here for a meeting. Pritchard said they were expecting me, but I haven't seen a person in days. At least I think it's been days. I fall asleep, and when I wake up, there's food and water. And it's good food. But how do they know when I'm asleep?"

I ran my fingers over the rope around her ankle and then pulled on it. "It's unbreakable," she said. "I put all of my weight on it, and if a hundred and sixty-five pounds won't loosen it, then I don't think your bare hands will." She reclined and rested her head on a pile of clothes. "How did you get here?"

"I got your email."

"That was a couple of days ago, wasn't it?" She yawned. "I've lost all track of time."

"I've been tied up with other aspects of the project," I said. "When I called here, the receptionist told me you'd been working in the vault and that there was no cell phone reception. I thought it would be best to talk to you face-to-face, so I came here in person."

"You might as well get comfortable," she said.

Nancie appeared to be more than a little out of it. Instead of taking her advice, I stood up and walked around the room. "You're sure nobody hurt you?"

"Sam, I'm not joking. The service here is almost as good as the Four Seasons."

"You're being held captive in the basement of an auction house," I said.

"I said 'almost.'"

I found my phone and tilted the screen in front of me to illuminate our surroundings. Untraceable meant no data plan, so I couldn't download the flashlight app. The best I could do was hit the End Call button every fifteen seconds, giving us short bursts of a blue glowing light. As if things weren't dire enough.

"How are things at the magazine? Are you and Pritchard working well together?" Nancie asked. Her voice was soft and light, as if she'd taken a hit of helium and it was starting to wear off. I looked at her. The blue glow from the phone faded, but I could see her face well enough to see that her pupils were dilated. Whatever had been putting her under had slowed down her cognitive functions.

"Nancie, *Retrofit* closed. There's no magazine anymore. Pritchard Smith isn't who he says he is."

"That's not possible," she said. My news did not appear to cause anxiety. "Pritchard might seem like a snob, but he's completely dedicated to the work. He waived his salary for the opportunity. Did you know that? I knew this project would require more than what you and I could do, but I had to spend my time finding ad sponsors. I put out a call for an unpaid intern. When he showed up, I practically turned him away. He was obviously too qualified."

Something Jennie Mae had said tickled the back of my brain. "Nancie, did you tell Jennie Mae Tome that I'd be coming to her house to view her collection?"

"Yes. I knew you'd love it. But Pritchard was in the office before you and volunteered to get a jump start. I think he wanted to prove himself."

"The man you hired is a fraud," I said. "The real Pritchard Smith was a shady businessman. He was killed by his business partner. Somehow a skull, possibly his, ended up in Jennie Mae's wardrobe. That's what this guy is looking for."

"Sam! Stop it. I don't want to hear ghost stories." She put her fingers in her ears.

I bent down and gently pulled her hands away from her head. "Nancie, they're not ghost stories, they're the truth. It's all the truth. The *Retrofit* offices have been cleaned out."

"The files are gone?" she asked.

"Empty." I let the word hang in the air for a few seconds, hoping it would sink in. "Nancie, when did you first meet up with Tahoma Hunt?"

"Tahoma? I've known him for years. Why?"

"A few days ago, I found him in your office. He said he was waiting for you, but I didn't believe him. And he was just here, out front. Today. He said he thought I misunderstood why he was at your office, and I accused him of trying to steal the *Retrofit* bible."

"Did he deny it?"

"Not exactly. He said you were home sick and that you sent him to our offices to get it."

"I did ask Tahoma to get the bible for me. I was out meeting prospective advertisers, and I thought if I could illustrate what we were trying to do, I'd have a better chance of convincing them."

"Why didn't Tahoma tell me that?"

"Tahoma has a sketchy history. He's been accused of burglary, illegal entry, and theft of historical artifacts."

"He wasn't just accused, he was tried and convicted."

"He never fought the charges. His father is well respected in their Native American community, and after his last parole was granted, he chose to leave Utah so as not to bring shame on his family. He was raised with a lot of pride. If he thought you suspected him of theft, he would not have denied it. He would have walked away."

I was silent. In the past few years, I'd been accused of behavior that I wasn't proud of, and I'd gone to extreme lengths to prove I was innocent. Which one of us was right? The person who fought to prove themselves, or the person who was so secure in who they were that they didn't feel the need to prove anything?

"Does Bethany House know they hired a felon?"

"Elements of the Native American culture seeped into the world of fashion a long time ago. Tahoma's background demonstrated how passionate he is about protecting that culture. He worked for years as the curator of Indian Art at a small museum downtown. Bethany House recruited him, not the other way around."

Before I could stop it, an image of Cher from the Half Breed days flashed into my head but was quickly replaced by the memory of Navajo, Jennie Mae's white cat, wearing the turquoise-and-red beaded choker. What would Tahoma say about that?

"Does Tahoma know you're here?"

"I doubt it. The last time we spoke was when I asked him to get the bible." She shifted her weight and rested the side of her head against a dresser. "Sam, where's the bible now?"

I pictured the bible, hidden behind the box of Bran Flakes in the pantry of my kitchen. Considering Detective Loncar's preference for fast food takeout, I figured there was no harm of it being discovered. "It's safe."

"Two years," she said softly. "Two years of research, files, notes on collectors, contacts with aging designers and the seamstresses who worked in their ateliers. *Retrofit* is really gone?"

The answer was yes, but I didn't say it out loud. I was too busy thinking about what Nancie had said. Those files had been stolen for a reason. Tahoma had been in Nancie's office. And he'd been here at the Bethany House, the very location where Nancie had been—and I was currently—being detained. Nancie hadn't known that I was coming; she couldn't have told him to meet me here. I didn't know what he was after, but I wasn't yet willing to give him the benefit of the doubt. The *Retrofit* files documented more than just the history of fashion, and someone was risking an awful lot to find out what.

I settled in on the floor. "Tell me about how you advertised this job," I said.

"Just like I advertised for our other interns. The rest of my candidates were college kids from the Institute, students who wanted experience in fashion or in journalism. Kids like our receptionist. They could give me a couple of hours each week between their classes and homework in exchange for college credit."

New York City had FIT and Parsons The New School of Design. California had FIDM. We had I-FAD. The Institute of Fashion, Art, and Design. Nick had attended there, as had his maybe-former girlfriend, Amanda Ries. Most of the buyers at Tradava had graduated from there as well. It was well-known, highly respected, and the go-to place for up-and-comers.

"The guy you hired—how did you find him?" By silent agreement we chose not to call him by name. It would have been easier if we had, though no doubt karmically insulting to the real Pritchard Smith who had been reduced to a skull in a hobo bag.

"He called to find out if I'd filled the position, and when I told him I hadn't, he set up an appointment to meet in person."

"At *Retrofit*?"

"Yes. We hit it off immediately. He knew so much more than the college students did. When I asked him about that, he said he grew up around fashion. He said a friend of the family was a pattern maker for several designers and had one of the most comprehensive collections of samples in the world."

I shivered. I knew of one woman who could claim that same thing. Jennie Mae Tome. But she'd told me that she and the real Pritchard Smith hadn't had children. "We spent two hours talking about Halston. I told him my idea to do a print magazine to supplement what we did online. He was very interested in the concept, and I got caught up in his enthusiasm. I showed him the mocked-up bible so he could see my vision."

"You showed him the bible before he agreed to work for free?"

"He knew the job was a non-paying job. I told him I was sorry I didn't have more of a budget because he'd obviously be an asset to *Retrofit*, but that we were turning enough of a profit to only employ you and me."

I got the impression that at that moment, she regretted having me on the payroll. I didn't ask her to confirm or deny that fact.

"He said he completely understood and that he wasn't worried about income. He did ask that I kept that confidential, otherwise it would change the way you treated him."

"Did you tell him anything specific about me?"

"He asked if there was anything he should know about you to ensure you worked well together. I told him about your background at Bentley's and how you moved to Ribbon to buy the house you grew up in. He seemed to think that meant you were a small-town girl, but I set him straight."

"How?"

"I said you were something of a local celebrity and told him about the arsons, the hat exhibit, and the knockoff ring. He was most impressed when I told him you were the one who took down Patrick's killer."

Patrick, a one-name celebrity in the worlds of fashion and design, had been largely responsible for pushing me beyond thinking about changing my life and actually doing so. Over the weeks after I met him outside of Tradava, through a stream of unconventional interviews in parking lots and restaurants but never in his office, I came to see him as someone who could mentor me into a new phase of my life. But before I'd had the chance to officially work in his employ, he'd been murdered.

Pritchard knew all about my background when we met. "Did you tell him anything else?"

"Nothing important. He asked the questions you might want to know about your coworker but would be afraid to ask. Were you in a relationship? Did you live far from the office? Were you a cat or a dog person? He said those were the real questions. I thought it was charming."

Not. Definitely not charming. Not. At. All.

I sat back against the wall. My pantyhose had run in four different places, and I'd torn my blazer. I took it off, balled it up, and wedged it behind my head. I undid the bow at the neckline of my blouse and unbuttoned a couple of buttons. It was warm. If they were treating Nancie like it was the Four Seasons, why not turn on the air conditioner?

I stood up and kicked off my shoes, then wandered around the basement in my stockings. The cool concrete felt good under my feet. I had to move three racks of clothes out of the way before I found what I was looking for. The air conditioning vent, two feet over my head. No air came out of it.

"Are you warm?" I asked Nancie.

"Not right now. The temperature comes and goes, and sometimes it gets a little chilly. Why?"

"Because I think I know how to get out of here."

I looked around for something to stand on. The room was filled with racks and clothing, but nothing else. Even if Nancie hadn't been tied up on the floor, she probably would have found that corner to be the most comfortable spot in the room.

"Can you give me a hand over here?" I asked.

"Sure." She joined me under the AC vent. "I bet it's set to go on when the place reaches a certain temperature. I have mine set like that at home."

"Do you remember the last time it was cold?"

"It was a couple of hours ago, I think. I snuggled under a pile of fake fur coats and took a nap. When I woke, my lunch was here."

"That's how they're doing it. There must be something in the AC that makes you fall asleep. The AC kicks on, you fall asleep, they check on you and leave you food. The thing I can't figure out is how they manage to not affect the rest of the building?"

"Sam, that's crazy. Do you hear what you're saying?"

"Nancie, look around. You are in the basement of an auction house, surrounded by the private collections of some of the wealthiest people in the Tristate area. What part of this isn't crazy?"

She scanned the room. "If I were a size two, these would have been the greatest couple of days of my life."

I'd always suspected that fashion people had a distorted connection between size and quality of life.

I grabbed the grid in front of the vent. A few shakes, and it came loose. I handed it to her. "The receptionist led me down here. She said they were about to close." A low rumble started deep inside the vent. I held my hand up to the grate and felt the beginning of a cool breeze. "If I'm right about the AC, then we don't have a lot of time. I'm going to try to go through the vent and get us help."

"This is how you get involved in those situations, isn't it?"

"Nancie, this is not me getting involved in a situation. This is me trying to save our lives. Neither one of us knows what is going on here. What I do know is the person behind all this doesn't shy away from violence. This is not the time to judge me."

"Judge you? I was about to give you a raise."

Cool air trickled out of the vent. "Give me a boost instead," I said.

Nancie threaded her fingers together, and I stepped onto her palms and then up into the air conditioning shaft. It was narrower than I would have liked. For a moment, I wished I was wearing one of my new poly-cotton sweat suits.

The walls of the shaft were anodized aluminum. The surface was cold to the touch. I tied my scarf around my mouth bandito-style to filter the air and crawled on my hands and knees, making slow progress. I felt increasingly tired and dizzy as I progressed through the vent. I hoped whatever direction I was headed in, it was the right one. The vent turned a corner, and then another one, and then there was a slight decline. I couldn't shift or sit, so I continued. If not for the icy-cold aluminum against my skin, I would have closed my eyes and fallen asleep. Eventually, I came to a stop with a view of the lobby through a dirty white plastic grid.

The vent was ten feet above the ground. It seemed I was destined to hang from impossible heights. Worse, I'd have to knock the plastic grid out to jump, and once I came out, I wouldn't be able to reach the vent to replace it. Anybody who entered Bethany House would know I'd gotten out. Which meant I'd have to get Nancie out too.

I pressed my face to the plastic grid and gulped at air from the lobby. I felt the haze in my mind clear slightly. I smacked at the plastic until one corner popped out of the frame, then the second. A third whack and it swung like a microwave door. I threaded my scarf through the slats on the plastic, flipped over so I was on my back, fed the top half of my body through the opening, and slowly climbed out. As soon as my full weight was on the plastic screen, it snapped away from the wall and sent me tumbling to the ground. My blouse tore at the shoulder, and I was pretty sure I'd have a nasty bruise from where I landed.

I pulled myself up using the corner of the desk for leverage. I grabbed the phone and called my home number. Loncar answered. "Send a team to Bethany House in Sanatoga," I said. "They've been pumping something into the AC and holding a woman in the subbasement. I can get her out, but you'll find the evidence you need for when she presses charges." I hung up and stared at the calendar on the desk. There were reminders of auctions and notes for appointments to look at various collections.

And then I saw something that wouldn't mean anything to anybody but me.

Dentist 9:00 p.m. Listed underneath the reminder was the address where I'd met up with my source.

24

NOT A BAD IDEA

IT WAS A THIN CONNECTION. THINNER THAN GAUZE BACKSTAGE AT A Cher concert. But considering I'd never heard of a dentist who kept office hours at nine o'clock at night, I didn't believe it was a coincidence.

I opened and shut several drawers before coming across a janitorial key ring and a pair of industrial scissors. I ran to the elevator and flipped through keys until I found one that fit the control panel. I turned it half a turn and pressed the button for the subbasement. The elevator car descended and then came to a stop.

The doors opened to darkness. I removed one of my chunky heeled shoes and wedged it between the elevator doors to keep them from closing, stepped into the darkness, and hollered for Nancie. A few moments later she called back, her voice weak. I held my breath, felt my way to her, cut through the rope, and pulled her to her feet. We stumbled to the elevator. I kicked my shoe out of place and pressed the button for the first floor. My lungs convulsed with the need for a fresh breath. Nancie was quiet. When the elevator reached the main floor, I pulled her along behind me. We didn't stick around to talk to the police.

AGAINST MY BETTER JUDGMENT, I drove Nancie to her apartment. She lived in the upscale units across the street from the old Vanity Fair outlets, popular with the single, professional crowd. I declined her invitation to come in for a drink and suggested she pack a bag and get out of town for a few days. Nancie didn't have family obligations keeping her in town, which explained how she'd gone missing for several days and nobody but me had noticed. She looked like she still didn't quite believe I wasn't playacting. I wrote two numbers on the pad by her phone: my untraceable cell and Detective Loncar's direct line.

"Nancie, you need to call Detective Loncar and tell him what happened. And then leave town. There has to be some place you've always wanted to go. Now's a good time to take a spontaneous vacation."

She looked at the phone numbers. "Will the police help me get *Retrofit* back?"

"I don't think that's their priority," I said softly. I put my hand on her arm. "But when this is over, I'll help you." *Retrofit* had been my most recent job, but it had been her lifelong dream. I didn't know how else to console her.

After leaving Nancie's house, I drove in circles trying to figure out my next move. I was a little smarter than I'd been twenty-four hours ago, but not much. I needed a computer, and I knew where I could find one.

I drove to the vacant *Retrofit* offices. The Office For Rent signs were still on the doors, and a bunch of colorful flyers and coupons were stuck between them. The lights were off. I pulled my keys from my bag and entered. The last time I'd been here was the day I saw the offices had been emptied. I didn't know if I was being watched or not. That thought alone kept me on edge.

It's a well-known fact in fashion that if you dress the part—any part—people will treat you as if you belong. Appearances matter. A stylist can take your money and make you look like an insider even if you never touched an issue of *Vogue* in your life. This emptied-out office with For Rent signs on the windows was an illusion. The outside world had been led to believe, based on the way the offices looked, that Nancie had closed her doors. But it wasn't real.

The office had been dressed to look like it had been abandoned. I pieced together what I knew, established a timeline in my mind. Once Nancie had been hidden away in the basement of Bethany House, someone made it look like she'd skipped town. She hadn't been the one to remove evidence of the magazine's daily business. But the appearance of an abandoned business would throw suspicion on her in the long run. I doubted the rental company had been notified.

I doubted *any* of the companies who provided power, water, and trash had been notified. Whoever had cleaned out the files, shut off the lights, and taped signs to the front doors, had wanted people to think we'd gone belly-up. If I was right, the power, the water, and the internet would still work. I went to the breaker panel and flipped several switches.

I was right.

I sat in the dark at my desk, not wanting to leave signs of my presence. Pritchard's message to me, leaving my cubicle intact, had been his mistake. I remembered the notation I'd found on the calendar at Bethany House. If someone was meeting my source at the dentist's office at nine, I intended to be there.

Now I had to do something about my outfit.

The last time I'd gone undercover, it had been with help from

Dante. This time I called his sister. Cat Lestes owned Catnip, an off-price designer outlet that I frequented on occasion. She kept my measurements, preferences, and credit card info on hand for fashion emergencies, and seeing as I had a torn vintage blouse and one shoe, the emergency sirens were on high alert.

"Hi, Cat, this is Samantha. I need your help."

Cat was accustomed to me starting conversations like this and didn't miss a beat. "Sam, you will not believe what came in today. Dead stock from a denim company. High-waisted Calvins like Brooke Shields advertised. Remember them? You had to lay on the bed to zip them up? There are garbage bags full of them. I think they've been sitting in a warehouse since 1981." She laughed. "I'm thinking of having them used to recover the sofa and chairs outside of the fitting rooms. Now, what's the occasion?"

"Something non-descript. I don't want anybody to notice me."

"Cashmere jog suit? I have them in red, pink, and blue."

"Too noticeable. What else do you have?"

"I have two racks of gray tweed on clearance. Never let the fashion magazines tell you gray is the new black. I don't care how many shades E.L. James says there are, in my world, there's one: markdown."

"Are they boring? I want something boring."

"I'm not in the business of carrying boring clothes. What is this for? A costume party?"

"Not exactly." I dropped my voice. "I need an outfit that is the opposite of anything you've ever sold me. And I need you to deliver it to the dentist office on Penn Avenue before nine tonight."

"Have you been hanging out with my brother again?"

I ignored her reference to Dante. If he hadn't made it clear that he was interested in more than a mentor/mentee relationship, I would have called him. Maybe. If not for my reignited relationship with Nick. Heck, there were a whole bunch of reasons I had for calling or not calling Dante. Could he help? Probably. But Dante's presence would introduce a whole new can of worms into the salad called life, and salad was bad enough. Who wanted worms with it?

"Please, Cat? Price is no object."

The magic words. "What time is your appointment? Maybe we can have dinner afterward."

"What appointment?"

"With the dentist."

"There's no appointment." I debated how much to tell her. "Cat, this part is especially important. I need you to drop the bag of clothes into the Dumpster and then leave. Can you do that for me?"

———

I WAS LATE GETTING to the dentist. A group of guys climbed in the dead taxi at the red light by Lancaster Ave and didn't believe me when I said I wasn't a real cab driver. I dropped them at the closest brewpub, took the twenty they handed me, and left.

My source leaned against the exterior of the building. Her wig was askew. A cloud of cigarette smoke surrounded her, and a littering of butts covered the ground by her feet.

"You should have told me you were coming," she said.

"How did you know I was?"

"Call it a hunch." She inhaled from her cigarette. When she spoke again, the smoke exited her mouth in short bursts with each word. "A woman pulled in and tossed a bag in the Dumpster. Seemed curious so I looked. The bag had an envelope addressed to you."

"That was my friend. She's a big joker."

"Right," she said in a voice that suggested that she neither cared nor believed me. She tossed another butt onto the ground and almost immediately lit up a new cigarette.

"You know those things are bad for you, don't you? And they probably turn your teeth brown."

"I get free cleanings," she said.

Today she wore a plunging V-neck sweater tucked into a pair of black trousers. Again her boobs were hiked up and on display, and while there was no evidence of a bra, there was also no evidence that gravity had had an impact on her physique either. She appeared to have the same devil-may-care attitude toward the sun as she did cigarettes, because her cleavage was tan and spotted with freckles.

"What do you know about Bethany House?" she asked.

"The woman I work for was being held in their basement."

"Was?"

"She's not there anymore. She's someplace safe." I hoped.

"Bethany House is a front for stolen goods. They masquerade as a reputable auction house, but if you look at their books, they barely turn a profit."

I mentally kicked myself for not looking deeper into Bethany House, especially considering Tahoma's connection. "How am I supposed to look at their books?"

"Tell your friend the policeman. Have him get a warrant to search the place. If you had left your boss there and just called it in, the police would have found her and had an excuse to do it themselves." She tipped her head to the side and tugged on the bottom of her silver hoop earring.

"How do you know about him? Or that I didn't tell him?" I asked. "How do you know he isn't on his way here right now? Who are you?"

She stepped backward. "Don't try to find me," she said. "I'll contact you when I have something more."

She put out her new cigarette and jogged to the side of the building. Considering I knew where she worked, her dramatic closing line lacked the punch I think she'd desired. I waited five minutes before digging Cat's bag out of the Dumpster.

It was late, and I was tired. And hungry. And even though Cat had triple-bagged the outfit she'd left in the trash, I couldn't shake the scent of garbage. The last food I remembered eating was pizza with Nick last night. As far as last meals went, it was a good one. And if I remembered correctly, there had been leftovers.

I drove the dead taxi to Nick's old apartment, circled the building twice, and then parked in the back and went inside.

The apartment was in much the same condition as it had been last night. Snooping on Nick had lost its allure so instead, I stripped down to take a shower. Crawling through an air conditioning duct and Dumpster diving weren't exactly a day at the spa.

Between the bar of Irish Spring and the coarse loofah sponge that Nick had left in the shower, I scrubbed myself raw. I turned the water off and emerged from the cloud of steam. The words *I'm going to get you* formed in the condensation on the mirror. I screamed and slid the shower doors closed. But there had been more. I slid the doors open. *I'm going to get you some food. Check the kitchen.*

I needed a break.

I dried off and dressed in the clothes Cat brought me. A striped boatneck T-shirt, sailor pants, and a pair of deck shoes. In the bottom of the bag was a beret. Apparently to Cat, undercover meant dressing like Jean Paul Gaultier (or Popeye).

The clothes were both comfortable and warm. I wrung out my hair and then pulled it back in a loose braid to keep it off my face. When I was finished, I found my phone and called Nick.

"How did you know I was here?" I asked.

"I stopped in to grab a couple of boxes and heard you singing in the shower. I didn't know you sang in the shower. How'd you know I knew?"

"I saw the message you left on the mirror after taking a shower. It scared the crap out of me."

"I thought you were going to stay put today. Where did you go?"

"I think it's better if I don't tell you. I don't want us to get into an argument."

"Kidd, I told you, whatever you need, I'm there."

"Okay. I went to Bethany House and found Nancie tied up in the basement. I climbed through the air conditioning vents and came out in the lobby, where I made the connection between the auction house and my source."

He didn't respond. I waited a few moments then said his name a few times, just to make sure the call hadn't dropped.

"I'm still here," Nick said. "Do you want to know what I did today?"

"What did you do today?"

"I designed a shoe."

"You went shopping, too. You bought grapes and cheese." I closed the refrigerator and opened the pantry. "And pretzels! You bought me pretzels!"

"You just went from being the most complicated woman I've ever met to the easiest to please. Is that all it takes?"

"Pretzels? They're a start."

"I'll remember that. Are you in for the night?"

"I hope so. I don't know what to do next. Somehow the skull from Jennie Mae Tome's attic connects back to Pritchard Smith, Bethany House, and the *Retrofit* magalog, but I don't know how."

"Why not write an exposé? Technically, you're a reporter for *Retrofit*, right? You have a press card. You can use my laptop. Why not write an article about what you know, quote your anonymous source, and watch what happens? Just keep Loncar in the loop. Maybe you can set up a sting."

I smiled. Whether he'd realized it or not, Nick was starting to speak my language. "That's not a bad idea."

"Then I'll leave you to it. Good night, Kidd."

"Good night, Taylor."

The bag of pretzels was mostly empty by the time I clicked save on my exposé. I knew one person at the *Ribbon Eagle/Times*, Carl Collins. He was the reporter who had written the article about me that had given me local fame. What better time than the present to ask him for a favor? I called the main number and asked to be routed to his desk.

"Carl, this is Samantha Kidd," I said. "You know how you're always asking for a scoop? Well, you better sit down, because have I got a story for you."

25

SNOOPING

"Samantha Kidd?" Carl repeated. "What are you into now? Exposing sweatshop conditions in Philadelphia? Child labor in Allentown? Wait." His voice dropped to a lower decibel. "Duty-free garments coming in from New Jersey?"

"Not exactly. It has to do with a scandal that leads back to Bethany House in Sanatoga."

He laughed out loud. "Sure, and Sotheby's keeps a room filled with kids knocking off Picassos. Seriously, Kidd, what's the joke?"

"No joke. I was there today. They were holding a woman captive. An anonymous source told me."

"Whoa. Who's your source, Deep Throat?"

I pictured her plunging necklines. Deep V was more like it. "Even if I did know her name, I wouldn't reveal her identity."

"You need to get better at the game of reporting, Ace. You just let on that your source is a woman."

He was right. If I could convince him to print the story, whoever was watching me could easily follow me around and spot me talking to her. "This could be big for both of us. I need this guy to come out of hiding and make a mistake. You need a big story that could get you national attention. We could help each other."

"Why are you asking me?"

I weighed my options and settled on the humbling truth. "Because you're the only reporter I know."

"If I didn't know any better, I'd say you were a crackpot. But you're lucky, Kidd, because you have a track record for being in, shall we say, newsworthy situations. Send me your article, and let's see what we can do."

I hung up and read over my article before sending it. If Carl kept his end of the bargain and published it, this would set a chain of events into motion that would end this thing.

In some circles, fashion is a dirty word. In others, it's a hobby. But to the men and women of the industry, it's a way of life. Fashion represents who we were and where we've been. Curators and archivists have elevated fashion to an art form and dedicated their lives to preserving the styles of yesterday. But news of corruption at the esteemed Bethany House may change how people view the way we celebrate styles of the past.

Bethany House is an auction house that specializes in clothing, jewelry, and accessories. Founded in the 1980s, they've been the go-to inheritor of private collections around the Tristate area. They are the Sotheby's of Style. Or are they?

Rumors from an anonymous source claim they continue to hide their underhanded business dealings behind press releases about their acquisitions and news that all but the most fashion-minded would tune out.

I rested my fingers on the keys and leaned back. What else could I say? I could out Tahoma Hunt as being a felon, but that appeared to be old news. My coworker, on the other hand, had taken on more roles than an actress trying to land her first big break. He'd been the talented and connected overachiever at *Retrofit*, the surprise visitor in my office, and the gun-wielding sharpshooter who'd sprayed the Motel 6 with bullets—or so I thought.

The information I'd uncovered at the library spoke of a counterfeit ID operation, which led me to believe that the guy I'd worked with maintained the illegal business his dad had started and had even used it for his own purposes.

But by using the name Pritchard Smith, he was waving a red flag. He wasn't hiding his identity; he was putting it front and forward, trying to elicit a response from someone. Pritchard Smith —*either* Pritchard Smith—seemed to have no connection to Bethany House. But I knew it was there.

The short amount of time I'd spent in Fake Pritchard's presence left me with a keen awareness that I knew ridiculously little about him. I looked back at the article that I'd written. I put my fingers back on the keys and slowly typed.

The man at the center of this corruption goes by the name Pritchard Smith. He should be considered dangerous. Anyone with information on him should contact Detective Loncar with the Ribbon Police.

I saved the document and emailed it to Carl Collins before I lost my nerve. I included my untraceable cell phone number in the event he needed to reach me and closed with a request: *Let me know when this runs.*

I cleaned up evidence of my cheese, grapes, and pretzel meal, wiped down Nick's kitchen, and then used his bathroom. I dried my hands on his monogrammed towels and wandered back to the living room. I could have left. Maybe I should have left. But a part of me wanted to give Carl Collins a chance to email me back.

And a part of me wanted to find out what else I didn't know

about Nick. Especially why his monogrammed towels had the initials "D.T." Who was DT?

I'd like to say I wasn't proud of my snooping. I'd like to say that snooping around about my coworker had led to seven very good reasons as to why snooping, in general, was a bad idea. Seven very good reasons should have been enough to put me on the straight and narrow, reform me from the same idle curiosity that had led me to almost run a background check on him. On the other hand, if I'd done that background check, I'd probably have learned that Nick's full name was Domenic Taylor, a fact that I learned today because I found his notice of late payment for the electric bill under the coffee pot in the kitchen.

I was dating a man named Domenic who didn't pay the electric bill on time?

I put the bill back under the coffee pot. It wasn't snooping on my coworker, but it was snooping nonetheless. And it—my behavior—was Reason #8 that snooping was a bad idea: some behavior can't be stopped.

But it was too late. The poker games, the sax playing, the protein powder, the stash of signed and personalized Janet Evanovich books in the closet. Seeing Nick in his black plaid boxers. The late electric bill and his full first name. It was too much discovery, and it was addictive. I couldn't *not* snoop.

Nick had been the one constant in my life since I'd moved from New York to Ribbon. He'd been the normal guy, the rock that I thought I could lean on, the port in the middle of the storm, the flotation device that I reached for when I was in choppy waters. Even when things hadn't gone well, I'd projected a form of perfection onto him that made me feel not good enough, and then, by default, too difficult for him to handle. But every detail I'd found over the past few days had told me one thing. Nick was as human as I was, and I hadn't given him the chance to show me his flaws.

I went through the kitchen, opening and closing drawers, looking for I didn't know what. The angel who normally sits on my shoulder had taken a coffee break, and the devil was in full control. My excuse? What I was doing was good practice should I ever need to search someone's apartment without leaving a trace. Because if I left any evidence of what could be described as the actions of a crazy person, the door to a relationship with Nick would be closed, locked, and sealed with the six bottles of Gorilla Glue I found under his sink.

Who needed six bottles of Gorilla Glue?

I moved on to the bedroom. Brown corrugated wardrobe boxes lined the wall just inside the door. I raised the flaps on the first box and saw a wooden bar lying across the top, holding several zipped garment bags on wooden hangers. Nick's suits.

I pulled out one garment bag, laid it on the bed, and unzipped it. Inside was a chocolate-brown pinstriped suit of summer-weight wool. I slipped the blazer off the hanger and put it on, and then looked at my reflection in the mirrored doors of the closet that lined the south-facing wall. Even though the jacket was too big in the shoulders, too boxy throughout the waist, too brown for my colorful sensibilities, it was perfect, because it was the Nick I knew. The professional shoe designer with the sartorial style. The scent of his Creed Bois du Portugal clung to the fabric, a faint aroma that made me feel like the man I knew was in the room with me. It was enough to shake me out of my temporary insanity.

What was I doing? If I hadn't learned my lesson now, then I was incapable of growing, of changing, of becoming a better person. I didn't have to ruin my life because I had an opportunity to snoop. I could tell Nick something came up, and I could leave right now.

I took off the suit jacket, rehung it on the wooden hanger, and forgetting that the garment bag was on the bed, eased the closet door open so I could hang it inside.

Scratch being a better person. Because what I saw in the closet was enough to cancel out at least half of reason number eight. It was the most powerful evidence I could possibly have found to prove my instincts to snoop were correct.

On the floor, next to a row of hanging trousers, bound and gagged, lay Nick Senior.

26

—————

TOP PRIORITY

I DROPPED THE SUIT JACKET ON THE FLOOR AND KNELT BESIDE NICK'S dad. He was dressed in the same clothes he'd worn the night we'd watched the Son of Sam documentary. His wrists were pressed together, and his fingers entwined like he was praying. I tried to push my hands between his palms to find a pulse but had no luck. I pressed my fingers against his temple instead and felt a faint heartbeat.

"Mr. Taylor," I repeated over and over. "Wake up. Mr. Taylor, come on, wake up." He didn't respond.

I looked for a closet light, but the socket was empty. It was too dark outside to get any light from the window. My eyes had adjusted as much as they would, but it wasn't enough. I pried at the knot on his gag until it was undone and then unknotted the rags that bound his wrists and ankles. One by one, I unbent his knees and laid his legs out in front of him. He hadn't reacted, hadn't appeared to notice I was even there.

I ran out front and felt around for my untraceable phone. I pressed the 9 and the 1 before stopping to think about what Nick's dad's presence meant. Him being here was no accident. The poker game, the trip to Atlantic City, the hot tables and winning streak that kept him from answering his phone had all been made up. So had the message that he was okay. Whoever was stalking me had kidnapped him and made his life miserable to send a message to me. But how long had he been here? And why had he been brought back at all?

The fight. Whoever had done this must not have known that the fight was staged. He must not have known about the extraction by the parade location or the fact that the bearded, mustached, side-burned guy driving the Crown Vic was Nick. Which meant I *couldn't* be the one to find Nick's dad, because it would give away the fact that none of that had been real. It would bring the danger right back to the people I loved.

I called Nick.

"No names," I said before he had a chance to talk.

"If that's how you want to play it," he said.

"I'm serious—this is serious. You need to come back. Right now." I fought to keep the hysteria out of my voice but was unsuccessful.

"Are you okay?"

"Come inside and go directly to your bedroom. You'll know what to do when you get there."

I hung up the phone and called Detective Loncar. "Nick's dad was tied up in a closet in his old apartment. He has a pulse but it's faint. He broke his hip a few months ago so this can't be good for his recovery. I untied him, but I can't be here when Nick gets here or else whoever did this will know I called him, and it'll keep going—"

"What's the address?" Loncar asked. I rattled off the apartment number and cross streets. "Get out of there. Now. I'm on my way."

I filled a cup with water and carried it back to the bedroom.

Nick Senior was still unconscious. I set the cup next to him and put my hand on his hand. "Please be okay, Mr. Taylor. Please. I'll make this right. I promise. Just be okay." Tears streamed down my face, and my breath hitched in my throat. Headlights appeared outside. I didn't know if they belonged to Nick or Loncar or somebody else, but I couldn't risk being seen.

I also couldn't just leave Nick's dad there alone.

I climbed into the closet next to Nick's dad and wedged my shoulders between a guitar amp and a pair of skis. A row of men's tailored trousers hung in front of me. I kept my hand on my untraceable cell phone in case of emergency, pulled my feet back into the darkness, and wrapped my arm around my knees. Nick would show up. He'd take his dad to the hospital. Loncar would help him. When they were gone, I'd leave.

It was the best I could come up with, considering the circumstances.

The front door opened and closed. "Kidd?" Nick called out.

I slid the closet door closed in front of me and held my breath. Had he seen the dead taxi parked out back? Had he put two and two together and known I was still there? Had I made a grave error in not leaving when I had the chance?

I couldn't see anything past the hanging trousers. The pile of the carpet would mask the sound of his footsteps as he moved throughout the apartment. I'd told him to come to the bedroom. He was taking his time—taking too long. He didn't understand the urgency. I put my hand on the closet door to slide it open when I heard another voice.

"Mr. Taylor."

"Detective Loncar. Why are you here?"

"I got an anonymous tip."

"Where are you going?"

"The bedroom."

"I don't think that's a good idea—"

The voices grew closer. I tightened my arms around my knees and sat as still as I could. The doors in front of the end of the closet were open, and Nick Senior's legs stuck out front. As soon as Loncar and Nick entered the bedroom, they'd see him.

"Dad!"

Conversation was replaced by movement. From my angle, I watched hands reach inside the closet and grasp Nick Senior's shoulders. His body shifted, and I pictured Loncar slowly pulling him, legs first, out of the closet while Nick kept his head from moving about too much. I recognized Nick's hands, his shirtsleeves cuffed up once at his wrists, the hands on his watch glowing in the darkness of the closet. Nick Senior was reclined back onto the carpet. Nick's wrist bumped the cup of water, which tipped and spilled on his dad's face. Nick Senior grunted and then moved his head back and forth.

"What are ya doing?" he said. His voice was scratchy and dry, as if out of practice of speaking.

"Can you tell me your name?" Loncar asked.

"If you don't know my name, then you should get out of here before I call the police."

"Dad, he is the police," Nick said. "He needs to see if you know your name."

"Nick Taylor. Senior."

"Where are you?"

"By the looks of things, I'm in my son's apartment."

"How many fingers am I holding up?"

"Three. You want to tell me what's going on?"

"You need to get to a hospital. I'll call an ambulance. I'll get your statement later tonight, but right now, your health is top priority."

The voices shifted to grunts as two men helped the third stand up. I closed my eyes and said a silent thank-you to the powers that be. The sounds moved from the bedroom to the hallway. I rocked back and forth ever so slightly, praying Nick Senior would be okay. Sirens announced ambulances. Minutes passed where the only sounds were those of emergency technicians doing their jobs. I heard a door close, and then silence. I counted to three hundred as slowly as I could and then slid the door open and pushed the trousers out of my way.

Detective Loncar stood in front of the bed with his arms crossed in front of his chest.

27

UNDERSTANDING AND FORGIVENESS AND PRIDE

I HELD MY FINGER UP IN FRONT OF MY MOUTH AND THEN POINTED toward the door. Loncar squatted down in front of me. "They're gone," he said. "I would be too except I recognized the taxi out back as the one I thought I returned to the graveyard." He kept his voice low.

"Here's what happened," I said, matching his volume. "I talked to a reporter at the newspaper and told him I was sending an exposé about Bethany House. To smoke Pritchard and his partner out. I came here because I thought it would be empty and I'd be safe."

"I am not going to ask how writing an exposé for a newspaper led you to find Mr. Taylor tied up in the closet, because it appears as though whatever your reasoning was, it may have meant the difference between that man living and dying."

I felt heat climb my neck and then my face. Breathing became a little more difficult. Snooping didn't make me a good person. It was a freak thing that Nick's dad had been in here. And sooner or later the question was going to come up, how I knew, how I found him, how I managed to save his dad—

Loncar put his hand on top of mine in a fatherly gesture. "Ms. Kidd," he said. "Do not beat yourself up over whatever it was that led you to that closet door. You did the right thing." He paused and squeezed my hand. "Your boyfriend will understand."

I looked him in the eyes and saw understanding and forgiveness and pride. Loncar's wife and daughter had to be two of the stupidest people I could imagine if they didn't see how much this man deserved to be a part of their family.

After climbing out of the closet, I described to Loncar the condition in which I'd found Nick Senior. He took notes in his little spiral-top notebook and tucked it back inside his suit jacket pocket. He clicked the end of his pen and put that away as well.

"Do you have somewhere to go?" he asked.

"Can I go back to my house?"

"I don't think that's a good idea just yet."

I nodded slowly. It was after midnight, and I didn't much care where I went as long as I could sleep. I ran the options through my head: the motel where I'd been sprayed by bullets, the abandoned offices where I'd found Tahoma going through Nancie's files. I thought of my friends, who would readily offer their sofas for my use, but I couldn't trade their safety for mine.

There was one option, and as much as I hated it, I knew I couldn't hold up Loncar any longer. "There's one place," I said.

"Good. Keep your phone on and lock your doors. Whoever kidnapped Mr. Taylor brought him back because they didn't think there was value in keeping him. His return was either a message or a change in their game plan."

"Are you any closer to figuring out what my coworker wants or who he's working with?"

"Right now, I'm more concerned with making sure nobody else

gets hurt." Loncar climbed into a dark, unwashed sedan and backed out of the parking lot. He turned on his headlights and then pulled onto the shoulder. He wasn't going to leave until he knew I had left, too.

I packed up my phone and pulled the beret on over my hair. I left Nick's extra key on the kitchen counter and flipped the lock from the inside. Unless Nick left additional keys hidden inside a rock in his garden, there would be no temptation to re-enter. I climbed into the dead taxi and drove to the most remote place I could think of. The dead taxi graveyard.

The next morning, I woke in the back seat of the taxi. Sunlight streamed across the cars in the lot, casting them in brilliant yellow tones. I desperately needed a bathroom, and I cursed the decision to not hold onto Nick's spare key. Of all the opportunities to turn over a new leaf, this was not my best choice.

While this was not a normal hour for me to rise and shine, the cramped sleeping quarters had limited the number of comfortable positions one could find in the back seat of a taxi. And as soon as I found myself awake, memories from the previous night assaulted me. No way could I sleep now.

I got out and raised my hands over my head, the left and then the right, stretching out all the muscles down either side of my body. I tipped my head from side to side, too, and then shrugged my shoulders in circles, first to the back and then to the front. I stretched out my neck a second time and then walked across the lot in search of a public restroom or a Porta Potty. Men had it so easy.

Past three rows of taxis in need of tires on various parts of their vehicle, I found a small office. The doors were open, and a navy-blue nylon windbreaker rested on the back of the chair behind the desk. A series of hooks were mounted along the right-hand wall. I counted eight across and eight down, creating a perfect grid except for the empty spots by numbers twenty, twenty-one, and twenty-two. Key chains hung from each hook, marked with a small round tag with a number written on it. I picked up one set of keys and then looked out at the lot. From the ground, it would have been hard to identify any of the taxis. From the elevated position of the office, I could see that a number had been painted onto the roof of each yellow taxi as well.

Hanging on the wall next to the taxi keys was a long wooden block with the word "Restroom" written on it in thick black letters. Two silver keys hung from the end. I crossed the room and picked the block up. The restroom must be near. I left the office and circled the perimeter until I found the rusty brown door. The key fit the lock, and the facilities, while far from what I would have liked, were operable. When I was done I ran my hands under the sink water for well over two minutes, lathering up several times. I dried my hands on my sailor T-shirt and doused them in two pumps of goo from the jug of hand sanitizer that sat inside the door. Satisfied that I'd killed anything I might have picked up while inside, I let the door shut behind me and went back to the office to return the keys.

This time, the office wasn't vacant.

28

RELEASE FORMS

A SLATE-BLUE CAT CARRIER SAT ON THE DESK ALONGSIDE OF A MUG OF coffee. Steam rose from the mug, indicating it was a fresh pour. The door to the carrier was closed, but when I stepped closer and peeked inside, I saw long white fur. A small face looked up at me. Around the neck of the cat was a collar made from a turquoise-and-red beaded choker.

It was Jennie Mae Tome's fluffy white cat, Navajo.

I glanced around the interior of the small office. A brown leather briefcase sat on the floor next to the wall of keys. I would have recognized it even if it didn't have the letters P. S. monogrammed in gold next to the combination lock. It was the briefcase I'd found in Pritchard Smith's office last week.

Bells, alarms, and warning flags went off and were thrown. I grabbed the cat carrier. Underneath it was a sheet of paper with the words *demo 21—23*. I looked out the window. A large crane was parked next to the taxi where I'd slept. Giant metal jaws descended on it until the teeth tore into the roof of the taxi and lifted it into the air.

I grabbed the cat carrier, the briefcase, and the keys on the bottom corner of the wall and ran out of the office. The noise of the large crane drowned out any other sounds. I ducked behind the taxi on the end and strained to see the man operating the crane. If he was Mohammed's cousin who oversaw the taxi graveyard, then why would he have Jennie Mae Tome's cat inside the office with him? Why did he have Pritchard Smith's briefcase? Why would he be destroying the car where I'd slept? There should be no connection between those things.

With the thumb on my left hand, I flipped the round paper disc that was attached to the keys. It was marked #3. I ran into the sea of taxis and scanned the vehicles for a corresponding number. The cat carrier shifted, and Navajo howled. I raised the carrier to my face. "Bear with me," I said. "I have to find us a car." I held the carrier against my hip with my arm wrapped over the top of it. From the ground level, I couldn't see the numbers on the top of each taxi.

I set the cat carrier and the briefcase down and climbed on the hood of the closest taxi. Number eight. Next to it was number seven, and next to that number six. I hopped back down, grabbed Navajo and the briefcase, and counted out the cars until I reached number three. I jammed the keys into the door and unlocked it, and then set Navajo's carrier on the passenger-side floor. I tossed the briefcase on the seat next to me and started up the car.

The taxis were parked close to each other, and there was no way out without causing damage. I put the car into gear, pulled the steering wheel to the left, and stepped on the gas. The taxi lurched forward, and it rammed the side of the ones next to it. I nudged the obstructing cars out of the way until I was past the office and on the road. From my rearview mirror, I saw the crane in the graveyard holding a yellow taxi in the air. Moments later, it dropped to the ground. The glass in the windshield shattered on contact.

It was too early in the morning for that level of noise. Someone was bound to call the police, and if the call made it to Loncar, he'd put two and two together. I could give him my version of events during the inevitable follow-up.

My untraceable phone, the laptop, and my temporary identification were in that car. Again, I had nothing. Nothing but Pritchard Smith's briefcase, Navajo, and the key to dead taxi #3. There wasn't much I could do about returning Pritchard's briefcase now, but I could get Navajo back to Jennie Mae. I drove to her house.

Traffic was light. After snaking through the streets of West Ribbon, I turned and drove east toward Amity. I didn't know how I'd explain a visit at such an unusual hour, but if Jennie Mae was anything like me, she'd prioritize the return of her cat over sleep. I ignored the posted speed limits and blew through several yellow lights. I wouldn't have minded if a cop put on his siren and followed me there.

I pulled into the long gravel driveway and slowed considerably. A landscaping van was parked next to the house. The back doors were open, and a row of potted trees and shrubs were scattered about the driveway. I parked the taxi on the opposite side of it and climbed out. I picked up Navajo's carrier and approached the wide-open front door.

"Jennie?" I called out. "Miss Jennie? It's Samantha Kidd. I have Navajo." I stepped into the living room and looked around. The rugs had been rolled up, the collection of frogs had been removed from the shelves, and the cats were missing from the divan. The one thing that remained was the empty rocking chair that I'd sat in during our visit, loosely covered by the earth-toned afghan.

I set the carrier on the divan and opened the door. Navajo was scared. I cooed at her and blew kisses, and then reached in and pulled her out. She reached her paws toward my shoulder, and her claws dug into the flesh through my striped shirt. I stroked her fur and tried to calm her down while I looked for Jennie Mae or Mr. Charles.

"Jennie? Hello? Who's here?" I called. I carried Navajo to the kitchen and set her down by an empty bowl.

There had been so many cats here on my previous visits that I didn't understand how there could be one bowl on the ground. I found a can of cat food in the refrigerator and forked it into the bowl, and then filled a separate white china bowl with water. I pushed the bowl toward the opening of the pantry. Navajo's head peeked out. She buried her head in the food and made eating noises that reminded me of Logan.

I called 911 and told them about the empty house. I had no firm evidence that what I saw was illegal, but after the theft, I wasn't taking any chances. It seemed odd that someone had arranged for movers to pack up the contents of the house but that nobody was there. Was this going to turn out like Nick's apartment, with Jennie Mae and the rest of her cats hidden inside a closet?

I went up the stairs and stared into the attic. The trunks were gone, leaving dark rectangles on the floor where they'd sat. The room looked much larger now that it was empty. Sunlight cast through the window and painted golden stripes on the floor. I walked to the window, my footsteps creating a rhythm of dull thuds with each step. A week ago, I'd been standing among Jennie Mae's vast collection of fabulous retro fashion. Her racks, filled with runway samples and the accompanying Polaroids of how they were worn on the runway, had been a treasure trove of fashion history, the value of which might never be known.

I turned around and looked back at the empty space. Something was off, but standing in the middle of an empty attic as I was, I couldn't figure out what. I turned to the left and slowly let my eyes pan across the walls, the ceiling, and the floor. And that's when I noticed that the discoloration on the floor, the rectangle that I'd assumed had been where the trunk had sat, had nothing to do with fading light or shadows. The wood in that rectangle had been replaced.

I walked to that section of floor and dropped to my hands and knees. When I ran my palms over the wood, I detected an edge. I fished the dead taxi keys out of my pocket and inserted them in the narrow space between floorboards and pried at them until I was able to lift one. A shadow of turquoise caught my eye. My fingers slipped. I dropped the board and started over, this time wedging the keys underneath the board as soon as I lifted it high enough. With a little effort, I was able to wrench my hand under the board and push up on the neighboring one. It was tighter than the first, but with pressure on the middle of the board, it lifted. And I realized what had felt off to me when I'd first walked across the floor. My footsteps should have sounded hollow against the wood. Instead, they'd left a dull sound, muffled. Because the space under the floorboards wasn't empty.

The black silk robe trimmed with piano fringe was there, as were the paisley-printed dresses and suede skirts. But who would have put these garments here?

I removed more floorboards and found a stash of samples. The turquoise satin peasant blouse that I'd started to try on when I'd heard Pritchard coming up the stairs that first day was still half on its hanger as if it had been flung here and not folded and tissued and treated like the valuable item it was. I touched the beadwork by the collar. Tiny hand-rolled beads in shades of coral, white, and turquoise had been placed in a perfect pattern. The beads were so small that I could barely make out each individual one.

It was exquisite. The kind of garment that Nancie would have wanted us to use in our editorial. A piece that could go from a runway show forty years ago to the pages of *Retrofit* with a slight shift in styling. It represented every single thing Nancie loved, everything she'd dreamed of when she first dreamt up *Retrofit* and then planned the print magalog that would take it to the next level. After what she'd been through, Nancie deserved to have her editorial.

I pulled the turquoise blouse off the hanger and laid it on top of a white gauze scarf, and then rolled the scarf until it was a few inches wide. I tied the scarf around my waist and knotted it on the side. We'd been granted permission to photograph the collection and use what we wanted in our magazine. Jennie Mae had signed the release forms before the collection had been stolen. Nobody had to know this blouse hadn't already been removed from the premises. When we were done, I'd see that it was returned to Jennie Mae's collection regardless of where she lived.

But the clothes under the floor were a fraction of what I'd seen that first day. I reached my hand under the samples and felt around, discovering that the pocket of space was about five feet long by two feet wide. I sat back on the floor and looked around. No other sections of floor were discolored like this one.

The hidden clothes were part of a bigger crime. Had someone been stealing from Jennie Mae all along? Had the collection reached a point where the empty holes became noticeable? Or had the apparent theft of the clothes been a diversionary tactic? A smokescreen to focus our attention on the clothes when they'd never been stolen in the first place?

I was halfway down the stairs when it hit me. Pritchard had told Nancie that Jennie Mae signed the release forms, but where were they? Those release forms, if they did exist, were more likely than not in Pritchard Smith's briefcase. In the back seat of dead taxi #3, which was parked out front next to the landscaping van.

I ran downstairs to the kitchen and grabbed the phone from the wall mount. The cord had been cut. I picked up the cordless. The battery chamber was empty.

I tossed the useless phone to the counter. It clattered against the marble, and Navajo jumped by my feet. I glanced around the kitchen one last time. Navajo lowered her head and ran past me into the tall cupboard cabinet next to the back door.

"Come on, Navajo, we have to get out of here," I said. I eased the pantry door open and peeked inside. And what I saw changed everything.

29

GRAVITY

N AVAJO LAY ON TOP OF A CARDBOARD BOX FILLED ALMOST TO THE BRIM with clothes. Immediately, I recognized items that I'd seen in Jennie Mae's attic on my first visit. The box had a shipping label to Utah. Navajo looked at me, and I swear if cats could think human thoughts, then the one going through her little kitty mind was this: *These belong here, and I won't let anybody steal them.*

I was a person who had grown up with cats. Our family's first, Topsy, had been a Bengal kitty, colored with markings of orange, black, and brown. Next came Buddy, a calico, and then Murphy, an orange-and-white striped tabby. My favorite summer ever had been my fifteenth year, when two separate strays had chosen our yard for their litters. We'd gone from a one-cat family to a nine-cat family while my parents tolerated the interest my sister and I took in the care and feeding of feline squatters.

When I'd adopted Logan in New York, he'd been a kitten. He'd seen me through a lot and had become more than a pet. He was my family. If someone had found him abandoned, I'd want that someone to take care of him for me. There was no question that I would not leave Navajo alone.

I reached down and ran my hand over her head. She purred. I stood back up and fished the dead taxi keys out of my sailor pants. If I moved the car around to the back of the house, nobody would know I was there. I could get the boxes out of the house and into the dead taxi, and they'd be safe. I opened the back door and found myself face-to-face with Mr. Charles.

"Hurry," he said. "There's not a lot of time."

I backed away from him. "Where is Jennie? Where are the other cats?" I asked. "What have you done with them?"

"They already left. Come with me and I'll explain everything."

"No." I slammed the door in his face and flipped the dead bolt. He stared at me through the glass panes, and it occurred to me that if he wanted to get me, all he'd have to do was to break the glass. I backed away, slowly at first, until I saw him turn and move swiftly to the right side of the house. I turned around and ran through the kitchen, past the rocking chair in the living room, to the front door, and threw the lock on that as well. I leaned my back up against the door, my pulse racing.

When I heard a key slide into the lock and the tumblers shifting into place, I darned near jumped through the roof.

Mr. Charles pushed against the door. I pushed back, but he was stronger. I stepped away. The door swung open unexpectedly, and Mr. Charles fell through onto the exposed wood floor. I ran up the stairs even though I knew the way out was the window—I'd gotten through it before, and I could do it again. The floorboards that I'd peeled up were scattered across the floor. I ran across the floor to the window, flung it open, and climbed out.

This time I didn't spend time hanging from the shutter. I jumped to the drainpipe and wrapped my hands and knees around it. The drainpipe pulled away from the wall, so slowly at first that I didn't notice it. I clung to the metal tube, increasingly aware that the distance between the drainpipe and the ground was closing. It wouldn't have mattered if my last three meals were salad instead of pizza. Gravity was going to win this battle.

Mr. Charles stood on a patch of grass looking up at me. And my wily coworker, who had caused all the trouble from the get-go, snuck up behind him and hit him on the head with the butt end of a gun.

30

DIRT POOR

THERE WASN'T TIME TO CREATE A MASTER PLAN. AS SOON AS THE drainpipe got close enough to the ground for me to jump, I did. I tried to stay loose, but the impact knocked the wind out of me. I rolled away from Pritchard and stood up. Vertigo claimed my senses and kept me from running. I put both hands out, reaching for some point of contact so I could bring my senses back in line. My left hand connected with the dangling drain pipe that had continued its descent after I'd jumped. It pulled away from the wall and fell to the ground like a defeated dinosaur.

"I made it very clear that you were to leave me alone. I'll have to report in to Nancie that you do *not* follow direction well. You do *not* work well with others."

"You're not the boss of me," I said. "I mean, you're not my boss. Nancie is."

"Nancie. What a delightful woman. Giving me free rein on the basis of a background check and a waived salary."

"A fake background," I said. "You're not Pritchard Smith. You're a phony. You made up everything you told her about you. You don't deserve to work at *Retrofit*. You deserve to be behind bars."

He maintained his distance, but the gun trained on me kept me from making any sudden moves. "You're not one hundred percent correct," he said. "My name is, indeed, Pritchard Smith. And I am well versed in the history of Seventies fashion. Your knowledge comes from a college degree and a more-than-causal interest in the subject. I came about my knowledge through a more intimate route. I was born into it."

"Jennie Mae Tome didn't have any children. You have no legal claim to her clothing collection."

"Jennie Mae wasn't my mother, but Pritchard Smith was my dad. She chose her modeling career over her marriage, and he found companionship when she was away."

I thought about what I'd learned about the two business partners and the argument that had gone horribly wrong. "They didn't argue about business, they argued about a woman. Your dad slept with Gene Whitbee's wife, didn't he? *That's* why Gene killed him."

"How do you know that name?" Pritchard said. For the first time since I'd met him, he appeared surprised.

"Your dad and Gene were small-town crooks. They trafficked in stolen goods and manufactured fake IDs on the side. People suspected that Gene murdered your dad, but his body was never found."

"I'm impressed. Seems you know about more than just the history of fashion. I'm curious, Ess Kay, what do you think any of this has to do with *Retrofit*?"

I ran the facts as I knew them through my head. *Retrofit* had led us to Jennie Mae Tome's house. But the contact here wasn't through Nancie, it was through Pritchard. He needed the cover of legitimacy to obtain access to the collection in the attic. He'd planned all along to come here. *Retrofit* hadn't needed him; he'd needed *Retrofit*.

"You manipulated everybody and everything to gain access to this house. You're after the clothes."

"A clothing collection assessed at over four million dollars. I'd say that's worth more than a credit in a start-up magazine, wouldn't you?" He laughed.

Behind him, Mr. Charles lay still in the freshly groomed lawn. I didn't know how badly he'd been hurt or whether I could rely on his help to take down Pritchard. His lack of movement told me I was on my own.

A dark sedan pulled into the driveway. Dust and gravel kicked up as it neared. Pritchard tucked the gun into his waistband under his suit jacket and adjusted his vest to conceal the weapon. If not for Navajo, I might have tried to make a break for the dead taxi and flee, but I wouldn't leave Jennie Mae's white Persian cat behind.

Pritchard turned away from me and watched the sedan. It pulled up behind the dead taxi, and the driver's side door opened. Deep V, my contact from the dentist's office, climbed out. Without her highlighted wig and liberal makeup, she looked different, but still familiar. Today she wore a leopard-printed jersey wrap dress, cinched tight around her waist. A black-and-white zebra-printed bra showed above the low neckline, not by accident. "You should have listened to me," she called out.

"I tried to," I said. She slammed her car door and walked closer, stumbling slightly when the stiletto of one of her high heels sunk into the freshly mowed grass. I shook my head from side to side and gestured for her to turn around and leave.

She wasn't getting the picture. In about three seconds, Pritchard was going to be able to take both of us hostage. I looked for a weapon. The landscapers had cleaned up too well, the evidence of their work in progress being a scattering of trees in plastic pots that were evenly spaced out by the perimeter of the building.

"Get out of here," Deep V said.

"He has a gun," I yelled. "He knocked out one person and could kill us both."

She looked at him and then at me. And then as if in slow motion, she raised her arm and fired a gun I hadn't even seen her holding. Pritchard screamed and dropped to the ground.

"Are you crazy?" he yelled.

"Don't be a baby," she said. "It's a flesh wound. If you had taken care of her like we agreed, I wouldn't be here."

Pritchard curled into a ball and whimpered.

I took two steps toward her and then realized the gun was now aimed at me. I looked back and forth between them. How could I have missed the resemblance? It wasn't her outfit that made her familiar, it was the similarity in bone structure she shared with my coworker. She'd emailed Nancie with information about Pritchard. I'd replied, and she sent me off on a wild-goose chase that kept me away from the very house where I should have been spending my time. Deep V had been the one to send me to Bethany House and had fed me the information about Pritchard Senior. It was the notation on the desk calendar at the auction house that I pieced together her contact with them.

"These men need a doctor," I said.

"They'll have to settle for a dental technician." She came closer. I backed up. In a few steps, I'd be up against the wall and Deep V would have no trouble aiming at whatever part of me she wanted to hit.

"Gene Whitbee didn't kill Pritchard, did he?" I asked.

"Who cares? Pritchard Smith was a bum, just like my dad. They both got what they deserved."

My research indicated that Gene had died of natural causes, but

I got the feeling there was more to that story. "You couldn't have been more than a teenager when Gene died."

"My mom OD'd when I was sixteen. I took my brother," she glanced at Pritchard, "*half*-brother, and we moved in with Gene. He didn't think I was smart enough to use his equipment, but I watched and learned. It's too bad he died right after my eighteenth birthday. Maybe we could have been partners." She laughed.

"Whose skull was in the attic? Pritchard's?"

"Yeah. I can't believe you found it."

"How did it end up in Jennie Mae's sample collection?" Did it matter? Probably not, but I had to keep her talking. The longer Pritchard bled from his flesh wound, the less he would be a threat. I didn't know if I could take Deep V, but I wasn't ready to give up just yet.

"Pritchard left all kinds of equipment in Gene's possession. After the desert critters had at the body and left me with a mass of bones, I hid them in his boxes. I planned to dump them in a donation drop box where nobody would be able to trace them to me. But Gene was always such a pushover for a pretty face. When Jennie Mae came to Gene to see if he'd heard from Pritchard, he said she could take his belongings. She should have found the skull and figured out what happened. I waited a long time for that shoe to drop."

"She never unpacked the boxes," I said. "She kept everything in storage. Those boxes were a reminder that when her career took off, her husband left. She's been haunted by that her whole life."

"Which would have been fine if you hadn't come along. I thought Pritchard had taken care of you with a few threats, but when we found out you took the skull, I had to intervene. We thought we'd have all the time in the world to empty out her closets, but you changed that. It never occurred to you that I didn't get involved until after you took the skull to the police, did it?"

It hadn't. I'd been so busy trying to figure out what Pritchard was doing that I hadn't given much thought to anything else. "Everything you told me was a lie."

"I'm sure *something* I said was true," she said. She chuckled.

She moved closer to me as she talked. The gun never wavered. "My mom used to tell me about Jennie Mae, the successful model who had everything. Jennie Mae's husband was my dad, but we were still dirt poor. It wasn't fair."

"Why come here? Why now?"

"That's because of you. I lost track of Jennie Mae Tome, but I never forgot about her. When I heard *Retrofit* Magazine was looking for private collectors of Seventies memorabilia, I knew it was the perfect opportunity, a way in. I set my brother up with the right ID to get inside. We could have made millions selling off her wardrobe."

"But why use Pritchard's name? Jennie Mae recognized it right away."

"That was the plan at first. We were going to drive her out of her mind. We could have used that to our advantage if we had time. And then you came along. We had to back burner Jennie Mae and deal with you first."

"I was just doing my job," I said.

"Ironic, isn't it? How far we'll go to do our jobs. Becoming a dental technician was supposed to be a way to turn over a new leaf. And now, DNA evidence in the pulp inside a bunch of teeth in a skull is going to bite me from beyond the grave."

In the distance, I heard sirens. *Please let them be headed this way, I thought. Let them be responding to my 911 call.* A car turned into the driveway of the Tome house. I didn't dare look away from Deep V to see who it was. If it was the police, the sirens would grow closer. If it was a random car using the end of the driveway to make a U-turn as people so often did, the driver would never see us. We were easily a hundred yards away from the road.

But the car, a glorious, freshly washed, bright yellow taxi, drove all the way to the house. Deep V turned and looked, giving me just enough time to grab one of the potted trees by the trunk. I swung it as hard as I could toward the back of her legs. She dropped to the grass. The gun fell. The tree came out of the pot, showering Deep V with dirt. I kicked the gun through the grass toward the driveway and used the trunk of the tree to pin her to the ground.

"Miss Samantha?" Mo called out of his window, "I think this time maybe you need more than a taxi so I call the police."

Four cop cars, blaring sirens and flashing lights, pulled into the driveway, parking him in. Judging from his smile, he didn't seem to mind.

31

A PACKAGE DEAL

IT WASN'T UNTIL THE NEXT DAY THAT I LEARNED THE FULL STORY OF what had happened over the past week. Deep V, aka Natasha Whitbee, was Pritchard's older sister. She'd been seven when Gene Whitbee shot Pritchard Smith. She'd watched her father bury his business partner in the desert. Gene turned to alcohol to numb the memories of what he'd done. When their mom died of a drug overdose in the early eighties, she and Pritchard had been left to raise themselves. She dug up the skull and hid it in a box in the basement. Security, in case her father's murderous streak ever threatened their safety.

She watched and learned the ID operation and, after her father's death, reinvented herself. It wasn't until a Google Alert on Jennie Mae Tome popped up and let her know the long-hidden archive of Seventies fashion would become public thanks to *Retrofit* and Bethany House that she contacted her brother with a plan to steal the samples. She established her brother's background, and he wheedled his way into Nancie's trust.

While Pritchard had been tasked with logistics of the theft,

Deep V had been crafty in her pursuit of the skull. She'd taken a job as a dental technician with a local dentist, hoping to gain early knowledge if the police requested dental records to find a match. She distracted me by delivering a series of misinformation delivered in the parking lot outside her place of work. She'd manipulated me by tapping into my inquisitive side, something she learned after researching me just like I'd researched everybody else. Perhaps another reason why snooping was a bad idea, though I'd given up counting arguments against my nature.

Speaking of snooping, thanks to me, Nick's dad was going to be okay. Pritchard and Deep V had treated him much the same as they'd treated Nancie in the basement of Bethany House, so while being tied up and held against his will wasn't the ideal way to spend a couple of days, it hadn't been torture. Pritchard hadn't known about Nick's new apartment and had returned Nick Senior to the wrong location. Had I not happened along when I did, who knows how long he would have been tied up in the closet.

Tahoma Hunt had not been involved in any criminal activity. His past felony convictions had been accumulated during a time when he'd made it his mission to recover relics of his American Indian heritage. The very past that had seemed so suspicious to me had been the qualifications that made him an attractive candidate to Bethany House: someone who recognized the historical and cultural symbolism in garments and was willing to put himself on the line to connect buyers to merchandise.

The only thing Bethany House had done wrong was to leave their receptionist in charge of the office keys. Detective Loncar's team found cartridges of nitrous oxide, readily available at most dentist's offices, in her desk drawer, along with a small oxygen tank and instructions on how to care for Nancie. Deep V had bought her help with the promise of free dental hygiene. Somebody needed to seriously consider the ramifications of the health care crisis.

What I hadn't known was that when Navajo had gone missing, Jennie Mae had gone to the police. Her accusation of catnapping might not have motivated them to act, but my 911 call plus the hysterical report of a taxi driver did. Mo, after hearing from his brother the fate of dead taxi #21, told Detective Loncar how often he'd been driving me to Jennie Mae Tome's house. The coincidence had been far too great.

Loncar and his team arrived shortly after Mo pulled into the driveway, arresting Pritchard and Deep V and transporting Mr. Charles to the hospital for immediate emergency care. Navajo was reunited with Jennie Mae. The clothes in the attic floor were recovered. Loncar had left the keys to my house with an officer who in turn left them with the night nurse. I drove home and slept in my bed for the first time in a week. I had completely forgotten about the turquoise silk blouse hidden in the scarf that was tied around my waist until I undressed for the night.

***

THE NEXT DAY, I woke up early and on edge. I was one year older but back to square one in my quest for steady employment.

I showered and dressed in a pair of amber culottes and an ochre chiffon blouse with full sleeves. I hung a gold pendant around my neck and slipped on a pair of striped espadrilles with ribbons that laced around my ankles. I blow dried my hair without benefit of a brush, letting the curls pop up naturally, and then knotted the yellow paisley scarf over the top and tied it on the side. My project might have ended, but I'd become charmed by the style of the Seventies.

I had a long list of people to call and things to do, but one item rose to the top of the list. I called Eddie and arranged to pick up Logan at Tradava. Twenty minutes later, I was sitting in his office, one hand on a cup of coffee, the other stroking my chubby black cat.

"Dude," Eddie said.

"I know."

"You wanna talk about it?"

I was quiet for a moment. So much had happened in my small little world. The Seventies project, the trashing of *Retrofit*, being shot at, being trapped in the basement of Bethany House, crawling through the air conditioning vents, and being held at gunpoint. I'd learned a lot about the people around me, but I'd also learned something significant about myself. Pritchard Smith had been right: I did not follow direction well. How many times would I have been safe if I'd stayed put like Loncar, Nancie, even Nick had asked? But the isolation—the sense of being trapped, or of missing out on something—had been stifling.

The thing that had gotten me through it all were friends: Eddie, who'd taken care of Logan no questions asked. Nick, who'd been dealing with the nuances of moving in with his dad but had taken time out to take care of me. And possibly the most surprising of all, Detective Loncar, who had his own drama: the estrangement of his wife, daughter, and her new baby.

"I'll probably want to talk about it at some point, but right now, I'd rather hear about you. What's up with the junk food?"

He sighed. "Tradava got the idea to put out a monthly catalog. As part of my visual director responsibilities, they have me sitting in on the buyer presentations and styling the pages. In addition to dressing the store. And until they find someone to run that division, it's all on me."

"But junk food? That's what I do when I'm stressed. You usually turn to spinach and grilled chicken."

He shrugged. "I don't know. You seem invincible, so I thought I'd give your way a try."

"How's that working out for you?"

He looked down at his stomach. There was a pooch on top of his waistband.

I picked up Logan, slipped him into his carrier, and stood up. "Here's a thought. I work for a magazine that is currently without a home. I have a feeling my boss would be open to a conversation with Tradava on taking over this catalog of which you speak."

Eddie leaned back and pushed his blond hair away from his face. He laced his fingers together and rested them behind his head. "That's not a bad idea," he said. "*Retrofit* and Tradava working together. Your boss has the know-how and the contacts. All I'd have to do is style the pages."

I stood a little straighter. "You do know I have experience with that sort of thing," I said.

"You're suggesting a package deal?"

I nodded once.

"Exactly how many employees are there at *Retrofit*?" he asked.

"Two. And trust me, that's as many as we'll need."

EPILOGUE

From the desk of Samantha Kidd

Send birthday thank-you notes to:

1. Eddie: for 1-year membership to the sandwich of the month club
2. Nick: for arranging an "extraction" on my birthday because he thought it was an experience I'd enjoy
3. Cat: for 30% discount coupon to Catnip
4. Mo: for 1 complimentary taxi ride
5. Detective Loncar: for approving my new application to the Citizen's Police Academy
6. Logan: for sleeping on my head last night

PEARLS GONE WILD

1

———

MEN ARE RATS

"Men are rats!" Cat said. She threw a dinner plate into her kitchen sink, and it shattered on contact.

"They're not all rats," I said.

"Name one who's not a rat. Go ahead, name one." Before I had a chance to answer, she continued. "My husband is a rat. His bosses are rats." She grabbed another plate. "My brother is kind of a rat, don't you think?"

"Cat, I don't think it's my place to say whether or not your brother is a rat."

"He's a rat, trust me. You don't know because you chose Nick instead of him." She brought the dish down against the sink. It bounced off, unbroken. She looked at it, confused, and then turned it over and looked at the bottom. "Corelle. Well, that's not satisfying at all." She tossed it onto the counter, where it skidded until hitting a loaf of bread.

Cat Lestes was a local boutique owner, a friend, and one of those people who make you constantly feel rumpled because they're always immaculately dressed. I'd never seen so much as a hair of her striking red, asymmetrical haircut out of place...until tonight. Her husband spent more than half of his life on the road, and as if that hadn't been enough space, he'd told her earlier this evening that he needed a break. It turned out his definition of "break" differed from hers; he was moving out. Considering Cat was eight months pregnant, George's timing seemed suspicious.

"I'm pretty sure George is just going through a phase. Like last month when you said you wanted to run away and join a convent."

She picked up a mug and shook it at me. "Nuns don't have to deal with swollen ankles."

I stepped forward and put my hands on her wrists. "He didn't cheat on you, he didn't ask for a divorce. He's just asked for some space. He was probably thinking about the baby and about how his life is going to change."

She glared at me for a moment and then deflated like a balloon twenty-four hours after a twelve-year-old's birthday party. Her normally size-two frame shrank, causing her pregnant belly to protrude. It looked like a tiny nerf basketball had been strapped to her waist under her chocolate-brown knit dress.

"There are times to think about making more money and there are times to be there for your wife," she said. "He should have known that."

I pried the mug—the next about-to-be-broken item in her arsenal—from her grip and set it on the counter and then wrapped her in a hug. Cat was like me in that she wasn't particularly touchy-feely, but at the moment we both needed it.

When we pulled apart, I pointed to the living room. "You go sit down. I'll clean up in here."

"It's my mess," she argued.

"Let me do this for you."

She nodded and left me alone with the broken dishes. Cat lived in a split-level house in a residential neighborhood in Wyomissing.

Her neighbors were in the post-retirement, 65+ range and were friendly but not nosy. I often thought of myself as a woman who lived alone in a house probably too big for one person, but even before Cat's marital troubles, she'd been in a similar boat because of her husband's travel. Except now she had a baby on the way. I couldn't begin to imagine the pressures she felt.

As I collected pieces of broken dishes and glass from the floor, I heard what sounded like the local news coming from her TV. These days it was mostly stories about the weather or the occasional car theft from one of the malls in the area. Thus represented the city of Ribbon, Pennsylvania, where we split our time (and our residents) between do-gooders and criminals. At least that's how it seemed since I moved back two years ago. And here I'd thought trading New York City for small-town life would lead to a more peaceful existence.

Cat's proclamation that all men were rats landed on deaf ears thanks to my relationship with Nick Taylor. While her husband had let her down at a time when he should have been there for her, my love life was chugging along, hitting all the right notes.

Nick was a local shoe designer who kept an apartment in Italy, and shortly after my birthday in May, he'd left to meet with the factories about his upcoming collection. Our relationship was not without problems—many of which explained why we'd broken up once since making the shift from business colleagues (nine years) to on-again, off-again couple (two years)—but ever since I'd saved his father's life, Nick seemed willing to overlook the problems (inconveniences?) that came with dating me. And I understood the needs of his business and that spending six months out of each year in Europe was part of his life. But I'd be lying if I said I wasn't looking forward to Nick coming home for the holidays.

I found her broom and swept the broken pieces of china into the dustpan and then into the trash. Cat's kitchen—her whole house—was usually immaculate. I did a double take when I saw two errant grape tomatoes and a scattering of green peas in the dustpan. Maybe her housekeeping skills were relaxing, but at least she was still keeping up with her daily vegetable intake. That put her one step ahead of me.

"Stupid bastard!" Cat yelled from the living room. Moments later, there was a thud.

I dropped the dustpan and broom into the sink and ran to the living room. Cat was on the floor with her feet splayed out in front of her. Her dress was hiked up to her hips and between her knees was a partially empty bowl. Across the room, popcorn was scattered around the base of the TV.

"What's wrong? What happened?"

She pointed to the screen. "The news is doing a profile on the rat. 'Local businessmen do good.' That's a joke. He didn't do any good by leaving me. Just because he's helping his company hand out free ornaments tonight doesn't make him a saint. It's Christmas. Where are the stories about stolen cars and thefts at the mall? Where are all the shady Santas?"

I leaned forward and plunked the remote from her hand. "Are you okay?"

"Retail. Holidays. Pregnant. Rat husband. Keep up, Sam. I thought I could rely on the news to match my mood, but no. It's like they got tired of reporting on all of the retail theft, so they're looking for feel-good stories. The rest of the year, it's all politics, hate crimes, and misdemeanors, but when I need it? 'Local businessmen do good.' And these people call themselves reporters."

I sat down next to her. "Where are they—your mall?" Cat's boutique, Catnip, was in the Ribbon Designer Outlet Mall. "Is it a special shopping night? Are there discounts?"

"It's the lighting of the mall Christmas tree. Kenner & Winn are the hosts—that's the company George works for. If George was a good guy, he'd be here, not at a party handing out baubles. The news should focus on the stores, not the vendors. We're the ones who make it through the battleground of December shopping so people can have presents under the tree. But we're like the elves. Totally under appreciated." She threw another fistful of popcorn at the TV.

I bent down and corralled the spilled popcorn into a pile, and then, using both hands, transferred it onto a *Glamour* magazine that Cat had left open to the "Fashion Don'ts" section. I set the magazine on the coffee table and spun around to face her.

"I know this is going to sound strange coming from me, but I think you need to calm down." She stared at me but didn't say a word. "I know you're mad at George, and I understand why. But you can't let that anger spill onto everything else. Didn't the doctor warn you about your blood pressure?"

"Yes, but it's not like I can sit around and relax. Not now. There's going to be another mouth to feed, and I don't trust that rat to do the right thing. Employee turnover is at an all-time high. I tried to hire extra staff to take some of the pressure off me, but as soon as I train one person, another one quits. Yesterday one of my associates resigned at the end of her shift. She got an invite to go skiing for the holidays and is leaving tomorrow. I didn't even get two weeks' notice. Honestly, what is wrong with people? I told her I was surprised she even bothered to show up, and you know what she said? She wanted to make sure she got her last paycheck."

"That's not very professional. I hope she doesn't want a referral."

"People don't think of retail jobs as professions. It's what they do while they figure out how to do what they want to do. It's frustrating."

"You need to cut yourself a break. My vacation just started. I'll help out whenever I can, but now is not the time for you to try to be superwoman."

My work history post moving back to Ribbon had been spotty (at best). Earlier in the year, I'd been gainfully employed at *Retrofit*, a start-up e-zine that showcased current fashion trends and how they correlated to fashion history. My boss's big dreams of expansion had had disastrous results, and *Retrofit* was on its way to becoming yet another casualty on my resume, until an unlikely savior stepped in: Tradava.

Tradava was a mid-range retailer that actively pursued their share of the entry-level trend market. Their partnerships with design competitions and museum exhibits had kept their name in the news and their affiliation with mid-range fashion present. Their desire to produce a glossy magalog—a cross between a catalog and a magazine—led to a bit of creative thinking, and some smart person at the top of the food chain made the decision to buy *Retrofit* and bring us into the advertising fold.

Which meant I still had a job. Not just any job, either. One with health benefits and a 401K of my own. In the three months after my probationary period ended, I'd had a full blood workup, a physical, and an assortment of exams that covered the parts of me that needed to stay in working order. If medical came with a customer punch card like the sandwich shop, I'd be due for a freebie any day now.

I picked up the remote and cued up the guide. "Let's find something else to watch to distract you. Look—*Dial M for Murder* is on. Are you feeling Hitchcocky? Or maybe we need a rom-com."

"I think you're right," she said. She put her palms on the sofa behind her and slowly lifted herself off the floor and onto the cushion. She smoothed her red hair with her hands and then stood. "A distraction is a good idea." She crossed the room and picked up her handbag and then pulled out a laminated card and waved it at me. "You feel like a party?"

"You didn't say anything about a party when you invited me over."

"That's because when I invited you over, I didn't know we were going."

"Where are we going?"

"There. To the party. I should be there, not him. I'm the one who buys their product and sells it in my store. I want him to look me in the eye in a public place and let everybody know what he did."

"But I thought you said Kenner & Winn were jerks?"

"They are. And tonight they're the jerks who get to be the target to all of this misplaced anger."

I didn't get up. "Five minutes ago, you were breaking china. Maybe you need to sit still for a couple of minutes—"

"If everything had gone according to plan, I was going to be in the middle of a romantic dinner tonight. But I'm not. That doesn't mean I have to sit here like a big fat blob. I can have a life too, right?"

I looked down at my outfit. Navy sweater and blue camo pants. At least my boots had heels. "I'm not dressed for a party."

"You look fine," she said, providing further evidence that she wasn't exactly herself. Under normal circumstances, Cat had choice things to say about my occasional desire to shop the Army-Navy store (because blue camo is totally fabulous even if a non-hormonal Cat wouldn't agree).

"I think it would be better if we stayed in." I pulled my phone out of my handbag. "Pick out a movie while I call Nick. I'll make you a fresh bowl of popcorn when I'm done."

I slipped from the living room into her den. "Hey, Kidd," he answered.

"Hey, Taylor."

"How's your Friday night?"

"Touch and go. I'm at Cat's. She's...her husband...things aren't great right now. I'm acting as a calming force."

He laughed. "You're about as calming as a bed full of itching powder."

"I resent that!"

"Just saying you're not known for your ability to relax."

"I can relax as well as the next guy," I said. "What about you? Packing? Your flight takes off in a couple of hours, right?"

"Change of plans," he said. "There's a problem at one of the factories, and I can't leave yet."

"You're not flying home tonight?" My positive outlook waivered. I wanted to feel all the things you feel at the beginning of a relationship, but I couldn't help wonder if, ten years down the line, Nick would be restless just like Cat's husband. "Is it a big problem?

"If I want to stay on production schedule with my new collection it would be best to fix it in person."

"Have you told your dad?"

This past May, Nick's life had been flipped on its head when his dad, recovering from a broken hip, moved in with him. In addition to the newly negotiated domestic situation, it had brought Nick and I closer. I'd learned a multitude of quirks about him that raised eyebrows. He learned the truth about my daily caloric intake. And yet, we were still together.

"Tonight's his poker night. It violates the rules of their game to use cell phones."

"Sounds like you're going to come home to cheap beer and stale chips."

"You fixed the chip situation with the golden Chip Clip you gave him the last time you were over. It's his favorite thing in the house."

"See? There is no limit to the problems I solve."

"Kidd, there's something I have to tell you. I told a friend to crash here while I was gone, but now that I have to stay, well, I didn't expect to have a roommate."

"Two bachelors in Italy. Should I be worried about you cruising for Italian women?"

"Kidd, she's not a bachelor. She's—the friend—is Amanda Ries."

If I'd been standing in Cat's kitchen, I might have picked up that unbreakable piece of Corelle, thrown it onto the floor, and then stomped on it a few times. Instead, I stood up and punched the hunter green leather chair behind the desk.

"Kidd, you know she's just a friend."

That wasn't the point, and I knew it, and I was pretty sure he knew it too. "I think I hear Cat calling me from the living room. I have to go." I hung up before he had a chance to reply.

When I returned to the living room, Cat was sprawled out on the sofa. The screen saver for *The First Wives Club* was on the TV. The remote control dangled from her hand. I took it and clicked off the TV.

"Get your handbag. We're going out."

"What changed your mind?"

"Turns out you were right. All men *are* rats."

2

———

YOUR KIND

NICK AND AMANDA WERE COLLEGE FRIENDS WHO BOTH WORKED AS designers, though in different aspects of the industry. Their friendship, shared experience, and education had created a bond, and she was a part of his life. The rational part of my brain knew there was nothing going on between them and not just because he'd told me. But my irrational side taunted me with all kinds of images: Nick and Amanda together on a seven-hour flight. Nick and Amanda sharing a walk around Italy under a starry sky. And possibly the worst: Nick and Amanda sharing a margarita pizza. (I'm especially territorial when it comes to food.)

I'd had a spotty employment record after leaving my nine-year career as a designer shoe buyer for Bentley's New York and moving to Ribbon, Pennsylvania, and in that time, I'd taken on whatever fashion-related work I could find. During Nick and my off-again period, I'd helped Amanda mount her first fashion show. I'd committed to the project before Nick and I had broken up, and it had been important for me to honor my commitment. Things hadn't gone exactly as planned.

Nick's friendship with Amanda was something I'd have to learn to accept, just like Nick had to acknowledge my friendship with Cat's brother, Dante. But either time one of their names came up, the reaction was the same: jealousy. And if we didn't find a way to deal with that, any relationship we started would be doomed.

I pushed thoughts of Nick and Amanda in Italy (with or without food) from my mind and drove Cat to the designer outlets. "Tell me about this party."

"Tom Kenner and Don Winn are the partners who own Kenner & Winn. They're jewelry wholesalers. They're co-sponsoring a shopping night at the mall to promote their jewelry line. George joined their company a couple of months ago and took over their biggest territory."

"Kenner & Winn. How come I never heard of them? I was a buyer for nine years before I moved here."

"Their specialty is licensee deals. Designers sign on with them to source products, but most designers don't want you to know where they get their products from because you could just cut out the middleman and get the merchandise without the name attached."

The nine years that I'd spent as a buyer had been in ladies' designer shoes. Cat was right. I didn't buy directly from the factories, I bought from the designers. I could tell you a lot about how the shoe business worked, but the technical side was still something of a mystery.

"I never thought about it before, but jewelry must be a high-margin business."

"It is. There's no way to put a designer name on an item except on the packaging. You're getting double the mark-up for a designer name, and only the people who follow high fashion know whether your jewelry is Chanel or Saint Laurent or Oscar."

"This party is being sponsored by the men who import the product, right?"

"Yes, but don't worry, they're not fashion people. These guys are the ones with the money. They don't care about taste, they care about the bottom line. If I told them I wanted to start selling rhinestone-encrusted bras, they'd find a way to supply them."

"You've bought from them? For Catnip?"

She shook her head. "Not until recently. I don't carry precious jewelry, and even if I did, I always thought it was a bad idea for George and me to mix our work life with our home life. Shows what I know. If I'd been one of his clients, I might have known he was on the verge of a mid-life crisis."

"But recently, you placed orders from Kenner & Winn?"

"Yes. One of his accounts canceled an order of pearls because Kenner & Winn missed the delivery window. I've been working on a luxury strategy for Catnip, and George talked me into buying the canceled order."

"How's it selling?"

"It never had a chance to sell. It was stolen in a smash and grab. Merry Christmas to me," she said in a flat voice.

For those not in the know, a smash and grab is an in-and-out retail theft. The idea is that, if you're quick, you can break into a store, smash a glass case full of merchandise, grab as much as you can carry, and get out in less than a minute. Judging from where the security officers might be, even if they know a theft is taking place, you can be gone before they can catch up with you.

It's a bold way to steal. Most people get caught because they're either not fast enough or they get greedy and stay in the store too long. Sometimes thieves smash the first case they find and take armloads of items that have low resell value. That's one of the ways you can tell if thieves know what they were doing.

"Was anything caught on camera?"

"The camera is mounted to the opposite side of the mall by the main entrance. The alarm went off, but by the time the police showed up, the merchandise was long gone."

"They got everything?"

She nodded. "Black Tahitian pearl necklaces. You remember them, right? The only one they didn't steal was the one you asked me to put on hold."

I'd seen the necklace in question last week during a quick shopping trip. As much as I'd wanted to splurge on it, the comma in the price had been a good deterrent from adding it to my list of must-haves. It sounded like the thieves knew what they were doing.

WE ARRIVED at the Ribbon Designer Outlets, and I pulled up next to a twenty-something in a red jacket and black pants, exited the car, and headed toward a giant green tree. It was decorated in lustrous round ornaments that looked like oversized pearls and sparkling plastic gemstones. Thick ribbon printed with the Kenner & Winn logo had been loosely draped around the tree. Subtlety wasn't high on the duo's agenda. White twinkle lights wound through the branches, and two spotlights on the ground were aimed at the top just in case you somehow missed the monstrosity.

I followed Cat to the entrance. A woman in a soft, chiffon duster, coordinating satin tank top, and palazzo pants stood next to a man in a tuxedo. Her lashes were so long I felt a breeze when she blinked. The man held out a hand to Cat. She shook it aggressively, though I didn't think she had much of a choice.

"Welcome to the Kenner & Winn holiday party. I'm Tom Kenner. This is my wife, Joyce."

"Cat Lestes," Cat said.

Tom turned toward the woman next to him. She looked at her

husband first and then at Cat. Her smile seemed disingenuous, although whether it was Cat and my presence or boredom that caused the reaction, I didn't know.

"Cat. Is that short for Catherine?" Joyce asked.

"Yes," Cat said.

"And you are?" Joyce said to me.

Before I could answer, Cat spoke up again. "This is Samantha. She's my partner."

"She means—" I started, but Cat put her hand on my arm. Tom and Joyce looked Cat's pregnant belly.

"Nice to see your kind taking such good care of each other," Tom said. He put his hand on Cat's belly, and I felt her tense next to me. "Little one is going to be lucky, having two moms."

"Is Mr. Winn here?" Cat asked.

"Nope. We heard about some trouble with the exporter, and he lost the coin toss. He'll be spending his holiday in India." He chuckled.

Joyce looked past me and gestured toward a cluster of people more appropriately dressed than I was. She extended a braceleted arm with long, well-manicured nails and directed us toward a waiter handing out pre-poured flutes of pink champagne just inside the store entrance. Behind them, a woman in an ivory pantsuit worked a coat check booth. It wasn't until after we were inside the store that I pinched Cat's arm.

"Ow! What was that for?"

"Partner?"

"Business partner. Why else would I bring you here tonight?"

"Friend, associate, customer," I ticked off possible answers. "How come he doesn't know you're George's wife?" I asked. "Shouldn't he recognize you?"

"I've never met Tom or Joyce before. We haven't been to any company events for Kenner & Winn yet."

"Look on the bright side. He'll probably give you a set of hers and hers matching towels when you have the baby."

"They don't know I'm married to the rat." She looked over my shoulder and then scanned the rest of the room. "You don't see him, do you?"

"He's going to be here?" I asked. I dropped my voice to a whisper. "You're not going to cause a scene, are you?"

"Of course not. I'm a lady." She smoothed out her hair. "Go to the bar. You'll fit in more if you're holding a glass of champagne."

"I'd fit in more if you would have given me five minutes to change."

"I'm going to see what non-alcoholic beverages they have." She pulled her long silk scarf from around her shoulders. "You're creative. Do something with this."

I weaved through the crowd in search of a private spot where I could work a makeover miracle on my G.I. Jane outfit. Pearlescent balloons had been blown up and scattered around the floor and hung from the ceiling. The coat check woman pointed to a public restroom, and I went inside and into a stall to change.

I pulled my sweater over my head and then tied two ends of Cat's scarf around my neck. I tied the other two ends behind my back, creating a drape-front, open-back top. My bra was an eyesore, so I took it off, which created a whole other set of problems. I found a roll of fabric tape in the bottom of my handbag and used it to, shall we say, secure my assets with a trick I'd learned from a stylist. I re-knotted the scarf and jumped up and down a few times to make sure everything was going to stay in place. The door to the bathroom opened. I flushed the toilet (cover story) and waited until feet appeared in the stall next to me before I left mine.

My sweater and bra were too cumbersome to fit in my handbag. I looked for a place to stash them for later retrieval, but frankly, there was something a little skeevy about stashing clothes in a public restroom. I slid the window open and pushed the two items outside. They landed on a patch of brown grass behind a bare bush.

I washed my hands and ran my fingers through my hair. The other stall opened and a ghostly pale woman with full red lips and heavily arched eyebrows came out. Her jet-black hair was slicked away from her face, and a hibiscus was tucked behind one ear. She wore a skintight yellow strapless dress that was cinched with a red patent leather belt. After washing and drying her hands, she pulled a tube of lipstick out of her handbag and touched up her pout.

A small bundle wrapped in tissue paper fell out of her bag and landed on the floor by her red patent leather peep-toe pumps. I bent down and picked it up. "You dropped this," I said.

Her eyes went wide. She grabbed the bundle and held it for a moment. "Trash," she said and then shoved it into the bin in the corner. She left, and I followed her back to the party.

A few people swatted pearl-colored balloons back and forth with one hand while sipping champagne with the other. Aside from the brief introductions I'd had upon arrival, Cat was the only person I knew at the party. Cat didn't care that I wasn't an industry insider. What she did care about was whether or not I had steady employment, because a fair portion of my disposable income now went back to her store's bottom line. I helped myself to a flute of champagne and weaved through the partygoers, looking for her.

I shouldn't have left her alone. In the center of the party by the UP Escalator, Cat stood face-to-face with her husband, George. A display of gloves, hats, and scarves in bright candy shades provided a nice backdrop. George's lips moved, but I was too far away to hear what he said. He looked distraught, earnest. A shock of brown hair had fallen forward on his forehead, making him appear boyish.

In my head, I scripted imaginary dialogue for them. Him

apologizing. Her accepting. Him promising to do whatever it would take to get them back on track, her laughing off his fears.

He put his hands on her arms and leaned down and said something to her, and stood straight.

And she grabbed a drink from a passing server and tossed the contents in his face.

3

PARTY GIRL

I HELD MY CHAMPAGNE FLUTE ABOVE MY HEAD AND SQUEEZED through the crowd. By the time I reached Cat, her husband was gone. Partygoers had backed up and left a circle of space around her. "Did you see that?" one woman asked. "Hormones," said another, casting a judgmental look at Cat's belly. "I heard she left him for another woman," said a third.

Cat looked stunned. I put my arm around her and led her toward a quiet corner.

"I'm not ready to be a mother. I just threw a drink at the father of my baby! Why did I think I could do this?" Cat said.

"You are going to be a better mom than ninety percent of women who get pregnant. Yes, your life is going to change, but for amazing reasons. You're going to have a baby." I smiled. "That won't change who you are. It's going to magnify who you are."

"You think so?"

"I know so."

Her eyes dropped to my makeshift top and her forehead

wrinkled with a frown. "What about you? It would be easier if we did this together. Do you think you'll ever have a baby?"

My nervous system woke up like it had been plugged into an outlet and a cold sweat broke out on the back of my neck. Cat having a baby was one thing. I was pretty sure I knew where I stood on the subject, but the lack of serious relationships had lulled me into a false sense of never having to examine my thoughts too closely.

"Let's get you through your pregnancy before we tackle that issue," I said.

"You're right. You're not even married. Not that you'd have to be..." She looked at me again.

"Let me take care of you while you take care of little Andy or Jenny."

She pulled away. "Isn't that line from *Rosemary's Baby?*"

"We should leave," I said. "Walk with me to the coat check."

Cat looked at the faces staring at her. A few had the decency to look away. She turned back to me. "I'd rather not. Meet me by the exit."

I went back into the mall and collected our jackets. When I returned, Cat was seated on a low bench with an older man in a tweed suit and a full head of white hair. They appeared to be comfortable with one another. She held a champagne flute, but the beverage was clear. A wedge of lime had settled in the bottom.

"I have the coats," I said, holding them up. "Are you ready to go?"

"Sam, there you are. I want you to meet someone. Jim, this is Samantha Kidd. Sam, this is Jim Insendo. Jim used to own my store," she said.

I shook Jim's hand. "So you're our town sleuth," he said. "I've heard a lot about you. Are you hot on somebody's trail tonight?"

I smiled. "Nope, tonight I'm just a party girl." I looked around the party and spotted the woman from the bathroom standing with George. Maybe there *was* another woman. Things were adding up, but Cat didn't need to know the score. "Come on, we should get you home."

"So soon?"

"I think you should get some rest. It's been a big day."

"Okay," she said. She turned to Jim. "It was nice catching up with you. Call me if you want to get together for coffee. You know the number." She stood and set her glass on a display of perfumes. Jim smiled and then left us and walked to the bar.

"Do you mind if we go to Catnip before we leave?" Cat asked. "I want to check on the store."

"I'll meet you there. I need to get something from the bushes outside of the mall."

We both bundled up and left the party. Cat went toward the car and I split off to the right and around the side of the mall in search of my sweater and bra. She passed me as I was pulling dead blades of grass from my sweater.

When I reached Catnip, the exterior door was propped open with a rock. I went inside and found Cat straightening a display of colorful cashmere scarves and gloves. "I'm going to get something from my office. I'll be a minute." She tucked a strand of red hair behind her ear.

"Go do what you have to do. I'm going to the fitting room."

"Don't get distracted. We're only staying as long as it takes me to check the safe."

"How long is that?"

"Two minutes."

I could try on at least three outfits in two minutes. I entered the fitting room and stripped down to my fabric tape and panties. Before I had a chance to pull a fringed ivory dress over my head, I heard a crash.

I peeked out of the dressing room. A figure in baggy black clothes, gloves, and a knit ski mask stood in front of the jewelry case. He held a tire iron in one hand and a handful of thick pearl necklaces in the other. Broken glass was scattered on the floor all around him.

"Hey!" I yelled. I ran out of the fitting room holding the dress in front of me. He took off for the front of the store. Until that moment, I hadn't noticed that the gate wasn't closed.

I ran after him, but the lack of support in the ta-ta region slowed me down. Cat stepped out of the shadows, and the figure pushed her back. She lost her balance. I changed course and ran to her.

"Are you okay?" I asked. I yanked a blue puffer jacket from a nearby hanger and wadded it up under her back. She put one hand on her tummy. The color had drained from her skin, leaving it a ghostly shade. Her labored breathing came out in bursts like I imagined she'd learned in Lamaze class.

"Did you see what happened?" she asked.

"It was a smash and grab."

"You scared him away. Who knows what he would have done if he didn't see you."

I considered the style in which I'd chased after him: cotton panties and fabric tape. "I don't think he saw me as much of a threat."

A young man in a black uniform ambled up to us. He looked like this job was just his warm-up for a night gig as bouncer for the local cover band circuit. His head was clean-shaven and shiny—which indicated shaving probably didn't have a lot to do with his choice of hairstyle. I grabbed another puffer jacket from the fixture and pulled it on over my naked torso.

"Mall's closed, ladies. You need to leave." he said. From our position on the floor, I couldn't tell how tall he was, though his rotund physique made him appear on the short side.

Cat sat up. "This is my store. I'm the owner."

He looked annoyed. "Officer Aguilar. Mall security." He shook Cat's hand and then mine. "I heard a crash. Is everything okay?"

"There was somebody inside her store," I said. "He smashed one of her cases and grabbed her merchandise. He pushed her out of the way when he ran out of the store. That's assault. She's eight months pregnant and could have been hurt. So no, I don't think everything is okay."

That got his attention. He looked back and forth between our faces. "Do you need medical assistance?"

"I'm fine," Cat said. "We were at the party and came here to make sure the store was locked up properly."

"It's after hours. Everybody has to be out by eleven." He looked at Cat. "You know the rules."

"I know," she said.

"The thief was probably already here when we arrived and we just didn't see him," I said. "How would someone get in without you noticing?"

"We try to cover the whole mall, but with that party at the other end, there's a chance someone could have gotten past us. Or maybe they hid in the store after it closed. Were you the one who locked up?"

"No," Cat said. "I didn't even think of what time it was. It's the holidays and since I wasn't the one to lock up, I wanted to check on the store before I went home." Cat sat up and stared at the shattered jewelry case and the broken glass on the carpet. "What do we do now?"

"As long as I'm here, we might as well fill out the report." He pulled a radio from his belt and told somebody to override the lights in the rest of the mall. "Show me where this happened."

"I'll go." I stood up and held the puffer jacket closed with my fist. Cat moved from the floor to one of the ottomans that were positioned around the store for customers who needed a rest. Officer Aguilar followed me through the store.

I stuck to the aisles between fixtures. In the darkness, I felt the crunch of broken glass under my feet before I saw it. I grabbed a trash bin from the aisle behind the counter and then stooped down and collected some of the bigger pieces of glass, careful not to cut myself. The lights came on, and I blinked a couple of times while my eyes adjusted.

I wished the lights had stayed out.

The smash and grab was no longer the main concern. Sometime before Cat and I had returned to her store, before I'd ducked into the fitting room for after-hours shopping, before I'd interrupted a robbery in my underwear, Cat's husband, the rat, had been strangled by a pearl necklace and his body had been left behind the glass case that normally held her jewelry display.

As far as Cat's problems went, this one was on a whole other level.

4

GOOD COP

It was a much more official team that worked in Cat's store while we sat, wrapped in blankets, on a nearby ottoman. Emergency technicians had arrived shortly after my call to the police, but there was no urgent pace to their task. George had long since been dead.

By the time the police arrived, I was back in my sweater, camo pants, and proper undergarments. I'd convinced Cat to leave the broken cases as they were.

I knew a few things about crime scene investigation: one, don't touch anything. Fingerprints cast suspicion where I least wanted it. Two, considering my presence at the store, I would be questioned whether I wanted to or not. If lucky, questioning might end up giving me a detail or two. Third, be patient. Eventually, my old pal Detective Loncar would show up. After we caught up on each other's respective lives ("Hi, Detective. Is your wife speaking to you yet?" "Ms. Kidd. Keep out of my investigation."), I'd sit back and watch the routine: bagging evidence, collecting statements, photographing the surroundings.

It was safe to say we wouldn't be leaving any time soon.

A red-headed young man in a navy-blue suit, white shirt, and pink tie approached us. "Which one of you is Catherine Lestes?" He asked

"Me," Cat said.

"I'm Detective Madden. I'd like to ask you a few questions."

"Where's Detective Loncar?" I asked. Madden seemed surprised by my question. "We have a history," I added.

"Tahiti." He looked at his notebook and then at Cat. "Are you comfortable? Can I get you a cup of water or something before we get started?"

She looked up at him, her eyes wide and red. "Water would be great. Thank you."

"I'll be right back." The detective left us sitting on the ottoman. I was so surprised by his act of generosity that for a moment I went blank. And then I remembered it was up to me to coach Cat.

"Listen. He's going to ask you a bunch of questions about tonight. Tell him the truth—"

She interrupted me. "George is gone," she said. "Five hours ago, I hated him. I threw a drink in his face. And now he's gone. Forever." Her peaches-and-cream complexion turned red, and blotchy patches appeared on her throat. She put her hands on her belly and moved them in a circle.

The red-headed detective came back.

"Here he comes. Be cool," I said.

He handed her a small paper cup of water. "Are you okay here on that ottoman? Would you rather move to the sofa? You'll have better back support."

Cat sipped her water. "Thank you."

I interjected. "Detective, maybe you should talk to me first while Cat calms down."

"Ms. Kidd?" he asked. He looked at his phone. "I'll talk to you in a moment." He was quiet for a few seconds. I imagined him gearing up to go in for the kill now that he'd lulled Cat into a safe space. Instead, he kept his attention on me. "Do you think you could give Ms. Lestes and me a couple of minutes alone?"

"I—um—Cat?"

"It's okay, Sam."

"But don't go far. I'd like to talk to you when we're done," Madden added.

"Okay," I said. I stood up and walked away from them, stopping to turn around and look back twice. Madden sat on the ottoman next to Cat. His head was tipped and if I didn't know any better, I'd say he was laying the Good Cop routine on a bit thick.

———

I WAITED IMPATIENTLY for my turn to talk to Detective Madden, wandering around the portion of the store that the police had not cordoned off. I bypassed cocktail dresses and headed toward a display of ivory garments. Merchandising an outlet store wasn't as easy as working with new shipments, because the inventory often came in piecemeal. Cat had an exceptional eye for trends, though, and had learned to cherry-pick from her inventory to make strong display statements. In front of me, a wall of pale pink slats had been rigged with silver hooks. The dresses varied from ivory to winter white to beige to the palest taupe. Cashmere, wool, tweed, and silk mixed together to create a luxurious presentation. A neighboring fixture held strands of costume-grade pearls, perfect for achieving the layered look without the investment. An assortment of pearlescent shoes was set up on the corner. I killed time by trying on the shoes. It paid to have sample-sized feet.

"Excuse me, Ms. Kidd?" I turned around. Madden stood in front of me with a clipboard. "Before I get your statement, I want to reassure you that we've been through the store, and there's no longer a threat. Did you sustain any injuries tonight? Would you like to seek medical attention?"

"I'm not the one who got pushed out of the way of a fleeing murderer."

Madden made a note. "Can you tell me what happened here? Just a couple of sentences. In your own words."

"Cat and I came to her store so she could make sure everything was locked up properly. You probably know there've been some smash and grabs in the mall, right?" He nodded once. "We were already here for a party at the end of the mall. She thought it was best to check on her store before we went home. I was in the fitting room and I heard a crash. When I came out, a person was in front of the jewelry case with a tire iron. When he saw me, he grabbed the jewelry and ran. The mall security officer must have heard the crash, or heard me yell, or heard *something,* because he came in to see what was going on, and that's when we found George's body." I paused. "That was more than a couple of sentences. Sorry."

"That's okay. I want to hear everything you have to say, the whole story. We can take a break if you want." He made a few more notes. "Finding a body is a traumatic situation. Would you like us to call somebody to come pick you up?"

"Do you know who I am?" I asked.

He looked back down at his clipboard. "Ms. Samantha Kidd, right?"

"Right."

"Are you okay?"

"I'm fine. I'll drive Cat—Ms. Lestes—home tonight. You don't have to make special arrangements."

"Would you like some water before you go?"

I felt like I was out to dinner at the Olive Garden, not giving a statement about finding a body. "No, I think I'd like to get out of here."

"Here's my card," he said. "Call me if you think of anything else. Being present at a crime scene is a traumatic situation."

"You already said that."

"Oh, yes, I did." He looked back down at his clipboard. "Thank you for your statement, Ms. Kidd."

We walked back to where Cat sat in the shoe department. "Ms. Lestes, I'll call you when the forensic team finishes up," Madden said to Cat. "It's going to take us a while to make sure we collect all the evidence. If you think of anything else, call me. Here's my card."

Cat took the card and held it in her lap. She looked at the detective. "Thank you," she said. "I'll notify my staff not to come in until I hear from you."

He nodded at her. "Good night, Ms. Lestes, Ms. Kidd."

We walked to the car. Cat called her employees and told them what had happened. It was the worst possible time of the year for a boutique to miss out on business, but the unexpected tragedy had shifted her priorities.

Detective Madden had our names, phone numbers, and statements. There was always the chance that he'd have more questions in a few days, but we'd been forthcoming with our information. The absence of a lecture about not getting involved felt a little strange.

"It's late. Let's get you home and to sleep," I said.

"I can't go to sleep. I have to call my family, and George's family, and then they're going to come visit, and there has to be a memorial, and I don't have groceries, and—"

"Slow down. It's late and you need to go home and try to relax. You can call everybody tomorrow."

Cat put both hands up toward her face and swept her fingers under her eyes to wick away the tears that had pooled there. She tipped her head back and stared at the ceiling, and a fresh wave of tears trickled out of the corners of her eyes and dripped into her hairline by her temples. I felt for her. Here was a woman who appeared in charge of most of the time, and in the past twenty-four hours, life as she knew it had fallen to pieces.

"Sam, can you stay over tonight?" she asked in a small voice.

I thought about every reason I shouldn't: I had no pajamas, toothbrush, or change of clothes for tomorrow. Logan, my trusty feline companion, would be left with dry food and day-old water.

"Of course I can," I said.

I BORROWED a pair of PJs and made up the sofa. Cat went to bed. Even though my body was tired, my mind was unsettled. I lay on my side and stared at the mantel above the unlit fireplace. It was filled with framed photos on display, pictures of Cat and George from vacations and cozy nights at home.

There was nothing in George's expression that indicated his unhappiness. Nothing that hinted that this wasn't the life he wanted to lead. His broad smile, body language, and repeated public displays of affection with Cat spoke of the opposite of his actions.

I hated him for tricking her so thoroughly.

Twenty-four hours ago, this holiday season had had all the makings of being my best one yet.

Not anymore.

5

LIFEBOAT NO. 6

I'D LIKE TO SAY THAT I WAS THE PERFECT HOUSEGUEST, WAKING EARLY and starting breakfast for Cat, but even with the best of intentions, that wasn't the case. Whether or not she was trying to be quiet was a moot point after the shattering of glass woke me from a sound sleep at quarter after five.

"I dropped the coffee pot," she said. The puddles of brown liquid on the floor and the scent of freshly brewed coffee were explanation enough.

"You're not supposed to have caffeine."

"I made it for you."

"Then as a thank-you, let me clean it up." She protested, but I insisted. "I'll get coffee from the drive-through on my way home. It's no big deal."

Cat looked at me for a long moment and then started to cry. Small sobs at first, which grew into bigger ones. She didn't even bother wiping the tears away this time. Her face turned a shade of red I'd previously only seen in radishes. I scanned the floor for my shoes and pulled them on and then crossed the floor and hugged her. This time she held on like Molly Brown with a life preserver before climbing aboard Lifeboat No. 6.

We stood like that through the microwave timer and the teapot whistle. At each domestic sound, I patted Cat on the back and tried to pull away. She gripped me closer.

Seventeen minutes later (wall clock), she relaxed her arms. I stepped back and appraised her condition. She grabbed a kitchen towel and wiped her face, and then balled up the towel and carried it out of the room, leaving dark, coffee-colored footprints in her wake. Good thing she had hardwood floors.

I followed her to the living room and guided her into her favorite chair. "Sit. Relax. I'll take care of the kitchen. You should call your family."

* * *

AFTER CLEANING THE KITCHEN, resetting the microwave timer, and fixing Cat a mug of green tea, I drove home. I had no problem temporarily moving in with Cat, on one condition. Logan, the most faithful companion a girl could ask for, would move in with me. And assuming I'd woo him with treats, he'd probably agree.

On the drive home, I started a mental list of reasons why George might have been murdered. As morbid as it sounded, it was my way of trying to control an uncontrollable situation. This wasn't the first time I'd found a body. Not even the first time I'd found the body of someone I'd known. But this time, the victim was tied to someone in my life. No matter what the outcome of the ensuing investigation would be, the fact remained that Cat was a widow about to become a single mother.

The first thought to pop into my head was that George had been in the wrong place at the wrong time. But besides that being the answer with the least amount of closure, it also didn't fit.

George had gotten into a fight with Cat earlier that night, and he'd told her he was leaving her. So what had taken him to her store? Was there more to him needing space than an untimely midlife crisis? If it was merchandise he was after, he had access to far more valuable pieces through Kenner & Winn.

Did George have enemies? Or was there a secret that drove him to put distance between himself and Cat in the first place? And the scariest question of all: did his murder have anything to do with Cat, and if so, was she now in danger?

I'd gotten to know Cat over the past two years since first moving to Ribbon. We hadn't been instant friends, but a friendship had grown out of our mutual love of clothes. Over that time, I became a regular customer of her boutique, and she became an example of what normal people were like. I'd learned early on that her husband's job as a sales rep kept him on the road for about half of the year, which made girl-time the norm.

But for as much time as I'd spent with Cat while George was traveling, I hadn't spent much time with the two of them together and barely knew him at all. The thing I *did* know was that Cat hadn't taken his last name when they married. It was a decision that had less to do with independence than practicality: George's surname was "Stevens" and Cat preferred not to be confused with the artist formerly known as Cat Stevens.

Traffic around Ribbon had been thinning out gradually as we got closer to Christmas. This morning, the highway was light, and I made it home in under the usual twenty minutes. I pulled into my driveway and let myself in.

Logan stood next to his food bowl. He'd tipped the scales at fifteen pounds a few months ago, and the vet had put him on a low-cal, high-fiber diet. When that hadn't worked out, Logan and I reached an agreement. He could have the kind of cat food he wanted, but only a half portion. In a show of solidarity, I did my best to do the same, but between you and me, eating half a pizza isn't all that different from eating the whole thing.

I scooped half a can of high-protein fish parts into Logan's bowl and called my best friend Eddie at Tradava, the local department store and our joint employer. Eddie was a surfer-dude type who maintained a go-with-the-flow vibe on most occasions. He was as at home on a skateboard as he was in his VW Bug, but I'd never seen him as stressed as he was during the holidays. For the past month, his vocabulary had more expletives than *Scarface*.

According to the clock, he'd be somewhere between his second and third cups of coffee. "I shouldn't even take your call," he said in place of hello. "Vacation the week before Christmas while I'm stuck here round the clock. Last night, a tree fell over and pinned Santa. Destroyed three of the elves. I had to replace them with garden gnomes. If the store manager sees that, I'm done."

"Good morning to you too," I said. "Have you heard from Cat?"

"No. Why? She didn't go into labor early, did she?"

"Her situation is a little more dire than premature labor. Her husband was murdered last night."

"I have seven minutes. Talk fast."

I told Eddie everything I knew. "He left her yesterday. Like—left her, left her. Said he couldn't do the whole start-a-family thing, that he wasn't ready. She was freaking out, smashing plates, full on Connie Corleone from *The Godfather*. We crashed his party at the mall and they fought, but then later when we went to her store he was there. Dead. Behind a jewelry case with a strand of pearls from her inventory tied around his throat."

"I think I missed something. He had a party last night but was dead in her store? How'd he get from the party to her store?"

"You told me to talk fast, so I edited."

"Do you know how long he was gone? Or when he left? Or how he got there?"

"We don't know anything except he was in her store, strangled with a strand of pearls."

"Whoa. What did Detective Loncar say?"

"He's on vacation. The detective we spoke with was named Madden. He acted like everything was routine."

"You found the body and called 911?"

"Yes."

"Sounds routine to me."

"It's not like I expected a gold star, but a little positive reinforcement wouldn't hurt."

"Dude."

"I feel like Loncar and I have an agreement."

"You do. You agree to stay out of his investigations, and he doesn't arrest you for obstruction of justice."

"That was last year. I think we had a breakthrough around my birthday."

We were silent for a moment. "I don't envy her," Eddie said. "The holidays are rough for any retailer. Even in quote-unquote normal cities, the crime rate rises. At least once a year, there's a shooter dressed in a Santa costume on the news. People are shopping under pressure, employees are burned out, and stores are fighting for every sale we can get. It's not pretty."

It had started as a subtle shift, one that some stores never saw coming. Buyers, like I'd been when I worked in New York, had been the ones to determine what a store would carry. In a way, we were style curators, editing a designer's collection down from a sea of samples into a cohesive assortment that we felt our customers would want. But designers soon learned that if they embraced the internet, they could offer their entire collection to the world and let customers—*not* store buyers—make the decisions of what would be produced. Ready-to-wear, a market that could shift quickly, found it more profitable to go directly to the consumer and cut out the retailers. The accessories market had it harder because of materials and factory production schedules.

The changing face of retail meant good things for customers but not so good for stores. In the simplest terms of supply and demand, the scales had been tipped in the wrong direction. Profit, the money between what a store charged for an item minus the various costs of doing business, had been whittled down to pennies. The easiest way to make a profit was to lower the cost of an item, thus increasing the difference between the cost and the price a customer pays.

Ribbon, Pennsylvania was the first city to have outlet malls. But the one where Cat worked, the Designer Outlet Mall, had been different. It wasn't the kind that had been around since the fifties, offering girdles and surplus glassware and dungarees. It was the kind that promoted in-season trends and designer merchandise with the understanding that you'd pay less than if you shopped at a store like Tradava.

But places like Tradava weren't exactly pulling in hordes of customers anymore. A tough economy had caused most customers to tighten their belts—or stop buying belts to begin with. Subsequently, the retail stores slashed prices, and the outlet malls were no longer unique. Finding a way to gain a portion of a customer's wallet had gotten tougher than ever. It was part of my new challenge in the advertising department: how to promote the same trends that everybody else promoted while creating customer loyalty? Difficult, but not impossible.

"Do you think the murder is connected to the outlets?" Eddie asked.

"It's hard not to see the connection. Eddie, I'm worried. Cat's pregnant and hormonal and her business is at risk and now this. Logan and I are staying with her for a few days. I don't think she should be alone right now."

6

"THAT CRAZY BROAD"

I DRESSED IN A CREAM CABLE-KNIT TURTLENECK SWEATER, CREAM corduroy trousers with pale-pink suede knee patches, and pink lizard boots. I blow-dried my hair into a soft bob and filled an empty suitcase with enough clothes to get me into the new year. The doorbell rang as I was sitting on top of the suitcase to get it to zip. I ran downstairs and answered the door. A man in a FedEx uniform stood on my porch.

"Samantha Kidd?"

"That's me."

"Sign here." He shoved a black device at me, and I signed the screen with a thin black plastic wand. The signature wasn't anywhere close to accurate. He took the equipment and handed me a box. "Have a nice day." He turned and left.

I stared at the package. It was from the Apple store. I held it up to my head. It wasn't ticking. (It's good to be cautious.) Logan rubbed his back against my ivory pant legs, leaving a transfer of black fur on my shins. He looked up at me and meowed.

"We'll leave in a second." I pushed the door shut behind me and tore open the box.

Whatever I expected, a new iPhone wasn't it. I powered it on. There was one message from the one number programmed in: The Charming and Handsome Nick Taylor.

I bit back a smile. I wasn't a hundred percent on board with the Amanda Ries Roommate situation, but Nick got points for making me laugh. I cued up the message.

"Hey, Kidd, It's Nick." There was a slight pause. "Call me when you get a chance, okay? I don't like how things ended last night."

I pressed redial. One ring, two rings, three rings, four rings...

It was a little after seven. The six-hour time difference meant it was a little after one in Italy. The phone rang. And rang. And rang. As I was about to hang up, he answered.

"Nick? It's Samantha. I was hoping to catch you alone." I paused, cringing at the words spilling out of my mouth. "Not that I think you're not alone. Or are. I mean, there are a lot of Italians in Italy, so you're probably not alone."

"Kidd, slow down."

"Okay." I took a deep breath. "Hi."

"Hi. You got the phone."

"I got the phone."

"Before I left, you mentioned something about wanting to upgrade. Consider it an early Christmas present. Your personal, private, direct line to me. Whenever you want to talk. No matter what's going on, if you call, I'll answer."

"Don't answer if you're in the bathroom." He laughed. I turned and walked toward the sofa. "'The Charming and Handsome Nick Taylor?'"

"I may have been overselling."

"No, I think it fits." I sat down. "How'd you program me?"

"If *only* I could program you."

"You know what I mean. Is my number in your phone?"

"Yes. 'That Crazy Broad.'"

"You did not."

"You'll just have to wait until we're in the same city to find out, won't you?" He was quiet for a second. "Kidd, I'm sorry about last night. Are you okay with this?" he asked. "With Amanda staying here?"

Last night. Thirteen hours ago, I'd put Nick in the same category as Cat's husband: men are rats. I thought about last night, about finding George's dead body at her store. Hours before he'd been found dead, they'd fought, first at home and then at the party. Their differences had been over something far greater than letting a friend crash on his sofa. In terms of things to be angry about, this one was pretty small.

"I have to be, don't I?"

"It would make things a lot easier if you were."

"Okay," I said with more conviction than I felt. "What about your dad? Do you need me to check on him?"

"If you saw how he keeps the place when I'm not there, you might be scared away for good. Between you and me, he might have met a lady friend at the grocery store. Better give them their space."

"If that's the case, then we'll have a whole new set of problems when you get back."

"We'll figure it out. I know we both thought I'd be home by now. I'm sorry about the timing."

I stood in the doorway and stared out at the street. The curtains on Mrs. Iova's front window may have moved, and I squinted and stared for further evidence she was watching me. "It's okay," I said idly. "I understand. You're lucky the factories weren't closed."

"I had to call in a couple of favors. If I don't meet with them now, I'll lose a month of production." He paused. "So, we're good?"

"We are, but there's somebody who isn't." I chewed my lower lip for a second. Telling Nick about things of this nature hadn't been easy in the past, but I knew that not telling Nick would be worse. "You remember Cat Lestes, right? Her husband, George, died last night."

"Isn't she about to have a baby? That's beyond tragic. Was it stress? Heart attack?"

"No, Nick, it was murder." I left out the details about their fight and George telling Cat he was leaving her. "We found his body in her store."

Nick was silent. There was an ocean between us, but that didn't matter. I half expected a lecture and half expected him to hang up.

"Be careful, Kidd. I mean that. I know Cat's your friend, and I know your friends are like your family. And I know you're going to be there to help her through this. Just be careful, okay? Promise me that?"

"I'll be careful. I promise."

AFTER OUR CALL, I packed Logan into the car and returned to Cat's house. A short woman in a black wool coat and red scarf with snowflakes printed on it was leaving as I arrived. Cat was inside on the sofa, wrapped in a pink fleece blanket. Logan crawled out of his carrier, jumped up next to her, and began kneading the blanket folds.

"Who was that woman?" I asked.

"One of my neighbors. She saw the news and came by to drop off some food."

A shiny white plate filled with square-cut brownies sat on the glass coffee table in front of her. Small ceramic dessert plates sat next to the tray. "She brought you brownies?"

"She brought me a casserole. The fourth one today."

"You've had four visitors already? It's eight o'clock in the morning."

"I've been up since five. I needed junk food, so I made brownies after you left. Help yourself." I reached for a dessert plate and stacked two brownies on it. "The doctor wants me to eat more vegetables, so there's spinach and cooked carrots in them."

I put one of the brownies back. "How are you feeling?" I asked. "Any better? Any differently?"

"Better, maybe. I don't think I can cry anymore. Differently, I don't know. My parents are on their way from Florida, and George's family called this morning to find out when the memorial service will be. The phones won't stop ringing, so I turned them off. I've already gotten five emails from Fidelity about what to do with George's 401K. It's like an automated machine. 'Loved one dies—initiate sequence five.'" She wrapped the blanket around her a little tighter, and Logan meowed. "I feel like a fraud. He left me, Sam. He walked away from me and our marriage. Yesterday I hated him for what he did, and today everybody's suffocating me with what a great guy he was and how sorry they are that I lost the love of my life. I feel like I'm lying to everybody by not telling them our marriage was over."

"Cat, I need to ask you something." She looked up at me. "What did George say to you at the party that made you throw your drink at him?"

"He told me to go home. He said considering the circumstances, I was making a fool of myself. And then he threatened me. He said if I expected anything from him in the future, I needed to stay out of his business. I know throwing the drink was childish. I didn't even think about it. I was so angry with him I wanted to spit in his face!" Her eyes grew wide, and she clamped her hand over her mouth. Logan let out a long, low growl, as if he didn't like the direction the conversation had taken.

I picked Logan up and cradled him against my arm. I stroked the fur on his belly, which was still rather large thanks to the overeating situation. He closed his eyes halfway and purred.

"You had every right to be mad at him, and throwing a drink was a lot nicer than spitting in his face." Logan opened his eyes and meowed again. "I know what happened. You know what happened. But the rest of the world doesn't have to know. People want to support you right now, so let them. You need to let me help you. Except for some last-minute Christmas shopping, my schedule is clear."

Unlike Eddie, who'd been fighting a losing battle of merchandising standards vs. customer shopping destruction, *Retrofit for Tradava* had put the spring/summer issue to bed two weeks ago and my last-minute request for time off the week prior to Christmas had been approved by the director of marketing.

Merry Christmas to me.

"I can't expect you to spend your first real vacation helping me at my store. Not the week before Christmas." She ran her hand over Logan's head. "Besides, I already made arrangements for help."

"You hired someone to help with the funeral planning?"

"No. I called my brother."

7

———

FIRST-THINGS-FIRST STRATEGIST

Cat's brother Dante had made more of an impact on me than I would have expected. Between the two of us, Cat was the normal one. My friendship with her had grown from when we'd first met during a design competition, to our joint participation in a local publicity stunt, to my becoming a regular customer at her designer boutique. I'd had a brief flirtation with Dante during my breakup with Nick, though Cat had appeared not to care either way that the flirtation had been short-lived.

It didn't seem appropriate to ask the questions that sprung to mind: When is he coming? Where is he staying? Does my hair look okay? Especially since I was in a relationship with The Charming and Handsome Nick Taylor and had recently shown great maturity and acceptance about him sharing his apartment with Amanda.

I temporarily forgot about the vegetables in the brownie and ate it. It was surprisingly good. I reached for the plate and picked up another. There was a shave-and-a-haircut rap on the door. A couple of seconds later, a familiar voice spoke. "C'mon, Sis, I don't have all day."

Cat left the blanket on the sofa and answered the door. "It's about time you got here," she said.

Dante entered. He wore his trademark black leather motorcycle jacket over a faded zip front hoodie and T-shirt. His black hair was pushed away from his face, and his normally long sideburns had recently been trimmed. He carried a casserole dish covered in clear plastic wrap in one hand and a large black canvas bag slung over the other shoulder. Cat shut the door behind him. He dropped the bag on the floor.

Dante was a freelance photographer who occasionally picked up hours working for a private investigator. His background was slightly blurry: never been married, worked odd jobs, lived in Philadelphia. He was a flirt, a willing participant in my sometimes ill-conceived investigations, and a really good kisser. When Nick and I talked about Dante, it was mostly about the private investigator stuff. Otherwise we veered into the same territory as when we talked about Amanda.

Dante showed no surprise at seeing me. "Hold this." He shoved the casserole at me. When I took it, he turned to Cat and wrapped her in a giant, brotherly hug. "You okay?" He asked. Her head nodded against his shoulder.

When their hug ended, Cat took the casserole from me and went to the kitchen.

"So, Sammy the Kidd. How's your boyfriend?"

"He's good. We're good. Everything's good."

"Good."

"What about you? Everything good?" I asked. My vocabulary was going to require a good-ectomy if this kept up.

"Truth? I've been a little lonely."

"Somehow I doubt that."

He shrugged. "Believe what you want."

Dante was baiting me. He'd crashed my life about two years ago and had been in and out ever since. And I'm not going to lie. There was some serious chemistry.

But.

Yes, I was attracted to Dante. He was equal parts Marlon Brando and Adrian Zmed. (Don't even pretend you haven't seen *Grease* 2. You know what I'm talking about.) He was the stereotypical bad boy dressed in a black leather motorcycle jacket and tattoos. Except as I got to know him, I realized he was anything but stereotypical.

Dante kept me on my toes during the time we were together, but showed me we could connect on a deeper level too. We shared a bed but didn't sleep together. He told me about his son. I told him about my fears. It was an exciting week that opened up my world a little more than when life was about my career as a former shoe buyer and my ongoing flirtation with Nick. It gave me a taste of what life with Dante would be like.

Maybe that's why I ended things. I wasn't a hundred percent confident that anybody could have a life with Dante. He was a loner.

Dante could throw his belongings into a backpack and ride his motorcycle into the sunset. That wasn't the life for me, but the short time I'd spent close to his flame had made me view my life differently. I'd confronted the issues that had kept me from finding steady employment. I took the rose-colored glasses off and examined my life and saw what it was that I wanted.

Logan walked the length of the sofa and then jumped onto the floor and sniffed the bag Dante had dropped. Dante scooped Logan up and scratched his ears. Within seconds, Logan purred like a lawnmower engine.

"I missed your cat," Dante said.

"Sounds like he missed you too."

He carried Logan to a large club chair and sat down. "Okay, sis, what's the plan?" he called out.

Cat came back from the kitchen and sat down. "I don't have a plan. My whole life is falling apart and I'm trying to hold it together."

Dante looked at me. "I almost hate to ask this, but do you have a plan?"

"I'm more of a first-things-first strategist."

"What's the first thing we need to tackle?"

Cat replied. "Your priority is the store. Detective Madden called and said they released the crime scene." Cat's complexion turned a shade of green. "I'll be right back." She jumped up from the sofa and ran down the hall to the bathroom. Even though she slammed the door, it wasn't hard to guess what she was doing. (I hoped it had to do with the pregnancy or the thought of her store as crime scene and not the vegetable-laced brownies.)

I looked at Dante. "How much do you know?" I asked him.

"Not much. Talk fast."

"George told her he was leaving her yesterday morning. She didn't take it well. We went to his company holiday party last night. They got into a fight in front of a lot of people and then we left."

"And his body was found in her store later that night."

"Yes. When we got there, we thought we were alone, but we weren't. Somebody dressed in all black was there to rob the store."

"Burgle."

"What?"

"Robbers rob people. Burglars rob stores. The store was closed, so it was a burglar, not a robber. Man or woman?"

"I don't know. I keep thinking it was a man. He smashed the jewelry case with a tire iron."

"Did he see you?"

I nodded. "I heard the crash and saw him. I yelled and he took off. He shoved Cat out of the way and ran out the front gate."

Dante set Logan down and balled up his fist, and then slammed it into the back of Cat's brown leather club chair. Logan jumped down from the sofa and ran under the couch. I knew Dante was angry. I also knew he usually bottled stuff like that up and the reaction I'd just seen would be his only one. Frankly, I was a little surprised he'd reacted that much.

"I keep replaying things in my mind, but the thing I remember clearly is that the thief was just standing there, staring at the jewelry case. When I yelled, he grabbed the jewelry and took off."

"Why don't you know if it was a man or a woman?"

"He—or she—was wearing baggy black clothes, a ski mask, and gloves."

"Could have been a burglary gone wrong. Could be the burglar snapped and killed George in a trance. Your yell snapped him out of it."

I shook my head. "I could see that if it was a gunshot or a head wound but it takes a lot of effort to strangle somebody with a necklace and then drag their body behind a jewelry case. And the necklaces would only be strong enough if they were doubled over, so that requires a little more effort. This feels more deliberate."

"That does sound deliberate."

The door in the hall opened and Cat came out. Her lipstick was faded to a ring of faint burgundy around the outside of her mouth. Her red hair was pulled back into a high ponytail that had already come loose and was tipped slightly to the side.

"Sam, can you pack up the brownies? I don't want to deal with them after"—she pointed behind her—"that."

"Sure." I carried the tray of brownies into the kitchen and found a plastic food container and a corresponding lid. I packed all but two away and opened the fridge. The shelves were overflowing with glass dishes filled with casseroles. I did a little rearranging and then tucked the vegetable brownies in the lunch meat drawer. The way things were going, I had a chance of hitting the recommended vegetable intake for one day, and I wasn't going to blow it.

I rejoined Cat and Dante in the living room. He'd moved to the sofa next to her and had his hand on her back. "Are you sure?" she asked.

"You need to take care of yourself," he said. "We'll take care of the store."

"We?" I asked.

Dante looked at me. "Yes, we." He stood up. "Cat's going to the doctor and we're going to the outlet to clean up the crime scene."

We took separate cars. Dante drove a black SUV filled with vacuum cleaners and miscellaneous boxes of rags and jugs of chemicals. I took my late-nineties black Honda del Sol, a hard-top convertible with ridiculously low mileage thanks to the fact that for the majority of the nine years I worked in New York, it sat in a parking garage. My car was considerably zippier than Dante's SUV, and I left him in my dust.

The mall was hopping with holiday shoppers. I found a space at the perimeter of the lot and approached the building. Cat had given me the keys to Catnip, but I hadn't forgotten that on two separate occasions criminals had gotten inside when the store was locked. I was curious about the condition the police had left the place, but not so foolish that I charged inside alone. I waited on the sidewalk for a couple of minutes until his black SUV pulled up to the curb.

"Help me unload then I'll park and we can go inside." He climbed out and met me around the back.

"What'd you do—rob a sanitation service?" I asked.

"The PI I sometimes work for had me do crime scene cleanup," he said. "Good way to get first access to a crime scene. Cops do their thing, but you never know what else you can find. Sometimes you can tell where the cops focused their attention. Wait too long and you learn nothing."

"There are people who make their living doing this."

"And they're good. Too good when you're looking for evidence or clues. That's why it's best to do it yourself." He pulled two shiny vacuum cleaners out of the truck. One of them still had a tag on it.

"These look brand new," I said.

"They are. Crime scenes can be messy. Depending on what's at the scene, you won't want to waste time trying to clean up a vacuum. Easier to toss them when you're done."

I paused with one hand on the handle of the vacuum and a box of heavy black garbage bags under my arm. "How messy?"

"You said George was strangled, right? So we're lucky. It's a black bag job. No hazardous waste." He looked down at my feet. "You're wearing pink lizard boots."

"Do you like them?"

"They're not practical."

"I didn't know I was going to be cleaning a crime scene."

He pulled out his wallet and handed me a twenty. "Go to the camping store next door and buy a pair of sneakers."

"I can afford a new pair of sneakers," I said (proudly). "Besides, I don't think twenty dollars would cover it."

"Don't get caught up in what they look like. Go cheap."

"I don't wear cheap shoes."

"You're going to throw them out too."

"That's not how people are supposed to approach the purchase of new shoes."

Dante rolled his eyes. "I'll unload into the store. Meet me back here."

I walked to the mall entrance and then continued on to the camping store. An announcement came over the loudspeaker reminding customers of the gift wrap stations throughout the mall.

I asked a guy who looked like he'd been camping in the mountains for weeks before starting his shift for the location of the sneakers and was sent to the back corner. I found the clearance aisle facing the back wall and snatched a pair of marked-down rubber rain boots.

Twenty dollars. Sold.

I carried them to the checkout station. The mountain man waved me to his register. Up close, his look was more Hipster Hunter than authentic. A buffalo plaid shirt was buttoned up to his chin and half tucked in. The fray on his jeans appeared carefully placed, not achieved through wear and tear. Elmer Fudd couture, I thought.

I glanced around the store interior. "Have you seen any mall security officers? I need to talk to them." I asked.

Hipster Hunter scanned my items. "Why? Don't tell me you forgot where you parked your car. How do people forget where they parked their cars?"

"It's about what happened at the mall last night. Were you working? Did you see or hear anything?"

Hipster stopped scanning barcodes and studied me. He shook his head. "My night off. I heard about it this morning. Wild."

Wild? Not my word choice.

I yessed and noed my way through the transaction, turning down add-on items in order to get out of there faster. I knew the task ahead of Dante and me would be both time consuming and unpleasant, but I couldn't help wonder if we'd find something amongst the cleared crime scene that would help us shed light on who had murdered George.

8

SUSPECT EVERYBODY

AFTER I PAID, I CHANGED FROM MY PINK LIZARD BOOTS INTO THE RAIN boots. I walked back to Catnip through the warmth of the interior of the mall. The gate was down, making the store appear out of business at a time when the rest of the mall was thriving. An empty glass and chrome fixture sat outside the gate. It was a display case just like the one that had been smashed last night: rectangular with glass on the top, front, and sides. Chrome trim. Blond wood trim around the base and on the lockable drawers on the back. The drawers were unlocked and a set of keys were inside in a clear plastic bag, taped to the base with masking tape. More masking tape was wound around the outside of the case several times, and CATNIP had been written on the tape in sloppy handwriting. I left the mall and doubled back to the outside entrance and knocked. Dante opened the door.

"All set?" Dante asked.

"I guess. The new jewelry fixture is on the other side of the gate."

"First we clean. Take this," he said. He rolled a large Hepa-Vac toward me. "Concentrate on getting up what's left of the broken glass. The police got most of it, but the jewelry counter is right across the aisle from her shoe department. Cat won't want to take any chances on somebody accidentally stepping on glass with a bare foot."

"The police vacuumed? That was considerate."

"Trace evidence. That's the easiest way to make sure they don't leave a clue behind."

My heart sank. "We're not going to find anything they didn't, are we?"

"Is that why you're here? You thought you were going to find something they missed?"

"I'm here for Cat."

"But if you happened to pick up a clue that the police left behind, you'd be okay with that."

"Well, duh."

"Forget that. Police are only that dumb on TV. Our job is to get the store looking like Cat wants the store to look. So first, we go over everything again to make sure it's clean and safe. Then I'll replace the broken fixture so you can merchandise it. What the police did do was leave behind coffee cups. Throw them out. Pretend this is your store and you have to get it ready for business."

"Got it." I dragged the Hepa-VAC with me to the area where the case had been smashed, stashed my boots next to the shopping bags, and got started.

I needn't have worried about time spent with Dante. He went one direction and I went the other. As he'd said, the store was littered with used white disposable cups. I found an empty roll of trash bags in a drawer behind the register and searched the store for cups like I was a kid at an Easter Egg Hunt. Once I was sure I'd disposed of them all, I knotted the bag and set it by the front gate next to the rest of the store trash.

After coffee cup duty, I moved on to vacuuming. I worked by the store entrance. The gate between the entrance and the mall was in place, keeping our activities out of view from customers. I could hear the sounds of holiday shopping through the gate: snippets of conversation, the rhythm of footsteps passing by, and the occasional melody from the soundtrack that had been playing since the week before Thanksgiving. The news about George had been released and I was glad we were behind the metal gate. Knowing how people rubbernecked at accidents along the side of the road, I could imagine what they were whispering about the murder that had taken place inside of Catnip—I didn't need to hear it.

A couple of hours in, I took a break in the stockroom and brewed a pot of coffee. Clean plates for employee use had been stacked on a shelf next to the cups. I moved them to a more secure area, poured two mugs of coffee, and went back to the store. Dante rested against the wrap stand inside the jewelry cases. I handed him a mug.

"How's it going?" I asked.

"Police left the store better than I expected. We're lucky the gate keeps us hidden from the rest of the mall. This would take twice as long if we had spectators." He took a pull on his coffee. "What are your theories?"

"About what?"

"About what happened here."

"What makes you think I have theories?"

"You always have theories."

"Okay fine, I have theories. Do you want to take five and bounce them around?"

Dante raised his eyebrow slightly but didn't answer. I took it as a yes.

"Cat doesn't usually carry expensive jewelry. The merchandise that was stolen, that was an experiment. And not just any experiment. The merchandise came from George's company, Kenner & Winn. In the ten years that Cat and George were together, it was the first time she placed an order with him from any of the vendors he represented. She said he told her another account canceled the order, so he could sell it to her cheap. He convinced her to take the merchandise."

"So there's a connection to his employer and to another retail account."

"Yes. His employers would have known the merchandise was in Cat's store—at least, I assume there'd be a paper trail through invoices. Maybe the other retail account, too. It helps explain the theft, but not the murder."

"Who do you suspect for the murder?"

"You know how I am. I suspect everybody."

He smiled. "What else?"

"Someone on her staff could have been involved. It would be easy enough for one of them to make a copy of the key to get in after hours. And George—I can't help wondering about the timing of their fight. I agree with Cat—he was a rat for leaving her while she's eight months pregnant with his baby—but it had to take courage for him to speak up at all. He does what might have been the hardest thing of his life and then gets killed hours later. The timing seems suspicious. Did you know him? I mean, he was married to your sister. Did you see any of this coming?"

"I knew him, but not well. Holidays, mostly, and there was drinking involved. Seemed nice enough and got along with the family. He made my sister happy, but I know she wished he was around more. What about you?"

"I never knew George because he was always traveling. Cat said he'd been with the jewelry company for a couple of months. I thought maybe he changed companies so he wouldn't have to travel as much."

"You said George was at the party. Notice anything strange?" He leaned forward on the jewelry case. I stood opposite him on the outside. If the store had been open, it would look like he was trying to sell me something.

"At one point, Cat and George spoke. It looked like things were going to be civil, but then Cat grabbed a drink and tossed it in his face." I closed my eyes for a moment to recall the scene. "Later, before we left, I saw him talking to a woman in a yellow strapless dress with red accessories." I opened my eyes. "I notice stuff like that."

"What does it mean to you?"

"I don't know."

"Yes, you do. You noticed her for a reason and I'm guessing it's not because you're a fan of the ketchup and mustard color palette."

I thought back to the first time I'd seen her. "She and I were in the bathroom at the same time. She dropped something. I picked it up and handed it to her, and she threw it into the trash. Later, George was off to the side talking to her. My first thought was that the real reason George left Cat was that he was having an affair with that woman, but their body language didn't fit."

"Why did you two come here after the party?"

"One of Cat's employees quit after her shift was over, and Cat was afraid she didn't lock up properly. I wanted to get her out of the party without seeing George talking to the woman in yellow. We came here and interrupted the theft in progress. Right after the crash, I yelled and scared the robber-burglar person. He practically knocked Cat over when he ran out of the store."

He stood up straight and balled his fists. "She could have been hurt."

"I know. What I don't know is if the burglar knew she was

pregnant. The lights were out and she had her coat on. If it was somebody who knew her, then they would have known she was. If it was random or someone hired to do it, they would have thought she was in the way of their exit."

"Either way it's assault."

We were interrupted by the sound of someone rapping on the outside of the metal gate by the mall entrance. I followed Dante to the front of the store. Pieces of mail had been pushed under the gate and spread out in a display of light blue, pink, and white envelopes. The rapping started again, followed by a voice.

"Mall security. Anybody in there? You gotta get this case out of the way."

Dante stepped over the envelopes on the floor. "Hold on. I'll open the gate." He looked to the left and the right until he located the controls. I handed him the keys. He tried a few until one fit into the box. He flipped the handle to the left and the gate chugged and retracted. When it was halfway up, he turned the handle to the right. The gate stopped.

The mall was filled with customers. A few stopped what they were doing to watch us. Two women in matching pink knit hats with pompoms on top stood by a sign that advertised free gift wrap with purchases over a hundred dollars. One of them said, "Is that the store?" The other said yes. Dante had been right. If we'd had spectators while we were putting the store back together, it would have taken a lot longer.

Fortunately for us, the fixture was on castors. Dante ducked under the gate and pushed it into the store. The weight of the fixture caused it to sway to the left. I stood backward on the opposite side and guided it so it stayed on the marble path. Once we were inside, Dante grabbed the bottom of the metal gate and pulled down. It didn't budge.

"You two get that fixture in place. I'll watch the entrance," the security officer said.

"Let's go." We maneuvered the fixture down the aisle and past a table loaded with cashmere sweaters. It took a little effort to move it once it was on the carpet, but with one of us at either end, we were able to slowly nudge it into place. Dante left me to merchandise. About half a minute later, I heard the gate chug back into place.

For the rest of the afternoon, I worked on a new display in the jewelry department. Like most retailers, Cat kept her backstock locked in drawers behind the fixtures. What people often didn't realize was that vendors shipped merchandise in unglamorous plastic bags and sent velvet boxes and cleaning cloths separately. I unlocked and relocked four different drawers before I found the bags of pearl jewelry. The items were sorted by color in large freezer bags, and individual pieces were in smaller bags within.

I unpacked several thirty-six-inch strands of dull black pearls, and then matching bracelets, earrings, and rings. Another drawer search netted me display props: a mauve flocked velvet neck stand to show off a three-strand Jackie Kennedy–style necklace, a slightly inclined rectangular platform on which to arrange the long strand of pearls, and a couple of matching four-inch square pillows that I hooked the bracelets around. Earrings went on earring stands and rings on ring holders. When I finished fitting everything into the display, I moved to the front to see if my angles were all straight. That was the first of seven attempts before I achieved ninety-degree perfection.

Occasionally the scents of chocolate and cinnamon floated past me. Even though Cat's gate was in place, it was hard to get away from the ambiance.

By the time I finished, the cases were full with a meticulously placed assortment of pearl necklaces, bracelets, and earrings. It wasn't the valuable merchandise that Cat had planned to display, but a part of me wanted to see if a smash and grab happened again tonight—*after* the murder—and if the thieves knew the value of what they were stealing. All pearls look lustrous by night, even the knockoffs.

I locked what was left of the backstock in a drawer behind the counter and went looking for Dante. I found him outside Cat's office. "Are you ready to leave?"

"One last thing to do. Install a camera."

"The mall has cameras."

"Outside, and we won't be able to see what they see. This way, we'll have our own surveillance." He went inside the office and I followed.

Retail store space, when empty, was basically a giant box. Profitability was estimated by the square foot, and after taking out stockroom and fitting room space, there was little left for Cat. Her office was about eight feet square, with a tall filing cabinet set up along the wall she shared with the camping store next door. Bookcases filled with catalogs and binders of sales figures lined the back wall. Two chairs rounded out the furniture assortment: one behind and one in front of the wooden desk. Add in Dante and me, and the quarters were very, very close.

Dante dropped a duffle bag onto the chair in front of the desk. After unzipping it, he pulled out a couple of computer tablets.

"What are you going to do with those?" I asked.

"Program them to take pictures every five minutes. We'll see if there's anything suspicious going on around here."

"But you won't know if anything happens until you take them down and look at the pictures. By then the damage will be done."

He propped himself up against the desk. "If we want to find out who's doing something they shouldn't be doing, this is the best way to do it. We're not in this to strike back. If security was doing their job, this never would have happened." He tapped the screen a couple of times. "For all we know, they might be in on it."

"What will we do with the pictures?"

He finished tapping and handed me the tablet. "Put this on the second shelf so it's aimed at the door."

I held out my hand, and he set the tablet in my palm. When his fingers brushed mine, a shock passed between us. We both pulled away and the tablet fell to the carpet.

It landed right next to my rubber rain boot. He stooped to pick it up. I couldn't help but notice how close he was to my legs. When he stood back up, he glanced down to my pink suede knee patches on my pants, then up to my face.

He handed the tablet to me again. I went behind Cat's desk and climbed on top of it and then positioned the tablet on top of the filing cabinet. I arranged a plastic plant on one side and a short stack of catalogs on the other, hoping to conceal everything but the lens. I probably fiddled with it longer than necessary because I was going to have to ask Dante's help to get down and wanted to postpone that moment as long as possible.

"I think it's in place." I turned to face him, but was still standing on the chair. "Can you help me?"

"Sure."

I expected him to hold out a hand and guide me to the floor. I didn't expect him to wrap an arm around my knees and throw me over his shoulder.

He carried me out of Cat's office and then bent down and lowered me onto a large tufted ottoman. I pulled my sweater down and smoothed the creases out of my corduroys. Dante seemed to enjoy my embarrassment a little too much.

"The tablet will take a picture every five minutes for twenty-four hours."

Without stopping to do the math, I exclaimed, "That's like a thousand pictures!"

"Two hundred eighty-eight per tablet."

He went into the office and returned with an empty duffel bag. We moved the cleaning equipment to the exit. Dante went to the SUV and pulled it to the curb, and we packed everything in the back.

"My car's in the back row," I said.

"Climb in. I'll give you a ride."

He drove to my small convertible, sandwiched between two minivans. They hadn't left much space for me to get in or out, but that wasn't my primary concern.

No, I was more concerned with the knife protruding from the now completely flat back tire.

Cat's troubles didn't seem so unique.

9

LAW-ABIDING CITIZEN

THE TWO OF US STARED AT MY TIRE. I DIDN'T KNOW WHAT DANTE WAS thinking, but the thoughts running through my head were built of a string of profanities that would have made Eddie proud.

"Call the police," Dante said.

"The police? They're not going to change my tire."

"I'll change your tire."

"I can change my own tire."

"I'm sure you can. And I'm almost willing to say yes and let you freeze your butt off because it's sometimes fun to watch you think you can do everything yourself, but it's late, this is vandalism, and we need to get back to check on my sister. So you call the police, and I'll get started on the tire."

"You wouldn't believe how polite the cops were the night we found George. Watch this. I bet they offer to come out and give me a ride home." I pulled the Nick Phone out of my handbag and called the police. "I'd like to report an act of vandalism."

"In progress?"

"No, in my tire. Somebody stuck a knife in my tire."

"Is the perpetrator still there?"

"No, I came out to my car and there was a knife in the tire."

"At your residence?"

"No, at the Ribbon Designer Outlets."

"You can fill out a police report online. Do you have a pen?"

"A pen? For what?"

"I'll give you the website address."

"I'll find it myself." I hung up. "Something's up with the police department," I said to Dante.

"Why? Are they treating you like a law-abiding citizen?"

"I am a law-abiding citizen." I shoved the phone into my pocket. "Why don't you just drop me off at Cat's? I'll deal with the car tomorrow."

He stood up and studied me. "How come you're not spending the night with your boyfriend? Trouble in paradise?"

"Paradise is great. Nick's in Italy. I told Cat I'd stay with her for a couple of days."

"Sounds like we'll be getting cozy."

"'We'? I thought you kept an apartment in Ribbon."

"I sublet it to a couple visiting from France." A flicker of a smile twitched at his lips. "We've got all the makings of a slumber party."

"Change of plans." I held out my keys. "You can change the tire and then go stay at my house."

"It makes more sense for you to go home and me to stay with my sister."

"My cat is at her house. Home is where your cat is."

We exchanged keys. "You don't trust yourself around me," he said.

"You tell yourself whatever you have to so you can get through the night."

I didn't wait around to "help" him. I started the engine and pulled out of the space. As I approached the sidewalk that ran around the mall, I spotted a woman in a floor-length chinchilla fur coat. She looked toward the far end of the mall. I followed her gaze. Jim Insendo, the white-haired man who'd been talking to Cat at the party, headed toward her. She met him halfway, and they hugged. They were about fifty feet away from the SUV. Close enough to see her face light up but out of eavesdropping range. She gestured to Catnip a couple of times, and they shared a laugh. He handed her a small present. She held it carefully until they parted ways then tossed it in her oversized designer handbag. A car horn sounded behind me. I pulled forward and drove to Cat's house.

Her front door was unlocked. I found her in the kitchen with a green cotton apron tied over her pregnant belly. Logan had his head buried in a bowl of cat food, and Detective Madden sat in a chair by her dining room table. He wore a black suit and white shirt. Today's tie was marigold.

Floral arrangements in baskets were lined up by the back door. "What's all this?" I asked. I gestured toward the flowers, but it could be argued that the same gesture included Madden.

"They started arriving after you left. There's more, but the smell turned my stomach, so I put them out back." She pushed the curtain aside, and I saw a row of white plants and wreaths decorating her otherwise barren patio. "This one is from Kenner & Winn. It's the nicest of the bunch. I thought I should try to keep it for the memorial service." She adjusted a leaf and then looked at me.

Madden folded his hands and leaned forward on the table. "You're a well-liked woman, Ms. Lestes. Between the casseroles and the flowers, it's obvious."

She turned on the faucet and ran her fingers under the water. "I know a lot of people through the store."

"These are from customers?" I asked.

"Customers, vendors, neighbors, extended family." she said. "It was on the afternoon news. I saw it at the doctor's office."

I looked back and forth between her and Madden again. There was no tension in the air, but the detective showed no signs of leaving. The brown mug that Cat had almost broken the night of her fit was on the table, and a used tea bag sat nestled in a spoon to the right of the mug.

Logan lifted his head from his food bowl and licked his whiskers a couple of times. He turned and looked at Madden and then lowered his head and scurried out of the room with his tail low.

"I'm almost finished here, and then you can have my undivided attention," Cat said. "You like lasagna, right, Sam?" One hand was on a rectangular glass dish that was layered with large flat noodles, ricotta cheese, tomato sauce, and something green. The noodles, cheese, and sauce were identifiable at a fifty-foot distance. The green thing—a vegetable, I guessed—wasn't my area of expertise. I was pretty sure a vegetable couldn't ruin a perfectly good tray of lasagna.

"I love lasagna."

"Good. I added kale. You're okay with that, right?"

"Sure. I put kale in my lasagna all the time," I lied. "How did things go at the doctor?"

"I told her about what happened, and she said it's more important than ever that I meditate and try to establish a calm space." Cat slid the lasagna into the oven and set the microwave timer. "Detective Madden has been keeping me company while you and Dante were at the store. Where is Dante?"

"He's still at the mall. Somebody stuck a knife in my tire and he's changing it."

Madden set down his mug. "Did you file a police report?"

"I called and they told me to fill one out online."

"You didn't catch the vandals, did you? Get a description or a lead?"

"No. Why is everybody asking me that? Usually the police want me to stay away from criminals. Now you're all asking me if I caught one."

He chuckled. "It's taking all of our manpower to respond to the calls we get, so the chief determined some crimes were non-emergency. Vandalism is one. Sad to say it happens this time of year. Fill out the report online, and someone will follow up with you."

"Speaking of the crime wave, how's the investigation going?" (I didn't expect him to answer, but you can't blame me for trying.)

"It's going," he said.

"Detective Madden was telling me about the evidence they found at my store," Cat said.

"You were?" I was surprised.

"It's hard to say what was important and what wasn't, especially in a store that gets a lot of traffic this close to the holidays," he said.

"They found footprints," Cat said. "Isn't that right, detective?"

"Not sure if they're pertinent, but we did notice footprints that were deeper in the pile of the carpet than the other impressions we found, which indicates that the person might have been running. They were pointed toward the gate."

"How far apart were they?" I asked.

"The distance between the prints was also in line with the running theory."

"Anything else? What was the shape? High heel? Loafer? Sneaker? Man or woman?"

"Round-toed boot. Not conclusive one way or the other, but not a very large print, so I'm not ruling anybody out just yet." He took a pull on his coffee. "Ms. Lestes, you don't happen to own a gun, do you?"

Cat and I were surprised by the seemingly unrelated question. "Of course she doesn't own a gun," I said.

"Yes, I do," Cat said.

We both looked at her. "Let me guess. It's a pearl-handled revolver," I said.

"No, it's a Ruger LC9. George bought it for me. He said I should have a way to protect myself when he was out of town."

"Where is it now?" Madden asked.

"In a case under my bed. I admit I don't like owning the thing, but George said it was necessary." She looked at me and then at Madden. "I haven't fired it since the day my brother took me to the firing range to practice."

"When was that?" Madden asked.

"Three years ago."

"Why are you asking about a gun? Are you worried for Cat's safety?" I asked.

Detective Madden looked at me but his response was aimed at Cat. "Ms. Lestes, I'm going to need to see that gun."

Cat gave Madden the gun and he left. I excused myself and showered off the crime scene. When I came out of the bathroom, Cat was in her bed. A meditational podcast played from the phone on the side table. I went downstairs and wondered what the detective knew that we didn't. By nine thirty, I was asleep with Logan curled up next to me.

10

AUTONOMY

The next morning, I woke, showered again, and dressed in a white cashmere tunic, brown tights, and a brown tweed skirt. Cat was making leek pancakes and a green beverage.

"I can't believe you sent Dante to your house," she said. "He could have stayed here. There's room."

"Cat, I'm already sleeping on your sofa. Where was he going to sleep? The garage?"

"There are two sofas in the living room."

"I don't think that would have been a good idea."

"You don't trust yourself," she said. (Like brother, like sister?)

"I trust myself just fine."

"Have you told Nick?"

"About what? I didn't tell him about Dante and me going to your store. He has a lot on his mind, and I didn't want to stress him out further."

"Sam, the man has made it clear that you're a part of his life." She put her hands on her hips and the residual of uncooked leek pancake batter flipped off the end of the spatula. "Does that scare you?"

"'Scare' isn't the right word. I've gotten used to my autonomy, and for a long time it's been me making decisions about me. Reporting in to someone else doesn't come naturally."

"Calling your boyfriend to talk to him about what's going on in your life isn't 'reporting in.' It's communication."

"I know. I'm just not good at it." I sipped at my glass of green juice (the coffee wasn't ready, and frankly, I was afraid to ask what it was.)

"How come? How did you get to be your age and not know the fundamental rules of maintaining a solid relationship? You can't tell me you've never been in love."

"I was in love with Tommy, who took me to my high school prom. And Milo, the fraternity brother I dated for two years in college. And Sal from the deli counter across the street from Bentley's—no, I think I was just in love with his spicy salami."

She set the spatula down and looked at me.

"Not like that. He gave me free lunch meat."

"So?"

"So what? We didn't have all of this cell phone and social media stuff when I was in high school. Things were simpler then. You decorated somebody's locker and they asked you out."

"Yes, and when Tommy took you to the prom you had to walk uphill both ways. Come on, Sam, you're avoiding the subject. Forget high school and college and the lunch meat connection. You like Nick. You've liked him for over a decade. Now that you have him, are you bored? That's what Dante thinks."

"Dante talks to you about me?"

"I probably shouldn't have brought that up, but you know what I'm saying, right?" Cat asked.

"Don't you want to talk about the investigation? Madden told us all kinds of stuff last night. That was weird, right? Why was he so forthcoming?"

"I don't want to talk about that. If you tell me the store is ready to open, I'll go in and open it."

"The store is ready to open."

"I'll call my staff and we'll pretend it's business as usual."

"That's called denial."

"No, it's called finding a way to function."

"Well, not talking about past relationships is *my* way of functioning."

Cat flipped the pancakes. "I'm not trying to pry. I know Nick is important to you. I've seen it ever since I met you. But I also know my brother. He's going to buzz around you like a fly unless you swat him away. He likes what he can't have because it's a challenge. I've watched this my whole life. I love him because he's my brother, but that doesn't mean I don't see his flaws. If you want to date them both, then date them both. There's nothing wrong with that. But you better be honest with Nick."

"I don't want to date them both! How come we're still talking about me? Your problem is a lot bigger than mine."

"I'm not sure I agree with that."

She eased the leek pancakes off the griddle and laid one on each of the plates on the counter. We ate in silence. As soon as I was done, I excused myself and dug the Nick Phone out of my overnight bag. The battery was low, so I plugged in the phone and left it on the counter.

It was about forty degrees outside, cold enough for a scarf and jacket, but still unseasonably warm for December. If we didn't have snowfall in a week, it wouldn't feel like Christmas. Cat drove us to her store. The gate was up, and customers were milling about shopping.

A petite, scowling girl with blue hair and more than a few man-made holes in her head stood behind the case of pearls with the keys in her hand. Her pants looked synthetic, and her shoes were of the Herman Munster variety. She hollered out to get Cat's attention.

"Who's she?" I asked. I felt like I'd seen her before, but wasn't sure why. Her heavy makeup and high number of piercings made her look like a lot of other goths around town. In the quest for individuality, their style had turned formulaic.

"Shana Brice. My new assistant manager. She looks a little scary, but her recommendations were solid."

Empty black velvet-lined trays sat on top of the jewelry case, and clear plastic bags of jewelry sat next to them. The mauve fixtures I'd used were off to the side. I'd merchandised that case with the precision of someone with OCD rearranging a partially full container of eggs. Unless there'd been a rush on cheap pearl knockoffs in the past half hour, there'd been no reason to redo it.

Cat and I walked to the counter. "Hi, Shana," Cat said. "I didn't expect the store to be open already."

"I called the management office this morning to find out if we could get back in. They said sure, the police were done." She looked at me. "Are you new? I could use some help redoing this case."

"I don't work here. I'm Cat's friend. Samantha." I held out my hand to her. She looked at it and then kept working on the case. "What are you doing?"

She scowled at me, though I wondered if it was a natural expression or if the heavy black eyeliner and brow paint on her face created it. "I'm rearranging the merchandise. Somebody wasted this case with a bunch of cheap pearls."

Cat turned to me. "I thought you merchandised the cases last night?"

I nodded. I didn't want to explain my reasoning for using the inexpensive pearls instead of the more valuable inventory in front of Shana so I said nothing.

"We don't lock up the cheap stuff," Shana said. "It goes on the top-of-counter fixtures. Anything under two hundred dollars up top."

"Sam was just helping out," Cat said. "I didn't tell her our merchandising standards." She thanked Shana and turned away.

"Cat, there's mail here too," Shana said. She glanced at me quickly. "I don't know why it was on the counter and not in your office."

"That was me too," I said. I took the stack of envelopes from Shana and held them out to Cat. "The mail was on the floor at the front of the store last night, probably somebody pushed it under the gate. I didn't know where to put it so I figured it was best to put it where you'd see it."

"Good thinking. Shana, it looks like you have things under control. Sam, can you come with me to my office?"

"Sure."

As we headed through the store, the lights and the security gate by the mall entrance started to descend. I ran to it and threaded my fingers through the metal like Dante had last night. I yanked up, but the gate kept moving. I reached for the control panel, hoping the switches were labeled. Not only weren't they labeled, there weren't any switches. Inside the metal box was a tangled mess of wires.

I yelled to Cat for help. She ran to the control panel and flipped a switch under the wires. The screeching of the gate subsided and, moments later, it stopped.

There was one remaining problem. The toes of my pink lizard boots were dissected underneath it.

11

BUSINESS AS USUAL

CAT HAD A PANIC-STRICKEN LOOK ON HER FACE THAT WAS AT ODDS with her chic red hair and elegant green dress. "Are you okay?" she asked.

I was a little shaken up. I bent down and unzipped the boots and then pulled my feet out one by one. Fortunately for my future footwear choices, it was the pointy tip of the boot that had been damaged, not my toes.

A customer bundled up in an oversized gray coat stood next to the gate. "My packages are under there. Now I'm going to be late getting my kids. I don't have time to wait while you fix this."

I looked at the packages and then at the woman. She set multiple shopping bags on the floor while she'd stopped to sort through a display of Art Deco–inspired salt and pepper shakers.

Cat's professionalism took over. "I'll arrange to have everything delivered to you. Let me get your name and address." She looked at Shana and pantomimed writing something on a notepad. Shana ejected a length of register tape and brought it and a pen to Cat. "Your address?" Cat asked. The woman didn't answer. "Are these gifts? We'll arrange complimentary gift wrap along with the free delivery. Now, your name?"

The woman provided her name, address, telephone, and probably would have given her Social Security number and blood type if she thought Cat would throw in a few extras. Cat handled the issue gracefully, the true hallmark of customer service. When the woman was gone, Cat gave the information to Shana. "Call a delivery service and wrap these. I'll call maintenance to deal with the gate."

I followed Cat to her office. She sat behind her desk and called security. "This Catherine Lestes at Catnip. Yes, that's the store. The security gate malfunctioned. Customers are trapped inside." She paused. "Yes, I'd say this is more of an emergency than a lightbulb out in the ladies' room." She slammed the phone down. "I should have kept the store closed. Did you see the crowd out there? Those people aren't shopping. They're just here to see the freak show. And lookie! Faulty gate traps people in store. We just gave the newspaper their follow-up story."

"Cat, that wasn't a faulty gate. You saw the jumble of wires in the control panel. That was sabotage, and you need to call the police."

Tears formed and fell, and she swiped them away. "Darn hormones," she said. "I never cried this much before I was pregnant."

"Who has a key to the store?" I asked.

"Everybody on my staff. I want them to trust me." Neither of us mentioned the irony. "What am I supposed to do? I can't do everything myself, but I can't trust anybody either."

"Cat, don't you think it's suspicious that all of this is happening now? The thefts and the vandalism? In the same week your husband was murdered?"

She went pale. I paused for a moment, expecting her to tell me to stop talking about the murder. I took her silence as encouragement to continue. "Dante and I cleaned the store last night. The gate worked. Those envelopes," I pointed to the mail, "were under the gate. Whoever delivered it did so between the murder and the police releasing the crime scene. It's one more thing that's out of order."

She opened the top envelope, pulled out a sheet of paper, and then handed it to me. "It's the invoice for the pearls that were stolen," she said.

I scanned the page. Cat's payment terms were Net 30. It was common practice for distributors and designers to set up payment terms with existing retail accounts. "Net 30" meant that Cat was expected to pay in full thirty days from the date on the invoice.

"When did you place that order?"

"A couple of weeks ago when George first told me about the pearls."

To hear Cat tell it, George had done her a favor by cutting her a special price on his inventory, but I couldn't help wonder if he'd been motivated by something else. Breaking off a ten-year marriage the month before his wife has their first child wasn't the action of a man afraid of his future, it was that of a man who was desperate for an escape hatch. He was one of the few people who knew the full value of the inventory at Cat's store and knew exactly where she'd merchandise it. I wondered again why he was at the store the night he was killed. It was starting to look like he'd been in on the theft all along.

Cat interrupted my thoughts. "I should never have placed that order. Business as usual is an expression for a reason."

"No. The way to get ahead is to take risks, and if you wanted different results, you had to try something new. Your instincts were on target. You never could have predicted what happened."

I set the invoice down as a different idea came to me. "Didn't you tell me you worked here before you bought the place?"

"Yes, from Jim Insendo. You met him at the holiday party, remember?"

"Why'd he sell?"

"He hit a point where it wasn't fun for him anymore. He wanted to have time to travel. He sold the store to me in a turnkey transaction."

"Why was he at the holiday party?"

"He was in business for a long time, and sometimes he consults for companies."

"But you said you never ordered from Kenner & Winn."

"Jim did, but I didn't. When I bought Catnip, I took over the store with the inventory as it was, but as we sold out of his inventory, I found new resources. That's been my favorite part of owning a boutique. Why so curious about him?"

"No reason."

I hadn't given much thought to seeing Jim on the sidewalk outside of the store. He could have been shopping or visiting friends at the outlets. And I could already tell Cat wasn't the type to sit around and theorize about the murder, but too many seemingly random things were happening for me to ignore them. I would have liked to call Eddie, but the needs of the visual department had kept him busier than Santa's elves.

Cat pushed the invoice back into the envelope and set it in her inbox. We left her office, and she pulled the door shut behind her. Two men in brown coveralls worked on the gate by the mall entrance. Shana directed customers to the door that exited onto the sidewalk. Cat joined the workers, and I wandered down the aisle. Until Dante showed up with my keys, I was stuck in the store.

Thanks to Tradava, I had both money and time to burn, a rare new circumstance. Add in that I hadn't even started my holiday shopping, and the decision to hang out at Catnip was a no-brainer.

I idled by a table of cashmere sweaters and considered how

wrong it would be to shop for myself and not the many people on my list. Just as I was about to continue on to the men's department, I got distracted, but not by merchandise.

The woman who I'd seen outside the mall last night with Jim walked into Cat's store. She was wearing the chinchilla coat. She shrugged out of the coat, revealing a beige crocodile blazer underneath. I quickly found Cat arranging and pointed the woman out. "See that woman? She was hanging around your store last night after Dante and I left."

"Which woman?"

"That one. Right there. In the beige crocodile jacket."

Her eyes grew big. "I don't see anyone other than Lela."

"Who's Lela?"

She pointed directly at the blonde. "Lela Sexton. My top associate."

12

SYMPHONY OF WOOD AND METAL

I LOOKED AT THE BLONDE AGAIN. "HOW COME I DON'T KNOW HER?" I asked. "I shop here all the time."

"She worked here when I first bought the store, but one of those big luxury stores in King of Prussia recruited her and she left. Now she's back, and the timing couldn't be better. Remember I said somebody quit the other day? Lela called and asked if I had any openings. She's not management material but knows how to sell, and she buys enough to keep the lights on."

If Cat wasn't going to wonder why her associate was sneaking around the mall after dark, then I was. Cat went back to her office and I approached the jewelry counter. I pasted on what I hoped was a friendly smile. "Nice jacket."

"Thank you. It's one less thing to lock up at the end of the night."

I decided to play dumb. "You work for Cat? We haven't formally met. I'm a friend of hers, Samantha Kidd." I held out my hand.

"Lela Sexton." She offered up her fingertips to shake, just like

Joyce Kenner had. Who shakes a hand like that? Was this a thing I hadn't read about on social media?

Lela glided toward a couple of customers who had wandered into the store. If Cat was paying her associates enough to buy crocodile blazers, then maybe I was working at the wrong retailer.

I watched Lela from afar. It wasn't just the expensive jacket that made her stand out. Her taupe silk shell and matching skirt, her thick gold necklace with the single pearl pendant, her gold chain belt...it was understated elegance. Most people didn't know how to do that. And for sure most people who knew how to do that weren't looking for work in an outlet store, even with Cat as the owner.

I hid behind a display of sunglasses. As I tried on pair after pair, I fake-looked around for a mirror while keeping my eyes on Lela. She was at home in the store. Her keys didn't jangle around her wrist like most sales associates who work in stores that lock up their pricey merchandise, but rather hung from the end of a chain belt that she had slung around her waist. She smiled at everyone and assisted them as if she were the hostess at a cocktail party. There was no air of retail angst in her; she made the job look like the prize in a popularity contest. I pulled on a pair of round purple frames and glanced at her feet. She was doing it all in three-inch heels.

I didn't know what I was hoping to see, but this picture of perfection never slipped up. When the customer rush subsided, she stepped out from behind the cases of jewelry and walked toward me. I unfolded a pair of silver frames and pretended to admire myself in the mirror, even though they weren't right for my face.

"The plum ones would suit you better." She handed me a pair with a three-digit price tag. "I noticed you trying to get my attention, but I couldn't get away. It's tough when it gets busy and there's no one else around. Cat needs more staff."

I thought carefully about my choice of words. "Maybe she can't find people she can trust."

She looked at me like royalty who'd been challenged by one of her subjects. "She said that?"

"No, just my theory."

Her eyes stared into the sunglasses that were perched on my face.

"You should consider those frames. They set off your cheekbones nicely." She excused herself and walked away. She'd turned my surveillance mission into a need for high-priced eyewear.

She was good.

I AMASSED a pair of cashmere socks (for Nick), a purple scarf (for Eddie), and seven sweaters (for me), and then, feeling guilty over my obvious one-for-you-a-whole-bunch-for-me shopping strategy, put it all back. Dante came into the store while I was rehanging the socks. As soon as he saw me, he headed my way.

"Cashmere socks. Wow, that's an intimate gift. Who's the lucky fellow?"

"My brother-in-law," I lied. I held out my hand. "My keys?"

He pulled them from his pocket. He put his left hand under mine and placed the keys into my palm with his right. He closed his right hand over the top of mine, making a hand-and-key sandwich that was not altogether appropriate. I balled up my fist around the keys and pulled my hand out.

"Do you always keep your house at a steady fifty degrees?" he asked.

"Um, no?"

"I didn't think so. Your pilot light was out. I fixed it, but still had to dig a couple of blankets out of your hall closet. Cat called me when you two left this morning, and I went to her place." He pulled a cell phone out of his pocket. "Is this yours? It was charging in her kitchen. My sister is anti-Apple, so I know it's not hers."

It was the Nick Phone. I took it and clutched it to my body. "Yes, it's mine. You didn't look at it, did you?"

"Why? Did you use it to take selfies in your underwear?" He pretended to try to see the screen and I blushed.

"No," I said. "Thanks for changing my tire and taking care of my house."

"No problem. Just be careful—you're driving on a donut. You'll want to get a real tire on that car soon."

I left Catnip and drove home. It was early, but I was tired. I had every intention of taking a bath, putting on my pajamas, filing the vandalism report, and crawling into bed.

Plans can change.

The door pushed open when I stuck my key into the lock. The living room was dark but lights were flickering in the kitchen. I stood still, listening for unusual sounds. The house was eerily silent. And then, footsteps. Coming down the stairs.

I ducked into the coat closet and pulled the door shut behind me, wondering if the perpetrator was aware of my presence. My heart pounded in my chest so loud I was certain it could be heard down the block. The vacuum cleaner handle caught on the hem of my skirt and then slid underneath it.

The footsteps stopped. I'd spend the next twenty-four hours in the closet if it was necessary, but sooner or later, I was going to have to get out of there. The front door was a few feet away, and if I was lucky, I could make it to my car and drive away before my intruder could get to me.

The vacuum cleaner handle was cold against my tights. I shifted my weight and stepped on the hem of a trench coat. The coat fell from the hanger. The hangers knocked against each other in a symphony of wood and metal. Whoever was outside the closet had to have heard.

I unsnapped the vacuum cleaner extension and aimed the angled end like a weapon. Shadows formed below the door. It was just a matter of time until I was exposed.

13

HOT MAN

"Kidd, are you going to come out anytime soon, or do I have to refrigerate dinner?" Nick's voice asked.

I opened the door and stared at him. He had one hand on either side of the door frame. The sleeves of his taupe sweater stretched across his shoulders and chest and hinted at muscles underneath the argyle pattern. His curly dark-brown hair was mussed up in a way that suggested he'd slept on it, and he had a two-day beard growth. But it was his eyes, his root-beer-barrel colored eyes, that got to me the most. They searched my face, crinkling at the corners with the faintest hint of a smile when he took in the vacuum cleaner attachment weapon.

"You're back? You're here? How is it that you're here?"

"I persuaded the factory owner to show up early and then caught the red-eye. Surprise." He leaned down and kissed me. "I missed you."

He'd spent his night on a red-eye so he could be with me. He had come straight here from the airport. He was standing in front of me, in the flesh. Not in Italy. Not with Amanda. And had he just said something about dinner?

"Not that it's not entertaining to watch you converse with the voices inside your head, but can you give me an indication of how long that's going to last? I need to figure out if the chicken parmigiana is going to burn."

"You seriously cooked dinner?"

"I seriously cooked dinner. Take off your coat, put away the weapon, and join me for a glass of wine."

I did as told, though not because I was good at taking directions. I was shaking, and only some of it came from the terror in the closet. I'd seen Nick in a tuxedo and in jeans, and he looked good either way. Today he was rumpled, and he wore that well, too, like Indiana Jones in Italian adventure clothes.

I tossed both the coat and the vacuum attachment onto the sofa, gave him a quick smile, and went upstairs to my bedroom. It wasn't until after I returned, comfy in jeans, silk shirt, and cashmere socks, that I joined him in the kitchen. There were a lot of questions I wanted to ask, and most of them ran along the why-are-you-home-so-soon? and did-Amanda-come-home-with-you? variety.

Dinner, I was happy to discover, wasn't just a box of pasta and a jar of readymade sauce. Instead, I was greeted with two plates of appetizers: melon wrapped in prosciutto and fresh sliced tomatoes and buffalo mozzarella garnished with basil and drizzled in olive oil.

"Is all of this in season?"

"Do you care?"

Good point.

I opened a bottle of wine while he tended to the delicious-smelling entrée.

"You're game for chicken parmigiana, right?"

Secret rejoicing—except, "Did you put any green vegetables in it?"

"Why would I put green vegetables in chicken parm?"

"Never mind." A few minutes went by while I sipped my wine.

Nick moved around my kitchen as if he'd done it a hundred times. "I have to admit, I'm a little disappointed in your reaction."

"To what, dinner? I'm totally impressed." I'm not that stupid. I knew exactly what he was referring to.

"To my being in your house."

"I've been trying to figure out a good way to broach that subject."

Just then, the Nick Phone rang. Being that Nick was the only one who knew the number, I didn't answer. Nick picked up the phone and glanced at the display. He didn't move for a moment. He set the phone down.

I picked up the phone and turned it toward me. The missed call had come from "Hot Man." I switched the ringer to off. "Telemarketer," I said.

"Sure." Nick stood up and checked on the chicken.

I grabbed the phone and went to the living room. I pressed the message replay button and held the phone to my head. "Sam, it's Cat," said the message. I relaxed ever so slightly. I couldn't explain "Hot Man," but I could explain Cat calling me. "I'm still at the store." Papers rustled in the background. "Call me back. Okay? Soon."

I poked my head into the kitchen. "I need to check on Cat. It'll take me a minute."

Nick nodded his head but didn't look up.

I called her at Catnip. "It's Samantha," I said.

"I tried to call you at my house but you weren't there. Where are you? And how come Dante has your new number and I don't?"

"I'm at home. I was going to get a change of clothes, but Nick surprised me."

"I thought Nick was in Italy."

"That was the surprise. He's here. He was here when I got here."

"Then where's Dante?"

"How should I know?"

"He said he left something at your place. I thought he'd be there by now."

I froze. If what Cat was saying was true, there was a very good possibility that Dante was either on his way over or was already here.

I looked over my shoulder. No Nick. I crossed the room and poked my head into the kitchen. He was bent over the oven peeking inside. "Everything okay?" I asked.

"Yep. We have about half an hour until it's done." He closed the oven and came over to me. I held the phone face-in toward my shoulder. He put his arms around my waist and smiled. "I was thinking about taking a shower to freshen up before dinner."

"Good idea," I said. "I mean, sure, go ahead. You know where it is."

He moved his right hand up toward my face and cupped my chin. "Do you want to join me?"

Before I could answer him, I realized that the tinny sound I heard was Cat's voice coming from the phone. I stepped backward and held up my finger, and then put the phone to my head. "Cat, I gotta go."

I fumbled with the screen until I found the End Call button, and then set the phone (facedown) on the counter behind me.

"You go ahead," I said. "I, um, wasn't expecting company, and my bedroom is a mess. Not that we're going to be in the bedroom, but I should make sure there aren't any panties lying around. Not that I throw my panties around. I mean—"

Nick pressed his finger to my lips. "The clock is ticking. I'll shower in the hall bathroom." He removed his finger and leaned down and kissed me. I temporarily forgot about the Dante problem.

The Dante Problem!

Dante had spent the night, and now he was on his way over to get something he'd forgotten. There had been no evidence of Dante in my living room or kitchen. What did he leave behind? And where was it?

I waited as patiently as I could (not very) until I heard the sound of running water coming from the bathroom at the top of the second-floor landing. I crept up the first two stairs, and then a hand clamped over my mouth from behind. A second arm circled my waist and lifted me from the stairs, pulling me backward.

14

———

BE STEALTHY

THE STRONG ARM AROUND MY WAIST PIVOTED AND SET ME ON MY living room floor. I spun around and looked at Dante. His hand was still over my mouth. He leaned close and the scent of cinnamon came off his breath.

"If you don't want Loverboy to find out I'm here, you better be quiet."

I grabbed his hand and pulled it away. "How did you get in here?"

"I came in through your garage. I've been on the other side of that door for the past ten minutes."

"Then you heard..."

"Yep." He grinned. "I was hoping to hear more."

I glared at him. "What did you forget?"

"My leather jacket."

"I've never once seen you without your leather jacket."

He shrugged. "Must be Freudian. You know, like my subconscious wanted an excuse to come back."

"Where is it?"

"In your bedroom."

"You slept in my bed?"

"I told you it was cold. I thought being in your bed might warm me up."

"You have to leave. Now."

"I'll leave as soon as I get my jacket." He started up the stairs and I grabbed his arm.

"No way, José. You go out front. I'll get your jacket." I yanked him backward (he barely budged) and charged up the stairs two at a time. His leather jacket was folded neatly on top of my pillow.

Forgot, my fanny.

I pulled a pillow out of its case and stuffed the jacket inside and then threw it over my shoulder like Santa Claus. The water in the shower turned off. I ran downstairs and looked for Dante. He wasn't there. I opened the front door and was hit with a blast of cool air. Cat's car was parked in front of my neighbor Nora's house next door.

Great. Dante had disappeared, and I had his (recognizable) leather jacket in a pillow case in my house. Like that was going to be easy to explain. I tossed the pillow case out the front door and it landed in the bushes by the front porch. I shut the door just as Nick came down the stairs. His hair was wet, and he rubbed a towel against the side of his head.

"It's cold down here," he said.

"The pilot light keeps going off. I should check it. You wait here." I ran past him and down the stairs to the cellar.

Dante stood at the bottom of the stairs. His arms were crossed over his chest. He raised both eyebrows. "My jacket?"

"It's out front in the bushes. In a pillow case." He stood watching me, not moving, not reacting. "I had to think fast. Nick finished with his shower, and I didn't want him to find you here."

"Why not? Nothing happened. Nothing's happening. This..."

He dropped his arms and moved away from the closet door "Is completely innocent. Right?" He gestured back and forth between us and walked straight toward me.

I put my hand palm-side out. "Right. But still, you have to leave. Go out the garage door and be stealthy. And call your sister. She's looking for you."

I returned to the kitchen. Nick had changed into a gray turtleneck sweater and brown slacks. His face was clean-shaven. He opened the oven and pulled out a clear Pyrex dish that immediately filled the room with the scent of tangy tomato, melted mozzarella cheese, and chicken. I temporarily lost track of everything in my life and closed my eyes, inhaling the scent. I could get used to this.

An hour, half a bottle of wine, and the most spectacular dinner that had ever come from my kitchen later, I moved my napkin from my lap and set it next to my empty plate.

"You have a choice. Coffee or ice cream," I said.

"You have room left for ice cream?"

"I always have room for ice cream." I smiled. "But point taken. Coffee, it is."

Nick excused himself. As soon as he was out of the room, I grabbed my old phone and the Nick Phone and worked on syncing my contacts. One of these days, I'd delete the numbers I no longer needed, but then again, you never know when you'll be driving through New Jersey and want to call ahead to your favorite pizza joint to place an order. When the process was finished, I called Cat.

"Hi," she said. "The store's busy, so I can't stay on the phone for too long. It's like what happened gave me free publicity. Everybody wants to shop at the crazy lady's store."

"Nobody thinks you're crazy."

"*I* think I'm crazy. Why wouldn't they?"

It was hard to argue with logic like that. "Listen, about tonight, I think I'm going to stay here," I said.

"I figured as much, what with Nick coming home. Enjoy your time together. This is my problem, not yours." She paused. "Maybe I'll stay at the store overnight."

"Cat, I don't think you should be pulling an all-nighter at the mall. What about Dante? His night should be wide open."

"He said he had plans."

"Trust me. His plans fell through. You are going to stay home and get a good night's sleep in your bed. You owe it to little Andy or—"

"Don't finish that sentence."

"You owe it to your baby. And Logan's at your house. He's very good at keeping people company."

"So you're going to stay home with Nick tonight, and we're just going to cross our fingers that the store will be okay?"

"I have something different in mind." I hung up and poured two cups of coffee and turned around. Nick stood on the other side of the counter.

"Is that decaf?" he asked.

"No."

"It's late. Coffee will keep us both awake. Not that I mind, but the time change is going to catch up with me sooner or later."

I handed him a mug. "Let's hope for later. I just volunteered us for overnight surveillance."

"'Overnight surveillance'? Sounds like fun."

"At the mall."

"You mean...oh. I thought that was a euphemism. The mall has security guards and cameras for that."

"Yes, but we don't know if we can trust the security guards, and the cameras are on the opposite side of Cat's store."

"You're serious."

"I'm serious." I ran my fingertips over his forearm. "I'll make it worth your while..."

He grinned. "I'm afraid to ask how."

Nick had, at times, opposed my involvement with the criminal element. He'd helped me out of one jam, fought with me over another. We'd broken up over it and gotten back together because of it. His agreeable nature tonight was mildly suspicious.

It didn't matter, though; one way or the other, the night would be fruitful. My late-night investigation might turn up some new details for Cat, and I'd get to spend the night with Nick. Bonus points: because we'd be out of the house, he wouldn't discover that Dante had slept in my bed last night.

All in all, it was a win-win.

15

PRIVATE ROOM

Twenty minutes later, Nick and I sat in the cab of his truck, watching both customers and employees trickling out of the outlet center. We parked on the side where Cat would have exited; there was no reason for that other than it being the most familiar to me. If something happened on the back side of the building, we would need a second night of investigation.

Overnight surveillance was serious business. Before we left, I changed from my jeans and silk blouse into a black cowl-neck sweater, pink camo pants, and heavy black boots. So far, Nick was being a trooper. My handbag did contain a Swiss army knife and an odd assortment of gadgets that I carried for potential emergencies just like this one, so I still felt adequately prepared.

"Bring me up to speed on this investigation," he said.

I couldn't tell if he was taking me seriously or not but filled him in on the highlights of the problem anyway: the smash and grab, Cat's argument with George at the party, the burglar in the store, and George's body behind the jewelry case.

"If this was all about the jewelry theft, then why kill George? He left her earlier that night. Was he involved with someone else? Was this a crime of passion? But then was the smash and grab an odd case of timing?" I finished.

"You love this, don't you?" Nick asked. "Not what happened, but this part. The questions and the evidence and the search for answers and justice."

"Doesn't everybody?"

"No. I can safely say that most women your age would not be sitting in the front seat of a truck conducting overnight surveillance on an outlet mall in forty-degree weather the week before Christmas."

"I guess that makes me unique."

"You're telling me." He reached across my lap and pulled a small black case out of the glove box. He waved his hands up and down the case like a magician prepping for a magic trick and then extracted a pair of binoculars from the case and handed them to me.

"Do you always drive around with binoculars in your glove box?"

"Only since I started dating you."

I held the binoculars up to my eyes. After a few seconds, I dropped them back to my lap. "Forty degrees?"

"Somewhere around there."

"You didn't happen to pack any blankets too, did you?"

"When I planned to surprise you, I changed into clean clothes at the airport. I picked up the ingredients for dinner on the way to your house. I didn't want to be presumptuous about what might happen after that—although if anything happened, I figured your house would have the necessary accoutrements."

"So no blankets."

"Next time I'll be more prepared."

I checked the clock on the dash. The camping store was still open, and if the temperature dropped at a rate of two degrees an hour, then by midnight, it would be... I looked away from the clock. I'd never gotten the hang of those "two trains leave the station at the same time" math problems, and this calculation was on par with that.

I turned to Nick to see if he'd been watching. But despite sharing almost a full pot of coffee, Nick was asleep. His head was nestled between the window and the side of his head rest. His arms were around his body. The cab of the truck was cool and, with no engine running, getting colder every second. I took off my coat and tucked it in around him. His eyes opened halfway and he made a sound that I interpreted as "thank you."

Jetlag may have driven Nick to doze off in the cab of the truck, but no coat, half a pot of coffee, and the responsibilities of a surveillance had left me wide awake.

It was nine-thirty. I had about half an hour before the mall closed for the night. Half an hour to get to the camping store to buy a blanket (and look for suspicious activity, because as far as cover stories went, the blanket ruse was pretty solid.)

I hopped out of the truck and jogged through the parking lot toward the entrance. If we needed a flashlight, flare, or any other emergency items, I would be sure to find an assortment in the camping store as well.

I asked a grungy looking clerk for the location of the blankets and was sent to the back corner of the store. Still shivering from my walk through the parking lot, I added a propane heater to the pile, along with a thermos, flashlight, and a couple of pink metallic D-clamps. They seemed like things I should have on hand in case of emergency too.

I headed toward the register. Hipster Hunter was working again. I stacked my items on the counter and held out my credit card.

"Is there any place around here where I can get some hot chocolate?" I asked.

"There's a chocolate stand by the department store at the end of the mall, but the cups are kiddie sized."

"I mean for the thermos."

"Oh. Head out the exit and turn right. Go past the novelty sock shop and turn left. They have hot chocolate at the coffee shop, but you better hurry. It's closing time, and nobody likes staying after hours."

When my shopping was complete, Hipster Hunter walked me to the door and pointed down the mall. He handed my bags to me and pulled the metal gate into place as soon as I left. I draped the handles of the shopping bags over my arms and walked as fast as I could considering I was now prepared for a polar expedition.

The hot chocolate stand was closed by the time I reached it. I cursed to myself. I left through the mall exit and was about to cut through the parking lot to Nick's truck when I saw Aguilar, the rotund security officer who'd checked on Catnip the night we found George's body, loitering on the sidewalk outside of Catnip not fifty feet away from me. I dropped down and hid behind the end of a public bench, squinting through the darkness at him.

Aguilar's presence should have been calming. Nick and I were there to keep an eye on the store, and apparently, we weren't the only ones with that idea. I should have felt better knowing mall security had taken an interest in protecting Catnip, but something about the officer had felt off from the first moment he'd come to check up on the store after we'd interrupted the burglary in progress.

His hands were in the pockets of his jacket, and he looked from the bottom left corner of the door frame, up to the top left corner, across the top and then back down the right-hand side. He stepped past the door and peered into the bushes. A truck lumbered past.

Aguilar lit a cigarette and sat down on a bench not unlike the one I hid behind.

It could be he was just doing his job, keeping an eye out on a store that was involved in a recent crime. Or—

The door to Cat's store swung open, and a woman came out. She locked the door behind her and then headed to Aguilar. I recognized the blue-black dyed hair and the shine on her pleather pants immediately. An oversized black leather jacket with the collar turned up hid most of her face, but that didn't stop me from making an identity. I was looking at Shana Brice, Cat's assistant manager with the crappy attitude and the Herman Munster shoes.

As I watched, she set a shopping bag by her feet and locked the door to Catnip. She turned back around, reached into the bag, and pulled out a brown bundle. She tossed it in the trash can and then walked along the sidewalk to the end of the mall.

When Shana vanished from view, Aguilar stood up. He put out his cigarette and then went to the trash can. He reached inside and pulled the bundle out. He stuck it inside his brown flight jacket and pulled up the zipper then jogged across the lot to a beat-up car, climbed in, and drove away.

I crossed the parking lot to Nick's truck and yanked the door open. Nick was asleep, his head resting against his window. His right leg was stretched out along the seat. I moved his leg and tucked a blanket around his waist. His eyes opened slowly.

"Come here," he gestured with his head, and without thinking about a master plan, I slid over to him. His arm wrapped around me. I pushed thoughts of Shana and Aguilar's suspicious behavior to the back of my mind and the next thing I knew, Nick and I were kissing.

His hands moved to my waist, and one thing led to another. The steering wheel was behind me. The windows fogged up, and even though we were parked in the lot outside of a shopping mall the week before Christmas, it felt like a private room. And because it felt like a private room, we did things that should have been done in a private room. I may have thought briefly about the placement of the Ribbon Designer Outlet security cameras, but I don't remember. Nick had been out of town for far too long, and to be honest, I was a little distracted by what he was doing with his hands.

Once our X-rated activities came to a close, I felt around the floor boards for my panties. The insanity of the holidays had officially infiltrated my world.

I snuck a look at him. He was buttoning his shirt. He held his hand out, and I grabbed it and sat up. My foot had left a print in the condensation inside of his window. He didn't seem to notice. He put his fingers under my chin and raised my face so I was looking at him. "It's been eleven years since I first saw you on a street corner outside of my showroom trying on samples that fell out of the back of my truck."

"Eleven years since I saw you in your Rocky T-shirt. I thought you were a delivery man."

"I thought you were the first woman I'd seen who could pull off a bucket hat." He smiled at the memory and put his arm around me. "It might make me seem like less of a man to admit this, but that's the first time I've ever done—*that*—in a truck," he said.

"Me too."

We kissed again, which set us off toward round two. I put my hands on Nick's chest. "Focus. We have to focus. We're here to focus," I said. I held the binoculars up to my eyes, but the windows were too fogged to see out.

Nick cracked his window. "Give it a minute. It'll clear." I nestled under his arm and stared at the mall.

I DON'T REMEMBER the rest of Nick and my surveillance mission. What I remember next is being shaken awake inside Nick's truck. We were parked in front of my house.

"Kidd, wake up," Nick said.

I pulled away from the crook of his arm and sat on my side of the truck, blinked a few times, and ran my fingers though my hair. The clock on Nick's dashboard said five forty-seven. It was dark, but the glow of the sun peeking up from the horizon cast the neighborhood in a pinkish-orange glow that matched my favorite Instagram filter. After a few labored breaths and wide-eyed blinking, I looked at him.

"What are we doing here?"

"You live here."

"I know that." Another labored breath. More for emphasis than anything else. "What time is it? Why aren't we inside? Why aren't we in bed?"

He raised his eyebrows.

"You know what I mean. Why aren't we on surveillance?"

"I don't know. We were in the truck, and then we...and then that's about it. I woke and you were curled up next to me under a blanket I've never seen before." He ran his hand over the red plaid blanket on his lap. "I'm hoping you can tell me?"

"You fell asleep before I could tell you. I went into the camping store for supplies." I blinked several times and thought back over what else I recalled. "The security officer was outside Cat's store."

"That's good. That means he's keeping an eye on things."

"Yes..." The details came back to me slowly. Aguilar outside Catnip. Shana exiting the store and throwing something away. Aguilar taking it out of the trash and then leaving. There was something odd about that. "You don't remember anything?"

"When I woke up, you had your elbows propped on the dashboard. You appeared to be very focused on your task. It wasn't until the binoculars dropped from your hands that I realized you fell asleep while holding them."

"I fell asleep while on surveillance?" I asked. Talk about letting yourself down.

"It was as much a surprise to me as it was to you," he said. "I had four cups of coffee on the flight home from Italy because I thought I was going to have to keep up with you." He yawned. "It's good to know you're human."

"So that's it? You didn't see anything suspicious?"

"Kidd, it was five o'clock in the morning. The most suspicious thing in that parking lot was us."

I held my hair back away from my face. "Why are we here and not inside?"

"Because I thought it set a bad relationship precedent for me to go through your handbag in search of your keys."

I pulled my bag up to my waist and dug around the interior for my keychain. It wasn't there. I tried to remember if I'd grabbed it when we left. I looked at the house and then froze. Not because of the temperature but because someone was moving around my living room.

16

SO THIS WAS HOW IT FELT

Nick noticed the activity inside my house too. He hopped out of the truck and stepped in front of me, using his arm to keep me back. We crept the few steps necessary to get to the front door, but circumstance wasn't on our side when it came to being unseen. The door pulled open and we found six strangers in my living room adjusting lights and placing the finishing touches on a Christmas tree. Correction: five strangers and Eddie.

Eleven months of the year, Eddie was my best friend, confidant, and occasional voice of reason. During December he was more like a figment of my imagination thanks to his responsibilities at Tradava, which was just one of the reasons I thought I was being *Punk'd*.

"What's going on here?" I asked.

"I think the words you're looking for are 'thank you for decorating my house,'" Eddie said, undaunted by the rising tone of my voice. "You're so busy helping Cat that you didn't put up so much as a twinkle light, let alone a tree. My visual staff is fried, and we needed an off-site project. So, voila. A new tradition."

"I grew up here. I've had more Christmases in this house than any place I've ever lived."

"So an old tradition. Either way, you're now ready for the holidays."

Nick came out of my kitchen with a wooden tray filled with mugs of coffee. I doubted the caffeine was going to get in the way of sleep, so I took one just like everybody else. Eddie's team packed up random items they hadn't used and left one by one, touching base with him on what time they'd get to the store and where they should start working. Nick hovered next to me, watching them make their exit. When everyone but Eddie had left, Nick handed me his empty mug and asked for a refill.

I went to the kitchen and filled the mugs to the brim, sipped a few sips from my cup and refilled it again. I was returning to consciousness, which started to become a problem when I recognized words like *keeping her away, good timing,* and *not yet.* I set the mugs down and went back to the living room in time to see Eddie pull a set of keys out of his cargo pants and set them on the Halston book that sat on my coffee table.

"You had something to do with this?" I asked Nick. "Is that why you agreed to go on surveillance with me?" My eyes went wide. "Is that why we...in the parking lot?"

"You did what in the parking lot?" Eddie asked.

"Never mind," Nick and I said in unison.

"Dude," Eddie said. "I have to go. We did Cat's house before yours. I'm on call all day. You're on your own." Eddie looked at me, at Nick, and then back at me. He shook his head and left.

"I get the 'keeping her away' and the 'good timing,' but what did he mean by 'not yet'?"

Nick crossed the room in about three strides and tipped my face up to his. Before I knew what was happening, he kissed me.

At first his lips just brushed over mine, then connected. When the kiss ended, he pulled away from me and ran his hands gently down my cheeks to my neck, then over my hair. His pupils were dilated, darkening his eyes. He took my hands and walked me to the sofa, and then sat down next to me.

"Kidd, I don't know what to do about you. You're in my head. You're in my shoe collection. You're not the kind of woman I want to fool around with in my truck in a parking lot outside of a mall."

"There's another type of woman you want to do that with?"

"That's not what I mean."

"Nick, I'm not going anywhere. You've seen what my life's been like since moving back to Ribbon. Our relationship is the most stable thing I have. I don't want that to change either."

"So if I were to, maybe, make things a little more permanent, you'd say yes?"

"More permanent like how?"

He let go of my left hand and reached into his jacket pocket. He pulled out a small black velvet box. Suddenly I wasn't all that tired. A burst of electricity shot from my heart out to my fingertips and my breath caught. Nick dropped my other hand and opened the box. Inside was an engagement ring with a single square cut diamond nestled against a pale pink satin interior.

"More permanent like this."

A cocktail of emotions cycled through me, excitement and nervousness and happiness and nausea. I felt my hands shake and I balled them up to stop them. After a few seconds, I looked from the ring to Nick.

"You had that with you all night?" I asked quietly.

He nodded.

"Even when we..."

He nodded.

"And you're asking me to..."

"I'm asking you to marry me, Samantha."

"You didn't call me 'Kidd.'"

"It didn't feel like a 'Kidd' moment."

I didn't know anything about my future. What I knew was that I'd moved back to Pennsylvania to live in the house where I grew up because I'd felt like my life in New York wasn't me, but the happiest I'd been during the nine years I'd spent climbing the Bentley's New York corporate ladder were the days when I worked with Nick. Ever since I'd left, I'd been searching for something, a place where I fit. That need to find something had led me into a lot of dangerous situations, and even though I'd managed to come out of them alive, each time, I was left wondering what I was really looking for. I'd had career and financial security when I was in New York, but that hadn't been enough. Nick was offering me something different. An acceptance of who I was and a promise for the future. I put my hands on his forearms and leaned in to kiss him.

I saw a new emotion in his face, one I hadn't seen before. Vulnerability? Hurt? Why was I hesitating? Why hadn't I just grabbed the ring and said yes? I knew I wanted to. I'd thought about it more than once, and if he looked on the Chinese food takeout menus in the junk drawer, he'd even see that I occasionally doodled the initials "SKT" to see what my monogram might look like.

"I'm scared," I said. It came out closer to a whisper than words.

He set the ring box on the floor and pulled me to him. I put my arms around his neck and his were around my back, and we hugged closer and longer than we ever had before. I could feel my heart beating hard in my chest—or was it his?—and I realized that this was the most secure I'd felt in a very long time.

"I don't want to scare you or rush you." he said in a soft voice next to my ear. "Just know that I love you, Kidd. I love your craziness and your impulsive nature and your need to try to fix other people's problems. I love your loyalty and your style and your sense of humor. When you put yourself in dangerous situations, I wish I didn't love you so much, but I do. I've been in love with you for a long time. Nothing is going to change that. You don't have to give me an answer right now."

I felt his embrace relax, and I pulled away from him. He picked the black velvet ring box up from the floor and set it into the palm of my hand.

"Where did you get the ring?" I asked.

"It was my mom's."

Emotion and exhaustion overwhelmed me. "Thank you for asking me," I said.

He caught my face between his hands and held it. Our faces were close. He leaned in for a kiss that was less innocent than the others. The fear and nausea left my body and a couple of new sensations took over. I hadn't felt this with my prom date or my college boyfriend or Sal from the deli counter across the street from Bentley's. So *this* was how it felt to be in love.

My body was sending clear signals that it was ready, willing, and able, but my brain sent up a warning flare that our first time together had been in the front seat of his truck in a parking lot and maybe going round two on my living room sofa with the curtains not quite shut wasn't a good follow-up performance. To be honest, I'm not sure the thought was that fully formed. What I was sure about was at least one of us needed a shower and that one of us was me.

Nick didn't appear too surprised by my gentle resistance.

"Not now," I panted.

"I know you're right," he said. "But—"

"But you know I'm right."

"I thought I was the voice of reason in this operation?" he said. He stood up and tucked his shirt into his jeans. I sat up and adjusted my bra. "I'm going to head home and spend the day with my dad. Chop down a tree, buy some presents. Do the whole men-at-Christmas thing. Talk to you tomorrow?"

"Sure."

"Take your time, Kidd. It's a big decision, and I want you to be as sure about this as I am."

17

WHAT DOES THIS MEAN?

I gave Nick a ten-minute lead and took off last night's surveillance clothes (was my sweater on backward?). I showered and dressed in a taupe scoop neck sweater, brown leather leggings, and brown wedge-heeled sneakers. I transferred my wallet, phone, keys, and lip tint into a small cross-body bag. I blow-dried my hair upside down and then slipped in a quilted brown leather hair band. Twice I slipped on the engagement ring and admired the way it changed the look of my hand. Okay, three times. It was my version of dragging my big toe through the water of the deep end before jumping in.

As tempting as it was to climb into bed, I needed to check on Cat and Logan. I grabbed a couple of cans of diet cat food, pulled on an ivory car coat, and left.

Like just about everything else these days, the weather was pretending to be something it wasn't. The temperature was in the forties and would no doubt climb during the day. Trees were bare of leaves and lawns were the color of uncooked wheat pasta. Aside from the occasional light display in a neighbor's yard, it did not feel like the holidays.

I parked in Cat's driveway and, after tapping on the front door, let myself in. Logan was curled up on Dante's black leather jacket in the middle of the sofa, and Cat was in the kitchen.

"Good morning," she said. She seemed to be in good spirits. "I'm making banana-avocado-yogurt smoothies for breakfast. Want one?"

"I think I'll just have coffee. I didn't get a whole lot of sleep last night." I debated telling Cat about Nick's proposal and the truck incident, but it didn't feel like the right time. She had her own issues to worry about, and my news might upset her.

She pulsed the blender a few times and then turned it off. "You shouldn't have had to worry about me. It's my problem, and I need to figure it out. I should never have involved you."

"Cat, you're eight months pregnant. Whether or not this happened, you would have needed my help with the store, and even if you didn't ask me, I would have volunteered. You're about to become a very busy woman, and I think right now you should be resting."

"I talked to the detective last night," she said.

"Where?"

"He called. He said he wanted to come over today. He said a couple of people told him about George and my fight at the party and that raised questions in his investigation."

Warning bells went off in my head. "What did you tell him?"

"I told him about everything—George's meltdown and how scared I am about having this baby." She put her hand on her belly. "He said I didn't have to talk to him if I didn't want to, but I want this to be over."

"Cat, when he said you didn't have to talk to him, did he ask you if you wanted a lawyer to be present?"

"Yes, but my lawyer was George's friend. I don't know if they know how he was feeling. I don't know if they knew this was coming."

"Um, Cat, I don't think what George's friends think of you should be your biggest concern. It sounds like Detective Madden is looking at you as the main suspect," I said. Cat picked up the blender of avocado-banana-yogurt mixture and poured it into her mug. She took a sip and stood very, very still, not saying a word for upwards of a minute. "Are you okay?" I asked.

She turned to face me. Her unfocused eyes moved up my sweater until she reached my face. "No. I am definitely not okay." She grabbed the blender and dumped the contents into the sink and then tossed the empty blender in on top of it. Droplets of green goo splattered out and landed on the backsplash and on her apron. She threw her towel onto the counter and stormed out of the room.

My first instinct was to follow her. I got as far as the doorway when I stopped to think about things from Cat's point of view. In the past four days, she'd gone from being a happily married wife about to give birth to her first child and celebrate her ten-year anniversary to facing life as a single mom while mourning the death of her husband. He'd left her, and then he'd *left* her. There would be no hope for a reconciliation, no explanation for his decision or for his timing. For the rest of her life, Cat would question whether George's friends knew of his dissatisfaction, whether there was something deeper at the root of his change of heart. I didn't think she was the type to let other people's opinions shape her view of herself, but it would make it hard to reach out for help from people she no longer trusted.

When I'd first moved to Ribbon and started my life over, I'd felt alone. Cat's new reality was ten times more challenging than mine had been. I'd survived my circumstances, but I hadn't had the extra burden of a baby on the way.

And the most frustrating thing of it all, the one thing that none of us were saying because of how it would make us appear, was that Cat couldn't be mad at George anymore. Her "Men Are Rats" rant prior to the party had been her knee-jerk reaction to being left in her third trimester by a man who selfishly said he was leaving her when she needed him the most. Nobody would have questioned her anger. But they'd fought at the party at the mall, and that was the single most damning evidence against her. Who knows how many people saw her throw her drink in his face. George had brought her wrath onto him by his actions, but when he was murdered, everything changed. George became the victim, not Cat.

And we still didn't know why.

I wandered into the living room and sat down next to Logan. He looked up at me and meowed. I ran my hand over the top of his head and scratched his ears. I picked him up and carried him to the fireplace. He put his front paws over my shoulder. Again, I looked at the photos on the mantel. The last one was of Cat when she'd just started showing. She and George stood next to each other. One of his arms was around her and the other was on her tummy. The look on his face was pure joy: eyes wide, smile even wider. Cat looked at him, and he looked at the camera, and anybody who saw that photo would think this baby was going to be born into the best marriage ever.

I set the photo facedown and noticed something taped to the back of the frame. It was a piece of white paper wrapped around a small, lumpy object.

I should have left it alone.

We both know I didn't.

I peeled the tape away from the frame and unwrapped the object. It was a tiny gold key. A poem had been typed on the paper:

Roses are red
Violets are blue
This life has been perfect
With just me and you.

Below the poem, written in George's handwriting, was a personal note:

My Dearest Kitty-Cat, Our family grows by one! No matter what happens, you'll never be alone as long as I'm alive. There are no words to say thank you for what we have so I won't even try. Love forever and ever, George.

P. S. Look in the flue!

"What's that?" Cat asked from behind me.

I looked up suddenly and closed my hand around the key. "It's —it's—" I searched her face as what I'd just read sank in. I was never intended to see this. Cat was.

And if what I thought was correct, it changed everything. I held the paper out toward her. "You need to see this."

"I can't take any more bad news."

"It's not bad news, I promise."

She crossed the room and took the paper. Her red hair fell forward while she read it, hiding her expression. It wasn't a long note, but she stared at the paper for a very long time. A large fat tear plopped onto the paper. Finally, she lowered it and looked at me. "Where did you find this?"

"It was taped to the back of the last photo on the mantel." I held out the key. "It was wrapped around this."

She took the key and turned it over in her fingers. Slowly, she crouched down and peered inside the fireplace. She reached her hand up into the flue and moved it around. Her body tensed for a moment, and then she leaned forward more and pulled something out. It was a small box wrapped in paper with little pink and blue bows printed on it.

"How did this get in there?" she asked. I didn't reply, because it seemed we both knew the answer.

"If you had started a fire, it would have been destroyed."

"It was a joke. George baby-proofed every square inch of this place, and I asked him how he was going to baby-proof the fireplace. He said not to worry—that he had something special in mind for that."

She walked to the sofa and sat down and then slowly tore the paper away from the box. Inside was a small antique jewelry box. Cat fit the key inside the lock and opened it. A tiny ballerina spun to the tinkling tune of *Love Story*. Two small boxes were inside. One had a tag that said, "Pearls for baby." The other had a tag that said, "Pearls for mother."

A mother-of-pearl-handled baby rattle was inside the first box. A thick strand of the most glorious pearls I'd ever seen was inside the second. A certificate of authenticity was nestled inside the box under the necklace.

Slowly Cat closed the box and looked at me. "What does this mean?" she asked. Tears streaked her face and moistened her shirt, but she didn't sob. She already knew what it meant. She just needed me to tell her.

I stooped down in front of her. "It means George wasn't a rat."

"But he said he needed space. He told me to leave him alone."

"I don't think he said that because he wanted to. I think he was trying to protect you."

"From what?"

"From whoever it was that killed him."

18

DO AS I SAY, NOT AS I DO

After finding the hidden present that George had left behind, there wasn't much to say. Cat let go of the emotions that had been building up inside of her and cried on my shoulder for the better part of an hour. For once, I knew to keep my mouth shut. Of all of the situations that I'd been through, this one was unprecedented.

"I can't do this," Cat said. "I can't. I can't give up my store and be a stay-at-home mom. I can't stay at the store and raise a baby. I can't let the police arrest me for my husband's murder and plan his memorial service at the same time. I don't want to give birth in a prison! And I can't let somebody get away with taking him from me and destroying the memories of my marriage."

"So don't."

She looked at me. "Don't what? Which one?"

"All of them. Any of them. Aside from the baby, that's how I feel almost every single day."

"But it's exhausting."

"I know. So don't focus on the can'ts. Focus on what you can do. Like me. I can get a job. I can take care of Logan. I can eat a salad for dinner once a month. Stuff I can control. It's not much, but it helps me deal with the other things, the things that feel impossible."

"So where do I start? Because right now it's all so overwhelming, and I can barely breathe."

"You have to be the one to figure that out," I said.

"I can't."

I didn't say it out loud, but she was kinda stepping on the whole concept.

"Cat, remember back when I first moved to Ribbon, I was hired to work at Tradava and my boss was killed? And how people suspected me?"

"Yes, but you proved them wrong."

"And you know how I proved them wrong? By accident. I didn't know what I was doing. I suspected everybody. I suspected you."

"Me? Why would I kill your boss?"

"I don't remember my reasoning. I felt like the walls were closing in around me and I was going to lose everything I had and it was supposed to be a brand-new life and before I even got out of the gates, it was over. I thought I was being framed. And I didn't trust anybody, and I made a lot of accusations that could hurt people. If you knew then that I told the police that maybe you killed Patrick, we probably wouldn't be friends right now."

She stared at me, either processing what I said or wondering if she could return the favor by connecting me to the murder of George with means, motive, and opportunity. Finally, she looked down at the pearls in her lap. "I never realized how you felt when that happened. I was so mean to you. You came to my store and I kicked you out. It never occurred to me that you were fighting for your life. I'm a bad person. A bad friend."

I might have let Cat believe that I didn't remember my reasoning, but the details of that time in my life were as fresh as if they'd happened yesterday. I'd gone to Cat's store because I suspected her and nobody would listen to me. I'd planned to try to catch her in a lie or an admission of guilt, to get evidence to take to the police. I hadn't seen her as a person who had problems of her own, but as a person who could take the heat off me with a little redirection. Neither one of us was innocent in this scenario.

"That's all in the past," I said. "Let's concentrate on what we can do to help you out now."

"Sam, tell me what to do. Please? Until this is all over, make my decisions for me. When I met you, you were a hot mess. No offense."

"None taken." (Ish.)

"But now you have it all. Career, relationship, friends, pet...I think you even lost a couple of pounds recently."

If there had been any recent weight loss, it had been thanks to Cat's vegetable-at-every-meal approach to her pregnancy. And if I had anything to say about it (which it seemed as though I was about to), I was going to put a stop to that right now.

"Are you sure about this? Because if I do this, it's only going to be until George's murderer is caught, and I'm only doing it if you don't question what I tell you to do."

"I've never been more sure about anything in my life." She put her hand on her pregnant belly. "Even this."

"Okay, for the foreseeable future I make your decisions for you, starting with this. Get a fresh banana."

"A banana? You never eat bananas when you're stressed."

"You're right, but I'm making *your* decisions for you, not *my* decisions for you."

"That's not what I asked you to do."

I signed. "Get a bag of pretzel shells and meet me in the living room. We're going to recap what we know and then come up with a plan."

My experience with the local police had resulted in an unexpected friendship between me and the lead homicide investigator, Detective Loncar. The last time we'd "worked" together (he'd insist on the quotes if he read this), I learned his daughter had recently had a baby but his wife, unhappy with him, had kicked him out of the house and asked for a trial separation. Loncar had never liked my involvement in his cases, but we'd broken through the initial gruff detective/amateur sleuth phase.

One of the many problems with this case was that Detective Loncar wasn't around. If I could talk to him, I could gauge how serious the police were about Cat as suspect. I could offer up counter theories. He might not want to hear them, but once they were out there, he wouldn't have a choice.

I had no experience with Detective Madden prior to his arrival at Catnip the night of the murder. He was acting like the nicest guy in the world, but if he thought Cat was guilty, nice wouldn't matter. He'd talk to everybody, collect evidence, and build a case. And once he felt his case was iron-clad, he'd go to the judge for an arrest warrant.

If I looked at things the way Madden was, I saw a pregnant, hormonal wife and a dead husband. I saw pearls from said wife's store knotted across said husband's throat. I saw witnesses who could place the wife at the same party where the victim was, describe a public argument, and place her at the scene of the murder during a window of time that I couldn't account for because I was looking for my bra in a bush outside of the mall. If Madden was already asking Cat if she wanted a lawyer present, I had a feeling he'd be meeting with the judge to get a warrant for her arrest sooner rather than later.

But with the exception of the time I'd spent creating/retrieving my garments, I'd been with Cat. I knew she couldn't have done it. Which meant:

A)Somebody else had a reason to kill George;

B)Somebody else wanted to make it look like Cat did it;

C)We had little to no time to figure out who.

Good thing I liked a challenge.

"Cat, last night I saw Shana outside your store after hours. And before you say anything, I know it was her—with her blue and black hair and her largely synthetic wardrobe, it would be hard not to recognize her."

"So she was outside my store. She worked the late shift and probably parked on that side of the mall."

"She threw something away in the trash bin outside of your exit."

"We usually put the trash by the gate in the mall for the cleaning crew, but after the gate malfunction, she might have made other arrangements."

"But remember the security officer who came into your store the night of the party? Aguilar?"

"What about him?"

"How well do you know him? He was rude to us when he first came into your store after the crash. Does he always act like that?"

"I know some of the mall security guards, but not all of them. They don't like the store owners because we blame them when we're robbed, but they say we should have better loss prevention measures. I think Aguilar was new, though, because I don't remember seeing him before the night of the party. Why?"

"Last night he was outside Catnip. He took whatever Shana threw out."

"He took her trash?"

I nodded. "Normally I'd say you should talk to outlet security, but considering they're possibly involved, I'd go straight to the police."

"Is that what you would do? Call the police?"

"Do as I say, not as I do," I said. "That detective on the case—Detective Madden—call him. He's in charge of the investigation."

"But we don't have proof that anybody did anything wrong. You said yourself we couldn't just go around accusing people without proof."

"I said that?" She nodded. "Tell him you have reason to believe Officer Aguilar is involved, and then tell him what I saw."

"And how do you want me to explain that you were hanging out in the parking lot outside of my store?"

"Don't mention that part. Call him and invite him over. Show him the baby rattle from the fireplace. Let's see how he reacts and figure the rest out as we go."

19

IT'S COMPLICATED

THIS WAS THE LEAST RELAXING VACATION I'D EVER HAD. BETWEEN Cat's troubles at the outlets, an unfamiliar detective, and Dante's general Dante-ness, I was more stressed than the day I had to present end-of-season projections to the CEO of Bentley's. Plus, Logan had fought back on the diet by eating one of Cat's casseroles that had been left out, and I was out one pair of pink lizard boots. Nick had provided the singular shining spot in a week of pre-holiday chaos.

With Cat at home resting, it was left to me to keep an eye on those who were minding the store. I headed to Catnip. Shana was behind the register and Lela was close by, folding a table of sweaters. She saw me, dropped the sweater, and walked away. "I'm taking my break," she said to Shana.

She wore another of her expensive outfits. Today it was a taupe tweed skirt suit that may or may not have been Chanel, a crisp white shirt, and a belt with a gold H in the front—instantly recognizable as Hermés. It was as if she'd been given a list of luxury brands to flaunt in front of her co-workers and customers.

I'd heard of looking the part, and between the designer wardrobe I'd accumulated while working at Bentley's New York and the more recent acquisitions from my employee discount at Tradava, I had complete confidence in my personal style. This woman made me look like my wardrobe came from a dollar store. Cat had mentioned that Lela's spending habits helped the bottom line, but that didn't mean she didn't feel entitled to extras on the side. Even the priciest items become affordable when you implement a five-finger discount.

I watched Lela leave the store and then ducked into the lingerie department.

"Excuse me, do you have these in any other colors?" a woman asked.

I recognized the voice and turned. Joyce Kenner, the wife of half of Kenner & Winn, stood next to me. She held an assortment of lace panties that were clipped to individual clear plastic hangers. Shopping for intimate apparel fell under "personal business," and from the looks of the assortment in her hand, Mrs. Kenner's business was booming.

"Mrs. Kenner," I said, "Joyce. I'm Samantha Kidd. I met you at your holiday party. I was with Cat Lestes."

She looked confused for a moment, and then recognition struck. "Oh yes, you're Catherine's partner."

"We're not partners like you think."

"I certainly hope you're not planning on breaking things off with her because of the baby," she said. "Whatever your problems are, I'm sure you can work them out."

"It's—complicated."

"Honey, doesn't matter if it's men or women. It's always complicated." The corners of her mouth turned up but the smile didn't reach her eyes.

"No, Joyce, it's not complicated like that. Cat is married. Was married. Her husband worked for your husband's company. George Stevens?" I expected her to respond to the name. At her blank look, I continued. "He was murdered a few nights ago, right here in the store. Didn't your husband tell you?"

"My husband doesn't bring details about the company home with him."

"But it's been all over the news. That and the usual retail thefts. I don't see how you could have missed it."

"I don't share society's fascination with murder and homicide. It's unseemly." She stood straighter. "About Catherine, Tom led me to believe the two of you were a couple. I didn't mean to imply anything."

I put my hand on her arm. "It's okay. Cat's going through a hard time right now, and she can use all of the support she can get. Imagine, eight months pregnant and now this."

Her eyes narrowed for a moment. "Eight months? That would mean—last April?"

"I imagine so. I never stopped to do the math."

"Poor thing," she said. She took my fingertips in her hand and squeezed. "Do let me know if there's anything I can do to help your friend out." She glanced at the assortment of panties in her grip and then, as if realizing she had no idea why she'd wanted them in the first place, handed them to me and walked away.

It struck me as odd that Joyce Kenner didn't know about the murder at the outlet. Not only had it been on the news, but George was part of the Kenner & Winn family. He'd been strangled with a necklace that had been outsourced by her husband's company. Not that I expected talk of murder to be dinner-table conversation, but this seemed like something that might transcend "pass the salt."

I returned Joyce's selections to the appropriate fixtures and headed to Cat's office so I could adjust my leggings. Once I closed the door behind me, I tugged at my waistband until the crotch was back into place. I pulled down my sweater and squeezed through the narrow space between Cat's desk and the file cabinet and dropped into her chair for a moment. I leaned back and studied the office. The ceiling consisted of pop-out, off-white cork tiles positioned on top of a gray metal frame. My old buying office at Bentley's had the same kind. It was handy for birthday parties when we needed a place to hang balloons, because while the metal frame was rigid, the cork tiles lifted easily. One party had us celebrating an engagement by dangling ring pops from the metal grid with colorful ribbons.

Happy memories of working at Bentley's had helped fade the recollection of the sixty-five-hour work weeks. I remembered the office camaraderie that we had, even though the job had held its stressful moments. The close-knit team I assembled seemed capable of rising to most challenges and having fun between the crises. Funny thing, I hadn't thought about that job in a couple of months. Now I was remembering it as though I'd been a fool to leave.

The walls of Cat's office were soft yellow. I was willing to bet she'd been responsible for the color choice and not Jim. My eyes traveled around the office, looking at the Erté print on the wall, the mirror that hung on the back of the door, and the file cabinet propped back against the wall. Our hidden camera was positioned between a pile of books on fashion and style, and I cringed while I realized that Dante would see me hanging out after hiking up my tight pants. As long as I managed to keep my embarrassing moments less than five minutes long, I had a chance to go unnoticed.

Or, I could go back through the pictures and delete the incriminating ones and nobody would be the wiser.

I stood on top of the desk and reached for the tablet. I discovered a new vantage point, one that let me see the top of the wooden cabinets that lined the wall behind Cat's desk. I stared at a small collection of crystal frames that sat off to one side and a stack of invoices held together with a large black binder clip. A cluster of awards for best sales promotion that were seriously in need of dusting. A framed sketch signed by a fashion designer with a personalized note to Cat. I picked it up and ran my hand over the glass. That was better. Then I noticed movement reflected in the glass.

I looked around, making sure I was alone. The overhead lights were all the same as they'd been when I entered. The computer screen had long ago defaulted to its screensaver, and the small desk lamp was off. I heard a scraping sound overhead and looked up.

One of the ceiling tiles was out of place. I reached up and pushed on it ever so slightly. Like every ceiling tile I'd ever seen, it lifted with minimal pressure from my fingertips. I moved my hands to the tile to the left. Same result. There was one tile left that was within my reach, and it wasn't sitting properly on the metal grid. I gently pressed on it, but it didn't budge. I applied a little more pressure, but nothing. I checked my footing and then stood on my tiptoes and put both hands on the ceiling tile and pushed up. The tile shifted, and a cascade of pearls pelted me on the head.

20

LOOKIE-LOOS

THE UNEXPECTED SHOWER OF JEWELRY CAUGHT ME BY SURPRISE, AND I yelled. I swatted at strands of black pearls as they fell on me, flinging some away. I lost my balance. My right foot knocked the inbox off the desk, and papers flew everywhere. I dropped to a squat and gathered up as much of the twisted and tangled jewelry that I could.

There was a knock on the door. On instinct, I stuck my left leg out and corralled the remaining jewelry from the desk and slid it across the surface in a sweeping kick like a character in a Quentin Tarantino movie. The door to the office opened and Cat's former boss, Jim Insendo, peeked inside.

"Cat?" he asked. His eyes went wide at the sight of me in a fighting crouch on top of Cat's desk. If exercise had been more of a priority in my life, I might have been able to get back up from the squat. As it was, I tipped myself to the right and slowly brought my left leg around to the front. I shifted my right leg so I was sitting on top of the desk with both legs dangling in front of me. Only slightly less suspicious in terms of things-people-do-in-the-boss's-office.

"Cat's not here," I said. "Jim, right? I'm Samantha. We met at the Kenner & Winn party."

"Samantha, that's right." He reached forward and shook my hand. His full head of white hair had initially thrown me off, but up close, I saw he was younger than I'd originally thought. He couldn't be a day over fifty, and even that was a stretch. Must be nice, getting to choose retirement a full fifteen years before the rest of the working masses.

His eyes flicked over my shoulder for the briefest of moments but then returned to my face. "Do you know where Cat is? I brought some paperwork for her." He held a flat white envelope.

"She's at home resting. I'll take that." I held out my hand and took the envelope. He didn't let go right away, and for a moment we engaged in a passive tug-of-war. When he released the envelope, I tucked it under my arm. "I'm sort of helping her out around the store."

"I thought you worked at Tradava? Isn't working here a conflict of interest?"

I studied him. His normally jovial expression was less relaxed, and in its place was one that told me Jim Insendo didn't miss very much. I didn't know what Cat had told him about me. I pushed myself off the desk and stood in front of him, making him take a step backward.

"I'm on vacation," I said, conjuring up a smile. "Cat's had a troubling time lately and I'm doing her a favor. No pay, no benefits. Just a friend helping a friend. Isn't that why you're here?"

"Something like that."

There was something about him that seemed out of place. We stood like that for a few seconds, him fidgeting with his pockets, me crossing my arms and then dropping them to my sides to look less defensive.

Jim looked behind me again, his brows slightly furrowed. "Did I hear a crash?"

I smiled. "I knocked over her inbox. Klutzy, I guess." I inched my way forward until we were standing awkwardly close together. I pretended everything was okay but was pretty sure a necklace was caught on my shoe. Jim finally stepped back, and I kicked my foot a couple of times. The necklace dislodged and flew under the desk. I kept inching forward, making Jim move back, until we were out of the office with the door shut behind me.

"I have to take care of some things for Cat, but I'll tell her you stopped by."

"Make sure she gets that," he said, pointing at the envelope.

"I will." I scanned the store, looking for someone I could trust. Shana was by the registers, but she wasn't exactly on my trustworthy list. Dante, however, stood by the front of the store next to the control panel to the gate. I raised my chin and caught his eye and then tipped my head ever so slightly toward Cat's office. "Would you excuse me?" I said to Jim.

"Sure. I think I'll do some shopping while I'm here."

Jim walked away. I looked at Dante again. He hadn't left his post. I bypassed the cocktail dresses and headed toward the front of the store.

This time of year, the store should have been in complete disarray thanks to desperate customers who tore apart displays in order to find last-minute gifts, but that wasn't the case. Just like Cat had said, the customers who entered weren't there to shop, they were there to gawk. Between the theft and the murder, Cat was going to post a loss this season. The news had put her store on the map, but the people wandering through were the lookie-loos who wanted a story to tell on Christmas morning.

I reached Dante. "When did you get here?"

"About half an hour ago. Cat said you were here, and I called you, but you didn't answer."

"I found something in her office. Come with me." I turned around and led the way. I didn't say anything until after we both were inside the office with the door locked behind us.

Dante turned toward me. "You got my attention," he said. He was closer than I'd anticipated. "Though I question your choice of setting." He looked from my face to the camera.

"I came in here to get something from Cat's desk. The ceiling tiles were out of place. I climbed up on the desk and pushed on them and that fell down." I pointed to the other side of the desk at the pile of jewelry.

"'That?'" Dante put his hands knuckle-side down on the surface of Cat's desk and leaned across. He stayed like that for a few seconds.

"I'm no fancy former private investigator like you, but if I had to guess, I'd say 'that' is the jewelry somebody stole the night we found George's body. What I don't get is how somebody ran out of the store but then got it back into the ceiling in Cat's office." I picked Cat's desk phone up from the floor and checked for a dial tone.

"Who are you calling?" he asked.

"Detective Madden. This relates to the case, and he needs to know."

He put his hand on my wrist. "Does Cat know about this?"

"No, but she should. You need to get your camera out of here and find out how this happened."

The dial tone shifted from a steady one-note to a rapid beeping. Dante let go of my wrist and leaned too close for comfort. He reached behind my head and picked up the camera and then stood back up. "Keep me in the loop," he said and then left.

The number to the Ribbon Police Department was almost as

familiar as my own, though there were definitely times when my first instinct hadn't been to call it. I guess that hadn't been my first instinct this time either. When the desk sergeant answered, I asked for Detective Madden.

"He's interviewing a suspect. Whatcha got?"

"This is Samantha Kidd," I said, wondering if it would ring any bells.

There was a pause on the other end of the phone. "What are you calling in reference to, Ms. Kidd?" he asked.

"I need to talk to the detective about the murder at the Ribbon Designer Outlets. I found something he should see."

"You're calling about evidence in a murder investigation?"

"Well, sort of."

"Is it or isn't it?"

"It is."

"I'll let him know. What's the best number for him to reach you at?"

That's it? "Hold on," I said. I found my handbag and fished the Nick Phone out from the depths. There was a missed call from "Hot Man." I swiped the notification away from my screen when it occurred to me that I didn't know my phone number. There had to be a way to find out from the phone, but there was a faster way to get the information. I called Nick.

"Hey, Kidd," he answered.

"Hi. I don't have time to talk. What's my phone number?"

"Shouldn't you know?"

"I know my old number but not my new number and the police are on the other line—"

"The police? I'm coming over."

"I'm not at home. I'm at Catnip. I'll explain later."

"Do you have a pen?"

"Yes, tell me when you're ready." He rattled off a series of numbers. "You know my number off the top of your head?"

"It seemed important."

I smiled. The blinking light on the base of Cat's phone reminded me I had a desk sergeant on hold. "See you tomorrow."

"About tomorrow—" he started, but I cut him off.

"I gotta go." I hung up and took the desk sergeant off hold. "Hello?" I asked. "Are you still there?"

"No wonder Loncar took a vacation," he muttered. "Ready when you are."

I repeated the number for him and he repeated it back to me. After hanging up, I left the office. I locked the door behind me and looked up just in time to see Jim turn around and leave.

It seems he'd been keeping an eye on the office the entire time I'd been inside.

21

THAT JESSICA FLETCHER SHOW

I went to the register where Shana was refilling the shopping bags and shoved the envelope from Jim into my handbag. Today Shana wore a black pleather vest over a turtleneck and a pair of tight black jeans. A small chain dangled from a piercing in her left nostril and connected to another piercing by her eyebrow.

"When's Cat coming in?" she asked.

"She's not. I told her to take the day off and I'd watch over the store."

"Why?" she asked. "You're not part of the staff. I'm the assistant manager. If anybody should have been asked to step up and put in more hours, it should have been me."

"You're right, Shana. You do bear a certain responsibility for the store." I looked over my shoulder. "Weren't you the one who worked the night George was murdered?"

She went even more pale than her usual shade, probably making her more attractive to other goths. The blue streak in her hair stood out in stark contrast to her extra-pale skin, and dark-purplish-blue circles under her eyes became prominent. We'd been alone in the store when I joined her, but a woman with a basket of colorful leather gloves now approached. Retail rules dictated that we press pause on our confrontation until we could take it off the selling floor.

"Excuse me," the woman said. "Is one of you Samantha Kidd?"

"That's me," I said. "Can I help you?"

"Not me, but you can help that gentleman over there." She pointed to the front of the store where Detective Madden stood. The collar was up on his long loden-green trench coat, and his red hair curled against it in the back. He held up a hand in a mock salute.

"What is he doing here?" Shana asked. If she went any more pale, she'd be invisible. I was certain she was hiding something, but I didn't know what.

"The detective? How do you know him?" I asked.

"Wasn't he on the news?"

"Probably. He's here because I called him," I said. "I found something that I thought he should see." I glanced down. Shana's hands were shaking. She balled them up and shoved them into the pockets of her vest. I looked back at her face, making no secret that I'd observed her very suspicious body language.

I met the detective at the front of the store. "Detective Madden," I said. "Thank you for meeting me."

"I got here as soon as I could. Dispatch said you found evidence that we missed?"

"I didn't say you missed it. I found something I think is related to the case. Truthfully, I don't know what it means, so I called you. It's in Cat's office."

"Lead the way."

As we walked through the store, I wondered if Cat had told him about the present George left behind for her. The gesture told me much about their relationship, but would the detective see it the same way?

"How are you holding up?" I asked. (Just being polite.)

"I have to tell you, I wasn't happy about getting assigned to this case. The week before Christmas, nobody wants to have to investigate a murder. And this case—it's a lot. Pregnant woman left by her husband days before a major holiday." He shook his head. "It's no Hallmark movie, I can tell you that."

I was surprised by the detective's apparent interest in discussing things. "You have to admit this is a tricky case," I said.

"How so?" he asked.

"There's the burglaries and then the murder, but aside from the victim being both the store owner's spouse and the supplier of the merchandise he was strangled with, what's the motive? Add in what I'm about to show you in Cat's office, and you'll see what I mean." I paused in front of the door and studied him. "Detective Loncar would have told me to mind my own business by now."

"Detective Loncar did that for your safety. I don't think that's as much of a concern in this case."

"I agree. You should be watching out for Cat, not me. Have you talked to the security guards? And the staff? And George's employers? I know you talked to Mr. Kenner, but have you talked to Mr. Winn? I could try to arrange a time for everybody to come here so you can follow up with them."

"Mr. Winn is out of the country. He has travel papers and passport stamps and hotel confirmations to back that up. His alibi is sound."

"Oh."

"Ms. Kidd, I appreciate your help. I'm sure your friend appreciates your help too." He looked behind me. "But I can't help wondering if you aren't trying to help your friend out a little too much?"

"Cat didn't do anything. I was with her the whole night. Even if she did fight with her husband, she didn't have time to kill him."

"You were with her the whole night? You didn't, say, leave her alone at the party while you went to the mall bathroom? Or after the party to retrieve something from the bushes outside?"

"How do you know about that?"

"Or go to the fitting room to try on dresses while she was inside the store? That was your statement. Weren't you in a fitting room at the time when Mr. Stevens could have been killed?"

"I was in the fitting room while somebody smashed the display case and stole a bunch of Cat's jewelry."

"You're right, that is what you told me."

"Cat couldn't have done this. You don't think George would have struggled while she was strangling him? He's not the most physically fit person in the world, but if he were fighting for his life, he'd be able to overpower her."

He crossed his arms. "They told me about you. The other officers. Said it was a matter of time until you made a call to us. I thought that only happened on TV, like in that Jessica Fletcher show. My mom loved that."

"Detective Madden, if the other officers told you about me, then they must have told you I've helped the city, not hurt it. Detective Loncar approved my application to Citizen's Police Academy shortly after my birthday in May."

"Have you attended?"

"Not yet. I finally got a job and haven't had a lot of spare time."

He grinned. "Maybe you should thank Loncar for that too."

"I got that job on my merits, thank you very much," I said. It occurred to me that in the short distance from the front of the store to Cat's office, our conversation had gotten derailed. "Detective, with all due respect, I think when you see what I found inside Cat's office you'll realize there's something very off about this case."

We stopped outside the closed door. He tried the knob, but I'd locked it. I unlocked it and stood back, gesturing with an open palm for him to try again. He opened the door and stepped inside. I peered over his shoulder. Everything was as I'd found it: the mess of necklaces that had fallen from the ceiling now scattered on the floor behind the desk. The ceiling tile slightly out of place. The chair pushed back, away from the desk, into the bookcase behind it.

"I came in here to—well, I needed a moment alone—and I heard something coming from the ceiling."

Madden looked up. "Is that how you found it?"

"Not exactly. I climbed onto the desk and put my hands on the ceiling and the tile shifted and all of this jewelry fell out."

He stood back. "Can you show me how you did that?"

"Right now?"

He nodded. I went to the side of the desk and climbed on, and then stood up. I stretched both arms up over my head and, using my fingertips on the ceiling tile, lifted it and shifted it slightly out of place. "I did this," I said, "and then all of that stuff fell on me."

"Why is it on the floor?"

"Somebody came to the office and I didn't want them to catch me, so I flung the jewelry to the desk and kicked it to the floor."

"Who?" he asked. He never looked away from my face.

"Jim Insendo. He used to own the store. And he's strong—strong enough that, unlike Cat, he could have overpowered George. Do you need me to spell his name for you?"

"Not necessary." Madden looked up at the ceiling and then at the desk and the floor, and then back at me.

I was still standing on the desk with my hands on the ceiling tile above me. "Can I get down now?"

"Sure." he said. He held his hand out to offer assistance, but I squatted and then shifted and then climbed down the same way I had the first time.

"This changes things, right? Whoever stole this stuff the night of the murder got back in here and tried to hide the evidence. They know if you follow the theft, you'll likely find them, so they found a way to get the evidence back so you can't make that connection anymore."

"I suppose that is one way to look at it," he said.

We were on the same page! "Have you narrowed down the suspect pool now that you have that footprint in the carpet? Maybe you'll find something in here. Do you want to seal the office so you can dust for fingerprints? I'll watch the door if you need to go to your car for equipment."

"There's no need for that," he said. "Ms. Kidd, I applaud your loyalty to your friends. That's what I said to the officers who told me about you. It's rare to find someone who is so willing to stand up for people she cares for."

"Thank you," I said. I couldn't help the ominous feeling that crept over me. "It is important for me to help my friends. Especially someone like Cat. She has enough to deal with right now. She doesn't need this."

Detective Madden leaned close to me. "I'm pretty sure you set this up to incriminate someone who works for Ms. Lestes. The jewelry in the ceiling, the surprise discovery when nobody else was around. You just demonstrated how easy it would be for you to have done it yourself. Like I said, I applaud your motivation, but that doesn't change things."

"I'm not sure I like what you're implying."

"Then I'll come right out and say it. I think maybe there was no burglary. I think you helped Ms. Lestes hide that jewelry in her ceiling to make it look like there was another crime in play. But if that's the same jewelry you claim was stolen the other night, I'll have no reason to believe anything except that she stole it herself to cover up the evidence of killing her husband."

"Why would she kill him?"

"Maybe she didn't want to deal with alimony and child support. As a widow, she gets sympathy and access to her husband's benefits."

"Cat's not like that. She wasn't sitting around plotting how to strangle her husband. Besides, how could she physically have done it?"

"Easy. George Stevens was shot. The pearls around his neck had been added after he died."

The gun. That's why he'd asked if she owned one. "But I was there. I saw him, and there wasn't any blood."

"Ms. Kidd, I'm afraid the details of the murder are part of an ongoing investigation, and I can't share anything else with you."

Great. Detective Madden's Good Cop act was slipping.

22

NOTHING'S REAL

Traffic around Ribbon had been gradually thinning out over the past week. Vacations starting early, people heading out of town. Once I escaped the magnetic pull of the shopping mall, it was smooth sailing to my house.

The temperature in the house was cool. I kept my jacket on and went downstairs to check the pilot light on the furnace. My dad had a routine with the appliances in the house. Put the instructions in a Ziploc bag and tuck them into some nook or cranny close by. This way, in case of emergency, anyone could have access to the original operating manuals. Besides, in the case of a house with a previous basement flooding problem, the Ziploc baggie protected the instructions against the elements. I felt around the front and side of the furnace until I found the yellowed plastic package and quickly scanned the directions to learn what I needed to do.

A set of hinged metal doors were hidden on the lower left of the furnace. Inside I saw a small piece of pipe—no larger than the width of a cigarette—that the instruction manual identified as the pilot light. This was supposed to be throwing off a blue flame. I wasn't brave enough to stick my fingers underneath for confirmation, but there certainly wasn't a blue flame, or anything else, coming from that little piece of pipe.

I consulted the instruction manual again, wondering how exactly I was supposed to go about lighting anything without burning my fingers or potentially setting the room on fire. Their drawing suggested that I was to use a super long match. Now, where exactly was I supposed to find one of them?

A couple of expletives later, I found a small matchbook, a long stick, and a fire extinguisher. There was probably a better method than the one I was about to embark on, but I'd played the scenario out in my head, and it seemed like this would work. A quick look at the heavens, or ceiling as the case may be, a short request for the help of St. Jude, patron saint of impossible situations, and I implemented my plan.

I talked to St. Jude a lot.

One more review of the plan. Light the match. Light the stick. Light the pilot light. Blow out the flame on the stick. Use fire extinguisher if necessary.

Now: action.

Match lit: check.

Stick lit: check.

Pilot light lit: check.

Flame blown out: check.

Of course, I forgot to turn the opposite way when I blew out the fire on the stick, so I blew out the pilot light too.

Second attempt.

Match lit: check.

Stick lit: check.

Pilot light lit: check.

Turn around to blow out the stick.

Drop the stick when I see Dante leaning against the door

watching me.

OOPS! Now I need the fire extinguisher!

While I fumbled to remove the pin, he crossed the room and stomped on the flame. It hadn't had a chance to do anything but burn further down the shaft of the stick since it landed on the exposed concrete floor.

"How long have you been standing there?" I demanded.

"Long enough." He stepped closer to me, took the matches, and lit the pilot light. "I think you'll be surprised with what I found on the computer tablet."

"You found something? Good. Because we have a new problem." I told him about Detective Madden's reaction to the pearls in the office. "He seems to think that Cat and I lied about the burglary, and if we lied about that, then what else did we lie about? And he's tricking Cat into thinking he's a nice guy, but if he arrests her, he is definitely *not* a nice guy. Not."

"Come with me." He headed up the stairs, and I followed. When we reached the kitchen, he turned and went up the next flight of stairs and turned left toward my spare bedroom. "I set up a second camera on top of the cabinet behind the desk. It picked up the file cabinet where the original camera was, plus the door and a little of the desk area. You want to see what I found? Other than the shot of you disrupting our surveillance."

"It was an accident."

He picked up a photo that showed me looking directly into the camera with my hands on either side of it. The angle made my hands look like those of a giant.

"I needed a moment of privacy."

"It's private here," he said playfully.

I felt myself stiffen. It was the same feeling I'd had from the first time I'd met Dante but different. Him as cat, me as mouse. The nervousness, the unsettled feeling, the sense that he'd gotten under my skin when I least expected it.

"How did you program your number into my phone?"

"You're switching gears."

"My cell phone. When I left it at Cat's house, there was one number in it. You brought it to me, and there were two. How'd you do that?"

He smiled, and then, realizing I wanted an answer, crossed his arms. "I found an unlock code on the internet. It was a joke."

"I know. But what's the deal with us, Dante? You show up here when it's convenient for you. You don't keep in touch, and you say it's because I didn't call you. How come you never call me?"

"You're in a relationship."

"If that fact meant anything to you, you wouldn't have programmed 'Hot Man' into my phone. Face it, you're a loner. You want to show up, crash the party, get what you can, and then vanish. Nothing's real."

"You think nothing in my life is real?"

"How would I know? You dole out information about your life like you're dealing a hand of poker with a marked deck. You let me know what you want me to know." Being around Dante felt unstable—like how I'd felt so many times while trying to get my footing on this new life. Trying to find my place in the world. I'd cycled through being a person who knew how to handle things in New York to a person who could barely keep it together in Ribbon. Holding Cat's hand through her ordeal had reminded me what it was like when I knew who I was.

"How many new friends have you made since moving back to Ribbon?" Dante asked. "Do you know your neighbors? Have you been to a town hall meeting or gotten involved in any local events? When's the last time you saw your family?" He studied me for a second. "If one of us is a loner, it's you. I'm going to let you sort out the photos while I check on my sister. Don't make any rash decisions, Samantha."

"What do you mean by that?"

"It means I serve a purpose in your life, and we both know it." He put his hand around the back of my neck and pulled me toward him, crushing my lips with a long kiss.

I pulled away. This wasn't the first time Dante and I had kissed, but if I said yes to Nick's proposal, then it would be the last. My pulse raced, and I had trouble keeping my balance.

Dante left the room and went downstairs. I stayed behind and swiped through the pictures on the tablet, not able to concentrate. I set the tablet on the desk and followed him downstairs. Dante opened the front door. The Nick Phone rang in the background.

"Let me know if you find anything," Dante called up the stairs and left.

I went to the kitchen and grabbed the phone from the charger. It was Cat's store. "Hey, sorry. What's up?" I said. There was silence. "Hello?" I was about to hang up and call her back when her strained voice spoke.

"Are you with Dante?"

"No, he just left. I'm at home."

"Can you get to the store as soon as possible?"

My blood went ice cold despite the warmth of the newly ignited furnace. "Is everything okay?"

"Not exactly," she said. Her voice wavered. "There's been another murder."

23

A TEMPORARY FOG

"Who—where—when?" I asked.

"Aguilar. He was in my office—in my chair," Cat said. Her voice shook.

"How did he get into your office without you knowing?"

"I don't know, Sam, but the police are here and they're asking questions I can't answer. Detective Madden said he wanted to talk to you. Can you get here too?"

"I'll be there in twenty minutes."

Police cars and an ambulance were parked willy-nilly by the curb outside of Catnip. Lights swirled and uniformed professionals moved about. A crowd of onlookers had formed on the sidewalk, but police kept them from seeing much. It was safe to say that Cat wasn't going to be doing any more holiday business today.

Detective Madden stood outside of the store on the sidewalk with Cat. Today's necktie was light blue. Cat had a thick blanket wrapped around her shoulders, and her makeup was gone. I parked and approached them.

"Sam," Cat said. She dropped the blanket and threw her arms

around me. I felt her shoulders shake. I looked at the detective. He nodded at me.

"What happened?" I asked. "I thought you were going to stay at home and relax."

"I had to get out. I kept staring at the package you found in the fireplace and thinking about George, about why he told me he was leaving me. It didn't make sense. I kept sitting there, trying to make it work in my mind, but I couldn't. And I knew you were with Dante, so I came here. I thought maybe I could work on something to take my mind off things."

I bent down and plucked the blanket from the ground and then held it around Cat's shoulders. "Can we go inside?" I looked at Madden. "I think she should be sitting down."

"She wanted fresh air," he said.

"Sam, it was horrible. I went to my office to work on next month's schedule, and he was just sitting there in my chair. His face was puffy and red, and there were pearls tied around his throat, just like George."

"But the pearls—" I looked at Madden. "I thought you collected them as evidence when I found them earlier."

Cat looked back and forth between our faces. I'd called Dante to come and get the camera, and I'd called Detective Madden. None of us had thought to tell Cat about the merchandise showing up or what the detective implied when I told him. I honestly couldn't tell if that was a good thing or a bad thing.

"The necklace around his neck was from the Kenner & Winn shipment," she said. "It was a long strand of black pearls. The ones you asked me to hold for you."

"How do you know?"

"The hold tag was still attached to it."

A uniformed officer poked his head out of the store and called the detective over. He excused himself and walked just slightly out of earshot.

"Sam, why is this happening? What did I do?" Cat said.

"Shhh. Did you talk to Dante?"

"Not recently. Why?"

"Okay, I have to talk fast. When I came to the store today, I went into your office and one of the ceiling tiles was out of place. I moved it and a whole bunch of pearl jewelry fell on top of me. I called Dante. He took the cameras, and I called Madden."

She looked relieved. "So my merchandise was returned? That's a little bit of good news, isn't it? When all of this is done, I have a chance to make up the sales, at least." Her brows pulled together and she looked confused. "But where did you put the jewelry? Lela didn't say anything about it when I came in."

"Lela wasn't here. Shana was. But I don't know if she knows, because I told Detective Madden. He said—he thinks—he made it sound like I could have put the jewelry in the ceiling to make you look innocent. He thinks there was no smash and grab the night we found George and that this merchandise showing up was just a way to corroborate that story to make you look like a victim."

"But I wouldn't do that!"

"I know. Everybody who knows you knows you wouldn't do that. There's one problem."

"What's that?"

"Detective Madden doesn't know you."

An EMT pushed a lumpy white gurney out of the store, and the officer asked Cat if she thought she could make a positive ID. I squeezed her hand in an attempt to give her strength and stood close to her while they pulled the sheet back.

There was no doubt that we were looking at Officer Aguilar. I looked away from his glassy eyes and focused on his name tag still clipped to his security guard uniform.

Cat stared at his face for a few seconds, and then her small hands balled up into fists. She turned to Detective Madden. "You think I did this? I'm a small, pregnant woman. How would I strangle him and get him into my office without anybody seeing? How would I strangle someone who knows me and then get his body behind a jewelry case? Can't you reenact the crime and see that it's impossible?" The blanket dropped from Cat's shoulders a second time. "Follow me," she said. "I want to show you something."

She went into her store and headed to the jewelry counters. Madden followed her, and I followed Madden. When she reached the aisle between the jewelry department and the shoe department, she turned to face him. "You're about George's size." She reached up for his throat, but her pregnant belly kept her from being able to touch his neck. "How exactly would this work? Oh, wait—I lassoed him, right?" She yanked a necklace from a top-of-counter fixture and held it taut between her hands. "How did I do it? Like this?" She stood on her tiptoes and pressed the pearls into his throat.

Detective Madden's eyes widened. He put his hands on her wrists and lowered them away from him. Two uniformed officers came over and stood on either side of her. Madden looked at them and shook his head slightly.

"Cat," I said in a low voice. "Give me the pearls."

As if coming out of a temporary fog, her expression changed from anger to fear. She looked at the pearls in her hands and at the faces of the officers around her. She dropped the necklace to the floor. Customers collected by the mall entrance watching the show.

"Nothing to see here, folks," I said. Madden and I shared a long look. "Detective, is there someplace we can talk?"

One of the officers led Cat to a nearby ottoman. Madden picked up a briefcase and pulled out a clipboard. He read something on it and then looked up. "You'd like to add something to your statement?" he asked.

"Last night I saw Mr. Aguilar come out of the mall and loiter outside of Catnip after hours."

"That's his job," he said.

"That's what I thought, too, but he acted funny. He looked around the door to Catnip and in the bushes next to the employee entrance. Eventually he sat on the park bench, and Shana Brice—Cat's assistant manager—came out of the store and threw something away. Aguilar took it."

"Do you know what it was?"

"If I knew what it was, I wouldn't be so cryptic. It was dark, and I was cold."

"What were you doing in the parking lot after hours, Ms. Kidd?"

I blushed, remembering exactly what Nick and I had been doing. "I forgot where I parked my car," I lied. "Detective, I know you know Cat and her husband argued at the party the night of his murder. That's all it was—an argument. Their life was about to change significantly, and he was looking forward to that. He bought her a mother-of-pearl baby rattle and a strand of the most gorgeous pearls you've ever seen, and he hid them in the house so she wouldn't know. She had no reason to want him dead, but somebody else did."

IT WAS MORE than a few hours before we were able to leave, not because the police wanted us to stay but because Cat was in no shape to walk. While we sat back, observing the activities around us with nothing other than our thoughts as distraction, Cat brought up something that had been niggling at the back of my mind.

"Should we tell them about the camera?" she asked. "They're going to find it sooner or later."

I'd been thinking about that camera. Now more than ever I regretted asking Dante to take it away. If it had still been in place, we'd have pictures of who did this.

A numbing feeling started in my torso and then radiated outward through my arms and legs. The tablet was at my house. I'd gone through a portion of the pictures on it. Now, I wondered at the coincidence of the pearls in the ceiling and the body in her office. They had to be connected.

Cat looked at me, eyes wide. "Why did your face just lose all color?" she asked.

I lowered my voice to just above a whisper. "We need to get to my place and look at those pictures."

I DROVE to Cat's house. She packed an overnight bag while I cleaned Logan's temporary litterbox and packed him in his carrier. Minutes later, we were en route to my house. Cat was in unchartered territory, and while being in her house might have provided certain comforts, I suspected the reminder of her life with George around every corner would be worse than coming with me.

Plus, the shock that goes with finding a body—and realizing that somehow you're now mixed up in a murder investigation—is not always easy to process. That it happened in her store—not once, but twice—made the crimes more personal.

I parked in the driveway. As soon as we were inside the living room, I let Logan out of his carrier and he took off. We tossed our coats on top of the sofa and went into the kitchen. "Want anything? Food? Drink?"

"Vodka," Cat said.

"No, seriously."

"I am serious. I want vodka. But since I can't have vodka, I'll take a glass of cold water. Serve it in a martini glass so I can pretend, okay?"

"One water in a martini glass coming up." I dug out the glasses and filled them from a pitcher I kept in the fridge. "The computer is upstairs."

"Let's go." Apparently, the illusion of a martini gave her enough courage to face the details behind the dead body in her store.

She headed up the stairs and slowed as she reached the landing. "Which way?" she asked.

"Turn left."

The last time Cat had been in my spare bedroom, I'd been using it as a walk-in closet. Racks of off-season clothes had taken up the majority of the space around the small desk that held my PC and printer. In the days between employment opportunities, I'd been forced to assess my wardrobe for value and had even sold off a few choice items in order to make my mortgage payment, a process that had pained me greatly. Nobody would treasure those late-nineties satin cargo pants the way I did.

Since then, I'd packed up the garments and stored them in the closet, safe from moths and Logan (he had a thing for cashmere). The desk had expanded thanks to a plank of wood from Lowe's and a couple of wooden sawhorses and was in an L-configuration. I'd upgraded to a twenty-two-inch monitor (it was better for shopping on eBay) and an assortment of colorful Sharpies separated into clear vases from the Dollar Store.

The tablet computer that Dante had dropped off sat next to my printer. A thin cord connected the two. I jiggled the mouse to wake up the computer and clicked through the images as they appeared on the screen.

"You don't think we have a picture of what happened, do you?" Cat asked.

"I don't know. Do we even know what happened? You told Detective Madden that you found Aguilar in your office. How did he get there? Did anybody see him go in? Why was he in there? Has mall security ever gone into your office before? It looks suspicious. Especially after I found the pearls in the ceiling. Did Madden check Aguilar's footprint? Could he have been involved in George's murder? Everything about it points to him not being there, because you invited him in."

"That's a lot of questions," Cat said.

"Remember how I told you he was hanging around your store after dark? And that Shana threw something away and he took it out of the trash? That's weird, right? I mean, now that he was found dead in your office."

She lost more coloring. "I'm going to be sick," she said. She ran to the hall bathroom and threw up. The faucet turned on and off. When she returned, she apologized.

"For what? This thing bothers you. That's good. That means you're normal."

"But you can talk about it. You can look at crime scenes and ask questions and suspect people. Why can't I be more like you?"

"Cat, I'm not eight months pregnant." Hearing Cat talk about wanting to be like me cast my whole life in a different light. "I am suspicious by nature," I said. "You know what else? I eat junk food and make decisions other people think are bad. That's who I am. That's not you. I need you to be the person you are: strong, reliable. Practical. Cautious."

"But you get things done."

"I won't let you risk your life because you think you're doing what I would have done."

"But we have an agreement."

"That's not how life works. You be you, and I'll be me. Okay?"

"Okay," she said. I could have sworn a shroud of relief settled in over her shoulders.

"Look carefully at these photos. Tell me if anything looks out of place," I said. The first few images showed Cat entering her office, sitting, working. Business as usual with no big surprises. It was the next series that caught my attention, and hers as well.

We stared at pictures that documented an affair. They grew increasingly intimate, starting with two people entering the office and ending the series with a photo that showed a woman who wore very little under her chinchilla coat. Although knowing her spending habits, I guessed her lingerie cost more than outfits modest people wore in public.

Cat's eyes widened, and she put her hand to her mouth in surprise. "Are they going to...?"

"I'm pretty sure they are," I said. "And judging from your expression, you're as surprised as I am to see that Jim Insendo was using your office to have an affair with Lela Sexton."

24

THE WALL OF OBSERVATION

I SELECTED THE INCRIMINATING PHOTOS AND CLICKED PRINT. THE power button blinked orange, and an error message on the screen indicated that the cyan toner was out of ink. I dug a backup cartridge out of a bin and replaced it. The printer recalibrated and then chugged out the photos.

Cat grabbed the stack as they printed and handed them to me. I tapped them on the corner of the desk to line up the edges, and then we moved to the kitchen. Cat bent over and breathed into a paper bag. I called Eddie at Tradava.

"Cat's in trouble. Big trouble. She needs our help."

"Roger that," Eddie said. "I'll be there as soon as the store closes."

Cat pulled a bag of Fritos out of a very large tote bag, dropped the bag onto the sofa, and tore the bag open.

"Are you sure you want to eat like that?" I asked.

"I can't drink. I can't sleep. I can't take Valium or Xanax or Ambien. I spent the morning planning a memorial service for the husband who left me, and I can't see my feet." She put a handful of Fritos into her mouth and crunched. "Besides, you would."

"Cat, sit down."

She clutched the bag like Linus with his blanket. I sat next to her. "You've just been through a traumatic situation. There's no doubt about that. I know exactly how you're feeling. I've been there. You barely knew me at the time, but I did exactly what you're doing now."

"What exactly am I doing now?"

"You're trying to hide from the situation. You're hoping it will go away. Don't you remember when I came into your store for the first time and was on a bender of a shopping spree? I wanted to distract myself. Just like you're doing now. You don't want to think about it, so you're trying to do whatever you can to pretend you didn't discover a dead body in your store. Not just one, but two."

I had to say it, to point out the facts, while I had her attention. When I spoke the last words, she reached into the bag of Fritos.

"Sooner or later you're going to have to do something. It doesn't matter what. You can close the store for the holidays. You can list it for sale. You can sell the house and move. It's your life. You deserve to know what happened, but you don't deserve to be a spectator on the sidelines, waiting for someone else to wrap up the details."

She didn't let go of the bag, but she didn't pull out more corn chips either. A minute passed. It felt like an hour.

"What do you suggest?"

"We make some coffee—leaded for me and unleaded for you— and go over the photos. Start a timeline of everything that happened. Figure out where we have questions and how we can get answers. Come up with a plan."

Another minute passed. She ate another handful of Fritos. My talk hadn't done a bit of good. But then she placed the bag on the table in front of her and looked me straight in the eyes. "Do you have any green vegetables?"

HALF AN HOUR LATER, Eddie arrived. He held two pizza boxes in one hand and a cardboard four pack of Birch Beer in the other. Wedged under his arm was an oversized Post-it board, and his cargo pants fought his belt thanks to the Sharpies bursting from the pockets. He pushed past us with a few unintelligible grumbles.

"Hello to you too," I said.

"No time for hello." He handed me the pizza boxes (green peppers and basil for Cat, extra cheese for Eddie and me, pepperoni on half to peel off and give to Logan for putting up with us) and took a bottle of Birch Beer out of the cardboard container. He then shoved the remaining three bottles at me. "Fridge." While I refrigerated the soda bottles, he opened up the Post-it pad, tore off a large sheet, and stuck it to my wall. He pulled a Sharpie out of the pocket of his hoodie and wrote *Suspects* across the top. He repeated the process two more times, writing *Motive* and *Means*. He pulled a bottle opener from his other pocket, popped the top off the birch beer, and swigged from the bottle. When he finished, he pointed at the wall. "Do your thing."

"My thing?" I said. "I don't have a thing."

Cat grabbed the crinkled brown paper bag and started breathing into it again. I pointed to the living room. "Eddie, we need to talk."

Once we were on the other side of the wall, I turned to him. "My 'thing'?" I said, using finger quotes. "In case you haven't noticed, this is no dream. This is really happening!"

"That's from *Rosemary's Baby*, isn't it?" Eddie asked. "You better not let Cat hear you quote that movie."

"I already did," Cat called out from the kitchen.

I put my hand on Eddie's arm and led him to the other side of the Christmas tree. I plugged in the electric train that ran around the perimeter of the tree stand and dropped my voice to just above a whisper. "I'm going to talk fast to get you caught up. Don't interrupt me."

"Go."

"Cat's husband didn't leave her. He left her but then she found a present from him that indicates that he didn't plan to leave her, so now we think he pretended to leave to protect her."

"Not abandoned—check."

"But nobody else knows that because right after we discovered the present, I went to Catnip and found the stolen jewelry in the ceiling of Cat's office."

"Stolen jewelry found—check."

"I called the detective to tell him what I knew, but he doesn't know about George not leaving Cat, so he not only still thinks she has motive, but now he thinks I hid the jewelry in her ceiling to make it look like somebody else is involved."

"Falsifying evidence—check."

"No! I didn't falsify anything! But he thinks I did because he doesn't know about the baby rattle in the fireplace."

"Baby rattle in the fireplace." He paused. "Dude, you officially stumped my decoder ring."

"That's the present George hid in the fireplace. A baby rattle and a poem. And a pearl necklace for Cat that cost more than my car. But now the security officer who I think maybe helped steal the jewelry in the ceiling is dead, and Detective Madden doesn't want to hear about baby rattles and roses being red. Maybe there's a conspiracy at the mall. Or there's a lunatic Santa on the loose. Or maybe one of the other boutique owners is offing the competition?"

"Slow down, Bugsy," Eddie said. He held up his hands like

claws and put them on either side of my head. "You need to take all that and sort it out. Because somewhere between the baby rattles and the roses and the pearls and the whatever else you have in there is the answer."

IT DIDN'T TAKE LONG for us to turn the kitchen into a makeshift war room. I was starting to wonder if it made sense to set up an actual crime lab in the house. Not that I was terribly upset about covering up the blue floral wallpaper, but the giant tear-off sheets of notes that now surrounded the room gave it a graffitied look. Stephen Sprouse meets Martha Stewart.

Cat went to the restroom. We'd finished the pizza, so I refilled Eddie's and my coffee and emptied a fresh bag of pretzels into a bowl.

Eddie bit into a pretzel. "She's doing better than I expected," he said.

"There are a lot of people checking in on her. A lot."

"Like who?"

"Her family, George's family. The neighbors. The company George worked for. Her refrigerator is filled with food that other people brought. How do people know what she likes? Or what she wants to eat?"

"That's what people do." He snapped off another piece of pretzel and chased it with black coffee.

"They do what?"

"They bring casseroles. Stuff that can be frozen so she won't have to worry about cooking. Maybe her close friends will take over her daily errands like laundry and dry cleaning."

"Aren't we her close friends?"

"Yes, but Tradava's got me so busy there's not much I could do other than decorate her house and hire a maid service to clean for her twice a week."

"You hired her a maid service?"

He shrugged. "I wish I could have done more." He took another swig of coffee. "You're helping her with the store, right? That's big."

"I guess so. I'm just trying to be a good friend."

I hadn't heard the toilet flush or the stairs creak, so when Cat spoke behind me, she took me by surprise. "What's this?" she asked. She stood in the doorway. Her palm was face up and the velvet ring box with Nick's engagement ring sat in the center of it.

"It's an engagement ring."

"Nick asked you to marry him?" she asked. Her voice was strained.

"Yes, but I haven't given him an answer."

"You didn't tell me?"

"I didn't think you'd want to hear about that, not now, not with everything that's happened."

Cat set the ring box on the bookcase next to her. "I have to go," she said. She pulled on her coat on the way to the front door. I looked at Eddie, expecting him to say something.

He crossed his arms over his chest. "Nick proposed, and you didn't tell us?" He stood up. "Cat, hold up. I'll give you a ride."

"Wait!" My chair tipped backward as I stood up and chased after them. "You're crazy busy with Tradava and Cat's got this whole baby-George-pearl thing to worry about! I was trying to be a friend and support you both. Why are you mad?"

The front door was open and Cat was halfway to Eddie's VW Bug. The street lamps were on, backlighting flurries of snow that blew through the wind. Fluffy flakes melted into her red hair on contact. She turned around and faced me. "You're trying so hard to be a good friend but you know what you forgot? How to be a good friend."

"Cat—"

"I lost everything, Sam! My whole life. Don't think pretending you don't have a life makes any of this easier for me. I don't need you to figure out why George died, because that's not going to bring him back. It's not going to change anything."

"But—"

"Do you know what I need? I need life to feel normal. I need for you talk to me about Nick's proposal or complain about your job or calculate how many pairs of satin cargo pants you need to sell on eBay to pay the mortgage. I need you to eat an entire pizza and have room for ice cream. I need to know that some things change and some things never will. Do you get that? Do you even understand why I'm hurt?"

I looked at Eddie.

"She's right, dude," he said. "That thing about you saving Nick's dad's life around your birthday? I had to read about that in the paper. If you want people to bring you casseroles when you need them, you're going to have to learn to open up."

"My life is an open book! You two know everything about me."

Cat crossed her arms. "When's the last time you had sex?"

"Excuse me?"

"We're sharing. Friends share. And I'm going to need something personal to make up for this. So, when's the last time you had sex?"

I exploded. "Two nights ago, in the parking lot of the Ribbon Designer Outlets. It was the night Nick came home from Italy and I convinced him to come with me for overnight surveillance on your store. We got distracted. And oh, by the way, that was our first time, and he proposed the next morning, and I'm not sure what to make of the timing. Are you happy now?"

Across the street, the front window curtains moved to the side. Mrs. Iova, my occasionally nosy neighbor, stared out at me. I glared at her and then turned around and stormed back into the house.

The kitchen was a mess. Logan was on the dining room table sniffing for leftovers. I moved him to the floor and cleaned up the empty bottles of birch beer that lay scattered about. My hands were shaking. The front door opened but I didn't turn around. It wasn't every day that I told the whole neighborhood about my love life, and, frankly, I was a little embarrassed.

"Well, that should be good for a couple of casseroles," Eddie said. He was alone. I looked at the window. "She'll be in in a second. Her phone rang, and she wanted some privacy."

"Nice concept."

"Dude, did you hear anything she said to you out there? Because she's right. You're amazing and loyal and you help us all, but the reason we're friends is because you're kind of a mess."

"Thanks a lot."

"Listen to me. I'm a mess too. I'm a single guy who spends three quarters of my life at my job. I don't even have a pet. The most exciting thing to happen to me this month was to win an auction of an original red Devo Energy Dome on eBay."

"You mean one of those flowerpot hats?"

"Energy Dome, dude. I could have gotten a flower pot for a lot less."

"You didn't tell me about that."

"Because that being the most exciting thing in my life is pathetic. But you and Nick? That's been over a decade in the making."

The front door opened a second time and Cat walked in. This time she wasn't alone. Detective Madden was behind her.

"Ms. Kidd," he said. He stepped forward and held his hand out to Eddie. "Detective Madden."

"Eddie Adams," Eddie replied.

"He called," Cat said to me. "I gave him your address and told him to come here."

The four of us stood around my living room. Detective Madden was the last person I'd expect to show up at my house tonight, but I was having a hard time regrouping on details of the investigation thanks to Cat and Eddie.

"Detective, would you like a cup of coffee?" Cat asked.

"Do you have decaf?"

"Yes. Follow me." Cat headed toward the kitchen. When she passed me, she reached out her hand and put it on my hand and squeezed. I looked at her face. She smiled a genuine smile that let me know we were going to be okay. I squeezed back. She let go, and Madden followed her into the kitchen. About two seconds later, Madden asked, "What's all this?"

Oh, crap! The wall of observation!

I ran into the kitchen. Cat handed Madden a mug of coffee. Madden thanked her and looked at the giant Post-it sheets on the wall. His eyes scanned from the left page to the right, pausing on the photo of Lela Sexton in her lingerie. Between the scene out front and the wall of observation in my kitchen, any secrets about what I'd been up to were pretty much out in the open.

"Don't mind the mess," I said quickly. I grabbed the packages of giant Post-its and covered the existing wall of observation with blank sheets. "We're helping Cat work out her staffing issues."

He held his mug, but didn't drink from it. "Sorry to drop in unexpected, but I thought you'd want to know we ran tests on your gun and it came back clean. Hasn't been fired in some time."

"I already told you that," Cat said.

"And I appreciate your honesty, Ms. Lestes, but I hope you understand we have to follow procedure. You can pick it up at the station at your convenience."

"I don't want it. I never wanted it," Cat said. "Is that all?"

"No, there's something else. A pretty significant break in our investigation, although I'm not sure what it means yet. Ms. Lestes, your store is going to have to be closed indefinitely."

"I haven't been back, not since the second murder," she said. "I already told my staff, so there's no reason anybody would try to open the store until I contact them."

"That's just the thing. A member of your staff threw us this new curve ball."

"I'm sorry, detective. I don't follow."

"Your assistant manager, Shana Brice, came to see us this afternoon. She said it's time she told us the truth. And then she gave us a full confession."

25

TOO CONVENIENT

"Shana killed my husband?" Cat asked. She sank into a dining room chair. Eddie stood behind her and put his hands on her shoulders.

"No, ma'am, she confessed to the burglaries. Seems she and Mr. Aguilar have been stealing from the mall on a pretty regular basis. Small, petty thefts originally intended to help complete their holiday shopping that turned into a way to profit on the side. Mr. Aguilar got her into the mall after hours. Ms. Brice committed the thefts. She put the stolen merchandise in a bag and threw it out in a public trash can. Mr. Aguilar retrieved it from the designated spot, and they reconvened after hours to divvy up the goods."

"But Cat started to carry more expensive jewelry," I said. "A fact Shana would know because she worked there. She'd know where it was kept and how much it was worth. Even if it was locked up at night, she'd be able to get at it."

"She said she learned the true value of the new merchandise at the party that night."

"Shana wasn't at the party," Cat said.

"She was the woman in the restroom," I said slowly. Now I realized why Shana had seemed familiar to me when I first met her at Catnip. "I didn't put two and two together. She was all dressed up, not in goth attire. Her hair wasn't blue, and she took out her piercings."

"I think I still would have recognized her," Cat said.

"When I saw her talking to George, I feared the worst—that maybe he was having an affair—so I kept you distracted so you wouldn't see her."

"The two of them had gotten away with smaller thefts for weeks," Madden said, "and had a false sense of confidence in the simplicity of their plan. Ms. Brice could have stolen the jewelry during her shift, but that night she waited until after the mall closed. Aguilar told her security would be busy with the party. He volunteered to cover the rest of the mall so she wouldn't have to worry about being caught. It was risky, but the temptation of stealing merchandise of that value was too great. For someone who carried a healthy amount of credit card debt, the take was potentially life-changing."

"And the murder? How did she do that?" I asked.

"She claims she didn't have anything to do with the murder. We drilled her about that pretty well, and her story never changed. She was in the store. She smashed a case of jewelry with the tire iron. That's when she saw the body. You screamed, and it snapped her out of shock. She was afraid you were the killer. She grabbed the jewelry and ran, knocking Ms. Lestes out of the way in the process. We checked her footprint against the print we found in the carpet, and it's a match."

"Why didn't she say anything before now?"

"For the past several days, she kept quiet because her

confession didn't cast her in innocent light. But when Mr. Aguilar was found dead in Ms. Lestes' office, she looked at things differently."

"She thought Cat killed George?"

"That is her opinion. She came to us to point the finger at Ms. Lestes."

I didn't like it. Cat was at the store the night George was murdered, but so was Shana. Cat had access to her office, but so did Shana. The person who could have fingered Shana as having been there was Aguilar—who was now dead.

"What do you think?" I asked Madden.

"I have to admit, her statement confuses things." He set his mug down on the table. He zipped his coat and pulled on a hat. "I'll be on my way now. Heard there's a storm coming. Oh, Ms. Kidd, we caught the vandals responsible for your flat tire. I never saw your report, but I thought you'd want to know. You three take care." He shook each of our hands and then left.

I wasn't buying Madden's whole "just happened to discover" this and "thought you'd want to know" that. It was all too convenient.

We returned to my dining room table. I took down the blank Post-it sheets, and we stared at the wall of observation. Even after several rounds of "Here's how Shana did it," Eddie remained unconvinced.

"She described in detail what was stolen," I continued. "She even said I almost caught her. She dropped a necklace in the public bathroom the night of the party. I picked it up and handed it to her. She told Madden she was scared I figured it out so she panicked and threw it away right in front of me."

Reasoning through the rest of the details raised a whole other set of questions.

"Cat, how much of your jewelry assortment was stolen?"

"A lot."

"No, you misunderstand me. What's the value? Ballpark."

Her eyes rolled up toward the ceiling, and her head bounced back and forth while she did some mental math. "About thirty-four thousand dollars retail, unless you want cost."

"I thought you owned an outlet. How come you have such expensive stuff?"

"Technically it's an outlet, but I prefer the term 'off-price retailer.'"

"What's the difference?" Eddie asked.

"An outlet sells last season's merchandise, stuff that's been severely discounted because it's not current. I get that merchandise from jobbers—people who buy end-of-season merchandise from department stores. I usually buy entire lots of product sight unseen. The jobbers sell it by a piece count. Like, two hundred pair of jeans, or thirty designer handbags, or something like that. There's always a gamble with jobbers, because if the price is right and the description sounds good, I'll take it, but it's mine to either sell or throw away."

Eddie got up and refilled his coffee.

"What about the rest of your inventory?" I asked.

"Mostly off-price. I go to market and visit with designers and vendors. Sometimes they end up with overruns of merchandise that didn't sell, that they produced to meet minimums. Sometimes stores negotiate inventory returns to them for various reasons. If I have good relationships with the vendors that I want to carry, they know they can call me and I might buy that inventory discounted. That way they're getting more than if they had to sell it to a jobber or at a sample sale."

"What about the jewelry? Didn't you tell me you came up with a luxury goods strategy recently and that's why you bought the pearls from Kenner & Winn?"

"It was something like that. I noticed about a year ago that there weren't any good jewelry stores in the designer outlets, so I started bumping up my average price to test the waters. Nothing too classic, but pieces I found in the market. A few designers were willing to work on consignment. The merchandise sold, so I gradually built up the category. I knew I could go to the five-hundred-dollar range. George's inventory was a risk. Those pieces were a couple thousand dollars cost, even with a discount. I told you my terms were Net 30, so I had thirty days to pay the invoice. The risk was whether I'd sell the jewelry before the bill was due. I thought I could because of the time of the year."

Eddie returned, and he and I exchanged glances. I knew what he was thinking. "So you don't normally carry this much jewelry?" he asked.

"Oh, God no. I usually have a couple of necklaces and earrings and an assortment of bangles. Very minimalist. I arranged through the outlet center to have extra jewelry cases put into the store so I could carry more merchandise this month."

"Did the rest of your assortment change much? Because of the holidays?"

"No. Like I said, it's an outlet, but also an off-price store. I change the way I merchandise some things, but other than the jewelry, it's still the same."

"Who else knew about your business strategy?"

"I asked Shana to come with me to select the merchandise. I thought it would be a nice opportunity for her since she doesn't get out of the store much." She looked dazed. "I tried to help her with her professional growth, and she thanked me by stealing from my store and then implicating me in the murder of my husband. What kind of a world do we live in?"

Eddie leaned forward. "What do you think about this?" he asked me. "Do you believe Shana's confession?"

"I don't believe anything any of these people say," I said, gesturing toward our wall of observation. "Shana confessed because it was the safest thing for her to do. But I saw her talk to George at the party. And before you say it, it wasn't like she was talking to her boss's wife. They *knew each other* knew each other."

Cat spoke in a low voice. "I told George I was going to Catnip after the party. I think he went there to tell me what was going on. You took a long time to get to the store because you had to get your underwear out of the bushes, remember?"

I pointed a finger at Eddie. "Don't ask."

He held both hands up in mock surrender. "Dude."

"Shana was there to steal from you. She knew the lights would be out, and she thought you were at the party. Maybe George knew what she had planned. Maybe he went to stop her. He could have overpowered her. He could have pulled off the mask, and maybe she killed him because he could identify her." And then she realized she could easily frame Cat for everything. Everything was falling into place.

We hashed things out into the wee hours of the morning. I told Cat and Eddie to go to sleep, but my mind was alert. I didn't want to tell either of them, but Shana's confession still troubled me. Why had someone knotted the pearls around George's throat after shooting him? And why hide the merchandise in the ceiling if she intended to confess? There were other details just slightly out of reach in my mind, details I knew I was missing. The information felt like chapters pulled from several different novels.

I let Cat and Eddie sleep while I tossed and turned. They needed sleep. Eddie was exhausted thanks to the grueling hours he kept at Tradava. And Cat was living through a nightmare. It was like she and I had traded lives: me with the solid job, the promising relationship, and the financial security. Cat unexpectedly on her own weeks before having a baby, her store on the brink of financial ruin. For as long as I'd known her, I'd thought she had it all. If everything could change in an instant, then wasn't the illusion of security a farce?

26

SEXED-UP MURDER SUSPECTS

There would be no sleeping in on my vacation. I woke first and left Cat and Eddie a note. Eddie's VW Bug was in the driveway, so I took his keys and drove to the closest bagel store. I bought breakfast sandwiches for each of us: eggs Florentine (spinach) for Cat; egg white, gluten-free (no flavor) for Eddie; and double bacon, egg, and cheese (yum!) for me. The wind was picking up, and I struggled to keep the VW in my lane.

It was too early for the color the sky had turned. A snowstorm was definitely coming. Nostalgia tugged at my heart. It would be nice to have the world blanketed in pure white. Mother Nature's way of hiding all of the imperfections on the landscape of life.

I turned right at the restaurant on the corner and drove down the street, lost in thoughts of snowmen and icicles. It was the navy-blue sedan, parked where Eddie's VW had been, that pulled me back to reality. Who was visiting now?

I approached the front door with caution. I shouldn't have left Cat alone, even for a few minutes. The doorknob turned easily under my hand, which meant someone had left it unlocked. I entered and called out a tentative hello.

"In here," Cat replied from the kitchen.

Jim Insendo sat across the table from Cat.

He pushed his chair back and stood up. "Samantha," he said. "Nice to see you again."

"Sure. I mean, you too." Considering the photos I'd seen of him and Lela, I had a hard time making eye contact. "Where's Eddie?"

"In the shower," Cat said.

"If I'd have known you were coming, I would have gotten you a bagel."

"Don't apologize. I don't eat bread," He said, holding both hands up. "With what happened at the store yesterday, I thought maybe you forgot to give Cat the envelope I gave you. I called her, and she invited me here. I hope you don't mind."

"Of course not," I lied. Everybody knew I loved having sexed-up murder suspects sitting around my dining room table. Especially ones who don't eat carbs.

He turned to Cat. "Think about what I said. It might be exactly what you need." He buttoned his coat and picked up a brown wool hat from the table. "I'll let myself out," he said. "Bye, Samantha."

I waited until the front door closed behind him to drop into the chair across from her. "He gave me something to give you. I forgot. I'm sorry." I craned my neck to read the papers in front of her from my upside-down angle. "What is that?"

"It's an offer to buy back the store."

"From Jim?"

She nodded. "He said he's been thinking he made a mistake when he sold me the store. He's bored. He never expected that. I guess that's the thing about retail. It's a high-stress, fast-paced job, and certain types of people are drawn to it, but the burn-out rate is high too. People are happy when they get out, but in time they discover this huge gaping hole in their lives because suddenly everyone isn't coming after them to solve their problems."

"Is that how he described it?"

"No, that's my interpretation," she said.

I powered up the tablet and swiped through the pictures of him and Lela quickly and then slowed by the ones after both had left. About twenty images later, I spotted something we'd missed.

"Look at this. These pictures are from after Jim and Lela left."

I spun the tablet Cat's direction. We'd already seen that Jim and Lela had been having an affair, conducted, at times, in Cat's office. We had *not* seen Lela return to the office by herself. But the camera had caught her rifling through Cat's desk.

"Didn't you say Lela used to work at the store?" I asked.

"Yes, when Jim owned it."

"How often does she go into your office?"

"I never knew she did until now."

"What do you think she's doing?"

"No idea."

"Did she know about your jewelry strategy?"

"No, but I told Jim," she said. "At the party." She dropped her eyes. "I just wanted someone to talk to."

"Today wasn't the first time he's brought up buying you out, is it?"

"No," she confessed.

"Did Jim say anything about Lela?" I stood up and approached the wall of observation. We'd labeled Lela a suspect and had pinned an incriminating photo of the two of them about to bring up the natural shine on Cat's desk. The photo was missing, as was the sheet with Lela's name.

"I thought it best not to let him see we knew about that. When he arrived, I asked him to wait out front for a second. I said I was getting off the phone, but I came in here and took the notes down."

"Good thinking."

Cat silently stared at the table. "I talked to my parents last night. Their flight was canceled because of the weather. As soon as this is over, I'm going to go stay with them."

She looked at me. The events of the past few days had taken their toll on her, and it was starting to show. There were dark circles under her eyes, her peaches and crème complexion had taken on a dull gray shade, and her normally erect posture had converted to slumped shoulders. She seemed defeated. How could she not? Every single thing she knew about her life had changed—except for the one thing that was going to change in the next month. Cat was the one person who seemed to have it all, but in the blink of an eye, she was on the verge of having nothing.

27

POWER OUT

THE SNOWSTORM STARTED SOMETIME DURING BREAKFAST. AT FIRST, IT was a couple of flurries. We gathered around the windows and watched, temporarily distracted by the miracle of nature. Thin flakes turned into fatter ones that coated the street. After forty-five minutes, it was undeniable. Our stretch of unseasonably warm weather in December had broken, and this storm wasn't going to subside for a while.

"I'm due at Tradava," Eddie said. "I'm senior management and probably the closest person to the store. Somebody has to be there to decide whether to open or close, and if I leave it up to one of the merchandise managers, they'll argue that we need the sales." He pulled on his thick ski jacket. "Cat, do you want a ride?"

"I'm not on the way."

"No, but if we leave now, I can get to your house and back to the store pretty quickly. If we wait, the roads are going to be too slick."

They collected their things and left. Logan jumped onto the arm of my chair and climbed to the top of it. He ran his head across my nose and then gingerly stepped onto the white windowsill and lowered himself. Logan loved snowstorms, as long as he wasn't required to go outside in them.

I cleaned up as best as I could and then sat at the kitchen table and stared at the wall of observation. Could Shana be telling the truth? I didn't know. But if Shana truly believed that Cat was responsible for the murders, then both of their lives were in danger.

Despite the coffee, the questions, the snowstorm, and the general sense of unease, I fell asleep on the sofa and woke to the sound of knocking on the front door. The room was dark. I got up and turned on the lamp on my end table. The switch clicked, but nothing happened. I moved to the wall and tried the dimmer. Nothing.

The knock continued. I moved to the window, cupped my hands around my eyes, and looked outside. Nick's truck was in my driveway. The rest of the neighborhood had been blanketed in white, creating an innocent setting. It was odd how peaceful it appeared in direct contrast to the crime wave at the outlets.

I opened the door and let Nick in. "Why's it so dark in here?" He was bundled up in a cranberry hat, plaid scarf, and navy-blue pea coat.

"The power must have gone out." I flicked the light switch a few times to demonstrate. "How'd you get here?" I asked. "I mean, I know you drove, but it looks pretty bad out there."

"I have snow tires on my car. You okay? I tried calling a few times, but the call went straight to voicemail."

"The battery was low. I plugged it in, but if the power went out then it couldn't charge." I headed to the kitchen. "Do you want some coffee? It's probably cold, but it's relatively fresh."

Nick hung his coat on the back of a kitchen chair and set his hat, gloves, and scarf on the table. His eyes swept over the walls, taking in Dante's surveillance photos, the scribbled identifications, and our lists of clues, notes, and questionable activity. I was about to repeat my question when he replied.

"You need a shower. I'll get the coffee."

Alrighty-then.

The steaming water caressed my aching shoulders and back, and I found myself becoming more aware of how little quality sleep I'd gotten of late. My mind became a blank canvas, absorbing the relaxing sensation of the shower beating down on me. Eventually the water turned cooler, a sign that the water heater was getting low. I got out, dried off, wrapped my hair in a towel turban-style, and pulled on a plush robe.

The long shower had a side effect on me. Not only had it relaxed my muscles and settled my brain, it drained my last drops of energy. I was dizzy from the change in temperature and needed to sit down. I pulled the covers back from the bed and crawled between the sheets, resting my head against the pillow. I just needed a few minutes.

IT WAS DARK. I didn't want to be awake. I shut my eyes and nestled further between the cozy down covers. A pair of arms encircled me, and I let out a quiet, sleepy moan as I readjusted my position. About a half second later my eyes popped open, and I went rigid. Nick was next to me.

He pulled me close, holding me as though he wasn't going to let go. We lay like that for a while, no questions, no answers, no danger.

I told him about the last twenty-four hours: Shana's confession, Detective Madden's visit, George's hidden presents left behind in the fireplace, Jim and Lela's affair in Cat's office. Every time I hesitated before sharing more details, he gently encouraged me to continue. It felt good to talk to him, to let it all out.

When I finished (more like when I finally paused for air), I wondered what was going through his mind. The longer we lay in silence, the more I worried that I'd said too much. Logan, not one recognize a moment when he saw it, howled for his dinner.

"I think you better get up and feed your cat."

"Can't we stay like this for a couple more minutes?" I mumbled, ignoring the persistent cries from the floor.

"I'm not sure that's such a good idea."

"Logan's on a diet. He's not going to starve."

"I was referring to you being very naked underneath that robe. Unless you want to conduct some more overnight surveillance..."

28

____

NEED MORE TIME

"Who are these people?" Nick asked. We were in the kitchen. After our bedroom tryst, I dressed in a leopard-print cashmere lounge tunic and pants. We each held a flashlight aimed at the wall of observation. I'd also dug up a laser pointer that doubled as Logan's favorite toy and used it to pinpoint different facts.

"That's Jim Insendo, the man Cat bought the boutique from, and that's Lela Sexton, one of Cat's employees," I said.

"They seem to like each other."

I nodded. Standing in the kitchen bringing Nick up to speed on the investigation was one thing, but staring at the intimate photos of Jim and Lela, especially after just climbing out of bed with Nick, was a little uncomfortable (in a good way).

"What's their connection to Cat's husband?"

"It's complicated. Jim used to own Cat's store. He offered to buy the boutique back from Cat just recently. See that picture of Lela leaving Cat's office? We think she might have planted something on Cat's desk, or taken documents from her office, so she would be more prone to sell."

"Is she? Considering selling the store?"

I nodded. "I can't tell if it's because she wants to or if everything is getting to her. The week before Christmas is stressful for anybody who works retail. She's got so much extra piled on top of that stress that who knows why she's doing what she's doing."

Nick scanned the wall. "Kenner & Winn...the jewelry wholesalers? Why did you write their names up there?"

"We don't have pictures of them."

"What do they have to do with this?"

"George worked for them. How do you know them?"

"Industry connections. I meet a lot of these people on the accessories circuit. So the pearls that were stolen from Cat's store the night of his murder came from their inventory?" Nick asked. I nodded. "Then they knew the value of the merchandise at the store."

"Yes."

"Do you trust them?"

"Seems doubtful they'd be involved. Why rob the store of merchandise they could get on their own? Why commit murder at all? If it's about the pearls, they can mine more."

"You think pearls come from a mine like diamonds?" He smiled.

"You know what I meant. Winn's been out of the country this whole time. And Tom Kenner offered to pay for all of George's funeral services and three months' salary to help Cat."

"Let's get back to Cat. Somebody went out of their way to pull her into this."

"That's what I originally thought, but now I'm not sure. The more I think about George, the more I wonder why was he killed? It doesn't make sense that it was a case of mistaken identity, because why else would he have been at Catnip that night? Somebody arranged for him to show up, and whoever that was must have planned to kill him. If it's about George, that's one thing. But the security officer was murdered too. What's the connection between them? Anything? Or was it totally random?"

Nick leaned back. "Are you seriously entertaining that as a possibility? Because if that's the case, we can forget the whole thing and go out for pizza."

"Don't try to distract me with pizza. I've considered it as a possibility, but not seriously, and here's why. The pearls showed back up in Cat's office. They were stashed in the ceiling. And Aguilar was strangled with a strand of pearls that I had on hold, and if I had them on hold, then they couldn't have been stolen in the smash and grab."

He stared at me. "You were going to buy the necklace that the security officer was strangled with?" Our eyes connected. "Do you think that's a sign?"

"No, I think it's bad clothing karma that came back to haunt me. Maybe because I once wore knickers." (This was not the first time I'd considered the implications of once wearing knickers.) I chewed my lip. "But I think it means something."

Soon enough the coffee pot was empty and because of the storm there would be no calls for takeout. Nick walked to the pantry and scanned the shelves. I was embarrassed that I had no food and said as much. My comments were unanswered.

"Keep talking," he said.

"About what? My lack of food?"

"No, about the investigation. Things you've figured out." He pulled a couple of cans from the shelves and set them on the counter. Confused, I tried to regain my earlier train of thought but failed.

"What are you doing?"

"Making us something to eat."

"I don't have any food."

"You've got plenty of food. You shop like you're preparing for a zombie apocalypse." He held up two cans of spinach. "You expecting Popeye?"

This whole meal thing captured my interest, much to Nick's amusement. He turned toward me with his hands propped on the counter.

"I left some parmesan cheese in the fridge. We need to eat it or it'll go bad. I'm going to make pasta and spinach pesto. Will that be to your liking?"

"Sure, yep, sounds good. You can do that without electricity?"

"You have a gas stove and a battery-operated coffee grinder, right?"

I was starting to feel like I had MacGyver in my kitchen. "Right."

While Nick moved about the kitchen, I poured a small bowl of milk for Logan. Nick filled a pot with water and set it on a gas burner. He drained a can of spinach and dumped it into my coffee grinder with olive oil, juice from half a lemon, minced garlic, and some grated cheese. I let him cook in silence while I fished candles from the junk drawer.

Sooner than expected he brought two steaming plates full of pasta tossed in a green sauce to the table and sat down across from me. Not a moment too soon, either, since my stomach let out a massive rumble. We spent the next few minutes eating.

"Is there anything you haven't told me?" he asked.

Dante's face popped into my head. While it might not have been what Nick was asking, it was something I had to confess. "The photos on the wall were taken by Cat's brother. Dante. He's been helping us—her. Us." I paused. "He kissed me two nights ago."

Nick slowly nodded. He set his fork down and put his elbows on the table and then rested his forehead against his clasped hands. A few seconds later he looked up at me. I laid my arm out on the table with my hand open toward him. He dropped his arm and took my fingers in his. I never looked away from his eyes.

"Nick, I think maybe we're not ready for the next step."

"Are you saying no?"

"I'm saying I need more time. Does this change anything?"

"Not for me."

WE FINISHED dinner and turned our attention back to the wall of observation. I stood next to the giant Post-its and tapped the notes and photos one at a time, giving Nick the necessary bullet points.

"Every suspicious thing we've come to see, hear, suspect, or learn is written up." A thumbtack fell out of the wall, and a still shot of Cat's office fluttered gently onto the table.

"Let's see if I get this. This is Jim, the former owner, and he's with Lela, one of Cat's employees. And they seem to be having an affair. Is he married?"

"I don't know."

"Okay, so that may or may not mean anything. Who's the punk girl?"

"Shana Brice. Cat's assistant. She confessed two nights ago."

"If she confessed, why are we talking about this?"

"Because she confessed to stealing the pearls, not the murder. She said she and Aguilar had been stealing all along but that George's body was in the jewelry case when she got there."

"Do you believe her?"

"Not sure. She said she and Aguilar conspired to steal the pearls. When Aguilar was found dead, Shana got scared and confessed." I shook my head. "Why say anything at that point? If the goal all along was to steal the pearls, then she was in the clear. Why bring them back to the scene of the crime? Why go to such lengths to hide them once they're there? And who killed Aguilar?"

"It's almost like there were two different crimes committed that night," Nick said. I looked at him. We stood facing each other for upwards of a minute. "What?" he finally asked.

"That would explain a lot. Assuming Shana was the thief, she looked...confused. She held a tire iron that I'm pretty sure she used to smash the case. She could have whacked George. Why would she strangle him?" I was excited by this new theory. My voice picked up, and I thought through other details out loud. "She would have had to smash the case so it didn't look like an inside job. It's like *My Cousin Vinny!*"

"There were no metallic mint-green convertibles. There were no cans of tuna. How is it like *My Cousin Vinny?*"

"There were two sets of people in the store. The first person killed George. I don't know who, when, or why, but he strangled George and then left his body behind the jewelry case. The second person, Shana, was there to steal the pearls. She broke in and went to the case. She probably knew exactly which case to smash, so she did, but after the crash, she noticed the body. And when I yelled, she turned around and looked at me. She knew I saw her. Even though she was wearing a black mask, she might have thought I could identify her—and now it wouldn't be in conjunction with a smash and grab, it would be with a murder."

Nick picked up the thread. "So she took off," he said. "And after the fact, with an investigation in full swing, she tried to get the merchandise back to the store to eliminate the evidence."

"She didn't just try, she succeeded."

Nick crossed his arms. "So it's possible Shana's telling the truth that she committed the thefts but not the murder. Do you believe her?"

"Yes, well, no."

"That's clear."

"Shana—and all of Cat's staff—has access because they have keys. Jim has keys because he's the former store owner and Cat never changed the locks. Aguilar had access to the mall master keys. What if..." I chewed my lip, wondering how crazy Nick was going to think I was when I said this next bit. "What if Shana wasn't trying to hide the pearls in the ceiling? What if she was trying to return the pearls to the store and just didn't have a chance to finish what she started? Like she gained entrance to the store through the ceiling?"

"Kidd, people don't go crawling through ceilings."

"River Phoenix did in *Sneakers*."

He uncrossed his arms and put his hands on either side of my face, bent down, and kissed me.

"What was that for?" I asked.

"Sometimes with you, there are no words."

I refilled our wine, and we sat next to each other facing the wall of observation. "Everything Shana said makes sense. It is entirely possible that she was there to steal the pearls."

"And her partner, Aguilar? Could he have done it?"

"He came into the store after the crash. So in the case of George's death, I can't get him there."

"They could have killed him earlier."

"True, but then why kill Aguilar? And then why confess at all? Which brings me to Jim. He had a way to get in, and he seems awfully persistent about getting the store back. If it's about running a store, he could just open a different boutique and become one of Cat's competitors."

"You think there's something about that particular store that he's after."

"Yep. I think we're missing something about Catnip."

29

BETTER AT DISCOUNTS

"YOU MEAN, WHY IS CAT'S STORE SO VALUABLE?" NICK ASKED.

"Yes. And is it the contents of the store or the *location* of the store?"

"Assume we're missing something about the location. It stands to reason that it's in one of these pictures. Tell me again how—" Nick paused for a fraction of a second. "Cat's brother got these pictures?"

"Dante programmed computer tablets to take pictures every five minutes."

"How many tablets?"

"Two."

"That's five hundred seventy-six pictures a day."

"How did you do that?" I demanded.

"What?"

"That math. Right there. Without a calculator."

"Twenty-four hours times sixty minutes an hour divided by five-minute intervals times two."

"Maybe I'm better at discounts." I unlocked the tablet and

handed it to Nick. "You can swipe through the images we didn't print."

"Where's the other one?"

"Upstairs in the walk-in closet, on the desk."

He handed the tablet back to me. "I'll be right back."

I studied the pictures while he was gone. He was right; there had to be something we were missing about Catnip, and it had to be right in front of us. I stepped on a thumbtack, cursed, and stooped to pick it up. While I waited for Nick's return, I squeezed between the unoccupied chairs on the far side of the table. It was a tighter squeeze than when I tried to get between Cat's desk and file cabinet in her office. I was going to have go back on the Logan half-portion diet for a while.

I stuck the thumbtack into the wall and noticed something we'd all missed. Between the early set of photos and the later ones, the file cabinet in Cat's office had moved. Dante, Cat, Eddie, and I would never have noticed it. Our investigation had become so distracted by the players in the photos that it had never occurred to us to stop and look at the backdrop: Cat's store and office. But once I did, it was obvious the answer had been there all along.

Other than the location of George's body, Cat's office was the epicenter of the suspicious activity: The necklaces turning up. The location of the affair. Lela stealing something from Cat's desk. Aguilar's body.

When Nick returned to the kitchen, I told him what I discovered. "Cat's office furniture was moved. Look." I pointed to the file cabinet in one photo and then in another. "We have to go to the mall and find out why. We've got to see what's behind that file cabinet."

"How are you going to get into the store? Do you have keys?"

"Yes, but I need to talk to Cat first." I grabbed my phone before remembering it was dead.

Nick held his out to me. "Do you know the number?"

I pulled out my old phone and looked up the number in my contacts. I accessed the call log on Nick's phone. The most recent call made was to "The Future Mrs. Taylor." I snuck a peek at him to see if he was watching me. He was. He smiled like we shared a secret the rest of the world knew nothing about. I smiled back and felt warm and tingly all the way to my toes.

Focus, Samantha.

I called Cat. "Sam? Is everything okay?" she asked.

"Yes and no and yes. I'm here with Nick, and we figured something out. Did Detective Madden release the store to you yet?"

"Yes, but with the storm coming, the mall's closed. Why?"

I looked at Nick. "Do you mind if Nick and I check on it? I still have your keys from the night Dante and I reset the store." Nick crossed his arms and frowned slightly. "Okay, thanks." I hung up. "We cleaned up after the police released the crime scene. You were in Italy with Amanda. I don't want to hear a word."

"What? I didn't say anything."

I changed into jeans and a turtleneck sweater, pulled on Moon Boots and a white puffer jacket, and followed Nick to his truck.

It took longer than usual to get to the outlet center. I plugged my Nick Phone into his cigarette lighter. Even though the streets had been plowed and showered with salt, Nick drove with caution. Several traffic lights had defaulted to flashing red. The mall was dark, as were the surrounding streetlights and holiday decorations.

The parking lot was mostly empty. A couple of cars remained behind, covered by snow. I pulled on pink mittens and a matching hat and held my coat closed by my neckline. Falling flakes had multiplied, and the wind blew them at an angle past my face. I jumped out of the truck.

I tried to walk faster, but the snow hindered my progress. Nick caught up with me and grabbed my elbow. I pulled away, but he had a tight grip. I slipped and fell. Nick landed on top of me.

"Stay down," he said.

Gunshots punctured the air. I heard a pop and a sizzle. It was cold. I wriggled around to get out from under him but quickly realized he had me pinned. A car drove past us and lost control in a wide spin around the side of the mall. We jumped up and ran as fast as possible to the entrance. I fumbled and dropped the keys twice before unlocking the door.

"Give me your phone," Nick said.

I held it out. Nick flipped to the contacts, paused at one of the names, looked at me, and then pressed the screen. "Unlock the door," he said to me. "I'll be right back." He turned around. I couldn't hear his voice. A few seconds later he hung up and handed the phone to me.

"Cat's office is on the left side of the store." I pointed. "Come with me."

The door to Cat's office was open. Nick turned on the flashlight and aimed it up. "You said the pearls fell from the ceiling, right?"

"Right."

"Then let's see what else is up there." He climbed on the desk and pushed two of the cork tiles out of place. He did a pull-up from the metal frame. He stayed there for a few seconds and then dropped back down to the desk.

"Give me a boost," he said.

"Let me go. I'm lighter."

"Don't take this the wrong way, but can you do a pull-up?"

I rolled my eyes. I stood on the desk and laced my fingers together. Nick put his foot on my hands and did another pull-up and, with the resistance I provided him, was able to climb up. He disappeared into the ceiling.

"Hey, River, see anything suspicious?" I asked.

His voice came back muffled. "I knew you were going to say that."

While I waited, I stared at the carpet. There was a faint impression, slightly off-center from the base of the filing cabinet. I looked up at the ceiling. "I found something down here," I called.

I set my phone on Cat's desk and tipped the tall metal file cabinet to the right, revealing a faded square of drywall behind it. I applied pressure on the square, and it popped out and fell backward.

I grabbed my phone and stepped through. On the floor in front of me was a strand of black pearls. They were far more lustrous than the ones I'd put on hold. I aimed the light at them, and they took on a greenish-blue cast. I scooped them up and shoved them into the pocket of my coat.

I was inside the camping store where I'd bought my rain boots for my night with Dante and the blankets for my night with Nick. Slowly, I crept forward, stumbling thanks to the clunkiness of my Moon Boots. The retractable metal gate that separated the store from the mall was open. A beam of light cut its way through the dark interior. I hid next to a display of men's plaid flannel shirts and strained to see who was with me.

Joyce Kenner.

She aimed her flashlight at the ground. I was struck by the odd manner that she held it, until I realized it was taped to something.

A gun.

It was tiny. It looked like a toy. I didn't know squat about guns, but I couldn't see that one inflicting enough damage to take a life.

But in a match of gun vs. pearl necklace, gun would win. I needed the element of surprise. I crawled backward past a camping tent and called Nick. A few seconds later, his ringtone sounded from somewhere above me. Joyce pointed her gun/flashlight at the ceiling and fired. The bullet zinged off a length of exposed pipe. I couldn't let her shoot again—not at Nick, who had no idea we were down here.

"Get help," I whispered into the phone and then stood up. "Looking for something?" I asked. Joyce turned toward me, and the gun-flashlight followed. "You've gone to a lot of trouble for a strand of pearls that you dropped behind a file cabinet."

She seemed surprised to find me there. I didn't know if Nick had heard me. Why hadn't we called the police when we arrived? When the shots were fired in the parking lot? Even if Nick could call them now, would the weather keep them away?

I pulled the black pearls out of my pocket. "These aren't like the other pearls George placed in Cat's inventory, are they? They don't look like regular pearls." I rested them in my open palm. "They don't *feel* like regular pearls."

Joyce lunged forward and grabbed for the necklace. I swung my hand out of reach. "Cat said the order she bought from George was worth about thirty thousand dollars retail. The whole order." I held up the necklace. "I'm guessing this strand is worth a bit more than that, isn't it?"

"Give them to me." She lunged toward me again, and again I yanked them back. "Two people have died over that necklace. What makes you think you won't be number three?"

"Out of curiosity, what *are* they worth?" I was stalling for time to give Nick a chance to get away. Joyce had acknowledged the murders. She had no intention of letting me walk away.

"It took five years to produce that necklace," said a weak voice from the floor behind her. I craned my neck and saw Tom Kenner leaning against a wooden picnic table. The light from my phone illuminated a dark shiny substance on the thigh of his trousers. "They're natural pearls produced from wild oysters. Gem quality. That strand is worth close to a million dollars."

30

IT'S ABOUT TIME

"You—shut up!" Joyce yelled at her husband. "You did this when you slept with that woman. You were supposed to fix this. Now I have to clean up your mess." Joyce looked at me. "Give me the necklace."

"You'll get the pearls when I get answers," I said. "Why did you kill George? What did he do to you?"

"She didn't kill George. I did," Tom said from the floor. "I had to."

I thought about George lying on the floor behind the jewelry counter with the pearls tied around his neck. "You shot him, but he didn't die. That's why you had to strangle him with the pearls."

"Poetic, don't you think?" Tom said. "I made every arrangement to get that necklace through customs, but George outsmarted me. When it ended up in his wife's store, I had to get it back."

"You killed George over this necklace?" I asked.

"That necklace was for me," Joyce said. "My husband made a very big mistake when he cheated on me. For a million-dollar necklace, I could forgive the affair."

I didn't know if Nick had gotten my message or not. The bullet Joyce fired had bounced off the ceiling, but if she fired again, things might be different. There were twenty feet between us. If Joyce rushed me, I wouldn't get away.

My mind flashed over the emergency supplies in my pockets. Rope. Duct tape. Scissors.

Scissors.

I reached into my pocket and felt around for the scissors but kept talking. "And Aguilar? Why kill him?"

Tom spoke. "If he'd told me where to find the necklace, he might still be alive."

"He was a criminal," Joyce added dismissively. "He deserved to die."

I looked back and forth between Tom and Joyce Kenner. Tom, who had killed two people, now bleeding on the floor of the camping store from a gunshot wound inflicted by his wife. Joyce, who showed no signs of distaste over her husband's actions or pain. They were both certifiable.

Joyce stepped forward and aimed the gun at me. "Now give me the pearls."

"Fine," I said. Before I could rethink my actions, I pulled the necklace out of my pocket and sliced through the silk cord on which it was strung.

Both Joyce and Tom's eyes went wild and crazy. "No!" Joyce screamed.

Individual knots between the pearls kept them from scattering around our feet like I'd wanted. I gripped the necklace tightly in my left hand and snipped through the silk cord at randomly spaced intervals. I grabbed at the end of the cord and pushed against the lustrous black pearls. One by one they slid over the knots between them and fell, bouncing against the cold marble floor and scattering wildly. Joyce tossed the gun to the floor and dropped to her knees, clawing at the rapidly scattering orbs. Several rolled into the stream of blood that trickled out of the wound in her husband's thigh.

I grabbed the gun and aimed it at Joyce. I knew I couldn't pull the trigger.

"NIIIIIIIIICK!!!" I yelled. "I need heeeeeeeeeelp!"

The Lycra of Joyce's catsuit displayed a lean, muscular body that had been kept hidden under palazzo pants and caftans. This was no pudgy middle-aged wife. This was a woman who took great pains to fight the aging process with perky man-made breasts, sandblasted porcelain skin, pearly white teeth. But it would take a lot of high-priced stylists to make Joyce Kenner regain the appearance of a society lady after this. Suddenly, the pile of lingerie made sense. She was a desperate wife somewhere past middle age, watching younger women get the attention she once received. She was down but not out.

Her hand shot out and caught me at my knees. I fell. She crawled over me and pressed a wool blanket into my face. "Why are you protecting her? She's a tramp. She's having my husband's baby. She's destroying my life!"

She pressed the blanket over my nose. I couldn't breathe. I turned my head one way and then the other. She didn't let go. Her knees were on my arms, and I couldn't move. Where was Nick? Had she shot him? I closed my eyes and felt dizzy from the lack of oxygen.

And then the weight of her lifted, and the blanket was pulled from my face. Nick dropped down beside me. I put my hand on my throat and gasped for breath. Joyce stood up and ran. Her foot caught on the pearls that were scattered on the floor, and her feet shot out from under her.

Nick grabbed a bundle of black tree-climbing rope and

wrapped it around Joyce. He knotted the ends and secured her to a fixture with D-Clamps.

"You heard me," I said between ragged breaths. "You were in the ceiling. I didn't think you'd come."

He put his hands on either side of my face. "Are you kidding? That's the first time you ever asked me for help." He pulled me into a hug. "I'm a firm believer in positive reinforcement."

Finally!

Before I knew it, sirens pierced the air. I unlocked the mall doors and watched a squadron of cop cars and an ambulance pull into the parking lot. Several cops and EMTs filtered out of their cars and charged into the building. Tom Kenner was moved to a gurney and rolled out. Joyce Kenner was handcuffed. Nick and I sat by the camping display, his arm around me, a blanket not dissimilar to the one I bought the night of our "overnight surveillance" wrapped around us.

And then a voice I hadn't heard for the past five months said, "Quit it with the cuddling and tell me what you're mixed up in this time."

In the two years I'd been back in Ribbon, I never thought I'd be so happy to hear that voice. I looked up at dear, sweet, ornery, tan-from-Tahiti Detective Loncar.

Nick leaned close to my ear. "I hope you don't mind. I called for backup after the gunshots."

I smiled at Nick and then gave Loncar my most stern expression. "It's about time you came back from vacation," I said.

31

THAT'S IT

THE NIGHT BEFORE CHRISTMAS, WE GATHERED FOR A PARTY AT CAT'S house. Cat had recovered from the past week. She was dressed in a vibrant purple dress and the pearl necklace George had left behind in the fireplace. Her shiny red hair framed her face, and her smile, which had been in hiding for the past week, now reached her eyes. If all went as planned, her baby would arrive in a few weeks. The glow of pregnancy had eradicated any residual negativity from George's death.

Eddie adjusted tinsel on Cat's Christmas tree. Dante sat on the sofa drinking eggnog. Nick was in the kitchen assembling a plate of hors d'oeuvres for us to share. Other people mingled. Both Cat's and George's families had finally arrived thanks to a break in the weather. Neighbors who'd been stopping by all week with casseroles now enjoyed a glass of champagne. The vast array of sympathy flowers had been layered with colorful red poinsettias and lent a cheerful backdrop to the party.

I was dressed in the ivory fringed dress that I'd tried on the night we found George's body. The hardest part of the evening had been accessorizing, since the dress called for several long strands of pearls. In deference to what had gone down, I forwent the pearls and wore a band around my hair with a small flower on the side. My only other accessory was Nick's engagement ring.

Christmas had come way too quickly this year. I'd been so preoccupied with Cat's situation that I'd barely noticed the dates changing on the calendar. My vacation had sped by in a blur of early mornings, late nights, crime scene clean-up, and suspicion. When Nick had tactfully pointed out that the holiday was in two days, I swore he made it up. It hadn't taken much more than a cross reference to the closest four desk calendars to prove him right.

One, he could fake. Four sent me into a panic.

"Don't worry about it," he'd said. "The holidays are about being with friends and family, not about presents. I'll help you forget about what happened."

What happened.

Tom and Joyce Kenner had enjoyed a long marriage and a certain lifestyle thanks to his business. But Tom had risked that marriage on more than one occasion by having affairs on the side. Joyce pretended to look the other way as long as Tom made it up to her with jewelry, but this last time was too much. When she found out he had a dalliance with an employee from the mall, she threatened the kind of divorce that would leave him rubbing two pennies together trying to make a nickel.

So Tom did what he always did. He faked the paperwork on a valuable necklace to get it through customs. He canceled the order to the retailer, intending to declare the merchandise a loss and give it to Joyce instead. The value of the necklace was close to a million dollars, but to Tom it was worth the price of forgiveness.

But George, his newest sales rep, was eager to be successful. Unaware of the true value of the necklace, he convinced Cat to buy the canceled order for Catnip so his new employer would be out nothing.

Tom threatened George about the necklace. During his interrogation, Tom admitted to telling George to get that merchandise back or he'd never see his baby. He'd planned it all along: meet at Catnip after the holiday party, get the pearl necklace. But Shana burgled the store, and I caught her in the act. Later, when the stolen pearls were discovered in Cat's office, Tom knew somebody was on to him. He could no longer expect the police to link the burglary to the murder. He tracked the thefts to Shana and Aguilar and committed a second murder, hoping Shana's confession would lead him to what he was after. Aguilar would have made a better scapegoat, but one small detail kept Tom from killing Shana instead.

His affair had been with her.

Shana, unaware of the value of the missing necklace, had given Tom the *other* necklace from Kenner & Winn left in the store: the one I'd put on hold. Tom used it to strangle Aguilar. If I had thought more about that and less about clothing karma, I might have realized Shana knew more than she'd admitted. The million-dollar necklace I'd destroyed inside the camping store had been dropped when Aguilar tried to hide the stolen jewelry in the ceiling of Cat's office.

George, not willing to risk the life of Cat or his unborn child, faked the fight with Cat and told her he needed space. I liked to believe he planned all along to reconcile with her when things blew over. Nobody saw murder coming—especially people who lived on the right side of the law.

As for Joyce's rant when she attacked me? I had myself to blame. When I'd found her shopping for lingerie at Catnip and told her Cat had gotten pregnant in April, it coincided with Tom's latest discretion. Cat moved from the "pregnant lesbian" column to the "scheming other woman" one. In Joyce's mind, destroying Cat's life was simply payback for an affair Cat had never had.

The doorbell rang, but Cat was caught behind a throng of family members and neighbors. She signaled to me to answer it. When I opened the door, Jim and Lela stood outside. I invited them in. Jim helped Lela out of her chinchilla coat, and I looked away, remembering what she'd worn (or not) the last time she'd removed it. Tonight, she was tastefully dressed in a red wrap dress. Even under the jersey, or in spite of it, I could tell the woman had a great body. Maybe that's why she was comfortable parading around in her undies.

"I wouldn't mind seeing you in one of her outfits," a voice whispered in my ear.

"I don't see what's so special about a wrap dress," I countered.

"I was talking about her *other* outfits."

I turned around and faced Dante. "I don't think I own an outfit like those."

"Shame." Dante handed me a flute of champagne. As I held the glass to my lips, I watched him take notice of the engagement ring on my left hand. "So that's it," he said.

I shrugged. "That's it."

"He's a lucky guy," he said. He tapped his flute of champagne against mine and walked away.

I threaded my way through the crowd toward Nick. He stood by the tree, talking to Lela and Jim.

"What I don't understand is how you came to think I had something to do with the murders," Jim said.

It was Lela who answered him. "Honey, we have been acting a little suspicious. It wouldn't take much for someone to think we were up to something. Consider it from their point of view."

"And then we saw the pictures from my office," Cat said.

"What pictures?" Jim asked. "Oh, no. You installed a camera in your office? How much did you see?"

"Let's just say we saw a more than a business meeting," Cat said tactfully.

Lela turned beet red and slapped Jim's arm playfully. "I told you it was icky," she said.

Jim put his arm around her. "From now on, only your place or mine. Until we agree on a house that can become ours." She turned her face away from him and he kissed her on the cheek.

"I'm sorry I suspected you," I said. "Someone was going after my friend, and I couldn't let that happen."

Jim smiled. "Maybe someday you'll think of us as friends, too."

"Remember, Jim, Samantha is a very good customer," Cat said. "You might want to make sure 'someday' is sooner rather than later."

I looked at Cat. "What does that mean?"

"Didn't they tell you?" she said. She had a hand on her very pregnant belly. "I'm selling the store back to Jim, and he and Lela are going to run it together. When we thought Lela was taking something from my office, that was Jim's offer. He was afraid the paperwork would get lost, so she took it and gave it to him, and he gave it to you."

"Are you okay with that?"

"That store was a part of my life for a while, but it's time to move on to something new."

I leaned in close and whispered in her ear. "Full-time mom? Are you sure?"

"I'm sure," she said. "Now, come with me. I want you to open your present."

"You didn't have to get me a present."

"Oh yes, I did. I hope you don't think it's weird." She pointed to a flat box under the tree. I picked it up and shook it. The contents rattled. Cat giggled. I tore off the paper and opened the box. Inside was a suite of black pearl jewelry: earrings, bracelet, and necklaces. I slammed the box shut.

"They're knockoffs!" she said. "But they're perfect with that dress. I couldn't let you not accessorize because of me."

I added the jewelry to my outfit and hugged her. Nick put his arm around me. The party pulsed with a level of merriment and joy we all needed.

The party broke up hours later when the snowstorm started up again. Nick popped his head into the room to see if I was ready to go. He held my coat in his hands.

"Go ahead," Cat said. "You've earned a Merry Christmas as much as anybody."

"Are you going to be okay? There's been a lot of change in your life in the past week. A week ago you said all men were rats."

"Isn't it wild how things turned out?" She put her hand on her throat and touched the pearls. "My husband didn't leave me. You're marrying Nick. And my brother is moving in to help when the baby comes."

"Wild" didn't begin to cover it.

EPILOGUE

Nick invited me to spend Christmas with him and his dad.
After presents had been unwrapped and champagne had been
drunk, he held out his hand. "I have one more present for you, but
it's in my bedroom."

"Your dad is asleep in his recliner!"

"My dad knows about the present. He helped me get it ready."

Curiosity took over.

"Trust me," he said.

I followed him to his bedroom. A giant box, about six feet high
and six feet wide, sat in the middle of the room wrapped in a
mosaic of wrapping paper squares. A large tab dangled from the
top of the box with lettering that read *PULL HERE*.

I pulled the tab, and the box fell open like a drawbridge. Inside
were stacks upon stacks of white boxes, all labeled with Nick's
signature logo. There were too many to count, but I hadn't seen that
many matching shoe boxes together since the day I'd stumbled
upon Nick's delivery truck in New York City eleven years ago.

"You were my muse. My inspiration. This whole collection was about you. I wanted you to be the first person to have it. *That's* what kept me in Italy."

I'd like to say Nick got something special that night too, but he didn't.

He fell asleep long before I was done trying on shoes.

THE KILLER FASHION MYSTERY SERIES

Killer Fashion Mysteries

Designer Dirty Laundry

Buyer, Beware

The Brim Reaper

Some Like It Haute

Grand Theft Retro

Pearls Gone Wild

Cement Stilettos

Panty Raid

Union Jacked

Slay Ride

Tough Luxe

Fahrenheit 501

Stark Raving Mod

Gilt Trip

Ranch Dressing

Murder Italian Style

ALSO BY DIANE VALLERE

Madison Night Mysteries

"Midnight Ice" (prequel novella)

Pillow StalkThat Touch of Ink

With Vics You Get Eggroll

The Decorator Who Knew Too Much

The Pajama Frame

Lover Come Hack

Apprehend Me No Flowers

Teacher's Threat

The Kill of It All

Love Me or Grieve Me

Please Don't Push Up the Daisies

The Glass Bottom Hoax

Sylvia Stryker Outer Space Mysteries

Murder on a Moon Trek

Scandal on a Moon Trek

Hijacked on a Moon Trek

Framed on a Moon Trek

Warped on a Moon Trek

Material Witness Mysteries

Suede to Rest

Crushed Velvet

Silk Stalkings

Tulle Death Do Us Part

Sheer Window

Contesting the Wool

Costume Shop Mystery Series

A Disguise to Die For

Masking for Trouble

Dressed to Confess

Mermaid Mysteries

Dead in the Water

Non-Fiction

Bonbons for your Brain

ABOUT THE AUTHOR

National bestselling author Diane Vallere writes stylish, character-driven mysteries that blend clever clues, sharp wit, and heart. Her stories span contemporary small towns, the glamorous mid-century past, and retro-inflected worlds, all anchored by strong voices and sparkling intrigue.

She is the editor of the Agatha Award–winning essay collection Promophobia: Taking the Mystery out of Promoting Crime Fiction. Diane studied art history at the College of William and Mary and spent years in luxury retail before trading fashion accessories for accessories to murder.

She currently resides in Pennsylvania.

instagram.com/dianevallere

DIANE VALLERE

where style meets sleuthing

or visit
dianevallere.com/books

Polyester Press